Tchipayuk

Tchipayuk
Or the Way of the Wolf

Ronald Lavallée

translated by
Patricia Claxton

Talonbooks   Vancouver   1994

Published with the assistance of the Canada Council

Talonbooks
201 - 1019 East Cordova
Vancouver, British Columbia
Canada V6A 1M8

Typeset in Goudy by Pièce de Résistance Ltée., and printed and bound
in Canada by Hignell Printing Ltd.

First Printing: March 1994

Tchipayuk was first published by Éditions Albin Michel S.A., Paris.

Canadian Cataloguing in Publication Data

Lavallée, Ronald, 1954-
    [Tchipayuk, ou, Le chemin du loup. English]
    Tchipayuk, or, The way of the wolf

    Translation of: Tchipayuk, ou, Le chemin du loup.
    ISBN 0-88922-338-6

    I. Title. II. Title: The way of the wolf. III. Title: Tchipayuk, ou,
Le chemin du loup. English.
PS8573.A7924T33 1994   C843'.54   C94-910118-4
PQ3919.2.L38T33 1994

PREFACE

In 1886, the Canadian government invited Isapo-muxica, Chief of the Blackfeet, to visit the great cities of the East. He was stunned by the experience. He had never left the foothills of the Rockies before; how could he have imagined that there were so many white men on earth? He had always considered them a weak if vexatious race. Now he could not get over the number and might of the city people. The Canadians, he told a chronicler, had even captured the stars of the sky in order to light their streets at night.

We like to imagine that the Canadian West was the scene of a terrible clash between two cultures, the ingenuous one of the New World and the awesome one of the Old. In truth, there was no clash; there was mutual rebuff, two ancient cultures turning their backs to one another, refusing to see each other. Europeans and Indians might come into contact, even collaborate, yet each side kept essentially to itself. The explorers were surprised that the Indians were not more curious about customs on the other side of the ocean. And when I was very young I knew missionaries who, for all their many years among the native peoples, knew nothing of their ancestral beliefs—on principle. Even today, plenty of politicians both white and Indian keep exploiting a comic-book impresssion of the other: Red Man, indolent and quarrelsome; White Man, greedy and heartless.

The fact that Canada escaped the bloodbaths that stain American prairie history owes less to British fair play than to the Métis. They were the guides, interpreters, and traders who breached the silence between their uncommunicative cousins. Would there have been a Little Big Horn if Custer had listened to his Métis guide, Michelet Bouyer? Without deliberate intent, perhaps, the Métis defused the worst of the confrontations. Until the day, that is, when they themselves raised the flag of revolt; the only ones among the Canadian native peoples to understand white society, and paradoxically the only ones to declare war on it.

For over a hundred years, they have been considered traitors for their War of Resistance ("rebellion," according to Canadian historians). They alone had sullied the noble dream of Canadian expansion; they would not soon be forgiven. Dispossessed of their farms, treated like children by a legal system that refused recognition of their competence to govern themselves, they drifted back into the vicous circle of poverty, alcoholism, and lack of self-repect from which they had just begun to emerge.

I was among those who profited from their decline. The land my parents farmed in Manitoba had belonged to a Métis family sixty years earlier. Our French-Canadian parish had supplanted a village of semi-nomadic Métis hunters who, it seems, had themselves supplanted Crees and Sioux. Occasionally — not often — one of my schoolmates would bring to class an Indian arrowhead or club unearthed during plowing. We were not very interested in these artefacts; we saw much more impressive things in the movies. About the country's first inhabitants we knew less than nothing, for as far as we were concerned the country's first inhabitants were our own great-grandparents. Those who had been there before they arrived were forgotten.

Or almost. No one who had Indian blood in the family acknowledged it with good grace. Having a Métis grandmother was considered a congenital blemish. It might be said behind a hand that So-and-so's grandfather had dried his meat in the old days, or smoked kinnikinnik (willow-bark tobacco); it was rarely heard from So-and-so's own mouth.

In villages inhabited by both French Canadians and Métis, things were no different. The *"Sauvages"* generally lived on the village perimeter, sat in the back pews in church (or stood), and as far as possible married among themselves. When my great-uncle learned that his daughter had fallen in love with a Métis lad, he considered it his duty to apprise each of his brothers and sisters discreetly so as to lessen the scandal. Not all reacted as did Georges Trudeau, my grandfather, who, having grasped the nature of the problem, told his brother that "the Métis's every bit as good as your Gloria!" The usual response was swift rejection of such suitors; the Métis were reputed to be spendthrift and tuberculous, neither of which was desirable in a son-in-law.

We were hypocrites, no two ways about it. We glorified the memory of Louis Riel, the Métis leader, because he was French-speaking and Catholic and had been hanged by the English-speaking Protestants. He was our hero, the symbol of French-Canadian resistance. We loved Riel; we despised his people. I don't remember a single person remarking on the incongruity of this.

I began writing *Tchipayuk* in 1979. The characters I was going to create had lived just a hundred years before. There was no shortage of eye-witness accounts of one kind or another. The Hudson's Bay Factors, the first administrators of the North West, had left voluminous correspondence. The missionaries, chronically shorthanded, had bombarded French and Canadian seminaries with petitions, to which they added thrilling descriptions of the countryside. There were already tourists in the persons of English lords and German barons who, between hunting forays, crisscrossed the wilds jotting down notes and making sketches. Also official emmissaries. In 1857, the meticulous Henry Hind was sent out by the British government to take the first recorded measurements of the backcountry regions. He counted everything he saw: the portages on the rivers, the degrees of slope of the mountains, even the French Canadian voyageurs' paddle strokes (3,600 per hour). He underestimated the extent of the Great Plains, true enough, but their magnitude is difficult for anyone to grasp, even today.

There were the personal stories of the old folk, told in their own voices and preserved in archival sound recordings; not very reliable as to details, but rich with feeling. There is no one left today who can brag personally about buffalo hunting or skirmishing with the Oglallas. Still, the memories of the oldest still alive reveal the tenacious vitality of the old-time Métis, their patient clan loyalty, the grace of their resignation to Nature's dictates, and always the earthy Métis sense of humour that sees things for what they are.

For a while there will still be the inimitable prairie French impregnated with Cree and Ojibway known as Métchiffe. It is rarely heard any more. It has been been so roundly censured by "real" French speakers that it has gone underground. The young people spurn it. Their elders only speak it in private. Like Marie D., a gentle, elderly lady of rotund proportions, in her cabin in an aspen grove on the Manitoba-Saskatchewan border. At the sound of a tape recorder switching on she immediately became unilingually English; my half-hour of coaxing and reassurance thereafter made no dent in the bulwark of a hundred years of ridicule. Similarly with Daniel M., who simply would not let me hear his French, however hard I tried to tell him that in Paris my own had made plenty of people wince.

Three hundred years have passed since Europeans penetrated (or invaded) the North American continent. We have still not progressed beyond half-hearted mumblings of goodwill. No terrible clash. Not yet. No joining of hands, either. Europeans and Amerindians are still strangers to one another.

Ronald Lavallée
Gaspé, February, 1994

TRANSLATOR'S NOTE

Ronald Lavallée has researched his material for this book among primary sources and contemporary newspaper articles, ensuring the authenticity of countless details, from the interior of a teepee to flowers on the prairie, to Saint Boniface Cathedral before the fire that destroyed all but the façade, to dress and hairstyle in late nineteenth-century Montreal. He has also travelled through all of the countryside he describes, the better to describe it.

The early French penetration of the continent has left a surprising number of familiar terms and placenames in English, some adapted first from Indian tongues. While a French origin for the word "coulee" is easily recognizable, I wonder how many English speakers realize that the sled driver's command, "Mush!" was originally (and more sensibly) *"Marche!"* The word *"Sauvage"* in the French and particularly Canadian French of this period most often bore no pejorative overtones; it simply meant "Indian." This is how I have translated the word unless context indicated otherwise.

The spelling of Cree words in either French or English is phonetic. Without being exhaustively systematic, I have modified some of these spellings to accord more with English than French phonetic conventions. I have left acute accents in certain words as an aid to pronunciation.

Ronald Lavallée has made a fair number of changes in his underlying text of 1987, some for the paperback and two book club editions and others for this edition. They are mostly excisions of passages or words that he has judged redundant or needlessly digressive. Some obtain greater accuracy, in geographical orientation for example, or the customs and attitudes of the period. Both plot and characterization remain unaltered.

I wish to express my gratitude to Ronald Lavallée for his patient cooperation throughout the consultations I have had with him. I also wish to thank Sister Pauline Martin who has provided me with guidance on religious terminology, and Jane Osterland, a prairie native who has helped me resolve some hesitations over prairie terms. I have consulted numerous reference and other works and would like to acknowledge the quality and quantity of information I have obtained from several: Rudy Wiebe, *The Scorched Wood People* (Toronto: McClelland & Stewart,

1977); Stewart Symington, *The Canadian Indian: The Illustrated History of the Great Tribes of Canada* (Toronto: McClelland & Stewart, 1969 [prepared at the request of the Department of Indian Affairs and Northern Development, Ottawa]; Mason Wade, *The French Canadians* (Toronto: Macmillan, 1955); W.L. Morton, *The Kingdom of Canada* (Toronto: McClelland & Stewart, 1963); Craig Brown, ed., *The Illustrated History of Canada* (Toronto: Lester & Orpen Dennys, 1987); M.H. Scargill et al., *A Dictionary of Canadianisms on Historical Principles* (Toronto: W.J.Gage, 1967); D.G.G. Kerr, ed., *A Historical Atlas of Canada* (Don Mills: Thomas Nelson & Sons, 1966). The translations of verse by Louis Fréchette and Octave Crémazie are mine.

For the original French version of this book, Ronald Lavallée won the Prix Champlain 1988 (Canada), the Prix Riel (Manitoba), and the Prix Jules Verne (France). His novel was also chosen for special editions by two book clubs in France.

There are those better qualified than I to judge, therefore, who consider this book to be more than just another historical novel. I hope that readers of this translation will agree.

Patricia Claxton
Montreal, February, 1994

PART ONE

The Prairie

1

Okaskatano-pisim, the Freezing-Over Moon, rose pale as a woman corpse over the embattled night. The prairie was in tumult. The high brown grasses clicked their frozen stalks.

The child ran, not daring to look back. The path was narrow. The grasses caught at his legs and beat on his chest. Try as he might to run on tiptoe, his moccasins pounded the ground. It was terrifying. The evil spirits live below ground. When they hear footsteps on their roof they come up to look.

Askik Mercredi began to cry. He was six years old and had been betrayed. His mother had shaken him awake, stood him up near the ill-fitting door, roughly pulled on his anorak and then, without a word of encouragement, even with a hint of irritation because he took a while to find his winter moccasins (he went barefoot in summer), shooed him out into the night.

As if a boy of six could brave marauding spirits.

As if there were no *wetiko*.

A moist gust of wind struck him from behind. He forgot about being cross with his mother. Fat clouds were turning to silver, fraying to shreds before the moon. Bits of grass were flying about in the darkness, striking him in the face.

What would he do if he met the wetiko?

He came to a stop. The path led steeply down into darkness. Here a coulee cut deep like a cleft in the prairie. Down there in the ravine there were willows whistling. Willows and what else? Askik ran back and forth on the brink, whimpering like an anxious puppy. Then he swung about. Face twisted with fear, he ran back along the path, yelling

3

at the top of his lungs. He no longer cared what his mother would say. All he wanted was to see the warm red glow from the parchment windows of the house.

But deep down, Askik knew he would not run all the way home. His mother would insist on knowing why, and for the first time in his life he knew he would be ashamed to admit being afraid.

He slowed his pace and then stopped altogether. He returned with heavy heart to the ravine, did not listen to the willows, plunged down into the coulee, stumbling in his haste, then scrambled up the other side and quick as a sparrow crossed the brink and was safe.

Pale lights from the other side of the Red River showed through a thicket. The Scottish colony. Askik opened his eyes wide the better to decipher the shadows, whether path or prairie in this blustering wind.

A shelter of squared logs loomed abruptly on his left and he heard the peaceful breathing of cattle. Now he could just make out the trees beside the river. A house with all its windows dark slipped by on his right. A cart was singing in the wind, shafts held high. Thump, thump, thump went Askik's moccasins, running through the dreams of things asleep. Men's possessions sleep as their masters do. Only grasses and sullen moons stir up the night.

There were now two deep ruts in the path: the road to the colony. Anxiously, Askik reviewed his mother's directions. "A big stone house after three streets, on the left, with windows like water." It was hopeless, it was all muddled in his head! He'd never find the house, he'd get lost for certain, and it was all his mother's fault. He was too little to be travelling alone.

The ruts led away before him like two blue furrows. The grass was cropped short. There were certainly cows hereabouts. Cows are reassuring, but Askik could not see one anywhere.

The path bent to the right, toward the river, through some dark woods. The boy hesitated, but followed on. The forest floor sloped steadily down toward the river. Askik's moccasins kept slipping on the half-frozen leaves. Gusts of wind blew like torrents through the tops of the trees. The path took another sharp turn and stopped at a cabin lying squat and humpbacked against the river. There was not a single window. The peeled logs ran from one end of the house to the other without interruption.

What kind of man lives in a house without windows?

A door creaked. Something was coming out! Askik screamed. He backed away, hit a tree, tried to run back up the path but missed it,

4

plunged along the river bank, tripped and fell with a loud snapping of branches.

"Who's there?" a suspicious voice called.

Askik picked himself up. He had scratched his hands and took care not to hurt them further.

"Is somebody there?" called the voice, now alarmed.

"*Ehé*," Askik said miserably, "*Nina*, it's me."

"Me? Who's me? C'm 'ere where I can see you. Where are you?"

The old man stood in the door of his house, one half of him red with firelight, the other half swallowed by darkness.

"*Astam outa!* Come closer!"

"I'm going to St. Boniface," said the boy, though he no longer believed it. Those stone houses had to be an incalculable distance from this godforsaken river.

"The town! At this hour? The *bourgeois* are all asleep. Are you going to wake them up?"

"Maman wants the priest."

The old man put a hand behind the boy's head and led him into the cabin. Inside, it was like a sibling of Askik's house — a hearth of rounded stones, an earthen floor, a storage chest that served for sitting on, a wooden bed with a heavy red blanket. But no buffalo robe by the fire.

"There's no children here?" Askik asked in astonishment.

"No, *mon bonhomme*," cackled the old man. He pulled on a heavy, rather greasy leather coat. He studied the boy out of the corner of his eye. He had been raised the old-fashioned way and to him it was sinful to pry into the business of others. Well, what of it? Toddlers don't go asking for priests at night without reason.

"*Astam!*"

He hooked the door carefully behind the boy. The moon was giving the river a glassy grey-blue overlay. The man took three long strides and then bent to untie a boat.

"C'mon now, get yerself in!"

The boy climbed into the boat. He had never been on water and was afraid the old man was going to send him off by himself, but the ferryman pushed off vigorously with his foot and hopped in after, then picked up the pole. Standing there against the stormy sky, he looked as big as a tree. Askik was not afraid when the wind whipped at the water and made the *tsiman* rock.

"What's the river called?"

"The Seine."

"Does it cross the Red down there?"

"It don't cross it, it empties in it."

The prow of the boat glided onto mud. A pathway came to the water's edge.

"Take that there path," the ferryman said. "It takes you to the town. When you get there, look fer a stone house by the cathedral. Wait — you seen the cathedral? Guess not. It's a big buildin' with a big bump on the roof. When you got the priest, come back. I'll take you back over. Got that, boy?"

Askik nodded and quickly scrambled up the steep path. The woods were less dense than on the other side and gave way almost at once to the prairie beyond. Funny kind of prairie. The grasses were cut short like spindly stakes. Askik was afraid for his moccasins; his mother was very strict on that score. The Métis call their moccasins "frowners" because of the design sewn on them. Askik thought it an allusion to his mother's face when she was making them.

He ran beneath the gaunt arms of a cross, through a line of poplars, and found himself among the outermost houses of the colony. He looked everywhere for the cathedral; he saw nothing but shacks similar to his own, but so many he was astonished. Could there be this many men on earth?

He came to a windy square bordered with maples. Blowing leaves and dust were raking the street and they filled Askik's eyes. When he opened them again, he beheld a miracle. As the moon came out from behind the clouds, the cathedral emerged from the darkness, its whitened walls becoming luminous, its windows glowing, its roof glinting subdued blue reflections. He heard a whispering behind him, turned and saw a dried-up hedge, and behind it a big house. It was made of stone.

He climbed the wooden steps unenthusiastically and, since he had never seen a door knocker, knocked on the door with his fist. He kept knocking and knocking. He was cold and sleepy and began to cry again, thinking that the people here weren't much interested in little boys and would probably leave him on the doorstep till morning. The ground in front of the house was a seething checkerboard of light and shadow. He knocked harder, adding weak, plaintive supplications, but to no avail; his knocking was swallowed up in the dark corridors inside, leaving the sleepers undisturbed.

At last a faint light appeared in the window. It flickered, seemed to be going away, then grew until it blazed, and revealed a horrifying thing.

There was no parchment across the window; a waxy, fluid face was looking at him from behind a ball of fire. Askik, who had never seen glass or oil lamps, turned to run away. But the great door clicked and swung open. A titanic woman stood on the threshold holding a lamp. She was in nightclothes with a shawl about her shoulders and a scowl on her face. She glared down at the intruder; the small brown face streaming with tears, the frightened-rabbit eyes, the jet-black hair, all infuriated her.

"What d'you want?" she barked.

Askik did not care, he was grateful to her for showing him a more or less human face.

"I want... the priest."

"The priest? Which one? This is the bishop's house. The e-pis-co-pal palace." She pronounced the words with head slightly thrown back, the better to savour the majesty of the place. She was proud of her position and vocabulary. "There's more than one priest here," she added.

Askik had not anticipated this eventuality. He lost his temper. "Maman wants the priest," he yapped back at her, as though it were unthinkable for anyone to defy his mother's command.

She slammed the door in his face. The light moved away and for many minutes the extraordinary windows remained dark and icy, like the Seine. Then the light returned, accompanied this time by a man's voice. The door opened, an arm sheathed in black reached out, and Askik found himself as if by magic in a room whose walls were white and smooth. Where were the logs?

There was a floor of gleaming wood, a coloured carpet, engravings on the walls, furniture covered with cloth and leather, and best of all the wondrous oil lamp, reposing nonchalantly on a small polished pedestal table, its glittering light reaching even into the corners of the room.

The housekeeper was there, glaring homicidally at the boy, but she no longer concerned him. Everything around him was novel and enchanting. He was dazzled by the bishop's vestibule.

"Just a little savage that ain't never seen nothin'."

"Madame Berthier, I beg you!" The priest's voice was older than his face. "Sit down and be patient a minute," he said to the boy.

Askik turned questioningly to the housekeeper, who translated.

"Apé! Sit down. Keyam apé! Keep still."

Obediently, Askik hoisted himself gingerly onto a chair with arms, a green cloth seat and feet like a dog's. The housekeeper, humiliated, remained standing at attention, though she could not repress a shudder of horror to think of the fleas the child was probably carrying. To say nothing of that deerskin anorak, which would surely leave a smell of smoky animal fat on the chair.

The priest returned wearing a woollen coat, and bending over the boy asked him if he had come for a priest for a sick person.

"*Ahkoseo nimouchoum*," Askik replied

The priest turned to the housekeeper.

"His grandfather's sick," she said. "A pagan, more'n likely."

The priest seemed not to be listening and began wrapping a scarf around his neck. The housekeeper, in remorse for her uncontrollable fits of temper, tried to help, but pulled the scarf so tight that the priest thrust her away to avoid being throttled. Then she tried to make amends with chatter.

"Anyways, its a shame to be goin' out at night for dyin' folks that don't never show their nose in church. Then d'you even know how to get there, *mon bon abbé*? You'd be better off t' wait till daylight. Old folks don't kick off quick as all that."

"If the boy found his way here, Madame Berthier, he knows the way back."

"Him? He's just a baby!" She added to this a quivering whimper, conveying the conviction of being unloved and unappreciated.

The priest gave parting directives from the doorstep.

"Leave a candle and matches at the door. Then put out the lamp and go back to bed. Breakfast at the usual time, Madame Berthier."

The housekeeper closed the door muttering that monseigneur's schedule wasn't going to be changed by no young whipper-snapper anyhow.

Two shadows strode through the sleeping village, the small one ahead, the tall one following, leaning into the wind. Askik had let go the priest's hand; since he was the guide, he would lead. To his great surprise, retracing his steps was easy. The houses, the poplars, the cross and the meadow were all where they were supposed to be, as manageable as well-behaved children. Askik made only one mistake, in fact, missing the path when they came to the woods. The priest thought it understandable since the night was so dark; the path must be close at hand. And indeed, Askik discovered it almost at once.

When they came to the water's edge the priest hailed the ferryman. The two adults exchanged pleasantries during the short crossing. Askik was too busy remembering the rest of the way home to listen, or he would have learned that his companion's name was Teillet, Abbé Charles Teillet.

The ferryman told them of a shorter way than the one Askik had come by. The priest arranged for his return crossing and then climbed the slope behind the boy.

The prairie was lying in wait. It attacked the line of trees the minute Askik emerged. Dry leaves crackled like grape shot. Branches clashed. His confidence wavering, Askik turned to make sure the priest was not far behind. They collided. He drew back abruptly and then was filled with shame and set out anew.

The path became grassier. Then it disappeared. The priest walked at an even pace, breathing only slightly harder than usual. Except for the rustling of his cassock, the boy would have thought he was all alone.

At last they saw the mottled glow of a parchment window; then a cabin standing in an earth yard, a barrel, a broken basket, a wooden door showing light between its planks. Askik lifted the latch and entered without looking back at the visitor. The priest was more formal, removing his hat and waiting for Askik's mother to receive him at the door. An old man was sitting on the floor by the fire, propped up awkwardly against a large wooden chest, head back, mouth open, phlegm rattling in his throat.

The clouds thickened in the sky. Okaskatano-pisim gave the prairie one last wink and covered her face for the night.

2

The housekeeper was right. The old man was not ready to decamp. He had done exactly as he pleased on earth and saw nothing to be gained from a change.

Determination availed him nothing, however. Six days after the extreme unction, death claimed him in the early hours, just as he was allowing himself a few winks after a night of vigilance.

Anita Mercredi assumed an air of mourning, more or less, but was relieved to be rid of him. Not that she lacked respect for her elders. On the contrary, she had cared dutifully for her father-in-law, had endured equally his fits of senile temper and his flashes of carnality. It was just that the old man's time had come.

Anita recruited her neighbour to assist in washing the body. Madame Gingras brought her six-year-old son to be with the two

Mercredi children, whom the inconsiderate corpse had already driven outside.

It was one of those fleeting afternoons in winter when the sky slips surreptitiously from pale to dark grey, from daylight to darkness. There was a heavy layer of snow on the ground, but since the frost had not yet set in, the children's feet were soaked. They played some improvised games at first, then squabbled from boredom, then finally gave up and loitered about by the waiting coffin of unfinished wood. It had turned cold when Madame Gingras, who was strong and corpulent, came out and picked up the coffin bodily.

"Go and play," she snapped and took the coffin inside, banging it against the doorposts. Disobediently, the children stayed lolling against the house with their hands behind their backs. Minutes later they were called inside. The old man was resting peaceably in his box, wrapped in a buffalo robe. The neighbour was giving the orders.

"Kina, you," she said to Askik, "take the other end with your mother."

Askik and his mother, not being as husky as their neighbours, had drawn the feet, but they still had difficulty lifting their end. Passing through the narrow door, both of them bruised their hands and elbows on the door frame.

They put the coffin on logs on the north side of the house.

"He'll keep better outside," Madame Gingras said, and hurried off home. Anita Mercredi had not thanked her. They both had children to bring into this world and family old folk to see off into the next. The services each provided to the other always depended on their being reciprocal.

Anita began preparing supper. She was expecting to feel pleased to have got an unpleasant job over and done with, but a germ of unease was at work inside her.

She put pieces of pemmican to melt in boiling water. Handling her knife like an axe, she chipped pieces off a chunk of the dried meat and flicked them into the pot, where they sank to the bottom. The thick brown purée bubbled, sputtering greasily. It was not the best pemmican. It had been taken too late in the season, but hunting was so poor these days, you had to kill the animals when you could find them.

Anita took the pot off the fire and put the cast iron kettle in its place. She adored tea. She poured the steaming pemmican into three crude bowls, each with a wooden spoon beside it. The Mercredi family did not live lavishly.

The children had had a whole afternoon of idleness to stir their appetites. They attacked their dishes like young sled dogs, slurping down the hot sauce and chewing their bannock with mouths open. Their mother's thoughts wandered. With an adequate supply of sweetened tea, she could spend hours in conversation with herself, silently or out loud. She would stare at a wall (never a window, she might see a shadow there) and endlessly recount episodes from her own life. She never pictured herself as beautiful or rich or respected. The lot she had drawn seemed to her quite interesting enough already.

That evening, Anita was thinking about Death. She was terribly afraid of the *tchipayuk*, the spirits of the dead. You could hear them at night sometimes, making eery sounds like the sobbing of a child, pickaxe blows on nights of frost, or a cart driver's call to his horses on a deserted road.

It was said that tchipayuk could not harm the living, but Anita was not so sure. She would shudder at the very thought of hearing one.

And yet, fearful though she was, she gave no thought to the body lying just beyond her walls. He did not worry her in the least. For her father-in-law, she had done her duty. Scolding him had become so natural that if he had appeared at the door in his buffalo robe, she would have told him off and sent him back to his box. Senile old men make poor ghosts.

There were no clocks in the house. When she became too sleepy to think straight, Anita knew the day was over. The fire was slowly going out. The children were asleep, rolled up in buffalo robes that smelled of wood smoke. The earth by the hearth was flat and warm; she would not be able to resist sleep herself much longer. Regretfully, she put away the tea in the chest that served among other things as a larder, then went to the only bed there was in the house. The covers were pulled back to allow the straw mattress to absorb as much heat as possible. When she lay down she made the bed slats creak. She snuggled herself up to her nose in the thick buffalo hair and began to doze off, but suddenly her eyes flew open wide in fright. She knew now what was bothering her; she had never before spent a night in a house without a man. For the first time she missed her father-in-law, who was lying in the dark as she was, but on the other side of the wall. There was only one way now to get to sleep, and that was to close her eyes and pretend that nothing had changed.

However, some fateful force drew her eyes to the window. Surely there was some monstrous shadow out there, and if there was not she would have to watch until dawn for fear one should come. She buried her head in the buffalo robe so as not to look, but not being able to see made her even more afraid. Was that a stirring in the air, mere steps from the bed? She expected at any minute to hear the blood-curdling scream that would find her in the midst of one of the tales of horror told by Métis storytellers.

She threw back the bedcover and looked panic-stricken at the window. The parchment showed as a grey square in the black wall. The wind was making the house creak at the joints. The poplars were whispering over the roof. Shaking and bathed in sweat, Anita pulled the cover back over her. She waited a long time for sleep to come.

3

It was Askik's first time in the church. When he entered, he uttered such an awestruck "Oh!" that the congregation had to stifle snickers. A woman muttered that it was pagans people had taken the trouble to come for. Anita heard. Not Askik. The Mercredis' cabin was so poky and dark, the cathedral so immense, and white, and luminous. The polished floor of the choir reflected the light of the tapers. Golden letters hovered over the altar. Blue reflections fell on the benches under the windows.

Anita hesitated at the foot of the central aisle. She was late. The coffin was already at the front of the church and the tapers were lit. The snow was melting off her boots, making a puddle, embarrassing her. A little water on an earth floor makes no difference, but here...!

A giant of a man in a wolf coat rose in one of the front pews and beckoned to her. Deeply grateful, Anita hurried down the aisle with Askik in tow and slipped into her brother-in-law's pew. Raoul Mercredi was considered a sophisticate by his Métis kin because he lived in St. Boniface. The cathedral and fort were familiar ground to him. He did not mind occasionally giving an uncultured relative the benefit of this experience, but liked to receive considerable gratitude for it. Anita did not disappoint him.

On his knees, squeezed inconsiderately between the two adults, half-suffocated by the fur of his uncle's coat, Askik was furious. His view of the church was blocked. If he tilted his head way back he could just barely make out the letters on the vaulted ceiling, but in this position his eyes would not hold their focus. His elders were praying and paid no attention to him. In spite, he looked at the ugly things about his uncle: the head and neck, thick as a fire-log, the strong jaw with its deep blue shadow. Raoul Mercredi had the air of a hard-nosed trader who keeps his eye peeled when the merchandise is weighed. This was exactly the way he wanted it. Twenty years of trading with the Indians had made him rich, hard, and deeply distrustful. Unlike most of his kind, he had an instinct for saving and investment. While his old cronies were still wearing themselves out on portages, he was living the life of a master in the colony.

He was not used to kneeling. He stood up on the kneeling bench; he could see better that way. The coffin with its tapers on either side was only paces away from him. The white spruce box was covered with a cloth of black brocade with silver threads.

He was turning his attention to other parts of the church when his uncle, without opening his eyes or missing a syllable of his Hail Mary, put a hand on the boy's shoulder and pushed him back down on his knees.

The congregation rose. The priest had entered. Askik was indignant to see everyone doing exactly what he had not been allowed to do moments before.

He was overwhelmed by what he saw next. A resplendent creature in dazzling robes was intoning breathless airs, turning his back to the congregation, turning around to face it, holding out his arms, crossing himself, and hiding his face against the brilliant altar cloth. Two pink-faced boys festooned in lace, hands joined before them, kept one on either side of the apparition. One of them had red hair, an ultimate miracle that dumfounded Askik. He looked anxiously at his uncle. Impassive. His mother too seemed unperturbed. *Mouchoum...* was still in his box. Everybody, living and dead, was behaving as if this vision were nothing more than natural.

And then the indescribable happened. Without any signal from the apparition, without anybody calling, *Apik!*, the whole congregation bent at the waist and sat submissively on the pew benches. Askik renewed his acquaintance with his uncle's fur coat. He had resigned himself to seeing only the heads of the faithful when suddenly, up near the ceiling, the apparition rose out of an enormous goblet of carved wood. What extraordinary ways they had in this place!

Now the priest was speaking in a normal voice, and Askik recognized him. He was his companion of the other night, the Abbé Teillet.

At first, Askik swelled with pride to be friends with so remarkable a man. Then he was disappointed that the apparition had turned out to be just a man you could walk with and be a guide for.

The priest talked a long time. Askik understood Cree better than French and was soon bored. Eventually the former apparition came down from the goblet and the ceremony continued in accordance with its mysterious rules. To Askik, the mass amounted to this: he saw nothing sitting down, his knees hurt when he kneeled, and standing up made his feet cold. During the week the cathedral was heated only enough to dispel the frost. When the people said their responses, their breath rose with the incense.

The tapers were more impressive now. The wind had drawn a curtain of snow over the whole countryside. Only an anaemic light was filtering into the church from outside, whitening the windows and fading before it reached the vaulted ceiling.

The body was taken out by a side door, not for reasons of race or rank but because the great front doors were rarely opened in winter.

"Hail, Mary, full of grace..." When he came to "Holy Mary, mother of God,..." the priest covered his face with his scarf and let the congregation continue without him. The sudden cold had crystallized the melting snow. The air was full of ice particles that stung on the skin and tinkled on the coffin. Abbé Teillet smiled grimly behind his woollen scarf. "Our cassocks are too thin and our halls too cavernous," he had said to his fellow seminarists one day in Trois-Rivières when they were grousing about being cold all the time. Pray to be spared the Red River, my friends, he was thinking now.

When they came to the grave, the pallbearers began to argue. Teillet approached and looked down, and saw that the hole was half full of snow. The other mourners arrived, wondered about the delay and complained bitterly when they learned the reason. Two grandnephews of the dead man seized the shovels left standing in the mound of earth and jumped down into the hole. Someone suggested leaving the snow and lowering the coffin down onto it, for surely it was not very deep, to which the verger objected for fear of a collapse come spring. Besides, the shovelers were making headway. Raising a minor snowstorm themselves, in fact. A few minutes more and all was back in order in the grave. The coffin hovered briefly over it, then descended, with the ropes singing through mittened hands. The box gave a hollow sound when it touched bottom. Abbé Teillet finished rapidly; his parishioners were cold. He closed his missel with a slap and signalled to the grandnephews, who had warmed themselves emptying the grave and now set cheerfully to filling it. The coffin resounded to the shower of frozen lumps of earth at first, then fell silent. In no time a mound had formed over the dead man. The crowd now scattered like leaves in the wind. "God rest his soul. We've done our duty."

The snowstorm was now well under way. Since there was no question of Askik and his mother going home, his uncle was obliged to invite them to stay. The two adults and the child walked briskly along the river road and once past the convent turned away from the river. Raoul Mercredi lived in a house of squared logs, built in the traditional manner for these parts and enlarged twice to keep pace with the growing fortune of the master. The outbuildings — granaries, warehouses, and below-ground pemmican houses — were mostly empty, which was further sign of wealth. The goods and supplies they had contained had been shipped by canoe to the Athabaska trading posts before freezeup. Raoul Mercredi, former trading post agent, onetime outfitter and illicit fur trader, had maintained lucrative ties with the Hudson Bay Company. He kept the Company's posts supplied and the Company paid in cash. He infringed the Company's monopoly by trading furs to the Americans, and the Company closed its eyes and received the benefit of his influence among the Métis. This excellent arrangement, this pooling of interests, had made Mercredi a rich man. He had just ordered new carts for his biggest ever spring harvest of hides. He had no shadow of doubt that the buffalo would be there for his benefit.

4

The storm blew itself out by midnight. In the morning, a fog had frosted the trees and was obscuring the village.

Askik shivered as he walked along the river road, eyes fixed on the few paces of deeply rutted snow he could see ahead of him. The river groaned; ice was forming. Sometimes the thin new layer cracked, the report rolling and echoing like a pistol shot.

The severe Grey Nuns' convent loomed into view by the road. A bell sounded inside.

Carelessly, Askik put his foot in a slushy hole. The ice at its surface broke and cold water seeped through the worn stitching of his moccasin. He jumped, then continued walking. His mother was going to be pleased with him now!

The fog had flattened the cathedral. All you could see of it from the road was a blue outline, as flat as a card.

The boy left the road. He walked through the churchyard, past the stone gravemarkers, and came to the wooden crosses.

A human shadow was moving about in the fog. Askik hid behind a tree. The shadow was going and coming among the crosses, bending low at every other step. A Native, Askik thought, seeing the red blanket in which the woman was wrapped from head to foot. She was gathering the twigs that the storm had scattered about on the snow. When her arms were full, she took the branches to a fresh grave on which a small fire was crackling. She scolded at the fire under her breath and went to gather more fuel. The stealth of her movements, the furtive glances she kept throwing all around, betrayed guilt. Now she sensed that someone was watching, and looking up saw the boy peering from behind his tree. Askik recognized his mother.

She beckoned. The small fire on the grave whistled and smoked with its wet twigs. When the boy was close enough to hear, she whispered, "It's to help Mouchoum see his way on his journey."

"Hasn't he gone already?"

"It ain't four days yet. The day after tomorrow, just after sunup, the time he died, that's when he'll go. He'll take the Way of the Wolf and go up to heaven.

"But *tandé* Mouchoum? Where is he now?"

Anita shrugged and gave a vague wave of her hand. While waiting for the time for his soul to rise from the earth, Mouchoum was wandering.

"Can you talk to him?" Askik asked, remembering her mutterings.

"I was askin' him not to keep hangin' round, to go to heaven now, 'cause he's been well-looked after and well-buried.

"So what if Mouchoum doesn't want to go?"

Anita said nothing. That would be all she needed.

Mother and son then went gathering twigs under the trees, and found enough to feed the flames for another hour. Finally Anita announced that it was time to go. The verger might catch them at it and tell the priests, she said.

Askik felt his cheeks grow hot. So what they were doing was wrong? The bishop's vestibule, the cathedral, the mass, all that wondrous light, returned with the sharpness of despair. He resented his mother's putting him at variance with the priests.

Anita pulled the red blanket closer about her, a gift from her sister-in-law, (who was kinder than the husband, let it be said in passing) and called Askik. He, sulking and silent, trailed far behind his mother till they were well out of St. Boniface.

5

The autumn hunt was poor. Long trains of Red River carts were seen returning half empty. Fewer carts than started out besides. A growing number of Métis families were not returning to the settlement, remaining for the winter in the wooded hill country along the American border, where game was still abundant.

Though the Métis still did not suspect as much, the buffalo were disappearing. There had been lean years in the past, and then the herds had returned more abundantly than ever. Some of the Métis believed, like the Indians, that the buffalo come up out of the earth in springtime, like the flowers and springs of water. Some years there were less. That was all. When *les hivernants*, the winterers, headed for the surest hunting grounds, they thought simply to live out a bad spell until the herds returned in force. What they were doing in truth was pursuing the frightened remains of a vanishing species.

The cart trains brought home more than meat, moreover. Packs of hungry wolves followed them to the gates of the colony and then prowled about the farms, devouring cattle and forcing the men to be exhaustingly vigilant.

Askik, oblivious to these hardships, was now going to school. His first appearance in the town had been noted. The day after the funeral, a teaching brother had called at the Mercredi house, and after a terse lecture on the necessity of education had departed with the family's elder son. Askik quickly became accustomed to the whitewashed walls of the college, and oil lamps and glass windows soon lost their fascination for him. For months to come, however, he would remain in awe of his teacher, Étienne Prosy.

Pale and wraith-like, with bad teeth and imperfect vision, Prosy looked like one of those sickly plants one finds under old bales of hay. A virgin celibate, he was imbued with excessive romanticism. He liked to go to the window in the middle of a lesson and lean in dreamy pose on the sill, gazing outside with an intensity that would melt the heart of a horse. Too bad the body did not match the sentiment. The window was so low and the teacher so tall that in this favourite pose he would be bent almost in two, pointing his bony posterior at the ceiling. No one in the class would laugh. The Métis pupils, who knew nothing of Chateaubriand or Vigny, who dreamed only of hunting and horses, were as solemnly and quietly polite toward their teacher as their fathers would be. They did not share his tastes and retained little of his lessons. Not one of them would dispute the value of history or literature, but few indeed were interested. Askik, however, was one of those few.

He had changed. His eyes and head were filled with numbers and religious images. He was not yet hoping to join the ranks of priests and teachers; his pleasure was simply to be in their shadow, burning to serve them and intolerant of the slightest opposition to their will. In his eyes, Prosy even took on the stature of a young god. And Prosy, all too happy to find a disciple in this land of two-fisted men, let the overflow of himself pour out upon the boy. He taught him the rudiments of Greek without following up, reprimanded him more severely than the others because he gave him more of his time, and kept him after class to read poetry to him. Between two tiresome poems he would slip some lines of his own, to see if the child might suddenly light up, struck with their power. Alas, the boy's face would remain impassive. Askik would listen studiously. He would be vaguely conscious of the rhyme, but could find no pleasure in this jolting speech. He made no apology for not liking poetry much; maintaining a respectful silence at such times was good enough.

For Prosy, it was good enough just to be listened to. He almost always kept his pupil very late. Askik would watch through the window as evening approached, and for all his deference toward poetry would fidget until Prosy let him go with a magnanimous but disappointed smile.

He would run all the way home. His mother did not like to be alone at nightfall. The path had grown shorter since his first excursion to the town. He knew the farms on the way to the river by heart, never mistook the path when he came to the woods, and chattered easily to the old ferryman, who for his part was no more talkative than when they had first met.

However, on the other side of the Seine was the prairie, which defied familiarity. When daylight became darkness within its vast compass, the prairie became what it always had been: powerful and inhabited. On its massive flanks, beneath the bottomless skies, what was one small child? Askik ran along the path like an acrobat on a tightrope, looking neither sideways nor upward, while all that ancient world was awakening around him.

Each night he marvelled that the walls of the house kept standing up to the winds and the spirits, for even home was no longer a safe haven. Anita, more suspicious than ever, was relying on him increasingly. Whether she looked on him as his grandfather's successor, or considered him endowed with new authority since he had been going to school, she had taken to confiding her secret fears to him and insisted on reassurance. For her, the bark of a fox, the cracking of a tree, a flare-up in the fireplace were all messengers from an invisible world.

"D'you think it's a dead person?" she would ask, her eyes as big as saucers, and the son, so as not to be frightened himself, would reply with new-found wisdom that most likely it was not. At night, while his mother snored, the six-year-old master would lie awake, listening.

In St. Boniface he was safe. There were no spirits in the clean, rectagular rooms of the college. Whenever Askik thought about the wetiko, he pictured him on the other side of the river, crouching in the underbrush, watching for him on his way home from school. It was inconceivable that the cannibal demon should set foot on the priests' domain. There were angels and demons in St. Boniface too, indeed, but they seemed a more manageable lot than the tchipayuk.

And so Askik was now leading a double life. Like a traveller who goes back and forth between two hostile countries, never speaking in one of his business in the other, every morning he crossed the frontier between the primeval and the new. He never mentioned tchipayuk in St. Boniface or poetry to his mother. He was the only one who saw prairie and town at odds.

Friday. Askik Mercredi had scurried away with his usual trapped-rabbit face. Étienne Prosy was left alone. The afternoon was quickly giving way to night. The stove at the front of the classroom, from which a stovepipe ran the whole length of the room the better to distribute the heat, had stopped roaring. The teacher did not need to put on his coat; he had been wearing it for several hours. He left the chilled room, closed the door, which had no lock, and stood for a moment on the covered porch. This porch was round like a tower and raised by ten steps. It was prodigiously admired by prairie children, who love any elevation, however slight. From the top of the steps, Prosy looked down at the colony like a judge at a prisoner. He was not in a forbearing mood. The low-lying buildings on the flat banks of the river, the black roofs against the unanimous grey-white of the prairie and sky enraged him. What paucity of imagination to live in a place like this!

The poet, muffled up as best he could, set out with heavy step. The snow crunched under his feet. The cold was painful. Less painful, however, than the sight of those dirty shacks and frozen wastes. What was he doing so far from everything that counted? For the nourishmnet of their inner lives, others could draw on cities full of grace, green country-sides, streams that really gurgled. There was not even a certain rusticity to redeem the Red River.

He loped across the courtyard of the bishop's palace, bounded up the steps in two strides and entered the building, where relative warmth reigned. He lived here by necessity; rooms to let were few and far between in St. Boniface. The vestibule was completely dark, completely silent except for a faint rattle of dishes from the kitchen.

On the way to his room, Prosy met the bursar, the Reverend Father Gervais, who was armed with a green-bound ledger of impressive size. The diminutive cleric's head was on a level with Prosy's chest.

"Is Monsieur Prosy doing us the honour of arriving in time for sup-per?" he barked in a squeaky voice, glaring at the teacher through his thick glasses.

Prosy drew himself to his full height, which was considerable.

"What a pity Monsieur doesn't apply himself as industriously to attendance at holy offices," the bursar continued.

"My work keeps me in my room, as you know."

"Ah yes, your work. Speaking of that, let me remind you that you burned three candles again last night."

Prosy turned his eyes to the window, letting a contemptuous smile play on his lips. It was too much for the bursar, who had been enduring the teacher's arrogance for weeks.

"Look at this," he cried, opening his ledger to columns of figures. "Since September you've used fifteen pounds of candle wax. The chapel doesn't use more than that! D'you think that's reasonable?"

He thrust the ledger under the teacher's nose. His hands trembled but his eyes were triumphant, the look of a prosecutor with a damning piece of evidence. It was a look that made Prosy bristle. He was letting himself get upset. He had promised himself he would not bicker with the fellow any more, but the bursar kept on.

"Monsieur cannot abide the company of simple priests, of course. Monsieur has to shut himself up alone and burn candles, while Monseigneur himself spends the evening in the common room."

The sally hit home. Prosy valued his solitude as he did his life. Without this time spent by himself in his own kingdom of thought, insanity would surely overtake him. Besides, he detested any kind of intimacy. This custom among the priests of digesting together after dinner filled him with horror. The very idea of the bursar forcing him to adopt it infuriated him. His chin trembled.

"Father," he began in a choked voice, "I remind you that I am an employee of your order, I am not a member of it. You cannot oblige me to participate in your communal life. I have not taken vows..."

"God is wise indeed."

Prosy fumed; the presumption of this dry little stick of a cleric! His fingers curled; he had to restrain himself from sinking them into his adversary's pale throat.

"Monsieur," he retorted, deliberately avoiding the humiliating "Father," "put on those airs if you like with the Métis, who cannot see through your deceitful hypocrisy, but do not, I pray you, speak to me of God. Not of the God who forbids commerce with Mammon..."

"That's not right, that's not right!" squawked the cleric, now beside himself. "I won't have you lecturing me! 'He that is faithful in that which is least is faithful also in much.' That's what the Gospel says! Freethinker! Freemason!"

"Pharisee!"

Their raised voices brought the housekeeper running. There was so little excitement in the poor woman's life. She arrived so clearly expecting to enjoy the altercation, however, that both men were ashamed and thereupon parted. Disappointed, she returned to her oven, wiping her hands on her apron.

Once in his room, Prosy rushed to the window to offer his overheated brow to the breezes, but the window was so firmly frozen shut that he had to make do with throwing himself on the bed. Staring at the ceiling, his head cradled on a bent arm, he decided he was coming down with a nervous fever. Artists beset with trials are subject to nervous fevers.

The schoolmaster was healthier than he appeared to be. When dinner time came, since the fever had not progressed significantly, he went down to eat.

6

Askik cracked an imaginary whip over twelve imaginary dogs. His sled flew through the fresh snow. The harness bells jingled cheerily over the prairie.

"*Yé!*" he shouted as he entered the turn leading down to the Seine. "*Cha!*" he barked when he came to the old boatman's cabin. He set his feet down between the runners of the sled, and leaving the dogs yapping and jingling, went to knock on the door of the cabin.

"Who's there?" called the ferryman.

"*Nina!*" replied the boy in surprise. "Askik! I want to cross."

"Well, go 'head, boy. The ice is set."

The door remained closed. Askik was perplexed.

"Monsieur Laurendeau! *Nenatawé* to school!"

"Who's stoppin' you? To the right o' the boat, the ice is good."

The boy went to the river's edge. The boat was turned upside down on logs and was gathering snow on its bottom. There were footsteps leading away across the river. Gingerly, he ventured a few paces. The snow creaked like old leather, but held. He went a little farther and then turned to look back. The bank was already far behind. What if he fell through? But this was no time to change his mind. It was as risky to go back as to go ahead. Moving only one foot at a time so as to stay as light as possible, he pushed on to the middle of the river, where the wind had bared a patch of slate-blue ice. Great white bubbles were moving about under this alarming window. Askik crossed it, lifting his feet high like a goose walking in the snow.

Once safely on the far bank, he raised his arm and brought it down sharply, shouting "*Ouiskache!*" to set his sled speeding through the woods. Through the narrow band of trees flew the sled and team. As the dogs burst into the open with their muzzles pointed toward St. Boniface, hell-bent-for-leather like twelve fleeing devils, Askik suddenly found himself face-to-face with a stranger. Dogs and bells vanished as if by magic.

The man was short, ill-dressed and ill-shaven. His moccasins were patched. His striped woollen tuque was unravelling in places. There were stains on his blue coat. His sash was faded. But he bent down to address the child with a familiarity meant to be reassuring.

"Well! A Company runner! You got far to go, little man?"

His smile showed sparse, yellowed teeth. He had the same Canadian accent as the priests, but otherwise was not at all like them.

"Where you come from, lad? The Bourbon?"

No reply.

"Farther'n that? The Rabaska, then?"

The boy nodded so as not to offend.

"From the Rabaska? I knew it! Ha ha ha! Seriously, fella, where'd you really come from?"

Pointing with his mitten, Askik indicated the other side of the river.

"Over there? There ain't many folks over there. I gotta know yer pa, lad. Hey, whacha bet I know yer pa, eh? Wouldja bet yer sled? No? His name's Jérôme Mercredi, ain't it?"

Askik started in surprise despite himself.

"Aha!" exclaimed the stranger. "That's it! Jérôme Mercredi's yer pa. He's a Company runner too, ain't he?"

The stranger had knelt with one knee on the snow and was holding the child firmly by the shoulders.

"Y'know who I am?" he demanded, shaking the boy gently. "Urbain Lafortune. You're gonna remember that name. You're gonna tell yer ma you met Urbain Lafortune, and he said to tell 'er that 'er man's gonna be home for la Saint-Jean, St. Jean Baptiste Day. You got that, lad? Yer pa's gonna be back fer the first hunt. Hey boy, got that?"

Askik nodded. The man gave him a slap on the back and stood up.

"Ha! A real li'l Méchif! Don't talk no more'n a firelog!"

When Askik had moved away several paces, the stranger called after him in a harsher voice, "Hey boy, yer pa really is Jérôme Mercredi, ain't he?"

The boy turned and nodded vigorously in reply and then fled. The stranger stood watching him for a time as though still in doubt, then disappeared beneath the trees.

The schoolyard was deserted. Askik was late. He ran up the steps of the tower and opened the first door, which led into the coat room. He hung up his leather anorak among the cloth coats; he was one of the few pupils who still dressed Indian fashion, which was deeply humiliating. Then he slipped out into the corridor between the two classrooms. The door of his classroom was ajar. He could see the bent heads of the boys and hear Master Prosy's abrupt voice. He shrank against the wall. He had never been late before. When it happened to others, which was often, they would come in nonchalantly, excuse themselves if Prosy insisted, and while he scolded would sit down as though nothing had happened. Askik could not face it. Pride and shyness made his legs weak. Yet he could not stay in the corridor, either; the big boys' schoolmaster might come out and find him. Would he go home, pretend he had been sick? His mother would not care. He was still deliberating when the door opened wide. Prosy stood towering over him, framed in the doorway against the light.

"Monsieur Mercredi, when you want to fool your teacher, you don't go by beneath his windows!" He seized the boy by the ear, dragged him grimacing into the room and deposited him roughly in his place. The other boys had turned around and were watching the scene with interest. A few snickered.

"Punctuality, gentlemen!" Prosy cried. "Punctuality! The guarantee of success is a well-ordered life. Doing the same tasks always at the same time of day, that's what gets a man ahead. Rid yourselves once and for all of that hereditary indolence of yours; it produces nothing, leads to nothing, is good for nothing. What will your future employers say if you don't get to work in the morning with the rest? Who wants dawdlers and slackers?"

Huddled on his seat, his face scarlet, Askik choked back sobs of rage and indignation. He accepted taunts and bullying without a word, but this was the first time anyone had laid a hand on him. No other pupil had been disgraced this way. It was a betrayal too, which made the insult doubly wounding; Askik was the only one to have shown the schoolmaster a kind of loyalty. When the noon bell rang, he left with the others rather than linger with the teacher as had been his habit.

7

Askik learned about counting the hours. It made the winter seem even longer. He learned to dread getting up, to watch the sun following its course through the windows at school, and to stretch out his evenings. He learned that life is divided into hours of dreary, unpleasant work and hours of leisure, the latter to be cherished and prolonged. He would wait for Sunday all through the other six days of the week. When his day off came at last he would begin it early.

Since he had begun going to school, he had also been going to mass. The fathers insisted on it. The path to St. Boniface, although it was the same, seemed more cheerful when it was not leading to the college. He would arrive in the town when the sky was still red and greet the church as it emerged from the shadows. He loved its heavy doors, the smell of candlewax and incense wafting about the icy vestibule, the little stove at the back, at which he would gratefully warm his hands. Mass began at eight o'clock as the January sun began peeking over the roofs of the houses. The dark knave lit by tapers brightened progressively as the ceremony went on. When all was bathed in white, airy light, it was time to go home.

When he opened the door of the house he would hear his mother telling him to close it quickly so as not to let in the cold. The house was dark inside; the single parchment window gave a light that was yellow and dense. The place smelled of smoke and chamber pot.

The family almost always breakfasted on sagamité, a purée of corn and animal fat. Otherwise they would make do with bannock. Bones, crusts and rind ended up in a corner of the cabin. When the pile got to be a nuisance, Askik would carry the refuse out to the coulee. The foxes and coyotes would eat what they wanted and the spring floods would carry off the rest.

Fed and warmed, Askik would take his anorak from near the fire, where he had put it to warm, and leave the house. He would follow a path beaten in the snow through the poplars to the coulee, where cliffs of snow had been raised by the wind. A few feet from the edge, he had dug a wide, deep hole and covered it with branches and snow, leaving only a small hole in the middle for ventilation: his own private house. It was round and completely invisible from the surface and its only entrance, from the coulee, could be sealed during his absence with blocks of snow. He could light a tiny fire inside with embers brought from home, about one candle power, which was enough to provide light and keep him more or less warm. He had learned the hard way that a bigger flame would cover the walls of his refuge with ice and make it uninhabitable. On the walls he had scratched pointed window shapes, as in a church. When there was a fire, they stood out in dark lines like the ribs of a vault against the glistening snow.

Here in this retreat, Askik spent his Sundays. He would go out into the coulee to gather twigs and reeds, and return to warm himself and sit daydreaming. He would watch the patterns of light and shade made on the walls by the flames and think about the future when he would no longer be a child, when he would live in a great, white house, when life would be the way it should be, straightforward, and clean, and full of light.

At night while Askik slept, others in the colony were dreaming their own dreams of a better life.

Raoul Mercredi would think about the forthcoming profits from the next hunt, and pour himself a congratulatory glass of rum.

Étienne Prosy would angrily trim a candle wick and recopy his most recent poem for a journalist friend who had not asked for it.

Anita would dream of Anita.

8

H.B.C. "Here before Christ," the Company employees used to say. There was truth in it; trade had come before Christianity to the inhospitable shores of Hudson's Bay.

The scarlet flag with white letters hung as if frozen over the squat walls of York Factory, the old Fort Bourbon under the French. It was forty-two degrees below zero, but since the sun was shining and the winds were calm, the factor had ordered the men to go out and get some exercise. Guns had been distributed to the best shots in hope they might bag something to eat other than smoked fish. So while its men stomped about on the taïga, the fort was almost deserted.

Jérôme Mercredi had had a better idea. He had found a warm fire blazing in the principal store and settled down there in a chair with his feet on the fire rail and a pipe in his teeth as if for the rest of the day.

A Company clerk, an Orkneyan, had drawn a table close to the fire and was doing his accounts with obvious ill humour. The Métis paid him no attention; in his mind, dour and Orkneyan were one and the same thing.

Mercredi was pleased with himself. He had just made the journey through the forests between Ile à la Crosse and York Factory in record time. When he was three days' journey from the coast, a terrible cold spell had set in and he had given up trying to sleep because he had to get up every ten minutes to keep his circulation going. Two days from the coast, in the middle of the night, he had been wakened by furious barking. An old, emaciated polar bear had smelled the sled dogs under the snow. Mercredi put a musket ball in the bear's haunch and the bear made off. Unfortunately he had had to shoot his lead dog, his best, because the bear had disembowelled it with a swipe of its claws.

Nevertheless, on the third Tuesday in February, which would go on record as the coldest day of the year, Jérôme Mercredi had arrived like a bolt from the blue in York Factory. The employees could barely conceal their astonishment. The factor of the post was bundled up in woollens that day despite the fire burning in his office. When he received the accounts and orders from the faraway Athabaska posts, he whistled in admiration.

"You're a devil, Mehkwedi," he said in his laboured French."

The Métis immediately had cause to feel recompensed for the cold and danger he had endured. The factor filled his tobacco pouch and ordered that he be fed and given a bed. The stores advanced him moccasins, gunpowder and shot.

Now, Mercredi stretched out his legs contentedly, warmed to the bones by the comforting heat of the fire. The store smelled of pitch, hemp, leather and tea. The smoke from his pipe rose in graceful, fragrant spirals. His eyelids closed for long minutes at a time. Sometimes he made an effort to listen to the scratching of the clerk's pen, to bursts of laughter outside, to the crackle of the burning logs. At other times he thought about the hunt he had decided to undertake in the spring. When he was in the woods, there was powerful attraction in the prospect of life on the plains, engaging in hunting and risk-free smuggling. At present he was hesitating, weighing the pros and cons. The life of a runner was hard: treacherous ice underfoot in spring, flies in summer, the cold, the blizzards and endless silence in winter. Runners died young, sapped by attrition and alcohol if not killed in a quarrel or frozen to death just outside a fort, having staggered out in a drunken stupor. Some had the good sense to escape, like Urbain Lafortune, whose example Mercredi had sworn he would follow. Still, it was not so simple as all that.

How many of the Red River Métis could walk with their heads high into a factor's office and share his tobacco? What other occupation in the world offered the satisfaction of criss-crossing the wilds, bearing the Company's colours?

"Think plenty on it," he told himself, gazing into the flames. At his son's baptism, when the priest had asked the father's profession and he had answered, "Hudson's Bay Company runner," the curé himself had looked up from his register with a look of admiring curiosity. A Company runner had a superhuman aura. In popular imagery, he was close to those roving spirits that fly over the back country, at once everywhere and nowhere, brother to the wolves. Jérôme Mercredi cherished the image. Polished it with care. He wore a hat of dark wolf fur, a buckskin coat down to his calves, and his very own mark of distinction, a *ceinture fléchée* as black as night. He was recognized in all the posts of the high country. Ha! That devil Mercredi!

Slam! The Orkneyan had closed his ledger and opened another with corresponding delicacy. He eyed the Métis with righteous indignation; the slothfulness of the brown races filled him with deep repugnance. Mercredi yawned more widely than necessary, clacked his tongue twice, and slumped further down in his chair with an "Umpff!" of self-satisfaction. The clerk returned to his calculations, muttering a little louder and faster than before and calling down the ire of all the Celtic demons on the Métis's head.

Mercredi studied his neighbour. Queer duck all the same, he thought. The Company had been recruiting personnel in the Orkneys for so long that the islands' inhabitants had come to think they had an hereditary right to employment, a privilege they were not about to share with anyone else. They were hard workers, persevering and sober. The Company had done well to choose them, but now was recruiting elsewhere, for the Orkneyan villages had joined forces to obtain higher pay. London was not amused. The Company was turning increasingly to the Métis, who were far less sober but far more accommodating. And while the Orkneyans cravenly stuck near the coast and saved every ha'penny with a view to returning to their blessed isles, the Métis roamed the whole North West for half the pay and spent their money in the Company's stores.

Mercredi got up to stretch his legs. He sauntered over to the window and looked out into the courtyard. The Company had a knack for making every post look like all the rest. The same lumpish buildings, same walls, same flagstaffs. Two gentlemen in fur coats and beaver hats were strolling arm in arm. One of them would give a familiar little pat to a cannon each time he passed it every two minutes, as if wooing its protection against the savage hordes lurking in the surrounding taïga.

"*Ouais ben*, I teenk I go sleep now," Mercredi said, turning back to the industrious clerk.

All of Scotland's most prickly thistles might have been contained in the clerk's glare. He was beyond oaths; he let a godlike resignation rise up in his breast. Since there was so little justice on earth, bring on the Judgment! The thought of watching the papist Métis roast brought a hint of a smile back to his pale lips.

"By all means. Why don't you do that?" he cooed, the better to launch the half-breed on the road to damnation.

No doubt about it, that's a queer duck, Mercredi thought. With a philosphical air, he ambled away to the bed the factor had designated for him. Generous, appreciative factor.

By good fortune, he woke in time for supper. He ran his fingers admiringly through his hair, replaited a braid, smoothed his moustache tenderly with his fingers, and went to share with the others his pleasure in knowing what a handsome fellow he was.

He met with disappointment. The dining room was icy cold, despite the cannon balls heated red-hot that were hanging at the windows. The diners were all scowling; fish was the fare, for the hunters had returned emptyhanded. The amiable Doctor Peterson had seen a lame polar bear in the distance, but thinking it best not to disturb it had decided to take refuge behind a rock. The worthy doctor was the only one to find the fish exquisite and the dining room perfectly comfortable. The others thought him mildly off his rocker.

Mercredi dined between an untalkative Englishman and a Scotch Métis who was careful to distinguish himself from the French Métis by opening his mouth only to put fish in it.

The meal did not last long. The men swallowed their lukewarm tea in silence and left for bed. Mercredi's good humour was dampened. With a twinge of wistfulness, he remembered those summer evenings in the canoemen's camps when the Métis would forget their day of toil and laugh, joke and dance fit to unhinge their ribs.

His lively imagination, however, was devising a way to brighten his stay at the fort and at the same time boost his prestige. Tomorrow, at first light, before the worthy doctor and company had scared off all the wildlife for miles around, he would slip outside, kill a bear, and offer a feast in honour of the factor.

He began chuckling into his cup. The factor would invite him to sit at the head of the long table and give a short speech of thanks, while among the diners would rise a murmur of admiration for that devil, Mehkwedi.

The two gentlemen and the factor had put down their cups and left the room. Mercredi's eye followed them to the door with such paternal goodwill that he did not at first see the chief clerk standing beside him.

"Yes, Monsieur?" he said breezily. The chief clerk, secretary to the factor, was a young Englishman with fair hair and pink cheeks. Mercredi could not help liking him.

"Monsieur Mehkwedi, you'll leave at dawn tomowwow for Nohway House. Ouah guests have pwessing wecommendations for the intendant theah. You will weceive the dispatch in the mohning."

Mercredi could not believe his ears.

"You'll take the Hayes Wiver, of course," the chief clerk continued. "We have some things for delivewy to the agent at Oxford Lake..."

"But Monsieur le secrétaire, I had a very hard journey comin' here. Gimme time to breathe!"

"I think the factah has wecompensed you well for that journey, Mehkwedi. The Company doesn't pay you to sit awound. You're a wunner, so you'd better wun. Hee hee hee! How's that fo' a pun, eh? You don't get it? I'll explain..."

Mercredi exploded.

"Don't gimme any of your damn bad jokes, *garçon*! You ain't the one that's gonna freeze 'is ass off in the bush!"

The young man with the pink cheeks stepped back a pace, visibly shocked at Mercredi's language. In London he had been advised to treat the natives kindly but firmly. The time had come to use that advice.

"Now that's quite enough, Mister McWeedy! We'll have none of that! I must wemind you that you have obligations to the Company. And advances you've weceived and not wepaid, too, I believe. In wecognition of yo'ah past sehvices I shall fohget this incident, but I wahn you, don't let it happen again. We don't tolewate that kind of behaviah , do you undahstand?"

In the eyes of this very proper young man Mercredi read that, when all was said and done, he, Mercredi, was only an unwashed Métis, only good enough to run errands for gentlemen in fur coats and beaver hats.

The chief clerk paused at the door and added, with all the dignity his twenty-three years could muster:

"I don't think it necessawy for this convahsation to weach the eahs of the factah, do you? I shall expect you tomowwow at dawn. Good night, Mehkwedi."

Mercredi and his dogs were ready well before sunup. The next to appear was the chief clerk, who handed him the important dispatches with a "Good mohning, my man" worthy of the haughtiest of London clubmembers. Then came the two gentlemen arm in arm, delighted to be seeing a real sled-dog team and its colourful driver. Finally, the factor came looking for his two visitors to take them for breakfast. As he led them away toward his quarters, he threw back over his shoulder, "Bon voyage, Mehkwedi!"

"Hee-aah! *Marche!*" shouted Mercredi, and left York Factory vowing never to set foot there again.

9

Anita, who had been afraid to be alone without a man, learned when her husband reappeared that she could do without one after all. As usual, Jérôme Mercredi returned emtyhanded. By some Orkneyan feat of magic, what he bought from the Company always exceeded the pay he received from it.

Two days after his arrival, Mercredi went to Fort Garry to ask for credit. The first buffalo hunt was approaching and he had neither cart, nor ox to pull one, nor horse, nor provisions to eat. He might have asked his brother Raoul for them, but he knew Raoul to be miserly with money and liberal with displeasure.

Askik and his father left the house around noon. It was a sunny day but the wind was still biting. The sodden prairie smelled of earth and wild grasses. Everywhere, as the snow melted, there were sounds of trickling water draining toward the river. The creek had become a torrent and had to be crossed by two logs laid across it.

The Mercredis were not the only ones on their way to the fort. At the Red River they found a small crowd waiting for the ferry. McDougall, the ferryman, was dangerously overloading his raft but still could not keep up with the demand. The colony's titular boatman had several times come close to losing his permit; his ferry was rotted, his boat leaked and he was drunk every day of the week. He claimed never to have lost a passenger.

When Jérôme's turn came to board, he announced with breezy confidence, "I ain't got a sou, garçon, I'll pay on the way back." McDougall, like a bear only half-awake, motioned to him to get on and keep quiet. The passengers, packed together in a dense square, had their feet awash the whole way.

The ferry crossed the Red River diagonally, heading upstream to the mouth of the Assiniboine. Here, at the confluence of the two rivers, stood Fort Garry.

The four-sided fort was protected by a wall of stone and beams twenty feet high. At each corner was a short, sturdy tower. There were three gates: the main or South Gate opened to the wharves on the Assiniboine and gave access to the warehouses in the fort. The North Gate was prettier and opened only for people of quality. Visitors without rank or merchandise customarily went to the East Gate. This was where the Mercredis went.

Near the gate, a small group of women and children huddled together in silence. Their buckskin clothes and woollen blankets were black with smoke. They wore no ornaments of any kind, except that the women had a trace of ochre along their hair partings. Askik pointed them out to his father, who said, "Chipewyans, down from the Bay." Askik thought he had misunderstood at first. These poor, shy creatures were Chipewyans? When his mother became exasperated with him, she would threaten to sell him to the Chipewyans, who lived on the barren lands and ate their children to keep from starving to death. He stared openly at the silent children, wondering why they did not run howling away from their mothers. He had imagined the Chipewyans to be quite different.

The walls of Fort Garry concealed another, more impressive town than St. Boniface. The high, imposing stores and the warehouses and employees' houses formed another rectangle inside the fort.

The town was swarming with people, and all of them were there for the same reason: to get credit against their take in the upcoming hunt. The Company needed pemmican for its far-flung trading posts. The Métis needed the Company's imported merchandise.

In the main store, men were crowding against a wide counter that ran all around the room and kept the customers separated from the merchandise. Clerks were coming and going between the counter and the storage shelves behind, bringing and displaying the goods requested and recording purchases. In the corner near the door was an ageing, sour-face clerk behind a wicket, to which Jérôme Mercredi pushed his way through the crowd.

"Well," growled the clerk, "you had enough of bein' a runner, Mercredi?"

"Plenty! I thought..."

"That you'd go huntin'."

"*Kah!*"

"So of course you need gear..."

"That's it!"

"Yeah, Yeah. So what all d'you need exactly?"

"Well...ever'thing."

"Everything."

"A cart, an ox, a horse, a gun, powder, shot, food, and yeah, blankets for the wife and kids."

The clerk pursed his lips. "I'll let you have the powder, shot, food," he said, "and yeah, I'll be generous, the blankets too."

Mercredi bristled. "Hey, looka here! What good's all that if I can't get me t' th' hunt? You gotta let me have a horse!"

"No horse."

"Well then, gimme the cart."

"No cart."

Mercredi looked around him despairingly, made a brusque move toward the door, turned back again and banged his fist on the wicket shelf.

"The Company owes me that stuff!"

"The Company don't owe you nothin'. Maybe you owe the Company, even. Want me t' check?"

Jérôme tried pleading.

"You can gimme a gun, that ain't too much t' ask."

The clerk pursed his lips again, as if torn between generosity and his trader's instinct.

"Guns cost a lot, and huntin''s bad..."

"I'll give you whatever price you want."

"It's the same price for everybody. All right, then, the gun too. I hope you get t' use it."

"Don't you worry 'bout that!" Jérôme laughed like a child while the clerk made out the credit note. "We're gonna bring back some cow, plenty of it," he declared. Enough to make ever'body sick."

On his way out the door, Mercredi senior did a little jig at the top of the steps. He would be back later, with a cart, to get his goods. Now to find the cart.

Father and son crossed back over the river, for free, and set off at the run for Antoine Gingras's farm. Under the trees some porous snowbanks were still hanging on. Purple crocuses were pushing through the floor of rotting leaves. As he ran, Askik kept looking for the crows that were cawing in a distant thicket.

Jérôme was mulling over the business he was going to have to do. Renting an ox and cart was going to cost him four big bags of pemmican, called "taureaux" in both French and English. Robbery. A man could make a cart himself in a week.

From a distance, Antoine Gingras's yard looked like an enormous beaver dam, such was the tangle of shafts, rails and wheels of carts. Gingras chartered cart trains plying between the colony and St. Paul in the United States.

The "King of Carts" was in the stable watching an ox being shod. Short, paunchy and ruddy-faced, straw hat pulled down to his eyebrows, he greeted the Mercredis politely.

"Heard tell you was back. Couldn't believe it. You left yer job with the Company?"

"There's more'n the Company that counts. A man wants to be 'is own boss sometimes."

"That's for sure. This your boy?"

"The oldest. Got another at home."

"*Pittaw*. Congratulations."

"*Kinanaskomitin*. Thank you. It's business I'm here for, though."

"Well, now!"

"I reckon to go with the first hunt, an' I thought you might like t' go into business with me."

Gingras dropped his chin to his chest. An unnecessary precaution; his power of concealment was total. His lips betrayed not a shadow of a smile. It was laughable just the same. Jérôme Mercredi proposing a partnership to the King of Carts? Gingras pretended to be thinking it over.

"What would be my part of the deal?"

"An ox and cart."

"All right. Three taureaux."

"Three taureaux! That's robbery!" Mercredi was surprised and delighted to be getting off so lightly. Perhaps things were less rosy for Gingras than people said. But he persisted.

"Two taureaux, no more!"

Gingras pretended to be undecided. Just so he could let it be known that not even Raoul Mercredi's relatives could afford his usurious prices, he was giving the gear away.

"All right," he said, looking defeated, "come by again tomorra. I'll have what you need then."

Mercredi was certain now that a fortune awaited him. Laughing, he wrang his new partner's hand. Gingras did not invite him to drink to the deal.

Now for the horse.

A cayuse trained for buffalo hunting can penetrate a herd, dodge charging bulls and manoeuvre close to the fat cows. In the midst of a stampeding herd of buffalo, a man's life is worth no more than his mount.

Try as he might, Mercredi really could think of no one who might lend him a horse. But since nothing in this world is gained by despairing, he found a tune to whistle and stepped briskly along to the next farm.

It was less prosperous than Gingras's, but tidier. The round-log house was on a rise of land, out of reach of spring floods. A long strip of black earth stretched all the way down to the river.

This was a disappointment. Hunters rarely have such fine fields. And indeed, when the master came to the door, Mercredi realized that here was a genuine farmer who was in the habit of letting others do the hunting for him.

The Mercredis set out once more. By now night was approaching. Convinced that he could not sleep a wink without having his equipment complete, Jérôme quickened his pace. Not far away there was another farm where he had never been, but where there might well be a spare horse.

Minutes later they saw the grey end of a house through the trees, and an orange glow from a window. The yard was empty. The door was closed.

Jérôme knocked heartily. A woman came to the door, a naked child clinging to her leg. She was beautiful, perhaps twenty-five, well-rounded without being heavy, hair black and shiny, teeth white and even, a coppery complexion. But her patched and faded clothes showed that he had knocked at the wrong door again. Poor people do not have fine horses.

More children came to cluster about the woman, filling the doorway. Not one of them seemed to have a complete set of clothes.

"*Tansé*," Mercredi began, "is yer husband here?"

"No, he's gone."

"Can me'n the boy wait fer 'im t' come back?"

"He ain't comin' back."

"Oh..."

Mercredi cleared his throat. Though it was pointless to continue, he did anyway.

"Y'see, I need a horse for the hunt. Would you have one to rent?"

The woman did not react to the absurdity of the question. She simply looked down at the little heads clustered around her. Mercredi stepped closer, leaned a hand on the door frame and with a flirtatious tip of the hip assumed a less businesslike air.

"So's somebody goin' huntin' for you this summer?"

"No." She spoke softly. Though she kept her eyes on the ground, she did not seem troubled.

"How d'you manage with so many kids? You gotta have a man to feed all them. You got family hereabouts?"

"No."

A small girl, dressed a little more warmly than the other children, appeared from behind the house with an armful of deadwood. She stopped short when she saw the strangers but showed no more emotion than her mother.

"So you ain't from round here?" Mercredi pursued.

"From St. Laurent," the woman replied.

"Yer husband too?"

"Yes."

"He's gone back there?"

"I don't know."

Askik, still standing in the middle of the yard, was extremely uncomfortable. The little girl with the wood kept looking at him, saying nothing, making no faces, totally impassive. She had slightly dusky skin, hair the colour of café au lait, brown eyes. There was a smear of mud on her cheek. She was wearing a clumsy hooded cape that showed a cotton dress so worn, so thin that in places the cloth had simply vanished.

"So what d'you live on?" Jérôme had forgotten about the horse. Instinctively, he smoothed the hair at his temple as he moved closer.

She did not reply. Mercredi now ventured the clincher.

"Mebbe I could bring you back a little somethin' from th' hunt, eh? Think you could use that?"

"Ehé."

Mercredi smiled broadly and put a hand to his moustache. For the first time she raised her head and looked him straight in the eye. She did not smile but did not seem displeased either.

"In fact, I'll come by tomorra on m' way back from the fort. I'll bring a bit o' tea. Mebbe some sugar even. Wouldja like that?"

"That'd be nice."

"Good, good. Well, now, it's late. I think we'll be gettin' on home. C'mon boy."

Askik gave the little girl in rags a last defiant look, which she did not return. He and his father strode out of the yard, two men with business to attend to. When they had gone a little way, Jérôme turned back toward the house, which he was beginning to consider half his already. He was startled to see that none of the family had moved a muscle, the mother, children, or the little girl with the wood; they were all still watching in complete silence. Jérôme gave a quick, abbreviated wave and walked on, muttering to himself, "Queer one, all the same..."

But the thought of coming back the next day brought the smile back to his face. Whistling his favourite jig, he set his course for the Seine and commended himself for a day well spent.

Arriving at the river, he bellowed loud enough to wake the fish, "Laurendeau, c'm here!" The ferryman never hurried, and even less when asked to. He came at his own sweet pace.

"You plastered, Mercredi?"

"Not a bit," Mercredi replied jovially, "ain't got a drop in m' body."

When they reached the other side, the old boatman took them to his cabin without a word. He found an earthenware crock, uncorked it and put it on the trunk, then sat down Indian style.

"I swear I ain't drunk," Mercredi protested, "but if yer invitin' me t' take a drink, I'll drink t' yer health."

Laurendeau took out his pipe and packed it methodically. When a man fills his pipe it means he is ready to listen. Mercredi recounted the events of his day in detail: the Red River crossing at the hands of McDougall, his victory over the parsimonious clerk, the really shameful deal he had put over on Gingras, and finally the more nebulous one he had struck with the beautiful stranger.

All this took some time. When it was over, Laurendeau knocked out his pipe on the edge of the trunk.

"If I got it right," he concluded, "you got no cayuse. If you got no cayuse, how you gonna feed yer girlfriend?"

Mercredi stared at him for a moment, looking foolish, realizing the truth that he still had no horse. Not that he had forgotten; the seriousness of it had temporarily escaped him.

"I'll find one," he declared.

"The hunt leaves day after tomorra."

"Yeah, yeah, but there's gotta be one horse left in the colony." There was a note of panic in his voice.

Laurendeau prepared a new pipeful of tobacco and, bending over it, added reflectively, "Seems Ormidas Choquette got hurt huntin' this afternoon. Got shot by accident, seems like."

Jérôme was not listening. He was wrestling with a terrible problem. Without a horse, he could not go on the hunt on his own account. And he was going to need a great deal of meat to repay his debts, feed his family, feed the beautiful stranger's family, and smuggle some to the Americans. He was about to wish he still had his job with the Company when Laurendeau repeated, louder this time:

"I said Choquette got hurt"

"Whazzat?"

"Choquette can't go on the hunt."

Mercredi was already on his way out the door. He stopped to call back from outside, "Keep the kid till I'm back. He won't give you no trouble."

Askik was left alone with the boatman, who sniffed noisily, spat, and returning to his pipe growled, "Shut the door."

Having crossed to the other side of the river once more, Mercredi ran like a hare. Sweat and alcohol were muddling his vision and his heart was thumping, but he kept going. His arrival at the Choquette house was greeted by thunderous barking. A large watchdog planted its teeth in his pants, but he sent the hound flying into the shadows. The dog was returning to the attack when the door of the house opened. Mercredi entered. He offered to supply the family with meat in exchange for which the family would lend him its horse. Choquette, lying in bed with his thigh wrapped in bandages, took some time to decide. Mercredi's reputation as a buffalo hunter was still to be made, and his manners left something to be desired, but the hunt was about to begin. In the end, urged by his wife, the wounded man gave in.

Choquette had nine children; Mercredi had incurred an onerous debt with this new agreement. Still, the former runner had had such a really superb day that there was no doubt in his mind that he could feed all St. Boniface all by himself.

10

The rain fell as though the heavens had opened never to close again. The cart train — two hundred carts, six hundred men, women and children — had halted in a small wood, of which not much was left; firewood was getting hard to find. The children were hungry. All over the camp, their wails rose from the sodden, smoke-filled teepees. Everything inside was wet and dirty. The women cooked wild turnips and reed tubers. The men sat all day long staring through the streaming entrances of their hide-covered dwellings. Once in a while the weather would seem to be clearing, usually to the west, and the news would sweep the camp, a wave of hope. The curtain of rain and fog would lift slightly, revealing a tree or butte previously unseen, then reclaim the territory so briefly glimpsed and once more close it off to the camp.

On the morning of the tenth day, the Prairie Council met as usual. The twelve councillors, all respected hunters elected by their peers, were the judges and generals of the group. They controlled the activities of the camp. They had not been able to agree for several days. Some wanted to break camp and head north to the Pembina River, where the people would find wood to keep themselves warm. The rest, the majority, advocated staying put, waiting for better weather, then proceeding south in search of the great herds of buffalo. The whole camp waited in silence. The people too were divided.

The Council meeting dragged on. Toward the end of the afternoon, teenage boys posted outside the Council teepee reported that the hunters from St. François were threatening to go their own way. At this news the six hundred Métis were more depressed than ever. It was a serious thing to divide the camp, a violation of tradition, a guarantee of ill fortune. The taboo dated from the time of the wars between the Métis and the Sioux, when the Red River hunters never ventured out on the prairie except in strength.

That evening, a cold wind broke up the fog. Askik left the camp with other children in search of fuel for the fires. Normally the Métis burned buffalo wood, dried dung, but the rain had made it unusable, so the children were looking for buffalo bones left from previous hunts and scattered by wolves. Askik had found only one porous vertebra when he heard a voice say, "There's bones over there."

He turned and saw the little girl of the other evening. She was wearing the same blue hooded cape and looked no cleaner than when they had first met. She pointed to a clump of trees in the distance and repeated, "There's bones over there." Askik just stared at her, speechless with surprise. Impatient, she stepped forward and knocked the vertebra out of his hand. "*Astam!*" she commanded.

They set out together. It took them a half hour to reach the poplar grove. It seemed a very long way to Askik; he was afraid the fog would close in again, although he did not dare admit it to his companion. He sensed that she was older and above all more strong-willed than he. As they aproached the trees, he saw that the grass beneath them had not been trampled, which he thought odd. They searched in the grass and found an almost complete buffalo skeleton. A wounded animal must have come and hidden under the trees and died here.

As he gathered an armful of bones, Askik watched the girl out of the corner of his eye. When her face was turned away, he asked his question point blank.

"When did you come here before?"

"I didn't never come here before."

"How'd you know there was bones here, then?"

"I knew."

Askik let the matter drop. Remembering their last meeting, he asked, "Is your maman with you?"

"No, I'm workin' for the Gauthiers."

Askik said nothing. He was impressed. He had never earned a penny himself and this girl already had a job. Bending low, arms hidden to the elbows in the grass, she was working quickly, throwing the bones into a pile behind her.

"How old are you?" she asked without straightening.

"*Tebakop.* Seven."

"You still live with your parents?"

Askik was mortified but had to admit that he was still living like a little boy.

The girl lifted a bundle of bones, perfectly sorted and tied. When Askik stood up, half his bones fell at his feet. Calmly, the girl put down her bundle and remade his. Once all was ready they set out for the camp. When they came to the edge of the trees Askik uttered a cry of despair.

"*Ahuya!* I knew it was too far!"

The fog had closed in again. Night was falling.

Nothing deceives more completely than a prairie fog. Earth and sky are indistinguishable. Things that seem far are close. What looks familiar is not. You run from landmark to landmark and recognize none of them. Métis children lost in a fog would not infrequently stray away from the camp and be eaten by bears.

"We should wait here," Askik said. "Papa will come and find us."

But the girl walked off with confident step, erect despite her load of bones, her hair streaming behind her.

"Not that way!" Askik cried.

But she replied, "*Astam!* Come on!"

Half an hour later they saw the hide-covered tents and the ravaged wood. Grimy smoke hovered among the teepees. The girl stopped abruptly and turned to Askik.

"If you need *nina*, I'm in the third teepee from the end. Then she introduced herself: "Mona *nitissinihassoun*." She pronounced it "Mounna," in the Métis fashion.

Askik blinked stupidly and nodded. She walked away, taking her bundle of bones to her employers, head high, cape slapping vigorously against her bare, grubby legs.

The next morning, though the drizzle continued, the hunters from St. François and St. Paul left the camp. Those remaining watched them leave apprehensively or enviously, but everyone knew that an era had passed; the Métis of the old days would have avoided the breakup.

Two days later the sun showed its face, making brief appearances at first. Then it stayed. The diminished cart train pushed on south-westward over increasingly difficult terrain. The rich prairie of the Red River gave way to a meagre layer of soil over sand-covered rocks. The scouts' horses came home with ragged hooves. The prairie, no longer flat, rose and fell in impressive green and brown waves. In the hollows, swamps and sloughs defied passage and forced numerous detours. The grass was shorter and sparser in this parsimonious soil; the oxen and horses took longer to graze.

There were ducks nesting in profusion in the hollows, but since the Métis had no shotguns and had not learned to shoot birds on the wing, they did not catch many.

The farther the column went, the higher rose the hills and buttes. Some of the elevations had crowns of bare rock. Sometimes, in early morning or at dusk, antelopes and muledeer appeared at their crests, profiled against the sky. The hunters brought home only a few of them. A swift horse was needed to take this game, and it was impossible to kill more than one antelope at a time. Since meat taken en route had to be divided among all the teepees, each individual received next to nothing from these meagre kills. Only the slow, heavy buffalo could feed such a throng, but there were none to be found. The Crees and Sauteaux accompanying the Métis said that Moustous had gone back underground. At night they made the camp ring with their songs and drumbeats, imploring Kitché-Manitou, the Great Spirit, not to let his prairie children perish.

For famine was now close by. Reeds and turnips were not enough. Rose hips were hard to find. Sometimes the children would catch a prairie dog, but this required a lot of patience and yielded little meat.

One afternoon of torrid heat that muddled one's vision as well as one's thoughts, when it was more than high time they should have found some "wild cow," a scout appeared on a hillcrest and gave a triumphal cry as he spun his foaming horse.

The young Wolf had found a herd of a hundred animals moving westward, a half-day's ride away. They seemed jittery. Thomas Legardeur, the Métis leader, frowned to hear this report. Ain't no sure bet, he thought. A spooked herd could move fast. Not so his carts.

Despite the hunters' increasing frustration, Legardeur waited until evening, hoping for news from the other scouts. Perhaps the herd sighted was a breakaway fragment of a larger one. But when evening came and the last Wolf had returned, he called the Council together. The twelve councillors heard the scout's description of the herd's location. Men who knew the country well were called and questioned. These illiterate hunters had prodigious visual memories. Piecing together the buttes, thickets and ravines remembered by each, the Council charted the countryside and formed a plan of attack.

Although the moon was already high, the flag had not been lowered. The whole camp was standing by. The oxen remained unhitched but were wearing their harnesses. The horses, lightly watered and fed, were not asleep. At long last, after a time that seemed endless, the crier emerged from Legardeur's teepee and announced the Council's orders.

The Wolves set out again at once to pinpoint the herd. The hunters, divided into two groups, would ride all night so as to be in position to attack at daybreak. The carts would arrive around midday and the butchering of carcasses would begin.

The ten captains and their soldiers galloped about the camp, shouting to the men to hurry. In the Mercredi teepee, confusion reigned. The gun, the saddle, the bullets, all the equipment so carefully stowed and cherished for weeks had somehow managed to slip into the farthest, most inaccessible corners of the cart. Jérôme was beside himself. His flustered wife was turning everything upside down and defending herself resentfully.

"Where'd you put the horn, mother?"

"I ain't touched it!"

"And my food bag, *tandé?*"

"Look under the big pot."

"Under the big pot? *Ahuya!* What kinda place is that?"

"You're the one gets everything in a mess."

"*Nina? Nina?*"

A captain spun his horse near the cart.

"Mercredi! Get movin' or we'll leave without you!"

"Askik," Jérôme yelled, "where's my gourd?"

The Choquette horse peevishly laid back her ears. The uproar was getting on her nerves. Jérôme flung himself into the saddle, jerked on a rein and disappeared with a fairly convincing "Hee-yaa!" Having spent his entire youth in canoes and behind dog teams, however, he was an indifferent horseman.

The first carts were already pulling out. The hunters gathered outside the camp to hear the plan of attack. It was thought that the herd would spend the night in a bowl with a coulee on one side and lines of hills around the other three. One group of hunters, led by Lelièvre, would cross the creek and ride up the ridge to the west. The other, under Legardeur, would ride down from the ridge to the north.

It was a crime to shoot before the signal was given. This was a law known to everyone, but a reminder before the year's first kill was thought opportune.

In June the sun never sleeps, the Métis say. It never gets totally dark. The horses were able to move at a trot, sometimes a canter. The uneven ground caused them to stumble from time to time, however. This put the Choquette horse in very bad humour. She would add a well-timed buck to each stumble in hope of unseating her inexpert rider, dip her head abruptly to pull the reins from his hands, and snort violently to loosen the saddle girth. Jérôme was not unaware of his mount's evil intentions, however, and was vigilant.

He was sorry now to have spent all his youth in the forest. He felt inferior. The Métis were the best horsemen in the world. The Americans of the North wanted to hire them for their war against the Southerners, the English wanted to send them to fight in South Africa, and some do-gooder had even dreamed of taking them to Mexico to liberate the poor. Mercredi was unhappy not to be as fearsome as his companions.

After riding for three hours, the Lelièvre group stopped to rest. A few of the horses began to nibble grass; most were tired and stood motionless with their heads drooping. The men lit pipes but not a fire, and sat smoking and calculating the distance they had covered. It was a fine night. A raw wind blew down from *Natakham*, the Land of Waters. The sky was clear, the prairie grasses rustled pleasantly. The men savoured the pleasure of being many and powerful in the night's immensity. After some brief talk in hushed voices they fell silent, faces turned to the wind, eyes blinking from the tobacco smoke, hands dreamily clutching their guns. The starry vault of the sky dipped slowly westward. There remained perhaps two or three hours of darkness.

Lelièvre stood up. "*Tetapitanne*, on your horses," he ordered quietly.

The spell was not broken. On the contrary; the horses seemed to be sharing the peacefulness of the moment with their masters, allowing themselves to be mounted without snorts or whinnies. No one was figuring the time or the distance now. The party had entered the buffalo's orbit.

The sun was rising. Meadowlarks and kildeers were calling to one another from one butte to the next. A herd of pronghorn antelopes appeared briefly on a hillcrest, then dispersed as if by magic. The hunters pressed on, hands ice-cold, thighs warm against their mounts, nostrils full of the smell of sagebrush and horse.

In the distance the men could see two ridges and a line of willows suggesting a creek. Was this the place? Two weary scouts trotted slowly to meet them. They said the buffalo were still in the bowl where they had spent the night.

To cross the coulee, the men were obliged to dismount and coax their horses across. The Choquette horse went willingly enough, which allowed Mercredi not to look foolish. Both Mercredi and the horse had trouble climbing the steep, crumbling bank on the other side, however. Once the party was across, Lelièvre struck out for the west butte, keeping to the hollows as much as possible.

The sun was almost yellow when the men caught sight of the buffalo, a small brown patch on the green and yellow carpet of the prairie. Jérôme Mercredi poured powder into the muzzle of his gun, put a ball on top and rammed it. Only the first shot was rammed. Once the attack had begun, recharging had to be done in the saddle, where using a ramrod was impossible.

The hunters were ready, holding their muskets upright, butts propped on their thighs. Lelièvre kept waiting. He had pulled out a telescope and was scanning the north ridge, cursing to himself. Where the devil was Legardeur? Each moment lost increased the risk of something going wrong. A whinney too much, a ramrod dropped on a stone, an accidental shot could frighten the herd and stampede it beyond the reach of the tired horses. At last Lelièvre saw a horseman, then two, then sixty lining up silently across the north ridge. He put his telescope away. When he saw the line in the distance begin to move, he brought his raised hand down and his line moved off also. Across the whole front of horsemen, there was not a murmur. Total silence was the absolute rule. Lelièvre signalled threateningly to a few youngsters who were brashly getting ahead of the others; they fell back into place. When the line reached the foot of the hill, Lelièvre spurred his horse to a trot. For Jérôme Mercredi, this pace was the most painful. Out of the corner of his eye he saw the Legardeur group advancing on the other side of the bowl. He shot an anxious glance at his neighbour, who returned it. Were Legardeur's men going to reach the herd first?

The cows and calves were still grazing at the bottom of the bowl, but a large male, alerted by ground vibrations, had raised his nose. The wind told him nothing. A buffalo has sharp ears, however. Shaking his massive head, the bull gave an angry growl, stalked halfway around his herd, stopped dead and snuffed the air, then broke into a run. The other males formed a cirle around the cows and calves, pawing the ground and snorting loudly. The whole herd began to turn slowly like a huge wheel, bellowing and bawling, then suddenly broke into a run toward the south-west. Too late. The horsemen were only twice musket range away and closing fast. It was now that skill would tell.

Jérôme slipped a handful of bullets into his mouth, taking care not to swallow any accidentally. He gave the horse her head as he searched for a good fat cow. Picking one's animal in the cloud of dust was not easy.

The first shots rang out to the east. They were ahead of us, the bastards, Jérôme thought. He saw a heavy cow running hard to his right, took off after her and narrowly missed colliding with another horseman who had chosen the same target. The two men glared at each other, mouths full of bullets. Mercredi spurred his horse straight for the cow and slipped between two young bulls, which seemed not to notice him. The dust was suffocating. The cow's fat rump was drawing closer. When he was only a few feet away, Jérôme lowered the musket barrel, aimed behind her ribs and fired. The cow collapsed, blood spewing from her mouth. The superbly-trained horse swerved abruptly to avoid her, taking Jérôme by surprise. He felt himself rise from the saddle. He was falling! His right foot groped for the stirrup but his knee had now slipped under the horse's belly. He clutched at her mane and heaved himself back into the saddle. He had very nearly swallowed a bullet!

Now he was in the middle of the stampeding herd. Across the mass of brown humps he could see the shadows of other horsemen galloping through the dust. He lifted the barrel of the musket, poured some powder down it, spat a ball in after it, tapped the butt on his saddle to seat the wet ball in the powder, and searched for another victim. There was a young cow running with head down on his left. He was separated from her by some calves and bulls. He considered shooting over their backs, but it was risky when the bullet had not been rammed. He should get closer. He manoeuvred through the herd, looking for openings, threading his way among the animals. A big bull touched his leg with its horn. Little by little Jérôme approached his target. He had to drop the rifle barrel and fire immediately, before the bullet rolled too far from the powder. Oh, the beautiful cow! His eyes caressed the sandy fleece, saw the flesh throbbing, there behind the ribs where the bullet would enter. His finger curled around the trigger.

Then the cow disappeared. Jérôme took too long to realize what was happening. His horse fell into the void with a cry of terror and crashed onto the seething heap of animals at the bottom of the coulee. The bellows were deafening. The ragged banks were crumbling. Shots kept ringing out. Jérôme picked himself up out of a muddy stream. Hoofs and horns were flailing the air all around him. A gigantic brown cataract was pouring over the edge of the coulee, crashing to the ground with grunts and cracking sounds. The animals that were getting up were charging about on either side of Mercredi, droves of them scrambling up the crumbling banks and falling to the bullets. Only a few reached the crest and disappeared. Others rushed this way and that like crazed bees in the bottom of the coulee, lunging at anything that moved, trampling, disemboweling even their own calves.

The thundering of musket fire and hoofs went on a few minutes longer, then suddenly it was over. There were sounds of animals breathing their last. A crow cackled. Willows cheerfully waved their branches. Bit by bit, the astonished men gathered speechless in a line on the bank and looked down at Jérôme Mercredi. Never, never had they seen anything like it.

The buffalo lay in confused heaps, their thick brown pelts filthy with blood and grey mud. And amid the dead and dying animals, Jérôme stood with arms dangling and dazed eyes peering from his muddy face, as motionless as a picture of Daniel among the lions. He had seen the buffalo returning beneath the earth, the plunge of souls into hell, and was not yet sure he had survived.

When the carts arrived early in the afternoon, Mercredi's adventure was the talk of the day. Anita quickly grasped the important part: her husband had killed only one cow, the gun had been retrieved in two pieces and the Choquette horse had been caught but was lame. Jérôme, however, wanted none of his wife's whinings; he himself was still dazzled by his miracle.

The men had begun the butchering. They placed a buffalo on its front knees and stretched the back legs out behind, removed the hump first (a delicacy), then slit through the hide all the way down the backbone. The women cut the meat into strips and took it back to the new campsite, where they lay it to dry on green-wood racks. They built smoke fires to drive away the flies and hasten the drying. The children carried gourds of water to the men, who were streaming with sweat as they worked. Some of the men chewed buffalo muzzle cartilage to lessen their thirst.

When evening came, they left the coulee. The camp had been pitched at the foot of the line of hills. Humps and tongues were roasting over wood fires; the Métis were going to have a feast.

Since he had only one cow to butcher, Jérôme Mercredi had spent most of the afternoon finding another gun, which he bought for a quarter of meat. He therefore had only three quarters left, yet he thought this sufficient to allow him to entertain for dinner. He invited two other families from among the least fortunate in the camp. Oscar Ferland had killed only one heifer, for his rifle had exploded on the second shot, a frequent accident during these hunts when reloading had to be done by guesswork. Louison Champagne, a tightlipped, violent young man with a wife and a baby that was not his, had returned emptyhanded. His horse had fallen at the very beginning of the run. He had refused the invitation at first, thinking it motivated by pity. He accepted when he learned that his host had a plan to compensate him for his bad luck. The men stretched out on their blankets and smoked their clay pipes while the meat cooked.

Meanwhile, Askik was battling the mosquitoes at the bottom of the coulee. His mother had sent him to draw water for supper. Others had been there before him and the flat banks of the stream had been turned into a muddy mire. He could not get near the water without sinking in to his knees. He walked a long way looking for a firm footing. The coulee's bed was a tangle of rushes and willows. It was dark down there. At every few steps, red-winged blackbirds would rise, chattering furiously, and flap over the head of the intruder, then settle back down among the rushes when he had moved far enough away. The mosquitoes traced zigzags in the sky. Try as he might to drive them off, they kept attacking his shoulders, neck and ankles.

He was getting to firmer ground. The bank was now a little higher off the water. The boy approached the stream, hoping to find a promontory from where it would be easy to fill his bucket. He was parting the rushes in front of him as he walked and suddenly stumbled into a dark, hairy body.

He jumped back, dropped his bucket and scrambled away as fast as he could go. But the buffalo was dead. A young male, lying on its side. It had not been spread out for butchering; either the hunter had found a better carcase or the wounded animal had come and died here out of sight. Its eyes were still shining. Its blue, swollen tongue showed between its yellowed teeth. There was a little blood clotted on its lower lip.

Askik returned slowly, watching the animal, ready to run at the slightest quiver. But the buffalo was truly dead. Its legs were curled up in running position. Its muscles had hardened under the skin. Its belly was distended.

Askik had seen carcases before, surrounded by men, being twisted, pulled, skinned, cut into pieces. But never left alone. Never still. Never so absolutely still. The stiffened muscles filled him with wonder. How could this buffalo be so inert? Was there nothing left of its strength? Not even enough to make a nostril quiver, or an ear twitch? Had life drained out of it all at once?

Askik walked around the carcase and dipped his bucket in the water. He had to try several times because the soft leather kept flattening against the surface of the water. He was lifting the bucket out three quarters full when, at the other side of the coulee, he saw a pair of shining eyes, which blinked out immediately. A grey shadow slipped quick as lightening into the willows. The wetiko? Other long, swift shadows were moving silently along the opposite bank. *Mahikanak!* Wolves! Askik looked quickly along his side of the gully. Nothing was moving there. Carrying his bucket, he retraced his steps, making as little noise as possible. He had reached the foot of the coulee's side when he heard a series of loud splashes behind him. The wolves had located the carcase and crossed the stream. Once up on the prairie again, he thought he saw dozens and dozens of grey shadows on the other side of the coulee, hurrying to the charnel house down there at the bottom.

The fires of the camp flickered brightly against the dark hillside. Askik moved along as best he could, the bucket hitting his legs, his arms aching. As he entered the camp, he thought he saw Mona working near a fire, but kept on without speaking to her. He was ashamed to be carrying his bucket so clumsily.

"You took your time about it!" his mother exclaimed when she saw him. He had better things to do, however, and went at once to find his father. Jérôme was smoking with his guests. His face darkened when his son announced that he had found a dead buffalo and that the three men could still butcher it if they hurried.

"The Métis don't eat carrion," he said abruptly.

"But it was killed *anouhsse*, today!" Askik insisted.

"Bull don't digest so good. Don't you worry, *monhomme*, we'll find cow, plenty of it."

Jérôme turned back to his guests to resume his account of the morning's events, but Askik's determination was growing.

"If you don't find no more *bôfflo* at least you'll have this one," he said.

Jérôme was angry now. Was he going to butcher an animal spurned by another hunter? Admit to everyone that he was incapable of shooting his own meat?

"Askik, *awasse!*" he snapped.

He turned back to Champagne and Ferland. "Is Legardeur God the Father?" he said to them in Cree. "Who put the bourgeois over us? They talk French, they can read, so does that make 'em better hunters? Long as they lead the hunt, they get ever'thin' and we get nothin'."

The "bourgeois" in Red River parlance were the Métis who were most like the Whites, sending their children to school, practising a single religion and working the soil. Thomas Legardeur was a bourgeois. Jérôme Mercredi was not.

"Legardeur don't need buffalo to get through the winter. He's got stuff to live on at home already. But what are we gonna do if we don't find no buffalo, eh? Boil bark? Suck our fingers? 'Course not. We'll work for Monsieur Legardeur. It figures. For starvation wages, that figures too. We'll be eatin' bannock an' snow.

Champagne and Ferland remained impassive. Mercredi had promised them a plan. They were waiting for it. The preamble was a bit long, but the Métis are patient folk.

"There ain't no more *bôfflo*," Jérôme said finally in a hushed voice. "I knowed that this mornin' in the coulee. I dunno how t'explain it. I seen the buffalo fallin' like rain — gave me a turn, I can tell you — and I heard like a voice talkin' inside o' me. Ehé, a voice tellin' me, 'These are the last of the race'."

"Was it in Cree or French?" Ferland interjected.

"French. Edjercated French."

"Oh," Ferland said, leaning back against the cart again, although nothing was proven.

"Then what?" Champagne wanted to know.

"There ain't no more buffalo," Mercredi repeated. There'll still be little herds like the one today, but that ain't no good when there's so many families. We gotta do like th' Indians o' the North, break up into small groups." And speaking more softly still, he leaned toward his neighbours and said with an air of finality, "Follow me. We'll go by ourselves; I'll take you t' find cow."

Ferland and Champagne exchanged astonished looks. That Mercredi should have a vision was not so surprising. The best hunters

49

dream of their prey, everyone knew that. But Mercredi was no great hunter; why would the *manidos* do him such a favour?

"How you gonna find cow?" Ferland asked.

"I got guidance. Them that follows me will eat."

"What about the rest?"

Mercredi looked down at the ground and kept silent.

"What?" breathed Ferland. "All of 'em?"

Mercredi said nothing.

"You sure you can take us to the buffalo?" Ferland persisted.

Silence. The time for explanations was past. Champagne believed. A murderous manner is no guarantee against credulity.

"When do we go?" he asked.

"It ain't allowed," Ferland objected.

"The St. François bunch left."

"They followed their *okimaw*."

"*Pittaw!* Mercredi's gonna be our *okimaw!*"

The individual in question kept his eyes fixed on the ground. Ferland was wavering.

"There ain't no rush," he said at last. "Hafta let the cherries ripen."

Champagne's face twisted with anger. Mercredi was about to protest but the roast was ready. The palaver was postponed. The men unsheathed their knives and helped themselves straight from the spit, cutting thick slices of meat from the surface so as to let the rest roast some more.

After dinner, Askik climbed up on the cart to look at the fires of the camp. There were at least fifty, turning the teepees orange and laying out ceilings of smoke at their peaks. Cries and laughter rose all around. It was irresistible. Askik scrambled down from the cart and went wandering about the camp.

In front of each dwelling, jovial faces were lit up by a great fire with its charge of meat. The grownups sat in a circle around the fire. The small children ran back and forth around them but did not venture beyond the firelight's reach. The adolescents flitted from one teepee to another, appearing and fading away in the darkness, trying to scare each other.

Askik went to look at all the fires in turn. Each was an island surrounded by darkness. In the dark spaces, dogs lay gnawing on bones, poles were there to trip the unwary and bullies waited for victims to pummel. On the shadowy fringes of the camp, elusive as phantoms, lovesick adolescents waited for girls who never came. Grandmothers were keeping a sharp eye on granddaughters.

The Sansregrets were the camp's biggest family. There was much animation around their fire. Children came from other teepees to join their circle. Brown faces and jet-black hair reflected the glow of the fire.

"What's the moon made of?" one of the littlest asked, pointing up at *Tipiskawi-pissim.*

"Nothin' at all!" exclaimed a waggish fellow with a beard. "It's *Nokoumisse,* the grandmother who went up to the sky to keep an eye on us."

"Get on with you!" a woman protested laughingly. "D'you wanta make a pagan of my little boy?"

"The moon's a world like this 'un," ventured a hunter of more serious bent, "but its ground shines instead o' bein' black."

"What makes it shine?" the same child asked.

The hunter begged off with raised hands. An explanation was offered by another.

"Well, I heard tell it's a great big rock flyin' through the air."

"*Tché!* Ho, ho, ho!" A torrent of laughter and sarcastic remarks fell on the theorist's head.

"You ever see a rock that flies?"

"It don't fly very fast."

"We'll see if there's a ricochet," a young joker cried, aiming his gun at the moon.

"No, no, no! *Tcheskwa!*" shouted the others, feigning terror. "The bullet will come back at us!"

"But what's it made of?" the same little voice asked.

"Mouchoum! Mouchoum!" a chorus of voices called. "What's the moon made of?"

There was silence while the family patriarch, Simon Sansregret, rested his head on his cane and pondered at length.

"The moon?" he croaked at last. "The moon...dunno."

The young folk had stopped waiting for answers and were amusing themselves apart.

"Y'ever been *outa* before, Mouchoum?"

"*Isa,* of course he's been here before!"

"Was that when *Kokoum* was here?"

"Where's Grandma now?"

"In heaven."

"In the Old Man's house."

"In the Sand Mountains."

"Come now!" a woman interjected. "Your Kokoum's in heaven. She was a Christian!"

"*Hé kiyam!*" growled the bearded hunter. "It's all the same."

"Ti Toène, you here?" called a man passing by.

"Look for 'im round the Lépine teepee."

"There's one won't die of thirst tonight!"

A hunter caught sight of Askik in the shadows. "Hey there, lad," he called, "did yer father get over his accident?"

"Ehé!"

"Didn't come to no harm?"

"*Namona*, no," the boy said, drawing away several paces. His father's adventure was not an entirely glorious one, he perceived.

"Damnedest story I ever heard," the hunter continued. "Fallin' into the cows then gettin' up without a scratch!"

"Hey, there's better'n that," the bearded hunter said. "I once seen a man get stuck with a bull's horn an' fly thirty feet in the air, then get up and run off soon's he hit the ground."

"You remember Pitt Simard?" a slow-speaking oldster put in. "Ol' Pitt fell off 'is horse right on top of a cow. He grabbed ahold of her pelt an' stayed on top of 'er till the herd went away, then 'e killed 'er."

"Musta bin hungry!" a young fellow said scornfully.

"Anahow, there ain't a young'un alive would do that these days," the old hunter concluded.

"T'ain't true!" the youngster said indignantly. "We're just as good as you old guys."

"Okay, okay! Don't get the bit in yer teeth."

"Where's ol' Pitt now?"

"Buried at Pimbina Mountain. Didn't want no churchyard. Had his own ideas, he did."

"He believed in the Manitou?"

"Didn't believe in nothin' at all."

"How many cows you killed in your life, d'you figger?"

"Oh, I dunno," the ageing hunter replied. In the days I worked for th' American army I killed a lot. But in them days there was more to kill."

"Oh, there's as many now, only they ain't in the same place no more.

"Where they gone then? There's still *bôfflo* in Judith Basin an' in the mountains. If y' ask me, when there ain't no more there, there ain't goin' to be none nowhere."

"Aw c'mon! There's a thousand times more buffalo than hunters."

"An' each hunter wants to kill a thousand. And we're doin' it all wrong too. Instead o' killin' the cows in autumn when they're through

milkin', we take 'em in spring when they're with calf. That's two generations dies at the same time."

"But we always done it like that."

"Well, we ain't gonna do it much longer."

The scraping of a fiddle sounded through the night, an off-key jig
calling a challenge to every other musician in the camp. Out of the far
corners of tents and carts, more fiddles appeared and also guitars, jew's
harps, rattles and spoons. The bearded hunter struck up a tune on a
mouth organ. Others put drums to warm by the fires to shrink the skins
and give them more resonance.

Suddenly there were ten different airs playing at once. Dancers
were silhouetted against the flames. Groups formed and reformed. The
sounds of dancing, drumming and singing mingled until dawn. When
the Métis finally retired to their beds, it was their neighbours' turn to
make a racket: the wolves too had eaten well; they performed such a
joyful concert that they kept the Métis awake until sunrise.

The next morning, a detachment of American cavalry crossed the
gully and approached the camp. There had never been an incident
between the Métis and the soldiers, but relations were always tense.
Washington only barely tolerated the presence of "British" natives on its
territory.

The soldiers stopped well outside the camp, not far from the Métis
horses, which were being guarded by teenage boys. Their commander, a
young lieutenant of imperious manner, rode into the midst of the Métis'
buffalo-runners. Legardeur mounted his horse so as not to be on foot
when he came face to face with the American, and rode out to meet
him. He took with him Thomas McKellar, a Scotch Métis who spoke
English.

"These your horses?" the lieutenant asked, continuing his inspec-
tion without waiting for a reply. "The Sioux had thirty stolen two days
ago. Know anything 'bout that?"

Legardeur had the question translated and replied in the negative.

"You got Crees with you? Assiniboines?"

"They didn't leave the camp."

"Yah, I bet. Where you headed?"

"South-west."

The lieutenant stood up painfully in his stirrups. The long ride had
made him irritable. He was beginning to be anxious again about his

future. He was not one of those mama's boys from an Eastern private school who breeze through promotions without ever setting their asses on anything more mobile than a pivoting office chair. He had been born on a wretchedly poor Vermont farm. Had enlisted in the cavalry at the age of seventeen. In the Dakota Territory he had had more promotions in five years than he would have had in fifteen on the east coast. To get a transfer, however, he had to keep peace in his district. The Sioux were restless, there were Crows roaming all over, and the arrival of Métis hunters only added to his problems.

"I don't want trouble, understand?" he said to Legardeur. "The Sioux are to the south-west. Stay clear of 'em. If you mix it up with 'em I'll hafta intervene. And I got other things to do 'sides that."

"We won't go nowheres near 'em, sir."

"Yah, sure," the American said, turning his mount. Wearily, he urged his horse to a trot and went to join his dust-covered bluecoats. The lieutenant did not like the Métis. In his opinion, they had the vices of two races: lazy like the Indians, grasping like the whites.

"If the Sioux are t' th' west, we'll head due south," Legardeur growled when he returned. "No point lookin' for a fight."

The last battle between the Métis and the Sioux had been at Grand Coteau in 1851. The two nations had lived in peace since then. There had been moments of bad blood — the first man hanged at the Red River settlement had been condemned for the murder of a Sioux ambassador — but the truce had held. After the massacre of white colonists in Minnesota in 1862, the Sioux had crossed the border in great numbers. Once in the North West, they had learned to humour the British authorities and their Métis subjects to avoid being deported. The truce had been fragile, nevertheless. The Sioux considered the half-bloods to be intruders. The two nations stayed out of each other's way.

Legardeur called the Council together and suggested breaking camp as soon as possible. The weather was warm and dry and the meat was drying quickly. The carts would move on in two days.

The news was welcomed in the camp, but especially by the Mercredis, who were in dire need of meat. Jérôme was jumping for joy and for a few hours forgot his plan to leave the camp. Besides, he had not seen Champagne and Ferland again; they were avoiding him.

The resurgence of optimism was not to last. In the language of the Cree, the south is *Nimita*, Without End. The cart train penetrated deep into the limitless prairie and found no buffalo. In the hollows, the grass grew as high as a man because the there were no longer buffalo grazing there. Clouds of mosquitoes rose from this dense vegetation, for the ground beneath it did not dry. The excitement of the first hunt evaporated like dew in July. The grumbling in the teepees resumed. Legardeur was wrong to be pushing south, it was said. People began to imagine and then to talk about the easy, luxurious life the St. François dissidents must be leading on the Pimbina River, though there had been no word from them.

Jérôme Mercredi sensed the leader's authority waning and became his harshest critic. Now he missed no opportunity to trumpet his discontent. He was attracting attention. The hunters began to think as he did, that hunting on such a large scale was unworkable, that the group must divide into smaller units. The more so since each man was convinced that only he knew where to find the buffalo herds.

Legardeur alone was admitting that he did not know. He became increasingly isolated. By day he rode ahead of captains who were no longer responding to his calls. By night he huddled at the far side of his teepee, stirring only to hear the reports of the scouts.

Fresh, cold air swept in under the raised sides of the teepee. Curled up under his woollen blanket, Askik sensed rather than watched the sky pale progressively. A kildeer uttered its first call of the day. The Choquette horse scratched herself against the cart. From the other end of the camp came the ring of a cooking pot. In a minute the family would have to get up, shiver, light a fire of wood and dung, take down the tent, prepare breakfast, hitch up the oxen and carts and set out once again.

The camp sounds grew louder. At first the women had greeted each other in low voices but now were calling from one lodge to the next. An ox was demanding water. A fire crackled. The fragrance of wood and burning dung wafted among the teepees. Finally, to disabuse any who were hoping it was still nighttime, the crier brought his hoarse, hateful voice to evey corner of the camp.

"*Lève! Lève!* Everybody up! Get ready to push off! *Waweyik!*"

Jérôme Mercredi crawled on all fours to the teepee entrance, threw open the hide door, stood up and stepped out with joints cracking and urinated with his back to the neighbours. He was heaving a manly sigh of satisfaction when he saw a little white cloud form at the end of his nose. Surprised, he looked up at the prairie; it was white with frost.

"Mother!" he called sharply. *"Astam outa!"*

Anita put a tousled head through the teepee door. "What's the matter?"

"Look!" her husband replied, waving at the frosted hillsides. "Autumn's here!"

After breakfast, Mercredi saw Champagne and Ferland approach side by side, hands in pockets. It was Ferland who spoke, Champagne as usual signifying his agreement with grunts.

"Ain't goin' good," Ferland began. "Summer's nearly done and we ain't killed nothin' yet."

"That's what I said already," Jérôme said, sucking on his clay pipe.

"What we gonna do?"

"Go."

"When?"

"Wapahé, tomorrow."

"You had a dream? You know where there's buffalo?"

"That'll come."

Ferland was still unsure. He had been hoping for more convincing arguments. But Champagne concluded the matter, overcoming his usual silence with a major effort.

"It can't go on. We'll go *wapahé.*"

"Okay," Ferland sighed. "Where we goin'?"

"North ... west," Mercredi announced, with a pause to allow inspiration to provide him with the direction. North-west, toward the Souris."

"Monsieur Gauthier's talkin' about goin' with your father," Mona said. The wind was flattening the grass and lifting the girl's hair.

"That's bad," she added in an expressionless voice.

Askik and Mona were sitting at the top of a small butte. Behind and below, the camp was having its midday snooze. Before them, the prairie rolled away in humps and folds. Askik was twirling a sprig of grass between his thumb and forefinger.

"They won't find no *bôfflo,*" Mona said, making clouds shift by closing one eye and then the other.

"Do *you* know where the *bôfflo* are?" Askik asked.

"No, but they have to stay with the others to find any."

"How d'you know?"

"*Nikiskenten.* I know."

Askik threw away his sprig of grass and let the matter drop. He was getting used to her way of saying, "I know."

Mona closed both eyes and shut out the clouds so that she was present only for the wind. The mild air still bore a hint of the morning's frost.

"D'you think I'm pretty?" she asked suddenly, turning to Askik.

The boy looked at her carefully. Her face was round, almost chubby, with almond eyes, her body slightly on the heavy side. Pretty? Not as much as some other girls. But Askik thought she was pleasant enough to look at, and he was not yet of an age where compliments can be costly, so he replied, "Ehé, not bad."

"You know," she said with a serious face, "if we travel together you're gonna hafta to listen to me."

Askik bristled. There were too many people getting it into their heads to tell him what to do.

"Why do I hafta listen to you? You ain't my mother!"

"I can help you."

"I don't need no help," he said gruffly, pulling a new sprig of grass. He resented her acting as though she were older. Now he was sorry he had told her she was pretty, seeing that she was taking advantage of it.

"I dreamed about you last night, you know," she said.

"What kinda dream?"

"You were sittin' in the dark," she began in a near whisper, "and you were cold, you were shakin'. There was something behind you, I don't know what, I couldn't see. But you couldn't see neither an' you didn't wanta look."

Askik had an icy feeling in his stomach. He wanted to shut her up.

"*Tché!* That's a girl's dream!" he taunted. "Who cares what you dreamt!"

But Mona kept on. "I called to you but you wouldn't get up. You was too scairt."

Askik flushed. "It ain't true! I weren't scairt!"

"I wanted to help you but you wouldn't listen," the girl said plaintively.

"I don't need no help from you! I ain't no baby!"

"I cried an' cried, but you wouldn't come!"

Askik stood up. The conversation was getting uncomfortable. In the distance, the boys watching the horses were laughing. Askik realized that he could not be seen in company with a girl. Pretending interest in looking at a badger hole, he ran down the side of the butte in leaps and bounds. When he turned around, Mona was watching him with an expression of reproach.

Then a hitherto unknown demon took hold of Askik Mercredi and he ran off, shouting as he went, "An' it ain't true you're pretty!"

He went straight back to the camp. His parents were asleep under the cart, shaded from the sun. Askik went and hid up front, between the shafts. Chin on his knees, eyes shut tight, he tried with all his might to disappear for ever. When he thought enough time had passed for his disappearance, he opened his eyes and there once again were the grass, the sky, the shafts, and the ox, affably chewing its cud. Was he going to stay a little boy all his life? In his nightly dreams, being seven never prevented him from leading a satisfactory life. Why was real life so different? He felt worthy of respect and was ignored, capable of great deeds and was held down with menial chores. In his dreams he never lost his temper; he was just and generous because everyone looked up to him. In real life, everyone behaved like his master. No wonder he was bad tempered sometimes.

That evening, Ludger Gauthier, Mona's employer, came and sat at the Mercredis' fire. He was a fat, greying man who exuded a strong animal smell and was renowned for incomparable belches. He had nine children, debts, and carts that were never full. He had heard about Mercredi's visions. He had no faith in them at all, but was anxious to return northward. He had come to verify that this was the visionary's intention. Ferland and Champagne arrived on his heels.

The Mercredis' teepee was old, its hide covering thin. When Askik turned toward the wall he could see the silhouettes of the hunters sitting together around the fire outside. He had not been much interested in his father's plan, but now he hoped it would be abandoned. He sensed that Mona's dream had to do with the defection being readied, that the one would not happen without the other. A dream can be laughed at in daytime, but it weighs heavily when darkness closes tight around the fire. Why had Mona seen him in the dark, frightened and trembling?

Askik looked through the teepee entrance. Against the vault of the black sky, a solitary pine clinging to a butte stood out blacker still. Under its branches shone Scorpio, the friendly giant which the cart train had been following, but on which the Mercredis would be turning their backs in the morning.

Jérôme Mercredi was mistaken when he expected to slip away unnoticed. His ox was not yet hitched to the cart when half the Council appeared, breathing threats and maledictions. He stayed calm and did not respond as he went about his preparations. There was only one disappointment, in fact; at the time of departure, only a dozen carts joined his own. He had expected a more impressive following. The anger of the chiefs had weighed. A Métis is free to go where he chooses, except during a hunt.

The dissident families retraced their steps of the day before as they left the camp. They turned their backs to the south, their faces toward the Land of Waters.

Askik, to his displeasure, was walking with the rotund Mathias Gauthier, son of Ludger. Mathias had two passions: hunting prairie dogs and wrestling. Wrestling kept him amused all morning. He would grab Askik and hold him in a headlock until his own arm hurt, then release him with a growl of triumph. He knew a lot of other holds, but none gave him more satisfaction. Askik would wince with pain and hold his tongue. Each time Mathias let him go Askik would give a friendly little chuckle as if he found it all very entertaining, but would add in a voice of reason that that was enough. He would as well have reasoned with a bear. The fat boy would stay quiet for a few minutes, arms hanging nonchalantly at his sides, then without warning would rush his victim with his little eyes gleaming and apply a hold with all his might. Mona was walking alone. Askik would have preferred her company, but was too afraid of the taunts he would have drawn from Mathias.

When the cart train stopped at noon and each family turned to its own meal, Askik thought he was delivered from his tormenter at last. Mathias, however, had discovered prairie dogs near the camp and without further ado declared war on them. Askik was conscripted as a matter of course.

Laying seige to a prairie dog village requires some knowhow. It was an art at which Mathias was a genius of sorts. From the location of holes, he could judge the layout of tunnels and the depth of the nesting chambers. He had rodent instincts.

As the boys approached the town they heard the shrill whistle of a lookout. By the time they reached the first burrow there was not a prairie dog left on the surface.

"They've gone," Askik sighed, pretending to be sorry. "We'll come back later."

"Shaddup," Mathias said calmly, squatting on his heels. He waited, keeping a sharp eye on the town.

A blistering light fell from the sky. The horizon shimmered. Eddies of sand and dried grasses chased across the prairie. The birds were silent.

There was a puff of dust from a hole. A prairie dog had come to the surface, seen the boys and retreated in haste. Mathias moved from his place with stealthy steps, beckoning to Askik to follow.

"Stand here, *outa*," he ordered. "Take this stick. When I give you the sign, bang like hell."

He fished a noose from his pocket, tiptoed thirty feet away, laid the small lasso around a burrow entrance and moved away, playing out the cord. He lay belly down on the ground and, with an imperious wave of his hand, commanded the offensive to begin.

Askik began to bang half-heartedly on a mound over the burrow, hoping the inhabitants would see through the manoeuvre. Mathias glared at him and bent his arm as if crushing an imaginary cranium. Askik banged harder. A small, tawny muzzle appeared suddenly in the snared hole a few inches below the lasso. Askik stopped his banging. The animal went back down the hole. Mathias looked daggers at him. Askik began to bang again; he was getting tired of this.

Below ground, the banging coursed along the walls, penetrated down to the chambers, resounded through the tunnels. As though a giant's heart had begun to beat in the middle of the village. The frightened animals crouched in the farthest recesses of their dens. One, a lookout come up prematurely, was trembling in the tunnel entrance within view of the light. It advanced and retreated nervously, its tiny feet barely touching the vibrating earth. Behind, the dark tunnel throbbed like a living creature. Above, a circle of blue sky. The animal darted forward. The string closed about its throat, instantly emptying it of breath. Its claws lost contact, it saw the sky, the sun and the ground rushing to meet it. Mathias swung it at the end of the string a second time and smashed it on the ground.

Askik came and looked reluctantly. The prairie dog was twitching, one black foot vainly kicking. Its light brown fur was crusted with dust and blood. An eye hung out of its socket.

"We might as well go," Mathias grumbled. "The others know it's dead. They won't come up now."

He untied the noose and hurled the animal afar.

Three days later they came to a muddy stream choked with willows. While the adults put up the tents, the children gathered firewood and also stones to hold down the sides of the teepees. Mathias stamped about in the mud, unearthing reed tubers. Askik and Mona went to dig wild turnips on the prairie.

Askik had resolved to speak nicely to Mona, out of friendship and also because the Gauthier children treated her contemptuously. Mona's mind was wandering, however; she was not working well and barely listened to him. She kept looking up to gaze at the surroundings with a puzzled look, as if trying to recognize a place that she had already seen but which had changed. Finally, holding a dozen wild turnips in her apron, she strode away, back to the camp. As Askik watched her pick a path through the willows, he had to acknowledge that, with her boyish walk and outgrown dress, to him too she was a bit absurd.

The daylight faded earlier than usual. As night fell, so did a fine, cold rain. For the first time since spring, the Métis lit fires inside the teepees. There was a touch of autumn in the cooler air.

Bundled up in his buffalo robe, Askik wondered what place Mona had been given in the Gauthier teepee. She would surely have to sleep by the door, where it was cold. The Gauthiers were not nice people, he reflected.

He thought he was not asleep, yet already was dreaming. It was morning. The whole camp was up. The Gauthiers, however, were not in sight. Their neighbours shouted to them to hurry, but none of the family stirred. At last Askik's papa went to the door of the silent lodge, lifted the leather flap, and invited Askik to put his head inside. There in the darkness, Askik found the corpses of the entire family, a dozen bodies wrapped in their blankets.

He woke with a start. The rain was pattering on the hide walls. His parents and brother were asleep. A few embers were glowing in the middle of the teepee. He decided he would stay awake the rest of the night so as not to have any more dreams. Whereupon he promptly fell asleep again.

The next morning, Jérôme undid some of the wooden pins that held the door of the teepee closed, put his head outside and received a cold shower on the back of his neck. It had stopped raining but the tent was still streaming wet. A blue-black ceiling hung low over the prairie. A raw wind drove Jérôme back inside. He raked the ashes off the fire, threw on some new sticks and ordered his wife to prepare a big helping of rubaboo, pemmican in broth. He had decided not to wake the camp;

this would be a slack day. Only too happy not to be called, the other hunters did not even come to find out what was up. Breaking camp in the rain, when the hide tents are wet and heavy, is best avoided.

After breakfast, when Jérôme was filling his pipe, the Mercredis heard steps approaching. It was Mathias with beaming face. He and his father were going hunting in the woods; they were inviting the Mercredis to go with them. Grudgingly, Jérôme began to stir his stumps. He had hoped to spend the day staying warm, but how could a chief let a hunting party leave without him? Askik, for his part, was far from keen to go tramping around in a wet forest. But since Mathias was going with his father, how could Askik not go with his? So the Mercredis father and son hid their resentment as they pulled on their high moccasins. Askik had gathered bullrush down for lighting the fire, but there was not enough for stuffing his moccasins. He foresaw that his feet were going to be cold.

As they approached the Gauthier's tent, they saw Mona standing with her arms crossed over her chest, gazing at the prairie. Ludger Gauthier came out, spied her and scolded her harshly.

Hey, *fifille*, I don't pay you to hang round doin' nothin'! Go in! Help yer mistress!"

Mona shuddered and went in without a word.

"She's half crazy," Gauthier said. "She was blubberin' in 'er sleep all night long. A real wild one...but with a mother like that..." Then, turning his nose to the wind, he said, "Okay, I think we gonna have a real good hunt."

The hunters walked along the coulee for over a mile. They came to a hill cut in two by the stream. On the far side, the narrow band of willows swelled into a small forest of poplars and scrub oak.

"If we gonna do it right we gotta go up both sides o' the creek," Gauthier proposed. "Me 'n the boy, we'll go over t'other side. You two go up this here side."

It was not a hunt that Gauthier was proposing, it was a competition. And Gauthier was an impressive deer hunter. Jérôme let no emotion show.

They separated. Gusts of wind brought showers of cold water down from the treetops. The underbrush was wet. The Mercredis' legs and feet were soaked in no time. On the other hand, the damp ground made it possible to move noiselessly.

Jérôme had plenty to do. He had to pick a path over the broken ground, point out dead wood to keep Askik from walking on it, detect wind shifts and search the ground for animal tracks. He stopped every five paces to listen to the sounds of the forest, alert to anything other than the whispering of leaves — a step, a bush stirred, the snap of a twig — that would betray the presence of game. He was soon rewarded. A deep, hoarse cough came from the depths of the woods.

He signaled to his son to hide and stay put. Askik crouched in a small hollow behind a poplar. His father stood motionless for a few minutes, scanning the shadowy underbrush. He took some down from his pocket and released it in the air to determine the wind direction. Then he advanced, moving from bush to embankment to tree-trunk, body hunched and knees bent, deeper into the woods, from which came no further sound. Askik lost sight of him.

Left alone, the boy was soon bored. For a time he let himself be amused by the indecipherable letters traced by the topmost branches of the aspens against the grey clouds. He followed the ridges in the bark of the tree with his finger, even tore off some strips to uncover bugs. He pulled apart a rotting log on the ground beside him, digging out handfuls of crumbling wood. But these were dull diversions. His thighs and ankles began to ache. He longed to kneel, but the moss everywhere was sodden. He was sorry he had destroyed the log because he might have sat on it. Finally he turned around and squatted on his heels, leaning back not very comfortably against the trunk of the poplar.

Jérôme, meanwhile, was up to his neck in a clump of ice-cold dogwoods. With his head high and his body motionless, he looked like a watchful goose. His eyes were busy, however, looking this way and that, searching for prey through the rain-blackened trees. He was about to resume his stalking advance when he spied a pale flutter some distance away in the woods. Now he concentrated his gaze on a spot which at first had seemed deserted. Gradually, as his eyes adjusted to the shadows, he spotted a buck with antlers held high. Jérôme suspected it had seen him, but seconds later it lowered its head to graze. Jérôme counted to five before it raised it again to look about warily. When the animal bent to graze again, the man quietly cocked his musket, stood up and moved forward, counting. At four he froze but did not try to hide. The buck raised its head, pricked its ears, and then, perceiving no movement, returned to its meal. All it could see while grazing was the ground. Jérôme kept approaching his target, freezing every four seconds and taking care never to look the animal straight in the eye. A deer may not recognize a motionless man but, like all wild animals, is alarmed by a direct gaze.

It took forever. When the buck turned toward him, Mercredi could barely resist putting the rifle to his shoulder and firing. He held back, however, until he was fifty feet from his target. He waited one last time for the animal to lower its head, then took aim. The damp gun smelled of steel and grease. The wind was dropping. Three...four...five. The buck raised its head. Mercredi pulled the trigger.

The soft click was muffled at once in the moist air. The gun had misfired. The buck rose like a bird, beat twice with its legs, and flew away into the forest.

"*Cré bâtard de vieux fusil!*"

Mercredi leapt to his feet, shook the wet powder out of the pan, and listened. The buck had doubled back and was passing upstream to his left. Mercredi swung about, ran to the first clearing, poured a new charge and knelt on one knee.

A yellow-brown streak burst out of the woods followed by a crash of hoofbeats and snapping of branches. Askik turned, aghast, and all at once saw the deer, the gun, the puff of smoke and the poplar spewing fragments above his head. He did not hear the shot until afterwards, when he was already face down on the ground.

When he lifted his head, he saw his father kneeling in a small cloud of smoke, looking utterly stunned. Jérôme dropped the gun, staggered forward a few steps, then rushed to Askik yelling, "Did I hurtcha, lad?" He looked so terror-stricken that Askik was embarrassed for both of them. Hunters, they were supposed to be! His father threw himself on his knees and clasped him tight against his black, wet braids.

Jérôme had no heart left for hunting now. The misfire, the deer doubling back rather than running straight, the near tragedy, all were evil omens. There was sorcery in the air. Jays were chattering despite the bad weather. A hare loped calmly across their path as though they were not there. A poplar hurled itself about as they approached as if trying to break from its roots and flee their presence. Jérôme remembered that Gauthier had lived for years with the Ojibways, who could cast spells on plants and animals.

They must quickly find an open space, he thought. He went down to the stream, but the grey water was dispersing among the trees; there was no dry bank to walk on.

Caw! Caw! Caw! The harsh cries now came from the other side of the coulee. Jérôme turned back.

"*Astam*, lad!"

Father and son cut straight through the underbrush, the shortest way to the prairie. Grasses twisted around their ankles, twigs caught at Jérôme's braids, an owl brushed the side of Askik's head. It took an eternity. When they broke out of the woods at last, the heavy grey sky seemed incomparably airy and refreshing.

"We didn't get nothin'!" Jérôme declared to his wife as though announcing a wonderful piece of news. The teepee smelled good inside: leather and fried fat. The fire was crackling, the baby laughing. "Put on the pot, mother! I'd like some tea."

Jérôme had not even finished pulling on his dry moccasins, however, when he heard a angry voice outside.

"Mercredi! C'm out here, *charogne!*"

Gauthier's trousers were plastered to the knees with mud, his hands were scratched, he had burs all over, even in his beard. The only clean, tidy thing about him was his gun, which he held cradled in his arms like a sleeping baby. He was irritably fingering the trigger.

"You get anythin'?" he asked sourly.

"*Namona,*" Jérôme replied. "Where was you?"

This was not a good question. Gauthier exloded. The muzzle of the gun turned partway toward Mercredi.

"You know bloody damn well where I was! I was chasin' yer goddam buck!"

"You catch it?" Jérôme asked innocently.

Gauthier stepped forward and stood nose to nose with him. "Don't you act smart with me!" he yelled. "Yer a goddam conjuror! You knew I was a better hunter'n you, that's why you sent me yer blasted buck. It's you sent the *bôfflo* away. Admit it, *charogne!* You wanna starve us so you can have our souls!"

Mercredi was so stunned he could find nothing to say. He kept his eyes on the fat, dirty finger quivering on the trigger. The other hunters ambled up, drowsy from a morning of idleness. Gauthier turned to address the whole camp.

"Listen here, all o' you! Judge fer yourselves." He gestured at Mercredi. "This swine an' me, we made a deal to go huntin'..."

He recounted to the impassive circle that he had heard the voice of a deer and had tracked the animal quietly for half an hour before finding it in a clearing. He had fired from fifty feet, as good as point blank for a hunter of his skill, but instead of falling dead on the spot the buck had fled. Gauthier had followed it easily by the trail of blood on the leaves and ground. He had been vexed to think of the meat going to waste, then was amazed to have tracked the animal so far and still not found the carcase. The buck complicated the chase with long detours through bramble patches and mudholes in which Gauthier sank up to his knees. After an hour, dirty and torn and out of breath, he had found his prey at last by a slough. The buck was still standing but its muzzle was hanging in the mud; its eyes were glassy, its flanks were heaving feebly and there was blood oozing from its mouth. Gauthier was going to recharge his gun but decided to save a bullet. As he approached he unsheathed his long knife, already cursing the distance he was going to have to walk back with his load of meat.

Then the buck had suddenly raised its head, eyes bright, ears pricked. Opening its mouth as if to laugh, it had sped away like an arrow.

"He laughed at me!" Gauthier cried shrilly, carried away by excitement and anger. "He turned round goin' in the woods and I swear there weren't a mark on his body! But I'd wounded 'im an' I seen the blood. Look! *Kinawapamik!* I still got some under my fingernails!"

His listeners, now uneasy, hovering on the edge of fright, told him that he must have seen wrong.

"Listen t' me now!" cried Mercredi. "It's not me that sent the buck, but I saw 'im."

He told his story in detail and denied all responsibility, but stopped just short of denying that he was a conjuror. After all, when a chief can inspire a little fear...

When he had finished, other hunters recounted at length that they had felt forebodings arriving here. Even those who had suspected nothing now remembered some vague anxiety.

"There's a *mahtsé-manito*, an evil spirit hereabouts."

"A tchipay! Prob'ly an old Native who liked comin' here t' hunt."

"Don't have t' be. Could be sumpin' in the earth. There's bad places just like there's bad people."

"I say it's a warnin'."

"Unless...it's the Deschamps," an old man put in.

The group fell silent. All the Métis knew the legend of the Deschamps family. Quarrelsome, immoral people. During a summer hunt, the Deschamps sons had shot down a captain. The next morning the whole family was found — men, women and children — dead in their sleeping robes. Their teepee was carefully closed from inside. The bodies bore no wounds. The deaths remained unexplained.

"What, you say it's here they died, Mouchoum?"

"Oh, I don't say right here," the old man replied, "but somewhere in this country. They'd pitched their camp near a coulee. It's my father tol' me. He was there. And the Deschamps didn't have no marks on their bodies neither. Like yer buck."

This was more than enough. Three minutes later it was being said in all the lodges that the camp was pitched on the very site where the Deschamps had died. It was also being said that Jérôme Mercredi was a conjuror, which on reflexion surprised no one.

11

When they crossed a ridge several days later, the Métis saw a curious butte like an animal's heart turned upside down.

"It's the Petit-Coeur!

"Naw, it ain't!"

"I tell you it is! I come this way once when I was a boy. It's the Petit-Coeur."

"Yer wrong. The Petit-Coeur's near the Missouri."

"The Missouri? Could it be...?"

Eyes turned to Mercredi, who did not deign to reply, although deep inside he was shaken. It might be a mistake, too. There were plenty of buttes with fantastic shapes, and none of his men had yet hunted west of the watershed. So this did not have to be exactly the Petit-Coeur. But whenever he looked at it, darkened as it was by distance, pointed among rounded hills, something wrenched in his gut.

For two whole days the butte weighed on the Métis' minds and hearts. They kept looking up at it to measure their progress and being discouraged to see it still so far away. When they lost sight of it during descents it remained on their minds. When it came back into view from the heights it would seem not to be a single inch closer. The prairie here rolls up and down like a blanket shaken in the wind. The yellow-brown hills in their zigzag line against the sky are numbingly tedious. The south slopes, gnawed by erosion, burned by the sun, allow for easy climbing. Only sparse grasses, yuccas, and small, round, flat cactuses called Missouri snowshoes grow on them. The north slopes, on the other hand, are more protected from the sun and passage is hampered by ash trees, scrub oak and shrubby willows. The slightest depression capable of holding water is choked with vegetation. Advancing through this maze of thickets, ups and downs leading nowhere and half-dried swamps takes an angel's patience. But more than the obstacles, it was the Métis' secret fears that made their steps heavy. If the butte were the Petit-Coeur, if the Missouri were near and the Red therefore so far, if the snow came early, if the children were cold, if the butte were really the Petit-Coeur, how many of them would return from the prairie?

Jérôme rode at the head of the column like Legardeur before him, absolutely alone. He dreamed of the forests of the North, their teeming game, their pure, cold springs. He longed to curl up in the bosom of a shady forest. He felt only indifference for the yellow, naked butte that weighed so heavy on his companions' hearts. He could not understand their worries. If God wanted to save them, they would live. If not, what did it matter?

The horses stopped even before anyone pulled the reins. After a moment of silence, someone spoke the obvious.

"Ehé, this is it. The Missouri."

And that was all. Calm, shallow, dotted with sandy islands, the Missouri unfolded its wide valley across the landscape, careless of what it might mean to this handful of hunters gazing upon it. The Métis did not know what to think. What they had feared was proven beyond argument; they were even farther south than they had expected. They had barely begun the journey home. Yet the valley was so fresh and joyous compared to the parched prairie that they could not resist a moment of cheer.

The river flowed over a bed of white sand, bordered with willows and plains cottonwood. On the dry ground behind there were real oak forests ringing with birdsong. This was where the Métis pitched their tents, in a grassy wood that sloped in terraces down to the river. Although they were no better provisioned now than in the morning, they allowed themselves a feeling of relative plenty. A river and a wood made all the difference for these hunters of the plains.

As the day approached its close, Jérôme felt a need to draw aside to pray and dream. The sullen faces being shown him by his neighbours made the call the more urgent. He resolved to climb a butte and there fast until God brought him counsel. He even considered following the example of the Indians, who would slash their arms and legs to draw sympathy from the spirits, but he decided this would be going too far. He called his wife.

"Tell them," he said, "to be up before the sun and ready to march soon's I come down from the butte. Tell 'em I'll pray while they sleep."

Anita grudgingly did as she was told. She did not relish her new role as wife of a prophet. She had the impression that the Métis women snickered as she passed, that even the little girls were making fun of her in imitation of their mothers. Neverthless, she went from tent to tent announcing her husband's plan, although she did not add his order to be up before dawn. She knew better than he the limits of her neighbours' tolerance.

As Jérôme and Askik left the camp, the neighbours watched impassively. Few doubted the power of dreams. But the spirits are touchy; perhaps Mercredi had offended his protectors by omitting some observance of rite or morality.

The woods rose toward the prairie in successive levels like giant steps, each step a phase of thousands of years in the excavation of the valley. Beyond the woods was a butte rising steeply, marking the edge of the prairie. Its base was densely covered with grass. Its top was almost bald. The Mercredis arrived at its summit as night fell. Jérôme chose a big flat rock. He gestured to Askik to go and settle down somewhat apart, and to keep watch. In order to learn. Askik unrolled his blanket at the foot of a buffalo berry bush, whose red berries are excellent in jelly but bitter in the natural state. He picked a few handfuls for dessert after his dried meat.

Night began. A warm wind climbed the superheated flanks of the butte. Jérôme tried to put himself in a pious frame of mind but was distracted from his prayers at first by the spectacle of darkness invading the valley, the stars appearing from top to bottom of the sky, and the crescent moon lighting up midway.

He prayed for a dream. He closed his eyes and, reconstituting the landscape obliterated by the night, searched for buffalo on its hills and in its woods. There were none. He cleared his mind and allowed another, unfamiliar landscape to take form, to see if this one contained a herd. Still nothing. He opened his eyes and raised them to the heavens, and said another, more ardent prayer.

"We been wanderin' for a long time about the country, and we ain't found nothin'. I don't understand. You feed the Natives and even the Americans, who are Protestants, but to us Catholic Métis, you give nothin'. Would you let us starve to death? That would make your enemies happy. Would you make a joke of your church? When you spoke to me at the bottom of the ravine, I didn't complain. I told the others what you wanted. They laughed at *nina*. The councillors wanted to hurt me. Why did you protect me if you was gonna destroy me on the prairie afterwards? How did I know we was comin' to the Missouri? I trusted you. Let me see some *bôfflo*! Dear God, you put more stars in the sky than grass on this hill. What's a dozen cows beside all that?"

A night hawk with slender, pointed wings plunged into the valley after flying insects. Askik methodically sucked strips of dried meat, softening them with his saliva.

Jérôme kept praying. "So what you gonna do with your *bôfflo*? Give 'em to the wolves? Drown 'em in the sloughs? Let the mosquitoes eat 'em? Why'd you put 'em on earth if it wasn't t' feed us? So why're you hidin' 'em? I don't understand you."

He kept on interminably, whining, arguing, threatening, carrying on as he would when dealing with a Company store clerk. Pester and thou shalt receive. The wind that was blowing over the hill was now cold and raw. The scent of sagebrush, musky in the heat, was now sharp. The moon was sinking. Askik had rolled up in a ball under his bush and was sleeping fitfully. In the east, the sky was no longer entirely black. Jérôme stretched out on the flat rock because his back hurt and the rock warmed it. He lay with his face to the stars, nervously muttering incantations, bone weary but unable to sleep. Sleep is not forbidden to someone in search of a vision. It is even good to sleep to make oneself more accessible to the spirits. But this jumble of pale stars was putting him on edge, for they made no rhyme nor reason.

Then all of a sudden he saw his mistake. Why had he not seen it sooner? It was so blindingly obvious! They were not stars but hills, forests, rivers, more sparkling and diaphanous than usual, true enough, but every bit as unmistakable. A wondrous landscape in which every blade of grass shone like a firefly! Mercredi felt a surge of joy so great that it lifted him off the ground and projected him straight as an arrow toward those airy hills. A fantastic ascent! He was flying at incredible speed. His jacket — he should have buttoned it — fluttered in the wind and his splendid moustaches were plastered against his cheeks. He steered between the buttes, flew over lakes and swamps, overtook a flock of luminous ducks and saw a river so sparkling, so exuberant that he wanted to leave everything behind — camp, horse, wife — and spend the rest of his days beside it.

"*Tcheskwa!* Stop!" But in the twinkling of an eye he was past the river. He was going faster and faster. The wind whistled in his ears, his long tresses pulled at his scalp and the end of his nose was beginning to freeze. Up and up and up he flew. He saw a lake, and near the lake a wood. And near the wood, tiny points of light that were growing exceedingly fast. For Jérôme Mercredi was now traversing space in a magificent arc, which is to say, he was plunging toward earth.

"Ayeeee!"

But instead of shattering into a thousand pieces, he skimmed the ground at dizzying speed, and saw that the tiny points of light were in fact buffalo.

The like of these buffalo he had never seen before. Their manes were a mass of stars. Heavenly bodies glittered in place of eyes and at the ends of their horns. Their tails formed constellations. The animals were moving slowly like the seasons, yet were powerful and full of grace. To Jérôme they were beautiful, and he himself unsightly. Tears came to his eyes. He uttered a sob of love and gratitude toward these magnificent creatures for admitting him to their presence.

When he came to himself, he was lying on his back with his eyes wide open to the stars, and the tears were running down into his hair. He wept from joy and longing. He thanked God and the Buffalo for the honour he had received. He vowed never again to kill a buffalo without making an expiatory offering. He asked to be allowed back to that wondrous land after his death. He came close to asking for an imminent death, but changed his mind, thinking that in a few hours he might regret it.

"Askik! Askik! We can go down! It's time t' go, *monhomme!*"

The sun was rising over the rounded hills and the faraway Petit-Coeur. Mercredi lost his temper briefly when he reached the camp and found the tents still standing, but he was so sure of the buffalo now that he let his followers sleep, and even went to bed himself.

He was just dropping off to sleep when he heard a watery slap-slapping. Sounds like a family of big beavers, he thought with a smile. A shot rang out. He grabbed his gun and dashed out the door of the teepee.

Everyone was running down to the river. A steamboat was passing, its paddles methodically slapping the water and its funnels spewing enormous grey plumes. The Métis were shouting angily at a string of Americans idling about on the promenade deck. The Americans had been relieving the monotony of the voyage by shooting at anything that moved on the river banks. One of them had just killed a Métis horse, no doubt taking it for a bald buffalo or an unusually elegant elk. The guilty party, a dandy in a green suit and brown bowler, gave a smiling apology. The owner of the horse demanded compensation but the dandy, placing a hand delicately behind an ear, pretended he could not hear. Finally he spread his arms as if to say, My dear fellow, what do you expect me to do?

This was too much for the Métis. An opening volley of shots chased the Americans inside. Delighted with this unexpected diversion, the gentlemen took up positions at the windows. A running battle ensued, the Métis darting from tree to tree and the vessel making full steam ahead for the American fort upstream. Just as the Métis cause looked all but lost, agitation and the need to keep his head down got the better of the pilot. The boat came to a stop on a sand bar with a dreadful grinding sound. The Métis raised a shout of triumph. The pilot reversed engines. The seething water turned muddy and the vessel panted like a tired ox but did not budge. The gentlemen were no longer laughing. Finally a white tablecloth appeared at a dining room window and waved limply, signifying surrender.

While the Métis congratulated each other for being the first of their race to win a naval victory, the gentlemen took a collection among themselves. They engaged a black boy to swim to shore and give twenty dollars to the owner of the horse.

"Wah! Wey!" the Métis cried as they saw the black boy emerge from the water. So enchanted were they by his colour that they wanted to keep him. The boy was terrified, however; they had to let him go.

12

They marched and marched from dawn to dusk, cursing at their tired animals, not even stopping midway through the day for fear of winter overtaking them. The last traces of greenery were fading from the prairie. Above the brown reeds in the marshes, ducks were making trial flights before taking off for the south. Higher still, wild geese were passing day and night, their great V formations slicing through the sky every day, grey and sunny alike.

The land was progressively flatter. As the cart train drew away from the Missouri, it moved along the great plateau separating the rivers that flow north and south. Here the prairie was less rugged and richer, dotted with marshes and lakes. The scouts carefully scanned the periphery of each lake, for according to Mercredi the buffalo would be found beside water.

Jérôme himself was no longer sparing any effort. He was in the saddle at dawn and kept scouring the countryside until the campfires were lit. Between him and the Choquette horse, a silent pact was now in effect. Perhaps the mare had finally realized that she would not be going back to St. Boniface without buffalo meat. She had stopped her bucking and mock sneezing. To Mercredi, she seemed to be putting some verve into crossing hills and skirting thickets, as if in a hurry to see buffalo slaughtered.

So Mercredi took her seriously one morning when, emerging from a small wood, she refused to take the direction he wanted, pricking up her ears and snorting crossly. Mercredi pricked up his own ears. After a moment he heard the voice of an angry male buffalo, half rumble, half roar. A quiver of pleasure coursed the horse's body from nose to tail. Ears upright, she turned abruptly and headed for the camp. Jérôme almost fell off. He had wanted to get closer to the herd in order to count the animals. But then, perhaps the mare was right to go for reinforcements.

When the Métis saw the Choquette horse approaching at breakneck speed with her rider hanging on for dear life, they almost expected to get the news from her.

"Bôfflo!"

"Tandé? Where?"

"That way."

"How far?"

"Dunno."

"Long way?"

"Not very."

"Lotta help that is!"

The carts came to a halt. The hunters got ready with grim determination. The women, old men and children stayed out of the way and kept quiet. It all smacked too much of the last chance. Askik approached Mona as she watched the hunters ride away.

"Are they gonna to bring back cow?" he asked.

"Mouats nikoskenten. I don't know."

The men nearly botched it. A young bull and two cows were chewing the cud on the south slope of a hill, out of the wind and separated from the herd. The hunters rode over the crest of the hill almost on top of them. Fortunately, the frightened animals fled not toward the herd but in the opposite direction.

To prevent this from happening again, Mercredi climbed the next line of hills on foot, leaving the man next to him in charge of his horse. Before long he spotted some forty buffalo at rest beside a small lake, as he had seen in his dream. An enormous bull was holding off half a dozen young males that were persistently sniffing out the females. The mating season had begun. No sooner would the bull tackle one of the young rascals than the others moved in to circle the cows, waiting for one to come into heat.

"Poor ol' fella," Mercredi murmured as he scrambled back down the hill, "you got too many wives. I'm gonna take some, make it easier fer you.

The hunters had dismounted.

"They're over the next butte," Mercredi said quietly. "Four gun-shots off. Lyin' down, most of 'em."

"But we got the wind in our backs," Gauthier growled. I say we gotta gallop right straight into 'em afore they smell us."

Everyone nodded agreement, and Mercredi assented. The line of horsemen charged up the hill, over the summit, and down into the basin on the other side. The bull, surprised in the midst of chasing off a rival, froze in seeming disbelief, then bellowed and began rounding up his herd. The cows and calves scrambled to their feet, kicking up small clouds of dust.

The hunters were only two gunshots away and their horses were gaining rapidly on the lumbering buffalo. The big bull turned, raised its tail and charged the hunters. Mercredi felt his heart leap into his throat. This brown monster was nothing like his star-studded *bôfflo*. God, long's he don't come at me! he thought. But the bull went for Gauthier, who was obliged to use his rammed shot to put a bullet just above its muzzle.

The Choquette horse was performing wonders. Coming to the ring of young bulls that were providing a primary line of defense between the cows and the hunters, she headed instinctively for the less agressive ani-mals and slipped between them. Realizing that they had been bypassed, the bulls turned abruptly and abandoned the cows to their fate. A few more strides and the mare was among the cows and calves, which kept running with heads low, intently, as if running required total attention. Jérôme spied a good sized female, aimed behind her ribs and fired. The animal dropped dead, its lung shattered. The horse chose the next vic-tim while her rider reloaded. It was already time to fire again before Mercredi had finished tapping the butt on the saddle. Another buffalo crashed to the ground. With one less ball in his mouth, he could speak some words of appreciation to his mare.

"Nife wo'k, girl! Yer pweddy good!"

The cows were scattering. No way to follow all of them. He had to choose. Mercredi glanced at a young animal, medium sized, not too speedy or too far away. He turned the horse's nose toward his victim and kicked hard with his heels to show her clearly what he wanted, and began recharging. The horse hardly needed so much telling. She easily overtook her prey, even without the hill they were starting up. Buffalos are poor at running uphill; Mercredi found himself beside the cow before he had finished recharging. He was still juggling his powder horn as the mare and buffalo ran neck and neck down the other side.

Suddenly he heard galloping hoofbeats approaching. Another hunter was after his cow! No way! He spat a ball down the muzzle and, taking the risk of not tapping it home, lowered the barrel to take aim at the cow. A ball whistled past his ear.

"Goddam fool," he yelled, turning to look at the reckless hunter. He nearly fell out of the saddle. A big, half-naked devil on a piebald gelding was recharging his gun with an embarrassed grimace. A Sioux! The Indian was staying behind and to the left. Mercredi could not shoot him unless he turned to face backwards in the saddle. He'd let others try that. He braced against the stirrups and yanked on the reins with all his might. The horse came to a stop with a whinny of indignation. The Indian, taken by surprise, kept going. Mercredi raised his rifle, aimed at the Sioux's back, and fired. The rifle exploded with a deafening blast. Mercredi found himself in the grass.

When he sat up, Sioux and buffalo had vanished over the next hill. He smelled something odd; putting a hand to his face, he discovered that his right eyebrow and lashes were missing. Even his moustache felt less ample. The horse was chewing on her bit; the jerk on the reins had cut her mouth. The exploded rifle was smoking in the grass.

There was nothing left to do but go back to camp, hoping not to meet any more Sioux. Jérôme saw no others. In fact, when he rejoined the Métis, he discovered that he was the only one to have seen the Indian. Naturally, no one believed his story. Everyone thought his gun had blown up through his own clumsiness and he had invented the Sioux story as a coverup. Fine *okimaw* he was! A disaster with every hunt! And whoever saw a chief look like that! Half his face like a plucked goose and his cheek burnt all red and black from the powder!

"Hey, Mercredi!" he heard someone call. "That spirit you hear talkin' to you, is it Pakkosus maybe?"

Pakkosus is the spirit of misfortune. The hunters were in good humour. They had not forgotten who had led them to the buffalo, but while they followed his advice they could also laugh at him. The spirits sometimes choose to speak through fools. No one knows why.

That evening the Mercredis ate a stew of oesophagus, tongue and hump. As always in the rutting season, the meat tasted slightly of wild onion. They ate alone; Jérôme had no wish to entertain anyone. He was the one who had seen the buffalo in his dream, who had found the herd and been attacked by a Sioux warrior. He deserved to be feasted and was being ridiculed.

When the rest of the family had lain down to sleep, Jérôme lit a big fire of grass and willow boughs. Into it he threw sweet hay and sagebrush to perfume the air. Then he unsheathed his knife, cut into pieces a woollen blanket bought that spring, and offered it piece by piece to the flames and to the Buffalo. When the last piece of wool had been consumed, he looked up at the stars and there was peace in his soul. It was very cold.

The drying fires were revived in the morning. For part of the day the children were again put to work gathering deadwood. As soon as there was enough, the boys took off on a chipmunk hunt.

In autumn, chipmunks roam the forest in search of seeds and nuts and store them underground. They are quick and wary and difficult to get near. The boys lured the animals into the open by sucking noisily on the backs of their hands. Then, yelling and shouting, they drove them up into the trees, where chipmunks are ill at ease. They shot them down with blunt-headed arrows, taking care to shoot against the treetrunk so as not to lose the arrows in the forest.

Askik loved the sport. His whole being rejoiced at the sight of a tiny chipmunk, cheeks bulging and paws quivering. When he lifted his bow with the animal chattering at him from high in the tree, when he let the cord roll from his fingers and felt the arrow fly, his heart would beat with terror and fascination, as if he were both hunter and hunted. When the broken little body fell to the ground with limbs in spasm, however, he would almost be sorry to have killed it. Yet if he had not killed he would have been branded as an incompetent. A Métis who cannot hunt must sponge off his neighbours.

After the hunt, the boys lit a fire and roasted their tiny game. It was customary during these feasts to discuss the affairs of the camp, as if the hunters gathered around the fire had been shooting buffalo instead of rodents. The merits of hunters, cayuses and guns were argued heatedly. A stranger hearing the names l'Heureux, Le Brave and Tonnerre might wonder which were weapons and which were horses. Among the boys, however, each name was greeted by catcalls and compliments too. A swift steed brings honour to its entire family — both horses and humans.

But a rifle that explodes brings shame. When the hulking Mathias saw that Askik had three chipmunks skewered on a stick while he himself only had two, he unkindly brought up the episode of the previous day's hunt.

"Hey, Mercredi! Lucky yer arrow didn't go off in yer face like yer pa's gun!

A salvo of jeering laughter met the dig. No doubt about it, the big boy knew how to twist the knife! Askik, busy browning his chipmunks, had not expected this. A surge of fury seized him. He wanted to leap at Gauthier, hammer him with his fists, but had to hold back. Mathias was too big and strong. Askik's chin trembled and tears of rage and helplessness welled up in his eyes. He wanted to speak up, crush his enemy with sarcasm, but when he opened his mouth what came out was a quavering, ludicrous sob. Mathias howled with laughter.

"Go ahead an' cry, baby!"

"*Tché! Tché!* Crybaby Mercredi!"

"His pa has dreams!"

"Then he don't know which way to go!"

"Crybaby! Crybaby Mercredi!"

It was more, much more than Askik could bear. He let his chipmunks drop in the fire, seized his bow and an arrow from behind him, took aim at Mathias's right eye and drew the string with all his might. Mathias turned ashen. Horrified, the others fell silent. Finally the silence was broken by a voice; a steady, dispassionate voice.

"Gauthier, shut yer mouth."

Askik lowered his bow. The others turned their eyes back to the chipmunks. Someone retrieved Askik's skewer and handed it to him.

The boy who had spoken offered a terse explanation. "That gun was ours," he said. "Mercredi bought it from my father. It was a good gun, but he had to shoot without ramming. Things like that happen."

And that was all. The conversation resumed, avoiding the subject of guns. Only three of the boys remained silent: Mathias because he was afraid, Askik because he was ashamed, and Charles Ross, the boy who had spoken, because he was not much given to talk anyway. He had black hair like the others, but parted on the right like an Englishman. He was reputed to be a good hunter, though he never brought back more than two or three chipmunks, even in spring when it was not unusual for a boy to kill twenty. Yet it was said that he had killed a deer.

When the meal was over, Askik returned to the camp. He did not see Mathias hiding behind a tree until the big boy stepped out at the last minute and blocked his way. Although he was head and shoulders taller than Askik, he did not lay a hand on him.

"You're gonna pay for that, you little creep!" he hissed.

The women took turns at the fires through the night to hasten the drying. The smoke rose straight up. The sky was clear. "*Witahkayaw*," the old people said as night fell. And indeed, the cold became so intense that the women had to light another fire, a blazing one, to warm themselves by. A neighbour came to wake Anita several hours before dawn. She and two other women walked from one smoke fire to the next, smothering the flames with dry branches or reducing them with cold grasses so that the meat would dry but not cook. The sun, when it rose, found the prairie silent and covered with frost. There were no birds left.

Anita returned calm and happy to her own fire. Her companions had talked to her nicely, normally, as they used to do. All it took for the women to get along was to have the men asleep.

Jérôme threw back the teepee door flap and emerged, shivering.

"Did it freeze?"

Anita gave no reply. All he had to do was open his eyes; the prairie was glistening. Jérôme squatted in front of the fire, holding out his hands. He looked old this way, with his stubbled chin, rumpled face and tangled hair. Still, he was in good humour.

"I had a big sleep, *ma vieille*!"

His wife remained silent.

"I dreamed about St. Boniface. And Montreal!"

"You never been to Montreal!"

"I was there last night. Heh, heh! What d'you think that can mean, eh?"

Anita held her tongue, fearing some crazy new scheme.

"*Monéong!*," Jérôme sighed, turning his back to the flames to warm the seat of his pants. "I always wanted to go an' now it's for sure I'll go. 'Cause I dreamed it. But why'd I go to Montreal, d'you s'pose?"

He thought for a minute. Maybe to represent the Métis... in the government, perhaps. This was a stunning idea; it had never occurred to him before. The Red River was not a part of Canada, but the Canadians might like to hear the views of a French Métis. Or a Métis ambassador.

"An ambassador!" he shouted gleefully. "I'm gonna be an ambassador!"

"Shut up! The neighbours will hear!"

"So what? I dreamed about Montreal, that's gotta mean somethin'. Hey! Maybe I'll be goin' there for business. Maybe I'm gonna be rich! That's even better'n bein' an ambassador. Hooo-ee!"

"Be quiet I tell you!"

"I'm gonna build a big house beside the bishopric. Eight chimneys! Loadin' dock at the gate t' take in goods. Whatcha got to say 'bout that, woman?"

He laughed loudly, as happy as a child waiting for a gift.

After breakfast the men went looking for more buffalo. They killed a solitary heifer that must have got separated from the herd during the hunt three days earlier. Too far away, they saw a dozen pronghorn antelopes which scampered off, flashing alarm signals with the white hair on their rumps. After this, nothing.

"Don't get it," Gauthier said as he watched them escape.

Ten years earlier there had been as many pronghorns as buffalo. The two lived side by side in perfect harmony. The buffalo ate the grass and the pronghorns fed on the broad-leaved plants. There were not that many men on the prairie, so why were the herds disappearing?

So as not to delay moving on, the Métis did not dry the meat from the heifer. It was distributed among the families, who ate it on the spot. The next morning they broke camp.

They thought at first it was just a clump of trees between two hills. They would have gone on their way if not for something white waving at the top of the tallest tree. Scouts sent on reconnaissance found a circular enclosure made of branches. Poles were laid from the top of the palisade to a mast planted in the middle, converging like the spokes of a wheel. A dance lodge, built that very year, judging from the leaves still clinging to the branches.

When Mercredi entered the lodge — on foot because the Choquette horse refused to go in — one of the scouts had already climbed the ceremonial mast. There were some offerings of cloth hanging from it, but young Sansregret was not interested in these. The thing he coveted was attached to the very top: a white buffalo hide. The Indians held an albino buffalo to be sacred. It belonged to the Sun, the Great Mystery. It was a singular blessing for a hunter to kill a white buffalo; he would keep the hide until the following spring, when he would offer it to the Sun during the Dance of Thirst.

For the Métis, a white buffalo skin had a usefulness of a different kind. An albino hide was worth a dozen others at a trading post. Sansregret was not well rewarded for his pains, however; once the hide was down on the ground, it became clear that the birds and elements had left it in lamentable condition. Great patches of hair were missing and the skin was dry and shrivelled. Sansregret kept it anyway, hoping to cut a saddle cloth out of it. He was warned that despoiling a Sun lodge could be dangerous, but the brash young man just laughed. Jérôme Mercredi briefly considered ordering him to put the hide back, then let it drop.

Two days later he was sorry. A scout appeared on a hilltop and threw a handful of dust in the air, which meant, "There are many." Mercredi did not need an explanation.

"Do the circle!" There was not a cry, not an oath. The Métis gathered their children, unhitched their oxen and arranged their carts in a circle, rims of the wheels touching, poles passed between the spokes to block the wheels, shafts pointing out. The animals, women and children took refuge in the centre of the circle and the men took up firing positions outside, behind stacked pemmican bags and barrels of water. The women dug trenches for the children.

Sioux warriors began to mass on the hills. It was time to go and talk. Mercredi asked several men to go with him. He put Askik in the saddle behind him. The Sioux, he thought, would appreciate this gesture of confidence.

In such circumstances, the hardest part was arriving in one piece before the chiefs. The Métis passed between phalanxes of young warriors who would not have spurned a good fight. The braves shouted insults or showed their bared behinds in the hope of provoking the Slotas, the Greasy Ones.

Jérôme kept cool. The more Sioux there were, the less the insults rankled. Calmly, he called the scout who had given the alert.

"Where's their camp?"

"A bit farther. On a river."

"What river?"

"Dunno. Didn't look very close."

"Gauthier!" Mercredi muttered out of the corner of his mouth that was farthest from the Sioux, "Is there a river over *outa?*"

"The Souris, I think."

"This river o' yours got cover?" Mercredi was anxious not to fight in open prairie.

"Not much. Flat banks. No woods. Lotta mud."

"Gonna be great."

When the procession arrived at the final hilltop, Askik felt his father become tense. He leaned out to look and saw more teepees than he would have thought possible. The Sioux camp was immense; five or six hundred lodges in a depression deep enough to hide them from sight a thousand yards away. Some of the teepees bore mystic designs; most were brown all over. In spite of the fine weather, a thin layer of smoke hung over the camp, produced by hundreds of drying fires. The contours of the village followed the bends of a narrow, wooded river, which was not the Souris but a tributary, the Rivière aux Hivernants.

A horde of naked children and yellow dogs poured out of the village and surrounded the Métis, making an incredible din. A good sign. The Sioux would not attack among their children. It was not reassuring to the Choquette horse, however; a half dozen scrawny mutts were sniffing at her hocks.

When they entered the camp, Askik saw a familiar sight: blackened meat on wooden racks, women pounding pemmican on old buffalo robes, boys carrying bows and dead rodents, men sitting smoking their pipes outside their tents. There was the same smell of butchered meat as in the Métis camp, except that here it was tinged with a strong smell of coffee; in the Métis camp it was tea. These Sioux teepees were lived in all year round and so were better maintained. There was more buckskin clothing and a more pronounced liking for braids. Otherwise, this was much like a Métis camp. To Askik, a second disappointment: he found he was no more frightened by the Sioux than by the Chipeweyans.

Jérôme Mercredi did not share his son's disappointment. He was very frightened by the Sioux. And his anxiety took a leap when he found himself facing the chief of the camp.

All the Métis recognized Standing Buffalo, who had spent several months by the Red River in 1863 and again in 1865, after the massacre of white colonists in Minnesota. The arrival of the three thousand Sioux had thrown the Red River settlement into a state near panic. The intruders had behaved irreproachably, but the Company management, goaded by the local press and backed by a strong Métis militia, had forced them to leave. One of their lesser chiefs, Little Six, was invited to dinner by some traders; drunk, drugged and bound, he was shipped off to the Americans, who promptly hanged him. Today, the Métis had to hope that Standing Bull was not one to bear a grudge.

The chief proved to have an accommodating memory. He invited the Métis emissaries into his teepee and passed the pipe. Askik was assigned to an unprestigious place to the left of the door. When his neighbour received the pipe, he drew on it several times and then handed it over Askik's head to another Indian. Askik was insulted.

Standing Buffalo genially recalled his sojourn in the land of the Great Mother, as the Sioux called Queen Victoria. He opened a bark pouch and spread out some fifteen George III medals conferred on his ancestors for ignoring the American Revolution. He informed the Métis that he was like them, a British subject. A compatriot, practically. He even declared that some day he would return to the Red River, which on reflexion boded ill for American colonists.

Standing Buffalo's lodge was more luxurious than the Mercredis'. The seams were in better condition, the hide thicker. There was a richly decorated inner lining to ensure air circulation and prevent condensation. Medicine bags hung from the wall. On a rack over the fire, pieces of meat were cooking or drying, depending on the height they were placed at. All around the fire, the ground was covered with furs. Standing Buffalo's lodge was made of perhaps fifteen buffalo hides. Métis lodges rarely took more than six. Only a very wealthy man could afford to move a tent this heavy.

The chief enquired where the Métis were bound for, asked politely whether they had had good hunting, sighed with them over the penury of game, and told them to say hello to the Bishop of St. Boniface, whom he called his good friend. In 1863, however, when the bishop had asked him to go back where he had come from, Chief Standing Buffalo had paid no attention. Of this, no one reminded him. The Métis finally took their leave.

As he left the chief's teepee, Jérôme came face to face with a big devil he had seen before with a piebald horse and a gun. The Indian grinned from ear to ear. He thumped Mercredi on the back and recounted their adventure to the audience at hand, laughing till tears came to his eyes. He was remarkably voluble for an Indian. After drying his eyes and for the fifth time describing the look of astonishment on Mercredi's face on finding that he was being pursued, he took Jérôme's arm and led him away, still chattering. Jérôme realized that his new friend was taking him home. So as not to give offense, he did not resist. The other Métis stayed outside Standing Buffalo's teepee, keeping close to their horses.

Fortunately the big devil lived close by. When they arrived at his teepee, he disappeared inside and came out with a rolled-up buffalo robe, which he offered to Mercredi, explaining that it came from the cow they had both been hunting. Then he laughed uproariously again. Mercredi was beginning to find the joke rather stale, but the Indian would not let him go until he had memorized an approximation of the name Jérôme Mercredi. He was a young brave, newly married. His lodge was tiny.

When he rejoined his Métis comrades, Jérôme saw with displeasure that two others had turned up, Louison Champagne and Jules Sansregret, in the wrong place at the wrong time as usual. When he saw Sansregret's saddle pad, he nearly measured his length in the dust. Was it his imagination, or was the albino hide really blazing in the sunlight? His mouth went dry and his heart rose up his throat as if trying to jump out. Fortunately, Sansregret had stayed in the background and the Sioux had not yet recognized their sacred buffalo hide. But the Métis were as good as dead and scalped the minute a single Sioux laid eyes on it.

Mercredi kept walking, stroking his new buffalo robe as if relishing its lustre, but also looking Gauthier hard in the eye. Gauthier, sensing something new, looked about and lit for the barest instant on the albino hide. While Mercredi began his speech of thanks, Gauthier glided up to Sansregret and ordered him in French to leave the camp, covering his saddle pad as best he could with his coat. Sansregret and Champagne, feigning boredom with their leader's speech, moved away on their horses as if to look around the camp, but in fact headed back to their own camp.

When night came, Mercredi called Sansregret before the Prairie Council and beat him black and blue with his fists and feet, taking care, however, to spare his teeth. Sansregret put up a minimum of defense and quickly recovered from his punishment. The buffalo skin was buried in one of the trenches dug by the women.

The glow from the dung fire was barely reaching the crinkled walls of the teepee. The sun was not yet up; the days were growing shorter.

"Askik! Mikiki! *Wanisgak!* Get up!

Anita shook the children in their buffalo robes. The baby Mikiki whined and seemed about to cry. Askik got up at once and approached the fire. He was dressed and had his moccasins on. The cold wind was driving the hide walls hard against the poles.

"Up! Up!" Anita dragged the whimpering baby from under his cover; he was like a baby mouse being snatched from its nest. "Sit here near the fire," she ordered. "And stop cryin'!"

The leather teepee door lifted. Jérôme entered. It was grey-black outside.

"All set, mother. The cart's hitched. Forget breakfast. We'll eat on the way."

The children were wrapped in their buffalo robes and shooed outside while their parents took down the tent. All over the camp, hides slithered down ash uprights and the tents flattened on the ground, like great grey birds settling low in the grass. Oxen backed willingly between the shafts, impatient to be on the march and warming up. In the distance, Askik recognized Mona heaving a large pot into the Gauthiers' cart. The first carts to be ready were getting under way. Soon the only remains of the camp would be a dozen glowing fires, surrounded by teepee stones.

Anita and the baby were sitting in the cart. Mikiki was making faces at Askik, who had to walk. The baby's real name was Michel. His grandfather had named him Mikikinuk, Turtle, after the little fellow had tried to stun a terrapin with his tiny fists. A good sign, grandfather Mercredi had said; he liked his *nossimuk* to have character. For Mikiki, seeing his elder brother walking when he himself was enthroned above the ox was hardly displeasing.

But Askik was happy. It felt good to walk, his head and shoulders warm under the fur and his legs and face stinging with the cold. When he turned around he could see many other cowled children walking beside carts as he was. The littlest were tottering under the weight of robes too big for them. It was a good thing the oxen were slow.

"Askik," his mother cried, "*petsak!* Watch where you're walking! You'll get tangled in the wheel!"

The wheel was taller than he; so grey, so full of cracks, yet it turned with such verve over anything growing in its path. Does a wheel get tired of turning? Does it ever get discouraged by all that distance ahead? Askik wondered if the wind were still drawing sparks from the abandoned fires at the campsite. Is a piece of land unhappy when it's not lived on?

He heard shouts and pounding hoofs. Sansregret and Champagne passed like the wind, yelling to urge on their galloping horses, whose hoofs were already barely touching the ground. A race, involving a bet, no doubt, between the two most impoverished hunters in the camp. The Métis shook their heads as they passed. Sansregret reached the next hillcrest first and shouted a triumphant "*Kah!*" Champagne scowled in resentment.

"Here, Askik, eat."

Anita passed the bannock and dried meat through the bars of the cart. The boy ate the bannock first because it was easier to chew and he was hungry. The meat tasted of wood smoke.

Sansregret shouted something to them from the hilltop, pointing toward the horizon. Champagne had his back to them and seemed absorbed by a sight still invisible to those below.

"*Wey?*" those below called. "What is it?"

The horsemen riding ahead galloped up the hill. When they reached the top they regrouped and seemed to be conferring.

Askik could no longer contain himself. He threw his robe and breakfast into the cart and took off at a run. He saw other boys doing the same thing. A flood of pride and excitement took hold of him. He had the heady feeling of running toward danger. He wanted to be there first. He wanted to be noticed.

The men had dismounted. The Choquette horse had turned her rump to the wind and from the sullen look in her eye seemed to be saying, Now we're in for it! Askik wove a course between the legs of men and horses and looked down over the prairie.

An opaque curtain had fallen over the farthest reaches of the plain, a great grey wall that hid the hills in their march to the horizon.

"Fog?"

"No. Too cold. Too much wind."

"Rain?"

"Too grey."

"What d'you think, then?"

"Snow."

"Don't look like snow to me."

"It's snow all right."

"I say it's fog."

"Too much wind."

"Here maybe. Not down there."

The carts toiled up the hill, their passengers one after another calling, "What's going on?" The replies were confusing. *"Kimwan. Mispoun.* It's raining. It's snowing."

"We'll find out soon enough anaways," Gauthier muttered.

The smoky wall came steadily closer as they watched. The hills and ravines in its way became hazy, then grey, then disappeared.

The oxen did not stop when they reached the top of the hill but started at once down the other side. The hunters remounted, their eyes fixed on the approaching grey wall. Each time they came to the top of a rise it was closer, only a few hills away now. Soon there was only flat prairie between the first carts and this wall that was as grey as a wild goose. The whole sky was darkening.

At first there were only tiny flakes, darting about like gnats and melting the instant they fell. Then came the regular troops, fat, soft flakes driven diagonally by the wind and falling methodically, in earnest. The snow began to accumulate among twigs and roots that were no longer warm, on reeds and rushes in the sloughs, on the covers over the carts. It fell in long white streaks slashing through the air. The horses hung their heads and blinked. Askik did likewise so as not to be blinded. He heard angry voices coming from the powdery white obscurity ahead.

"Gotta make camp. Wait fer it t' pass."

"What if it don't pass? Without firewood we'll croak from the cold."

"But we can't see nothin'. In the time it's gonna take to find wood..."

"C'mon now... (Askik recognized his father's voice.) We'll stop soon's we get to some trees. We'll find some."

"I told you we shoulda loaded up with wood back at the river."

"Well, now it's too late," Mercredi replied. "No use talkin' about it."

"No use talkin'! It woulda been more use if you'da tried thinkin', then we wouldn't be in this mess."

"You dream 'bout *bôfflo* but not snow, eh?"

There were other voices with just as bitter words. Mercredi made no reply, just rode with his head high, the hurt showing in his eyes. Askik pitied his father. He resolved never to put himself at the service of men. One day, he thought, when everyone needed *him* to save them from a horrible death, he would remember his father and block his ears.

The storm rolled over the Métis like a millstone over grain. They bent their heads before it, made themselves small. The children were

86

rolled up in their robes under the cart covers, which flapped in the wind. The teenage boys gathered and put on a front of joviality. The big wheels that had been creaking and squealing all summer now turned with a muffled, unreal sound—enough to make every last Métis lose confidence.

Shadows loomed through the storm: stunted willows in a marshy depression. The wheels cut deep into the soft, wet earth. There were fragments of ice mixed with the mud. The cart train skirted the depression, watching for a denser stand of trees. The falling snow made it so hard to see the edge of the slough that the carts were sometimes moving on firm ground and sometimes on a thick mat of reeds and icy water.

"Go to windward so we can get out o' the water."

"No! We'll lose the slough. We gotta find wood."

Askik had begun the day so well that this slough was a real comedown. His feet were soaked. His fingers were blue with cold as he held the fur robe close under his chin.

"*Mistikwak!* Trees!"

Slender poplars battered by the storm. Little underbrush. Ground denuded all around. Nothing to break the wind. The men consulted and decided to stay neverthless. It was becoming dangerous to keep on; no one could see anything.

They put up the tents around the stand of trees so as to have firewood close at hand. Working feverishly, Jérôme and his wife raised the three main teepee poles and anchored them firmly to the ground with strong rope. Then they added ten more poles and with the help of long sticks slipped the hide covering over the framework. Jérôme left his wife to organize the inside. He unhitched the ox and led it into the trees where other animals were already huddled together. Before leaving, he patted it sadly on the shoulder, just above its big black patch; weakened by days and days of forced march, the animals would not all outlive the night. With its placid gaze, it told him it was accepting whatever would become of it.

The Choquette horse was less philosophic. As soon as her bridle was off she rammed her way into the middle of the herd as if determined to put up a fight to save her skin.

Inside the teepee, Anita had swept the floor so that the thin layer of snow would not melt under the Mercredis' bodies when they lay down, but there remained a carpet of wet, pungent leaves that promised to be no more comfortable. In other circumstances, the family would have laid a floor of rushes or evergreen boughs, but the few branches that Jérôme brought back were needed for heat. There was no time to lose. The copse was already full of shadows moving back and forth, rummaging as he was under the snow and shaking the trees, hunting for deadwood. Somewhere an axe was biting into a poplar. Despite the cold, Jérôme was breathing hard and sweating. He needed to lay in a good supply of wood; the night was going to be long.

The storm was worsening. There were no separate snowflakes now; just continuous, luminous blizzard broken only by whirling eddies. The copse was small, yet Jérôme could not see the teepees on the other side. When he went home to warm up he found a hearty fire blazing in the middle of the tent.

"Are you crazy?" he shouted at his wife. He pulled half the burning sticks from the fire and stamped out the flames against the wet leaves.

The fire was now half as hot. The baby began to whine, then stopped when he saw his father's glowering face. The two children were sitting side by side on a tea chest; Anita could not bring herself to lay a robe on the wet ground. Jérôme stood for a moment as if warming up at the puny fire, then went out to look for more wood.

A gust of wind lifted the skirt of the teepee and blew a handful of snow inside. Anita ran outside. There was no prairie or stand of trees out there any more, just stark, moving whiteness that penetrated clothes and stung the skin. Anita piled earth and snow on the lifted edge of the teepee. It only took a minute but already her fingers and ears were hurting.

Now she was truly afraid. Her children did not have winter clothes. There would surely be a shortage of wood. It would not be the first time a Métis camp had been wiped out on the prairie by an early winter.

"Dear Lord God, save us! Gentle Virgin, protect us! Don't let us freeze to death. What good would it do?"

She let out a sob of terror. The teepee's sides flapped as if it were a living thing. The blizzard whipped viciously at the poplars. How could the camp survive such fury?

"Why us, Gentle Virgin? We've had such little luck this summer. Let us get home!"

"What? What's that you said?" She had not seen Jérôme approach. His arms were filled with wood for the fire. His moustache was white with frost.

"We're gonna die, Jérôme!"

"Aw, c'mon now, woman!" Jérôme forced a little laugh. "*Pittigwé!* Go inside 'n make yerself some tea, you'll feel better after."

And indeed, as soon as she had closed the teepee's door flap to the blizzard, she felt reassured. The walls kept billowing and flattening, but the poles were standing firm. The children had taken off their moccasins and, laughing shrilly, were holding them steaming over the fire. Anita spread out the old buffalo hide on which she pounded dried meat, set up her tripod and put on some water to boil.

The storm lasted a night and a day. All this time, or close to it, the children did not leave the tea chest. The small fire only just prevented the ground from freezing, and whenever the Mercredis lay down they would soon be up again, perishing with cold and humidity.

Jérôme tried to dream again of the wondrous buffalo that had brought him to this country, but they eluded him. He blamed himself for this; anxiety was preventing him from making himself wholly available to them, he told himself. His mission seemed so onerous now and he was so disheartened that all that night and the next day he sat by the fire with his head in his hands, not speaking and eating almost nothing. His breathing would deepen occasionally and he would sleep, then the least little thing would waken him — a child's cough, a gust of wind, the fire crackling. On the second evening he began to think the wind was lessening. Several hours later, around midnight, he woke from a bad dream and all was silent. The storm was over.

He threw some wood on the fire, intending to go back to sleep. Instead, he drew his knees up under his chin and gave rein to his worries. They had survived the winter's first storm. That was good. But they still had quite a few days' march, through the snow, in summer clothes. And how many oxen would be left to pull the carts? How many horses? He stepped over his wife, who wakened, drawing in her breath with fright.

"Go back to sleep," he told her. "I'll be right back."

"You'll get lost!"

"The storm's over."

"Virgin Mary! *Egossani!* We thank thee!"

"Go to sleep."

The stars were twinkling through the poplars. All around the copse, pale yellow lights pulsed in the teepees' hearts. Mercredi fought his way through the soft snow. He heard crunching sounds as oxen shifted from one hoof to another. The small herd made a black mass surmounted by vapour plumes. How many animals were dead? He began to count the humps in the snow, moving from one to the next, poking with his hands and feet. If he found a mane under the snow he subtracted a horse from the camp total. Otherwise it was an ox. Next he slipped in among the living animals. Their warm breath smelled of sour grass. His ox had survived. As dark as it was, Jérôme thought he saw a glimmer of friendship in its great brown eyes. The Choquette horse, on the other hand, pretended not to recognize him.

The losses were not so heavy. Four horses. One ox. They could still pull through.

"Mercredi!"

Askik and Mikiki were leaving the camp when Mathias hailed them.

He swaggered toward them, hands in his pockets, trailed by half a dozen sniggering teenage boys.

"Where you goin'?"

"Go get wood," Mikiki replied proudly, pointing to a clump of trees not far off. This was the first time his mother had allowed him to leave the camp without her. Anita had wrapped him in one of her shawls to keep him warm. Its pompoms bounced against his high moccasins.

"Naw, Mercredi, you know there ain't no wood left there, it's all gone already. Gotta go farther'n that. Follow us."

Askik hesitated. He had promised not to take his brother farther than that first clump of trees. But what could he say to Mathias? That he was under orders from his mother? That he was not his own master?

"Mikiki," he said, "go see Maman."

"*Mouats!*" The younger boy looked aggrieved but he stamped his foot and held his ground. "Mikiki go get wood with Askik. Maman said!"

"Another time, Mikiki. You'll go another time."

"*Mouats!*"

The big boys snickered. Askik lost his temper.

"Mikiki, go back! *Kiwé!*"

"No! Go get wood with Askik!"

Askik seized the little fellow by the shoulders, turned him around and pushed him hard toward the carts.

"*Awasse!* Go!"

Mikiki turned, howling with rage and despair.

"No! Maman said!"

He looked absurd, his face creased, his cheeks bathed in tears, his mouth twisted. The big boys laughed out loud.

"*Awasse!*" Askik picked up a lump of earth and made as if to throw it at his brother.

Defeated, crying his heart out, the little boy turned and headed back toward the camp. The fringe of the shawl dragged behind him.

Mathias led off with resolute step as if they had a long way to go. The little group crossed coulees and climbed hills, jumped half-frozen brooks and passed thick clumps of trees. Askik, still embarrassed over his brother's behaviour, did not dare ask why they were not stopping for wood. When they had skirted three clumps without sign of stopping, Mathias himself felt obliged to offer an explanation.

"Spruce," he said. "There was scouts saw spruce t'other side o' that big hill over there. It's spruce burns best."

Askik nodded, though it was not clear to him why spruce was that much better.

The sky had clouded over again, but the day was mild. The snow clung to the boys' feet and the prairie smelled of wet earth, as in spring. It took some effort to remember that this was really late autumn and winter would soon be settling in.

Finally they arrived at the big hill the scouts had talked of. On the other side they found a deep ravine bordered by spindly dogwoods. Askik could see no spruce anywhere. Without a pause, however, Mathias slithered to the bottom of the ravine, clinging to the willows as he went. Once there, he led the group along the dry creek bed, poking into the bushes like a dog following a scent. The ravine twisted and turned and doubled back like a tracked animal. Finally, Mathias dove into a bush shouting, "Come look what I found!"

Between the roots of a pussy willow, he had found an open hole big enough for a beaver.

"What is it?" Askik asked.

"A badger hole. We can catch one."

"Where's the spruce?"

"A bit farther, but we got time."

"Maybe we should go get the wood," said Askik. "The men are gonna wanta leave."

"Nah, baby. If we come home with a badger it'll be better'n wood."

Askik could not see how a badger would be better than wood, but from the way the boys were jostling around the burrow, whispering excitedly, apparently it was.

Mathias revealed the plan of attack.

"*Mistanask* has got two doors, one down here an' one up there on the prairie."

He climbed the steep side of the ravine with surprising agility, considering his corpulence, and disappeared. The others could hear him searching about in the trees at the edge of the ravine.

"Got it!" he cried. "Found the back door. Come up, you guys. No, not you, Mercredi."

He threw down a handful of dried meat.

"Put that in front o' the hole, then go hide on the other side of the coulee. The badger'll smell the meat. When he comes out, you yell. Then we'll yell down the hole up there so he'll be scared t' go back in. He'll try'n run off in the coulee an' we'll kill 'im."

"But that's not all we got to do!" Askik said sensibly.

"It won't take long, but we gotta make the badger think we left. Everybody hide an' keep quiet."

The boys disappeared at the top of the bank. Askik squatted in the underbrush across from the burrow. He heard a few more twigs cracking, then silence. He would have to wait.

Mistanask had probably smelled the meat but had not yet made up his mind to come out. Askik imagined him, a grey mass in his black hole, muzzle twitching with greed, every hair standing on end in fear. He remembered the cruel black claws that badger pelts are adorned with, and a little shudder ran up his spine. He groped quietly in the snow and came up with a good stout stick. This would be his weapon. He imagined what was to come. The badger, twice as big as usual, its eyes glinting with rage, would leap at him with wicked, wide-open jaws. Askik could feel its claws sinking into his arm, its fangs biting through his hand, but he kept beating it with his cudgel, stupendous, resounding blows. His awed companions took flight, more frightened by his ferocity than by the beast, leaving him alone with his awesome adversary. Then as night fell he returned to camp, exhausted and pale from loss of blood, the badger draped across his shoulders. Contemptuously, he flung it at the feet of...

An owl hopped out of the burrow. Askik could not believe his eyes. Just a little owl! After all this time! With the carts getting ready to leave! He was going to shout, "Mathias, come see your badger!" but he hesitated. Maybe the owl was sharing the burrow with the badger. Owls do live with prairie dogs. The bird pecked absently at the meat, looking about for the source of the gift. Eventually its yellow eyes came to rest on Askik. The boy tried to keep as still as the trees, but his legs began to shake in that squatting position and he had to shift his weight to the other foot. The owl flew away.

Askik did not know what to do. If he left his post and there was still a badger in the burrow, the others would be furious. If the burrow was empty and they waited too long, they would have to go home without any spruce.

Askik stayed a long time there in the bushes. The owl came to light on a branch and, keeping an eye on the boy, began bobbing its head at him. For a time the boy watched it, then wearied and turned his eyes back to the burrow. Secretly, he prayed to Mistanask to come up and get it over with. Then he cursed him heartily, with no better result.

How long had he been hiding in this ravine? It made no sense. His parents would be furious. Holding up the cart train like this when winter was threatening to sweep over them all! Taking great care not to break any twigs, and without taking his eyes off the burrow, he backed his way up the bank. When he reached the top he looked up long enough to wave to the others. The opposite side was deserted.

At first he thought it must be the light. The winter sun cast long shadows, darkened the underbrush. But no, there was no one there.

"Hey!" His voice resounded in the cold air. He crossed the ravine. He found the boys' footprints in the snow but could not follow them once out of the underbrush. There the ground had been swept clean by the wind. The frozen earth did not show any prints.

"Mathias!"

He knew that the others would be spying on him, hoping to see him cry.

"We're gonna be late! They'll be waitin' for us!" He was being very reasonable.

A bird sounded a few notes.

"Mathias! You bonehead!"

The silence astonished him. Not a snicker, not a hint of movement. Nothing but the slithering of the wind over the big hill all gold and white.

He started walking. They would come out for sure when they saw him leave. But when he reached the top of the hill he was still alone.

The winter sun was turning great swaths of the prairie to gold, leaving the hollows and north slopes in shadow.

"Mathias!" He put some annoyance into it, in case there was someone to hear it. In truth, he was already feeling more fear than anger. Look as he might in all directions, he could not see the camp.

The cold drove him from the hilltop. He took what seemed the most likely direction. Once he was on the move, his fear dissipated. Just the movement of his legs seemed to rouse a sense of direction.

He began to enjoy walking again. As he passed a colony of amaranth, he gave each spike a mighty slap to make snow and seeds fly. He followed the tracks of a hare that was heading more or less toward the camp. He thought angrily about Mathias and the others, who had long since been home and were pretending innocence while the grownups were fuming over the delay, for which he alone was now responsible. His father must have been taking a lot of curses.

He consulted the sun. It could be about noon.

He hesitated at the edge of a very deep ravine. He did not remember it. But the prairie is big; a ravine can look different and change direction many times. He crossed it and kept going.

A bit farther on he came to a slough ringed with willows. The frozen mud supported him more or less. He searched among the cattails and found some grackle and hummingbird nests. He kept the biggest. As he was about to leave the slough, he came upon the massive tracks of a grizzly among the reeds. He ran out from under the trees with his heart pounding.

Over the next hill he fell on a small lake where the water was not quite frozen. Some ducks circled the lake, swearing crossly, and disappeared. Askik could not remember this lake, either. He examined the surroundings and realized that he had veered too far to the left. He headed right, keeping the sun at his back. Although this last precaution seemed critical, it was more instinctive than reasoned. He tried to remember the position of the sun in relation to the ravine where he had watched for the badger, and how the ravine lay in relation to the angle of their arrival, but all this was very complicated and pointless since he was convinced that he would come to the camp any minute now. Here and there he spotted landmarks that looked familiar — the pitch of a slope, a patch of sagebrush, an angular granite rock. All confirmed that he was on the right track.

Still, how long the way home seemed! Each time he came over a hill he was sure he would find the carts on the other side, and each time there was another expanse to cross, another hill to reach. He threw away the stick he had found in the ravine. A few steps farther on he dropped his birds' nests. Now he hated them all, the stick, the nests, the sloughs, the prairie. The prairie most of all. His legs ached. His hands were cold. Thinking he was thirsty, he picked up a handful of snow, but it tasted of old hay. He was neither cold nor hungry, in fact. All he wanted was not to be alone any more.

The wind was stirring up the clouds again, driving them together, stitching them back into one solid piece. The sun resisted for a time, then disappeared. The white and ochre prairie turned brown and grey again, and smoky. Evening was coming. Winter was coming. Askik quickened his pace, throwing anxious glances westward. How fast the day was dying! His father must have sent some Wolves out to look for him. If he called they might hear him. But what would he call? Maman? He would be laughed at. He thought for a moment and then cupped his hands and called at the top of his voice:

"Over here!" And so that there should be no mistake, in case someone else was lost on the prairie, he added, "It's me, Askik"

He listened, sure he was going to hear galloping hoofs or the report of a gun. He looked all about the horizon in case a rider had come to the top of a hill. There was no one. The icy wind was biting at his ears and fingers. In the west, the clouds were salmon coloured. Already the hills were melting one into the next, the ravines and sloughs quietly vanishing.

He began to run. He had so little time left. If he reached a high point perhaps he would see the fires of the camp. But if walking was difficult, running was exhausting. As the snow cooled it formed a slippery, breakable crust. Askik fell so often that his elbows were bruised. When he came to the next hilltop he searched in every direction for the great fire that his parents would not have failed to light and would keep burning until he was home. A whole mountain of precious wood was going to disappear because Askik Mercredi had neglected to pay attention to where he was going. His ears began to burn. Still, the fire might light up close at hand after all. Then he'd be there before the first pile of wood was consumed, he'd come out of the shadows whistling softly, as if returning from a little stroll, and he'd ask innocently, "What's going on? Is somebody lost?"

A patch of wild flax rattled at his feet. The prairie had shrunk. The black hills pressed in on the child from all sides, except in the west where a little light hung on. There was no fire, no moon, not a single star. Perhaps his parents were waiting for total darkness before lighting the fire. Askik begged them aloud not to wait any longer. He wanted not to be alone any more, wanted to know that they were still thinking about him. He imagined his father throwing precious wood on the fire; things were going so badly for him already, without this. He thought about his mother and the comfortable smell of leather and tea she exuded. Finally he thought about Mikiki, whom he had spurned. He wanted to throw himself on the ground, hammer his head with his fists, really hurt himself so he could feel a bit sorry for himself. Bitterly, he swore never to listen to Mathias again.

But what was the good of making resolutions for the future? A dark and ominous night was filtering out of the North Pole and trickling down to the prairie. To the west, there remained only a pale grey line with the farthest hills profiled against it. One rose much higher than the rest. Was it the big hill they had visited that morning? With all his heart, Askik wished he were there. That hill was dear to him, almost like home, because it was familiar. The cold wind blurred his vision. With his arms wrapped around his body, hopping up and down on his ice-cold feet, he began to cry, quietly so as not to be heard by all the things that come out at night. Why was there no fire? What were his parents thinking of? Didn't they want him any more?

"Papa!" he sobbed loudly in fear and anger.

He stopped abruptly. He had just seen a cone wedged between two hills, as black as the hills but surmounted by a tuft of sticks. A teepee!

He uttered a bleat of joy. To think he was this close to the camp! He careened down the hill, stumbled, slid all the way to the bottom on his knees. He was up in a twinkling, running for all he was worth, yapping like a happy little fox. How hungry he was! How good the pemmican was going to taste! How beautifully he was going to get along with Mikiki from now on! He'd tell him about the bear tracks and the younger boy would be wide-eyed. Askik was laughing already.

He stopped dead. The ghostly shape before him was indeed a teepee, but it was alone. No camp. No fires. Just this one Indian lodge, painted with mystic designs. A wide black band symbolizing the Earth ran all around the base. A red circle, the Sun, flamed brightly near the peak. Between them were symbols of dreams and of the teepee's owner. The door was fastened from outside. Two lances trimmed with eagle feathers were planted in the ground, flanking the door. There was no sound from inside.

Askik approached cautiously, listening. He was passing the lances when he was startled by a whirring sound; a ceremonial rattle was hanging among the eagle feathers, swinging in the wind.

"*Tansé?*" he said shyly. "*Nekowatsin,* I'm cold. May I come in?"
The ear of the teepee clacked in the wind. There was no smoke.
"D'you know where our camp is?"

No answer. Askik looked around. Perhaps the owner was away
hunting. There were no footprints in the snow. The man had perhaps
been gone several days. And how was one to know whether or not he
would be back tonight? Could Askik wait? He was shivering with the
cold. If he went inside the teepee he would be out of the wind. He
would not disturb anything. If the hunter came home and found him
there, he would simply need to explain, tell him that he had been freezing and had no choice but to come inside. Judging by the painting and
the lances, the owner was a man of quality who would not refuse to take
in a little boy who was cold.

Askik went to the door of the silent teepee. He looked around him
one last time, and seeing no one, removed the first pin at the bottom. It
was difficult; the leather eyelets had stiffened. A drum attached to the
outside wall tapped gently against the hide. Feeling braver, the boy
removed a second pin, then a third. He lifted the leather flap and
looked timidly inside.

"Is anyone here?"

He put his face closer. A smell of moldy earth escaped from the
teepee, the mustiness of an ill-kept cellar. He let the flap drop and drew
back brusquely. He wanted to run, but where to? A poplar whispered
somewhere in the shadows, but without flintstones, what good would it
do to have wood? The wind blew into the teepee through the half-open
door and billowed the walls. He must close it again to keep the snow
out. He stood rooted to the spot. Should he go in? Or leave? He decided
to leave. After all, he wasn't really so cold. And how did he know the
camp wasn't just steps away. Better to walk than wait.

Resolutely, he turned his back on the teepee and hurried away.
The wind whistled in his ears. The snow crunched under his feet. He
would walk all night, until daybreak.

He went less than a hundred paces. He could see neither sky nor
earth any longer. He was walking in a very small circle of shadows
through which tufts of grass, rocks and bushes passed. Each stride
brought him into a different world. He felt the ground dip under his feet
but did not know if he was coming to a slough or a precipice. His pace
slowed, became more tentative, then stopped altogether. Was the great
grey bear also walking in the darkness?

He turned around and after a few minutes of anxious searching found the lone teepee again.

He hung back a long while before going in. The rattle and the drum did not seem to like the idea. The poplar in particular seemed to disapprove, whistling loudly as if to say, I can't see you but I know what you're up to, wretched child. Such hostility was unnerving, but now Askik was too cold to cry. He could not feel his fingers or feet any more and his thighs were as hard as stone. Reluctantly, he grasped the flap of the teepee and lifted it once more. This time there was no musty smell; the wind had done its job.

Askik slipped inside, keeping close to the wall so as not to go a foot farther into the lodge than necessary. He squatted near the door, which he left partly open, and for a long time stared stubbornly at the grey bar made by the opening, not daring to look around him. Then, when his eyes had become accustomed to the darkness, he began to examine the inside of the teepee. There were parfleche bags and bark baskets on the ground. More lances. A shield hung from the poles of the tent. And in the middle, where the fire should have been, was a shadowy, voluminous shape. A curiously large object for a teepee, which normally houses only portable things. A wall, or a giant container, Askik thought. He could not really tell. What was behind that wall, or in that container? A shiver ran down his spine. He curled up, not taking his eyes off the mysterious shape. He felt something rumple under him; it was a blanket. Carefully, he gathered it up and covered himself with it. The wool was dusty but soft and warm, like new.

He settled back against a pole and prepared to wait until morning. He would not allow himself to sleep. He would keep watch until dawn, tense like a hare, ready to leap through the door at the first sign of movement behind that wall. Or inside that container.

But fatigue works furtively. It began by undoing the knots in the boy's stomach and legs, then rounded his back against the hard ash pole and coaxed him to lean against the elastic leather wall of the tent. It slowed his breathing and bent his head. It ventured finally to close his eyes; he started awake, heart in his mouth. Then it began again, patiently, persistently, ten times, twenty times, and each time took less time to get the better of the boy.

Askik slept. He continued his vigil in his dream, however. It was even better, because here he was neither cold nor sleepy. He could see as if it were daylight. He sat straight and effortlessly, dressed in beaded clothes, armed with his lance and shield. Outside, the drum and rattle beat in unison. In the centre of the room, the great grey mass danced and twisted. The faster the beating rhythm, the more the mass rippled with humps and creases.

Suddenly it became small and muscular. A badger appeared, spitting angrily, its yellow fur bristling, its eyes flashing with rage.

"*Napeo*! Man!" it hissed, "What are you doing here?"

Askik remained calm and stared at the beast. What were those fangs and claws to him? He no longer had to defend himself. The badger lost countenance, backed away, and spitting hate, turned back to clay.

The dance resumed. The drum and rattle filled the teepee with their thunderous pulsing. From the heart of the mass there came a cavernous growl. Now the formless clay grew short, thick legs, a low-slung belly and a heavy, evil head.

"*Napeo*!" roared the bear. "What are you doing here?"

Askik did not raise his shield, did not grasp his lance. He was motionless and full of wisdom. His arms felt dry and stiff, his eyes could see without opening. Why should he need arms or eyes, lance or shield? He no longer had to reply. The bear roared, shrivelled up like a frozen plum, and turned into a grain of clay dancing on the blankets on the ground.

Then suddenly the ball of clay burst into a thousand demons and ghosts, which began to whirl above Askik's head, all vociferating angrily in their hideous voices:

"*Napeo*! What are you doing here?"

They created such a tumult in the air that Askik could feel their long grey locks flicking at his cheeks. Cheeks as dry as parchment. Yet none of this upset him. He no longer had anything to fear.

The boy awoke. The great grey mass was there before him, motionless. The rattle and the drum and the wind had fallen silent. It was freezing hard. Although Askik rolled himself up under his woollen blanket, he was cold all the way through to his innards, to the roots of his hair. He had lost all feeling in his legs. He was freezing to death. He thought of the scouts who would find him this way, rigid and hard like an animal dead in a trap in winter. They would take him back to his mother, stone dead but still sitting, ready to take his place by the fire. He was surprised he was not afraid. He was even impatient to go back to sleep, though it would certainly be to die. What good would it do to fight it? Who was going to save him?

The great teepee disappeared, or rather became transparent, for Askik was again the centre of his circle. He saw the sparkling, snow-covered prairie stretching all the way to the horizon. He saw the brightly shining sun, but also the moon and stars, though it was broad daylight. A great wolf with creamy pelt was standing before him.

"*Napeo*, what are you doing here?"

"I'm cold," Askik complained, rubbing his arms.

"Me too," replied the wolf, but it moved not a hair.

"I'm hungry," the boy countered, holding his stomach.

"Me too," the wolf repeated, but it did not lick its chops.

"I'm all alone," the boy whimpered, pointing at the endless prairie."

"Me too," replied the wolf without looking at the prairie.

"I'm lost!" Askik cried, lifting his arms in exasperation.

"I'm never lost."

A violent shudder woke him once more. He was stretched out on the ground yet could not remember lying down. A faint light had filtered into the teepee; it would soon be daylight. But it was too late. Not only his legs but his whole side turned to the ground were frozen. The cold was rising toward his heart. He thought about his mother, who was more childlike than he himself and would probably cry for him. He thought about Mathias, who had killed him, but found this an uninteresting subject. He briefly felt like crying for himself for dying alone and so young, but then his emotions fled and left him calm and dispassionate.

He was relieved to fall asleep again, happy to leave at last and promising himself a little visit to the camp before going up to heaven.

But he was wakened again by an old man's voice, a warm voice from the grey mass in the middle of the teepee.

"*Nikosis*, my son, what are you doing here?"

Askik raised himself on his frozen elbows.

"*Nikosis*," the voice repeated, "what are you doing here?"

"I'm lost," Askik replied.

The grey mass remained silent, as though it had not heard.

"I am lost!" Askik said more distinctly with a touch of annoyance.

"No, you're here."

A blinding light flooded the teepee. Askik saw a face framed in fur looking at him through the door and speaking in words he could not understand. He was going to reply politely that he was dead and would soon be out of the way. Instead, he rose off the ground. He hovered briefly over the great grey mass, which turned out to be a low enclosure of clay around a white head wearing feathers.

Everything that followed — the bright daylight, the crisp air, the piebald horse, the rough shirt rubbing his cheek — all of it vexed him in the extreme. Never would he have expected his ascent into heaven to be so prodigiously long and complicated. Then he remembered that he would still have to roam for four days before taking the Way of the Wolf, and he grudgingly resigned himself to the inconvenience.

A woman was making him drink a bitter decoction that tasted of catnip. Did he have a fever, then? Askik saw two women, Indians. The one who was giving him the drink was young. On the other side of the fire was an old woman bent over her sewing, humming in snatches. Askik observed further that the teepee was richly furnished, that the door was rolled, the sun was shining outside, and there were cries of children coming from all around the tent.

The fever left him gradually. His waking and sleeping moments faded one into the other without his taking note of them. Strangers came in or stopped at the door of the teepee just to look at him. Each waking brought new faces. The young woman talked volubly to the visitors, as if giving reports on the patient, while the old woman nodded her head and uttered satisfied cooing sounds. One of the intruders, a fat woman with an imposing stomach, even made so bold as to poke at the patient's cheeks and limbs.

When evening came at last, the young woman let down the entry flap and put wood on the fire. Not wanting to be waited on any longer by women he did not know, Askik sat up, though he was still light-headed. He wanted to thank his two companions, but they made signs to him to wait.

Minutes later, a man and two teenage boys came in. The boys had their hands in the meat pot as soon as they were seated. The father was more polite and turned first to his guest. He spoke a little Cree and Askik learned from him that, years ago, he had been to St. Boniface in company with a Sioux delegation. He seemed to have pleasant memories of the visit, of the cathedral in particular. It was true that a Sauteau had killed one of the Sioux, but the Métis had obligingly hanged him.

The Indian offered meat to his young guest, who accepted without enthusiasm. The Sioux then served himself, and after satisfying his hunger somewhat, explained how he had found Askik three days earlier while hunting.

He had left his lodge in the early morning to look for mule deer, having seen their tracks the previous day beside a small lake. Arriving at the lake, he had hidden and waited part of the morning without seeing anything. When he finally left his hiding place, he had found the prints of a great grey bear in the mud. The grizzly is the only animal feared by the Sioux. The hunter wanted to make sure the animal was not prowling around his village, and so followed the bear's tracks over the snow-covered prairie. To his astonishment the tracks were joined by those of a child. The Indian had pushed on, increasingly surprised at the direction the trail was taking. Finally he came to the foot of a small hill, where the child had hesitated at length, walking in circles. This was a sign that he did not know he was being followed, or that he was far ahead of the bear.

From the top of the hill, the Indian had immediately located the burial teepee that he himself had helped put up the previous autumn. He was not surprised to see the tracks leading to it; he had had a feeling they would. The bear's and child's tracks continued together as far as the door, which was partly open. Fearing witchcraft, the Indian hesitated. He lifted the entry flap with the end of his club: the child and the old man were untouched. The grizzly had circled the teepee three times, and had not entered.

"So I've only been here three days!" Askik exclaimed in Cree.

"Ehé."

"So maybe my parents aren't far away."

"They're at the Souris River. Our young men saw the carts this afternoon. I'll take you back tomorrow if you're feeling better.

A long silence followed. The teenage boys, having copiously stuffed themselves, were lolling against willow-bough backrests. Although they were too well brought up to stare openly at the visitor, they kept stealing curious glances in his direction. One in particular seemed consumed with impatience. Even the father seemed disappointed not to have heard Askik reveal more about his adventure. Not wanting to put direct questions to him, which would be impolite, he tried a different approach.

"The man you shared the teepee with was a great chief. He had powerful dreams."

"I dreamed in that lodge," Askik said, much ashamed not to have anything more extraordinary to offer. Then, since they were all listening attentively, he continued.

"I dreamed of a badger and a bear and demons, but I wasn't afraid.

Then I dreamed of a wolf, who told me he was never lost. And after that I heard a voice.

"Tell us about this voice."

"It was the voice of an old man. It was a kind voice."

The old woman uttered an exclamation of satisfaction and looked around triumphantly at her family; a look that clearly said, I told you so!

"This is my mother-in-law," the Sioux explained, "the wife of the ancestor who protected you from the bear. He was the one who spoke to you in your dream. He was a great chief."

The old woman looked lovingly at Askik. He felt he had been adopted.

As soon as he woke the next morning, the old woman brought him some marsh marigold tea to unblock his nasal passages, for the fever had given way to a cold. Then she offered him some pieces of meat cooked in a spicy sauce. She must have risen very early to prepare such a feast. Askik had never eaten dog meat, although it was widely appreciated on the plains; he enjoyed it.

When it came time for him to leave, she presented him with an embroidered bag that must have belonged to her husband, in which she had put some dried meat of the finest quality, as well as some medicinal herbs for Askik in case his mother might not have them.

"*Kitom kawapmitin*, I will see you again," he told her politely, and added, "Kokoum," which, when translated, brought tears to the old lady's eyes.

Askik was sorry to leave the Sioux village. He had a brief urge to ask his friends to keep him, to teach him the Sioux ways of hunting and fighting, but then he remembered that if he was to become a man of stature in his own community he would have to go back to school and finish his education. He resolved to invite his Sioux friends to St. Boniface once he had a big house with white rooms and windows of glass.

13

The carts had waited a day and a night for Askik before moving on. Jérôme Mercredi had not wanted to leave; the hunters had deposed him by a crushing majority. Grizzly tracks had been found near the big hill; no one doubted that Askik was dead. The cart train left without him.

The Métis were not lacking in compassion, but they were all afraid of freezing to death. Jérôme searched the prairie for two days and two nights. He arrived at the camp, hungry and dejected, to learn that Askik had been found by the Sioux.

The Métis were camping by a wide, shallow river, the Souris. This river put them at a *demi-bauche*, or two weeks' journey, from the Red River. Most of them would not in fact be going that far, having decided to spend the winter in the high wooded hills separating the prairie from the parklands.

They crossed the Souris in the early morning when the mud was still firm. They were making better time now because there were no hills and they could travel in a straight line. Knowing that they were so close to their goal gave new vigour to men and beasts alike.

Four days later the sky cleared and they could see a thin blue cord on the horizon, very pale, very hazy. This was enough. An explosion of joy broke out at the head of the cart train and spread all the way to the tail, which is to say, all the way to the Mercredis. When he heard the shouts, Askik climbed into the cart and, hoisting himself up on the rails, got his first look at Turtle Mountain. At first sight it was nothing to get excited about. It was in fact just a modest wooded and lake-dotted escarpment. But bears and deer lived there all year round, and the buffalo and elk came there seeking winter refuge.

The carts came to a stop in a big stand of aspens at the foot of the mountain. That night would be their last on the prairie, where they had been for five months, from mid-June to mid-November. They had endured rain, heat, mosquitoes, frost and snow. They had wandered aimlessly, guided by visions and memory, had brushed with hostile nations, endured privations of many kinds in their pursuit of the buffalo. And yet on this last night of their wanderings, there was no celebration. The camp was silent. The families huddled about their own fires; no one went visiting. Brother and sister, husband and wife barely spoke to one another. The silence was briefly broken when a scout arrived, returning late after getting lost in the woods, to announce the presence of a sizeable village of Métis and Cree on the mountain. Even this news failed to shake the Métis out of their despondency. Perhaps they were thinking of their half-empty carts. Perhaps, gloomily putting two and two together, they were finally beginning to believe that the great hunts were now things of the past. They had been hearing it long enough...

Still, for all the hardship it brought them, the prairie was their home, their mother. How could a Métis not spread his wings come spring, shaking off his troubles like an old winter coat, not roam the hillsides and ravines in search of the bearded buffalo, not feel the sting of the wind and shiver beneath the stars? Could all this be coming to an end? Would the Métis never again know the mingled smell of horse, sagebrush and offal? Why had the good Lord made the buffalo and the Indians if there were to be no hunting and warfaring? These Métis men and women had never learned what it was to live in one place, to wake up every morning to the same things to worry about; they could only guess at the duties and conventions that rule the lives of sedentary peoples.

Askik stayed alone by the fire outside. He threw sticks on the flames and watched the sparks fly up into the sky. Some extinguished a few feet up and others flew so high that Askik wondered whether they had gone out or risen too high for him to see any more.

Someone was coming. He heard footsteps, then saw a figure, a clumsily patched cape, then Mona. He had not seen her since his return to camp.

She was thinner. She looked even grubbier now than when she had left St. Boniface five months earlier. Clearly, the Gauthiers left her little time for personal hygiene. But as usual, she bore herself with composure that verged on carelessness. Perhaps she really was a little crazy after all.

"*Tansé*, Askik," she said in that rather flat voice, "I'm glad to see you back."

"*Kinanaskomitin*." Askik was embarrased. His adventure was the last thing he wanted to talk about. However he added, because it was true, "You were right, it was like in your dream."

"I know," she said.

"Are you going to St. Boniface?"

"No, the Gauthiers are stayin' here."

"And your mother?"

"She can't be in St. Boniface no more."

"Where d'you think she is?"

"I don't know."

"You can't stay with the Gauthiers all your life!"

Mona was no longer listening. She was gazing up and over the teepee at the tall, naked aspens swaying slowly in the wind. Behind the trees, the mountain was just visible, blacker than the night.

"What about you, Askik, what're you going to do?"

"I'm goin' back to school."

"*Kekwan ochi*, why?"

Askik hesitated briefly before revealing his plan, but he was burn-ing to tell it to someone. And then, there are things you can say to a woman without fear of being made fun of.

"I want to be educated," he replied. "I don't want to be afraid of nobody no more. I want to live in a big house, like the priests. I want..." He stumbled; it all seemed so unlikely, here beside a fire on the prairie, with Mona. "I want to be a great man!" he whispered at last.

Mona turned to look at him, showing no surprise whatever. "You will be, if you want to," she said simply. "But maybe you won't want to."

"Are the Gauthiers mean to you?"

"I can't complain. Who else would keep me?"

Askik felt a surge of pity for this girl whom nobody wanted.

"When I'm a great man you can come and work for me, Mona. You'll be at home in my house. You'll be well paid. And you'll be able to wash every day."

Mona looked down. Was she blushing? The flames were already giving a glow to her face. Proud of his future generosity, Askik con-tinued.

"Anyway, you can't spend the rest o' your life with Mathias!"

Mona reacted with spirit.

"Mathias ain't bad, Askik. He didn't think you'd get lost when he left you on the prairie. He just thought you'd get home late. He didn't sleep that night, he was so afraid, you know." Then in a low voice she added, "Mathias is very kind to me."

Askik felt a pang of jealousy. Not that he wanted Mona to himself, but it pained him to hear compliments paid to another. Particularly when they were paid to his enemy, Mathias Gauthier.

For a long time there was silence between the children. Askik began to poke at the fire, as if it needed to be well stirred in order to burn.

"Will you come an' see me before you leave for St. Boniface?" Mona asked.

"Ehé! Yes, yes!" the boy blurted without looking at her.

"It's always me that comes to see you. You don't never come an' see me."

Askik remained silent.

"I'm glad you came back, Askik. I was afraid, too."

"*Tché*" replied Askik, his eyes on the ground, "I ain't no baby!" When he looked up, she was gone.

Through meadows and clearings, along a winding trail where the men dug in the snow every ten paces to make sure they were still on the path, the carts slowly climbed up the Turtle's carapace. As darkness fell, which is to say, in mid-afternoon, they came to a pretty lake ringed with maples, aspens and birches. There were nets set under the water.

Minutes later the Métis saw smoke. As they made the turn around a final bend in the lake, they came to a large village of houses and teepees among the trees at the water's edge.

"*Tagosinok!* They're here!" someone called.

Suddenly the village was full of people. Everyone was coming to greet the newcomers: women with shawls hastily thrown about their shoulders, men come straight from butchering, their hands red with blood, old men warmly clothed trailing behind the rest, sucking on pipes gone cold; children most of all, swarming toward the carts as though bent on annihilating their occupants, then becoming tongue-tied with shyness on arriving beside them.

"Hello there, folks!"

"Why, it's the Gingras family!"

"*Tansé,* cousin!"

"Where've you come from?"

"Did you have good huntin'?"

Some Cree families milled about outside the circle of Métis, excited by the vistors' arrival but finding no Crees among them.

"No, not much *bôfflo* this year."

"Ah yes, it was the same fer ever'body."

"Seems the Legardeur bunch had a bit more luck."

"What's that? We was part of the Legardeur bunch! We went off on our own 'cause we hadn't found nothin'."

"Well, we don't know for sure, but it seems Legardeur found a big herd near Devil's Lake.

The men of the cart train gathered around the informative villager, who was sorry now to have talked so much.

"What's goin' on?" Gauthier demanded, pushing his way through the crowd. He had been behaving like a king since Mercredi's deposal.

"Legardeur found a big herd near Devil's Lake!"

"He couldn't've!" Gauthier retorted. "We'd already gone a long way past Devil's Lake and Legardeur was headin' due south!"

"I mean, Legardeur didn't find nothin' in the south," the villager continued. "He turned round an' come straight back north."

Gauthier's face flushed. So Legardeur had changed his mind! If he had done it sooner there would have been no split and everyone would have had good hunting. And while Gauthier was as responsible as anyone for the breakup, in his eyes there were now two guilty parties, first Legardeur and then Mercredi, who had taken everyone in with his talk of visions. Not that Gauthier had ever believed in them, but still, he felt he had been duped.

Mercredi, meanwhile, was having an embarrassing encounter. A man had stepped out of the crowd and seized his horse's bridle, exclaiming, "This here's my brother's horse!"

Recognizing a Choquette — why was it they were all built like buffalos? — Jérôme admitted humbly that the horse did not indeed belong to him, but the other kept vociferating, inviting the whole village to listen.

"You was s'posed to bring 'em back meat! That's three months Ormidas been watchin' for you now. He got nine kids to feed. An' you, you skunk, you was gonna stay here on the mountain fer the winter!"

Jérôme quickly got off the horse. People were beginning to watch. Two or three men were already walking toward them, clearly not intending to mind their own business.

"Look here, Choquette," Mercredi said in a low voice, "we didn't find no cows. Not enough, anaways. It ain't my fault, there just ain't no *bôfflo* no more."

"There's enough fer yer own family!"

"Only just. Barely. But yer wrong, I'm not stayin' on the mountain, I'm goin' straight back to St. Boniface."

In fact, the idea had never occurred to him, but once he had said it, it seemed to him as good as any other. The devil take hunters and hunting! He would go back to trading.

"There ain't no buffalo in St. Boniface, fella." Choquette growled, closing his fists.

There were two or three snickers from the villagers.

Jérôme clenched his teeth. That was enough. He had had more humiliation than he could take. If Choquette started a fight, he'd kill him rather than let himself be whipped. He sought one last time to avoid the fight. He lied.

"I ain't goin' t' St. Boniface t' hunt. I'm in business with my brother Raoul. I'm goin' t' collect my share."

Choquette said nothing. His brow creased in doubt.

"Well, why'd you go t' the prairie this summer?"

"To hunt one last time. I knew the *bôfflo* was goin' for good."

His story was having effect. People were listening closely. He decided to head off the questions.

"When I come down from the north last spring, I didn't wanta spend my money. I borrowed fer my huntin' gear."

He was gaining ground. He could tell from the confused looks on the faces around him. He laid it on some more.

"Raoul and me done a deal together, but we ain't told nobody."

Mercredi was surprised himself at the effect his lies were having. The others were backing off a little, their scorn changed to awe. But why were they looking at him that way? One of them apologetically ventured the next question.

"And you ain't heard nothin' from your brother since that?"

"Er, no," Jérôme said, wary of a trap. "How could he…"

"Mercredi," Choquette said breathlessly, "Yer a rich man!"

"What?"

"Yer rich, I said!"

"Hey, c'm' on," the others cried, "tell 'im!"

"Yer deal worked," Choquette said. "I admit I didn't believe it. When we heard Raoul was sendin' cart trains to Judith Basin, nobody could believe it. Then when we heard that his…that *your* hunters were only takin' the skins, they were leavin' the meat, we thought he'd…we thought *you'd* gone off yer rockers. But *torrieu!* You was right! Yer rich!"

And everyone confirmed it with vigorous nodding of heads.

The rich man's head was spinning. He did not know his brother had sent out a hunting party. Judith Basin was at the end of the earth. And what was the point of only taking the skins? He played it safe.

"I'm glad t' hear it…gentlemen."

His listeners were not used to hearing themselves addressed as "gentlemen." They were now convinced.

"You made a fortune on the American market," piped up a rotund little French Canadian who seemed slightly better informed than the rest. "How'd you know they needed skins?"

"Well… gotta keep yer ears open."

"Hee-aw!" cried the husky Choquette, landing a slap on Mercredi's back that almost deserved an apology, "Gotta keep yer ears open! *Cré* Mercredi!"

Approving laughter rose from the group. Now each was vying with the next to be the most familiar with the rich man. The rotund French Canadian bubbled with admiration, eyes sparkling.

"Who'da thought of it? Sellin' buffalo skins fer factory drive belts!

That's havin' a head fer business!"

Mercredi nodded affably. He even removed his hat to allow all to see his head for business. He would have given a lot to know what a drive belt was, though.

Anita had been watching her husband's mutation from hunter to industrialist and did not know whether to preen or hide. When Jérôme had returned penniless from the North, she had supposed that he had squandered everything. Had he had the foresight instead to entrust some money to Raoul? If so, he might have realized some kind of profit, without exactly becoming rich. About her brother-in-law's competence, Anita had no doubts.

"Okay now, if you'll excuse us, night's comin'," Jérôme said modestly. "It's time I put up our tent."

"No, no!" Choquette exclaimed. "You're gonna stay with us. I got a wood cabin. You'll be nice an' warm there."

"Thank you, I don't wanta put you out," Mercredi protested politely. The last thing he wanted was to be beholden to one more Choquette.

The other was not about to back down, however. What? A rich man living in an old teepee? The very idea! Jérôme was obliged to give in. Choquette was right. Who would believe in a rich man living like a Native? So he let himself be led away by his host, and found himself leading a parade of smiling, excited people.

Askik followed at a distance. People of the cart train smiled approvingly at him or plucked at a villager's sleeve to point out the heir. He had begun to enjoy it, then he passed the lead cart. The Gauthiers, father and son, were eyeing him suspiciously, which was enough to make Askik himself begin to doubt his good fortune. Mona stood apart from the Gauthiers, watching him with an expression of amusement.

The Choquettes' cabin was so crammed with people when Askik arrived that he could barely squeeze his way inside. He surmised that his parents were sitting by the fire with the master of the house. Everyone else was standing. Bursts of laughter made the walls of the little house shake at times, but Askik could not hear the witticisms that provoked them. Soon Choquette stood up and, opening his arms like a church statue, begged the visitors to kindly leave.

"The Mercredis are gonna eat now, so you go an' eat too. Monsieur Mercredi appreciates you payin' yer respects, but you mustn't tire 'im out. Go home now. *Bon appétit.* Sleep well.

The villagers filed out, talking and gesticulating. A few feet from the door, the Choquette sons were putting up the Mercredis' tent.

"Whew!" Choquette breathed when everyone was gone. "They got their hearts in the right place, but they don't know when t' lay off."

Jérôme, on the contrary, was sorry to have them gone. He was afraid that Choquette would now launch a close interrogation. Choquette was convinced of Mercredi's good fortune, however, particularly since he had been the first to apprise him of it.

"What I figger," Choquette began, offering his guest a clay pipe with a whole stem, "what I figger is you prob'ly got more deals you're thinkin about."

"How's that?" Mercredi could not help noticing that his host's own pipe had only a little stub of stem left.

"Well, I daresay you got more plans, more things up yer sleeve."

Jérôme did not like the familiarity. In front of the others, Choquette had addressed him as *vous*; now it was *tu*. But he gave no sign of having noticed and closed his eyes with an air of gentility, as if contemplating further riches.

"I mean plans that'll make money," Choquette pursued.

"Hmmm. *Maskouche, maskouche.* Maybe."

"An' I daresay you'd let a family that's your friends in on the deal. A family that lent you a good horse. A family..."

"You talkin' 'bout your brother?" Jérôme asked innocently. Choquette coughed.

"Not exactly. Well, it's the same family. I practically trained that horse myself."

"It's you you're talkin' about, then."

"You got it!" Choquette replied, giving Jérôme a slap on the knee.

"You got money?" Jérôme asked.

"Hunnerd American dollars."

"What? Where'd you...?"

It was Choquette's turn to close his eyes slyly.

"I know, a hunnerd dollars is birdshit to a Mercredi, but I daresay a hunnerd dollars, put in the right place an' with a friendly eye kept on it, I daresay it could bring in a nice little sum."

"*Maskouche, maskouche.* Only..."

"Only what?"

"We ain't in the habit of doin' deals outside the family, y'know. We don't work with jus' anybody."

This was being rather cruel, but Jérôme had no intention of burdening himself with another debt. So what if he had to spend the night in the tent! However, instead of becoming angry, Choquette lost countenance.

"No, no! Don't get me wrong! I'm not askin' to be yer partner. I know I ain't got that kinda money. I'm just askin' you to take my money an' put it in yer business and' pay me the interest."

Jérôme made as if thinking about this. And he was thinking hard, sure enough, but about something quite other than what was being proposed. He drew two or three times on his pipe and then leaned toward Choquette, who eagerly leaned toward him.

"Y'know, Choquette, money's always got a story to it — all money."

The other nodded without understanding.

"Y'know there's money that's clean and money that ain't."

Another nod. Still no comprehension.

"Y'know we can't take any money without knowin' where it come from."

Choquette opened his eyes wide. Now he understood. How pleasant it is to learn from able people! He put his mouth to Mercredi's ear and whispered:

"I found it on a dead man."

"A dead man?"

"An American. On the prairie. Killed by Indians. Assiniboines that wanted 'is horse. They took the horse an' left the money. Y'know, it ain't everyone that's given a head fer..."

"An American?"

"For sure," Choquette murmured huskily.

"How d'you know?"

"Dunno."

"I accept."

"Hah!" Choquette roared, making his wife jump. He seized Mercredi's hand and pumped it furiously. Jérôme gave him a suitable smile and wondered what he would do with the hundred dollars.

After supper the hangers-on and the curious returned, traipsing in and out of the house all night long, insensitive to Choquette's sour greetings. The whole village was staying awake, excited by the hunters' arrival and the Mercredi family's wealth. There was much running from house to house and jostling on the narrow paths through the snow.

Askik stayed on a stool by the fire until the small hours of the morning. When he was fed up with blinking his eyes to keep the smoke out and ward off sleep, he took his buffalo robe and went outside. The air was clean and as brisk as cold water. He entered his teepee, disturbing the Choquette boys. They made way for him with haste and respect, although Askik was younger than they. He fell asleep without thinking about it, happy to be back in the fresh air and in his own tent.

For two days, Jérôme Mercredi did nothing but receive visitors. His renown had spread to the other villages on the mountain; people were coming from all corners to consult him. They would tell him their problems or ask him to settle their differences. He would listen, tugging at his right braid with a learned air, then render judgments and advice, which the visitors bore away with beaming faces. A man who can make drive belts out of buffalo skins must be right about things of lesser difficulty.

By the end of the second day, however, the number of petitioners having diminished and Choquette's patience reaching an end, Mercredi was obliged to think about returning to St. Boniface. He was not sure what he would do there, but it might look suspicious for him to linger so far from his fortune.

And so he went in search of a cousin by marriage who was living in a nearby village, a short, potbellied man of forty or so, who for three days had been basking in his relative's glory from afar. He had not dared to go and pay his respects for fear of not being recognized. When he saw Mercredi coming to seek him out, therefore, he was so flattered he agreed immediately to take Anita and Mikiki under his roof.

"Y' see, cousin," Jérôme said, "I'm gonna hafta travel fast and far this winter. That's business. An' then," he added, looking the breathless little man straight in the eye, "fam'ly's fam'ly. Ain't no one gonna say you couldn't do us another favour come spring that'll be worth more t' you. Right?"

"Right, right!" the cousin replied with a knowing look. "An' yer older boy, you don't want I should keep him too?"

"No, Askik's gotta go back t' school."

"Of course. Business..."

"Takes an edjercation."

"Right."

And the two men exchanged a long handshake in view of the whole village. The little man was delighted at last to be beginning the life of prestige and influence he had always dreamed of. Jérôme was pleased to have a relative associated with his future successes.

As always when he took an idea into his head, Jérôme would not rest until it was realized. That very night he announced his plan to his wife, who protested vigorously. Anita wanted to go home to St. Boniface. Jérôme explained that he did not have the time to complete the journey by ox and cart. By midwinter he would send a carriole and dog team to fetch his wife and baby. The prospect of entering St. Boniface in a carriole like a Company lady tickled Anita's fancy, and although she did not really believe in her new wealth, she allowed herself to be persuaded.

On the morning of the day of departure, once everything was folded and stowed for the last time, Jérôme took his wife to the cart and sat her on a bag of pemmican. The cousin took the reins. Everyone realized that Anita was acceding to a new condition in life and would never again have to lift a finger. The cart moved off at once along the little snow-covered pathway leading to the other village. Jérôme mounted the Choquette horse, had Askik lifted on behind him, and with a final "Gentlemen," galloped off in the opposite direction. The onlookers went home with the impression of having personally witnessed an occasion worth remembering.

It took Jérôme and Askik two days to cross the mountain. The snow was deep. At times the trail disappeared from sight. The horse kept stumbling on buried branches; her riders had to walk part of the way. They came to the forest's end at the close of the second day. Once again the prairie stretched away before them, ghostly pale in the dying daylight.

"That's it, lad, the worst's over!"

They camped in a grove of aspens and the next morning struck north-east. They reached the Assiniboine River in a single day, and then had no further need to worry about firewood. Five days later they were in sight of St. François.

An old man ferried them across the river. Pieces of ice hit the sides of the raft, which made the ferryman spit in disgust.

The village was built along the river; each cabin overlooked the water. Except for the dogs that barked furiously at the travellers' heels, the streets were deserted. Half the houses were not emitting any smoke. Jérôme chose one that was neither too wretched nor too well-kept. He knocked at length on the door. No reply. Surprised, he went to the next house and knocked, then to the next. At last a door was opened. The owner, a young man with bad teeth, agreed to take them in.

Their host had been one of the St. François dissidents, the hunters who had been the first to leave Legardeur's camp. He whooped triumphantly to hear that the remaining group had later split a second time. He remained morosely silent when he learned that Legardeur had nevertheless succeeded in feeding his followers.

A heavy smell of musk and herbs filled the cabin. The walls were covered with dried plants and vegetables, animal skins and wooden tools. The floor was carpeted with thatch, which grew abundantly in the nearby marshes.

This cabin, although much like all the others Askik had seen, had a wild and warlike air besides, which was characteristic of St. François. It contained more arms than tools, more furs than cloth. The village was the Red River's outpost, the first rampart between the Métis and the Sioux. Its inhabitants lived on a perpetual war footing, preferring a brief and exciting existence on the prairie to the dreary certainty of dying old in St. Boniface. They prided themselves in being the most pugnacious, the most stubborn, the most refractory of the entire Métis nation.

But St. François was withering away. The Sioux who came this way were now only refugees. The buffalo herds were at great distances, drawing the hunters to wintering places far from the village. The vast White Horse Plain around the village was empty. Empty of game, Indians and Métis.

The Mercredis' young host complained about his summer's hunting. He also complained about his horse, his wife and his rotting teeth. He was a terrible whiner, in fact. Jérôme thought two or three times that he was about to ask for money. He did not do so, however; either he was shy about it or the Mercredis' shabby dress had convinced him that it would be pointless.

The next morning the Mercredis departed with relief. Once out of the village they followed the river. The wind had left only a thin layer of snow on the ground and the Choquette horse cantered along easily and steadily, blowing vapour from her nostrils. Askik was no longer hanging onto his father for all he was worth; the seven-day ride had turned him into an able horseman.

At midday they went down to the river to drink. While the horse tried to graze through the snow, father and son hungrily ate what was left of their dried meat. This was hardly wise; a sudden storm could still strike and keep them on the prairie. Nevertheless, Jérôme had decided that they would be home that day. Foreseeing trouble, according to him, amounted to inviting it.

He had been right. The weather was superb. The snow-covered prairie was dazzling; it was cold enough to invigorate without being uncomfortable. What a pleasure it was to ride for hours on end with nothing else to do but watch the vegetation go by, and yet have the feeling of having accompished something worth while!

The sun was sinking. It had become colder already when in the distance they saw a new line of trees beginning to block the remaining light; just a grey thread against the now pale sky.

"The Red River, Askik!" Jérôme shouted. "Look, it's the Red River! You can even see the roofs of the fort!"

Now father and son could barely keep still in the saddle. The horse seemed to be moving at a snail's pace. They both had an urge to jump to the ground and run as fast as they could.

And yet, when they were almost there, when they could smell the wood fires of the colony, a thought occurred to Jérôme and he pulled on the reins. Would it really be a good thing for him to enter St. Boniface in broad daylight? He was returning without meat, without ox or cart, and with a hundred American dollars that did not belong to him.

Kicking mightily with his heels, he steered the horse into the woods. Crouching among the trees, huddled together and shivering, he and Askik waited for nightfall.

They slipped into town in complete darkness, avoiding dogs and windows like two Sioux on a questionable mission. When they arrived at the edge of the Red River, it took them some time to find the ferryman; they discovered him dead drunk and snoring under an overturned boat. McDougall snorted, mumbled "Damn cold!" and lumbered down to his delapidated raft. The horse put a hoof on the shifting timbers and recoiled with a whinny.

Jérôme clapped a hand over her muzzle. "Shaddup, goddam nag!" he hissed.

McDougall opened a suspicious eye but said nothing. When they arrived at the other side, Jérôme was about to apologize for not being able to pay, but McDougall was already staggering off toward the collection of packing cases that served as his second sleeping quarters.

The Mercredis moved along beside the Red River, staying in the woods until they had passed the presbytery and convent, then struck into the open, across to Raoul Mercredi's house.

They went to an outbuilding where there was a light. Looking through the window, they saw an old hired man smoking his pipe by the fireplace. Jérôme knocked on the pane.

"Who's there?"

"Mercredi."

"Monsieur Raoul?"

"No, Jérôme. Is my brother home?"

"Ah, good evening, Monsieur Mercredi. Yes, your brother's in the house. Wait an' I'll open the door. We'll put yer horse in the stable."

"Don't bother, I'm leavin' again right away."

But the old man was already outside.

"The carts brought a lot o' wolves back this year. Horses gotta be shut up."

He took down an oil lantern and went to the fireplace to light it.

"Yes, a lot o' wolves, Monsieur Mercredi." And when he had adjusted the flame in the lantern he added, "This way, folla me."

"There's wolves every autumn," Jérôme observed.

"Yes, Monsieur, but there's more'n ever. For me, that's the best proof there ain't no more *bôfflo* on the prairie."

A strong smell of sawdust and tar struck the Mercredis' nostrils. They were coming to a building that was paler than the rest.

"A new warehouse," the old employee explained. "Business is good fer the master. Here we are."

He put the lantern on the ground and, pulling with all the strength in his bent body, opened the stable door. A wave of moist, manure-scented air wafted out. The Choquette horse opened her nostrils wide and trembled with pleasure.

"I'll take care o' yer horse, monsieur," the old man said. "Go straight ahead t' th' house, but go in by th' front door."

Jérôme and Askik crossed the courtyard. There was no light showing through the windows of the house. Jérôme banged hard three times on the door, thinking that he needed to waken the servants. A woman came immediately, however. She let them in and then disappeared with the candle, leaving them in darkness. A few minutes later she called to them from the next room. Askik thought her voice familiar but could not see her face. She led them through a sucession of rooms all in a line and left them without a word at a door under which a little light was showing. She had held the candle at arm's length all this time, so that they could not tell who was leading them.

Raoul Mercredi had established his office at the far end of his long house. It had a door that opened directly onto the courtyard, but this was reserved exclusively for the master's use. He insisted that visitors arrive by the main entrance. Having to walk through room after room of the big house, he believed, was an inducement to humility. Raoul was seated behind his highly polished desk, surrounded by papers and ledgers. To his young nephew, he looked even more impressive than ever.

"Ah, there y'are," he said unaffectionately at the sight of his brother. "The hunt was good?"

"Not specially. We got as far as..."

"Don't bother. I heard all about it. So you take yerself fer a chief these days?"

"They asked me to lead 'em."

"Why?"

Jérôme hesitated. Was he going to talk about his visions? The brass lamp threw a harsh light on tied-up bundles of letters and a number of ledgers standing at attention on a shelf. Everything about this room said severely, Come, come, no idle fancies here! Jérôme held his tongue.

"All right," Raoul said, "what you got to pay yer debts with?"

"I got a bit."

"How much?"

"Hundred dollars."

Raoul raised his eyebrows. Jérôme hastened to explain.

"It belongs to another man, but I thought if I invested it with you I could make a profit, then keep part fer myself an'..."

"Stop there! First yer gonna pay yer debts."

Raoul Mercredi stood up. With his short-cropped hair and clean-shaven face, this brother was heavier and more powerful than the one with moustaches and braids.

"Leave the money here. Go home. Come back an' see me to-morrow night. I'll think o' somethin'. Stay out o' sight till then. If yer creditors hear you're back, they might come and make a nuisance o' themselves."

"How about tomorrow night?"

"We'll talk about yer future."

"All right!" Jérôme exclaimed. This was exactly his own intention. "Can I go out this door?"

"Why?"

"To go an' get my horse at the stable."

"*Your* horse?"

"The one I borrowed from Choquette."

"Leave it, I'll send it back to Choquette tomorrow. With some o' that money o' yours to pay off the debt."

Jérôme wanted to protest. Paying off Ormidas Choquette with money borrowed from his brother was really too absurd. Too absurd for him to dare explain it to Raoul.

"So I gotta walk home?"

"You afraid o' the dark?"

Jérôme was about to leave when a thought occurred.

"By the way, what're drive belts?"

"Drive belts make machines work in the factories o' the East.'"

"An' they're made o' buffalo hide?"

"It's cheaper'n canvas."

"So you got rich?"

"Middlin' rich."

Jérôme's eyes glowed with delight. One day he was going to be middling rich too.

"All right, enough talk," he said briskly as if he had other things to do. "Good night, Raoul. I'll be back tomorrow night. I got some proposals I'm gonna make you. *Astam, Askik!*"

"Jérôme!"

"Yes?"

"Go out by the front door. Leave the candle here."

When his brother had left, Raoul Mercredi sat for a long, long time at his mahogany desk imported from St. Paul, with his solid brass lamp, his ink pots and his ledgers with tooled leather bindings. His eyes roamed over the maps hung on the walls, stopping at Judith Basin next to the Rocky Mountains, where Métis and Indian hunters were spitting *his* lead balls into *his* rifles to shoot down *his* buffalo. Then he traced the slow progression of the carts descending like a rich flow of blood toward the Missouri. He counted all those hostile nations — Siksikas, Kahnas, Arikaras, Piegans — blandished by his agents and bought off to let his cart trains pass unimpeded. At the Wolf Point fort, other employees were loading tens of thousands of hides onto the steamboats that lumbered off toward St. Louis and the industries of the East.

He had put everything at risk, laid everything on the line. Now he was in the process of becoming immensely, fabulously rich. So rich that his neighbours did not suspect even a hundredth of it. And all because he had been patient, had not thrown his money around the minute he had begun to have some success. He still wore a peasant smock and a *ceinture flèchée*, still ate deer and wild rice. Just like his fellow parishioners, who thought they could still impress him by arguing over puny little debts.

He had bought warehouses in St. Paul and chartered a steamboat, and was preparing to inundate the Red River colony with American products, which were not as good but cheaper than the English merchandise that arrived via the difficult Arctic route. He would build a big house of sawn lumber, the colony's first, with wood shingles, sash windows and polished floors, like houses he had seen in the United States. Then, to confound those imbeciles who thought that grass and trees grow only where Nature puts them, he would surround his house with green lawns and transplanted evergreens. Importing a fine tree and planting it in the wilds, what better way to convince his neighbours of the incalculable gulf between their own little projects and what he had already achieved.

Having thought on these things, Raoul Mercredi came to the inescapable conclusion that his brother was an imbecile. When he had heard that Jérôme had caused the breakup of the hunting party, was calling himself a visionary and chief, and more recently had been passing himself off as Raoul's partner and putting on a rich man's airs, Raoul had cursed his fate. He had muzzled his own family, created a zone of silence and respect around himself, but this ridiculous brother was beyond his control.

Now, however, he was regarding this as a natural affliction. Heaven had crowned his endeavors with success; could he decently be sour about this one little thorn in his side? Jérôme was the small cross he must bear, the aggravation that gave value to all the rest. This might even be his last obstacle, the ultimate test of his ingenuity. He decided to consider Jérôme a write-off, like the bribes he had paid the Indians: an unaccountable liability, but a relatively minor one. Opening his ledgers and reviewing his order forms, he began to resolve the problem of his brother, energetically and with gusto as with any other business matter.

Meanwhile, the object of his attention was gaily bending an elbow with Urbain Lafortune, the old voyageur he had worked with in the North. The Mercredis had discovered him at the old ferryman's cabin at the Seine.

"Laurendeau?" Lafortune said when inquiry was made of his predecessor. "Laurendeau gone las' spring."

"Dead?"

"Jiss gone. Had enough o' lookin' at people. I figger he went t' live in th' bush."

"At his age?"

The two men had a good laugh over the old eccentric.

"*Cré diable!*" Mercredi exclaimed as he entered the cabin. There was hardly room to move; the whole cabin was filled with the framework of a large canoe. The huge wooden skeleton was upturned on trestles. The first pieces of birchbark had already been sewn in place. Lafortune glowed with pride.

"Whaddya say, Mercredi? Ain't she beautiful?"

Jérôme slid his hand along the smooth keel.

"Ehé, sure is. What you gonna use it for?"

"Come spring, I'm gettin' outta here. I seen more'n enough o' this Injun-ridden country. Next spring I'm goin' back t' Lower Canada."

"To Lower Canada! By canoe?"

"I done it plenty o' times arreddy."

"When you was twenty!"

"I ain't in no hurry. I'll take my time. Listen t' me good, Mercredi — an' you too, boy," he said, taking Askik's head in his hands, "good thing fer you to learn a thing or two from what yer elders bin through. Listen t' me. All that time I was in the North, I saved my money. I ain't rich, no sir, but I got enough to finish my life in peace. Not here. There ain't nothin' here. I'm gonna go home. In my own canoe. Won't cost me nothin'. I'll even take a bit o' cargo to earn me a little. When I get to Lower Canada I'm gonna get me a job as a handyman in a convent, or a monastery. Jiss a little job fer the food I eat. Ain't gonna ask for pay — like I said, I got what I need t' keep me alive — but I'll live in peace, with Christians round me..."

Lafortune bent his head brusquely, as though choked up by some untold sorrow. Mercredi, uncorking the rum jug, wondered if his old mate hadn't become a little crazy.

"Listen t' me, boy!" Lafortune repeated, gazing despairingly into Askik's eyes. "Dontcha do like me! Dontcha go wanderin' round far from yer father'n' mother. Honour they father'n' thy mother, that's what the good Lord said, but how you gonna honour 'em if you ain't there? Know what I'm sayin'?"

Askik nodded, but Lafortune let go of him wearily.

"Bah! Is there jiss one real Christian in this whole goddam country?" And lifting the jug, he flung at Askik, "You jiss do what you like 'cause you won't finish up no better'n the rest. We're swine, all of us."

Askik went to sleep in a dark corner among wood chips and rolls of birchbark. The two men sat on the floor by the fire, bent over so as not to hit their heads on the canoe. Cheered by the rum, Lafortune fantasized with delectable details about his future life among the nuns: a soft bed, meals of beef and chicken, tender vegetables, fruits, cheese, wine, all the things he had dreamed of since he had had the unfortunate idea of enlisting as a voyageur in the service of a fur-trading company.

"Y'know, Mercredi, what I want most is to be round white women. Even nuns. At my age it don't matter no more. But Canadian women're more gentle, nicer company than Métis women. Can't tell ya why...."

"'Cause you can't remember," Mercredi chaffed. "You been too long in th' North West."

But Lafortune now seemed truly distressed and Mercredi said no more. The ghosts of all those years were back, hovering among the rafters of the cabin; years without parents, without women, without real friends. The two men turned to less painful subjects and thus whiled away the night in pleasant companionship. The sky was already pink when Jérôme woke his son. Lafortune took them across the river. His boat left a path of black water behind in the thin grey ice.

"Hey, Lafortune!" Mercredi laughed as he climbed the river bank. "How you gonna get yer canoe outta the cabin? It won't go through the door!"

"I'll make a hole in th' wall. It'll make an extra window fer the next one gets that rat's nest. Anahow," he said as he pulled away from shore, "there ain't gonna be no more ferryman. They're gonna build a bridge."

On that side of the river, Askik found the woods, the prairie and the ravine as they had been before. Nothing had changed. He felt no emotion to see his own roof approaching, except that the house looked uglier and smaller the closer he came. Too small even to build a canoe inside.

The door fell off in Jérôme's hands; mice had eaten away its rawhide hinges. They had also eaten the parchment over the windows. Inside, the floor and furnishings were covered with snow, dust and squirrel droppings. There was a hole in the big chest; when Jérôme and Askik opened it they found a family of mice nesting among their winter clothes. They chased the tiny animals off and put on their mouse-eaten coats.

They spent the day tending the fire and fasting. They had already eaten all their dried meat and Jérôme had forgotten to ask his brother for some.

When evening came, they returned stealthily to the town, like the hungry wolves which, at the same hour, were coming out of the ravines and thickets to hang around the stables. Askik wondered if there might not be other hunters as hungry as they, also waiting for darkness before coming to town. The woods could be full of them.

As they passed the school, Askik resolved to return there the very next day. Time was short. He was getting older and was no closer to being a great man.

A different servant opened the door to them — an older, heavier woman who was not afraid to hold the candle near her wrinkled face, though she might better not have. She led them to a room they had not seen before and put the candle down on a dining table.

"Eat," she said in a surly voice, "the master'll see ya later."

The Mercredis did not need to be told twice. There was a hot, greasy pea soup, smoked doré, cold venison. And a loaf of bread the like of which Askik had never seen. High, round and soft. So spongy that he thought he would suffocate with the first mouthful. It seemed to him tasteless compared to the bannock that his mother made. There was also butter. Jérôme showed him how to spread it on the bread, but to Askik it was too greasy. His father ate Askik's share, and all the rest of the bread.

When they both felt they had filled their stomachs to bursting, the surly servant appeared from a dark room, picked up the candle and ordered, "Fo!la me."

Raoul met them at the door of his office. He put a friendly hand on his brother's shoulder and led him to an armchair.

"Come in, Jérôme. Will you take a pipeful?"

"Don't mind if I do," Jérôme replied, delighted with the reception he was getting. When he had lit his pipe he settled back in his chair and said confidently, "All right, let's talk business."

"*Tout de suite!*" The elder brother walked around behind his desk and let himself down heavily in his chair. "Lemme see, lemme see" he muttered as he rummaged among his papers. "Yes!" he exclaimed after a minute, as if he had just discovered the one document indispensable to the success of their discussion. "Well, little brother, yer affairs ain't in great shape."

Jérôme's face fell. He had hoped for a more positive opening. Why dwell on the past? Raoul continued:

"I sent the horse back to Choquette, plus twenty dollars."

"Twenty dollars! Yer pretty generous, brother!"

"Twenty dollars to the Hudson's Bay Company — no generosity in this case; their accounts are well kept; they know what you owe 'em."

"But not what I gave 'em! The best years o' my..."

"Thirty dollars to Gingras for the ox and cart you left on the mountain. You got took on those, by the way."

Jérôme sucked savagely on his pipe, signifying protest.

"An' thirty dollars to a certain young thing you promised to support when you came back from the hunt."

Jérôme leapt from his chair and leaned over the desk. "There, you gone too far!" he whispered in his brother's ear so that Askik would not hear. "Give 'er somethin', that's all right, but between you an' me she ain't worth much. You don't know 'er!"

Raoul leaned forward in turn and into his brother's ear said in a hoarse half-whisper, "It was her opened the door to you last night. She's in the family way."

Jérôme let himself drop back into his chair.

"If I understand right, there ain't nothin' left of that hundred dollars," he said softly after a minute.

"That's right."

A ponderous silence fell between them. Jérôme kept expecting his brother to propose a solution. The other, hands folded on the gleaming surface of his desk, appeared to be waiting for Jérôme to reveal what he was planning to do. Between businessmen, of course. Jérôme cleared his throat and surrendered.

"Raoul, you got experience, you know 'bout money. I'd like you to tell me, to suggest, what you'd do, maybe, if you was in my place."

"Ah, that ain't easy, Jérôme. I ain't a chief. I don't have visions."

"They pushed me to be a chief. I didn't want to, specially."

"People gossip and that ain't what I heard."

"People ain't kind, for sure," Jérôme muttered bitterly.

"What's that?"

"Nothin'."

"All right. So, Jérôme, you want a job?"

Jérôme made a sour face. Had he talked about a job? If there was nothing better though, yes, he would take a job.

"I'm still tradin' in the North," Raoul continued in a less brotherly tone. "Furs ain't bringin in what they once did, but for a man wantin' to make a start, it can still be done."

Jérôme's heart sank. Make a start! He was thirty-five years old!

"What am I gonna do up there?"

"Buy furs. I'll outfit you, give you the trade goods. You can keep a third o' the profit. That's generous, so think about it."

"But that means I gotta spend the winter with the Natives again. That ain't no life! Ain'tcha got somethin' here? I dunno — office work...?"

"That's all taken. By men that's already shown their stuff — in the bush."

Jérôme was speechless. He did not want to beg for special treatment, but surely that was taken for granted between brothers.

"You ain't got somethin' more to the south, in Judith Basin?"

"Too late, too far."

"St. Paul?"

"No."

"St. Laurent?"

"Don't do business there no more."

Jérôme gave up. His head was spinning. He was like a fish that still believes he can spit out the hook as he feels himself being lifted from the water.

"If that's it...where you gonna send me?"

"By horse to Stone Fort. Then by boat to the Manigotagan."

"Yer hard on me, Raoul. Why so far?"

"If the fur trade was good all the way down to here, it would be better, of course. Tonight you can sleep with Lanthier — the ol' man who runs the stable."

Jérôme stood up. He was on his way out of the room when he turned.

"And the boy. What am I gonna do with him?"

Askik turned anxious eyes toward his uncle, who shrugged.

"Dunno. Park 'im with the priests."

A damp wind was blowing outside. The Mercredis found the Chemin du Roy and walked the length of the colony at a brisk pace. Askik had pulled up his hood but kept a hand over a large hole made by the mice. His father lamented bitterly as he walked.

"Dear Mother o' the poor, it's always the same ones gets it. Ain't I had enough hardship this year? Have I gotta die worn out? And gettin' treated like that by a brother...*Ahuya!*"

They passed the convent, its windows dark. The nuns retired early. Askik thought of Lafortune who longed to sleep in a convent. They came to the bishop's palace. Jérôme knocked at the door. Askik expected the scolding cook to come to the door, but it was an unfamiliar priest who opened it, a small, thin man in a shiny cassock. He looked the two visitors up and down from behind his thick spectacles.

"Are you...the curé?" Jérôme asked, uncertain that he needed a curé.

"I'm Father Gervais, the bursar."

"Oh. My name's Jérôme Mercredi." He began to put out a hand and then took off his hat instead.

"Ah, Monsieur Mercredi. We've heard a lot about you this last while."

"How's that, Father?"

"A hunter from Turtle Mountain told us about your good fortune."

"Er, well, you know Father, people exaggerate."

"Ha, ha!" The priest gave a dry little laugh. "Your brother's good at hiding his business deals too. You're partners, I believe."

"No. Well, yes. Just startin' tonight. Listen, Father, I'm ruined. I gotta leave again. My son..." — he pushed Askik toward the lamp — "started school with you last year. I'd like to leave 'im with you..."

"Why? Where's his mother?"

"At the mountain. She couldn't take no more. I couldn't bring 'er back with me."

"Well, well. What a shame," the bursar replied coldly, almost mechanically. His spotless spectacles projected darts of light. A smell of wax and good food wafted through the half-open door. The priest smelled of soap. In the darkness behind the oil lamp, Askik could see the glow of polished floors and furniture. He was ashamed of his father's lies, ashamed of his own dirty buckskin clothes. He tried to hide his mouse-eaten anorak. He pulled weakly at his father's sleeve; he wanted to go and never come back to this inaccessible house. But Jérôme kept talking.

"That's why I wanta leave 'im with you, Father."

"It's true that we sometimes take boarders, but they're children of poor families."

"I'm poor, Father."

"Poor?" the priest said in the same impassive voice. "I'm accustomed to business too, Monsieur Mercredi. Don't take me for a fool. You and your brother have made a fortune killing buffalo that your destitute brothers might have had for food."

"Father!" cried Mercredi, becoming desperate. "You don't understand!"

"I am this community's bursar, I remind you. And the son of a merchant. Do you think I can't see through your game? And yes, why are you leaving again?"

"I'm goin' to the North."

"To trade furs?"

"Sure."

"What with?"

"'Scuse me?"

"What are you taking to exchange for furs?"

"Ah...I dunno. The boats're at Stone Fort."

"Oh, so you don't know. Well, Monsieur Mercredi, I'll tell you. You're taking alcohol to the North. Just like your brother. You're turning the Indians against us the better to exploit them. You're working your less fortunate Métis brothers to death. And what is more, Monsieur Mercredi, you're trying to impose your son on us so he can take a poor child's place."

"I *am* poor!"

"And the drive belts?"

"What? No! Where'm I gonna to leave 'im?"

"With his mother. Or his uncle. Wherever he'll be spared your influence would be excellent, I should think."

"Father! You don't understand!"

"Better than you think."

The door closed. Jérôme stumbled on his way down the steps.

"There now, y'see!" he said to Askik as though the child were responsible for the misunderstanding.

Then he turned toward the windows of the bishop's palace and shouted, "I'm not rich, fer Chrissake!"

He gave a furious kick at a tiny tree — damnfool idea, moving trees! — and strode away.

PART TWO

The Forest

1

The boiling of the water alongside the boat soothed him somewhat. When he looked up at the woods filing by on either side of the river, however, Askik had a desolate feeling that he would never, never be a great man. Each dip of the oars was carrying him a little farther from St. Boniface, from school, and from his big house with white walls. He would never be rich or educated now. He would spend his life in the woods. Askik, trapper, trapper, trapper! said the oars. Trader! said his father's sturdy frame.

Standing among bales of merchandise, pipes clenched in their teeth, the Métis boatmen were plying oars three times longer than their own height. They had had to lower the sail since the wind was blowing straight over the bow. As they worked they kept looking up at the low clouds. Would it be rain or snow? One way or the other, they were in for it.

"Chabouillet, sing us a song!" shouted Jérôme Mercredi, who was always in good humour when departing for somewhere.

"Don't feel like singin'," Chabouillet grumbled. By their silence, the boatmen showed their agreement. They had thought their season of work over. Ice was already forming by the river banks. Was this the time to be venturing out on the water?

The boatmen were afraid of a freezeup. They had resolved to row all night, but the wind, which they called "la Vieille, the Old Woman," was playing tricks on them. The four heavy York boats had made so little progress that Mercredi and his men were obliged to camp the first night at the mouth of the Nipouwin, the River of the Dead, only a few miles from where they had begun. They pitched their canvas tents at the very spot where, many winters before, the Sioux had massacred a whole Cree village.

La Vieille flailed the trees all night. The next morning, while the boats picked their way through the channels and marshes of the Red River delta, a fine, oblique rain drove at them with the headwind. Once they were finally out on the vast waters of Lake Winnipeg, it obscured the horizon, mingling water and sky.

When Mercredi no longer knew what orders to give, Chabouillet took command. He had the boats hug the shore, looking for a spot that looked hospitable. When he sighted a broad, sandy beach, he ordered them to land. Mercredi, huddled brooding in the back of the boat, did not like the decision. He suspected Chabouillet of shortening the days, slowing the pace of advance, in order to have an excuse for turning back. The lake looked so disheartening, however, that he disembarked without a word.

The rain turned to sleet. Wading in water to mid-thigh, moustaches and eyelashes covered with ice, the men pulled tarpaulins over the merchandise. They put up their tents in the forest. Since they had no dry wood, they went to bed soaking wet.

No one slept a wink that night. La Vieille rattled the ice-coated trees. Branches heavy with ice came crashing down all around the tents. Sleet pellets pattered against the canvas. Askik, still dressed from head to foot in his new clothes, was bundled up under two woollen blankets but was shivering nonetheless. He could hear the men muttering in the other tents. Sometimes, despairing of sleep, one of them would declare aloud that he was going back to the fort the next morning. And yet at the first pale light, all of them were at the water's edge, miserable and bad tempered but ready to carry on and get it over with as soon as possible.

The lake would not allow it. Its shallow waters quickly became choppy. There was not the slightest hope of the heavy boats making way through the foam-capped waves.

Scouring the forest, poking under rock ledges and beneath evergreens, the men found enough dry wood to light a fire with. One of them, a lad of sixteen, came back from the woods in tears; he had slipped on an ice-covered log and sprained an ankle.

After a hurried breakfast of tea and barely heated fish, the men went back to their tents to wait for the storm to end. In the Mercredis' tent there were four men and a boy, cramped together, sullen and silent, listening to the monotonous sound of the waves. They did not go out all day except to stretch their stiffened limbs or relieve chilled bladders. Whenever one of them ventured beyond the trees and as far as the beach, he would sprinkle a bit of tobacco or shreds of cloth on the seething waters, and return impressed by the immensity of the lake and forest and the smallness of the white canvas tents flapping in the wind.

Toward evening La Vieille calmed. As if released from a spell, the men began to talk again. The tone was acerbic. Continuing, said Chabouillet, would be defying the spirits of the lake, who had given them a warning. Turning back, said Mercredi, would be a breach of contract and punishable by fine. But he saw clearly that most of the men were on Chabouillet's side. He therefore suggested that the spirits be consulted through conjury.

He sent for a Sauteau boatman, a shaman of sorts, who agreed to conduct the ceremony. All the men chipped in to pay him his fee in tobacco and rum. A tent with a stout frame was put up: four stakes firmly driven into the ground, joined by four hoops; then the frame was covered with tarpaulins and blankets. Small bells were attached to the main pole. When the work was done, Chabouillet tried to shake the tent, throwing all his weight into it. Not a tinkle came from the bells. Perfect!

After supper, once it was completely dark, the boatmen sat in a circle around the *djisigonne*. They were mercilessly critical as they watched the preparations, demanding total authenticity so that there should be no trickery. When Chabouillet tied up the conjuror, they demanded that the ropes be tied tighter. No one took any notice when the Sauteau complained that they were cutting off his circulation. Once the last of the onlookers had declared himself satisfied, the conjuror was pushed into the tent head first and the canvas was closed up behind him. One of the men threw some branches on the sputtering fire and a Cree finished warming up a drum.

Then there was silence. The men waited, eyes wide in fear and expectation. The most fainthearted were smirking; they would be the first to take to their heels.

At first the only sounds were the wind in the tops of the trees and the waves on the beach. Then there was an audible murmuring, wailing, humming; brief, rhythmic moans like an elk's in rutting season. And suddenly a trill, harsh and piercing, pulsing like a heartbeat and constant like the wind. The drum took up the rhythm. The conjuror's voice rose and fell, howling or humming, but always at the breaking point, barking like a coyote or bellowing like a buffalo. The prayer continued

133

for a long time. Would Mikikinuk the Turtle call together his manidos brothers, especially the Water Brothers, and enquire of their will? Would they deign to let the travellers pass? Would they take pity on them and prolong their days?

The song ended. Stopped short. The drum kept beating a little longer, then fell silent.

The ropes that had bound the Sauteau flew out of the tent and landed on the ground before the awestruck watchers.

In seconds the conjuror would place his hand on the lowest hoop. The spirits were arriving. Have pity, manidos!

The bells jingled furiously, the drumming resumed and redoubled. The tent shook like a leaf. The Métis drew back with cries of fear. Askik clutched his father's sleeve and held on for all he was worth. Incomprehensible words and grunts, growls and yelps emerged from the tent. The manidos were speaking!

"Holy Virgin!" Mercredi cried, sorry now to have gone over to the other religious camp.

The bells began to ring less dementedly. The tent's shaking was subsiding. It was over. A moment later the Sauteau ambled out and announced to anyone who cared to listen that the journey could continue. Then he sat down by the fire and in no time had consumed his fee. He was the only one who did not feel the cold that night.

The manidos kept their word. Seven days later the boats entered the Manigotagan estuary. A few miles from its mouth, the river became choked with ice. The boatmen were deeply grateful for this; in a flash they had unloaded the goods and, ignoring Mercredi's objections, pushed off again, anxious to regain the open water of the lake; a good north wind was blowing and they could raise the sails.

"But what am I s'posed to do here?" Jérôme shouted when he had run out of oaths.

"Go upriver," Chabouillet yelled, already far away. "There's Natives there. You c'n get *them* to move the stuff."

"How d'you know there's Natives?"

"Why wouldn't there be? Ha, ha, ha!"

"I swear t' you lad," Mercredi said, coming back to his son, "there's days when people make me sick."

Jérôme and Askik spent the rest of the day stacking their goods under tarpaulins, with the perishables in the middle — sugar, tea, tobacco, alcohol. As he lifted the hundredth keg of rum, Jérôme had to acknowledge that the grumpy little bursar had got it right.

When evening came, Jérôme took a stone and crushed the ends of half a dozen sticks, dipped them in hot pitch, and planted his flares in the snow around the pile of goods. They would burn all night, keeping animals out of the bales.

The Mercredis supped on smoked fish and tea; they had eaten nothing else since leaving St. Boniface. Askik went to sleep dreaming of the haunch of venison he had tasted at his uncle's. Jérôme lay awake a long time, listening to the sizzling of the flares. He did not really know what he was going to do the next day, did not know whether there were Indians nearby, nor where to look for them, nor how to bring his goods to them. He went to sleep and dreamed of deserted forests.

When he stepped out of the tent in the morning, he nearly fell over backwards. An Indian was peacefully smoking his pipe by the fire. As soon as Jérôme had recovered from his surprise, he spoke the usual greeting.

"*Tansé?* How are you?"

"*Monantow.* Nothing new," the Cree replied, then added politely, "*Kina maga?* And you?"

"*Monantow.*"

The Indian rummaged under the furs on his toboggan and brought out two skinned rabbits, which he presented to Mercredi. Jérôme lost no time putting them on a spit. After the meal, he presented a rope of tobacco to his visitor, who was clearly pleased. At last the Indian explained his presence.

Numeo had been hunting in the forest when from a high promontory he had seen four empty York boats moving under sail toward the open lake. He had been tracking an elk but gave this up at once and set out for the estuary. It was late at night when he arrived at the Mercredi's camp. He was happy to welcome his Métis brother and hoped he was bringing good things for him and the people of his village.

"Ehé, some very good things," Mercredi assured him. "Where's the village?"

"Not far," the Indian replied, mixing some *kinnikinnik* with the Brazilian tobacco.

"Can yer men take my goods to th' end o' the river?" Mercredi asked.

"Too far."

"I'll stop first at yer village, but I gotta get to Lake Manigotagan to trade with the bands round there. Can you help me get that far?"

"*Maskouche, maskouche,*" the Cree replied, savouring the excellent smoke. Perhaps there was indeed a way to do as the Métis asked. But the time had not come. Jérôme did not press the point.

They hid the goods under heaped branches and snow, and then went down to the river and set out on the frozen surface, keeping close to shore because the ice was still unreliable.

"Not far" in Numeo's language meant a walk of a good eight hours. When they came in sight of children and dogs frolicking at a big bend in the river, the winter sky was turning red. The village was almost invisible. A half dozen bark teepees, covered with spruce boughs and snow, looked as though they were trying to melt away among the rocks and trees. Jérôme was disappointed to see so few lodges. He could count on ten men at most to haul his goods.

Numeo's lodge was large and well built. The floor was covered with springy spruce boughs. The woollen blankets worn by members of his family, the iron cauldron and the steel knives testified to Numeo's skill at hunting; these things could only be bought from the Whites, and the only currency the Whites accepted was furs. Numeo's wife served them beaver. Numeo offered his guests the best part, the tail.

Numeo rose late the next morning. He took a leisurely breakfast and then settled into his willow backrest and prepared to spend part of the day smoking. Surprised, Jérôme reminded him that the goods had to be moved. The Indian did not stir a finger. After more than an hour of fruitless argument, the Métis lost patience and left the lodge, saying he needed some air. It was apparent that Numeo was not in need of anything. His less affluent neighbours would be more energetic, Jérôme thought.

However, in each of the lodges Mercredi visited, he was given tea to drink and told pleasantly that the time had not come, that his goods were safe. Defeated, he returned to Numeo's teepee.

For three days, life in the camp went on as usual. Hunters came and went. No one breathed a word about the goods and there was neither meeting nor preparation for departure. In desperation, Jérôme decided to leave the village and go to Lake Manigotagan on foot to recruit some Objibways there.

While it was still dark on the very morning he had decided to leave, he felt himself being shaken by the shoulder.

"Up! Time to go!" Numeo whispered so as not to wake his children. He was warmly dressed in skins and furs.

Jérôme staggered out of the teepee. A good thirty men with toboggans and dogs were gathered there in the darkness, ready to leave and waiting only for him. Numeo must have called on hunters from neigh-bouring villages. Some of them must have walked a fair part of the night to get here.

Just what I need! Mercredi thought sourly. He had been afraid of not having enough men to help him, and now he had too many. All these fine fellows were going to cost him the earth.

The Indians set out at a easy trot, laughing and joking. The younger men challenged each other to races, the dogs caught the spirit of it, and the empty toboggans rattled joyfully over the rough river ice. After several miles the pace slowed. High time, for Jérôme was on the point of collapse. A whole summer on horseback had left him unaccustomed to travel on foot. The men had covered half the distance before the tops of the spruce trees began to glow pink. Their high spirits had not diminished in the slightest. When they arrived, two young men were there; they had been sent by Numeo to guard the goods.

Jérôme swapped part of his stock for summer furs and old fur cloth-ing. Coat beaver, beaver fur that the Indians had worn against the skin, was still prized; the long coarse hairs had been worn away by friction and the short downy hairs were lustrous with the oil from human skin. However, most of the furs that Mercredi was buying now were still run-ning free in the underbrush. The Crees had already sent their autumn furs to Stone Fort; they promised to keep their winter take for him.

2

Hoping to do better with the Ojibway, Mercredi hired fifteen porters and took his goods upriver. He found a large hamlet of round huts four days' journey from the Cree village, and was assured by the inhabitants that there were other camps in the area. He decided to establish his headquarters here. He had a bark shelter built for his goods. Anything that could freeze was buried. For the rest of the winter, he roamed the region by dogsled or on snowshoes, accompanied or alone, buying, dis-counting, selling. In his bark warehouse, the goods sold were gradually replaced by bundles of frozen furs. Beaver, mink, fox, wolverine, wolf, fisher and bear; anything which, in Europe or China, would give assur-ance of being well-dressed in the skin of another animal.

For Askik, the first weeks in this village were difficult. He did not understand the Ojibway tongue. If he spoke Cree very slowly, he did sometimes manage to make himself understood. From the beginning, however, he noted strong similarities between the sister languages. Once his ear became attuned to the Ojibway pronunciation, he soon learned to imitate it.

His father had arranged to board him in the lodge of a young hunter, Niskigwon, who was an overgrown adolescent. However, the arrangement had been made without the knowledge of the man's wife, a tiny woman with a pockmarked face. From the very first day she let Askik know that he was unwelcome. The tiny lodge was already housing the young couple, a sister-in-law, an elderly parent and three small children. Askik found the three little monsters hard to take. They climbed on him, pulled his hair and poked sticks in his ribs. They thought it a great joke to throw his clothes to the dogs. His beautiful red tuque, a present from his aunt, vanished in a furious free-for-all of claws and fangs. Even the baby, when let out of his beaded papoose, beat at him with a squirrel skin stuffed with maple sugar. The two women looked on at these games and laughed indulgently. If Askik lifted a finger to defend himself, the mother and sister-in-law would shriek with alarm, pick up the children and run outside as though a bear had come into the lodge. Poor Niskigwon had no peace in his house. His wife jeered at him mercilessly, calling him a limp penis and soft shit. She had a gift for coarse remarks, in fact. One day in the middle of a tirade about his sexual performance, Niskigwon took off. Thinking he had left her, the wife covered her head with her blanket and began to weep bitterly.

A few minutes later Niskigwon reappeared at the door and announced that Askik was going to move out. The little woman unvered her head with a "Humpf!" of satisfaction, the children stopped their noise and the neighbours heaved sighs of relief. Niskigwon put his hand on Askik's shoulder and led him through the village with the air of a disappointed benefactor.

Askik was not sorry to leave, but as they drew near his new lodging he was overcome with despondency. This wakinogan was even smaller and more beggarly than the first. There was a tattered red blanket in place of a door. The lodge's birchbark covering needed renewal. Niskigwon left him at the door without a word.

Askik had an urge to take to his heels, get away from this village as fast as possible. Having to go inside this new lodge, beg a place there and suffer new whims and moods was going to be just too humiliating. What was he doing here among people who despised him? He had a mother — where was she? He was filled with despair by memories of school with its light-filled rooms and priests making the backs of big books crack with their clean hands. He took several steps toward the forest and stopped. Where would he go? St. Boniface was too far. School was in another world. And even if got there, who would want him? As he turned back toward the wakinogan, he thought about Mona. He had promised to take her into his service when he became a great man, but here he was just like her, with no future, no family, and no choice but submission to the will of hostile strangers. He felt so sorry for her, and for himself, that he let out a sob.

At once a cracked voice came from the wakinogan.

"*Pé-pitigwé!* Come in! And stop blubbering!"

The voice struck Askik like a slap. Someone had heard him crying. What were they going to do to him now? He had nothing to lose any more. He flung aside the dirty blanket and went inside, swearing to die rather than suffer the smallest indignity.

The lodge was filled with dense smoke. Askik dropped to his knees; the air was more breathable near the ground. At the far side of the wakinogan, an old woman was sitting with her eyes closed. Old she was indeed, very old. Askik had never seen such a wrinkled face. And how thin her skin was! So thin her teeth could almost be seen through her lips. She opened her eyes slightly. There was a feverish brightness about them. She spoke in Cree in a hoarse voice.

"I saw you come, little Métis. I need you. The others are afraid of Pennisk."

Askik did not know what to say. He felt the dry spruce needles dropping to the ground under his feet. The floor covering needed renewing.

"*Nipiy!*" the old woman muttered, pointing to a wooden bowl. "*Nipiy!*"

Askik took the bowl and went to the lake to draw water. He had to come back and borrow an old club to break the ice with. When he returned the second time he placed the bowl in front of the old woman, who sat looking at it sadly. Clumsily, Askik then put the bowl to her lips. He tipped it too much and a trickle of water ran down and spotted her buckskin dress. The sick woman did not notice. She drank several mouthfuls and then fell back against her backrest with a sigh of relief and exhaustion. Her head dropped sideways against her shoulder and she stared at the ground.

Askik went outside once more. It was getting dark. He gathered a new supply of deadwood, threw out the poplar logs that would smoke as they burned and lit a clean, hot fire. It made the lodge look even more ancient. The curling birchbark wallcovering was split in many places. Everything lying on the ground or hanging from the uprights was as antiquated and worn as the mistress of the house. The light from the flames revealed an astonishing number of herbs and roots, tied in bunches or plaited into thick braids and hung from the ceiling.

There was a cooking pot in the lodge but no food. Not knowing where to turn to find some, Askik went back to Niskigwon's.

It was dark by now. As he approached the lodge, the sound of voices inside stopped. His footsteps had been heard.

"Niskigwon, we're hungry," Askik called.

There was a brief silence and then he heard Niskigwon's voice.

"Was it her sent you?"

"Ehé," Askik lied.

There was movement at the bottom of the door and then a sizzling noise. A hot cooking pot had been put outside in the snow.

"*Kinanaskomitin*, Niskigwon."

"Don't come back, Métis. I owe you nothing more."

Askik chuckled as he carried the pot away. How things were changing!

The next morning he went to his father's warehouse and brazenly demanded an axe, fishing tackle and a gun. The Indian in charge of the goods hesitated. Jérôme had instructed him to open the cache only to his agents; he had said nothing about his son. The Indian gave Askik the axe and fishing lines and hooks, but refused him the gun. Askik also asked for tea and tobacco for Pennisk. He received these too and went away pleased.

He used his new axe to chop half a dozen holes in the ice in front of the village. He baited his hooks with birds' innards and attached lines to sturdy sticks laid across the holes. Next he turned to some nearby evergreens. He covered the entire wakinogan with spruce boughs, which would hold the snow, providing a layer of insulation. He laid a carpet of branches inside, to which he added some cedar because he liked its fragrance.

It was already getting dark on the big lake when he came back to his lines. He expected six big fish, which he would smoke or freeze. The first two lines had no bait left. The third had no hook either. The fourth had disappeared completely; all that was left was the stick across the hole. The fifth still had its hook and bait, but had caught nothing. There was only one left, the shortest because it was the last Askik had set and there had not been much line left. He was not expecting anything of a line that did not reach the bottom. Yet when he lifted the stick he felt the line go taught. In a twinkling his doubt changed to a frenzy of happiness. He threw away the stick and pulled up the line so fast that the fish practically slapped him in the face. It was a doré. Not an enormous one, but respectable. Laughing with delight, he gathered his lines and went back up to the wakinogan. He was famished, his mittens and moccasins were soaking wet, but he was satisfied. He was not missing school at all now. As he walked through the dark village, he observed with pleasure that there was no longer light showing through the cracks of his lodge, that now it looked only like a dark, bristly butte indistinguishable from the forest around except for the plume of smoke rising from the roof.

"*Hai!*" exclaimed Pennisk triumphantly when she saw the fish. She had not eaten all day either. With one stroke of a knife, she slit open the doré's belly and cleaned it, then wedged it in a split stick and planted it in place over the fire. The lodge filled with the smell of roasting fish, wood fire and spruce gum. The air became so warm and heavy that Askik almost fell asleep, even before tasting his fish.

Pennisk had strange manners. After the meal, she made a mix of red willow and the Brazilian tobacco Askik had brought, filled her pipe and then smoked at length, gazing into the embers in the centre of the lodge. She did not say a word all evening, gave no sign even of being aware of the boy's existence. Askik had expected a little more gratitude. He did not have time to wonder about it, however; the layer of spruce was springy and sweet-smelling, it was hot, and the air was thick with wood smoke and tobacco. He wrapped himself in a moose-skin robe with his feet to the fire and his head to the *pukkwi*, the woven willow that lined the inside walls.

In the middle of the night, he felt the air freshen around his head. He curled himself up in a ball under his robe, like a squirrel in its winter nest, and went back to sleep.

Then the old woman was patting his back and saying repeatedly, "Little Métis, time to get up."

Askik rubbed his eyes. Was it really morning already? He could see his breath. The old woman was poking the fire now. She was feeling better.

She brought him some steaming hot tea. "Drink this," she said.

Askik saw his lines and hooks carefully rolled up at his feet. The old woman had baited them with entrails from the doré. She began to speak precisely and with authority, as if it were imperative that Askik listen and understand.

"When you let out your line, don't let it go all the way to the bottom. Mikkikinuk the Turtle is still awake. He eats but doesn't let himself get caught. Don't fish in front of the village; go to the first bay to the east. You'll see rabbit tracks on the way. Follow them. You'll find the snares I set. I'm too weak to go. You go for me. Have you set snares before?"

Askik nodded.

"Good. You know the *agimak*, the ash tree? Take your axe. Find a branch this thick" (she closed Askik's fist) "and this long" (she indicated the length from Askik's left shoulder to the tip of his right hand). "Bring it back to me. Mind you don't wound trees needlessly. Be sure before you chop. When you've chosen the branch, put this tobacco at the foot of the tree to thank it for its gift to you."

It was still dark outside. Askik walked toward *Wabun*, the Morning, as Pennisk had instructed him to. He came to a massive rock with jack pines growing at its top. Then a dizzying descent to a marsh. There were rabbit tracks all over the snow. He found a shallow bay with a swamp at its end. He chopped holes in the ice near the reeds and let down his hooks. Then, on his way back, he followed the rabbit tracks and one by one discovered the snares that the old woman had set. These were loops of rope made of bark and were tied to the tops of saplings bent over and attached to the ground. A rabbit would catch its head or feet in the slip-knotted loop and the movement would release the sapling, which would spring back upright, taking the catch with it; up there, the rabbit was out of reach of carnivores on the ground.

The trap line wound this way and that through the forest, skirted swamps and rounded rocks. Askik often lost it and found only half the snares. The snow was deep in places. Each time he stopped to catch his breath, he was surprised at the silence of the forest. Sometimes the wind moved through the naked poplars. Most often he could hear nothing at all. Nothing. Just the barest, vaguest humming in his ears. Without thinking about it, he became more silent himself, breathed less noisily, placed his feet more carefully, to a point where his own silence alarmed him. To convince himself he had not gone deaf, he clapped his hands. Then at once was sorry he had given away his position. To whom? To what?

Whiskyjacks joined him. Impertinent birds that deserved their name of *Wesekechak*, Trickster. They moved along with him, flitting from branch to branch, chattering comments about him. Then in a wink disappeared again, so that he wondered for a moment whether he had imagined them.

He found an agimak in a hollow by a waterfall and carefully chose the branch he needed. He did not forget to leave the tobacco at the foot of the tree as a mark of gratitude. On his way back to the lake he found a green patch of Labrador tea and filled his pockets with it. He took three pike from the lake, coiled up his lines and went back to the village.

That evening when the grandfathers had lit their fires in the sky and their descendants had gathered around theirs on earth, Pennisk gave Askik a well-greased knife and showed him how to make a bow out of his ash branch, watching and correcting him meticulously. Not a child's bow but a man's, with a rounded face and a flat back. She herself was not idle. As she sucked on her stone-bowl pipe she stripped willow twigs, scraped off the inner bark and roasted it over the fire. This bark became kinnikinnik, Indian tobacco, which gives bite when added to Brazilian.

"Kokoum," Askik said as he worked, "how come you speak two languages? Are you Cree or Ojibway?"

"Don't say 'Ojibway'. That's what strangers call us. Say 'Anishnabeg'."

"Why d'you speak Cree?"

"Don't *you* speak two languages?"

"Ehé, Kokoum, but I'm Métis."

"Me too. In my own way. My mother was a Muskego. My father was Anishnabeg. I speak Sioux as well. But that's another story."

"Tell me about it."

"Another time."

"How old are you?"

The old woman gave a croak of pleasure and swayed back and forth on her scrawny haunches.

"How old? I don't know, little Métis. I'm very old."

"Did you never have any little boys like me?"

The joy that had lit up Pennisk's face faded all of a sudden. She looked down at the kinnikinnik, which was turning brown, and said softly:

"*Atoské*, little Métis. Work."

Their first conversation had come to an end.

She turned as silent as on the first day. When Askik tired of his work, he put away the bow and knife and said, "I'm going to sleep now, Kokoum." She did not even look up, seemed not to hear him. She kept smoking, pipeful after pipeful. Sometimes her still lips let fragments of song pass, barely whispered them, and the melody brought a brief swaying to her body. Her brown, wrinkled hands lay on the rough buckskin of her dress. She went to sleep sitting up.

3

A great cold settled over the land. At night the trees made cracking sounds like guns shooting. In the lodges, the old people tended the fires while the others slept.

Askik worked hard to open his fishing holes; every morning the ice seemed to be thicker. Still, the lake was generous. It gave him fish every day, if only one small yellow perch. There was no shortage of rabbits, either, and Askik wondered why he was the only one hunting and fishing in this part of the forest. One day when he was doing the rounds of his trapline, he found a fox hanging from one of his saplings. It was still alive, batting feebly with its paws, trying to reach and loosen the rope that was strangling it. It had probably been caught while following rabbit tracks. Its eyes were already glassy and it did not see the boy approach. Askik turned it on its rope and finished it off cleanly with one blow of his axe.

On his way back to the village he saw Niskigwon's wife going home with a bundle of branches.

"How are you?" he asked her politely in Ojibway, but she looked at him in alarm and without replying hurried away in the other direction. Askik remembered the lepers in the catechism and wondered if he himself had contracted a disfiguring illness.

Some children were playing at wetiko near the village. The biggest had tied some branches and dead leaves to his head and was hiding in a bush. The others ran around the bush, pretending not to see him, led by a teenager. When the wetiko bounded out of his hiding place, roaring and wagging his head, an explosion of terrified screams resounded all the way to the heedless village.

When Askik tried to join in the game, the cries rose in pitch, the excitement turned to terror, and even the wetiko ran off bawling to the village. The young Métis was left standing alone, dumbfounded, holding his dead fox. Now he was the one who was afraid. He whipped off his mitten and felt his face. His skin seemed smooth and his features normal. Had he changed colour? He crossed his eyes severely, trying to see the end of his nose; it was red because of the cold, to be sure, but not excessively. Perhaps it was the fox that had frightened them. He entered the village, deliberately passing in front of open doors. The women went inside when they saw him, taking their babies with them, and the men turned away.

He saw Pennisk standing outside her wakinogan with her face turned up to the sun and her eyes closed, squinting with pleasure. She at least was not afraid of him. She at least would tell him what had happened. He ran to her and breathlessly demanded:

"Kokoum, look at me!"

She bent her head, opened her eyes, and at once seemed concerned. Askik felt his heart drop.

"Rub your face, little Métis, you're frostbitten."

Askik broke into sobs. He had seen a Chipewyan with a frozen face, the end of his nose blackened and ragged like a rotting toadstool. This was the way he would spend his life. A repulsive monster. No one would love him ever again. He cried bitterly as he rubbed his cheeks. If only he had married Mona while he still had the chance! Who would want him now?

"Why are you crying, you little fool?" Pennisk barked.

"I'm ugly now!"

"If you're ugly it's not just from today. Your frostbite's nothing. Just patches, just barely white."

"But the others are afraid of me!"

"*Tché!* They're idiots. It's me they're afraid of, little Métis."

"Why?"

"I'm a Midé, a member of the *Midewiwin*, the Grand Medicine Society. They think the spirits turn me mad."

"I wanted to play with them."

"You can't play in this village."

"I've been nice," Askik protested.

"The nicer you are, the more they'll be afraid of you."

"Why?"

"D'you think the wetiko is like these children, howling and foaming at the mouth? *Tché!* The wetiko sits by the fire, shares his meat, gathers wood, draws water, hands out gifts. When he has won the confidence of his hosts, that's when he shows who he is."

Askik felt an uneasy shifting in the pit of his stomach.

"Have you ever seen a wetiko, Kokoum?"

The old woman smiled mischievously. "Why yes. You and me, little Métis!"

"They think we're wetikos?" Askik burst out laughing in disbelief.

"They're afraid that's what we'll turn into. They're afraid of a lot of other things as well."

"I'm afraid of the wetiko too," Askik confessed, serious again.

"Then you're as much a fool as they," Pennisk said, turning and going back inside the wakinogan. "Bring in your fox before it freezes hard."

The bow was almost finished. Askik was very proud of it. The white wood had a warm glow by the fire at night. When it came time to brown it, Askik almost refused to do it. It had to be done, though. The wood would be stronger after being heated. Later, the bow would be stained with red pigment. Pennisk was braiding a bowstring of nettle. She had a supply of the long fibres of this precious plant in her sewing bag. The Indians used so much of it that former campsites could be indentified by the abundance of nettle growing there.

She decorated the bow with feathers and strips of rabbit fur. She ordered ten arrows from a craftsman known for the straightness of his shafts. She fashioned a quiver of birchbark.

"They're too short!" Askik exclaimed when he saw the arrows. Indeed, compared to the great arrows of the Sioux, these of his looked like mere toys.

"You have to have short arrows in the forest," Pennisk snapped. The boy's fascination with the Sioux was irritating.

As soon as the bow was finally ready, Askik wanted to rush off into the forest to make the most of the remaining hours of daylight. Pennisk would not allow it. He therefore spilled his overflowing excitement in chatter, and Pennisk had to endure a deluge of boastfulness. He was going to kill bears, caribou, moose, elk, squirrels and wolves. He would pile up the carcasses and invite the villagers to help themselves. They would have to admire him. He could not understand how others could come home emptyhanded from hunting. Did they not have eyes for following tracks? Or heads for calculating the movements of the game? Age must be addling their judgment. What negligence! What sloth!

Good thing he was young! Good thing he was a Métis, descended from a race of hunters! He was going to kill only fine-furred animals. He was going to gather a heap of skins and sell them to the Company. He was going to go back to St. Boniface and send for his mother to keep house, and would resume his studies at the college.

However, he hastened to add, Pennisk had nothing to fear; he would keep a distant eye on her and send her whatever she needed.

The ungrateful old thing seemed not to have heard. Askik decided he would do this for her anyway. He went to bed early, exhausted by all his plans.

His excitement woke him well before daybreak. He left his fishing lines at home and passed by his rabbit snares without a glance. There were more important things for him to do.

At first he moved without plan, quickly, taking pleasure in the changing scenery. Then he slowed his pace, surprised not to have killed anything yet. He began to cross the high points more cautiously, searching the forest from the top of each rock outcrop; he studied the thickets before entering them. Still he saw nothing. When he listened, all he heard was the cracking of frozen trees.

And then, incredibly, the sun was beyond the crests of the trees. It was midday and all the animals in the forest were still alive. Askik could not understand it. The bow hung comfortably from his hand, the quiver bounced amiably against his chest and the arrows were beautiful, straight and lethal. Where was the game?

He turned back toward the village, not directly but taking a wide loop through the woods. He had never been so far away in the bush. He had to consult the sun and trees many times to check his direction. He even resigned himself to following a few tracks, most of which he did not recognize, but the tracks became muddled or disappeared on rocky promontories or wound endlessly this way and that through the forest until the boy lost patience. The afternoon was drawing to a close when he heard the village dogs barking. In desperation, he began to beat the underbrush in hope of flushing a grouse at least. There were none.

He entered the village after dark so that no one should see him, ate the rabbit stew that Pennisk had prepared, and went to bed without a word.

The following morning he went out into the forest again, with sore muscles but renewed optimism. He was no longer dreaming of carnage; one moose would do. The reasonableness of his expectation seemed like a guarantee of success. However, the frustration he had felt the previous day was soon back. He found the same successsion of empty marshes and thickets, the same clumps of whistling evergreens, the same tangled underbrush. Everywhere, just more dreary forest. Nothing had changed. He saw his own tracks from the previous day. There were no new ones crossing them.

He was now mightily bored with it all. For a change, and because he was itching to try his bow, he shot at a big poplar. The arrow shattered against the frozen trunk, leaving the iron point embedded in the bark, too high to retrieve.

Askik returned to camp earlier than the day before, disgusted with himself and his weapon. That evening he and Pennisk supped on a small piece of pike. It was all that was left.

He set out in search of game on the third day and came home emptyhanded once again. They dined on Labrador tea.

Pennisk made no allusion whatever to the young hunter's troubles. When she saw him come in without game she barely raised her eyebrows. She did without in silence, expecting nothing of him.

The boy, on the other hand, was on the brink of panic. He had expected to get by on instinct and was discovering with astonishment that hunting takes knowlege. He knew nothing of the habits of the big game. Rabbits were unreliable. As for Jérôme Mercredi's goods, the consumables they included were luxury items: tea, sugar and rum.

The more he thought about his fears, the more inevitable famine looked. His dejection was pitiful to see.

"You thought you were pretty strong, didn't you, little Métis?" Askik looked up at her, his eyes full of confusion.

"*Tché!* You're weak," she muttered, "the weakest of all."

Askik's temper flared. The old liar! Was she telling him she had known all along that he would fail?

"Then why did you give me that bow?" he cried.

"So you'd bring back meat."

"I tried and I couldn't."

"You never will. Not by yourself. You're pretty proud of yourselves, you buffalo hunters. You ride right into the middle of a herd howling like wolves and shooting at anything that moves. The only thing you're scared of is getting trampled by the game. Here in the forest you have to know how to hunt."

Askik said nothing. He bent his head to hide his tears of humiliation.

"Do you think you're master of all Creation?" Pennisk continued.

"Kitché-Manitou first created the Earth, plants and animals. Only after that he created Man, the weakest of all because in order to live he depends on all the others. But you, little Métis, you're like the Hairy Faces. You think everything belongs to you. You expect to kill animals on your own, without thanking the Creator who restores their number every night. And you're choosy, too. You want only moose, bear and elk so you can boast about it. Have you people forgotten everything? Don't you remember how the Earth was reformed after the great flood, thanks to the humble Muskrat?"

"Do not look down on any form of life. Respect all living things. Even the weakest have power of their own. And of all, you are the wakest. Anything you ever receive will be given to you. Take it. Show gratitude."

"Tomorrow you will do homage to the manidos. Then you will go back to your lines and snares."

From this moment on, Askik never left the village without his bow. However, he attended first to his lines and snares. After gathering his rabbits and fish, he went hunting other game.

He was barely beginning his education. Everything was a mystery. One morning he saw a snowy owl strike a weasel a few paces away. He shot his bow. The arrow pinned the two carcases together; he had trouble separating them.

Pennisk would not eat the owl. Owls, she said, were close relatives of Peaso the Thunderbird, a powerful protector of the Anishnabegs. Besides, she added, a snowy owl looks like a human baby once it is plucked. She offered a sacrifice of expiation to Peaso, muttering over the muddleheadedness of her young hunter. Talk about ignorance of the laws! She resolved to take Askik's education in hand.

At night when the wolves were harmonizing on the frozen lake, she would tell him the stories of olden days, of the Time when the Earth was still young.

4

Three nights in a row, the moon had a ring around it. The chickadees and whiskyjacks came and pecked around the lodges but were no longer chattering. There was no game to be found. Something was brewing. Pennisk advised Askik to come home early from hunting.

The sky was dull grey. On the high points a strong but surprisingly warm wind was blowing. Nothing else was moving. A couple of grosbeaks squabbling in a spruce tree were the only wildlife Askik saw. He found nothing at the ends of his lines, which was happening more and more often. His snares were empty; only one had been sprung, perhaps by the wind.

The forest was suddenly filled with fat snowflakes, still whirling from the buffeting they had received above. It was time to go home.

Retracing his steps, Askik saw the same grosbeaks devouring some tips of twigs. They, at least, did not seem afraid of the storm. The boy quickened his pace. The spaces between the trees were becoming hazy. The snowflakes were finer, more biting. The wind romped noisily though the upper branches. Sometimes a gust would hit the ground, raising a swirl of snow.

For all his resolve, when he emerged from the woods he had to stop. There was nothing but snow and torment. The lake had disappeared. From every lodge, the blizzard was whipping a long, powdery white stream, like the tail of a comet. Inside each hump of snow and branches, human beings were huddled, listening.

"Hai! I thought you'd got lost!" Pennisk exclaimed when she saw him come in.

It was very dark in the wakinogan. Pennisk must have had to dampen the flames because even the smoke was refusing to venture outside. Askik could see the old woman's breath.

The boy spent the afternoon by the fire, stirring embers and gloomy thoughts. The wind roaring all around the wakinogan reminded him of the winter's first storm that he had lived through on the pairie with his family. He missed them. He missed the Métis. Not that he disliked living with Pennisk; he was hunting and fishing when and where he pleased, just like a man. But the villagers here scorned him. And sometimes, though not often, his old dream of becoming a great man returned, spoiling his pleasure.

Pennisk had wrapped herself in all the robes and furs she possessed. She sat hunched over the fire, her pipe protruding from her hood, smoking constantly and listening to the storm.

"*Pipon*, ah, Pipon," the old woman muttered when the wind's howling reached new heights, "it delights you to rage against your enemy. You think you have crushed him. You beat him and he does not defend himself. He will come back to life. *Zigwon* will return from the south and drive you away again."

As if in answer to the old woman, the whistling of the wind rose to a shriek.

"Listen, little Métis, Pipon is wild, and do you know why? Because he quarrelled with Zigwon over a young girl. A long, long time ago."

She stopped. Her old eyes searched for the boy in the darkness.

"What's the matter, little Métis? Don't you like my stories any more? Why such a long face? You miss your parents? *Tché!* They're alive. Be thankful for that. You mustn't mourn for the living. Even though they're a long way away, your parents are walking and eating and sleeping, you know that. When they've gone, though, you'll wonder every day what they're doing, if they're happy or troubled, if they've safely passed the traps and pitfalls of the Way of Souls." Pennisk looked down at the fire. "You worry specially about the children," she continued, "specially about the children; will there be someone on the other side to take them by the hand and show them the way? There are so many evil spirits. No...never mourn for the living, little Métis, never..."

Perceiving that she was lost in her own thoughts, Askik reminded her of things that he considered more urgent.

"Kokoum, what am I going to do here?"

"You've learned a lot since you came. Don't you want to go on?"

"Ehé, but I wanted to learn other things."

"Like what?"

"I can read and write already..."

"*Hai!* I've seen their *masinahigon*. In some things the Hairy Faces are pretty clever, but mostly they're so ignorant! They walk with their eyes closed. It comes from working in metal. Evil serpents taught men about metal. Metal really is death; it puts the soul to sleep..."

"Kokoum!" the boy exclaimed, sensing the start of a new cycle of stories.

"Why d'you want to study the masinahigon?"

Askik was caught short. Why? To become an educated man, of course. But this was something the old aboriginal would not understand. Askik did not really understand himself what education was. What made the priests educated and his father not? What had they learned from their books that gave them such authority? Askik did not know.

He only knew that he wanted that authority. He decided to talk of more tangible ambitions to Pennisk.

"I want to build a big house," he said.

The old woman guffawed.

"Just look at those Hairy Faces!" she declared. I think Kitché-Manitou put them on earth to amuse us. Never satisfied. Their feet itch; they never keep still. Why would they ever have come to our country otherwise? They're always running, always got something new to do. Yet they want houses that are heavy like great rocks and are stuck in one place. So as to be somewhere else, I suppose."

Askik was stung. Let her talk all she wanted, this old savage in her hut made of branches!

"Aren't you warm and comfortable in the wakinogan?" Pennisk demanded. "Pipon can't get at you here. And if there's no game, are you going to leave your house where it is and build another? Why do you want a big house? To make you feel important, the way you wanted game? *Wigwasateg* the Birch has given his skin to shelter you. If you take more than you need in plants or animals, the manidos will take revenge."

"But the Indians trap furs for the Company!" Askik retorted. He was pleased to have found the old woman at fault.

"They're wrong!" She was angry now. "The Anishnabegs used to live at peace with the forest dwellers. They took only what they needed. In return, the animals let themselves be caught. Then strange, frightful sicknesses appeared. This is why the Anishnabegs lost faith in their medicine men. This is why they behave like blind things. This is why Kitché-Manitou has stopped remaking beavers and muskrats."

"Has he stopped for ever?" Askik asked, worried, picturing his profits shrinking.

"He's keeping them in the Land of Souls, waiting for the Anishnabegs to come to their senses, and for the White Man to tire of his metal."

"But you've got metal too!" Askik protested, pointing to Pennisk's knife in its leather sheath.

"Ehé. This knife has good medicine. It serves me well. I don't want any other. This pot too. I had another but it's dead."

"Dead?"

"Ehé." The old woman lifted the pot and touched it to the stones of the fireplace, making it ring. "You hear that? When a pot no longer sings, it's dead, its spirit has gone. Didn't you know that?" she asked with a mischievous grin.

"No, Kokoum."

"Can you do this?" She peeled a thin piece of birchbark from one of the supports of the lodge, moistened it in the steam from the kettle, folded it in four, and began to bite on it gently. After a few minutes of this chewing, she unfolded the bark and revealed a whimsical design of flowers, ferns and stars.

Askik immediately forgot his gloom. He clamoured for Pennisk to teach him this art. He spent the rest of the evening denuding the birch framework of the house, scalding his fingers, and making his jaws ache trying to imitate what Pennisk had produced, without really succeeding. His designs were muddled and blurred, his garlands looked like fat sausages, but he was pleased. His heap of designs grew at a furious rate.

Near the end of the evening, when all the birch in the house had been stripped and Askik was beginning to yawn and blink his eyes, Pennisk covered her ears and made a face.

"Oh, Pipon, Pipon," she exclaimed, "your whining makes my head hurt. Enough of your blubbering. My warrior's going to drive you off."

She took a twig, shredded one end and made a notch at the other.

"Take your bow," she told Askik. "Open the door. Put this arrow to the string, light the end of the arrow, and shoot it into the storm. Be careful not to hit the other lodges."

Askik opened the door of spruce boughs. A snowdrift had taken shape just outside. The night was filled with gusts of wind and swirling snow, faintly illuminated by the firelight from the lodge. Askik aimed into the torment and let the arrow fly. The wind seized the arrow. The flame went out immediately. He thought he saw another flame shooting into the sky from the village.

"Egosi! That's the way!" Pennisk applauded. "Now close the door before I freeze."

Pipon ran out of breath during the night. When Askik left the lodge in the morning, he could see the stars in the firmament. He was enchanted. At last he had learned something useful, something that would amaze his own people. Who else in St. Boniface could drive away storms?

The fishing in the small bay was a total loss. Pennisk was not surprised. The water dwellers liked to change camp once in a while, she said.

At the far end of the lodge there was a dusty heap of ropes, baskets and skins. Pennisk rummaged in it and unearthed a long package wrapped in bark. She cut a cord and unrolled a net made of willow bark. It needed repair, for which she had Askik help her. Handling the strips of willow soaked in hot water was not easy, but the bark net would rot less quickly than one of rawhide. While Pennisk regarded the water dwellers with all due respect, she thought it best to keep the advantage on her side. When the bark net was ready, she prepared a bag of food and announced that she would go with Askik to the new fishing site. If necessary, they would stay there several days.

They rose at first light. After greasing their faces for protection from the wind, they left the village, following the shore of the lake to the mouth of the river. The wind had laid long snowdrifts on the ice, but the old woman moved along with surprising vigour. Her cottony white exhalations were strong and regular.

"You know, little Métis," she said, puffing nevertheless, "when I was a girl I could run like an antelope. Even the boys of the village had trouble catching me. The first time I met my *nenapem* was in a foot race. I let him win. He was a good husband but a bad runner."

She tried to laugh but managed only a gasp.

"Where's your husband now?"

"Dead, little Métis, they're all dead. I'm the only one left."

"How about me?" Askik objected banteringly. "And how about the people of the village?"

"What's that?" she retorted with a look of surprise. "Did you see them this morning?"

"Who?"

"The people of the village."

"No."

"Then maybe they're dead too."

"What are you saying?" the boy cried. "They were asleep at home!"

"Ah, you think so but you don't know. You never know. You think you're as happy as can be, and then one morning it's all over. Everything's gone. Like the wind in the grass. Nothing's left of your life. Then what a stupid thing you are, there in that emptiness!" The old woman cackled with relish.

Askik loathed her. What a nasty old witch! Her stooped shoulders, the grey wisps escaping from under her robe, the sardonic smile, every-thing about her seemed to revel in morbid thoughts. No wonder the villagers shunned her!

A small island split the river into two channels. On the right bank they found a shelter of branches and the remains of a fire. So Pennisk was not the only one to fish here. There was a straight line of fishing holes along the ice. Askik had no trouble reopening them; the flow of water was swift and the ice thin. Pennisk unrolled her net and weighted it with stones. Then, with a long pole left there for the purpose, she pushed it through under the ice and then played it out, reaching through one hole after another until it was all in place.

They gathered their take once before nightfall. Pennisk attached a long rope to her end of the net. While Askik landed the net on the other side of the channel, she held this rope taut to keep the fish from dragging on the bottom. There were dorés, pike and perch caught by the gills in the tight mesh. Pennisk impaled them one after the other on a sharpened stick, where they would freeze. To lay the net once more, they simply crossed the channel and pulled on the rope.

They roasted two of the fish. Askik chose a doré. He picked off the piping hot flesh carefully with his teeth, turning the fish on its roasting stick in the way that other children, thousands of miles away, would eat toffee apples. Perfumed by the cedarwood fire, it was exquisite.

After the meal there was still tea. Pennisk radiated well-being, but said nothing. She assembled her pipe, filled it with sensual pleasure, and having lit it with a brand, sat dreamily watching the play of the flames. Although it was cold, the warmth of the fire was reflected inside the shelter. There was no wind.

When Askik had finished eating he began to count the stars that filled the black pools between the evergreeens.

"Kokoum, what are the stars?"

"Holes in the firmament that the light passes through. Others say they're the camp fires of the spirits. That makes more sense to me. If there was light beyond the firmament, there would have to be another sky over that, wouldn't there? Look, there's *Matotisan*, the Sweat Lodge. See the roof of the lodge? And you know what that is." She traced the sweep of the Milky Way with her finger.

"The Way of the Wolf!"

"The Anishnabegs call it the Way of Souls. Whatever you call it, it's the same thing."

Kitché-Pisim, The Great Moon of midwinter, was already rising over the forest, extinguishing the lesser stars.

"Be careful, little Métis! Don't look too long at the moon. She'll gobble you up if you do."

Askik shot a suspicious glance at the old woman. Was it true or was she joking?

"You don't believe me? Look. You see the little boy in the moon, carrying two buckets of water? He was a cheeky one like you. One night his mother sent him to get water; on his way back to the wakinogan, he kept looking and looking at the moon. It's pretty embarrassing to be stared at like that. To punish him for his rudeness, the moon made a prisoner of him. And there he is. He'll be there for ever. Do you want to go up there with him?"

Askik looked away quickly so as not to annoy the moon. But he kept turning the matter over in his mind. His parents had never warned him of this danger.

"Is it true, Kokoum?"

"What d'you mean, is it true?" she countered grumpily. "Don't you believe me? *Tché!* So go ahead and look, you impudent little boy, if you're brave enough, and let the moon take you! There'll be all the more fish for me!"

Askik studied her, looking for a sign that this was a joke, like the start of a smile or a quivering in her shoulders. She remained as still and expressionless as stone.

Then, with clenched teeth and defiant face, Askik raised his eyes to the moon. The old woman burst out laughing.

"*Hai!* You've got guts, little Métis!"

"You lied to me, Kokoum!" Askik cried, relieved to be still here on earth for all that.

"Oh, just a bit."

"I'll never believe you again!"

"Suits me. I won't wear myself out any more telling you stories."

Askik sighed. How could you argue with this woman?

"No, Kokoum, I want to hear a story."

"Well, well..."

"A scary story."

"What for? You won't sleep afterwards."

"Yes, I will. I won't be scared."

"So what's the point of telling you a scary story?"

"Kokoum!" Askik cried shrilly in exasperation.

"All right, all right. Wait while I think a minute... *Wah!* Do you know the story of Paguk?"

"No," Askik breathed, shivering already.

"He's the most unhappy of all the spirits."

"Even unhappier than the wetiko?"

"More miserable than that even..."

Pennisk went on to recount the story of a cruel, vain man who was transformed into a living skeleton, condemned to fly over the world for ever, weeping and crying out.

Askik had never seen a human skeleton, apart from the big bone that Mathias had claimed to be the leg bone of a Sioux, but one day he had discovered the decomposed carcase of a horse. He had only to imagine something worse than this memory to picture Paguk, lips blackened, teeth yellowed, strips of flesh hanging from his legs, a suffocating stench. Oh, how sorry he was to have asked Pennisk to tell him a story! It had been such a beautiful night. The darkness now closed in all around their tiny hut. What were they doing here, an old woman and a child, so far from the village and other humans?

"Hoo, hoo, hoo!" called an owl deep in the forest. "The owl is coming to get you," Anishnabeg mothers would tell their children. Askik began reciting an ave to arm himself against the spirit of the owl, then stopped so as not to vex the manidos. The relationships of the supernatural powers were still a puzzle to him, but he sensed that in the forest, at night, the manidos had the upper hand over the Virgin.

Pennisk and Askik lay down one against the other the better to keep warm. The old woman fell asleep at once, borne away by fatigue from the day and memories of travels in other days with her nenapem. Askik listened to her light, even breathing and felt the movement of her thin flanks through the moosehide robe. He tried to imagine what her life must have been like without a family or friends. For the first time he had a feeling of tenderness for Pennisk, mixed with pity. Hardly any wonder if her sorrows had unhinged her a bit.

The next day was a hard one. They went back and forth to the river to raise and empty the net, taking care not to break the mesh stiffened by the cold. They worked with bare hands so as not to wet their mittens. The fish would flap their tails a few times, then quickly turn as hard as rock.

Askik liked the work at first. It was fun to go to the river, gather a heap of green and grey fish and then go back with a sense of satisfaction to the warmth of the fire. He soon tired of it, though. However well he warmed his fingers and mittens, the heat was gone from them in seconds. His left heel became numb; he felt as though had a big stone under it when he walked. Pennisk was in a macabre mood; all she talked about was Indians frozen to death and discovered stiff as rods or half-eaten by wolverines.

Yet she had begun the day in good humour. She had dreamed of her nenapem and children, whom she had not seen for years. It had taken this fishing trip to bring back memories of them, she declared happily. She too was suffering from the cold, however. Her movements began to betray some stiffness.

That night, the northern lights spread in a jade green ribbon over the black forest. *Tchipayuk nimihituwok*, the Crees would say; the dead are dancing.

"Is it true they come closer when you whistle?"

"Who d'you mean?"

"The dancers."

"Silly prattle, little Métis."

"But they really are the souls of the dead. Why wouldn't they come if I whistled to them?"

"They're celebrating. They've gathered for a night of rejoicing. It's a sign it won't be so cold tomorrow."

"We're going to leave tomorrow?"

"Ehé."

"I want to go back," Askik confessed. He had had enough of being cold.

The old woman was usually impassive, but this time she made a sour, almost despairing face at the mere thought of going back to the village. Askik, surprised, said nothing.

The cold woke him well before dawn. He was hurting all over. The frost was gnawing at his muscles and he could barely move his legs. With effort, he lifted his head; the fire was almost out. Pennisk was sitting beside it with shoulders hunched, wisps of grey hair blowing in the wind. She was not moving at all. Askik had a horrible thought. Forgetting about the cold, he shot out from under his robe and seized the old woman's shoulder.

"Kokoum!"

She turned her head and stared at him vacantly. Askik's fear changed at once to fury.

"Why did you let the fire burn down?"

But she was already turning her head away again, as if he were only a bothersome gnat.

"Come on! Help me raise the net, then we'll go," the boy urged.

"Leave the net."

"Why? There are still fish in it," the boy insisted testily.

A small, impatient gesture was her only reply. Askik had to

manage by himself. When he returned from the river she was still staring at the smoking remains of the fire. He stacked the frozen fish impaled on their sticks with the bark net on the toboggan.

"Kokoum, it's time to go!"

The old woman looked up at him, undecided. Should she stay or go? Join her own or cope some more with the malevolence of the living? All through the night her soul had been pleading for deliverance. She could curl up in the snow. Let torpor take over. Drift off to sleep. The memories revived by this fishing trip had enchanted her at first, then filled her with despair. Could she have lived all these years without love, warmth, or consolation of any kind? Her rivals wished her dead. She was not sure she could withstand them to the end. Why allow them such a victory, then?

But what about the little half-blood? *Tché!* He had so much to learn! He called her "grandmother." It was something any child might do when speaking to an old woman, but with her, other children made an exception. The little Métis was the first to call her this. He would never understand. He did not know what awaited them at the village, and she could not explain to him.

"Come on, Kokoum! We must go!"

He was standing beside the toboggan, looking at her anxiously. Those frightened-rabbit eyes. Were all the Métis so anxious? I must teach him to be strong, Pennisk thought.

She stood up with an involuntary "Oof!"

"Go ahead, I'll come behind."

Happily, Askik set off, pulling the toboggan. The load was light, the snow firm underfoot. Later he might ask Pennisk to pull too, he thought. For the moment he forged ahead alone and with obvious pride.

Go ahead, little Métis, Pennisk thought. You're in a hurry to begin life. I hope they'll let you. You will be there for the end. You will escape if that is your destiny. If not, there will be two of us entering the Land of Souls; you will never find a better guide than I.

5

Starvation comes late in winter. When food supplies have run low, when game has gone far from the village. Some families were preparing to leave the lake and go to live in the forest when news of famine began coming from all around. A hawk was seen perching right in the middle of the village. A bad sign. For those who scoffed, there came another sign, a terrible one.

The hunter Tagawenin and his family were gathered around the fire, each deep in his own thoughts, when sounds of heavy footsteps came to their ears. The family all held their breaths. Outside, the dogs crept away from the lodge whining.

The footsteps stopped outside the door.

Tagawenin shuddered as he quietly loaded his gun. Should he open the door? He looked around at the other members of the family but all he saw was fear in their eyes. Getting control of himself, he flung aside the entry cover. A rectangle of light fell on the snow outside.

A porcupine was staring at them, eyes golden in the firelight. After a moment it turned around and went away with the unhurried steps of a placid man.

Tagawenin's wife fell face down in fright. The porcupine is the servant of the wetiko. He visits villages in winter, discovering families weakened sufficiently by hunger, then calls his master.

For several days the villagers forced themselves to laugh and joke to mislead the evil spirits. Meanwhile they watched one another anxiously, watching for the first signs of the madness that takes hold of the starving and turns them into wetikos, cannibals. Those with the least food pretended to have the most to keep from being driven from the village. Outlandish rumours flew from lodge to lodge. This one had driven away the game by giving the bones of a moose to his dogs. Another had made a pact with the evil spirit Matché-Manitou. Feverish incantations were muttered at night. Invisible spells and counter-spells flew back and forth over the lodges.

"There's sorcery behind it," the men told each other. Now Pennisk was hated even more than before. Who could say she was not the source of the evil? And what about the Métis lad she had in her lodge? Lewd rumours circulated about the two of them, spiteful bits of gossip repeated snickeringly, but regretted almost immediately; how could anyone be sure she was not hearing it all? There were those who claimed to have seen her sitting in the middle of her wakinogan, her ears grown long and pointed, listening to everything that was going on in the camp.

Even the strongest felt chills up and down their spines. There was only one thing to do about it, said the braggarts, touching a finger to their tomahawks. But no one went near the dilapidated wakinogan.

Askik had become used to unfriendly looks from the villagers and did not notice that the hatred had reached a new pitch. He saw a profound change in Pennisk, however. She stopped going outside altogether, even to warm herself in the sun as the weather became milder. She spent long days in the darkness of the wakinogan, muttering prayers or ruminating. At night, he endured the tedium of following her complicated rituals and listening as she endlessly repeated "Hey! hey! ho!", punctuating her chant with a tortoise shell rattle. At times she would bring out her *wayan*, a mink skin embroidered with beads and porcupine quills. This wayan was very old; each time she took it from her medicine bag it left behind another tuft of fur. Pennisk handled it reverently. Askik feared its power. Whenever she produced it, he would find an excuse to go outside and wait there until the old woman had finished her incantations.

One day on his way back from hunting, he found an assemblage of rawhide strips in the form of a spider's web fixed to a post a few paces from the lodge. He took it down and bought it inside to ask Pennisk what it was. She no sooner saw it in his hands than her face contorted with fear and anger. She snatched it from him crossly and went to fix it back on its post.

"Stupid little boy! That web protects us. If an enemy comes after me during the night, his soul will get caught in the web and the spider-manitou will eat him up. Don't touch it! It's powerful medicine."

But she herself did not trust it entirely. She was no longer sleeping, fearing that a conjuror might send spirits to carry away her slumbering soul. Whenever she dozed off in spite of herself, she would wake up seconds later with a snort, like a frightened horse.

She was constantly on the alert for any sign of sorcery: the howl of a dog, the cry of an owl, a sudden flare-up in the fire. And since these happened often, she would sigh and say bleakly, "There are so many, so many."

Then she would begin her fervent incantations once again, either to ward off invading spirits or to strike down those who were sending them, her rivals in other camps. She barely touched a little of the fish that was left. Her thin face became positively emaciated. Children were frightened when she went out to answer the call of nature, and so she began to go out only at night. The villagers took this to be yet further proof that she was in cahoots with demons. The famine at their doors inflamed their imaginations. Those who saw her out one night told of ominous shadows lurking in her company. A few days later, a frightened woman declared she had seen Pennisk with her head bloated and the ears of a pig, the hairless animal that was the colour of a White. That the Whites should be involved in this sorcery surprised no one.

It was now that a half-starved Muskego appeared, looking for alms in the village. The villagers drove him out savagely, fearing that he was a wetiko. How could a man wander about the forest without a supply of food unless he was feasting on his own kind? Harassed and cursed at, the intruder hung about the outskirts of the village for several days. Finally, weary of living, he went into the forest to await death. As he entered the shadow of the trees, he met a young Métis returning emptyhanded from hunting. The Indian immediately recognized the boy's blue hooded coat and red sash, the traditional dress of French Canadians and Métis.

Askik had more trouble recognizing Numeo. What a change! The plump and prosperous hunter who had received the Mercredis early that winter now looked like a beggar. His village was in a very bad way, he said. The game had disappeared the minute severe cold had set in. The little children had fallen sick in the chest. He himself had lost a child; he had no doubt he would find others dead when he returned home.

"*If* I return home," he added sadly. He had come to the Anishnabegs to buy food, but they were in no better straits.

"*Nisim*, little brother," Numeo whispered, "a wind of madness is blowing in this village. The people start at the slightest sound. They are not afraid to lay a hand on a stranger. An evil spirit is present here. We must both leave, little brother. Let us go to your father. He will have food for us."

"But I don't know where he is," Askik said.

Numeo looked chagrined.

"Then I shall die."

"*Ahi!* Why should you die? I'll give you fish, then you can go home."

"To watch my children die? I'd rather give up my soul here."

Askik desperately looked for an argument to turn Numeo's thoughts away from death. Then he spotted a wolf-dog from the village.

"We'll kill the dogs!" he exclaimed. "I'll help you. Then you can go home. On the way you might find a moose."

The Cree thought for a moment and found the idea a good one. The people of his own village had long since eaten their dogs.

That very night, Numeo and Askik set a trap for the village curs. They heated fish innards and hung them in the wind on the branches of a tree. At the first scent the hungry dogs were off into the forest, where they met with a hail of arrows. The yapping of the wounded dogs brought a few men out of the lodges, but not one of them ventured into the dark woods. "The old pig-head is eating the dogs," they whispered to each other.

Numeo finished off the dogs with a knife, then retrieved the fish innards for his soup. He left at dawn, his sleigh loaded with meat.

In the morning, the villagers counted the dogs and once again cursed the old sorceress who was depriving them of this last source of food. She was willing their death for certain.

"When you go into the forest, little Métis, don't think of the animal you're looking for. Look this way and that, pretending you're walking about without any real purpose. The manido will be fooled and won't warn the prey. When you kill, explain and excuse yourself. Animals have the right to live. They have the right to be respected. Don't break their bones. Don't throw their bones to the dogs."

Pennisk's teachings came pouring out between one incantation and the next, as if she must hold the manidos in respect all the while she was completing the young Métis' education. She would heat rolls of birchbark over the fire and unfurl them. On their reddish undersurface, Askik would discover fantastic scenes: fish, bears and sea monsters, gathered in great lodges for the Midewiwin ceremony. Or sometimes a simpler design, a great hooked line, branching seven times, the Way of Life.

A few days after Numeo's departure, a young woman, driven frantic by the cries of her hungry children, called her favourite dog, and taking a club smashed its skull.

At once the village was gripped by a kind of madness. In the time it takes to tell it, all the village dogs lay dead or dying. A few escaped into the forest, never to return. Everyone feasted that night. Everyone except Pennisk and Askik, who ate some fish remains.

A scrawny dog does not long nourish a family that lives entirely on meat. The situation was desperate. And so the chief called the elders together. The news met with approval in all the lodges. At nightfall the elders emerged, decked out in their finest furs.The young warriors followed them. The women and children watched through the cracks in the lodges.

Even Askik went outside to enjoy the spectacle, but some young braves saw him and began to cry out and point their fingers at him. Askik went back inside, his cheeks red with indignation.

Because their wakinogan was on the outskirts of the village, Askik and Pennisk could not follow the discussions. All they could hear was their tone. The sound of voices faded gradually as the night wore on.

The outbursts occurred less often. Then finally a last burst of voices suggested that the Council had dissolved.

Seconds later, Pennisk and Askik heard a dull "plok" over their heads. Turning away briefly from her prayers, Pennisk put a hand up to the roof branches. There her fingers felt the head of an arrow which an excited young brave had shot into her roof.

"The wetiko hunt has begun," she chuckled. She rarely laughed these days.

6

The spring so long awaited took everyone by surprise. One morning when he went outside, Askik sensed a change. Everything seemed to be just as it had been before: the snow crunched under his feet, the ice was firm. Yet there was moisture in the air, and the sky had lost its glint. A few days later *Jawano*, the South Wind, brought the smell of earth from far away. Teenage boys ran to the forest to watch for chipmunks and squirrels emerging from their nests. The men greased their guns and talked about *Maskwa* the bear, who would soon be waking. He would have to be taken as soon as he came out of hibernation, while he was still fat.

The winter was not over, not by any means. The lake would be imprisoned under its lid of ice for a long time yet. The humus floor of the forest was rock-hard. The geese were still far to the south. But everything was changed by the few drops of melted snow that trickled from the roofs around midday. The young braves lounged in the sun and dreamed of expeditions against the Dakotas, when they might distinguish themselves and perhaps even be judged worthy of a bride. The teenage girls brought their work outside, gathering in noisy groups. The old folk who had resigned themselves to dying decided to live a mite longer. Little children venturing outside the lodges for the first time were attentive to the spirit of the woods, who lets twigs fall to warn them of danger.

When the sun went down and the cold draped the trees in ice and the forest was lit with a thousand lights, the children took so long to come in that their frustrated mothers appealed to the scarer.

Disguised as a monster in rags, the scarer would prowl around between the lodges, face masked with white birchbark that glowed eerily in the twilight. The frightened children would scatter like sparrows. However, they had to scatter in silence; for every Anishnabeg, it had to become habit not to give away the location of the camp.

And when the children in their sleeping robes continued to chatter too long, a grownup might poke a foot inside the lodge, a spirit's foot — an old moccasin on the end of a stick. Only the very young were taken in by this ruse. For the older children, the parents would have to wait for an owl to call somewhere in the forest, and then whisper, "Shhh! It could be a Dakota!"

Askik wakened suddenly, his stomach in a knot.

The old woman was speaking loudly and rapidly, as if someone were in the lodge. He could see nothing. He groped his way toward Pennisk's bed.

"Kokoum! *Kitahkossin na?* Are you ill?"

Suddenly her wispy grey head was there in front of him and her mouth opened wide and she screamed, "The Sioux!"

Askik fell over backwards, rolled in the ashes and then hurled himself through the door without opening it. He found himself on all fours in the snow, his heart in his mouth. In the other lodges there was pandemonium. The men were rushing out with tomahawks and knives. The children inside were howling like wolves. But when the warriors saw the little Métis, naked, on all fours in the moonlight, they turned and barked sharp commands through the lodge doors. Silence returned. The men disappeared inside again, closing the entry covers behind them.

The light of the stars softened the folds in the snow, turned the evergreens blue, made the pale birches stand out. Askik did not want to go back inside. The gaping black hole of the wakinogan looked like an animal's lair. Pennisk had begun her babbling again. Askik considered spending the night outside, but the cold was gnawing at his toes. He went in and made a fire.

It took until morning for Pennisk to calm down. Words kept crowding through her lips in fragmented bursts, pouring like pus from a draining wound. Askik listened. Piecing together these maunderings and remembering what she had let drop about herself, he managed finally to picture the life she had led. There were large gaps, but the important parts were in place.

She must have had the typical Anishnabeg childhood: cherished, lavished with care and supervision. Once, only once when she was very small, she had strayed away from a hunting camp. She had wandered about the forest unafraid and then heard strange music, enchanting like the song of a kinglet, sad like the cry of a loon. She went toward the music and then heard men's voices talking in an unfamiliar tongue. She fled, leaving behind the Canadian voyageurs with their violin, not knowing that she had almost encountered another world.

At the time of her first menses, she retreated into the forest, as was the custom, and prayed to the spirits, alone in a tiny lodge. After several days of fasting, a horned serpent appeared to her, a magnificent creature that changed into a man.

"My girl, I am sorry for you," the serpent-man said to her. "Here is something to amuse yourself with." He showed her herbs, roots and green plants. Braving the protests of the older women, she ended her fast thereupon. It had been a powerful vision. Too powerful. The manidos who give liberally are sometimes the most jealous. Pennisk did not breathe a word of her vision. The village elders thought she had had the usual dreams dreamed by young girls, and did not press her. A woman does not need visions to be fulfilled; she is fulfilled through her children.

Pennisk was not an exceptional beauty as a young woman, but she was strong and a good worker. A nenapem was found for her, a life companion. She had her first lodge, her first child, and happily began the life lived by Anishnabeg women. She forgot her vision, content to leave such things to others. Her husband had little interest in the supernatural anyway. He was a skillful hunter and practiced the medicines of the hunt, but paid scant attention to other medicines.

Their happy, ordinary life came to an end one autumn morning when cries from the women of her village announced the arrival of the Sioux. Most of the Anishnabeg men were away hunting. Pennisk fled into the forest, a baby clutched to her breast and a toddler running behind. The children did not cry but kept looking up anxiously at their mother. As the young woman ran with them to hide in a clump of junipers, she came upon a party of Sioux prowling in the underbrush.

The two childen's skulls were smashed. Pennisk herself would have died on the spot if the Sioux had not lost three women in a Cree raid the previous winter. They took her away as a replacement.

She stayed fifteen years in the lands of the Sioux, roaming the parklands and prairies in accordance with the season and the movement of the buffalo herds. The first years left a blank in her memory. She was in a daze of grief over the loss of her family. Bullying from her captors made no impression on her. She was no longer Anishnabeg and not yet Sioux; she was nobody. For this reason she was given little to eat; for clothing she had to make do with the old skins that had lain underfoot in the tents. She did not wash and had to untangle her hair with her fingers; she stopped bothering about her hair. She slept outside with the dogs except when it was very cold, when she was given a place inside by the door. Even then, the others complained about her smell.

Her captors had turned her over to an old couple who needed help moving their enormous tent. At first the old man had been attracted to her and stroked her thighs with satisfied grunts. She was so negligent of herself and soon so dirty, however, that the old man lost interest.

That first winter, when the frost gave a brittle glint to the stars and the coyotes yowled with the cold, the slave expected to die several times. But how she cherished those nights alone, when she could dream of her chidren and relive her past!

She tried to escape only once. She was so weak and undernourished that finding her merely provided sport for the braves. Then they presented her with the scalp of her nenapem; she gave up all thought of going home.

Her ordeal ended one spring when the Santis went to Minnewakan, the Lake of Mystery, for the Festival of Virgins. There they joined the Yanktons, their cousins of the prairies, and the Oglallas, and even a few Assiniboines who kept moving nervously around the perimeter of the camp.

During the festivities, the young girls were invited to a feast. The men went as observers and were supposed to speak up if they saw a girl come forward whom they knew not to be a virgin. Disgracing a young woman without reason was a serious crime, however, and could be punished by death. No one raised an objection that day, and the girls passed the test triumphantly, cheeks and hair partings reddened with vermillion, braids wrapped in ermine fur and dresses shimmering with beads and coloured porcupine quills.

The whole camp joined in the battle of frills and furbelows. The married women loaded themselves with glass beads, silver medallions and copper rings. The braves attached skunk skins or wolf tails to their heels. The chiefs carried shields and gaily decorated lances.

The rage to decorate everything spread like a prairie fire. When they had bedecked their children, their husbands, their tents, their dogs and their horses, the Santi women looked for another challenge, and discovered Pennisk.

They bathed her in the lake, patiently untangled her hair and did it up with a metal comb bought from traders, and then dressed her up in clothes borrowed here and there. The result was quite picturesque. The Anishnabeg slave had become a multicoloured Sioux. Her masters were surprised to discover a rather attractive young woman with the round face of the peoples of the North, but pretty enough for all that.

Pennisk now began to be included in group tasks. During a berry-picking expedition, she met the two wives of Mato-Noupa, Two Bears, a minor chief of the Oglallas and a distant relative of her master. The young Oglalla women were intrigued by this stranger from a hostile nation. Pennisk responded as best she could with the few Sioux words she knew, and ingratiated herself with the Oglallas. When the festival ended, she set out for the plains with her new friends.

Until then she had known all her enemies by a single name, *Abwoinug*, but now she learned that the Dakotas, or Sioux, comprised several tribes. She had been the prisoner of the Wahpeton Santi, the People-of-the-End, who defended the eastern borders against the Anishnabegs and Whites. Now she was to live with the Oglallas.

At first she thought they led a very hard life. They were constantly on the move, except in winter, roaming a dreary and desolate prairie. While the Anishnabegs went warring once or twice a year, the Oglallas were continually on a war footing. Pennisk lost count of her enemies now: the Crows, Atsinas, Kiowas, Crees, Siksikas, Kahnas, Piegans, the treacherous Assiniboines, and sometimes even the faraway Kootenays. Who in fact did not bear malice toward the Oglallas? The camp slept with one eye open, ready at all times to repulse an attack or melt away into the night. Even the babies learned not to cry, so as not to alert enemy scouts. Warriors were constantly returning from the war path. The women would whoop for joy if they brought back horses, or wail lamentations if fewer returned than had departed.

Nevertheless, Pennisk soon found the heady existence on the prairies to her liking. The open space was exhilarating. Once she had heard the rumble of a stampeding herd of buffalo, she associated it ever after with rolling thunder or the roar of a waterfall. Even the perpetual danger of death raised the excitement of life a notch, and soon she was deeming it essential. Making war and hunting was keeping the people strong. Pennisk worked hard, applied herself to mastering the language, and gave everyone the benefit of her lovable disposition. During the first winter, she became Mato-Noupa's third wife. The first two received her with rejoicing, happy to have such a hardworking and obliging companion. Their husband progressed rapidly in the honours of war and hunting. A chief must distribute gifts and provide food for the weak; there was always work to be done.

The following autumn, Pennisk went outside the camp and, while her husband mounted guard at a distance, gave birth to a son. Barely three years after her capture, she became the mother of a Sioux warrior.

She used only the best bulrush down to diaper him. She decorated his papoose with beaded flowers, to the astonishment of her neighbours, for the only designs Oglalla women knew in this period were geometric.

When the child was old enough to walk, she put around his neck a little beaded bag containing a dried piece of his umbilical cord, for without it, according to old Anishnabeg women, he would spend his whole life searching for something. She traded weasel skins for tobacco, made a little pouch to contain it and hung the pouch on his back so that old folk might help themselves and bless the child. Even as he suckled at her breast, she dreamed that one day her son would conclude a lasting peace with the Anishnabegs.

Twelve years she spent like this. Years of glory for the plains Indians. There was only a handful of Whites in the country, mostly French-Canadian traders, who took Indian wives and did not disturb traditions. Their trade goods were welcomed, particularly tobacco and coffee. There were also the Black Robes. They were more difficult. Had God spoken to the Whites through his son, as they claimed? Why doubt it? But then why would the Black Robes not believe that *Wakan-Tanka* had spoken to the Indians through the mouth of Buffalo Woman, who had given them the sacred pipe? The Sioux had obligingly adopted certain Christian beliefs; they were shocked that the Black Robes did not return the courtesy.

The Whites were of no concern to Pennisk. She was busy with more important things. When her third child was born, her husband gave her permission to make her own teepee. The family had many horses; transporting a second dwelling was not a problem.

Pennisk had spent all her youth in birchbark wigwams. Now, learning from her sisters, she made her first teepee of skins. She chose summer skins because they were lighter, removed the hair with a scraper, soaked them in a gruel of brains and grease, and smoked them long and slowly. She bruised her fingers piercing the needle holes and worked long and diligently decorating the inner wall. She bought teepee poles of red cedar, a light and durable wood. She took endless pains over the backrests. She made them of willow stems, each of which she worked with her teeth to bend to an upright position. Finally she painted them and decorated them with red flannel.

When the day came to raise the teepee, her sisters presented her with cushions of leather and fur that they had made in secret. All was ready. The three main poles were raised, an elder prayed for the blessing of the Great Mystery, and the other poles and the hide covering were put in place.

Pennisk was radiant. The old women came and fingered everything, exclaiming over the fineness of the sewing and the straightness of the poles. The men looked at the creamy brown leather and imagined what mythical designs Mato-Noupa would paint on the teepee, for he was a man of powerful visions.

The first night, Pennisk gave a rich feast so that all the villagers would henceforth have pleasant thoughts when passing her lodge. In the course of the evening, she could not resist running outside several times to admire her teepee. She could hardly believe her eyes. The upper part of the cone glowed a beautiful warm yellow. The lower part, where the inner curtain hung, was in darkness. This curtain did more than facilitate the circulation of air; without it, the forms of guests would be silhouetted on the sides of the teepee, offering easy targets for enemies.

In such moments, with the prairie stretching away blue and grey in the moonlight, with the people gathered together all around her in their glowing teepees, Pennisk was almost happy to have been abducted.

Her Oglalla sisters laughed as they came to fetch her. "Come, you're neglecting your guests. Talk about house-proud!"

When one is happy, growing old is no cause for sorrow. The chronicle of winters unfurled its long spiral. Mato-Noupa became a great chief. Pennisk had children, a lodge painted with sacred symbols, and a herd of horses which she adored. Then came the Winter of Sores.

It was the first day of winter. Snow fell and did not melt.

The band was camped in a river basin west of the Missouri. Pennisk had surrounded her teepee with a windbreak of interwoven branches. A few steps away, she had stored pemmican and wild turnips in a straw-lined cellar. There was plenty of wood. The herds of horses found pasture in the clearings. There were fish in the river. The Oglallas were not fond of fish, but Pennisk relished it. She was preparing to rest from the hard work of summer.

Near the end of the day, some young hunters entered the village yelling at the tops of their lungs. They were brandishing blankets, guns and shields and were mounted on half a dozen stolen horses. They had come upon a family of Assiniboines travelling eastward and had killed them all. They were wildly elated. The Assiniboines had barely lifted a finger to defend themselves, they cried, the mere sight of the Oglallas had so demoralized them.

These words set the older folk to pondering. As treacherous as they were, the Assiniboines were Sioux nonetheless; they were not in the habit of sitting still and letting themselves be annihilated. And why would a family be moving about alone in enemy territory at the beginning of winter?

However, it is always good to have a victory. The drums sounded into the small hours and the people celebrated this easy triumph launching the winter's campaigns.

The fever broke out several days later. The babies died almost at once, their bodies covered with sores and their eyes full of pus. Pennisk lost her lastborn, the only girl she would ever bear. When the symptoms appeared in older children, the camp fell into a panic. Mothers did not sleep. Fathers stopped going out to hunt and hung around the lodges, dazed. Drums pulsed constantly, sagebrush burned in all the teepees, the medicine man was continually in a trance, contending day and night with elusive spirits. The old people died one after the other, sorrowing to leave their loved ones in such dire circumstances.

Then the illness struck the adults. Their bodies burning with fever and the itch, the sick would hurl themselves into the icy waters of the river. Those who emerged died a few hours later; others ventured too far into the water and drowned, not having the strength to return to shore. No one went to their aid. Anyone still healthy shunned the sick. Families avoided one another. Overwhelmed by this hitherto unknown malady, the Oglallas did not know what to do. What could they do to fight it? After a few days, the weeping and burial chanting ceased. Why weep? Why pray? They were all going to die anyway. The entire Oglalla people were walking the Way of Souls. And was this not a good thing when all was said and done? This must surely be a good time to waken from the lamentable dream of life. The earth was going to ruin since the coming of the Whites. Perhaps Wakan-Tanka had decided to regroup all his people in the ancestral lands of the beyond.

Like the others, Pennisk let herself sink into a state of apathy. But when her second son died and all she had left was her first, her favourite, fury seized her. She persuaded her husband to leave. The Assiniboines were fleeing east and therefore this evil was coming from the west, she reasoned. They must cross the Missouri.

It was as if a bubble had broken in the camp. The desire to live flared like a flame that had been smoldering under the sod. The camp broke apart and the families scattered in as many directions, each guided by its own inspiration.

There was no warring that winter. Handfuls of people wandered over the plains, leaving their dead behind like points in a dotted line marking their routes. When two groups sighted each other by chance, they would turn away. The wolves circled hungrily around these little clutches of humanity, but they themselves were sick, poisoned by the infected dead they had fed upon.

Around midwinter, the deaths ceased. The sickness passed. Astonished, the survivors took stock. It was neither the strongest nor the best who had survived. The cruel and capricious selection was the last straw for the Oglallas. If all of them had died, or only the weak or wicked, they would have understood that Wakan-Tanka had a plan. This unfair, purposeless slaughter horrified them. Some began to regard their medicine men with doubt. A few abandoned the religion of their ancestors altogether.

The following spring, the remains of the band arrived in small, ragged groups at the meeting place on the Cheyenne River. With the band reunited, there was not enough food. As long as the families had been roaming singly about the prairie, they had been able to live on hare, marmots and prairie chickens, but small game was not enough for a band of three hundred people.

Mato-Noupa, now first chief, called his Council together. There were too many young faces and the discussions dragged on needlessly. Still, the Council finally agreed to march north-east, which should enable the band to intercept the buffalo herds on their way back from their winter refuge in the wooded hills. When the Oglallas came to the Souris River Valley, the buffalo were waiting.

The succulent meat restored the people's zest for life. For the first time since the scourge, they began to envision rebuilding their society and resuming the life they used to lead. They had a capable chief, horses and arms, food and furs. In proper mourning for their dead, the men cut their hair short and the women let theirs hang loose; all of them coated their faces with white clay.

There were a few marriages and modest feasts. News gleaned over the course of the winter was exchanged. It seemed that the sickness had begun in the east. Assiniboines had brought it back after attacking some Anishnabegs. The Oglallas had contracted it in turn when they attacked the Assiniboines.

Pennisk was shocked to hear that it had come from her people and wondered where the Anishnabegs could have got it. However, she had too much to be thankful for to feel humiliated. Her eldest son had survived. He was thirteen, thought himself handsome, rode a horse majestically and behaved arrogantly toward his mother. In short, he was a consummate braggart. Pennisk took no notice. The living can learn and improve. Only the dead never change.

Some of the young people, their faces and souls scarred by the terrible sickness, were taking a new, more sober view of life. Most, however, were like Pennisk's son. For a whole winter they had expected the smallpox to end their short lives. Now that they had been spared, they swaggered and found fault insufferably; their parents looked on, hearts filled with gratitude.

The first skirmish with the Slotas, the Greasy Ones, occurred after the ice had broken in the spring.

The cart-men were coming farther and farther west on their hunts. They were encroaching on Sioux territory.

At any other time, the Oglallas would have mounted a war party to drive out the intruders. The men and horses were still weak, however, and the women needed skins to repair the tents and clothing. Mato-Noupa suggested that a fight be avoided. It would soon be time to cross back over the Missouri into more familiar territory. There were no Slotas beyond the Missouri.

The Council agreed, although there was heated argument. The young men, now disproportionately numerous in the band, wanted war in order to prove themselves. They had that right; a man who had not scored repeatedly in battle had no right to honours, did not rise in rank and did not interest women.

That night, after endless angry discussion in the Council, three warriors slipped into the ravine beside the camp, past the lookouts, and struck out across the prairie. They went on foot because Mato-Noupa had taken care to have the horses watched, precisely to prevent warring expeditions.

The young warriors returned brandishing scalps, a man's, a woman's and an old man's, the third pure white. It was honourable to kill women and old people because to do so their men had to be caught napping.

The adolescents gave the three warriors a noisy welcome and the women gave victory whoops, half laughingly; it was so long since they had done it. Mato-Noupa said nothing. He was glad to see the impertinent Slotas punished, but feared retaliation.

He proposed that the band immediately resume its march westward; he did not think the Slotas would follow beyond the Missouri. But the Council would not listen to him. Run away from the half-bloods? Since when? The people had been in mourning since autumn. Sorrow gnaws at the soul, undermines the people's strength. This victory must be celebrated so that the Oglallas might feel strong again. Mato-Noupa yielded to the popular will. One way or the other, the people would know their destiny.

Destiny spoke at sunrise, while the Oglallas were resting after the night's dancing. The warning cries of the lookouts were still ringing when the first wave of Métis swept over the camp. The pounding of hoofs and the guns discharging almost in unison threw the camp into chaos. Yet there were not many wounded, for the Métis were firing blindly into the tents.

After their initial confusion, the Oglallas regained the upper hand. They loosed a rain of arrows, while the Métis had to stop and recharge their long muskets. When the Oglallas launched their first counteroffensive, the Métis were already retreating in disarray.

Then the Slotas turned and fled, and a piercing cry rose from the ranks of the Sioux. The insolent Greasy Ones would feel the power of the Oglallas this very day! The Oglallas galloped in pursuit. They crossed one ridge, two ridges, then bore down on a poplar grove where the Slotas had taken refuge. Mato-Noupa saw the ruse but could not recall his men.

A deadly line of fire lit up the underbrush. The first line of Oglallas were flattened like reeds in a hurricane. The bewildered Indians rose from their dead horses and died in their turn. The survivors turned in circles where they were, unable to advance, not wanting to retreat, while the Métis recharged and fired again and again. Caught in the midst of the melee, Mato-Noupa knew he was living his final hours. It did not matter. What was left to love in the world? Nothing was the way it had once been. He saw his son in the battle and thought of sending him back to his mother, but who could say that destiny had not placed him here? As for the chief himself, his soul was already yearning for the Land of Lodges.

The Oglallas kept charging throughout the morning. The Indians would gallop to the edge of the wood and loose a volley of arrows, then charge back up the ridge. The Métis, well dug-in behind their rampart of earth and wood, suffered little from the attacks. The Oglallas, on the other hand, were leaving many men dead on the battleground.

"My friends," cried Mato-Noupa when the sun was already high, "look, we are achieving nothing. We have lost many young men to no purpose. I see my son among the dead. I do not grieve for him, for he died bravely, but I would have wished him to serve his people longer. Break off the attack! Go home! The Slotas are hiding in holes like rabbits and shooting us with guns. You shall have your revenge. One day, you too will have guns. Live, so that these Slotas shall die! As for me, I am weary and have vowed to go to the Land of Lodges this very night. Go home. But first, watch, I shall avenge you!"

And off he galloped toward the poplar grove, uttering a resounding, "Hokahé!"

Fifty muskets were trained on him as he approached. When the Métis realized the Sioux was heading straight for them, there was a moment of indecision in the trenches. One man stood up, uncertain whether to run. When the guns fired, Mato-Noupa's horse had already reached the edge of the wood. The man standing up had his head split by Mato-Noupa's tomahawk. Mato-Noupa gave up his soul in the bottom of a trench.

Just how Pennisk had returned among her own people, Askik never knew. After years of wandering here and there among the Anishnabeg of the South, she formed the conviction that the Horned Serpent, symbolizing medicine, had punished her for ignoring the vision of her adolescence. Some intensely jealous manidos will not tolerate other loves in the lives of their favourites.

Knowing this, how Pennisk came to study the Serpent's medicine was also a mystery. Perhaps she hoped for consolation in the supernatural. Perhaps, through the Midewiwin of the Dead, she only sought to guide the spirits of her children to the Land of Souls. When she involved herself in the occult sciences, however, she suffered the fate of all Midés; although her interventions were the final recourse for the sick and unfortunate, her calling isolated her from the people. The more powerful she became, the more she was feared.

She was already old when she undertook the long journey back to the forests of the North. She learned that her nenapem had not died at the hands of the Santis, as she had been told, but much later in a drunken brawl. The Anishnabegs had changed; murder among them was no longer rare. Devastating epidemics had made them doubt themselves and their traditions. They had begun to drink, and ruined themselves completely in order to buy diluted rum from the white traders. Their children went without food and clothing. Once the traders left their settlements, they would be overwhelmed with remorse and go into the forest in search of the life their ancestors had led. But every spring they would turn up at the trading posts, weary of living alone, hungry for diversion, forgetting the depredations of the year past or swearing not to repeat them. Futile vows.

To this demoralized, declining people, Pennisk brought the Midewiwin, which was still little known in the North. The Midewiwin teaches courage, integrity, and respect for traditions and for oneself.

But Pennisk was a woman. She was not listened to willingly. And the attractions brought by the Whites were irresistible. Hardly anyone dressed in the Indian fashion any more; cotton was more convenient than buckskin because it did not stiffen as it dried. Wool blankets were lighter and just as warm as moose hides. The young no longer knew how to use a bow. With a gun, they did not have to get near a timid moose; they could kill it from a distance, and the shot was not deflected by the slightest twig. When guns malfunctioned, of course, the Indians could not repair them themselves or make new ones, but would have to go back to the Whites, furs in hand. It was the same with all the new products; nothing was easily repaired; everything had to be replaced, and only the Whites could provide the replacements. Dances, feasts and religious ceremonies no longer played much part in the lives of the Anishnabegs, for families spent most of their time gathering furs, trying to reduce their ineradicable debts.

Pennisk's influence did not last long, moreover. The people soon came to fear her powers, exactly as had happened in the villages of the South.

7

Askik went to the door and pulled the entry cover aside. A blinding shaft of light entered the wakinogan, raising a cloud of vapour. All was strangely silent outside; were the villagers still angry over Pennisk's cry of alarm during the night? Did they not realize that she was ill?

176

"*Tché!*" the old woman said. "You still here?"

She pursed her lips bitterly. She was disappointed to be back; she had felt very close to the Way of Souls.

Awkwardly, Askik said nothing. He supposed her bitterness to be directed at him because she had been dreaming of the Métis who had killed her husband and son. For long minutes, both remained silent, she brooding over her disappointment to be alive, he searching for something he might say to excuse his people. Finding nothing, he took his bow and went out.

When he had left the village, he saw a small group of men talking together in the forest. He tried to slip away but they saw him. They were immediately filled with consternation. Some were terror-stricken; others looked at him with faces full of hatred. The group scattered.

Askik sighed. The villagers hated him, and now Pennisk was bearing him a grudge for being a Métis. Life was absurd.

He hunted all day without rest or food, longing to redeem himself. If only he could bring back a bear or caribou, all would be forgiven him.

He found not even the smallest grouse. The way home seemed three times longer than usual. He followed his customary path but took many wrong turns. When there is a moon, the snow lights up the underbrush. That night the sky was clouded and the darkness had a cottony consistency, distorting everything and making the shadows dance before his eyes.

The path became wider; the village was not far now. Suddenly a shot was fired just a few paces away. Askik stood riveted to the ground. The shadow of a man rose from the bushes, gun in hand. The man froze, then fled as fast as his legs would take him. A smell of gunpowder hung in the forest.

Askik raised one hand, then the other, and had to conclude that he had not been hit. Where had the shot gone? With his head blank and his knees shaking, he resumed his walk home.

Pennisk said nothing when he came in, yet she must have heard the gunshot. She served him some fish broth. He drank a few mouthfuls and then went to bed fully clothed, curled into a ball. What had happened that night seemed so outlandish, so improbable, that his primary reflex was to forget about it.

"Askik, get up!" The old woman poked two or three times at the boy's ribs with a stick.

"*Apé!* Sit up I tell you! You have to find them meat. They're crazy with fear. Take this."

She handed him her pipe.

"Smoke and pray."

Askik was not used to tobacco; after the first pipeful his head was spinning. He begged Kitché-Manitou to give him a stag or a moose, so that the villagers could eat and stop shooting at him. He addressed the same prayer to *Misoukoumik-Okmi*, Mother Earth, who never leaves her teepee so that the Indians may always know where to find her, and to *Nanabush*, who taught men to hunt. He presented requests every bit as respectful to the Holy Trinity, the Virgin Mary, and all the saints whose names he could remember. He searched his memory for other intercedents and since he could find no more began again from the beginning.

All this time, Pennisk was chanting, accompanying herself with her rattle. She would break off once in a while to sprinkle the fire with tobacco and rum, then resume her hoarse, breathless incantations. It looked as though she intended to continue all night. Askik, however, soon wearied of his prayers. The tobacco was making him feel sick. Pennisk's mumblings, her jerky movements, her old face screwed up in concentration, all seemed absurd to him. Discouraged, he went to bed and to sleep.

He woke at daybreak, saw that Pennisk was asleep, burrowed down in his now-cold robes and dozed off again. Then he saw a cliff, a rock face rising perpendicular out of the forest. At the foot of the cliff, he saw a small hole in the snow with a wisp of vapour rising from it. He saw — no, he smelled — a bear sleeping in a cavity under the snow. He heard a voice saying, "See, I give you this bear."

Pennisk had Askik describe the cliff and recognized it. She sent him into the forest.

Curiously, although the day was well begun, the village was quiet. There were a few people out and busy around the lodges. They either pretended not to see Askik or went inside. Yet what a lovely surprise he was preparing for them! In a few hours there would be a feast, and everyone, even the man who had shot at him, would be heaping thanks on him. He imagined the failed murderer coming with tears in his eyes to beg his forgiveness, filled with remorse for having allowed his mind to be warped by hunger. Askik, magnanimously, was waving the poor fellow aside and giving meat to his half-starved children, having reserved the choicest morsels especially for them.

Askik was so moved that his eyes blurred with tears. He quickened his step. He must still kill the bear, though in his mind it was already done. The bear had been given to him. All he had to do was go and get it.

The snow was heavy. He was too hot in his wool coat but when he unbuttoned it the cold, damp air made him shiver.

He found the cliff, a great grey sugarloaf rising over the forest. Some ravens with curved beaks were hopping about on the rock ledges, uttering their sinister "graa...graa...!"

Askik picked up a long stick. He would find the bear's air hole, use his stick to make him come out, then put an arrow in him.

He walked along the base of the cliff, watching carefully where he was placing his feet. But he saw no air hole. He retraced his steps, redoubling his attention. Every little depression in the snow attracted a poke with the stick. There was nothing. Perhaps this was the wrong cliff. There were several big rocks in this part of the forest. In fact there were dozens; there was a whole chain of rocky ridges winding through the forest. Seen from a certain angle, each ridge could be called a cliff.

His confidence shaken, Askik went and examined the neighbouring rocks. Then with heavy step he returned and walked one last time around the first rock, prodding at the snow with his stick. Not only were there no air holes, there were not even any cavities under the rock face. And why should there be? After all, he had not seen the bear in his dream, but merely smelled it. Fine dream! The cliff looked uninhabited anyway. The rock had a cleanness that banished all hope of finding a fat, dirty, stinking ball of bear under its flanks.

Askik sat down on a tree trunk, disappointed but bitterly relieved to be freed of this idle fancy. He had a terrible headache; it was past midday and he had had nothing to eat. He observed that the edge of the snow on the rock was moist and glistening. The rude squawks of blue-jays pierced the warm air.

Hmmf! It sounded like someone turning over in his sleep. Askik looked all around him but saw nothing. Oompf! There it was again, louder and more determined this time. A yellow-brown snout broke through the snow crust, then a black head, then a whole bear, emerging from under a big pine tree. Patches of snow and dead leaves clung to its black coat. The animal shook itself, snorting impatiently. Poof! Poof!

Askik remembered Pennisk's recommendations.

Brother, I need you, he thought as he drew the bowstring.

The arrow made the bear start but did not seem to jolt him out of his somnolence. He shuddered, took a step forward, then buried his nose in the snow and lay down again.

Askik approached cautiously. He saw his reflection in the big, half-closed eye. The tongue protruded delicately past the first teeth. The legs were extended to the full, as though the bear had stretched one last time before going to sleep.

"Forgive me, Maskwa!" Askik cried. The murder he had just committed horrified him. "You're so beautiful! You must have been happy to come out. I didn't want to hurt you, but the people of the village are hungry. They tried to kill me. They hate Pennisk. She doesn't like the Métis because they killed her husband and son. Papa left me with Niskigwon but Niskigwon gave me to Pennisk, who is sick."

He opened his whole heart to the dead bear. He told him all the things he had had to hide since coming to the camp: his fear and loneliness, his dashed ambitions. In the end he thought he felt a secret bond of understanding between him and the bear.

"Once more, I'm sorry. But tonight Kitché-Manitou will remake you and put you back on earth. You can make a new start. And if ever I meet you again, do this with your head "(Askik showed him how) "and I won't kill you another time. I promise."

Before leaving, he looked inside his friend's den under the pine tree roots. It was very small. Maskwa must have been cramped. No wonder he died with his legs stretched out.

Elated, Askik ran all the way home, but once among the lodges there was a problem he had not foreseen: who would he announce his news to? He saw a man renewing the branches on the roof of his lodge. When it looked as if Askik was approaching, the man hastily retreated inside. So Askik walked to Niskigwon's, because he knew no one else in the village.

"Niskigwon, are you at home? *Ki-apin na?*"

The lodge remained totally silent. Yet the toboggan and snowshoes were leaning against the outside wall; Niskigwon must be there.

"Listen, *nedji*, I've killed a bear. You can help yourself. The others too. Tell them that Pennisk prayed for them to have food, and that I've killed a bear. Tell them we aren't doing anything bad. There's no point shooting at us. If Pennisk cried out the other night, it's because she's sick. You should all be sorry for her, Niskigwon! She's lost two families. She's alone. She's afraid of the other sorcerers. And it's not my fault the Métis killed her husband and son."

He paused. He expected Niskigwon to come out and call the others to go and cut up the meat. He did not even care about being thanked. All he wanted was for the meat to be brought back before the wolves and wolverines ruined it.

"Come out, Niskigwon, there's no time to waste!"

He heard a woman's whisper inside the lodge, the crackling of a stick in the fire, then nothing.

Offended, he walked away, making the snow squeak to indicate clearly that he was going.

Inside the lodge, Niskigwon lowered the gun barrel, cursing himself for not having fired. But as on the night before, when the shadows had been playing tricks and had split the little Métis' silhouette in two and turned aside the shot, today as well Niskigwon found a good explanation for not having killed the half-blood. When he thought the enemy far away, he slipped out of the lodge and went to report the Métis' words to his uncle, an elder.

No one would believe it at first. A bear? Did she think them as stupid as all that? Respected hunters were returning emptyhanded, and a child kills a bear? And even if it were true, — anything could be done with sorcery, after all — who would want to eat this meat, the gift of a sorceress? All agreed that it was a cruel trap. Yet each was picturing a joint of bear turning above a fire, surrounded by little faces with sparkling eyes. The arguments became less categorical. No one doubted that Pennisk was a viper; that she had disposed of her own children and two husbands was hardly surprising; that she had then seduced a lad of the same race that had killed her family was in keeping with the rest. But why would Maskwa join forces with this demon? The bear is the first ancestor of the Anishnabegs, who call him "the Grandfather of us all." Would Maskwa allow his body to be used to poison his children? Was the old she-pig stronger than Maskwa?

The daylight faded; night came. Askik had hung around among the lodges all afternoon, hoping that his gift would be accepted despite all. Finally he went home in very low spirits, and dreamed of his bear surrounded by wolves and wolverines. In his dream he was crying over having killed the noble Maskwa for nothing.

Early the next morning he went back into the forest, determined to save at least part of the meat. What was his surprise to find a group of men at the foot of the cliff, laughing and arguing. The carcase was already completely cut up. Only the entrails and tongue had been eaten by wolves.

The men fell silent when they saw Askik turn up. After a moment's embarrassment, he stepped forward and picked up a paw that was lying on the snow, then turned and left. When he had gone a little way he heard the voices suddenly begin talking again. Niskigwon's was deep and menacing and brought laughter and cries of approval.

The smell of roast meat spread through the whole village. Laughter and the sounds of voices could be heard again through the walls of the lodges. Everyone was at the feast that Maskwa was giving. The women had been out to meet him with offerings of tobacco and alcohol. They had addressed him as "dear host," and thanked him for giving himself for the children, for the Anishnabegs hold him to be an intelligent man who knows when a hunter is on his trail and can either escape or let himself be taken.

Pennisk did not want to taste the bear's paw. Since joining the Midewiwin, she said, she had had a little bear in her throat who took ill when the flesh of his kind passed through.

She was not sitting by the fire now but was leaning against the south wall of the lodge, where some of the sun's warmth was filtering through. She listened to the festive sounds coming from the other lodges.

"You know, little one, the Anishnabegs used to laugh more. Things were better among us before the Hairy Faces came." She reflected a moment, then added, "Fiddles and cooking pots...that's not enough. Did they bring back Maskwa's head?"

"Yes, Pennisk."

"See that the skull is cleaned well and hung on a tree so the dogs don't desecrate it."

"There aren't any dogs left, Pennisk."

"Never mind," she snapped. "Maskwa has a right to honours!"

Askik looked at the ground. His companion was getting cantankerous. The way his grandfather had before he died. Was she also afraid to die?"

"Today I want to rest," Pennisk said. "They're revelling. Last night I felt their spirits crowding around the wakinogan. I heard the cries of the souls the medicine spider was eating. But they are many; they will be back. They're afraid of me, but they hate me even more. Did they speak to you, little Métis?"

"No, Kokoum."

"They'll leave you alone, though. They thought the meat was poisoned. They'll see that it's good and after that won't know what to think of you. And now that you've eaten, let me sleep a bit."

Encouraged by his recent success, Askik went out hunting again. He was no sooner in the forest than he saw a big hare jumping up and down to get a view of its surroundings. He could not catch it, but went and checked all his traps to be sure all the snares were well set. While walking on the frozen surface of a stream, he surprised a shrew scurrying about on the trickling bank. Laughing, he cornered it against a rock, seized it, and learned that shrews are poisonous. The shrew went his own way and Askik went his with a swollen finger. A flock of waxwings were plundering the powdery blue berries of a juniper.

He returned with hands empty but heart full, convinced that the spring thaw was not far off, that his father would be back soon to fetch him, and that the two of them would return to St. Boniface together.

But what was happening in the camp? The women were running from lodge to lodge with panic-stricken faces. A crowd had formed at the door of a wakinogan in the middle of the village. There were drums beating inside. From the questions being asked by newcomers, Askik gathered that a child was ill and it was feared that the sickness would spread.

He walked quickly past, sensing that he should get well away from the group. But he was seen. A deluge of hatred poured out at him.

"Sorcerer!"

"Poisoner!"

"So the old woman's not enough for you? Pig! You want our daughters!"

"A demon! A demon that goes after children!"

A young man picked up a stick from a pile of wood and flung it at Askik with all his might. The cries of rage redoubled.

Out of pride, Askik was reluctant to give ground. He would have defended himself but astonishment kept his mouth closed. A piece of firewood hit his shoulder. Another bruised him low on the face. He withdrew, eyes bright with indignation, nose bleeding.

The adults now went wild. The women especially screamed with rage and fear, teeth showing white in their scarlet mouths.

The crowd charged; the boy took to his heels under a flurry of sticks. When he had run halfway though the village, the young man who had started it all was the only one still after him. Out of breath, Askik turned around.

"Wait, *nedji!* What have I done?"

But the other rammed his knee into the boy's stomach, then sent him rolling with a solid punch to the side of his head. Winded, his ears ringing, Askik found himself face down in the snow.

The young man was about to attack him again but turned away when he found himself alone.

For a long, long time the air would not enter Askik's lungs. On his hands and knees in the snow, he opened and closed his mouth like a fish out of water. When at last he could breathe, he spent long minutes listening to his breathing and watching the blood dripping from his nose. The tempestuous noise in his head faded gradually. Finally, he pressed a handful of snow to his swollen lips and went home. Perhaps Pennisk could explain.

As he approached the wakinogan, he observed that the door cover was half torn away, that there was no fire inside, and that the old woman was silent. There were footprints in front of the door. Too many.

When he went in, all he could see at first were the embers glowing red in the darkness. Then little by little he made out the old woman's bare, splayed legs, the dress thrust up around her waist by the force of the fall, an arm bent awkwardly under her back, the head twisted to one side, the black streak running from her nose and staining her cheek.

Askik threw some straw on the fire. Then he saw the lump on her skull suppurating blood, the limp flesh of the thighs, the hairless pubes, the sinewy feet in dirty moccasins.

Was this what death was like? What about all those glorious murders in the tales of warriors? Askik had imagined epic struggles, heroic deaths, victims in icy repose. Here there was only squalor, degradation, obscenity.

The twitch of an eyelid. The slightest motion. Askik put his cheek near Pennisk's face and felt a faint breath. He dragged her to her robe, wiped the blood from her face but did not touch the wound. He repaired the door covering, then came and sat by her side.

8

She lived a few days more, suffering frightful pain in her head which, blessedly, left her only semi-conscious. At times when the pain lessened, she became aware of her surroundings and then seemed to take pleasure in talking. She was no longer the old Pennisk. Her deliverance assured, she was waiting patiently to rejoin her children. She liked to imagine a great lodge in the sky, where both her Anishnabeg and Oglalla families would be together. So convinced was she that she was walking toward youth that her gaiety of years past returned. Occasionally she even laughed aloud, remembering comic incidents in her life, or imagining her children's naughtiness in the other world — knowing them, they must have been setting the ancestors on their ears in her absence.

One morning when Askik was getting ready to go hunting, the dying woman called him back.

"Don't go out, *nitotem. Kawina wanawi!*" This was the first time she had called him "friend." Now she was no longer his Kokoum, his teacher, but a companion of like age. "As long as you stay here you'll be safe," she explained. "They won't dare come in. They're more afraid of me dead than alive."

"But I can't stay here for ever!" Askik protested.

"After I've gone, a man will come for you..."

"*Nipapa!*"

"I don't know. But wait for him in the wakinogan. If you go out and the little girl has died, they'll surely kill you."

"What little girl?"

"When you brought back meat the other day, a little girl ate some and fell sick. Maskwa is hard to digest after a long fast. Or perhaps something else made her sick. I don't know. The parents believed I had poisoned the meat and went yelling it all through the village. Imagine the panic. Everybody had been eating; the children had already stuffed their bellies. People went crazy. All those little darlings about to die! The only way to save them was to kill the sorceress."

"I heard them running this way. I was waiting for them. It was the little girl's father who hit me. I remember the club. Feathers, carved wood. Very pretty. My nenapem had one like that."

"Have you dreamed of the man who's going to come for me?"

"Ehé, don't worry."

"And what am I going to do after that?"

"I don't know, little Métis."

"But where's this man going to take me? I won't stay here, will I?"

"What does it matter? It's time you stopped depending on humans. You'll be a man soon. So far you've depended on your mother, or father, or me... From now on it's the spirits that will protect you, not humans. After I'm dead, you'll fast four days, praying all the time to be given a friend. The more you make the manidos sorry for you, the sooner one of them will adopt you. And if fasting the first time doesn't work, start another fast."

Outside, Zigwon was hacking at his enemy's walls, delivering the final blows. Levelling the snowdrifts, making the trees stream with runoff and pulling the buds from their slumber. Day and night the wild geese were passing, making the stars ring with their honking. The smell of grilled fowl hung in the air between the lodges. Askik nibbled at the remains of his bear paw, wondering why he was not hungry.

"Ah, little Métis," Pennisk said, watching him eat, "one day you'll come to my lodge to visit my children and me. And I'll make you a feast like the ones I used to make."

"Will we go to the same sky, Kokoum?"

"I don't know. I've been wondering that for a long time. They say that the entrance to the sky of the Whites is beyond the bitter waters, in England. I've heard say that the gate to the Land of Souls is over Michillimakinak, the First Earth. But where do the Métis go? I don't know. Perhaps they have a sky of their own. It's quite possible. But I wouldn't want to go there. I like your fiddles but not your carts; they make an awful racket. Where do the Métis go? It's an interesting question. Perhaps you can choose between the Indians' sky and the Whites'..."

"Then I'd take the Indians' so I could come and visit you."

"*Hai!*" the old woman chuckled.

"Kokoum..." the boy ventured, seeing her close her eyes.

"What is it?"

"Do you hate the Métis for killing your husband and son?"

"The Dakotas beat me then loved me. The Canadians gave me their sicknesses and their beads. The Slotas killed my son and then gave me another one. I have no preference."

"Do you think I should study the masinahigon and learn how to become a great man? Or should I become a hunter and marry Mona?"

Pennisk laughed heartily, at once ruing the sharp pains it set off in her head. Her wound was going to start bleeding again.

"It doesn't matter, little Métis."

"It matters to me!" Askik said indignantly.

"But it won't for long."

"What's the matter, Kokoum?"

Her face had become very pale. The ashen skin suddenly seemed to go limp and her features sagged.

"I'm tired. Let me sleep. I'll be better tomorrow." An opaque, dense pain had crowded in behind her eyes, smothering the light and draining all at once what was left of her strength.

The blue light of morning that was filtering through the snow-packed spaces in the roof was neither colder nor paler than the dead woman's calm, austere face. Pennisk had imposed herself on death with her eyes closed, her body straight and her arms lying in dignity by her sides. The wound on her head did not bleed.

When the boy woke, he knew at first glance that he was alone. Kneeling in his sleeping robe, he looked at her for long minutes, not knowing what to think. He wanted to pronounce a funeral chant, half sob, half warcry, of the kind the plains Crees would utter, but he did not know such a chant. He wanted to rush outside with his bow and kill Pennisk's enemies, but his hatred faded as quickly as it had come. Looking at the old stained dress, the tattered moccasins, he remembered that Pennisk had been alone and unhappy, and thought he was going to cry. But he was hurting too much.

The day passed. The night passed. Askik did nothing but sit by his old friend. Sit by her and love her. He loved her with all his heart.

He followed her instructions to the letter. On each hollow cheek he painted a brown disk with mushroom powder that she had prepared. He mixed vermillion with a little water and drew two red streaks from her ears to her mouth. He also drew red lines on her moosehide robe. Finally he took from its hook on the wall the medicine bag containing the terrible *wayan*. Through its old seams dropped a tiny white shell, the *midjisse*, which enters an initiate's body and kills it, then delivers it to the life of the Midewiwin. Askik had trouble lifting Pennisk's left arm, but having done so he placed the bag under it, beside her heart, as she had asked him to. Now she was ready for the spirit dance. Near her, the boy placed a bit of smoked fish, a knife and an extra pair of moccasins, as much as she would need on her four-day journey to the Land of Souls. Once there, she would find everything in abundance.

That night, Askik thought about his friend, young once more, walking the Way of the Wolf, the stars beneath her feet. Would she think with a smile of the little Métis who had outfitted her for the journey? Was she already hearing the celestial drums, far above, that call the spirits to the dance each night? What chants, what ceremonial whooping, would be heard in those spheres up there? Would Pennisk's little ones still be children, or men and women waiting to celebrate the arrival of a mother the same age as themselves? Oh, how he hoped that Pennisk was right, that the Métis really could go back and forth between the Paradise of the Whites and the Land of Souls, for he wanted badly to pay a visit to his old friend some day.

Soon he lost all sense of time. When there was no wood left, he covered himself with skins and got along without a fire. When he had eaten what food was left, he did without. He saw the passage of days and nights through the spaces in the roof, but did not count them. He gazed so long at the dead woman's immutable face that he thought time had stopped inside the birchbark lodge. Outside, people could quarrel, run around and grow old; inside, silence, cold and absence of needs were all there would ever be. He passed several eras thus, seeing forests grow, watching the seasonal peregrinations of the buffalo, and observing the multiplication of teepees glowing like lanterns in the sky.

In truth, it was only the fourth day when the lodge door was thrown open, the blanket lifted, and Abbé Charles Teillet put his head inside.

Abbé Teillet was in a hurry. He was anxious to get back to St. Boniface before spring breakup. Once the ice had broken, he would have to wait several weeks for the rivers to become navigable. He was returning from a tour of the North to assess the needs of missionaries among the Cree and Chipeweyans. It was more than high time his report reached Monseigneur's hands, since the usual petitions were due to leave any day now for the seminaries of Quebec and France.

As he entered the Anishnabeg village he was calculating the days it would still take him to reach the colony. No, he did not intend to stay, he told the chief; a priest would be sent to them during the summer when the village was at full strength. The chief did not press for one; priests interfere with commerce, quarrel with the medicine men and divide the people.

During the evening, however, Abbé Teillet sensed a malaise in the chief and elders that went beyond the suspicions born of religion. The villagers seemed anxious, excitable.

Before his departure the following morning, he asked outright if there were not something abnormal going on in the camp. After a moment's hesitation, the elders decided to consult him on a problem that was gnawing at all of them.

Several days earlier, they told him, a sorceress had poisoned a little girl of the village. The father, in a fit of rage, had gone to the dreadful old woman's lodge and beaten her brains out. The evil spell was broken: the little girl lived. Since that time, however, the dead woman's lodge had remained closed. There was no smoke coming from it and her Métis servant was nowhere to be seen. Some said that the half-blood had died of grief (he had been her lover); others said that the Métis was trying to bring her back to life. What did the Black Robe think? Should they burn the wakinogan and the Métis to prevent the sorceress from coming back to life? In that case, might she haunt the village? Or should they abandon this campsite for ever?

Abbé Teillet was not gentle with them. A winter in the bush had done nothing to soften his crusty nature. See where your pagan superstitions have got you! Look what rejecting Christianity brings! Sorceresses and evil spells! Idiocy! Murder and idiocy!

With the confidence of eighteen centuries of Catholicism, he strode off to the wakonigan of the sorceress, pleased with the chance to demonstrate the futility of their fears. But when he put his head through the door he gave such a cry of astonishment that the chief and elders grunted their satisfaction in unison. Will you believe us next time, Black Robe?

The Anishnabegs did not want this corpse in their burial ground. Askik and Abbé Teillet wrapped Pennisk in her moosehide robe and took her away on an old toboggan.

After a day's walk they climbed a rock promontory well back from the river and placed the body on a platform in some jack pines. There was nothing else they could do; the ground was frozen hard. Abbé Teillet said prayers for the repose of the soul of Pennisk, unschooled daughter of the Anishnabegs, who had died without the consolations of religion. When he had finished, Askik tapped him on the arm.

"She taught me a prayer and asked me to say it for her."

"Oh."

"Can I say it?"

"Yes, yes," the priest replied with a touch of irritation. All this was costing time. The longer he took to submit his report, the more Pennisks there would be dying in ignorance.

Askik looked up at his old friend, who was wrapped like a badly tied package in her robes and blankets. The jack pines whispered.

"Your feet are now on the Way of Souls," he recited. "Walk back along the trail. Return to where you came from."

Then he turned to the priest and added, "That's all."

"Come on then, Askik. You and I have a long way to go, too."

9

The Red River was covered in fog and the rising sun had the watery look of a half-cooked egg.

A few feet from the water's edge, a man was trying to sleep under an overturned birchbark canoe. He was restless. At times he would curl up, at others stretch out, kicking at his threadbare blanket. Finally, uttering a particularly loud curse, he rolled out from under the canoe, stood up and tried to shake out the dampness gnawing at his bones by hopping up and down. He hopped, rubbed himself, stamped his feet. Except for the pain that was contorting his face, it could have been funny.

"Christ! Holy Christ!

Lafortune had slept on too many riverbanks ever to warm up thoroughly. A residue of cold would always remain deep down in his body. All he could hope for was a good roaring fire when he got to hell. This is what he liked to say, anyway.

Next he stomped back and forth, slapping at his sides. A passerby might have mistaken him for a great aquatic bird limbering up its wings before take-off, but there were no passersby. The riverbank was deserted. The ferryboat was tied up. At the top of the bank, the colony was asleep, oblivious to Lafortune's woes. Why indeed should anyone care about him?

Why are some people continually dogged by bad luck? Two weeks before, Urbain Lafortune had demolished a wall of his house and brought out a canoe, round and blond and russet, like a loaf of bread fresh out of the oven. The spruce root seams, the pine pitch caulking, the green and yellow design on the prow, everything was painstakingly done, finished with care, perfect. Lafortune was going back to where he was born in a canoe twice as fine as the one that had brought him away forty years ago. Revenge of a sort.

All he needed now was a paddler and, most of all, a cargo to pay for the journey. The canoe route to Canada was no longer profitable, true enough; the American route by cart and railway had replaced it. Still, in normal times there was always a trader or merchant in St. Boniface who had packages to send, was not in a rush to have them reach Montreal and wanted to save a dollar or two.

In normal times, that was, for fate had turned against Lafortune. How? He did not really know. No one knew. All was rumour and speculation. It seemed the Hudson's Bay Company had sold the Red River colony to Canada — without letting the Métis know. Surveyors had arrived to prepare the way for Canadian colonists. They had stretched their chains across pastures and cultivated fields as if these pieces of land belonged to no one. Exasperated, the Métis had driven out the surveyors, driven out the new Canadian governor, driven out the English loyalists who came to restore order.

Such was the situation on this chilly spring morning with Urbain Lafortune pacing up and down in the mud. Behind the chalky walls of

Fort Garry, the Governor of the Hudson's Bay lay ill and confused, wondering whether or not he was still master of this country, while in his office a Métis chief was signing decrees and promulgating laws and not for a minute doubting his right to do it. The colony had closed tight like a trap; nothing and no one left it. The merchants were hiding their goods for fear of having them confiscated. Lafortune could find neither paddler nor cargo. And the season was getting on...

Plumes of smoke were rising in the blue-green sky. The women were getting beakfast under way. Some were coming out for wood and banging doors. A peasant passed on the road with his ox and cart. At every third step he spoke a gentle "Git along..., git along there" to the animal, but his gaze wandered everywhere else.

Lafortune was reminded by a loud rumbling that he had not eaten since noon the day before. Not very hopefully, he pulled up his fishing lines, then threw them back into the water without renewing the bait. He was sick of carp and catfish. Sick of this brown, sluggish river. Sick of his beautiful, useless canoe.

"Hey, Lafortune, you still here?"

McDougall had come out of his packing case hut. The old ferryman stretched carefully as if afraid he might tear his muscles.

"Oooo! Ahhh! Poor ol' bones! It's the fog, son, it's the fog that gets me."

"The fog's in there behind yer eyes, you no-good ol' drunkard."

"Ho, now! He's all on edge this mornin'! An' what've I done to 'im eh? So I drink, so what? I don't deny it. At my age there ain't much else t' make me happy. You'll find out."

"The devil take me if I ever git t' be like you!"

"Excuse me! I'd forgotten His Honour was gonna be livin' in a convent. It's gonna be busy today, Lafortune. If you gimme a hand we'll split the take."

"Busy, why?"

"It's today they're gonna shoot Scott."

"They're gonna shoot 'im?"

"Seems like."

"An' that don't mean nothin' to you?"

"What d'you want it to mean t' me, son?"

"Yer English, aintcha?"

"Scotch. It ain't me they're gonna shoot."

The old Scotchman began to muse out loud, the better to entice Lafortune.

"Today I c'n ask full price for ever'body. No exceptions. When they travel on business I don't mind givin' credit, but when it's to see a show, they gotta pay."

"So yer gonna get rich on the troubles of others. Bloodsucker!"

Which did not stop Lafortune from sitting at the bloodsucker's fire and sharing his coffee and bread. They had no sooner eaten their breakfast than the curious began arriving.

"Will it be today?" they would ask, putting on solemn voices as if to say, I'm not going for the entertainment; shootings don't amuse me any more.

"Dunno. Get in." the ferryman would reply.

Lafortune and McDougall worked all morning ferrying the sightseers, who no longer knew what to do with themselves once on the other side. They massed under the walls of the fort, milled about in front of the gates, called to the guards through the loopholes. The more there were, the more irresistible the crossing looked to those who had not yet crossed.

"*Baptême*, the whole o' St. Boniface is gonna be there!" Lafortune exclaimed as he hauled on the ferry rope.

"Not enough amusement in this town," the ferryman murmured, taking a penny from each passenger.

Some of the spectators were already crossing back again to St. Boniface, convinced that the execution would not in fact take place that day, when a young clerk in shirtsleeves appeared at the landing, looking for Lafortune.

"Urbain Lafortune?"

"That's me, young fella. What can I do fer you?"

"Monsieur Mercredi would like to see you."

"Jérôme!" Lafortune roared with a laugh. "Ah, that devil Jérôme! What a joker, sendin' an office clerk to announce he's back! If Jérôme's back with money in 'is pocket, there's a good time comin' up."

"*Raoul* Mercredi," the clerk corrected.

"Oh." Lafortune's face darkened. This was not so funny.

He followed the well-scrubbed clerk to a yard filled with new sheds. He entered the house, was roundly scolded by the housekeeper for his muddy moccasins and, to make a long story short, appeared barefoot before Raoul Mercredi.

Mercredi's bearing was that of a harried man who has earmarked a few minutes of his day for something he considers inconsequential. Nevertheless, he opened the conversation with some affable chitchat.

"Those imbeciles back from the fort?"

"Yes, they say the execution ain't gonna happen today."

"There ain't gonna be no execution. Take it from me."

With this the niceties ended. Mercredi came to the point.

"You're leavin' for Montreal and you're lookin' for cargo..."

It was not exactly a question, and anyway Lafortune did not feel compelled to answer. Mercredi's attitude galled him. While the Métis remained seated, Lafortune stood on the other side of the desk in his bare feet, not knowing what to do with his arms. He therefore crossed them, tilted a hip insolently and put on a scornful air as if to say, You don't impress me, fella.

"Suits me fine," Mercredi continued. "I got somethin' to send to Montreal."

Lafortune's face lit up. His attitude changed from devil-may-care to respectful.

"At yer service, monsieur. Will it be papers, furs...?"

"My nephew."

"Beg yer pardon?"

"I'm sendin' my nephew to Montreal."

"Not the little fella?"

"Not so little no more. D'you accept or not?"

Lafortune did his figuring. A nephew doesn't weigh much, can get across portages by himself and make loading and unloading easier. A nephew is fragile, on the other hand. Can get lost or broken. Not that easily replaced, either.

"You realize, monsieur, that the journey's gonna be long. An' hard."

"I know."

"There's dangerous stretches. Risks that can't be got round."

"I was a voyageur. I know all that."

"Men drown in the rapids..."

"And others die in their fields. Yes or no?"

"I gotta have the gear, plus fifty dollars."

"Twenty. For the gear and the food, see the clerk. Bon voyage, Lafortune. If you see my good-for-nothin' brother on the way, tell 'im I'm waitin' for his furs."

"But...where'm I s'posed to leave yer nephew?"

"Ask the curés. It's all their idea. 'Bye, Lafortune."

Mercredi was already poring over his papers. He looked up only to bark, "T'other door!"

Left alone, he tried to concentrate on his figures, which ordinarily were so fascinating. His mind was wandering, however. He stood up and went to the window, saw the insurgents' flag over the fort and swore aloud. When he built his house he had arranged for his office to over-look the fort, the cathedral of his new religion; commerce incarnate. At present, this view he had so wanted was giving him nothing but heart-burn. His sheds were filled with ploughs, scythes and forks; all was ready. When the Canadian colonists arrived, everything they needed to begin farming would be available at Raoul Mercredi's.

Then a little handful of fanatics gets it into their heads to put a stop to it, ruin it all in the name of this "New Métis Nation," as they call it. Fine nation! Half *canayenne*, half savage; half lazy, half shiftless. Mercredi snorted his indignation. He depised his race, though he would never have admitted it to an *Anglâ*.

Before sitting down again, he noted with sour satisfaction that the insurgents' flag bore the Union Jack in a corner. Even in rebellion, the Métis were submissive.

"You're gonna lose, you flock o' sheep," he muttered through his teeth. "When you don't know what you want, you lose every time. You hafta know what you want."

"It's a great, noble, fine thing that's happening over there!"

Étienne Prosy's thin, pinched face was flushed with enthusiasm. Only his nose, which was perhaps less political, was still pale. His eyes blinked rapidly behind glasses that begged for a handkerchief.

The teacher Prosy had been dismissed from the school. He was now associated with the local newspaper, which meant he was eating less regularly. When he met Askik on the main road, his trousers were muddied up to the knees in the manner of a man with no time to skirt around puddles.

"The meetings of the Provisional Government are held in the great hall," he told the boy. "Riel sits in the governor's chair. Ah, my dear Askik, you should see those hunters and peasants discussing a con-stitution, a Charter and laws! I haven't yet convinced them to adopt the Civil Code, but I might still succeed. Altogether, I think I've given advice that hasn't gone unnoticed. It's possible — all this is strictly between us, of course — that Louis Riel will call on me to head a min-istry. Education, perhaps. You see, Askik, the present councillors know the ways of this country and they're pretty straightforward in their speech and thinking, but the application of policy, whether it's internal or external, demands subtlety, skill. They can't do whatever comes into their heads. They can't settle all disagreements by wielding an axe. When they're dealing with the envoy of a foreign power — Canada, let's say — they need someone to put a reef in their demands, refine their griefs. Without giving ground on the essentials, of course; I'm adamant on that!"

Prosy bestowed an indulgent if somewhat melancholy smile on his former pupil.

"Ah," he sighed, "we've come a long way since our literary evenings of yesteryear, haven't we, my young friend? But I shall not be the first man of letters to do a spell in public life. Remember Lamartine and Hugo."

Askik remembered vaguely.

"And you!" Prosy exclaimed, about to leave but realizing that Askik had not yet said a word. "What do I hear? You're going to Montreal? At any other time I'd envy you, but at present, here is where things are happening. And the Sulpicians have an old-fashioned mentality that makes my flesh creep. It is the Sulpicians they're sending you to, isn't it? Never mind. You'll stand up to them. I saw unusual aptitudes in you at once and tailored my lessons in accordance. Who exactly is paying for your studies, dear boy?"

"A generous Montreal family," Askik replied; he had heard this and really knew no more.

"Ah, wealthy people. You won't be the first young Métis to have such benefactors. But you may be the last, once Sisters Scientia and Sapientia have arrived in this uncivilized country. And how are you getting to Montreal?"

"By canoe."

"Horrors! Cheaper, no doubt. Your uncle's idea?"

"The priests made him pay for the journey."

Prosy's face darkened once more. He bent toward Askik so that none but he might hear, although no one else was on the road.

"Your uncle is on the wrong side," he said. "It's known. It's been observed. Not by me," he added, straightening abruptly, "but by others who are quicker to judge, less lenient, shall we say. The axe-wielders, in a manner of speaking." He chuckled; he had discovered considerable wit since becoming involved in politics. "Goodbye, Askik. If I don't come to see you off, you'll know it's because I'm occupied with the affairs of the Nation." And as if to excuse the long strides that were already carrying him away toward the fort, he called back over his shoulder, "I'm going this instant to a meeting of the Council." Under his arm he had a sketch of the uniform that he hoped to see on the backs of the future Métis army. For there would surely be an army, he thought. It would be good to be Minister of Education; even better, Minister of the Army.

"Ain't never seen it! Never!"

It was the morning of the departure. Lafortune was loading the canoe and fuming. Not that the equipment provided by Mercredi was poor; it was excellent. Not that the weather was bad; there was not ripple on the water. No, the source of Lafortune's irritation was sitting peacefully by the fire smoking coarse tobacco mixed with kinnikinnik.

When Lafortune had informed Raoul Mercredi that he could not find a second paddler and the merchant had replied — through a clerk — that he would undertake to find one, Lafortune had expected a Métis or Canadian. Mercredi had sent him a Cree instead, a Muskego just newly arrived in the colony.

He had turned up one fine day, looking and asking for nothing, which in itself was suspect in Lafortune's eyes. He had walked around with his pipe in his mouth looking at the buildings and studying the chimneys, the clothes of passersby, the children's games and the way the women walked. He ambled through every open door, watched the blacksmithing under way in the forge, scrutinized what people were buying in the store, peered over the clerks' shoulders in offices, prodded the horses in the stables. He did it all with such artless curiosity that no one dreamed of driving him away. A clerk who was more alert than the rest asked him if he might like to see other, even more interesting towns; the Indian said yes. He was hired as Lafortune's second paddler.

"Never seen a savage got itchy feet. Never!" For Lafortune, it was clear. Indians, like deer, travel only by necessity. An Indian who travels for pleasure is an Indian with something up his sleeve. Perhaps the Muskego was going to take off and leave them somewhere on the way, once he got where he wanted to go. Perhaps he had a more sinister plan. Lafortune's hand moved instinctively to his belt, where he kept his dollars. The Muskego's eyes followed the movement.

There were voices at the top of the bank.

"High time," muttered Lafortune. His cargo was arriving.

Askik bounded down in a series of long jumps. Behind him, more sedate in his cassock, came Abbé Teillet.

"Numeo!" Askik cried in astonishment.

The Cree hunter almost dropped the pipe out of his mouth.

"*Nisim!*"

"What are you doing here, Numeo?"

"I'm going to see some country."

"What about your family?"

A look a resignation crossed the Indian's face.

"Gone, *nisim*, all gone. When I got home there were was no one in the village. I found our people in the bush. My children were all dead already. My wife wanted me to stay with her, but I hurt too much. She went back to her parents. And I'm going to see some country."

"Enough yakkin'," Lafortune barked. He was already in the bow of the canoe. "Get in!"

"Wait, Askik." Abbé Teillet put a medal on a leather thong around his neck. "It's Saint Anne," he explained, "the patron saint of the Métis and French Canadians. She'll watch over you."

The boy looked up at him, his eyes dancing with excitement and joy. It brought a twinge to the priest's heart.

"You're very young to travel so far, Askik..." He wanted to add, Aren't you sad to be leaving your father and mother?, but he held his tongue. After all, Askik was being sent to Montreal to remove him from the influence of his parents.

"Monsieur le curé!" Lafortune protested. "If we don't leave soon you can lend us yer snowshoes!"

The canoe was already pushing off. Lafortune was giving a final shove to the bank with his paddle — pushing off to Lower Canada, warm beds and soft women — when a figure appeared on shore, leaping like a hare and shouting at the top of its lungs:

"Wait! In the name of the Republic, stop!"

"*Cré maudit de baptême!*" Lafortune exploded. "We won't never get away!" Then his voice rose an octave in stupefaction. "Who in hell's that big beanpole?"

Prosy swooped clumsily down the bank and landed at the river's edge like an old, wind-battered raven.

"Askik!" he gasped, holding a package out across the water. "For the love of Heaven and the Nation! This is a collection of my articles on the present situation. Get them to the Montreal newspaper *Le Pays*. I tried to send them by the American route but no one would take them."

Askik took the package.

"We're off!" yelled Lafortune. He flailed at the water, swearing lustily.

"*Le Pays!*" Prosy shouted. "Somebody has to explain to the Canadians that the Métis are not rebelling; they're loyal subjects of Her Majesty. The Red River accepts marriage with Canada, but wants to discuss the terms of..."

Lafortune and Numeo were doing their job well. Askik could barely hear his former teacher. He twisted about in the canoe, trying to appear as if he were listening, but the position was uncomfortable. He gave up and turned forward again, shrugging his shoulders helplessly as though he could no longer hear.

At this precise moment, Lafortune gave a "Hey!" of disbelief. "Ah, no! Ah, *torrieu d'hostie!*"

He slammed his paddle flat on the water, choking with rage and humiliation. He wanted to throw himself overboard, weep, kill, yell, vomit. Never before had he suffered such shame. He, an old voyageur, had set off in the wrong direction!

"It's that goddam big *agrâ*, that beanpole got me all mixed up! Jiss hope nobody seen us! Ah, *Vierge Marie*, hope nobody seen us!"

The canoe turned about and shot off again like an arrow. When they passed their point of departure, Prosy began again to shout, fearing for his writings.

"Askik, Askik, what's happening?"

"Shaddap, ya goddam meddler!" Lafortune yelled.

There was laughter from both banks. A Métis guard sitting astride a wall of the fort called, "Wait, Lafortune, I gotta explain. There's two ways on a river: you can go up, or you can go down!"

Tears came to Lafortune's eyes. How embarrassing! What a way to end a career! But then, what did it matter, the old voyageur told himself. He was leaving for good and would never, never set foot in this godforsaken country again.

"Laugh, laugh all you like! I'm goin, you're stayin!"

Jérôme Mercredi arrived back in St. Boniface a few days later. He handed over a meagre package of furs to his brother — he had even oiled them to make them weigh more. He collected his pay and hurried away to retrieve his son from the priests. He expected to be castigated again by the brother bursar and was most surprised to be very politely invited in. He soon realized why.

"What d'you mean, to Montreal?"

They emphasized that Askik had talent, that he was learning nothing while running about the prairie and the bush, that a rich family in Canada had agreed to pay for his education, that such generosity could not be refused. Stunned, defeated by the arguments, Jérôme allowed himself to be shown to the door.

Once on the steps of the bishopric, he recovered his wits. He ran to the fort, bought a horse and galloped away from the colony at break-neck speed, heading for Turtle Mountain. He must find his other son before he too was snatched away. He would take his family far, far away from the arrogant Hairy Faces.

10

They camped that first night overlooking great Lake Winnipeg, the hub that led to the hamlets of the St. Lawrence in one direction and the frozen seas of the North in the other. To the west, lightning was illuminating banks of clouds. To the east, a veiled half moon hovered over the dark forest. In between, there were clusters of clouds and stars.

When thunder growled, the first thunder of the year, Numeo sprinkled tobacco on the fire. *Peaso* the Thunderbird had returned from the South, he explained.

"Where is he, Numeo?" Askik wanted to know.

"You won't see him. Peaso's hardly ever seen. He wraps himself in clouds. He makes his nest of stone on high mountains that are always in fog. *Nahtotao*, listen! That one had a deep voice; he's an old bird. In summer when the young are born, their cry is sharp and frightening. Sometimes the young birds hurt the Indians because they do not know their strength. But Peaso is the people's friend. Without him, the earth would be overrun with snakes."

Urbain Lafortune did not hear the thunderbird's cry and cared little what the Indian might be saying. He warmed his aching body by the fire and kneaded his limbs with tender care. The day had been hard; he was no longer used to paddling. His right arm throbbed with pain from his wrist all the way to his shoulder. His back was protesting the long hours kneeling in the canoe with no backrest. His legs, too long doubled beneath him, would not limber up.

"Time I put the paddle away, friends," the old voyageur murmured. "Time I retired."

Was he addressing his inflamed muscles or his two companions? Askik and Numeo thought he was talking to them and stopped talking themselves. Lafortune had nothing to add so there was silence. Each listened to the crackling of the fire, the rising wind and the distant roll of thunder.

Then Lafortune began to hum tunes from years gone by. Paddling songs. He reviewed them all and sang them softly, sadly because they were never heard any more. Who might he teach them to? This kid with a little girl's voice? This Native whose entire French vocabulary consisted of an energetic *Boujou*?

Ah, the days were long gone when the forests used to ring with those manly voyageur songs. When you were hauling canoes through fetid swamps, knee-deep in stinking muck and head wreathed in a swarm of flies, it all went better if you sang about limpid fountains and friends called Pierrot. And what Indian hamlet had not heard Canadian voyageurs returning from La Jolie Rochelle long before seeing them? From Montreal to the Ribaska, twelve thousand miles, twelve thousand songs. A guide who knew his business would willingly give up a strong paddler for a good singer; the right song struck up at the right moment could lift spirits and make paddles fly.

"They was men, they was!" Lafortune proclaimed for Askik's benefit. "Y'know what they used to say 'bout the voyageurs in them days, boy? Live rough, sleep rough and eat dogs! Ha!"

He threw his head back and pursed his lips. Askik expected him to howl like a coyote, but he merely uttered a heartfelt "Youppe!" in memory of comrades long gone.

"To tell the truth, boy, I ain't never ate much dog. From Montreal to Grand Portage we ate pork 'n' beans. From Grand Portage to the Red River it was Injun corn. From the Red River to the Ribaska it was pemmican. Them that went t'other side o' the Rockies ate salmon. I don't like fish none so I ain't never gone there. Weren't much variety but nobody died of it. Things was better in them days, boy. A helluva lot better!"

Lafortune was setting out to retrace in reverse order the route that had brought him to perdition forty years earlier. Each point, peak and waterfall reminded him of events that he had experienced himself or were graven in voyageur legend. He saw and smelled with the acuity of a man who will never be back, who is leaving the scenes of his youth forever.

He scanned the riverbanks anxiously, searching everywhere for traces of his old companions, afraid that none would be left. Each time he found the overgrown remains of a tracking trail, a rotting wood handrail, or (miracle!) a broken cooking pot, he would dance for joy. But like the Indians, the voyageurs had left few marks on the landscape. The forest had covered their tracks and there was practically nothing still visible. Occasionally, rarely, a spruce with three-quarters of its branches pruned would mark the beginning of a portage.

As for Numeo, he was seeing everything with similar satisfaction. He was familiar with parts of the country they were crossing through, at the beginning at least. He noted the growth of the trees, the collapse of certain stretches of riverbank, observed that there were more or less beaver lodges, exercising the prodigious visual memory of those who do not read the masinahigon.

Askik, on the other hand, saw nothing, or very nearly. Montreal monopolized his thoughts. What would the city, its schools and its churches be like? How would the city people dress? He had asked the priests the name of his benefactors. "The fathers at the college will know," Abbé Teillet had replied.

Askik was bringing no gift for his new family. Nothing. He had thought of begging a small bundle of furs from his uncle and had forgotten. His remorse over this was cruel and he even considered feigning illness so that Lafortune would be obliged to go back to St. Boniface. Forests and rock masses kept passing, however, and St. Boniface kept sinking further into the past.

Even Askik had to open his eyes to the succession of rapids and waterfalls, like the steps of a staircase along the turbulent Winnipeg River. Les Eaux-qui-remuent, la Rivière blanche, la Grande-Rapide, la Barrière; each had its share of memories and drownings. At Portage de l'Isle, crude wooden crosses marked where a freight canoe had overturned; not many of the voyageurs could swim. Askik discovered the crosses when he wandered away from the trail. They were grey and fissured and covered with vines and burr-cucumber. Names now illegible had been scratched into the wood.

Numeo and Lafortune had to paddle hard to make way against the current on the river swollen by the spring thaw. At each cataract the travellers were obliged to land and take the portage trail around the falls. Sometimes they had to search long and hard, for at the water's edge the portage entrances were blocked with reeds. Once in the trees, however, the trail would cut clearly through the brake. In some places the passage of thousands of feet had worn the forest carpet down to bedrock.

Lafortune never allowed the fragile canoe to scrape the river bottom; the pine-pitch caulking was too easily damaged. Its passengers stepped out into the water several feet from shore. They loaded and unloaded carefully; a package dropped or overturned could puncture the birchbark hull. Poles laid in the bottom of the canoe spread the weight of the load.

Besides food, blankets and clothing, Lafortune was carrying a package of contraband furs which, he thought, would help him buy room in a convent. This bundle of furs cost him endless anxiety. At each portage, he would get out first with his precious package, taking great pains not to get it wet. He would carry it himself on his back with the help of a tumpline across his forehead. Askik would follow with the paddles, rolls of birchbark for repairing the canoe, and Master Prosy's writings. Behind him would come Numeo with a load of food, breathing only slightly harder than usual. When they arrived at the other end of the portage, the men would go back for the canoe. Askik would stay to guard the furs. Each time, Lafortune would entrust them to him with entreaties.

"If you see an Injun, boy, even a long way off, give a yell," he would implore. "Them savages'd love to git their hands on my skins."

Askik would promise to be vigilant and he kept his word. He would faithfully scan the woods and even keep an eye on the vultures that circled over the treetops, perhaps watching for a single moment of inattention to swoop down and fly off with ninety pounds of furs.

Lafortune was not entirely wrong to worry over his skins. The boreal forest is immense, but its human inhabitants all travel the same water routes.

When evening came and a fire was lit for supper, Lafortune would become increasingly nervous. He would imagine the smoke wafting through the woods, attracting silent, invisible prowlers from miles around. In spite of marauding flies, he would put out the fire very early. By the time he finally fell asleep, he would be imagining a mute, malevolent horde surrounding them with eyes trained only on his furs.

For sleeping, he and his companions would overturn the canoe and throw a big tarpaulin over it, making a kind of tent without sides which allowed the flies in and only partly kept out the rain. They slept with their heads under the canoe. The bundle of furs would not fit under the tarpaulin. Lafortune tied some string around the bundle and attached the other end to his wrist.

The mosquitoes were too hungry to allow them much sleep. A hundred times a night, Askik would bury himself in his blanket, intending to stay there, then would begin to suffocate and come up for air. The mosquitoes went for the tender portions: ankles, neck, wrists. Sometimes one would get lost inside an ear and Askik would resort to desperate manoeuvres to extract it. Lafortune would lose his temper and cry, "Will ya keep still and lemme get some sleep, ya goddam brat!" Yet he himself could not keep still.

In the middle of the night the mosquitoes would disappear as if by magic, each insect searching out the underside of a leaf on which to pass the cold hours. By then it took the exasperated travellers still more time to get to sleep. Soon the stars faded, the mosquitoes limbered up their wings again, and it was time to get up.

Lafortune would open an eye, rest it on his bundle and shout, "*Lève!* Time to be up, men!"

Of the three, he was the most tired, yet the dawn of day, the sight of his furs and the prospect of soon being in Lower Canada gave him maniacal strength.

The first hours were the best. The canoe glided over the black waters; ducks flew by with flapping wings and bodies stretched out straight like arrows. Cranes rose nonchalantly at turns in the river. The serenity, the cold, the neutral light of dawn made the travellers feel fresh and strong.

These moments of grace did not last. Their bodies were imperfectly rested and soon rediscovered the aches and pains of the day before. The growing heat and monotony of movement destroyed their pleasure in the landscape. Paddling was boring and so everything else was boring.

Askik would feel lightheaded. The effect of the sun in the brown water made him drowsy. His eyelids drooping, he would be half asleep as he paddled.

At first he had wanted to change sides often to relieve his arms, but Lafortune barked, "Always the same side! That's the way you'll git used t'it." And in fact, after several hours of excruciating pain, the fire in his shoulder, arm and wrist went out completely. He felt his body move forward for the dip, felt the resistance of the water, felt the paddle lift out, but no longer had to pay attention to the operation. He was like a carter who lets his head droop and leaves his ox to get on with the job.

Every two hours Lafortune would shout, "Light up!" as if he were heading a brigade of twenty canoes. They would all ship their paddles. Numeo and Lafortune would light their pipes and Askik would trail his fingers in the water to see how fast they were moving. The canoe would glide a while with its headway, then be caught by the current and begin to slip back with it. All around they could hear the spring runoff trickling into the river.

The Winnipeg widened, became broad and calm, then opened onto Lake of the Woods. At Rat Portage, Lafortune flew into a rage with a clutch of Anishnabeg children who milled around the travellers, casting eyes on the bundle of furs. "*Awasse! Awasté!*" he yelled at them as they scattered and regrouped like a swarm of gnats. Older Indians were squatting against a hut of greyed wood that served as the trading post. The trading must have been done several days earlier; the effects of the alcohol were still visible. Most of the Indians were men; they were dirty, haggard, wrapped in dark blankets that had once been scarlet. Askik looked at his own shirt of flowered flannel and sturdy cloth pants and was profoundly happy to be a Métis and a Mercredi. He was young and educated and a friend of the priests. These Indians were old and dirty and were not going to Montreal. He had a future and they did not. They would never be great men. He was swept by a feeling of relief to have escaped a terrible stroke of fate. Yet at once a voice whispered to him that luck had nothing to do with it: his destiny was to go to Montreal; theirs was to squat beside this fort.

Lafortune insisted on getting as far away from the trading post as possible for fear of being followed. They paddled until late and stopped well after dark on one of the many islands on Lake of the Woods. It was a single huge rock with a few spruce trees growing on it. This was the first time they could sleep without fear of losing their food supplies to a bear; Maskwa does not always find enough in the woods to fill his belly in early summer.

Lafortune was melting some spruce gum for repairing the canoe. Numeo had replaced a broken seat with a piece of split wood and now was sitting by himself, listening to the lake.

"I know this place," he said tranquilly when Askik came to join him. "My eldest son was born near here. We had come for the fishing. There were many fish."

The wind rippled the moon's reflection on the water. On other islands in the distance, they could see the grey, toothy outline of tall spruces. These woods, these channels had rung with the cries of a woman in labour, the laughter of men at their nets, the chatter of children. The woman had gone, the children were dead, and the forest did not care.

There were few flies on the island; the cold mists over the lake kept them away. Askik went to sleep on a flat rock that was still giving off the heat of the day. He slept without a break all night and woke the next morning in the same position he had gone to sleep in. Lafortune himself slept so soundly that he did not see the sunrise. It was already light when he shouted his ritual *"Lève! Lève!"* They pushed off without breakfast in order to make up for the lost time.

The still-pale sky was clear. A layer of mist covered the water. Askik stretched his neck and looked about for the *memegwesiwok* that lived in this lake. Pennisk had seen them. The Water Spirits had canoes of stone, she said, which sank in an instant when the paddlers reached their underwater dwellings. Numeo scattered a little tobacco on the water, asking for help from the memegwesiwok.

It took them two weeks more to reach the Great Savanne Portage, where the waters flowing to Hudson Bay and to the Great Lakes divide. Summer was reaching its height. All along the dismal Rainy River the travellers saw not a single beaver, not the smallest gopher. The only life in evidence was the birds singing in the steaming woods; the white-throated sparrow's wistful five notes were so omnipresent they became obsessive. Bald eagles patrolled the riverbanks after fish, and kingfishers chattered in the tops of trees long dead and riddled with holes.

During the thirteen or fourteen hours of paddling each day, Askik had nothing to look at but the forest and Lafortune's back, which kept swaying back and forth, back and forth, as untiring as a steam pump. The voyageur had disproportionately broad shoulders and arms, a vestige of his youth when he could stroke sixty times a minute. Sometimes, without turning around, he would emit brief commentaries: "Worst time o' the year for travellin'. Like autumn better. River's dull. Ain't nothin' to see." During their smoking stops, he would allow himself to ruminate at more length. He still talked without turning around, so that the other two wondered whether he was talking to them or not. The closer he came to Canada, the farther back his memories took him.

"Believe it or not, I even prayed t' be a voyageur. My father was an *habitant* at Sorel. Lovely farm, good buildings. I was the youngest. I coulda had my inheritance, married, had children. But I seen the voyageurs swaggerin' round and goin' off t' th' Injun country. It turned my head. I wasn't ten and I was doin' novenas so I wouldn't grow no more. Big men don't work so good in canoes. I prayed to the Virgin, sayin', 'Let me stop growin'; let me leave an' go t' th' upcountry.' That's the only time I got my prayers answered.

"I was sixteen when I went. I left the village with a bunch o' bully-boys, all dressed up with feathers in our hats and proud to be voyageurs. We was playin' at bein' men. Thought we looked pretty good. The girls was all runnin' after us an' we was runnin' to where there weren't gonna be no girls. The guys that was stayin' looked pretty seedy that day; hicks, I thought, in their muddy clogs. I went an' they stayed. They got the farms, the old people, the women, the children."

He heaved a long sigh.

"My pa weren't pleased one bit to see me go. No sir! And my ma..."

He pulled a face.

"I hadn't been gone four days afore I knowed I'd been wrong. Us voyageurs wasn't such big shots on the job. The Scotch was the bosses, we was the paddlers. Fifteen hours a day. When we stopped at night, there was gentlemen we had to look after first. In daytime, the gentlemen sat in the middle o' the canoes and read books. When they got bored, they asked us to sing.

"When I done my first tour I come back to my village, to stay, I thought. But once I was home it was Ho, voyageur! Sing, voyageur! I had money in my pocket and nobody else in the village did. People kept askin' me fer stories o' the Pays d'en Haut. I told 'em pretty good an' in the end I believed my own lies. After that, I couldn't do nothin' but take off again. I even made myself think I liked it. I signed on for the Ribaska, 'cause the girls liked that. Ain't never seen Canada since."

Turning around at last, he glared at Askik.

"Yer lucky to be gettin' out o' here, boy," he snapped for the twentieth time. "See you get yerself in good where yer goin'! If I could start over, I'd never leave my father 'n' mother next time."

The first mishap occurred at Dead Men's Portage. The canoe was soaked with water now and was twice its normal weight. The men had to hoist it up and carry it right side up on rounded backs, one at each end. This time, Lafortune had trouble getting his end in place; the wet, slippery bark kept escaping his grip. After much grunting and cursing he set off, bent under his end of the load. The portage was two thousand feet long. At the far end, Lafortune waded into the water to his waist but could not muster the strength to lift the canoe off his shoulders. He bent his knees and sank in up to his neck, letting the canoe slip into the water. He emerged exhausted and trembling.

"We must rest now," said Numeo.

Anger flared in Lafortune's grey face.

"Rest? Yeah, you like yer rest, you Natives. You're pretty good at restin'. You're asleep at yer paddle, you let me do two thirds o' the work and then you wanna lay down and sleep at every portage. Great voyageurs you'da made! Work a bit instead o' loafin' round like a savage!"

He had intended to shout these imprecations but instead barely whispered them. He picked up the bundle of furs in his arms and tottered with it to the canoe, slipped on a stone, knocked the canoe away slightly and dropped the bundle into the water.

They now had to break the package open and dry the skins in the sun to prevent them from rotting. Without a fur press, it was impossible to bundle them all back into the same wrappings. Lafortune requisitioned the tarred canvas that had served as their tent, cut it up and made four packages. Repairing the damage done cost them two days, during which Lafortune kept a sharp and constant eye on his companions. Their conversations in Cree made him suspicious, and since there were now four bundles to protect, his distrust knew no bounds.

They came to a chain of small lakes surrounded by pine woods. By Lafortune's figuring, they should have reached the Height of Land, the divide. Yet the current kept running against them. They entered a bigger lake.

"This is it! I know where we are," Lafortune exclaimed. "It's Lac Brûlé, ain't no doubt about it!"

He was not really so sure, however. When an Anishnabeg canoe with elegantly curled ends approached, he called to Askik:

"Milieu, ask 'em where we are!"

The Anishnabegs politely received the pinch of tea that Lafortune offered them. The lake, they told him, was called Windigo. Lowering their voices, they explained that many years before, some starving Anishnabegs had eaten each other while wintering on this lake. Evil spirits still lived here, they said.

Lafortune was too old a voyageur to sneer at Indian beliefs, but this was not the answer he had wanted. Lifting his hand impatiently, he ordered the other two to get paddling. That night when they camped by the lake they found the charred remains of giant pines hidden in the underbrush.

"I told you so!" Lafortune cried jubilantly. "It's Lac Brûlé! The Height o' Land ain't far now! After that, the current'll be with us."

They made camp on a little beach of grey pebbles between the water and the forest. Lafortune was cheerful at supper. The next day they might reach Savanne Portage, where the voyageurs had built a log road across the swamp.

"A job and a half, that was, boy! I worked on it myself. Wait'll you see it!"

The colour faded from the sky. The lake turned grey, glassy. Newly wakened bats skimmed the surface of the water, drinking in mid-flight, then rose after insects. Arcturus was reflected in the water.

"What is it, Numeo?" Askik asked. The Indian had not said a word all evening. He seemed gloomy, although in truth this was not much of a change, since his expression was habitually solemn.

"This is not a good place," the Cree replied.

"Because of the wetiko?"

"There has been much trouble here."

"Pennisk wasn't afraid of the wetiko."

"There were Indians here who were hungry, *nisim*. The wetiko captured their souls. They became mad with hunger and killed each other. Perhaps they're still here, listening to us. Their spirits are not their own any more."

"They can't do us any harm," Askik protested. "We have plenty to eat."

"But these people suffered. This lake and the forest remember that there has been much trouble here. Look how they sulk."

A duck rose over the trees and flew away in the gathering darkness, quacking faintly. If I were a duck, Askik thought, I would not live here.

Since Lafortune had cut up their tarpaulin, they slept in the open. Askik tossed and turned for half an hour, dislodging inconvenient stones with his hip, a task which by hand would have taken five minutes. In the forest, two whip-poor-wills were trying to coordinate their syncopated songs. Nothing is more soothing than the whip-poor-will's call. Askik fell asleep long before the concert ended.

The next morning while they were crossing Lac des Mille Lacs, Lafortune almost stood up in the canoe and cried in excitement, "Boats! Boats! Look, Milieu, boats!"

Askik looked westward and, seeing the white sails, to please Lafortune cried, "I see them ahead!"

The old voyageur, however, was doubled up with laughter. He leaned over the water, held his sides, laughed till he was gasping.

Looking more closely, Askik saw that the sails were really shining rocks. Quartz.

"Ayeee!" Lafortune sighed as he caught his breath. Forty years he had waited to play this trick on someone else.

East of the Lac des Mille Lacs was the little Savanne River, which blocks up in summer, necessitating a difficult portage through swamp-land. The voyageurs of days gone by had laid a corduroy road of logs across the swampy mire. An exhausting job, but it did not occur to the Canadians, any more than to the Indians, to drain the swamp. What was there was there to stay.

This was what Lafortune had been so anxious to see. He had done maintenance work on it forty years earlier and wanted to find his very own section. There was a deep layer of water-laden moss over a base of soft clay, and everywhere dead birches and tamaracks standing stark and bare or blocking the road with their fallen remains. Young willows forced many detours and obscured the line of sight.

The travellers waded about for a long time before finding the wooden road. It was not much help to have found it. The logs were rot-ted and in places disappeared completely, swallowed up in the shifting ooze beneath. The travellers slithered and stumbled on the slimy, blue-green wood. Each time they lifted a foot out of the ooze, a sickening stench of decay emerged with it. Mosquitoes came out of the forest in clouds.

"We'll never get there at this rate!" Lafortune cried. "Let's get the canoe. We'll move ever'thing on one trip."

They put the furs and tools in the canoe and hoisted it up on their shoulders. The two men were sinking calf-deep and jostling each other as they struggled to free their feet. Lafortune was breathing heavily and painfully. When he tried to relieve an aching bone by shifting the canoe to a different position on his back, his torso was bent so low his long nose nearly skimmed the mud. The mosquitoes made thick, downy grey patches on his shoulders and arms.

With his load of food supported by a tumpline across his forehead, Askik's only defense against the mosquitoes was to blow sideways across his cheeks or shudder violently to dislodge those biting through his shirt. He was cross with the priests for having cut his hair; his neck was all bumpy with bites. Nothing stopped the gnats either, which got into his eyes and nostrils and bit him on the forehead and scalp, or the big grey horseflies which took devilish pleasure in tangling themselves in his hair.

"Ayeee! Stop! I'm stuck!"

Lafortune had a foot wedged between two logs. Numeo did not realize this and kept pushing from behind. Lafortune fell flat and the canoe crashed down on his right shoulder. Askik and Numeo rushed to help him, but the old voyageur was already picking himself up, spitting invective at the canoe, the mosquitoes, and Numeo for not stopping in time.

Rest here was impossible. The heat, the flies and the stench were unbearable.

"Milieu, Milieu!" Lafortune yelled, "c'm 'ere!"

He added a bundle of furs to what Askik was carrying already. The boy staggered under the load and would have put both hands to the tumpline to steady himself but could not because he was carrying Prosy's articles under his arm. He moved to put down the load and slip the papers inside his shirt, but Lafortune snatched them with a snarl.

"Devil take yer goddam papers! Git along, Milieu!"

Then, mustering all his strength, he flung Master Prosy's articles as far as he could. Having vented his spleen, he inspected the hull of the canoe and finding it intact resumed his ordeal with a high-pitched grunt.

Askik cast a guilty eye at the collection of articles. The wrapping was torn at a corner. Master Prosy's fine hand was slowly imbibing brown water. He could still retrieve the package; Lafortune was no longer paying any attention to him. The mosquitoes and the heat, however, had halved his capacity for judgement; the few steps it would have taken looked endless. Like the others, he had only one idea in his head: to get out of here. He fell into step with the two men, hoping never to see Master Prosy again.

Not two hundred paces farther on, Lafortune let out a cry of despair.

"Ahhh, friends, I can't go on!"

The bow of the canoe fell with a great splash into the mud. Lafortune staggered a few steps more. Even without his load, his body was bent and his face was ashen.

"Put down your bundles, *nisim*," Numeo ordered calmly. "Help me find wood."

In spite of the heat, they lit a fire, and when it had taken well Numeo threw on some leafy poplar boughs. A milky white smoke enveloped the travellers, temporarily protecting them from the flies.

"When I was young," Lafortune mumbled, "the Company paid us

extra to come this way. We was afraid of Savanne Portage; usta talk about it long afore we got here. And there was a road in them days, too! Oh, dear God, look at us!"

And indeed they were a sorry-looking bunch, their faces bloody and pouring with sweat, skin puffy with flybites, trousers shiny with grey mud.

"Oh, if only Prairie Portage is dry! Pray the prairie's dry!"

They drank a little warm water from an ox-bladder water bag. As soon as they left their fire the flies fell on them anew, the more ravenous for having waited.

Half an hour later they came to the edge of a small lake choked with bushy growth, crossed it, portaged again and were then on Height of Land Lake, a swamp that spills its water both east and west. This is the divide between two great river systems: to the east the Great Lakes and the St. Lawrence, to the west and north, the rivers leading to Hudson Bay and the Arctic. From this small wetland, half of Canada drains. It was here that the voyageurs of the old days used to "baptize" the "salt-pork-eaters," the canoemen venturing for the first time to the North West.

Luckily, Prairie Portage was relatively dry, the old-time voyageurs' trail negotiable. They climbed a steep slope through woods of white pine and after several hours, with increasingly frequent pauses, came into the open on a rocky height. Two hundred feet below was a lake. A lake like any other lake. Askik was disappointed. He had expected a change of landscape, perhaps even a city, since Lafortune had been so excited on the way up the hill. Instead, the forest stretched away forever, dark and rolling, broken here and there by a grey cliff or a sparkling expanse of water.

Lafortune seemed pleased, however. He leaned against a rock and smoked his pipe, enjoying the cool wind and absence of flies.

Suddenly he remembered Askik and cried, "Yer leavin' yer country, boy! This here's the end of the Terres d'en Haut. It's downhill from here to Montreal."

"Are we far from Montreal?"

"A month, month and a half. Depends on what the weather's like. Depends on La Vieille."

"Are we in Canada yet?"

"We're in Upper Canada."

"But..." Askik looked down at the forest below. "It can't be Upper Canada. It's lower down there!"

"That's 'cause we're still in the North West. Upper Canada's lower 'n the North West but higher 'n Lower Canada," Lafortune explained around the stem of his pipe. "It's only called Upper Canada 'cause it's higher 'n Lower Canada. Ain't got nothin' t' do with the North West."

"What's the matter?" Numeo asked, seeing confusion spread over the boy's face. Askik pretended not to hear.

Whatever Lafortune said, it was not true that the current carried them after they left the height of Land. They had to paddle as hard as before, except in the rapids where, for the first time, the water was flowing in the right direction.

The day after Dog Portage, where the forest dropped away four hundred feet, Lafortune cut out the smoking pauses and forced the pace all day long. Fort William was not far now; his plan was to spend the night there. The fort had been largely abandoned, it was true, but he said it would still be better than sleeping in the bush.

They made a rapid descent of the River Kaministiquia, running the rapids and accepting every kind of risk rather than set foot on dry ground. In the old days the heavy North canoes used to do ten portages and décharges on the Kaministiquia. Lafortune only did three.

"Paddle!" he would yell as the boiling waters approached. The two men and the boy would bend to their paddles and pull with all their might to send the canoe flying like an arrow over the turbulence. Rocks grazed the birchbark hull, the frame creaked, waves washed in, but the canoe conquered the rapids each time. Suddenly the travellers would find themselves in calm water, hearts pumping furiously, stomachs still rocking with the movement of the torrent. The men would laugh, their hair and shirts plastered to their bodies by the flying spray; Askik would bale the canoe with a big sponge, wringing it over the side with an air of triumph.

They did not reach Fort William that night, however; they had to camp on Mountain Portage, two hours from the fort. Numeo and Askik were hard put to persuade Lafortune to stop, despite pitch darkness that made navigation dangerous. They camped beside the portage trail on rough ground with stunted pine trees all around. It was a poor campsite. It was difficult to go ahead, however — the trail plunged into a dark ravine — and Lafortune would not go back even a step. The roar of falls on the river kept them awake half the night. The cataract must have been very close but they did not dare go and take a look at it for fear of going astray in the woods and falling off the cliffs. It had happened before.

The sky clouded over during the night. They were wakened by a fine rain. Sunrise found them sitting around a spitting fire, wrapped in wet blankets. They were soaked to the skin. The bundles of furs, however, were nice and dry under the canoe.

They set out as soon as they could see their feet. The trail dropped dizzyingly to the bottom of a ravine and was covered with brittle, treacherous red shale. Lafortune slipped on it and slid a good way down the slope on the seat of his pants. Surprisingly, he picked himself up laughing. Perhaps he had done the same thing forty years earlier. When they were finally at the bottom of the cliff after several descents to bring down all their gear, it was broad daylight.

"Off t' Fort William, voyageurs!" Lafortune exclaimed. "The worst's over."

They launched their craft with a resounding "Youppe!", crossed the calm surface of a small cove and turned into the current. As they did, the roar of the falls redoubled.

Askik and Numeo nearly dropped their paddles at the awesome sight. Even Lafortune, who had seen the falls before, caught his breath in wonder.

The Kaministiquia plunges a hundred and twenty feet into a cauldron of black rock. At the lip of the falls, the thundering water divides, split in two by a rock jutting over the void. The seething of the water fills the huge basin with spray. A dozen streamlets trickle all the way down the dizzy heights of the walls. The Canadians call this the "Great Falls"; to the Indians, because the rock splits the water, it is *Kakabecka*.

"C'm'on, *mes bourgeois!* Let's go!"

That morning their paddles danced. Lake Superior was very close and Lafortune had promised to take his companions to see the ruins of Fort William; they were beginning a day off.

Two hours later they heard the cries of gulls and felt the water deepening under the canoe.

"We're there, *les gars*," Lafortune shouted exultantly. "One last push!"

Redoubling their fervour, they rounded a final turn and ran plumb into the British Army.

11

The river was crowded with lumbering barges full of little men in scarlet tunics thrashing and splashing about. Oars were clashing, barges were colliding, while purple-faced individuals screamed commands.

"Well, I'm blowed..." Lafortune muttered.

When they perceived the brightly-painted canoe and and the three ragged travellers, the scarlet men thought they were being attacked. A pallid-faced young officer ordered his men to intercept the enemy vessel. Since his crew had to turn their craft around to do so, however, the offensive took time getting under way. Courteously, Lafortune brought his canoe alongside the barge. This took the young officer aback. He was not armed. Seeing that the three natives were not armed either, he seized an oar, held it across his body like a rifle, and pronounced:

"You're Fwench? I'm awwesting you!" And after a moment's doubt about his authority, "In the name of Her Majesty!"

"Milieu!" Lafortune barked. "What's he sayin?"

"I don't know," Askik replied miserably. "I can't understand English."

"Pwisoners, forward!" the youth ordered, pointing to shore. A small fort had been erected there.

"Let's go and take a look at that!"

With three paddle strokes the canoe reached shore. The barge and its crew were supposd to follow but instead wobbled off on an indeterminate course.

There was a constant throughout Garnet Wolseley's military career: his superiors were numskulls. He had entered the British army as a lowly ensign, his mother lacking the means to buy him a higher rank, and ever after was obliged to endure the witlessness of generals born to the calling.

In Burma, in the rebel-infested jungle, he had fought in white gloves and red tunic buttoned to the chin, as if on parade.

At Sebastopol, he had suffered the bitter disappointment of seeing the French better led and fed than the troops of Her Majesty.

At Peking, he had seen discipline fly out the window during the pillage of the Summer Palace, when the officers, clubmen born and bred, filled their pockets with treasures.

All over the Empire, he had seen signs of boundless venality, as if Bonaparte's defeat fifty years before had lulled Britain's rulers into permanent dormancy. The army was scattered among fourteen colonies; transportation was expensive and regiments were rarely up to strength. The men took concubines, raised chickens and never showed up at drill. The Imperial Army was going to the dogs while the seven ministries responsible for it quarrelled or refused to speak to each other.

Into this dangerous mess, Garnet Wolseley had attempted to introduce a glimmer of light. He published a compendium of rules, a handbook for ordinary soldiers, whose purpose was to counteract the ignorance of their officers. The War Office was not amused. Rare, in fact, were those in London who appreciated Wolseley's flair for reform. His enemies multiplied and his career stagnated. For nine years he had been in Canada, a colony where nothing happened. Thank God for the Métis!

The insurrection of the Red River Métis had not amounted to much in the beginning. The half-bloods, fearing loss of their farms and way of life, had been demanding a say in their country's annexation to Canada. Their pleas for consultation had been repeatedly ignored and finally they seized a crumbling fort and sent their new governor packing. Ample reason to send in troops, in Wolseley's mind, but oh, how the preparations had dragged on! The Prime Minister of Canada, Sir John A. Macdonald, had long held the Métis in suspense, and still he stalled. To go in or not to go in? Perhaps he never would have decided if Riel had not taken it into his head to shoot an Englishman. The expeditionary force had been called everything from punitive expedition to errand of peace, on the one hand to appease Ontario, which was demanding vengeance, and on the other Quebec, which was concerned for the French-speaking half-bloods. With great difficulty, seventy-seven French-speaking volunteers had been recruited in Quebec for the force. Seventy-seven out of a thousand was already too many, according to Wolseley, but the politicians had insisted; a question of national unity.

The troops were on the way, in any event. The expeditionary force was now encamped on the brink of the wilds, ready to strike out across five hundred miles of forest, hostile and largely uncharted territory. As soon as he learned of the arrival in camp of three travellers on their way out of the wilds, Colonel Wolseley ordered them brought to him. He instructed his aide-de-camp, a young teacher from Toronto, to put away the maps and have tea made.

The camp was surrounded by trenches and earthworks for fear of the Fenians. The three travellers entered it under armed escort.

Soldiers in suspenders and shirtsleeves were practicing loading six-pounder cannons. They moved one after the other, like dancers obedient to a group choreography. When the fuse touched down the men were standing at attention. Askik expected a detonation each time, but instead the men relaxed and gave one another congratulatory looks as if to say, We would have got 'em!

"Come in, gentlemen, come in!"

The voice came from a wooden hut. It was dark inside. Lafortune shook hands with a man taller than himself. The stranger had fair hair and a pink, balding pate. His moustache was darker than his hair and its ends were meticulously waxed and twisted. The assistant quartermaster general of Canada had a boyish air despite the baldness and the uniform. He was thirty-seven.

"Tea, gentlemen? Ah, our interpreter!"

An ageing soldier entered with heavy step: one of the seventy-seven French-speaking volunteers. The conversation could begin. The aide-de-camp sat at a folding table and prepared to take notes. Colonel Wolseley put his cup in its saucer and began.

"We are going to Fort Garry to ensure the peaceful passage of power from the Hudson's Bay Company to the Dominion of Canada. The United States denies us passage through its territory. We must therefore take the old canoe route. Since that route has not been used for nearly forty years, the information you can give us on water levels and the condition of portages will be invaluable to us."

"Beg pardon, monseigneur," Lafortune interrupted banteringly, "yer goin' all the way t' th' Red River in yer big boats?"

"Just so."

"With them little gentlemen we seen on the way in?"

Lafortune laughed loudly and long. Askik thought it shockingly rude of him. The tall gentleman with the moustache was so nice! The officer did not seem offended, however; in fact, he seemed not to have heard. The only one fuming was the aide-de-camp. The French Canadian interpreter was looking out the window.

"Yer not even gonna get up the Kaministiquia!" Lafortune cried, surprised at the officer's impassive expression.

"We will avoid it. My men are building a road through the forest as far as Lake Shebandowan."

Lafortune was not laughing now. He had gone up the Kaministiquia dozens of times, losing canoes and men. It had never occurred to him that the river might be detoured by a road.

"Okay then, monseigneur, what after that?"

"After that? Lac des Mille Lacs, Rainy Lake, Lake of the Woods, the Winnipeg River..."

Lafortune was flabbergasted. This Englishman was building a stretch of road and then he imagined all the rest was going to be a Sunday walk in the park.

"Some o' them rivers're dangerous! Specially the Winnipeg. Others are nearly dry..."

"That's why your information is going to be invaluable to us. But we'll get back to that. We'll have plenty of time, since you'll be doing us the honour of staying a few days with us. Tell me about the natives."

"You mean the Métis?"

"First the Indians we'll meet on the way."

"All quiet. Ain't nothin' t' tell you."

"Well, well... Lord Granville is mistaken then. We're not going to be massacred."

"Beg pardon?"

"Lord Granville is an eminent figure in London, where they specialize in the production of eminent figures. He opposed our expedition. You see, Mister Lafortune, people are afraid the Indians will exterminate us on the way and the Métis will annihilate us at Fort Garry."

Lafortune laughed again but this time there was a touch of servility in the laugh, a desire to please.

"Don't worry 'bout that. Riel won't fight."

"And why not?"

"He talks good, but he won't do nobody no harm."

"And yet he shot Thomas Scott."

"A varmint."

"An Englishman, sir," the colonel corrected with the same impassive face.

He put his cup down beside *The Meditations* of Marcus Aurelius and the *Imitation of Christ*. Askik admired his pink, clean fingernails. The colonel studied the rough clothes Lafortune and Askik were wearing. He did not seem interested in Numeo. He dismissed his visitors with an amiable wave of his hand.

As they left, Lafortune cheerfully accosted the Canadian interpreter with, "*Salut*, mate! Could you 'n' me be from the same neck o' the woods?" The interpreter was a small, greying man with a pockmarked face. He reddened and hastened away as if he had heard nothing.

"You could say a word t' me at least, ya bad-mannered bastard!" Lafortune yelled loudly after him.

The little man turned and hurried back. "Shut yer yap!" he whispered. "I'm gonna give you a piece of advice, fella: settle yerselves down near the river and don't move, specially at night. The camp's full of Orangemen."

"Orangemen?" Lafortune said, scanning the trees nearby.

"Englishmen, bonehead. They hate Frenchmen. Hate Indians even more. Specially Métis!" the interpreter hissed, glancing at Askik. "They're all in a hurry to kill Métis!"

"Waddya mean?" Lafortune said incredulously. "Yer toff's talkin' about makin' peace, no more'n' that."

"Pouah!" The interpreter spat on the ground with malicious pleasure. "They're gonna hang yer Riel. All 'is gang, too. I'm tellin' you now."

"Well, yer so good at tellin', tell us what business *you* got bein' here!"

The interpreter was already moving away with a shrug of his shoulders.

"Are they really gonna kill Métis?" Askik asked.

"Bah! If they shoot as good as they paddle..."

Lafortune spent the next three mornings in company with the expedition's commanders. He began to draw the route on their maps and became totally confused. He knew the lakes and rivers by sight; trying to follow them on paper got him all muddled. And so, tilting his chair back against the wall, eyes on the ceiling, he retraced his journey in reverse, recalling each portage, each marsh, while the officers wrote the information on their maps. They asked meticulous questions on the strength of the rapids, the steepness of the slopes, the depth of the water. They wanted to know particularly where each Indian band was located; they might as well have asked where the deer were in the forest.

Lafortune left out no detail, out of professional pride and wanting to please. Still, when they pressed him to say exactly how to find the beginning of this or that portage, he had to reply, "You'll find it when y' get there. You gotta look round a bit."

The commanders would frown and Lafortune would reproach himself for not noting those details on the way. Then he would add other details, providing plenteous information on all the real and possible obstacles awaiting the heavy barges. When he had finished, the maps were black with cautionary notes. Lafortune looked at them proudly, the commanders with alarm.

When he entered the colonel's hut on the fourth day, he saw the officers seated in a semi-circle, emptyhanded, with neither pencils nor teacups. This time there was no chair for him; he stood.

"Mister Lafortune," Colonel Wolseley began, "we have considered your comments and warnings. Perhaps we have underestimated the difficulties we will be facing. Perhaps you have exaggerated them. It remains that you are the last man to have travelled that route. You are in a position to save us a great deal of precious time. I must therefore ask you to accompany us to Fort Garry."

Lafortune remained smiling and affable long after the colonel had finished speaking because the interpreter was taking his time; when he came to the last sentence, Lafortune all but fell over backwards.

"Go back! I don't get it! Go back?"

As a plea it was weak, he was well aware, but astonishment tied his tongue. An officer with a very black moustache spoke up. He was a Canadian, not an Englishman, and so fancied he had a way with the people of the country.

"You will receive the same pay a boatman normally receives, and also a bonus — a generous one — for your guiding."

"And the satisfaction," Colonel Wolseley added, "of having served your country. You were born in Lower Canada, I believe."

Their words were no longer reaching Lafortune. He was seeing all his dreams tottering on the brink: the convent, the soft bed, the motherly cook. Gathering all his wits about him, he looked for a way out, and found one.

"Monseigneur, I'd really like t' help y' out, but it ain't possible. I'm travellin' with a Native an' a child. They'll be lost without me. I gave my word I'd get the boy t' Montreal."

"They'll take the steamboat to Toronto and the train to Montreal. I'll see to it."

"But I got business o' my own to settle in Montreal. *Commercial* business," Lafortune stressed, thinking he had touched a very English chord.

"Duty, Mister Lafortune, comes before personal gain."

Lafortune lost his temper.

"I worked like a dog all my life t' get the hell out o' the North West, an' now you wanna take me back there! Jiss like that!"

His anger did not survive the translation. The interpreter made his message unspeakably boring and embellished with polite turns of phrase.

"Come, Mister Lafortune," the colonel admonished. "I'm not asking the supreme sacrifice of you. You'll be back in Montreal before winter, I promise you."

Lafortune looked down at his feet. When he raised his head, his expression had changed.

"All right, monseigneur, I'll guide you, but first I'm gonna talk t' my companions. Hafta give 'em some advice."

"It would be better, I think, for you to wait in the fort. I'll send for the boy."

Askik found Lafortune squatting on the ground in the shade of a hut. There was a soldier on each side of the prisoner. Askik eyed their guns anxiously; he had not forgotten the interpreter's warning.

"Don't worry, Milieu, they're itchin' to go huntin' Métis, but they don't know what one looks like. It's bad, boy. Wolseley's takin' me back with 'im."

He was expecting a word of commiseration and did not get one. Askik was too young to understand other people's misery. Lafortune watched the gulls circling overhead and sighed.

"I ain't got the strength t' do the trip twice. Now I know I'm gonna die upcountry. I come pretty close to gettin' out, though. We done a good piece o' the way together, Askik. Now you two gotta go on without me. The canoe's repaired. Load it tonight and be ready t' push off first thing in the mornin'."

The French-Canadian interpreter was approaching with his insolent swagger. Lafortune talked faster.

"When you get t' Montreal, sell them furs — get the priests t' help — put the money in an account in my name. If I ain't back by the time yer twenty-one, the money's yourn."

He turned to the interpreter. "What you doin' here, snake? You dirtied yer own hole? Lookin' for another one?"

"Watch it, you!" the interpreter retorted, piqued. "A soldier counts for more'n a voyageur."

"Hey, a talkin' snake! Bet you never saw one before, Askik."

"The boy gotta go," the interpreter barked, a harsh edge to his voice. When he was angry his face went sickly pink.

"Okay, Askik, get out o' here. Explain to the Native. He's a good savage. I thought he'd cut out long afore this..."

"That's enough! Out!"

220

"Hey there, snake, what didja do before you got cozy with the English?"

"Yer lip's gonna cost you plenty, *mon maudit*. I can make things tough fer you on the trip!"

"It's gonna be tougher for you than you think, peasant!"

As he crossed the embankment, Askik turned one last time to look at Lafortune. The old voyageur was curled up with his head between his knees and his hands over his ears, refusing to see or hear these French Canadians he had been waiting all his life to be with again.

Walking down to the river, Askik met the soldiers coming back from drill — cheerful, pink-faced, blond or red-headed youths, happy to be soldiers, happy to be doing easy, pleasant, honourable work. They barely saw the Métis child, yet Askik was ill at ease. He sensed confusedly that his kind was not theirs, that he had more in common with the weak, broken Lafortune than with these young warriors. Their fresh colouring, strange language, congenital cleanliness, the ease with which they joked together, all intimidated him. He felt very small, very brown, very shy. He wanted badly to be back with Numeo, to be sitting by the fire in his old blanket that smelled of smoke and leafmold.

The need was humiliating. Numeo too was of the wrong kind. Feeling comfortable with Numeo meant recognizing that he would never, never be the equal of these fair-haired young men. He would never have their carefree superiority, nor the capacity for scornful amusement that creased the corners of their mouths so prettily when they passed the Anishnabeg families camping just outside the fort. Deep down, he acknowledged that they were right. Deep down, he revered them already. He was Métis, therefore he was different; he was less.

He returned to camp dejected. The very fact of returning to camp was a defeat, but what else was there to do? He spent the evening in a sea of doubt about himself and his future.

To cheer him up, Numeo began the unlikely story of *Wapos* the rabbit, but Askik wrapped his head in his blanket and lay down to sleep. The young Englishmen, he thought, would certainly not listen to a story about a rabbit.

It was well on into the night. Something had wakened Askik and he wondered what it was. A shadowy figure was darting from one side of the camp to the other.

"*Lève! Lève!* Move, you two!"

The shadow bumped into some bundles.

"I told you to load the canoe! Have I gotta do ever'thin' myself?"

"Lafortune!"

"Shhh!" A calloused hand clapped over the boy's mouth. "Shaddap, *torrieu*! Didja think ol' Lafortune was gonna let himself be had by a buncha shiny boots? A voyageur's smarter 'n a store clerk, like the pock-faced snake 'd say. Git on now, boy! Move!"

They loaded the canoe in two shakes, their hearts in their mouths. Each lap of water, each step was deafening. How could the guards not hear?

Now Lafortune and Askik were in the canoe, paddles held ready over the water. Numeo pushed off and hopped lightly into his place. The canoe flew, gliding noiselessly over the perfectly smooth water.

"G'bye, all you tightpants," Lafortune muttered as he paddled. "Bon voyage! Hope you get boiled good in them rapids. Hope the Ol' Woman dumps yer boats. Next time you put yer hands on a voyageur, watch out!"

The paddles slipped into and out of the water as silently as an otter dives. The canoe left behind a widening V which the moonlight accentuated. Were the soldiers even awake?

The two shores of the Kaministiquia sped by. Then abruptly the land stopped, as if halted by some sudden fear. The canoe braved on alone into Thunder Bay, the antechamber of *Kitché-Goumi*, the Great Lake.

The cool air was raising a thick mist silvered by the moon; Lafortune could see no more than two feet ahead of the canoe. Fantastic, luminous shapes kept forming in the mist — women in tattered blankets wafting across the cold water, old men with twisted arms descending suddenly into the depths. At times the travellers were paddling through an opaque cloud, at others crossing a black-water clearing surrounded by phosphorescent trees.

They paddled all night. The moon retired. In the middle of the bay the mist dissipated. Askik was exhausted and was dipping his paddle less and less deep. At Numeo's suggestion, he rolled up in the bottom of the canoe and went to sleep. Once in a while he would wake and see the canoe's rim and *watap* seams, the star-studded firmament, and Numeo's silhouette swaying patiently, resolutely back and forth over the water. As the sky was turning pink ahead of the canoe, a point of land came into sight, blocking their path: the eastern shore of Thunder Bay.

Beyond this point lay the vast expanse of Lake Superior. Lafortune had them round the point so they could land on its south-eastern tip in view of the lake. It was time to stop. As the sun heated the land, it whipped up winds on the lake's icy surface. Waves were beginning to rise.

The Canadian officer nervously studied the toes of his boots.

"They've gone, sir. The voyageur and the two Indians. Shipped out."

Wolseley turned an amused eye from his shaving mirror.

"Shipped out? You mean they've escaped?"

"Well...yes sir."

"Never mind, Lieutenant. I suspect our Mister Lafortune of exaggerating the difficulty of the route. Trying to get us to give up, probably, to protect his Métis friends. What d'you say, Lieutenant, can we get along without him?"

"Yes sir!" The Canadian officer departed, feeling better. Would Her Majesty's expeditionary corps really have to depend on a French-Canadian voyageur?

Pulling on the ample khaki jacket he favoured in defiance of all and sundry at the War Office, Colonel Garnet Wolseley went out to take the air before it came time for the meeting with his officers. The road to Lake Shebandowan was as good as finished. The force would soon be able to resume its march.

It was surprisingly cool. The summers are too short in this country, Wolseley thought to himself, but where else would one find this scent of spruce, these grey rocks covered with orange lichens, these foaming rivers leaping from unfathomable forests? Canada would haunt him to the end of his days.

His time had come, though he did not know it yet. As he paced the banks of the Kaministiquia, how could he know that Prussia had invaded France, that the French army was on the brink of collapse, that the British Parliament, frightened by the disaster across the Channel, was preparing finally to take action? Within a year, the military high command would be recast, the sale of ranks prohibited, the duration of military service shortened: all measures advocated by Garnet Wolseley and a handful of other young officers who looked upon war as a science. London had despised them, but was about to begin listening to them.

Fame and honour were in store for Garnet Wolseley, subjugator of the Ashanti, governor of Cyprus, conqueror of Cairo, liberator of Khartoum, commander-in-chief of all the Imperial forces. His very name became synonymous with success. In common parlance, "it's all Sir Garnet" came to mean "mission accomplished."

Yet his entire life was not unlike this expedition to the Red River. The expeditionary force was to cover five hundred miles of forest and rivers, farther than Napoleon from Niemen to Moscow; its heavy barges survived forty-seven portages and its soldiers became able boatmen. And it all ended in silence and heavy rain at the abandoned Fort Garry, because Riel and his Métis had fled. The Red River expedition, barely noted in the rest of the Empire, was very quickly forgotten.

And so Garnet Wolseley spent thirty years running from one skirmish to another, wasting his talents on the Empire's minor altercations. All his life he was to seek a fight worthy of those talents, and died on March 26, 1913, on the eve of the greatest war that human history had ever known.

12

They followed the north shore of Lake Superior, travelling mostly at night to avoid rough water and because Lafortune was a fugitive. They spent several days pinned down by the weather, stranded on a narrow, rocky beach, waiting for the lake to stop raging. In calm weather they paddled day and night.

To their left was a fearsome landscape: cliffs hundreds of feet high, thundering rivers surging through the depths of dark crevasses, smoking sulphur springs, caves through which the wind blew and moaned. To their right was endless water.

Ten days later they stopped at Pancake Bay. In the old days the voyageurs used to consume the remains of their flour here, since they knew they could restock in Sault Sainte Marie the next day. Lafortune made an exception to the rule. There were soldiers at the Sault; he did not intend to spend any time there.

It was after dark when they entered the Sainte Marie River, the link between Lake Superior and Lake Huron. Rounding Pine Point, they saw the lights of the American village on the right bank. The Canadian forest opposite remained dark and untamed.

They paddled quickly and silently. They were all but past the village when giant, shadowy shapes loomed ahead of them. The birchbark canoe was passing between massive vessels with heavy timber hulls and huge iron anchor chains. A steamboat was wheezing tranquilly at its moorings and giving off sparks.

Lafortune thought he had lost his mind. How could ships as heavy as these have passed the rapids? Numeo and Askik were awestruck. Where had these behemoths come from? How did they manage to float?

In the distance, on the American side, they saw lanterns moving and men coming and going by their light. Then they realized that something was moving above the men's heads, and were dumbfounded to see the masts of a ship, moving over dry land as it seemed, far from the river.

This was too much for Lafortune. He thought he was seeing the devil's work; he had never seen canal locks.

"Let's get the hell out of here!" he hissed. "Paddle, paddle!"

Minutes later, ships, locks and lanterns had all disappeared. The darkness was as complete and the river as peaceful as before.

"They dug a canal," said Lafortune, beginning to understand. Where the voyageurs had gambled their lives in frail canoes, gentlemen were now passing in iron ships. In his birchbark canoe which he drove with his arms, he felt ridiculous. Ridiculous and outmoded. Nothing was left of the voyageurs. Nothing whatever.

On Lake Nipissing he hunted and hunted for fourteen wooden crosses which, when he was young, marked the spot where an entire party had perished. These fourteen crosses were known throughout the North West. He did not find them. He thrashed furiously through the bushes and at nightfall came and sat by the fire, depressed and covered with grime.

A week later they launched their canoe onto the Ottawa River.

"Look, Askik," cried Lafortune, pointing to the left bank, "that there's Lower Canada. And over there on t'other side's Upper Canada." Askik was disappointed. There was no difference between the two shores, except that the hills on the Lower Canada side looked if anything a little higher than those of Upper Canada. Another absurdity, which he was careful not to point out.

The only dwellings they saw at first were poor huts: lumberjack shelters. Then a farm, striking in its isolation, with a tiny log cabin, a cow and a small cultivated field. The farther they went the less distance there was between habitations and the bigger the fields and herds of animals. Peasants hailed them in French from their barnyards: "Where've you come from?" The reply "the Red River" brought exclamations or astonished silences, especially from the elderly. A young man tending cows asked, "Where's that?" which was the last straw for Lafortune.

The journey's final days passed very quickly. Later, Askik was sorry to have taken in so little of this phase, and particularly to have paid so little attention to Numeo. The Cree hunter, hardly a talkative fellow at any time, became totally silent. When the village of Aylmer appeared with its sparkling church spires and shops and crisscrossing streets, the Indian showed as much surprise as Lafortune and Askik, if not more. He seemed to be looking on these new things with detachment, however, like a man whose thoughts are already elsewhere.

When the travellers returned from the village, Numeo asked his first and only question of the journey: "How many more days to Montreal, *nitotem*?" When Lafortune replied "Three," Numeo seemed content.

They paddled part of the night, passing huge rafts called *cages*, which were log booms floating with the current of the Ottawa to sawmills downstream. The *cageux* or raftsmen responsible for the delivery of the logs lived on the rafts in rough wooden shelters. When the three travellers were tired of paddling, they would haul their canoe up onto one of these rafts and sleep by a nice warm fire while the river bore them slowly closer to Montreal.

On the last night they camped at the foot of a series of rapids called the Long Sault, which they had run in the fully loaded canoe. The light of their fire made a scattering of shadows among the trees and threw pale glimmers up to the forest ceiling above. Askik had never seen such tall pine trees. "It's the climate," Lafortune said proudly. Since their arrival in Lower Canada, he had adopted the airs of a minor seigneur showing guests around his domain.

"This here's where Dollard des Ormeaux died, boy — him an' 'is companions. Massacred by the Indians. Killed a whole bunch of 'em first, though. Don't bother translatin' that for our Native, he wouldn't take it so good."

Lafortune kept fidgeting, bending and straightening his legs spasmodically as if not knowing what to do with them. He sucked nervously on his burnt-out pipe and cast longing eyes at the canoe. It would have suited him to paddle all night and be in Montreal at daybreak, but finding his way in the dark was another thing.

"You got no idea what it's like t' be homesick, boy," he sighed at last. "Forty years I spent in the North West. And there weren't a day I didn't long t' come back. I got a clerk t' figger it fer me: forty years, that's fifteen thousand days. Fifteen thousand days!" A look of disbelief crossed his face. "Fifteen thousand times I said t' myself I shoulda stayed home. No, you got no idea..."

He was silent for a moment, then continued.

"The worst was Christmas and New Year's. New Year's Day most of all. Stuck in a field of ice in a cabin no bigger'n my hand, not a woman in sight; sometimes I only had my dogs for comp'ny. And knowin' that back in Lower Canada that day my relatives were celebratin' and havin' fun t'gether an' maybe even talkin' 'bout me. Christmas, our men spent drinkin' and fightin'. That was their way of keepin' from dyin' o' loneliness.

"And there was some," he said softly, leaning closer to the warmth of the fire, "that couldn't take it no more or'd drunk too much an' made a deal t' go home fer New Year's Eve on the *chasse-galerie*. 'Take us to Canada, ol' Lucifer,' they said. 'If we ain't back by dawn, or if we hit a church steeple on the way, our souls're yours.' So they said the magic words and youppe! — their canoes flew off through the air with 'em."

Askik pictured the canoes of the *chasse-galerie* speeding over the forests and frozen rivers, covering twice in a single night the distance that had taken Askik, Lafortune and Numeo two months. The *canots de maître*, the great freight canoes, descended on the hamlets of the St. Lawrence, where the invisible voyageurs entered the festive houses. Near the end of the night, haggard and wan with weariness and grief, they boarded their canoes again and flew back as fast as the wind to the North West. A few men stayed, unable to tear themselves away from their homes, and were lost for eternity.

"We was wrong, boy," Lafortune concluded. "We shoulda all stayed here in Lower Canada with our fam'lies. What good did it do us, roamin' round the woods all our lives? We made the English rich, we made Métis, then we come home jiss as poor as we left."

Askik had a bad night. He dreamed that Master Prosy came and took him by the ear back to the Savanne Portage to find his manuscript. He woke at dawn, filled with anxiety. Fog had pervaded the forest; the pines looked even more massive than before. Far, very far away, a woodpecker tapped tentatively at a hollow tree. Numeo was sleeping noiselessly. Lafortune was tossing and turning, now with a grunt, now with a sigh.

The boy curled up under his blanket, his cheek against the fragrant forest floor. He was no longer impatient to get to Montreal, did not want to go to school, did not want to meet his benefactors. He wanted to keep travelling with Lafortune and Numeo, all the way to the seas of ice if necessary, far away from blond young men looking down their noses. Since he would never be like them, what was the point of learning to read and write? How would he ever become a great man if he could not even return a white man's gaze? He thought about Mona and felt a sharp pang of tenderness for her. She had understood all this. He did not really want to be a great man. His place was with her, among his own people. The forest here was too beautiful, he thought, too tidy. He longed for the scrawny trees, the tangled woods of the North West; not beautiful as here, but his people's own. He decided he would go back to St. Boniface.

A raven croaked hoarsely. Lafortune rolled onto his stomach, opened an eye, inspected the forest with puzzlement, then with a bound was on his feet.

"*Lève*, men! Up you get! We got a great day ahead o' us!" Then exuberantly to Numeo, "*Mino-gisigow!*" It was a measure of his good humour that he should venture a word of Cree. "It's our last day, voyageurs! Tonight we'll have supper in Montreal. In Montreal!"

And yet he made no move to leave. He was savouring these last moments. In a few hours he would cease forever being a voyageur. He could afford to take his time with this last breakfast in the forest, to sip his tea slowly while telling himself ten times, a hundred times that this paddle was the last he would ever hold, this tree with its gnarled bark would never see him go by again, this canoe overturned at the river's edge would never test the strength of his back again.

A torrent of angry scolding fell on them from overhead. A red squirrel was sitting on a branch, heaping abuse on the intruders.

"Look, *nisim*," Numeo said.

Askik barely gave a glance. He was not interested in squirrels. He knew now that his plan was absurd. Having come to the very gates of Montreal, would Lafortune turn around and go back?

"I like *Alikwatsas*," Numeo went on. "He's small, he's weak, but he's a great warrior. Hawks and owls attack him in the trees, foxes wait for him on the ground, but he does not hide. He stays in sight in the branches and shouts very loud. He's defiant and cunning. He could be as big as a bear, the way he runs on the ground. He has no weapon, but he is bold. He's not ashamed of his weakness."

The little animal had stopped chattering, as if listening to the praise. Askik looked at it more attentively. The squirrel impudently looked back at them both, its four feet braced apart, ready to leap in any direction.

Lafortune stretched and put his pipe in his pocket.

"Enough talk, men. It's high time I got home."

The remaining distance to Montreal was farther than Lafortune had thought. It was already late when they sighted an unpretentious chapel at the water's edge.

Lafortune was beside himself with excitement. "Sainte Anne!" he yelled. "That's the voyageurs' chapel. We came and prayed here before leavin'. It was here the voyageurs had masses sung before goin' off t' the *Pays d'en Haut*."

He snatched his bright-coloured tuque from his head, rose on his knees in the canoe, joined his hands and prayed fervently. "Thank you, Sainte Anne, for bringin' me home. It took you awful long but I'm grateful anaways. Goddam grateful! Oh Lord, it's the chapel!"

His cheeks were streaked with tears, his brown hands shook with emotion. He seemed ecstatic and anguished both at once. At last he picked up his paddle. Bareheaded, grey hair stirring in the wind, he began slowly to stroke again.

The sun was nearing the horizon when they reached the wharves of Lachine. Their journey was over.

Near the wharf was a large warehouse in which goods headed for the North West were once collected. A few hands were lounging about near the door, filling in the end of their day with talk. They were astonished at the sight of three voyageurs arriving in a birchbark canoe. Lafortune stepped out, took a few paces straight ahead, then stood still, eyes fixed like a sleepwalker. The oldest of the hands, a white-haired fellow, walked over to greet him.

"*Salut*, voyageur. You're home. Where'd you come from?"

"The Red River," Lafortune murmured.

"Ah! A man o' the North. Must be thirty years I ain't seen a canoe like that."

"It's a good canoe," Lafortune said, then sheepishly, "I shoulda put feathers on th' ends but I didn't have no feathers."

"Don't matter. Them customs ain't followed no more."

The setting sun was lighting fire in the dust over the hayfields. Great wagons loaded with hay were waiting by the sheds nearby. Lafortune had never seen anything so beautiful.

"Anybody expectin' you, voyageur?"

"Eh?"

"You got relatives, friends, who could take y' in?"

"No."

"Then you got an invitation fer the night. I was a voyageur too, but I ain't never gone to the North West."

"You did right, friend, you did right."

The two men were already walking away when Lafortune remembered Askik.

"The boy! He's gotta get to the Sulpicians' seminary."

"Nothin' easier," the white-haired man said. "Them wagons're goin' to the city." He turned to the hands. "Albert, find a place fer the kid."

Lafortune was being led away by his host when he heard a voice saying, "*Nitotem*, what will you do with the canoe?"

Numeo had stayed by the water with a paddle in his hand. He was looking at Lafortune with a half-smile.

"The canoe? What am I s'posed to do with it?"

Then, remembering that he had given Numeo nothing for his pains, Lafortune put his hands familiarly on Numeo's shoulders and said, "Yer a good Injun. I'm givin' the canoe to you."

"*Kininaskomitin, nitotem*, thank you." Numeo replied.

When Lafortune had gone at last, it was Askik's turn to ask a question.

"What are you going to do with the canoe, Numeo?"

"I'm going back home, little brother."

"You don't want to see Montreal?"

"No. I've already seen a lot. I'm going to go back to my wife. We'll never have any more children, but there are many Crees dying now. Perhaps there will be children who need us. If I go now I'll be home before freezeup. I'll buy food for the winter with the money I got from your uncle."

There were times when Askik was capable of acting unselfconsciously, without regard for appearances. He flung his arms around Numeo and clung with all his might.

"I want to go back with you, Numeo."

"No, you must stay. What is good for me is not good any more for you. Stay and learn the ways of the Hairy Faces. They are the ones who will decide everything for you now."

"But I don't like them!"

"You may like them some day. They're your relatives too."

"You wouldn't have made one of your sons stay!" Askik said resentfully.

"My sons were Muskegos. You're a Métis. Stay."

"I'm frightened, Numeo."

"Remember Alikwatsas, little brother. Be brave. One day you will visit my lodge and I shall be proud to receive you. *Kitom kawapmitin, nisim.*"

Askik sniffed back a tear and, realizing that the hired hands were looking on curiously, broke away from Numeo. The same voice that had spoken to him at Fort William was whispering now that it was shameful to embrace an Indian in front of Whites.

"*Kitom kawapmitin*, Numeo."

The carters spent part of the night at a tavern, a dirty, squalid, mud-splattered house by the side of the road. From his place atop the hay, Askik could see shadows moving behind the filthy windows. Inside the house was a woman whose loud, shrill laughter was almost always the signal for furious argument among the men. They did not leave until the small hours of the morning, having drunk and cursed themselves blind.

Bidou, the carter with whom Askik was travelling, seemed particularly black-humoured on leaving the tavern. He climbed up on the front rail of the wagon, slapped the reins savagely on the horses' rumps and, letting his head droop, lost all interest in his trade.

The faded hay that had been so comfortable at first was now covered with clammy dew. Askik thought of Numeo sleeping in the forest by a fire. Would Numeo have abandoned his little brother if he had known what kind of men he was leaving him to?

A rough hand wakened him. It was still dark.

"Yer there. Git off!"

Askik slid to the ground and banged his knee on a hard surface. Walking straight ahead, he saw an iron grille, took hold of it and stayed there. Bidou clacked his tongue. The wagon disappeared.

No one came by for a very long time. Now and then a dog barked in the distance, always the same one. There was a sound of water on the other side of the grating; was it a stream? Near morning, Askik heard a loud cry of fear, followed by a drunkard's mutterings. Then nothing more. His knee swelled and eventually stopped hurting; his hand, gripping the icy-cold iron, lost all feeling. Perhaps he managed to sleep in spite of all, for he did not see the towers of Notre-Dame emerging from the darkness. When he looked up they were already there, looming over him, glowering, black and dizzyingly high, higher than anything he could have imagined. He had no time to cry out, for the Bank then rose up on the other side, a stocky giant with massive shoulders and awesomely long stone teeth.

There is a special brotherhood among the carters who arrive very early at Bonsecours Market. They move about while others are still asleep and are the first to see what the night has left in the city's streets. That morning, one of them reported seeing a child clinging to the iron grille in Place d'Armes, a small brown child in old-fashioned clothes, clutching a buffalo robe. Laughter and sarcasm greeted the news. The lads heading out again past Notre-Dame promised to keep their eyes open, but of course there was no child.

PART THREE

Vieilleterre

1

"Please, gentlemen!"

A man no longer exactly young was calling for silence. Finally, despairing of being heard, he took an empty bottle and smashed it against the table. His companions were showered with broken glass, which drew another boisterous round of laughter and, eventually, silence.

"Thank you, my lords. I believe you know the cause of our festivities — Gauthier, dear porcine fellow, kindly get down off the table — We're gathered here, then, to bid a fraternal welcome to Sieur... what is it again?... Launay?... No?... Ah, *de* Launay!"

His listeners roundly booed the intimation of aristocracy.

"De Launay, then: country gentleman, student in his present estate, recent arrival in our city of Montreal, aspirant profligate at Les Trois Grosses Muses!"

The Speaker steadied himself against the table while a salvo of cat-calls greeted the Sieur de Launay's candidature.

"This worthy gentleman is requesting admission to our fellowship. His sponsor is Sieur Morin, his cousin. And Sieur Morin is known to be an egregious ass." Renewed applause.

"But what do we know of this de Launay?" As he spoke, the Speaker flung his arm in an arc, almost initiating a pirouette. His complexion was pale and his eyes bloodshot. It would have been a wonder if they were not, for there was more smoke than oxygen in Les Trois Grosses Muses.

"What do we know of him? Nothing! But devil take it, what d'you know of me?"

"Thrice nothing!" some revellers yelled.

"A fine blackguard!" others bawled.

Raising his voice above the others, the Speaker intoned,

"Therefore, gentlemen, I propose that we receive into our midst His Excellency de Launay!" He subsided heavily in his chair amid thundering cheers and bravos.

"Brothers," he beseeched hoarsely, "bring me drink. I am spent."

Ageing women, insensitive to the fine words, were placing big round loaves of bread and bowls of steaming *ragoût de boulettes* on the table. The diners fell upon the food with a rapacity that left young de Launay gaping.

"Unsheath your steel, monsieur," the Speaker cried to him, holding up his knife. "These dogs will leave you nothing!"

The newcomer inspected the grey meatballs floating in oily yellow gravy.

"To tell the truth I'm not very hungry," he concluded.

"Then you have made a wise choice of estate, monsieur, for students do not eat very often."

"Hmmf! Look at the fussy beggar," growled another diner, munching on his meatballs and bread. "D'ya really think this de Launay ever goes t' bed hungry? It reeks o' rich papa in here!"

Our Colin Clout's name is Martin," the Speaker said to the new initiate. "He's from the Beauce. Thinks our accent is pansy talk. Talks Beauceron himself."

"*Mange de la marde!*" Martin snapped.

"Done, my friend."

"Where's Mercredi?" someone called from the other end of the table.

De Launay gave an explosive little laugh, then excused himself, covering his mouth.

"Mercredi? Wednesday? What a funny name! Is he a negro?"

Martin stopped chewing, though his mouth was full. He seemed on the point of regurgitating in his plate by way of reply, but instead swallowed what was in his mouth at one gulp, then levelled a threatening finger across the table.

"Shut yer trap, fag! Next time you laugh at a friend of mine, I'll stuff yer skirts down yer throat, got that?"

"Mercredi has returned to his domains," the Speaker said in an effort to improve the atmosphere.

There was laughter. Martin gave a final growl and returned to his *boulettes.*

"Mercredi," the Speaker continued to de Launay, "is a member of long standing. A most remarkable figure whom I trust you will have the pleasure of meeting." The Speaker's mouth twitched with what might have been impatience; perhaps his witticisms were wearing thin, or he was feeling the indisposition that strikes drinkers around mid-evening before alcohol renders them oblivious.

"Mercredi," he continued more quietly, "arrived in Montreal fifteen years ago. He was found one morning clinging to the iron grillework in Place d'Armes. He had come straight from the Red River, by canoe if you please. He was not the first Métis to come and study here — Louis Riel was another — but Mercredi was very different. He spoke poor French and his baggage of beliefs made the good fathers' hair stand on end. Very shy. Never talked to anybody. Always alone. Never heard from his parents. In the dormitory one morning, the fathers found him sleeping on the floor; wasn't used to a mattress. When they took away his buffalo robe, he bit a father on the leg! Punishment didn't phase him a bit. At first the others called him 'the little savage', or 'the Métchiffe', making fun of his accent. He'd lash out any anyone, though, even the biggest boys, and since he never backed off till he was knocked senseless, they left him alone after a while. A wonder he didn't die of misery that first year."

"What about now?" de Launay asked. He was beginning to feel miserable himself.

The Speaker had stopped paying attention to him. "Mercredi's passion for learning was what saved him. He had a gift for languages. He already knew Cree and Ojibway, but they weren't on the curriculum. Do you know Cree, de Launay? In comparison, Latin is pompous gibberish."

"What about him now?" de Launay insisted. He was a major prizewinner in Latin translation.

"Well, Alexis Mercredi is now a lawyer's apprentice with Messieurs Leclerc and Juneau of Rue Notre-Dame. He fills his days with petitions and briefs and spends his time off, of which he is allowed considerable, at the estate of his benefactors, the Sancys of Vieilleterre."

De Launay sat bolt upright.

"He knows the Sancys?"

"He's their protégé. He didn't have much contact with them at first; didn't even know their name, I believe. He made his first visit to Vieilleterre only after the fathers decided he was presentable."

"And he's there now?"

"For the Christmas holidays."

"It's incredible! A Métis getting in with the Sancys, just like that!"

"Just like that," the Speaker confirmed. Seasoned observer that he was, he could taste the jealousy burning in de Launay's eyes.

"And what kind of future does your Mercredi think he's going to have?"

"With the Sancys' backing, what future might he not have? Lawyer, merchant, statesman..."

"A brown statesman!" de Launay guffawed, relieved at the absurdity of the notion.

"Brown I grant you," the Speaker broke in, "but rich. You're as milk-white as anyone could wish, de Launay, but do you have money?"

"It's not fair!"

"Everything has its price, my dear fellow. Mercredi has paid dearly."

It was late. The diners were retrieving their coats and arguing over half a dozen identical galoshes.

"Easy now, you oxen," the Speaker murmured as he wove his way toward the door. With a degree of solicitude shown only to him, his companions passed him a tuque for his head and a voluminous scarf.

"Well now," the Speaker said, "thought I had a blue tuque."

The group straggled along the dark dockside streets lined with warehouses and offices and emerged at the foot of Place Jacques Cartier. An icy wind was blowing down the hill.

"Lord, that's a cool breeze!"

Voices and snatches of laughter issued from an American-style saloon, the only establishment still open at this hour. Its windows wore a thick armour of ice. A man came out, staggered in two or three directions, then plodded up the hill toward Rue Notre-Dame.

"There's the sacrificial lamb. Follow me, me hearties!"

The students caught up with the stranger. He was heavily built, bearded and extremely drunk. With cheery slaps on his back, laughing at his inarticulate jokes, they steered him gently toward an ice slide that crossed the square downhill toward the river. They hunted about and found a luge with wooden runners.

"Your carriage is ready, Excellency. Ho there, lackey, give us a hand, pray!"

They sat their victim on the luge and, having advised him to hold on tight, launched him down the slide. The sled disappeared in the darkness, the man hanging on for dear life, chin on his chest. The students listened. The sled was going farther than they had expected. Finally there was a skidding sound and a dull "Oof!"

"Gentlemen," the Speaker pronounced, "I declare the session adjourned. Good night. Unpleasant dreams!"

The gathering broke up into small groups that quickly disappeared down the neighbouring streets. It was too cold to stand around and talk.

De Meauville — such was the Speaker's name — remained there alone for a few minutes. When he saw the drunkard limping back up the hill, he set off for his lodgings. He lived in the attic of a merchants' house on Rue Saint-Jacques. Of the group, he was the poorest. Yet in an age when all the young people were appending a "de" in front of their names, de Meauville had a right to his. He was an authentic noble, son of a seigneur ruined by the reforms of 1854, which abolished the seigneurial régime. Unfortunately his name was his sole asset.

It was deathly cold in the house; the owners were early to bed and the fires had been out for some time. De Meauville slipped into bed fully clothed. He pulled the tuque back on his head because the pillow was icy cold. A wan light was entering by the dormer window. It made him hanker for a smoke, though he was not sure why; there was hardly any stem left to his pipe.

"It really isn't fair," he thought to himself, inhaling the hot smoke. "Here I am, an ageing seigneur, freezing in third-rate rented lodgings, while Mercredi, grandson of Cree hunters and Canayen coureurs de bois, is warm and comfortable at Vieilleterre. Sacré Mercredi!"

There was a rustling under the table in the corner. A small rat climbed nervously onto the chair, then onto the table. It hunted for a minute among the books and dishes on the table, then froze, staring at the student with feverish eyes.

"Terribly sorry, Brutus, nothing to eat tonight."

2

"I'm not convinced, I'm not convinced. No, there's no point going over it again, I understand you perfectly. I'm just not convinced."

"But it's a golden opportunity, I tell you, uncle! The shares have been dropping for the last six months. Everybody thinks it's going bankrupt, no one knows it's going to be taken over by Luger Frères. You know the Stock Exchange. This kind of secret won't keep!"

"Yes, yes, but I don't have the cash in hand."

"What about your forestlands? Sell some! The Americans don't pay well, but you've got plenty of land."

"Standing timber's a sure thing. Your shares scare me."

The two men laughed together over their respective fears. They had argued the virtues of land versus stock exchange a dozen times this way. Eugène Sancy played the role of the great landed property-owner who was still a peasant at heart and distrusted scrip. His nephew Hubert, played the young businessman at ease with the stock exchange and technical innovations: the amasser of easy fortunes. None of it was real. The uncle possessed a seat on the Stock Exchange and the nephew owned land. In business, however, half the pleasure is in talk. Using arcane terms and understanding what the other means, tossing around theoretical millions and pretending they are real, is a game worthy of respect.

The two had retired to the study and were sipping port, feet propped on the fireplace rail before a cheery fire. Through the closed door they could hear the servants bustling back and forth with preparations for the Christmas *réveillon*.

"How is your sawmill going, uncle? You were having trouble with your foreman, I believe."

"It's all settled. Alexis is just back from there."

"Ah, your protégé."

"Himself."

Hubert studied the flames through his port. "A remarkable young man, that Mercredi, don't you think?"

"Exactly my opinion."

"But I'd bet the first time you saw him you had quite a different impression."

"How so?"

"He was a bit... unpolished."

"He had trouble adapting to our ways, but he's never shown ingratitude."

"He never talks about going back home?"

"Why would he? He's lost all trace of his family, while here he has friends, he has a future. In a few months he'll be able to plead in court."

"You're not afraid his colour will work against him?"

"He won't be the first French-Canadian lawyer to be a bit dark of skin. And he has no accent any more."

"What's his father?"

"A hunter, I believe."

"Strange. The father hunts and the son pleads in court."

"Our forefathers hunted too, not so long ago."

"Mmmm... yes. Does he think more or less the way we do?"

"Come now! He's not a savage!"

"Of course not, but his background's different; he's from another culture."

"No, there's no difference. At first, yes, he did have some odd ideas. One day he saw our cook pulling up carrots in the garden. He asked for some tobacco to put in the holes as a sign of gratitude to the earth."

The two men had a laugh over this.

"How about now?" the nephew insisted.

"No difference, I tell you. He's just like us. An honest-to-goodness *Canayen, un vrâ de vrâ*."

Eugène Sancy rarely stooped to popular parlance. When he did, he expected it to be noticed. His nephew responded with a smile that said, I know you use that language deliberately.

"But don't you think he's still, underneath it all — forgive me, uncle, but I can't find another word for it — still a bit of a savage, a bit unpredictable?"

"He's stubborn I grant you, but put yourself in his place. No family. Plunked down in a strange milieu. Surrounded by children who knew twice as much as he did."

"Lucky for him you took him under your wing, uncle."

"I've had no cause to regret it. Alexis is very helpful to me. And my wife loves him like a son. There's a good chance he'll become intendant of Vieilleterre one of these days."

"Don't you think he's spending a lot of time with my cousin?"

"Élisabeth? She thinks of him as a brother."

"And you, uncle, do you consider him a son?"

"Whoa, now, I wouldn't go that far..."

A servant came in to light the lamps; the daylight was fading. Madame Sancy came through the open door. She was a corpulent woman and taller than her husband, for which she was condemned for ever to wearing flat-heeled shoes. Her walk was the heavier for it. Unlike the two men, she spoke with the accent of ordinary folk.

"So, business is done in the dark now, is it?" she said.

"An economy measure, *ma tante*," Hubert said banteringly. "It saves on kerosene."

"My dear nephew, if you really wanta save money, start by changin' tailors. What you're wearin' would keep me in karrazin for a whole year."

"All right, I've got the message," Hubert laughed, then he turned to the servant. "Céline, bring me some scissors. I'm going to pare down to essentials."

By the light of the lamps, mahogany glowed and gilt and crystal sparkled richly. Hubert paid these things no heed; he was accustomed to luxury. What did impress him was the silence that enveloped the house and came to a focus here in this room. More than once, buy and sell orders originating here had convulsed the Stock Exchange and sowed consternation in Rue Saint-Jacques. Yet the serenity of Vieilleterre remained complete and unalterable.

"I envy you, uncle, living in the country."

"How it's snowing!" Madame Sancy exclaimed. "I hope the road stays passable."

"Alexis, it's late! I'm cold and supper must be ready. We have to go in! It's getting dark! We'll get lost!"

"We can follow the road."

"I'm cold!"

Askik laughed merrily. He was moving around a cedar tree, looking for the nicest, thickest branches. The children had already gone in with the Christmas tree; the only thing left was to gather cedar boughs for the crowns. Askik was taking his time because it vexed Élisabeth, and because he was in love with Élisabeth.

He had not always loved her; it was rather recent. On his way back from the Ottawa valley, he had thought about her in the same way he thought about the rest of the family, no more and no less. He had been curt with the coachmen all the way, insisting that they forego stopping to warm up at post-houses and taverns because he was impatient to be back in the big house at Vieilleterre with his friends. The roads had been blocked by the snow, however, and post-house keepers, expecting no further business, had given the horses their hay and retired to the warmth of their hearths. His coachman had even strayed off the road into the fields. In short, Askik had arrived very late at Vieilleterre. When he came into the house, all the familiar faces had been there to greet him, and yet, through some curious effect of weariness or destiny, he had seen only one. Among all these people laughing and jostling him and taking his coat and packages, there was Élisabeth. The others were only shadows.

She was the way he had always imagined her: tall, a little thin, her smile slightly mocking. She was wearing the grey dress covered with tiny roses that she liked best for weekdays. Her hair was done up at the back of her neck, the way she wore it when she had work to do.

She had not changed, yet when he looked at her he realized for the first time that he loved her, that she would be his wife, and this was how it had to be.

"Alexis!" the young woman cried, out of patience, "I'm going without you!"

"I'm coming, I've got enough now." Askik came out of the woods with an armful of cedar, wading to his waist in the light, fluffy snow. Élisabeth was waiting on the country road.

"Cedar smells good," he said, presenting her with a bouquet of it.

"This is a fine time! I'm half-frozen. Let's go in."

They walked briskly. The woods, the road and the meadows were disappearing gradually behind a blue-grey veil of snow and darkness. I could spend my whole life here, Askik thought. I could spend all eternity on this road with Élisabeth. Lighted windows pierced the darkness here and there. It made you feel good to know there were people around. It made you feel strong and supported.

"I hate December!" Élisabeth hissed. "It's always dark."

"I don't. Look how peaceful everything is. The trees and animals are asleep. Even the people are resting."

"That's just it," she pouted. "Nothing happens. I don't understand why papa insists on spending the holidays here, when it would be so much more fun in Montreal. At least there's something to do there in winter, instead of holing up here like peasants."

"What more would you do in Montreal?" Askik asked in the teasing, big-botherly tone that infuriates women.

"Oh, I don't know. Go out, read, talk, go to the theatre, go to balls, have friends in — all my friends are there!"

Askik was silent a minute, wounded that she counted his presence for so little. When he thought about it, though, he himself spent most of his time in Montreal, with the firm of Messrs. Leclerc and Juneau. He could hardly take offense at this.

"There are good things about the city, it's true," he said. He had just resolved to spend all his days in Montreal, just for her.

"Ah, there's the house at last!" Élisabeth cried. "I've never been so cold in my life!"

"What on earth kept you?" Madame Sancy exclaimed when she saw them come in. "Pépère has been waiting half an hour."

In truth, Pépère never waited for anyone. When Élisabeth and Askik took their places at the table, the old man had already downed half his soup. It was he, Albert Sancy (formerly Sansouci), who had laid the foundations of the family fortune by buying the seigneury of Vieilleterre. He had had nothing to do with its management for many a year, however. Whenever he took it into his head to intervene, it was almost always at cross-purposes; he would order the hemp brought in when the last hemp had been harvested ten years ago, or horses harnessed that were long dead and returned to dust.

The Sancys were having a light supper of soup and cold meat, in consideration of the heavy *réveillon* awaiting them after midnight mass. After the meal, they retired for some rest before going to mass.

When she left her bed several hours later, Madame Sancy glanced anxiously out the window and was pleased to see that the weather had calmed. The stars were still out of sight but it had stopped snowing.

"The good Lord's watchin' out for his feast day!" she proclaimed aloud. Then she turned to Céline, who was pouring hot water into a big wash basin.

"Is everything ready?" she asked.

"All ready, madame. I don't think I ever saw a finer goose."

"The children are up?"

"Yes, madame."

"Has Auguste cleared the entrance?"

"All the way to the fence. He says there shouldn't be no trouble with the road."

"Good, everything's ready then."

On the bed she had just made, Céline laid out a dress of burgundy taffeta trimmed with very dark lace. Madame Sancy had two thoughts as she watched her maid. First she wondered if the dress was really suitable for midnight mass. Next she reflected that Céline really was a jewel and wondered what she might do to keep this fine, resourceful girl in her service. Céline was a village girl. Though she spent all her time at Vieilleterre, she might well desert the family for some young farmer one of these days.

"How old are you, Céline?"

"Twenty-four, madame. Soon be an old maid," the young woman quipped.

Twenty-four, said Madame Sancy to herself. Pretty enough, though. Nice face. Healthy skin. Big breasts, men like that. Hair too black, almost Indian, but thick. Even my Élisabeth doesn't have as beautiful hair.

"Don't you ever think of marrying, Céline?"

"No, madame," the girl replied as she pinned a jet brooch on her mistress's bodice. Her answer was so clear and decided that Madame Sancy was almost reassured.

"Usually a girl your age wants to start a family."

"I'm fine where I am, madame."

"Your father drank, didn't he?"

"Like a fish."

That doesn't mean anything, Madame Sancy thought. A young woman can convince herself that all men are rotters, but there's always one comes along who looks like an exception. Then, having thought a little more, the mistress made a decision.

"Céline, is your blue dress clean?"

"Of course, Madame," the girl replied in surprise.

"Go and put it on. You're coming with us to mass."

"But... Madame... how about the *réveillon?*"

"Rosalie will look after it. Everything's ready. Go quickly and get dressed. Don't do your hair over, there isn't time, it's just fine the way it is. Go now! Go quickly!"

Céline withdrew resentfully. She had been waiting all day for this moment of peace when the masters would be at church. And what am I going to look like beside Mademoiselle? she thought as she reached her room. The village people will say I'm putting on airs, taking myself for a Sancy!

She pulled on the blue cotton dress that her employers had given her. Fortunately its neckline was high, dispensing with the need for ornamentation; Céline possessed no jewelry, not even the tiniest brass necklace. She gave her hair a couple of scornful brushstrokes and left the room after making a face at herself in the mirror.

"What you doin', all dressed up?" fat Rosalie exclaimed when she saw Céline come downstairs.

"What *you* doin'?" Céline retorted. "Go back to the kitchen and see nothin' gets burned. I'm goin' to mass with Madame."

Rosalie turned on her heels with the air of someone who has discovered a sacrilege. Céline was left alone. No one else had yet come down. She strolled twice around the hall and, finding nothing more to do, went and sat on a bench near the door. Instinct told her to run to the kitchen and save the sauces and pastries that Rosalie would unfailingly botch, but how could she prevent it, dressed in her Sunday best? The carrioles were waiting at the door. Through the frosted windows she could hear old Paradis lecturing the horses. One of them was jingling its harness impatiently; the big black one, Céline thought.

Alexis Mercredi entered the room.

"Is Élisabeth down yet?" he asked.

"No, not yet."

"You're coming with us, Céline?"

"Madame wants me to."

And then, as if they had been given the signal, all the Sancys came down all at once, laughing and gesticulating.

Élisabeth was wearing a pale blue satin dress of the same shade as Céline's but infinitely more fetching. Across the chiffon at her neck hung a string of pearls. Her blond hair was braided in a diadem, as if letting everyone know that she was no longer the little girl they had known until now.

When he saw her, Askik lost all self-confidence. She was not his little intended any more but a strong and beautiful woman of a breed he had sometimes seen at the opera, sitting in the expensive rows where English was spoken. He felt too young, too uncouth to possess so superb a creature as she, and yet, at his very core, he was already flushed with the glory of having such a wife. It filled him to overflowing, though he dared not speak to her.

"I congratulate you, cousin!" Hubert said, gallantly kissing her hand.

The parents looked on smilingly. Askik envied the young stockbroker's ease of manner. He himself did not have such facility, could never find exactly the right compliment or appropriate gesture. His charm, his worth, he told himself, was quite different. At such times he remembered his entire past and fancied himself braver and hardier than the men around him. They had pretty manners and could recite poetry from memory, but had they ever been cold and hungry, as he had been? At these times he became more silent, more gruff and sardonic, thinking he was making himself more interesting. In fact, people would wonder what had got into him.

Once outside, Askik moved to take the reins, but Madame Sancy stopped him.

"No, no, Alexis, you drive too fast. Sit there." She waved to the back seat. Askik complied good-humouredly, all too pleased to be recognized as a daredevil driver. But a moment later he was dismayed to see Hubert take the reins, with Élisabeth sitting at his side. Paradis set the footwarmers in the bottom of the carrioles, tucked the passengers into their bearskin rugs and, when everyone was ready, started up the horses with a gravelly "Heeyaah!"

The fresh snow offered no more resistance than down; the carrioles' runners glided over the ice beneath. On either side of the road, tall, grey, snow-dappled evergreens sped by. The passengers rode in silence, not wanting to expose their faces to the cold, each wrapped in his furs and his thoughts. Askik was thinking about Élisabeth. Never had she been so beautiful! He could see only her eyes, framed in fur, but they were the most enchanting eyes in the world. When she turned her head and gave a sidelong glance at Hubert, her graceful lashes made Askik groan inside.

I'd die for that woman, he declared to his secret self, and at once imagined a thousand ways of gloriously giving his life.

The village was almost in sight when he realized that Céline was sitting beside him. She herself had chosen the back seat, all embarrassed to be stepping into the masters' carriole. She had turned away her face and was staring stolidly into the darkness, her head leaning outside the sleigh as if to indicate clearly to onlookers that she was not part of this company. Askik could feel the warmth of her body under the rug. Her nose was rather long, her hair really very black, but she was pretty enough. At Vieilleterre, Askik often watched her as she passed. Her large breasts, her well-rounded hips excited him. Élisabeth never had this effect on him; proof, in his mind, that his love for her was pure.

Saint-Aimé-de-Vieilleterre was a large village with a mill, a store and a forge. It had been burned by the English in 1759. The villagers had rebuilt it on its old foundations but the seigneur had moved his manor to a more private location.

Although the Sancys were not nobility, in time they had acquired the prestige and certain of the privileges of their predecessors. The oldest or most obsequious of the villagers readily addressed Eugène Sancy as "monseigneur," which by no means displeased Madame la Seigneuresse. In the church, there was a special honorific pew reserved for them; the Sancys performed their devotions with the tombs of six seigneurs of Vieilleterre under their feet.

There was not enough room for Askik to sit in the seigneurial pew. He therefore had to follow the mass from the other side of the main aisle, beside Céline. The curé was shortsighted and had difficulty reading his missal, despite the oil lamps very recently installed. The little church was crowded to the doors with parishioners. The first mass gave them a foretaste of eternity, but when the second mass was about half way through it became necessary to open the doors and extinguish the wood stoves so that the congregation would not faint from the heat.

Madame Sancy did not understand Latin. She recited her rosary twice through, absent-mindedly turned the pages of her missal, and now and then said a heartening prayer. Then, judging that she had done her duty by the mass, she turned her thoughts back to her usual schemes. Her eyes tenderly caressed her pet project, Hubert and Élisabeth, who were sitting side by side, each as bored as the other. They were cousins only in name; Hubert had lost his mother while still a baby, and his father had taken as his second wife the sister of Eugène Sancy. Looking slightly away from the cousins, Madame Sancy's eyes fell on Askik and Céline.

In their sumptuous festive clothing, the Sancys made a splash of luxury in an assembly of homespun woollens. Élisabeth drew the gaze of everyone present, and was not unaware of it. Askik saw the admiring looks of the men and the envious glances of the women. He burned with indignation that he was not at his intended's side in place of this stodgy cousin. He would have liked all of Saint-Aimé to know from this moment forth that Élisabeth and he were a couple.

During the third introit, Céline began to feel unwell. The day's work, the heat in the church, the odour of unwashed bodies made her stomach heave. Askik noticed her rapid breathing and realized with irritation and alarm that she was going to be ill.

"What's the matter?" he asked, trying not to give an impression of intimacy between the servant and himself.

Céline bowed her head to make herself as inconspicuous as possible.

"I feel weak, but it'll be better soon," she muttered quickly, as if to excuse herself.

"You ought to go out and get some air."

"No, no! It's nothing." Get up in the middle of the mass and walk down the main aisle in front of hundreds of curious onlookers? What shame it would bring her masters! Waves of nausea assailed her. The oily smell was unbearable; if only the lamps were not smoking so much. Beads of sweat stood out on her forehead; she was doubled up and did not realize it.

When the mass ended, the congregation seemed to take forever to funnel out through the doors. In the vestibule, Céline was on the point of fainting and had to cling to Askik's arm in spite of herself. Askik had intended to move away, but when he saw that she would surely fall he resigned himself to supporting her to avert even greater shame. Both left the church totally mortified, she because she felt she was bringing ridicule on her masters, he because he was being seen with a sick servant in a homespun *capote* on his arm, while Hubert had Élisabeth on his.

When he helped Céline into the carriole, she murmured, "Thank you, Alexis," which to him was the last irritating straw. She always addressed him by his first name, never "Monsieur" as the village people did.

As she was getting into the sleigh, Élisabeth saw Céline slumped on the back seat. Askik was fidgeting impatiently several paces away from the sleigh.

"Is she sick?" she asked him, but he shrugged his shoulders as if to say, How am I supposed to know?

Askik was silent all the way home. On the front seat, Hubert and Élisabeth were laughing loudly, mimicking the curé's bumbling. From the other sleigh, Madame Sancy scolded them as a matter of form. When they reached the house, Céline was able to get out of the sleigh herself and at once went upstairs to her room.

3

The noise made by the thresher was enough to shatter windows. The heavy plank floor shook under the workers' boots. There were accumulations of chaff everywhere. It was cold and the husks were splitting away easily.

Askik had come to the threshing barn to inspect the new treadmill imported from the United States. A horse walking on a conveyor belt was turning a big bull wheel to drive the thresher.

"So it works better like that?" Askik shouted to the foreman, a gaunt little man whose nose and chin came close to meeting.

"Much better!" Auguste Paradis replied. "The mare hadda get used t'it — the noise frightened 'er, but we got round that by blockin' 'er ears."

The grey mare was plodding dutifully along on her treadmill, her ears plugged with wax-soaked rags.

They left the barn, dusting themselves off. Old Paradis had a fine layer of blond dust among the bristles on his chin.

"It's cold," Askik said. He never knew how to make conversation with the untalkative foreman.

"That's winter," the other rejoined.

They walked together in silence for a time.

"Ya know," said Paradis, "there ain't much point in threshin' faster if there ain't more grain to thresh. Part of the harvest stayed outside this autumn. We need more place t'put it. I been tryin' t' talk t' Monsieur Sancy 'bout it, but I ain't had the chance..."

"I'll speak to him," Askik said.

"I do my best, y'know, but I ain't the master."

"You'll get your storage."

"Good. You gimme some hope. It's time Vieilleterre had an intendant."

"I'm not the intendant."

"And while you're at it, remind 'im the sugarhouse burnt down last summer. If he wants sugar, it's time to build now."

"I'll give him the message, but I'm not the intendant. I'm going back to Montreal tomorrow."

"Hmmpf! Well, since you're goin' that way, stop an' have a word with Dubois up the road. His fences are a mess and 'is cows are into our barley whenever they git a chance."

"I'll remember that."

They had arrived at the foreman's house. Askik was about to go on his way when Madame Paradis came flying out, a shawl thrown hastily round her shoulders.

"M'sieur Mercredi, good day to you. Here," she said, handing him a package, "give this to Mademoiselle Céline, would you? It's a bit o' sewin' she asked me to do for Madame."

Askik took the package grudgingly. It was irritating to have a liaison between him and Céline taken for granted. That embarrassing scene after mass had started a buzz of rumours about them. It was even being said that Céline had come close to fainting during mass because she was pregnant.

"Tell 'er *bonjour* from me," Madame Paradis said, shivering from cold.

Askik turned his back and strode away.

"Queer duck," Madame Paradis muttered to her husband.

"He'll make a good intendant, though."

"I ain't so sure," she said as she hurried back to her kitchen, "once a savage, always a savage."

250

Askik put the package down in the kitchen. Céline was shuffling jars in the larder; he left without speaking to her. Taking a shortcut through the dining room, he met Rosalie, who was putting away a pile of freshly starched napkins. When she saw him enter, the fat girl stood up hastily.

"Monsieur Hubert left this mornin'," she announced, plainly consumed with curiosity. "A letter came askin' 'im to go."

"Left for where?"

"Montreal." And as if anticipating the next question, she added with a knowing roll of her eyes, "Mademoiselle Élisabeth ain't goin' till tomorra."

A rush of elation swept over Askik. Élisabeth was staying until the next day. They would be travelling together, then. She could have gone with Hubert but she wanted to wait for me, he told himself.

He flew like the wind to his room, picked up a book of poetry and threw himself full length on the bed. Though he tried to focus on the poetry, all he could hear was the tumult inside him. She loved him, there was no longer any doubt. She had chosen him. He had won! Hubert had gone back to Montreal with his tail between his legs, pretending business reasons. The cousin must have put his question the night before and been turned down.

He thought he would go wild with happiness. He longed to throw wide the windows and shout his victory to the whole parish. Instead, to calm himself he made an effort to absorb some poetry. How dull and pompous were these words compared to the feelings he was afire with! Finding nothing in this collection of poems that could faithfully translate this new and authentic joy, he jumped up, went to his desk, took up a pen and began feverishly to write; he fancied himself something of a poet. He traced in big, flowing letters the name "Élisabeth" at the top of the page, then, pausing at the first line of his poem, was surprised that the rest did not come by itself. He scribbled a few words and crossed them out. He was ready to burst with love yet his inspiration never progressed beyond, "My love, my beloved, my turtle dove..." He kept writing, scratching out, then crumpling sheets of paper three-quarters clean and flinging them savagely into the wastebasket. Little by little, by dint of scratchings out and paper consumed, his excitement waned. Finally, exhausted but now calm, he ceased his efforts.

On his way down to dinner, he was again feeling the serene, confident happiness he had known several days earlier. He chided himself for his doubt, for letting himself be upset by so little.

A lover loves the whole world. Passing Céline on the stairs, he gave her a look of warmth and kindness, forgiving her wholeheartedly for the embarrassment she had caused him. He hoped that one day she would know the same happiness that he was sharing with Élisabeth.

And yet, during dinner, Élisabeth said not one word and gave not one look intended for him alone: exaggerated discretion, Askik judged, but how could he tell her so? How radiant with excitement she was over tomorrow's departure! She was twice as pretty as she had been at midnight mass because she was turned out more simply. Her blond hair, drawn attractively to the back of her neck, shone like a beautiful fabric held near an oil lamp. She was bestowing smiles to right and left as she talked about the soirees, concerts and plays awaiting her in Montreal. In this torrent of chatter, Hubert's name cropped up rather often, but after all, Askik thought, it was a virtue to have a sense of family, too. He even felt a twinge of sympathy for the hapless cousin.

"Alexis," Monsieur Sancy said between slices of mutton, "You've been to the threshing barn? Things are going better?"

"Much better, yes, but we need more grain storage."

"So? Can we afford it?"

"Yes, although prices have been a bit weak this year."

"So have it built."

"And the sugarhouse?"

"That too. You can order the wood from the sawmill. Go and hire carpenters in the village tomorrow."

"But... I'm going back to Montreal tomorrow."

Monsieur Sancy pursed his lips, his fork suspended over his plate. Then he said, "All right," and went on with his meal.

After dinner, when Élisabeth and Askik had gone upstairs to pack, the Sancy parents stayed sitting at the table.

"What are you looking at me like that for?" Eugène Sancy said to his wife.

"You're not going to have me believe you don't know what the harvest brought in."

"I know what it brought in."

"Or that you needed more grain storage."

"I knew that too, but it's time to have our Alexis educated in these things, get him involved in seigneury business. Besides, he has a feel for the land, Paradis says so."

"Bah! Paradis!"

"A good man, but he's no accountant. That's why I need an intendant. If my plans work out, I'll have less time to spend on farming. I've been neglecting Vieilleterre. Somebody should be looking after it full time."

"Alexis sees himself bein' a lawyer."

"No, he belongs on the land.

"Then why are you lettin' him go back to town?"

"It's the off-season. I'll get him back for seeding. I want to work him in bit by bit. I've asked Paradis to bring him in on all the everyday decisions. As long as they get my permission for expenditures, of course."

"Élisabeth was very disappointed not to leave today," Madame Sancy remarked, coming back to her favourite subject.

"It wouldn't have been proper. If we send her with Alexis we won't have gossip. People think of Alexis and Élisabeth as brother and sister."

Askik could not sleep. How could he sleep when the next day's journey and his whole future promised so much? He had plans for such marvellous things and was impatient to begin. He had resolved to be an excellent husband and a gentle, wise father. He would become a great lawyer, and why not a great statesman too? He was sure he had the soul of an orator — or better still, a conciliator. He was the scion of two enemy races; who better than he could unite the disparate peoples of Canada? "Blessed are the peacemakers," he remembered with a shiver of excitement, "for they shall be called the sons of God." He gave something close to a sob of happiness and thanked God for having at last revealed his vocation.

His room seemed small and stifling. He snatched up his coat, slipped downstairs with as little noise as possible, and went out through the kitchen. A swirl of icy vapour formed when he pushed open the outside door. How cold it was! Not a breath of wind, not a sound. Everything was hard, rigid, frozen. The trees were not stirring a twig, lest they break the instant they moved. Even the glitter of the stars was steady.

Askik brushed the snow off a small bench under a massive elm tree. He chuckled to think of Hubert all warmly tucked up in his rich man's bed in Montreal. Hubert would certainly not have come outside on a cold night like this.

He took from his pocket an elegant little pipe that Madame Sancy had given him for Christmas. The burning tobacco's sizzle and the puffs of smoke he was sending into the night reminded him of another time.

"*Atsahkossak!*" he murmured, looking up at the stars. How far away it all was now! How far he had come since then! What an unlikely journey! Where were his parents? Were they still alive? Had they any idea what a prodigious course their child was embarking on? And Mona? He smiled. During his first years in Montreal he had often thought of that courageous little girl. Her example had comforted him. Where was she today?

The cold drove him from under his elm tree. Walking back to the house, he cast his eye about the countryside of this Quebec, so populated, so industriously worked, so human.

How good it is to be here! he thought.

4

The next morning he climbed into the carriole with the firm intention of declaring his love, revealing his plans for the future, and inviting Élisabeth to be part of it. Not for a minute did he doubt that she would be impressed by the generosity and grandeur of his ambitions.

Once settled in his place, however, he was overcome with shyness and said nothing. Élisabeth too sat silent, looking out the window in the door of the carriole, her thoughts on wings far ahead of the vehicle. Each tree left behind, each fence passed by, brought her a little closer to Montreal. She seemed to be trying to hasten the carriole's pace by sheer concentration; talking or reading would have been irksome distractions.

When the carriole stopped after barely a quarter of an hour, she flared up in protest.

"Why are you stopping?" she cried to the driver on the box outside.

"This here's the Dubois', mam'selle. The gentleman has to talk to 'em 'bout their fence-jumpin' cows."

"That's right, I'd forgotten," Askik said with a sigh as he got out. "I'll be right back."

What a relief it was to be outside! Their tête-à-tête had begun badly. Forging across the yard with hands in his pockets and head down, he almost collided with the neighbours' little cabin: unsquared log walls, roof of split stumps, canvas windows. The Dubois did not live opulently. Just beyond, surrounded by manure, was a shed that served for stabling cows and sheep. A few bony cows, muddy to their haunches, were rubbing against trees that they had long since debarked and killed. A lone sheep was trailing its feculent wool across the yard.

"Who's there?" a man called when Askik knocked at the door.

"My name is Alexis Mercredi. I'm here on behalf of your neighbour, Monsieur Eugène Sancy."

The door opened on a short, thin man with dishevelled grey hair. He was wearing dark trousers held up by suspenders. His underwear served as a shirt. On his feet he had woollen socks. Behind him in the semi-darkness, Askik thought he could see two or three human shapes.

"Whadizzit?" Dubois demanded gruffly. He spoke with a sound of popping bubbles, as if his lungs were full of mud. Askik could not keep his eyes off his thin ribs and the yellow hairs protruding from the neck of his union suit.

"Your fences are in bad shape, Monsieur Dubois. Last summer your cows got into our fields..."

"*Our* fields?"

"I am the intendant of Vieilleterre."

"First I heard o' it."

"It's recent. To get back to your cows, you're going to have to keep them on your side, so I suggest you repair your fences this spring..."

A fit of coughing suddenly had Dubois bent in two. In the time it takes to say it, he went scarlet. He kept gasping for breath, face crimson, veins standing out in his neck. For a minute Askik thought his neighbour was going to die on the spot. When Dubois finally straightened, he said simply, "Can't."

"Well then, your children?" Askik looked about in the semi-darkness of the cabin.

"Dead."

"You have friends, relatives. Organize a *corvée*, a fencing bee." Dubois did not reply. He stared at the visitor sardonically. Now that his eyes had become accustomed to the gloom, Askik could make out a woman sitting on the edge of the bed and someone very old, man or woman, wrapped in a blanket, head resting against the back of a rocking chair. He was worried about letting in the cold and made as if to enter and shut the door behind him, but Dubois blocked his way, not budging an inch. Anyway, it was barely warmer inside than out, and inside there was a pervading, insufferable odour of excrement. Obviously the old person was incontinent.

"Anythin' else?" Dubois demanded.

"Come now, Monsieur Dubois," Askik said, trying to look

compassionate. The man was pitiable, but he had to be reasonable. "You can't let your cows go wrecking your neighbours' fields. Put yokes on them, that won't cost anything. Hire a kid from the village to watch them..."

Dubois closed the door in his face, not brusquely but quietly, calmly as if his visitor had ceased to exist. Askik stayed standing in front of the door for a moment, not sure what to do. Then he retraced his steps across the small yard. The elms whistled mournfully among their drifts of snow. Far off in the fields, earth and sky mingled in the grey of winter.

"How dismal it is in the country!" Askik thought. "How cold it is!" He could not wait to be back among the lights of the city.

They set off again in bad humour. Élisabeth was indignant that she had had to wait. Askik thought she was put out because he had not declared himself, but his visit to the Dubois establishment had destroyed his desire to talk of love just now.

They entered the city at nightfall. As the streets passed, Askik's mood grew darker. The journey was ending and he had still said nothing, confessed nothing. Élisabeth, on the other hand, was growing livelier by the minute. She was naming off the streets, shops and restaurants, looking for familiar faces among the passersby, exclaiming over elegance of dress and pealing with laughter at garb which she found in poor taste. When they came to the wealthy neigbourhoods, she declared that there was nothing finer than these great, gas-lit houses behind their centuries-old trees. When the carriole stopped at last in front of the Sancy residence, she planted a sisterly kiss on Askik's cheek and, laughing happily, ran up the steps two by two.

Askik lived a long way from here, in the lower town. Nevertheless, he dismissed the carriole driver and set out for home on foot. The dark streets, the dirty snow, the dying daylight over the river perfectly matched his mood; he wanted to make the most of it all, to wallow to the eyeballs in his gloom.

What was his surprise to see a lank figure coming up the hill, thin as a scarecrow, dressed in a long black cape that flapped dramatically around him.

"Monsieur Mercredi," the man in black intoned, "good evening to you."

"Maître de Meauville," Askik replied, "greetings to you!"

"Does my presence in this neighbourhood surprise you? I'm on my way to Le Boeuf's, meeting friends. Join us."

It was less an invitation than a command. Askik accepted. He was suddenly craving to live, drink and cause havoc in revenge for his deplorable day. He seized his friend's arm impulsively.

"Dear Mercredi, I'd say you were in a mood to break dishes and jaws tonight."

"I'll settle for the dishes."

"Why stop at that?"

In his Grim Reaper costume, de Meauville's face was even paler than usual, while in the fading daylight Askik's skin looked almost black. Seeing the two of them approach, more than one pedestrian crossed the road.

"We're frightening people, brother Mercredi. Your Iroquoian demeanour is being noted."

Le Boeuf was Joe Beef, an Irishman, a former soldier of His Majesty, who had learned to cook in the trenches at Sebastopol. There were always two cauldrons steaming in his kitchen, one containing soup and the other meat. Dinner cost fifteen cents and a bed for the night could be had for little more.

The restaurant was full. Seated at long tables, a motley crowd was tucking away identical meals. Labourers, coal-handlers, sailors, stable boys and even a few newly-arrived and as yet unemployed farmworkers. Walking between the long rows, Askik and de Meauville smelled successively coal dust, horse dung, sawdust and wheat chaff.

A group of students had taken possession of one end of a table at the front of the room. De Meauville approached and, throwing back the hood of his cape with poetic flair, greeted them with a recitation from Louis Fréchette.

> And so we dreamed of glory, fortune, love...
> And, since for dreamers nothing is begrudged,
> We carved out fiefdoms in the moon above
> While off to supper on the cuff we trudged.*

No one paid much attention.

"I make no impression any more," de Meauville growled as he sat down. "Take my advice, Mercredi: never become an old young man, it bores people. There, that's my advice for the evening. Now I have a request: could you lend me fifteen cents? Thankyou, my prince. So, how was your sojourn at Vielleterre? Still smitten with your heiress?"

---

*Louis Honoré Fréchette, "Reminiscor."

"More than ever," Askik replied. Soup, stew and beer were being placed before them. "And I have every reason to believe she loves me too," he continued.

The Speaker made a wry face.

"Do you have proof she loves you?"

"No proof, but there are signs."

"Signs!" de Meauville snorted. "Impressions, likelihoods. Fancies riding on possibilities..."

"How do you know?" Askik was piqued. The Speaker was probably jealous.

"She has a rich cousin," de Meauville retorted, "very rich..."

"So?"

"So you've got nothing; a measly little apprenticeship to a law firm."

"I'm the intendant of Vielleterre."

De Meauville stopped, open-mouthed.

"Is that true? You're the intendant?"

"It's true," Askik muttered as if owning up to something shameful. "They're teaching me the business of the seigneury."

De Meauville appeared to be reflecting on this. His bantering attitude vanished and his face showed a rare directness. He leaned forward and gently placed a hand on his companion's wrist.

"That's very nice, Alexis, very nice. Congratulations. You're going to live in the country. I envy you."

"They want me to marry a servant."

"So... she's not a hag?"

Askik shrugged.

De Meauville tightened his grip on Askik's wrist.

"Do it! You've got no family and no money. Stop mooning over Élisabeth, they won't give her to you. Sancy's offering you a job. Take it. A wife? All the better! What are you afraid of? You won't be tied and bound to the land. Lawyers are needed in the country too. In a few years you've have your own farm, your own mill or your own sawmill. You'll be your own master."

Askik shuddered. He had been thinking big and he was being told to settle for much less.

"Hey, friend," de Meauville called to the waiter in English, "again beer!" He turned back to Askik. "I'm full of advice tonight, Mercredi. Here's one last piece. I'm giving it to you free, for nothing, out of love. At each stage of life a train comes by, Mercredi. You can get on board and accept what it brings you to, or you can let it go by. It won't ever come by again, though. Your train's in the station now. If you stay standing on the platform waiting for something better, you might end up sorry you didn't take the first one."

"You're talking rubbish, de Meauville."

"No. I'll recapitulate. The genteel birth you didn't have, the schooling you didn't have, the nicely turned ankle you spied one night at the ball and never got to fondle, you can't go back and fix any of that. It's done with. Finished. Get on with what's next!"

Askik was drinking too much, knew it, and ordered another pitcher of ale. The students too had pushed away their plates and were drinking hard. There was so much noise the customers had to lean across the table to hear and be heard. A carter was blowing his lungs out into a mouth organ while others were pounding in time on the table. As the ale and gin flowed, angry voices began to rise. The pungent smoke of coarse green tobacco hung about the oil lamps.

De Meauville gave up trying to make himself understood, either because he had lost hope of having Mercredi listen to reason or because he was tired of shouting. At the next table, some stalwarts were arm wrestling and bellowing like bulls.

"Mar-tin, Mar-tin, Mar-tin," the students chanted when they saw the burly notary from Beauce threading his way among the tables. They only dared poke fun at him when they were in their cups. Martin made a face and was about to leave, but when he saw Mercredi and de Meauville he came to join them. There were not enough chairs at the table; Martin took one from the neighbours, Irish immigrants who protested vociferously. He produced his tobacco pouch, filled his pipe and drew several puffs before speaking.

"Hullo, Mercredi. There's someone lookin' fer you. A bum was enquirin' after you at your roomin' house. Your landlady's been squawkin' all over the neighbourhood about it."

"What did he want?"

"Didn't say."

"Will he be back?"

"Didn't say that either."

The Irishmen were conferring, hands shielding their words and throwing malevolent glances at Martin.

"What's new?" the notary asked; for all his size and strength, he was inclined to leave the burden of conversation to others.

"Be advised," de Meauville said, "that you are addressing the intendant of Vieilleterre."

"Hmmm." Martin nodded approvingly.

"But monsieur isn't sure he wants the job," de Meauville continued.

Martin shook his head in disapproval.

"That's what I told him. They're even offering him a wife."

More approving nods.

"But monsieur wants the heiress."

Martin made a weary face, tilted back on his chair and gazed up at the ceiling.

"Well, worthy sir, what think you? Should he spurn the servant for the mistress?"

Martin thought for a moment and then took his pipe out of his mouth.

"One ass is as good as the next," he said.

"Crudely put, but true."

Thereupon, Martin disappeared. His chair slipped. He crashed to the floor with a resounding "whoomp." The students froze. The Irishmen split their sides laughing.

Martin was not yet on his feet when he threw his first punch. The victim took it full in the ribs and doubled up with a cry of pain.

The crowd exploded, in a twinkling split into Irish and French patriots. And providing unexpected spice, there were also some English sailors whom everyone could have a go at. Pitchers and curses in three languages were hurled. The donnybrook was shaping up to record proportions when Joe Beef, the tavern owner, came out of his private rooms. Seeing that the fire had got too hot to put the lid on, he called the waiter.

"C'mon Jimmy, let's get the girls."

The girls, who were having a nap in the cellar, were affectionate and playful and enjoyed nothing better than to come for a romp upstairs where all that exciting noise was coming from.

"Go to it, my pretties, have fun!"

The waiter was waiting nervously at the top of the stairs.

"Okay, Jimmy," he heard Joe Beef call, "open up!"

Jimmy did not need to be told twice. He shot through the door from the cellar, crossed the room in three strides and shut himself in the kitchen. The tavern's habitués took note of his move and began heading for the street. The rest were too busy giving each other black eyes to see the bears come in.

Malvina was the more mischievous of the two, which was why she wore a muzzle. When she saw two fighters locked in embrace on the floor, she rose on her hind legs, advanced a few steps and crashed down

260

on top of them. Mary, meanwhile, cleared the student section more methodically. She tackled one row at a time, delighting to see the bipeds leaping away like grasshoppers. She loped over to the door periodically to keep them from escaping too quickly. Yet for all her precautions, her fun was not to last; in the time it has taken to tell the story, the room had emptied and the worthy Joe Beef was putting a padlock on the door. The only customers left were the two combatants whom Malvina had knocked out, and they were no fun for anyone any more. Mary sat up on her haunches and voiced a protracted moan.

5

The tiny Rue Saint-Vincent is like a hyphen between the marketplace and the courthouse, between the commercial and contentious, if you will. In 1884, lawsuits were in fashion. From eight in the morning until six at night, the little street rang with the anxious steps of plaintiffs and respondents clutching writs of summons, vacant-eyed, absorbed in their own anxieties. And although the street was infested from one end to the other with lawyers and notaries, there were days when you would swear that half the pedestrians were hurrying to the premises of Maîtres Leclerc and Juneau. For all his splitting headache, Askik therefore had little chance of spending a quiet morning. As he entered the overheated office, a generous taste of ale crept up his throat.

"Well, if it isn't Mercredi!" exclaimed a tall clerk who was shovelling coal into the stove. "Your cheek's swollen. You must have been in a fight. And you're late."

Lecorbu loved to find fault with Mercredi. In the twenty years he had been drafting briefs and factums, procurations and contracts, he had never pleaded in court and never received an offer of partnership from his employers. His mania for detail and precise turn of phrase was his undoing. Scrupulous, hardworking and honest, he was the incarnation of the virtues that businessmen praise to the skies but which almost everyone does happily without. Lecorbu could not understand why his career had come to a standstill and resented a devil-may-care, imprecise and rather lazy Métis getting ahead of him.

"I hope you weren't at Joe Beef's last night," he sniffed. "There's going to be the devil to pay. Two men hurt. Beef's in court. It's a disgrace. A disgace! Are you ill, Mercredi?"

"Look, Lecorbu, I'm going to the Richelieu for a coffee. I'll be back in..."

"Tut, tut. What about Madame Gingras? Have you forgotten her?"

No, he had not forgotten her. He could see her already through the window, a plump little octogenarian walking up Rue Saint-Vincent, blowing at snowflakes that were impudently landing on her muff.

"By the way," Lecorbu said, "someone asked for you during your absence. A ragamuffin. Very dirty."

"Who was it?"

"He didn't leave a name. He said he'd be back. I haven't seen him since. Just as well."

Askik spent most of the morning untangling one of the innumerable wrangles between Madame Gingras and her debtors. When at last he could escape, he ran all the way to the Richelieu, leaving his coat behind to put Lecorbu off the scent.

The restaurant was almost empty. The waiters were setting the tables for lunch. Only a few idlers were lingering after breakfast. One of them, a young man with handlebar moustaches and a suit too pale for the season, wiggled his pince-nez in recognition. Askik frowned and pretended not to have seen him, but the other called, "Ho there, old boy!" so loudly that Askik hastened to join him, if only to shut him up.

"Mercredi!" Grandet exclaimed. "You're looking awful this morning! Waiter! Some coffee and very greasy eggs for this sinner! Had an eventful night? Hope you weren't at Beef's. The whole town's talking about it. I can hardly believe it: two scoundrels crushed by a bear! Ha, great fun! What strange customs we have!" As usual, his French was peppered with English words and phrases. "So," he continued, "you're not working today? Like me. Business is slow. Still, never mind, things will get better."

Askik was not in the mood to suffer optimists. "Why would things get better, Grandet?" he growled.

"Because they ought to, old boy! Ah, here's your breakfast. Will you allow me to go back to my paper? My cigar doesn't bother you, does it? Capital!"

Askik was trying to swallow a trial morsel of fried egg when Grandet sat bolt upright and gave a shout from behind his newspaper.

"Great day! Gordon's in the Sudan!"

"Who's Gordon?" Askik asked resignedly, pushing away his plate and pouring another cup of coffee.

"What?" Grandet cried, lowering his paper. "What? Charles Gordon? Chinese Gordon?" He looked up at the ceiling as if expecting it to come down on his head. "Come on, Mercredi, he's the Empire's greatest military commander."

"Grandet," Mercredi said, putting a hand over his eyes, "I've never met a French Canadian who takes more interest in the affairs of the British Empire than you."

"But we must! English, French, Métis, Indian — we're all subjects of Her Majesty, all servants of the Empire. Think of it — all these races united in a single civilizing and fraternal family! What a fine and noble purpose! Besides, you yourself, dear boy, have more connection with it than any of us."

"How's that?"

"Two years ago, when our army conquered Egypt, who was the commander?"

"Gordon?"

"Wolseley!" Grandet's tone was triumphant. "Sir Garnet Wolseley, the very man you met! The Sudan's a great desert bordering on Egypt. Its people have been fanaticized by a certain Muslim Mahdi. To ensure the safety of her new Egyptian subjects, Her Majesty has to pacify the Sudan. Who did she send to do it?"

"Wolseley?"

"Gordon!" Grandet's face glowed. "Gordon, who's a close friend of Wolseley. You see, it all fits together, and it all affects you personally!"

"Hasn't there been a battle there already?"

Grandet's face fell and he looked away. "Last summer, unfortunately. At El Obeid. Colonel Hincks and his ten thousand men, annihilated. Ten thousand brave men, fallen on the field of honour."

"How many men d'you suppose Gordon has?"

"He's gone there alone. The only way to answer those savages!"

"I hope they can appreciate that. If you'll excuse me, Grandet, I have to get back to the office."

"Of course, old chap! I've enjoyed our little conversation. We must do it again."

Askik was not out of the room before Grandet had his nose back in his news of the Empire, that vast amalgam of nations in which nothing happened that did not affect him personally.

When he returned to the office, Askik ran headlong into Lecorbu, who was visibly enraged.

"Mercredi! I demand that you rid us of that wretch! He's tarnishing this office and frightening the clients. Madame Ladouceur nearly had a nervous breakdown when she met him on the stairs."

"Who are you talking about?"

"That tramp who came yesterday. The one who's looking for you."

"He came back?"

"In your absence, which has been noted, let it be said in passing."

"He didn't leave any name, any message?"

"Nothing. In too much of a hurry. He kept looking over his shoulder. Very edgy. An habitual criminal, I'd bet my right hand on it. I've seen other ruffians of his kind. I didn't mince words with him. He won't be back here in a hurry."

"Quite right too. A criminal in a lawyer's office, that's not proper."

"Exactly! We practice good, clean law here!"

For several days Askik expected further sign of the stranger, then forgot about him. He was preparing his first case. It was a crashingly commonplace matter. In order to wake up the judge and sensitize him to the entire gravity of what was at stake, he had prepared an eloquent exposition in which he tied the circumstances of the case to the very basis of the Civil Code. "Your Honour," he was planning to say, "the integrity of the principles of Contract, of the Code and of Justice itself depends on your judgment." He was imagining a judge wearied and jaded by mean-minded bickerings and lawyers' platitudes, a judge saying to himself, If I hear *dura lex sed lex* once more I'll kill somebody; he was imagining this judge being suddenly reminded of the true meaning of his role and thereupon discovering fresh new interest in the case before him.

He admitted it to no one, but the feeling of being destined for a work of great import was constant these days. How otherwise could it be explained that fate had brought him out of the wilds, placed him in a rich and cultivated family, introduced him to the very inner workings of power, the Law and money? Could Providence have engineered such a meeting of capability and opportunity for nothing? He admitted sometimes, in all honesty, that it could all have been pure happenstance, that this extraordinary preparation might not in fact have an end in view, but it was hardly conceivable.

It was the kind of day best spent at home. The light of the sun had gone out in midcourse. Snow swirled about in darkened courtyards. The wind raced in from across the river, stumbled into the little Rue Saint-Vincent, kicked at the windows and passed on through with a scolding howl. Lecorbu had lit the lamps earlier than usual and was on his knees in front of the stove, trying to persuade the smoke to venture outside. Askik was sitting in boredom at his desk, his eyes blurring over a contract he was putting to rights. Even his own dreamy musings seemed colourless as this winter day drew to an end.

It was totally dark when an urchin bundled up in woollens knocked at the door, muttered a few indistinct words into the scarf tied around his face and disappeared.

"It's for you," Lecorbut said disdainfully as he handed a note to Askik; the paper was cold and crystals of snow still nestled in the folds.

Askik opened the letter, recognized the graceful hand of his friend de Meauville and read, "A miracle, brother, I have two tickets to Madame Albani's concert tonight. I shall await you at the Muses."

"Is it from the tramp?" Lecorbu wanted to know.

"Can you close up all alone tonight?" Askik asked him.

"Hmpff! I've been closing up the office for twenty years. Decide for yourself if I need your help."

"Apparently not," Askik rejoined, taking his coat.

A look of shocked disapproval crossed Lecorbu's face. "What, you're leaving this very minute? You haven't finished your work! Messieurs Leclerc and Juneau haven't left yet; they'll see that you're gone. They'll want an explanation from me." The old bachelor was spluttering with anxiety.

"Well, tell them I'll be in earlier in the morning," Askik replied.

He left the office whistling. Poor Lecorbu! Would he ever learn that bosses will forgive anything of employees who take advantage of them, and nothing of the old and reliable? Anyway, Askik owed his job to Eugène Sancy's influence. He was not afraid of his employers.

The law partners' carrioles were waiting at the door.

"It won't be long," Askik called to the half-frozen drivers. They raised their eyebrows as if to say, What do you know about it?

Askik was not wearing a scarf because he thought it childish. He was sorry for it as he walked the long distance along Rue Notre-Dame. With his head down and his hands over his ears, he did not notice as he passed the seminary where he had received the name Alexis.

"What's your name?" the priest had asked; he had the impenetrable accent of a Frenchman from France.

"Askik."

"That's your nickname. What's your name?"

"Askik."

"That's impossible. The priest who baptised you must have given you a Christian name. Think hard. Didn't anybody ever call you... Alexandre, Albert, Adelard, Alexis...?"

"Yes," Askik whispered.

"Alexis?"

"Yes." He liked the name, and since, where he had come from, one readily changed one's name with a change in condition, he quickly adjusted to Alexis.

"Alexis Mercredi..." the priest noted with satisfaction.

On stormy nights, as everyone knows, the signs over taverns swing in the wind, creaking poetically. The sign above Les Trois Grosses Muses was silent, rusted to its bracket. The faded letters spelled out an unimaginative name: À la Belle Fermière, À la Bonne Rincette or some such platitude as might appear half a dozen times on signs over the city's five hundred taverns. It was the students who had graced it with the name Les Trois Grosses Muses. Dead flies gathered dust in the window segments, the heating stove smoked and the three fat tavern-maid muses were ugly, but the students could do as they pleased there, pipes could be emptied on the floor, and constables rarely showed their noses.

De Meauville was sitting alone at a table by the hearth, sipping a hot scotch. He had draped his coat over the back of his chair and propped his boots on the hearth fender, a few inches from the soup cauldron.

"Ah, Mercredi! Happy to see you. I was afraid the big bad Lecorbu might have locked you up for the night. If you have no objection, we'll have a spot of dinner together before going to hear the illustrious Albani."

"Gladly. She's an Italian?"

"Canadian. A little lass from Chambly. She's made a fortune for herself overseas; it's an unappreciative country we live in. Here, I'll serve you," de Meauville said, stirring the soup in the cauldron. "This should save you a visit from the Furies. Well, my dear Mercredi, what's new?"

"Did you know that Gordon had entered the Sudan?" Askik asked gravely.

"How I'd love to be there!"

"All right, I'll let that one go."

"What I'm asking is what's new with you. In particular, I'm anxious to know if you're going to accept that job as intendant."

"That depends."

"That depends... on a certain young lady's plans for the future?"

"It amounts to that, yes."

"Have you talked to her?"

"No. Her parents are still in the country. I can't properly call on her in their absence."

"And as soon as her parents are back in town?"

"I'll get a note inviting me to dinner, as usual. I'll ask to talk to Monsieur Sancy. I'll let him know my intentions."

"You're going to ask for his daughter's hand?"

"No, not immediately. I want to... test the waters first."

"Excellent. I hope your eyesight's good."

"My eyesight? Why?"

"Our seats are in the last row."

They arrived late and had to grope their way to their seats in the dark. Marie-Emma Lajeunesse, alias Emma Albani, formerly of Chambly, Quebec, had begun the celebrated aria *La Somnambula*, which had sent her career skyrocketing outside Canada. Every last seat was filled. Braid, pearls and detachable starched collars were in evidence in the darkness at the orchestra level; in the boxes, like stars in the heavens above the common herd, there were diamonds. For the French-speaking on the orchestra level, the world-famous celebrity onstage was still Emma Lajeunesse, one of their own. The English-speaking in the boxes were seeing Madame Albani, an habituée at Court and personal friend to the distant, mythical Empress Victoria. The orchestra waited for the boxes to begin applauding first.

Askik was in seventh heaven. All he admired, all he coveted was here in this hot, stuffy theatre. He was elated to be sitting here among the bankers, industrialists and governors of Canada, like them enjoying a performance that nine-tenths of his compatriots would not have understood. The successive rows of the orchestra looked to him like rungs on a ladder. Even now he could see himself in the rows at the front, flanked by sons and daughters, with Élisabeth at his side. He would be nodding off to sleep after a hard day at Board meetings. She would smile indulgently and let him be. It would be nice to grow old this way.

He felt a surge of gratitude for these people who gave direction to the society, who led it, guided it and gave example. Could there be art without their knowledge of the world, traditions without their vigilance, music without their money? At once humbly and ecstatically, he reflected that he, Askik, would some day be called upon to serve them.

At intermission, once Madame Albani had left the stage, all eyes rose to the boxes. It was time to take a nobility count. No one bothered with knights any more; there were far too many, and some were even Canadian. Genuine aristocracy was the thing to seek out: rare, blue, imported blood.

Sooner or later, every gaze in the theatre eventually came to rest on the governor's box, with its swarm of English ladies in dark but sumptuous dresses, their daughters in cheerful colours and officers in black or scarlet tunics festooned with gold. Askik envied these young men their fine moustaches. The bitterest affliction of his life was to be beardless — a legacy from his Indian ancestors.

"Friend Mercredi," de Meauville whispered, "the time has come to turn your eyesight to account.

"How's that?" Askik demanded in a tone of annoyance; he expected more teasing, and off-colour too no doubt.

"In the first-tier box to the right," de Meauville pursued, "right by the stage. What do you see?"

Askik saw a young man barely older than himself in a Hussar's uniform, surrounded by a small clutch of admirers.

"Who is it?"

"A duke. One of Victoria's countless grandsons. On a sanctioned visit, far from his imperial granny. He's not the one we're interested in."

"De Meauville, you're going too far, I won't let you talk..."

Askik broke off in midsentence. Eugène Sancy had just entered the box and was having himself introduced. Well, he's in town after all, Askik thought in great surprise. Sancy turned, held out his hand toward the darkness and led forward... a dazzling Élisabeth. Her golden hair shone more brilliantly than any tiara.

When they saw her pass, the English ladies stopped talking and the greybeards adjusted their monocles. Only Élisabeth herself appeared unaware of the effect she was having. She went up to the duke, gave an off-hand little curtsey, and did not offer her hand to be kissed until His Grace held out his own. Everything about her seemed to be saying, I'm young and ignorant of the niceties of high society; I'm pleased to meet you but have no idea what your rank is. When the duke paid her a compliment, she turned to her father with a radiant smile, like a child asking if she may keep a present she has been given. She breathed such freshness around her, and with such artlessness, that the hearts of the sternest matrons felt the touch of a warm May zephyr. An elderly lady in the duke's entourage took her to sit beside her and told her her French accent was charming. Like a little girl with no thought yet of love,

Élisabeth gave the duke no further glance, but conversed happily with the elderly ladies, who became as lighthearted as she. The duke made a show of being interested in the many visitors pressing forward to be presented, eager to shake his hand, but as the women approached his eyes kept straying back to the pretty French Canadian. When the curtain was about to rise again, the ladies insisted she stay with them, shooing her father away and promising to take good care of her; the master of Vieilleterre went back to his seat alone.

When the houselights dimmed and the darkness descended on Askik like a balm. In the space of a few minutes, a violent storm had laid waste, devastated all inside of him. He heard Madame Albani's trills as if they were loud bursts of laughter coming from another room. Strangely, his outward behaviour continued to be perfectly normal; he kept exchanging small talk with de Meauville while all was crumbling within, kept on surveying the concert audience while hearing his own bellows of pain. What was his condition, then — the real one? Was he dying or was he unscathed? Stunned or indifferent? Should he leave the theatre whistling tuneful melodies or go and throw himself under a train? Rage, insouciance and pain took hold of him by turns in such dizzying succession that he could not pin any of them down. Like the colours on a roulette wheel. Perhaps he should wait until the wheel stopped on a single emotion and then decide. Indifference, I'll go out and have a beer. Pain, I'll kill myself.

As he left the theatre he saw the Sancy's carriole and team. Eugène Sancy was about to get in when he saw the young Métis approach.

"Ah, Askik, you were at the concert? Divine, wasn't it? What a voice!"

"I didn't know you were in town."

"We've been here a few days. You must come and see us. My wife will write you. Besides," Sancy added severely, "I have to talk to you; your employers are not pleased with you. But that can wait — it's freezing out here! Let's go, Georges. Good night, Alexis."

Élisabeth had said nothing. She had sat in the carriole with her face half-hidden in a woollen scarf, staring at Askik as if amused. Her shining eyes seemed to be saying, Did you see me? Wasn't I a sensation tonight? How I love this life!

When he saw her, Askik felt the wheel slow and then stop: pain.

De Meauville joined him. "Mercredi," he cried, "a grog to warm us up before bed. It's on me."

"Thankyou, no," Askik replied quietly, "I have to get to the office early tomorrow."

"Mercredi, are you all right?"

"Quite all right, de Meauville." And to prove it, he turned a steady and impassive gaze to his friend, a face in which absolutely nothing could be read. Another gift from his Indian ancestors.

He walked down Rue Saint-Paul as usual but when he reached his lodging he kept on going. He crossed the deserted wharves of the port and came at last to the St. Lawrence. What fury! The wind held absolute sway over the icy expanses of the river. What was merely gusting in the streets was tempest here. The snow raced through the darkness in clouds, like gigantic phantoms flying about the city's periphery. Askik thought of the things that had haunted his childhood, the wetiko, the tchipayuk that used to play in the fireplace in his house at night. He thought of how he had run from them, and of how he was rediscovering them now. A mere step away from Montreal and its concerts and lawsuits, Pennisk's and Numeo's First Earth was alive. Neither the banks nor the lawcourts, nor even the silly churches with their pretentious towers, would ever vanquish it. Askik turned to look one last time at Montreal, at those futile lights planted in earth that did not want them. Deep inside, he cursed the fate that had led him to this country, thrown him among these vainglorious strangers. He cursed the Sancys and their money, Élisabeth and her beauty, the English and their titles, the Hairy Faces and their waxed moustaches. Turning back to the river, he felt a painful longing for the prairies well up in him, the same stifling homesickness that had so often come to visit him in those first years at the seminary, and which he thought he had forgotten. He thought sadly of his parents, his house, his people.

I'm not very far away any more, he thought. Above this tempest lies the Way of the Wolf. Does it really lead to the eternal plains, to Pennisk's teepee? Why not? Why would the Hairy Faces be right about everything?

He went down onto the ice. How dark it was! He walked, looking for the big holes left by the ice merchants.

The snow was deep. He sank in at every step. He scolded himself for never having noticed where the icemen's sleigh tracks went. Even a man who wants to die can suffer from the cold. Pipon was having a ball. Askik put his gloved hands over his ears and soon his fingers were freezing too. Driving snow crystals slashed at his cheeks and forehead. His thighs felt like rock and his feet ached. When he turned around he could no longer see anything of the city; the snow had conjured it away. All the better, he thought. I'm lost. I'm alone. But where are those holes?

He walked and walked, each step an effort. The wind drew tears which then froze and sealed his eyelids. He took off his gloves to thaw the offending ice with his fingers, which were giving off less and less heat. He resigned himself to continuing with eyes half-closed, as if in a dream in which one senses approaching danger but cannot stay awake.

He stumbled against an embankment of snow and ice. There was a hollow on the other side. The icemen had spread straw on the water to keep the ice from forming too firmly.

That's it, he said to himself. Just have to jump. Have to go deep so the current will take me immediately. Can't be any chance of coming back. God, how I hurt! His half-frozen limbs screamed with pain. It'll soon be over, he promised them. No more cold, no more disappointments. He thought one more time of Élisabeth sitting in the carriole. Would she be sorry for her hard-heartedness? Would she blame herself for rejecting him?

But in fact, a voice inside him said, how is she going to know you killed yourself? That's true, he reflected. They'll think I just took off, went back to the Red River. I'll die for nothing. What a fool I am! What a failure!

But the voice spoke up again. Why do you say she rejected you? You haven't gone to see her, you haven't written to her. You're the one who has abandoned her.

"What about the duke?" Askik exclaimed. He clambered up the embankment and bent his knees, preparing to jump.

At the last minute, however, his body balked, the animal rebelled at the prospect of the icy water. If it was cold up here at the surface, what must it be like under the ice? The pernicious little voice persisted. Nothing's lost, nothing's decided, it said. Why does she have to consider you more important than other suitors? You should fight for her, win her, deserve her!

He turned his back to the hole and resolutely walked away. Suddenly he wanted to work whole nights through, rough up some pretty-faced dukes, command respect, create a huge fortune. The ice-sleigh track provided a firm, even surface. Soon he could see the lights of Montreal. I must have been walking in circles, he thought, surprised to have been so close to shore. Just hope I haven't frozen anything. This last was a galling thought. What good would all these new resolutions do if his face was going to be left deformed from freezing? What woman would accept him then? He covered his face with his hands and ran so hard that when he arrived home he was warm just about all over.

The next morning, he arrived at the office long before Lecorbu and worked so hard he surprised everyone.

6

The winter sun shone straight through the windows and illuminated nothing. The near-black woodwork, the grey marble, the khaki draperies soaked up the light of day like sponges. Over the door to the room, a yellowed engraving showed the empress forty years younger. The coal stove was roaring; the court employees were half-asleep with the heat and boredom.

The public benches were filled with tenants, grocers, investors, horse merchants. Some wore the self-righteous faces of victims; the rest showed the bravado of small-time cheats who keep working the same rackets and getting caught in the same traps. Both hunters and hunted were indignant to see their lawyers fraternizing on the other side of the bar while waiting for the judge.

"Stand! The Court is open. Monsieur le juge Duvernay is presiding. God save the Queen!"

A short man entered with heavy steps. His wig flapped against his flabby cheeks. He looked grumpy, not like a champion of justice preparing to punish the wicked but like a man not in the mood for work.

Each case was followed by the next with no change in tone. Plaintiffs and respondents came forward shyly, hat in hand. The lawyers talked incomprehensibly for a few minutes, the judge rendered his decision, and the parties left with their lawyers to have the judgment explained. Small justice for small grievances.

"Tremblay versus Lafontaine!" barked the clerk. "Who's representing the plaintiff?"

Askik cleared his throat. "I am... m'Lord." His voice was a thin, ridiculous tremolo. He was shaking from head to foot. This case which had looked so simple at first now seemed frightfully complex. He was sorry he had taken it. He was not ready for pleading. Lecorbu still knew best.

"Who's representing the respondent?"

"I am," a booming voice replied. A lawyer with a white mane and theatrical manner came to the lectern.

The judge rested his cheek on his hand. "Well, *maître*, what you got to say?" He had a peasant accent. He was nothing if not nonchalant.

"M'Lord," Askik began in a wavering voice, "My client, a butcher by trade, delivered on the fifteenth of July..."

"His name, *maître*."

"Beg your pardon?"

"Your client's name. He's got a name?"

"Tremblay, m'Lord, Arthur Tremblay."

"Go on."

"On the morning of the fifteenth of July, Monsieur Tremblay delivered two quarters of mutton to the restauranteur Albert Lafontaine, who left them in his yard. The meat spoiled, as is to be expected in midsummer. Monsieur Lafontaine refused to pay."

Askik was gaining confidence. He was even able to glance up at the judge now and then.

"This case, m'Lord, although simple in appearance, reflects profoundly on our civil law, and as I shall attempt to explain, on the very foundations..."

"You've got an acknowlegment?"

"M'Lord?"

"A receipt. Something acknowledging receipt of the meat."

"The parties had been doing business for years and got along without formalities. Moreover, if it had not been for the inexcusable negligence of the respondent, this harmonious situation would still pertain..."

"Does the respondent admit to receiving the meat?" the judge growled, turning to the other party.

The lawyer with the mane rose, turned back the cuffs of his gown with a flourish, pursed his lips and replied, "That the meat was in the yard, at a given spot, at a given time, we do not deny, but that there was negligence on the part of Monsieur Lafontaine, *that* we deny very emphatically."

"Was your client expecting the meat from the plaintiff that morning?"

"Mmm... yes, I believe so. But the meat was spoiled. *Mutatis mutandis*, that is."

"Well, seems to me your clients are both at fault. Monsieur Tremblay, in future get a receipt. Monsieur Lafontaine, you hafta look after what's delivered, eh? Okay, so I order the respondent to pay the plaintiff the price of one quarter of mutton. Court charges shared. Got that?"

The clerk nodded as he scribbled notes.

"You, *maître*," the judge said, suddenly turning to Askik, "you're new?"

"Yes, m'Lord."

"Next time do what counts first. Principles are fine. Receipts are better." The judge leaned toward the clerk. "Okay, how many left before lunch?"

Grandet was waiting at the door, pince-nez and cane at attention.

"Well done, old man! A promising start. What a mauling you gave that great booby! You're like me, you give 'em no quarter!"

"You've been pleading this morning?"

"No... no. I'm here poking round the cages. If the clients don't come to me, I track 'em down."

"You found some?"

"Two or three. A carpenter from St. Charles who knocked his wife's skull in with a hammer. Very promising. I've practically got it in the bag. So... lunch at the Richelieu to celebrate your baptism of fire?"

"Thank you, no, I've got work to do. Say, Grandet, what is it that attracts you to criminal law?"

"The drama of life, old boy! The passions of the lowly. The sordid details of life laid bare. The suspense of the accused waiting to see if he'll get freedom, prison or the noose."

"And it pays?"

"Oooh... moderately. But we criminal lawyers work first of all for love of our science. The courtroom is our laboratory." He gestured toward a closed door. "In this room, for example, a woman accused of killing her sister. She's ugly and the sister was beautiful. Both of them as dumb as their big toes. One day the ugly one pushes the beautiful one down the well and drops a rock on her head. The father thinks his beautiful daughter's skipped out and calls down all the devils of hell on her. A week later he finds the water tastes bad. The Crown prosecutor's asking for the noose, the defense is claiming insanity. Who'll win? Which one will outplay the other? And — though no one will ever really know — who's right? You have to admit it's more interesting than your butcher spats!"

"But it doesn't pay as well, does it?"

Grandet was pulling on a pair of kid gloves; very elegant and very ill-conceived for winter use.

"Mmmm... no," he allowed, examining the gloves on his hands, "it doesn't pay as well."

When he returned to the office, Askik found a note from Madame Sancy inviting him to dinner that evening. This was all he needed to make him feel on top of the world. Since his conversion on the St. Lawrence, everything had been working in his favour. His employers had praised him for his industriousness, he had pretty well won his first case, and now the Sancys were opening their door to him again. Even Lecorbu was showing him a little more respect, or at least was no longer sniffing audibly when passing his desk.

At six o'clock sharp, Askik put away his books and bid good night to Lecorbu with a very English mixture of curtness and courtesy, and hurried away. When he arrived home he flung open the door, ran up the stairs and was already on the second floor when he heard himself being called urgently.

"Monsieur Mercredi, there's a message for you!"

His landlady was waiting at the bottom of the stairs, a muscular woman with no sense of humour where propriety was concerned.

"I hope these here goin's-on are gonna stop pretty soon," she yelled. "Get your business with that bum over and done with and tell 'im never to come round my house no more!"

She handed him a rumpled piece of shapeless paper.

"He was gonna go away again like before without leavin' no word. I let 'im know what I thought o' manners like that. I told 'im to write down what he wanted to say and get the hell out. I don't want no police comin' to this house. This is an honest house, this is!"

Askik unfolded a piece of butcher's wrapping paper and read what was scrawled on it in barely legible pencil.

"A man wot wos gud ta ya long time go is in reel bad way an axed me tell ya. Cum to fowntin tmorro noon. Don let a gud frend down. Aint signin cuz I don wont no trubl."

"So is it sump'n important?" the landlady asked, pretending not to have read the note.

"Not specially. What did this man look like?"

"I told ya that already! Small, homely and dirty besides. Looked like a crook if y' ask me. I don't want no police here, mind."

"All right. I'll see him tomorrow. He won't be back."

Askik went up to his room. Who was this "gud frend?" What was the matter with him? Why did he have to communicate through such a beggarly go-between? He thought of all those who had helped or taught him since he had come to Montreal. They were all priests or merchants and none were likely to be "in a reel bad way." Something told him he should not be searching among his real benefactors, furthermore. He reread the note and frowned. The mystery was quickly becoming unpleasant. This unknown person was asking him to repay a debt of gratitude. What did he want? Money? Legal services? An introduction to the Sancys? Deep down, he was already feeling a germ of irritation with this impudent person who was so determined to collect for services long forgotten. And why choose a fountain as a meeting place in midwinter? Askik knew only one fountain, the one in Place d'Armes. He crumpled the note and threw it in the wastebasket.

His room was large and plainly furnished. His windows overlooked the Customs offices; if he craned his neck, he could see the harbour and the masts of ships caught in the ice. The furniture was sturdy, well matched and unpretentious. Madame Sancy had chosen an appropriate style for a young man who had reasonable means but had not yet made his fortune. Askik opened his armoire and took out a frock coat and trousers, a gold damask waistcoat, a white shirt and starched collar, and a black bow tie. The outfit had cost him a packet, but he was determined to be every bit as elegant as handsome cousins and visiting sprigs of nobility. He scrubbed his face with strong soap, gave his hair a thorough combing, then put on his new clothes, taking care not to crease anything. When the operation was completed, he looked at himself in the mirror and saw a young man typical of his race, taller than average, well-proportioned, with black hair and eyes. His healthy brown skin had a glow that stale office air and tavern food had not dulled. He was good-looking, he decided. And so he was.

Since everything was frozen in the streets, he had no fear for his trousers. He decided to walk and save the cost of a carriole ride.

As he left the house, he thought he saw a shadowy figure slip behind the corner of a building. The harbour was close by and it was not unusual to see vagrant sailors who had missed a departure. Most of these misfits took off for elsewhere with the coming of winter; this one might not have been able to ship out.

Askik walked quickly across Place d'Armes. I'll come tomorrow, he thought when his eye fell on the fountain with its ice-filled basins. Curiosity came to the fore and he thought briefly about his "gud frend" before turning his thoughts to Élisabeth. This time I won't be outdone, he promised himself. I'll play the calm, collected, confidant man. Women love men who don't need them. And if Hubert's there, I won't be shy any more. I'm taller than he is and stronger too. I'll make him feel my confidence. They'll see he's just a milquetoast beside me. Well... again!

A man had been hiding behind a hedge and, thinking he had been seen, had scurried away down a lane.

Someone's following me! Could it be the tramp, the messenger? Or a thief perhaps? Let him come! Askik gripped his cane with the spike tip.

He imagined himself arriving bloodied at the Sancys', a knife wound in his shoulder, but victorious, having knocked cold a notorious murderer. He would arrive escorted by constables... no, by the chief of police. He would be carried into the house where Élisabeth would dress his wound, fighting back tears but steadied by his courage. Now, here in the street, he turned, hoping fervently to be attacked, but there was no one to be seen. Where do the murderers go when you need them...?

He was surprised to see the Sancys' house so brightly lit. As he mounted the front steps he saw with bitter disappointment that the living room was full of people. He had expected to be the only guest and was discovering a large party in full swing.

"Alexis, here you are at last!" Madame Sancy kissed him maternally on both cheeks. "How nicely you're dressed, dear! You paid cash, I hope; there's nothing like getting into debt to ruin you young 'uns."

Eugène Sancy crossed through the entry hall, a tray of glasses in his hand and a flustered servant following.

"Alexis!" Sancy cried. "Happy to see you my boy! My, how elegant you are! As you can see, I'm doing the serving now."

The servant blushed all the way to her ears. "Monsieur took the tray out of my hands, Madame!"

"Thar, it's all yourn!" Sancy exclaimed with a guffaw, handing over the glasses. "Élisabeth, come and say hello to Alexis!"

Élisabeth wove a path among the guests and, smiling brightly, took Askik by the elbow.

"Here you are at last! Come quickly, there's someone here who says he knows you."

"Who's that?"

"It's a surprise."

"He's in the *grand-chambre?*" Askik asked, glancing suspiciously through the door.

"Now, Alexis," the young woman scolded, "*grand-chambre* makes you sound like a hayseed. Here we say *salon*. You're worse than Pépère."

The salon was full of light, music and mousseline. A quartet was playing reels and waltzes. Eugène Sancy knew nothing about music and had ordered light and lively things played. No whiny stuff. The greenhouse at Vieilleterre had been pillaged in order to put flowers on every table and in every corner. The guests were raising their spirits with champagne and sherry. They were talking loudly, not always listening to each other, and setting the chandeliers tinkling with their laughter. Élisabeth passed through the crowd with complete assurance, giving a nod here, a smile or pleasant word there. For all his determination, Askik was ill at ease. Everyone looked at him and no one wanted to look him in the eye. He was arousing curiosity; he felt like a rare species of animal, a well-trained savage in ceremonial dress. Me good Métis. Me talk good. Me not pee in spitoons.

There was a little clutch of people in the room who were not laughing and not even talking much, who even seemed bored. This was the group Élisabeth was leading him to. How beautiful she was! How she reigned over this company! At her ears were two diamonds set in gold; no doubt a present from her parents. Askik was feeling both the most intense happiness and the most excruciating anguish. The arm she had slipped insouciantly under his was round and pink and graceful; tiny blue veins were all but invisible under the skin. Her hands were delicate, lovely, yet she kept linking them any old way, as if saying, I know I'm beautiful and I don't need to pose.

"So... don't you recognize each other?" Élisabeth was smiling excitedly.

Askik was obliged to turn his attention to a thin, pale man sitting in the middle of the dull group. He felt something stir inside him; perhaps this skinny fellow was in fact familiar, but it was so irritating to have to share Élisabeth that he made no effort to recognize him. The man stood up. He was taller than Askik and had pock-marked cheeks, a razor-burned neck and bad teeth. He peered at Askik through thick glasses. He seemed as displeased as Askik with this meeting.

"Hello, Askik," the stranger said, using the Métis name. "Don't you remember me? Étienne Prosy."

Askik almost fell over backwards. For a moment he stood open-mouthed, looking at his former teacher. He heard Élisabeth chattering beside him and caught phrases like "great poet," "returned from exile," and "how small the world is," but could not retain the rest. He was afraid his whole past was about to be unwrapped and displayed to an audience hungry for diversion, but Prosy's demeanour was reassuring. He too seemed ill at ease; he too was anxious to draw a line through his years at the Red River.

Élisabeth, however, was launched on a campaign to animate this dour group, the one note of ennui at her party.

"It's incredible for them to meet again here, just like that, isn't it?" she said, addressing all the guests in the circle. "How long is it since you lost sight of each other?" she persisted, with the enthusiasm of a child asking for a story.

"Ohhh... fifteen years?" Prosy ventured. "More or less."

"Fifteen years!" Élisabeth looked around at the guests with an expression of delight. Her stratagem was working. Other guests were coming to join the group, glasses in hand.

"And you were Alexis's teacher? But what was that you called him a minute ago?"

"Askik," Prosy replied. He was becoming conscious of being the centre of attention. "I was very young myself at the time," he added.

"Askik!" Élisabeth laughed, putting her hand on the young Métis' arm. "You never told me you had a name like that!"

Askik forgave her on account of the hand.

"What does Askik mean?" she asked.

Askik wagged his head vaguely. "Nothing special, I think..."

"On the contrary," Prosy interjected, "the beauty of Indian names is that almost all of them have meanings. I've studied the Indian languages somewhat, you know. Askik, I believe, means "cooking pot," does it not?"

Everyone laughed. Not that there was unkindness meant, but all that wine was having an effect. And it's not every day that one meets a Cooking Pot Mercredi. Élisabeth laughed harder than all the rest, and with tears in her eyes amiably patted Askik's arm.

"Come on now," she scolded him, "don't take it seriously. Askik's an attractive name." And she pealed with laughter again.

Askik managed a little smile. He did not want to appear piqued. His boyhood name had another, deeper significance, but he was in no mood to hold forth. He tried to loosen his jaws, relax his hands and be amused.

"In general, native names are quite picturesque," continued Prosy. "The name 'Mercredi,' for instance, a deformation of the Scottish McCready or MacGregor, is colourful in itself but is also a singular example of predisposition. Since Mercredi, or Wednesday," he expounded lightheartedly, "is halfway between Sunday and Saturday, and the Métis himself is halfway between two cultures..."

This was becoming less amusing. Élisabeth steered Prosy onto another subject.

"Monsieur Prosy," she said to the assembled guests, "has just returned after spending several years abroad…"

"Alas, yes. I was associated with the provisional government in 1869. When the enemy arrived, I chose exile. In Chicago, in fact. But as you know, I continued to speak to my country through its newspapers, which earned me opponents of some influence here."

"Brave fellow, showing your face here!" said a cynical voice.

"A true love of nation, my young friend, is undaunted by threats."

Conversation thereupon stopped, and since the quartet chose this precise moment to change scores, an embarrassing silence fell over the room. Prosy glanced around him, realising he was losing his audience. He backtracked.

"Do you remember, Askik, how in the evening after classes you used to be afraid to go home? Because of — what was it? The wetiko?"

It was quiet enough for the whispered commands of the quartet leader to be heard, and then the music started and the guests turned away and began to talk about the snow and the coming summer. Élisabeth bestowed a magnanimous smile on the dull little group and fled to the other side of the room. Prosy had had his moment of glory.

Askik got up and went to find something to drink. He crossed the *grand-chambre*, being careful not to meet anyone's eye. He considered taking his coat and leaving, but indignant departures of this nature invariably fall flat. What should he do, then? Land two good slaps on Prosy's pale cheeks and throw him out in the snow? That would be overdoing it. After all, what had Prosy done except to remind people of what everybody knew, that Alexis Mercredi was a Métis? I was deluding myself, he thought; I'm the only one here who thinks of me as an elegant young French Canadian. Or else, perhaps the guests did not really think his race important. They had laughed at his childhood name the way they would laugh at their own schoolboy nicknames. He reproached himself for his inept reaction, for having seemed vexed or ill-tempered. He decided on a change of attitude. He recognized a lawyer with a rival firm, a young bilingual anglophone. He joined the group and tried to make himself pleasant. Because they insisted, he even told stories of his childhood. The ladies shivered deliciously when they pictured black bears coming out of their dens and wounded buffalo with heads down, charging Métis horsemen. This was how he spent the evening. Though he moved from group to group, the conversation would turn to his past every time. He resigned himself to it.

The clock struck midnight. The servants opened the sliding doors to the dining room, revealing a magnificent *réveillon*. The guests drained their glasses and moved into the other room, uttering Ohs and Ahs at the stuffed turkeys, lobsters, *tourtières*, *blanquettes de veau* and lamb chops. A gigantic bouquet of lilies reigned in the middle of the table.

Askik was tired but pleased with himself, convinced that he had once and for all exhausted the fanciful subject of his childhood. He felt no resentment whatever when Prosy joined him at the wine table in the deserted living room.

"I congratulate you, Askik. I see you're doing well for yourself." Prosy eyed his former pupil's gold vest. Askik observed for the first time that Prosy's clothes were clean but worn. His collar in particular was frayed.

"Was it you who sent me a message recently?" Askik asked.

"Absolutely not! I didn't even know you were in Montreal."

"You don't need my help?" Askik persisted in a low voice.

Prosy looked hurt. "I'll have you know, Monsieur Mercredi, that good fortune, particularly when undeserved, does not bestow the right to look down on those from whom one has benefitted in the past. It's true that my affairs are not going exactly well, but I provide for my own needs. And in that I derive a modest pride."

"Forgive me, you're right." Askik felt sorry for the pale, disappointed man. De Meauville would look like this one day, he thought. He handed a glass of wine to his former teacher.

"When did you leave the Red River?" he asked.

"A few months after you did."

"Did you ever see my parents again?"

"I'm sorry, no. Do you still have those articles I gave you?"

"Lost them in the rapids," Askik lied.

"Pity," Prosy sighed. "Of course, I wouldn't publish those childish pieces today. But as mementos..."

"Are you going to dine?" Askik held out his hand toward the dining room.

"Why not? But if you'll allow me a comment," Prosy rejoined, looking down at Askik's clothes, "flowered waistcoats are no longer in fashion. Believe me, a man of your race must avoid bright colours."

Conversation was going strong all up and down the table. The servants were darting in and out between the chairs like wasps at a picnic, bearing steaming bowls of vegetables and potatoes. Eugène Sancy was amazing everyone; his plate was never empty, his wife scolded and his neighbours cheered him on. Hubert, sitting far from Élisabeth, was scowling. Had Élisabeth finally put him in his place? Askik gave him a friendly smile. *Vae victis*, chum.

"I bet you never ate this well with the Sulpicians," bantered Robert Simpson, the young English lawyer.

Askik was about to reply when a fat young man interjected drunkenly, "Or in your wigwams." His wife was pinching his arm, but the fellow roared, "Whazza matter, he's been boastin' about it all night!"

Askik pretended not to have heard. "The seminary cooks at least kept me alive in that cold, damp, drafty place for fifteen years," he said.

"They say the seminarists come out educated or dead," Simpson pursued.

"Half and half, most of them."

"Talks damn well f'r a savage," the fat boor rumbled.

This time Askik stared him straight in the eye to shut him up. Wasted effort, for the man was too drunk. His wife, a thin blonde who had misguidedly done her hair in a braided coil over each ear, bowed her head and bit her lip in shame. Askik pitied her and turned away.

"Coz a real savage woulda said 'arf 'n' 'arf'," said the drunkard, laughing.

"Gérard, Gérard," Eugène Sancy called down the table, "you're going to embarrass our Alexis. Be quiet or I'll scalp you!"

The guests roared with laughter.

"Still," Sancy added, rising heavily to his feet, "Gérard has given me an opening for something I want to say." The guests stopped talking and all eyes turned to the affable host.

"My friends," Sancy continued, "my house is too big not to be filled occasionally. Thank you for coming. You'll want to know the reason for this celebration, and you will soon, but first I want to tip my hat to my friend Alexis — or should it be Askik? Whichever — to our Alexis who pleaded his first case in court today. A clear success: he neither won outright nor lost outright; he kept his client without being too hard on his confrères!"

There was laughter and applause from one end of the table to the other. Askik's neighbours slapped him on the back. Élisabeth clapped harder than anyone. "Bravo, Alexis!" she cried, beaming at him warmly.

"A first case," Sancy continued, "is always worth noting, but never more than today, because our Alexis was not born into a well-to-do legal family, or to wealthy farmers, or even to poor working people from whom he might at least have learned the rudiments of our language and culture. No, Alexis was born into another world, another culture, I

282

might even say another era. He has come farther in his twenty-four years than I have in my fifty-odd. I invite you therefore to raise your glasses to Maître Alexis Mercredi, advocate, friend of the Sancys, intendant of Vielleterre."

There was a scraping of chairs on the floor and a sea of glasses rose toward the ceiling.

"To Alexis!" the guests shouted.

"Here, here!" Simpson cried.

"A good lil' savage!" babbled the fat drunkard, nearly losing his balance as he got to his feet.

Askik thought he was dreaming. All these people with exquisite manners and sumptuous, elegant clothes were looking at him and smiling. He was discovering for the first time that he was liked, even loved, and admired. Élisabeth in particular was glowing with pride and happiness. How could he ever have felt uncomfortable among these friends? He *was* different to them, and he *had* come from very far away, but why should he be ashamed of it? It was his best personal asset. Never, never again would he want to hide his Métis origin. Oh, what great things he was going to accomplish for these beloved men and women! How proud of him he was going to make them! He was about to rise and attempt some words of thanks, but Sancy was still on his feet.

"My friends," Sancy resumed, "I've already kept you waiting too long. It's time to let you in on the reason for our rejoicing."

He stopped. He looked down at his wife, who smiled encouragement to him. Then he put out his hand and took his daughter's. Élisabeth lifted a radiant face, transfigured by joy and anticipation. Her eyes shone and her lips parted in a half-smile. When he saw the look the father and daughter were exchanging, Askik's blood ran cold; his mouth went dry and an unbearable ache seized the pit of his stomach. Never, never in his life had he felt such anxiety. He threw a panic-stricken glance at Hubert, but Hubert was glumly studying the pattern on the tablecloth. Half of eternity went by before Sancy finally spoke again.

"I'm happy to announce that in the coming national general election I shall be the Liberal candidate for the riding of Saint-Aimé."

A gasp of surprise rose from the assembled guests, followed by an explosion of applause. The men jumped to their feet, knocking chairs over onto the carpet and shouting, "Bravo, Sancy!" The women remained seated, clapping their hands and nodding approvingly at one another. The quartet struck up *"Il est en or!"* Sancy raised both hands to quiet his audience, and then, not succeeding, stood bowing modestly in reponse to the cheering.

"San-cy! San-cy! San-cy!" the guests chanted, already infected with election fever. In the Province of Quebec, it's a virus that's catching.

Askik was coming back to life. He applauded like the others, but his legs were shaking. For a few minutes he had had the horrible feeling that Sancy was going to announce his daughter's betrothal. Riding a wave of relief and gratitude, he clapped until his hands hurt. It took some time for him to realize that if Eugène Sancy were elected to Parliament, the whole family would be moving to Ottawa. His first thought was that this was another shift of destiny that was going to bring him closer to the seat of power. Then he remembered that Sancy had used the words, "Intendant of Vielleterre."

Never mind, he thought, I'll find a way. I'll be his personal secretary, I'll convince him that I'll be useful. I must go to Ottawa. I must!

"*Vive* Sancy, our M.P.! *Vive les Rouges!*" he shouted at the top of his voice.

The cheering abated. Eugène Sancy could finish.

"My friends, it's late. In the days to come, I shall need your help. Until then, good night and get ready for the fight ahead of us!"

A final cheer petered out almost immediately. Everybody was tired. The musicians launched into a rendition of *Bonsoir, mes amis, bonsoir* that was even slower than usual and riddled with wrong notes. Now the guests were in a hurry to leave. The vestibule seethed with scarves and galoshes and canes. Each time the door opened, a stamping of horses' hoofs could be heard outside.

"Goodnight, goodnight," Eugène Sancy murmured over and over.

"Come again soon, *y a pas de gêne*, don't be shy," his wife added.

Élisabeth leaned against a small table as she shook hands with the departing guests.

Askik did not take his coat immediately, but hung back as befitted an intimate of the family. He watched Hubert depart in his elegant mink coat without even looking at Élisabeth.

When everyone had gone, Eugène Sancy came back to the living room and poured himself a drink.

"Well, Alexis, my boy, what do you think of my plan?"

"Excellent, monsieur! I shall give you all the support in my power."

"I've been counting on it, my boy, I've been counting on it." Sancy winked at him. "To your health, Alexis."

"To yours, monsieur. You're going to need a secretary in Ottawa and I think I can..."

"The most valuable thing you can do for me," Sancy interrupted, "is to relieve me of running Vielleterre. Come now, my boy, why the long face? It's not going to be for ever. Just long enough for me to get settled in Ottawa, then we'll see..."

"But, monsieur..."

"Come, come..." Sancy said, raising a finger over his glass. "I'm asking you to look after my family assets for a time. That's not too much to ask, I hope."

He did not add, After all I've done for you, but the words were palpable between them.

"Good, good." Sancy saw that he had won. "Just for one summer, then. You'll see to the seeding and harvesting. When autumn comes, you'll be free. Agreed? Perfect! You may sleep here tonight if you like. Anyway, you decide. Good night, Alexis."

He climbed the stairs, breathing heavily through his nose. Askik, left alone, listened to the maids in the dining room, who were grousing as they cleared the table. It was always they who were the last to get to bed and, of course, the first up at daybreak. A tall woman came into the living room with a tray and stopped dead to find Askik there.

"My coat," Askik said, infusing the words with as much bitterness as possible.

7

Montreal never slept. It was impossible to go out without seeing announcements of sporting events, balls and concerts. Sleigh bells jingled until the wee hours and each morning employees arrived at their offices tired but happy. Torches burned on the river, where skaters, snowshoers and curlers came in throngs at all hours. The weather was cold and magnificent, and the whole city was in a carnival mood. Lent was approaching.

Askik was pleading in court every day and attracting notice. Most judges were less interested in probing the fine points of the law than in getting home. Askik took short cuts. He cited no authors, invoked only the most familiar jurisprudence and otherwise stuck to facts. Astonishingly, moreover, Maître Mercredi made a habit of being brief in cases he knew to be lost in advance. Occasionally clients were resentful of this, but lawyers and judges were filled with admiration for this young man who could lose with a minimum of talk. Moreover, he did not care whether he won or lost. His clients bored him with their problems. The more so since nearly all of them were liars. He had come to the conclusion that he would be rich only when he ceased serving the business interests of others and attended exclusively to his own. All his energy was now directed toward creating a small body of capital to invest.

He went less often to Les Trois Grosses Muses and spent his spare time instead at the Richelieu. The merchants and bankers came to appreciate the company of this young lawyer who had the good sense to listen to them. Even Judge Duvernay would give him a terse nod when they happened to be breakfasting at the same time. The judge never sat down alone; he ate and smoked with the high finance of Montreal. It was said that he had invested heavily in the Canadian Pacific Railway, which explained his constant ill humour.

Askik had become a closer friend of Elzéar Grandet, who was as penniless and as much an anglophile as ever. Still, however badly Grandet handled his own affairs, he was a marvel at understanding the affairs of others. No deal or setback occurred in Montreal without sooner or later reaching his long, idle ears. Through him, Askik knew all the city's financiers by sight and could find their houses on the mountain and identify their horses and vehicles in the streets.

He was also learning to understand *les Anglais*. Not that he had been unaware of their existence, for they had a finger in every financial pie. Until now, however, he had thought of them as a powerful but hazy background presence. Their conventions, ambitions and superiority were profoundly foreign to him. He set about learning from them, began with great difficulty to read their novelists, and rarely went out without an English grammar or a copy of the *Star* under his arm. In the English mentality, he found a composure and attention to concrete things that seemed to him lacking in French-Canadian Society. The French-speaking nationalists gabbled their indignation, harped on past injustices, threatened revolt; the English barely responded at all. Their power rested on solid foundations; they had nothing to fear from these loquacious Latins who considered it beneath them to sell peas or nails. And that was the real nub of the discord, Askik thought. The Scottish apprentice dreamed of founding his own business; the French-speaking student's ambition was to go to the bench or the altar. They were already master and servant. The first knew it; the second did not. Askik saw this.

Not that he saw no wrong in the English. Their newspapers oozed contempt for other races; their scorn for the Indians and Métis was almost beyond measure. But then, everyone looked down on the aboriginals. The French kept trying to make them over in their own image. Even Italian and Chinese immigrants spat upon the country's first inhabitants.

Askik stopped short of fawning on the English as Grandet did, knowing full well that he would never be admitted to their society. Deep down, however, he regretted having fallen on the side of the servants. He resolved to work hard, save his money and become his own master.

Yet how is one to save money when one has an Élisabeth to win? Askik had renewed his wardrobe, choosing clothes that were simpler and more conservative and, curiously, more expensive. Disregarding Madame Sancy's admonition about debts, he had finally replaced his old coat. A brand new pelisse of fisher fur and matching hat were hanging in his wardrobe cupboard. He took them out often, but had been waiting for the Carnival to wear them in public.

Not much light entered the Sancys' parlor. The windows were obscured behind heavy net curtains. A large palm tree, a symbol of Empire, stood grandly by a window. The piano, which nobody played, was covered with lace, photographs and bric-a-brac. The only sound came from a glass-domed mantel clock with discreet tick and gilt numbers.

How peaceful it is, Askik thought. What stability!

He was lying on the sofa in his shirtsleeves, with his hands behind his head. His gaze wandered, pausing now at the glow of a gas jet, now at the arabesques on the ceiling. Drowsily, his eyes came eventually to the back of the sofa and roamed through the tracery of leaves and vines cut in the crimson velvet. He traced tortuous paths, tried to retrace them back to where he began, got lost and dozed off.

Soft footsteps in the corridor, three gentle knocks at the door. Georges entered with a bowl of hot water and a towel. Askik sat up, rubbing his eyes.

"Thank you, Georges. Monsieur Sancy is back?"

"Yes, monsieur."

"And mademoiselle?"

"She came in half an hour ago."

"Oh my, oh my! I think I've mussed my shirt."

"That's nothing, monsieur. Eulalie will iron it again while you wash."

Georges left with the shirt over his arm. Askik wet one end of the towel in the hot water and scrubbed at his cheeks and forehead. He felt refreshed, strong, happy, in an excellent mood for the test awaiting him.

I must make her laugh, he thought. If she laughs, I'm saved. He pulled on his shirt, which was still warm from the iron, and carefully buttoned on the collar.

As he approached the dining room, he heard Élisabeth's airy laugh. I have a head start, Askik said to himself, she's in good humour.

Élisabeth had spent the afternoon at a friend's and was regaling her mother with new gossip.

"You remember the Lemieux girl? Her father owns mills at Gatineau. He's been hunting for a son-in-law. Well, he finally finds his pigeon — Alexis, come and listen to this! They invite the future husband and his parents to dinner, but that nitwit of a mother pulls her daughter's corset so tight to give her a waist that the girl faints into her soup! Can you imagine?"

Her story was interrupted by her own peals of laughter.

"Oh, that's sad!" Madame Sancy exclaimed before bursting into laughter herself.

After a minute, Élisabeth was able to continue, still gasping.

"Her future in-laws decided she was epileptic, so now papa Lemieux has to find himself another son-in-law!"

Askik laughed as best he could, although he thought the story rather pathetic. Still, anything to keep Élisabeth in this happy frame of mind. Eugène Sancy had entered the room.

"This is the kind of company I like!" he exclaimed. Hello, my darlings, hello Alexis. What's this horror story, Élisabeth?"

"Horrible but true. Julie told me."

"We shouldn't laugh at other people's troubles. That Lemieux put every penny into lumber. Bad business. Very bad."

"Eulalie," Madame Sancy called, "you can serve now."

"Well, I saw Judge Duvernay today," Sancy announced, unfolding his table napkin. "He had some very good things to say about you, Alexis."

"Of course!" Élisabeth chimed in. "Alexis is Montreal's best lawyer."

"What a grumpy fellow he is, though," her father continued.

"They say his affairs are going badly," Askik offered.

"The railway, yes I know, but he's worrying over nothing. The government won't let it go under. There'll be a subsidy or loan. Count on it. And that's what I told him."

"And how about you, monsieur?" Askik asked too seriously. "How are your election plans going?"

The question seemed to take Sancy by surprise.

"Er... fine, just fine... Say, I heard a good one at the club today. That old buzzard Renaud, the oil merchant, you know... he's gone into partnership. And who with, d'you suppose? Eh? You can't guess? Lecompte!"

"No! I don't believe it! Oh!"

"Ah, yes, exactly," Sancy crowed. "They used to loathe each other on principle. Now they're going into business together. Like it or lump it, that's the way it has to be these days! Naphtha's the energy of the future, but the Americans have the monopoly..."

"How about electricity?" Askik asked, hearing Lady Luck knock at the door.

"What about electricity?"

"The ice palace this year is going to be lit with electricity. They say it's stunning."

"In ice palaces, all right, but it's expensive. And dangerous. No, no, naphtha, I tell you. That's the gold of the future."

"Is it true, Alexis?" Élisabeth said, wide-eyed. "Lit with electricity? That must be beautiful!"

"It's going to be magnificent," Askik assured her. "I was by there today. They've poured a huge skating rink all around the ice palace. Saturday night, there's going to be a masquerade on skates."

Then, glancing around the table, he concluded energetically, "We should all go."

"Ho, ho!" Sancy guffawed. "My wife on skates! I can see it now!"

"Well, you better look again, *mon homme!*" Madame Sancy retorted. "Masquerades on skates are all right for the young folk."

"So we can go, maman?" Élisabeth asked. "I'll invite Julie."

"Don't see any harm in it," the mother replied. "Alexis can go with you. Eulalie, the soup!"

And that was all. Eulalie served the soup. For a time, Askik remained staggered by the ease of his victory. His first time out with Élisabeth! He ate hearty helpings of chicken, carrots, pastries, and tasted none of it.

Saturday. The minute he opened his eyes, Askik felt the day was going to last an eternity. It was early, much too early. He had nothing to do because everything was ready. The carriole was ordered, the restaurant was expecting him at seven o'clock, his clothes were brushed and pressed. He had already imagined his evening a thousand times had died a hundred deaths over each detail to be arranged. After painful debate with himself, he had even ordered a new pair of boots, marvels in red leather. Shapeless galoshes were for others. "Everything's ready," he murmured as he studied his face in the mirror. He had twelve more hours to spend fretting. Twelve hours to suspect that the carriole driver was going to let him down, to worry that the majordomo was going to seat them near the door, or that the bootmaker had got drunk. Twelve hours before seeing Élisabeth. Élisabeth! Was she as nervous as he? He could picture her in white fur, adorable and awkward on skates, leaning on him with all her weight. Enough to die with happiness!

He descended the stairs in his building, making each ancient step resound. Once in the street, however, where should he go?

De Meauville! he thought suddenly. De Meauville will go for breakfast, he's always hungry.

He ran, demolishing whole blocks in long strides and sliding at intersections. He narrowly missed being run down by a hay wagon. "Damn fool!" the driver yelled, struggling to calm his horses. With a peal of laughter, Askik took off once more. He had never in his life run so fast. Buildings flew by and pedestrians flattened themselves against walls as he passed. When he reached de Meauville's, he raced up the spiral staircase and flung himself against the door.

"Ho, friend de Meauville!" he called, hammering so hard on the old door that the hinges rattled. "A visitor, monseigneur! Get up! Get up!"

After several minutes of silence, the Speaker's face appeared at the door, looking a little cross.

"Come in, Mercredi," he said, recovering his composure. "I sense you're in a talkative mood."

"Let's go out, I'm buying you breakfast."

"No point," de Meauville sighed, going back to bed. "Monseigneur's not eating."

His face was grey and his eyes red. A green and yellow bruise made a sickly star above his right eyebrow.

"Evening at Joe Beef's?" Askik inquired, laughing.

"At the Muses, dear fellow. Can you believe it? Manners are degenerating."

290

"But you gave a few back, at least?"

"They get younger and younger, Mercredi, and all I do is get older. They hate me."

He did indeed look like an old man as he lay on his skimpy mattress, his hand over his eyes and his head down because it hurt less that way. The wallpaper over his head was peeling; the table was strewn with half-copied contracts and ends of candles gnawed by mice. In the single window, a pane was missing; a grubby rag was keeping out the wind. Pretentious and amateurish nude drawings were fixed to the walls.

"I think I'm going to change my way of life, Mercredi," the Speaker muttered. "Did I tell you? I might become a country schoolmaster. What do you think? Oh, forgive me... Here you are, bursting with life, and I'm boring you with the woes of a washout."

"Not at all!" Askik protested. He could find nothing to add.

"Well, go ahead," de Meauville said with a sigh. "What have you got to tell me?"

"I'm going out with Élisabeth! Tonight! To the Carnival!"

De Meauville opened one eye and studied Askik in silence. His headache soon forced him to close it again.

"My congratulations, Mercredi."

It was too laconic; Askik was stung.

"You still don't believe she could love me, do you?" he demanded. He thought but did not say, Because you're jealous.

With an effort, de Meauville sat up in bed.

"Don't be cross. I don't have all my wits about me. No, I wish with all my heart for you to be loved, but wishing is no guarantee. What more can I say? Old dreamers are cautious. Be cautious, Mercredi."

Askik was disappointed. He had come to share a vibrant, exciting piece of news, and his friend was talking to him like an accountant: prudence, caution, guarantees.

As if he could see inside his young friend's mind, de Meauville added sadly, "It was the *seigneuresse* my mother who taught me to pontificate. Perhaps if I went to live with the peasants..."

"In the Beauce, might it be?" Askik inquired teasingly.

The Speaker gave a child-like little smile. "Yes, perhaps. And you, if you feel like talking later, I'll be here all evening. *Y a pas de gêne*, as our Canayens would say."

"Thank you, this evening I won't have time. Is there anything you need? Food, coffee?"

"Thank you, no," de Meauville replied, lying down again.

"I can pay, if you're short."

De Meauville slowly waved a hand as if to say, Leave me alone. He had laid an arm across his forehead and his jaw was clenching and relaxing slowly. His lower face was as grey as his old dressing gown.

Askik took a single pace across the icy room to the door and turned one last time to his friend. What squalor, he thought; I must get him out of here. "So long, de Meauville," he called loudly, but received no reply. He went out, gently closing the door.

He spent the whole day waiting and was very nearly late for all that. The first hours seemed endless and the last few sped by in a twinkling. He returned late from the bootmaker's and had to dress in haste. He wondered if he had forgotten anything as he hurried downstairs and into the carriole. He was displeased with himself. The fisher coat made him look thirty pounds heavier, and his beautiful, expensive boots did not have the effect he had hoped with the fur. To give himself confidence, he imagined he was a rich, well-established merchant coming home in his own carriole. He was not feeling the serenity that attends well-heeled men, however. His heart raced, he had a knot in his stomach, and he felt depressed and elated both at once.

It was a magical night. Gas lamps threw circles of light on the snow, people were wearing smiles as they walked home, and even the horses were stepping with a lighter gait. The Carnival was about to begin. Passing through the city centre, Askik saw walls and statues of snow, and a little beyond, in Dominion Square, the still-dark crenellations of the ice palace. In a few hours, these deserted places would be alive with merrymakers and bonfires.

The carriole stopped. Askik walked up the path toward the Sancys' house. The snow squeaked under his new boots, coal smoke hung in the cold air, the stars twinkled between the high cornices of the house.

"O God," Askik prayed, "thank you for this world. Bless Élisabeth and me. Teach us to love each other."

The steps of the house were freshly shovelled. He was touched at this sign of care. He lifted his hand to enter without knocking, as was his custom, but changed his mind, thinking that Élisabeth might want to be informed of his arrival.

He let the doorknocker fall several times. No one came. He knocked with his fist. Still no response. The carriole driver coughed discretely into his mittens. Askik opened the door and went in. The vestibule and living room were dark and deserted. There was some light coming from the kitchen. He could hear voices upstairs. He mounted the first few steps.

"Good evening, is anyone here?" he called politely.

No one answered. He could still hear voices. It sounded like an argument. There were hurried footsteps back and forth between bedrooms. Askik was getting impatient.

"Hello! Can you hear me?"

The voices stopped. Footsteps approached. Someone lit a lamp at the top of the stairs. A maid leaned over the railing.

"Is that you, Monsieur Mercredi? What are you doing here?"

"What am I doing here? I've come to get Mademoiselle Élisabeth. We're going to the Carnival tonight."

The maid put a hand to her mouth, let out a shrill "Oh!" and fled. Stunned, Askik stood frozen on the stairs, his fur hat in his hand, his boots dripping on the Persian stair runner. He did not wait long. There were more steps almost immediately, accompanied this time by Madame Sancy, haggard and breathless. The stout woman descended the stairs, took Askik by the elbow and steered him energetically toward the door.

"Oh, my dear Alexis, I'm all upset. It's unbelievable, terrible... Élisabeth..."

"Is she ill?" Askik cried.

"What? No, no, she's invited to the governor's ball. The invitation just arrived this afternoon. How awful! Her dress! Her hair! So little time to get ready. Imagine! It must be the duke's invitation, we're sure of it. My poor Élisabeth's next to tears. Doing that to a young girl! Oh, those English!" The hapless woman raised her arms toward heaven.

She was beside herself, undecided whether to throw Askik out or weep hot tears on his shoulder. Her distress was paltry beside Askik's, however. He allowed himself to be pushed to the door, but once on the threshold he resisted.

"Élisabeth was supposed to go out with me tonight," he said.

"What?" Madame Sancy said, surprised at his resistance.

"Élisabeth and I," he persisted, "were going to the Carnival tonight."

Madame Sancy took a moment to understand, then struck her hand to her forehead.

"Oh, that's right. Forgive me, Alexis, I'd completely forgotten. With all this upset, you know... But you go on the Carnival yourself, there'll be someone you know for sure."

"But it was agreed. I've got everything ready. I've had expenses..."

"Expenses?" She had now shoved him into the vestibule. "Expenses for a masquerade? Oh, you silly boy! Well, my husband will pay you back, you know that perfectly well."

"How about the carriole driver?"

"Alexis, please!"

Her hand was on the doorknob. Askik was in despair. Why was he expressing himself so badly? Why did he talk about expenses and carriole drivers when all that counted was Élisabeth? Why was Madame Sancy pretending to be so dense?

"Élisabeth and I... were supposed to go out... together," he stammered.

"Listen, Alexis, you can see we're in a hurry and everything's going wrong." Her tone was firm and maternal. "Now you'll excuse us... Come back Sunday. Élisabeth will be here. She'll tell you about her evening and you'll..."

"No!" Askik shouted, practically in the fat woman's face. She stepped back, thunderstruck.

"Well, I never, Alexis! What's got into you? My daughter's invited to the governor's ball and you want me to send her skating at the Carnival? Well, I never!"

"She was supposed to go out with *me*!" Askik repeated stubbornly. "With *me*!"

Stunned, Madame Sancy said nothing. She observed for the first time the expensive coat, the new boots, the fur hat. From puzzlement, her expression turned to suspicion, then disbelief, then malice. The blood rose to her face.

"Are you crazy?" she hissed. "D'you think... my Élisabeth... with *you*?"

"Madame!" a maid called from upstairs. "Mademoiselle Élisabeth's crying. The bodice is too big!"

"I'm comin'!" her mistress yelled, then turning to Askik she barked in a voice of fury, "An' you, get out! I don't ever wanna see you here again, *charogne*! Out!"

Askik lost control, choked with loathing, could barely see. He wanted to hit, strangle. His voice shook as though he were about to cry.

"I'm just as good as you!" he yelled at the top of his lungs. "Just as good!"

Madame Sancy was livid with rage.

"Get out I said! You think I'm gonna give my daughter t' a savage? You're disgustin'!"

Eugène Sancy came running, wearing mules and dressing gown. He took his wife by the shoulders.

"Calm yourself, my dear, calm yourself! What's all this?"

Askik was ashamed. Ashamed of having raised his voice, ashamed of having made the worthy Sancy come running, looking rather absurd in slippers. He groped for a way to excuse himself. How indeed could he have thought... But it was too late. Madame Sancy levelled a trembling finger at him.

"He wants Élisabeth!" she yelled in a voice filled with revulsion. "He thinks I'm gonna give my little girl to *him*!"

"What is this, Alexis?" Eugène Sancy searched the young man's eyes, looking for a denial, an explanation.

"He wants Élisabeth!" the fat woman screamed.

To his credit, Sancy never lost his head. He drew his wife away several paces and spoke in a firm voice.

"Alexis, you can see the state my wife is in. Go now. I'll have you come to my office. Go, please."

Askik left, his fury deflated, his mind a blank. He even closed the door behind him. On the top step, he realized that he no longer had his fur hat; he did not care. How quiet it was out here! As he walked down the path, he saw the stars and the white cloud of his own breath.

It's cold! he thought, surprised. How could I not have noticed before?

He paused at the gate, uncertain what to do. His eye lit on a small bush half-covered in snow. It looked friendly. Its branches were frail and twisted; it must be cold, yet it was taking the trouble to be sympathetic.

"Monsieur," the carriole driver called, "my horses're freezin'! What we gonna do?"

Askik looked up quizzically. What to do indeed. Stay? Leave? Freeze? Kill? Bah!

"There's nothing left to do," he replied. "Take me home."

8

The roads were in appalling condition. The rain had carved channels in the ice and holes in the mud. The horses kept losing their footing and the coachman cursed with all his soul. Yet whenever he slowed their pace, a harsh voice from inside the carriage would call, "Faster!"

"You're gonna kill the horses!"

"Faster!"

The coachman choked back his anger and clacked the reins.

"Gee-up! Gee-up, or our intendant'll have yer hides!"

It was dark and smelled of damp horsehair inside the carriage. The window was constantly fogged; the intendant had given up trying to see outside.

Spring! he thought. What a depressing season! Where did all the sentimentality over spring come from? Probably France. Certainly not from here!

A wheel slammed into a rut and a jet of muddy water entered under the door. Askik's body was bruised from all the bumps and jolts. No matter, he was anxious to reach Vielleterre, to get things back in hand. Paradis' letter had not been reassuring. Preparation for seeding had barely begun. The ditches had been neglected and part of the land was in peril of being flooded.

The Sancys were in Ottawa. On learning that the master of Vielleterre would probably stand for election, the government had immediately offered him a senior post at Finance. It had been agreed that he would join the Cabinet on the death (imminent, it was hoped) of the Conservative Member of Parliament for Saint-Aimé. Eugène Sancy had driven a hard bargain and made it known to his intimates and journalists that if he was joining the government in power it was not to lay his liberal thinking to rest but to bring about change. Happily, at this juncture, friends of the Sancy family were swept by a wind of realism. Those who had applauded his espousal of Grit principles now cheered his joining the Tories.

When he had boarded the train for Ottawa, Sancy looked preoccupied, anxious, like a man about to shoulder an enormous responsibility. Reporters took note of this. They also took note of the politician's daughter, a young woman of great beauty who, it was said, had close ties with English aristocracy. Unlike her father, Élisabeth showed not the slightest reluctance to board the train.

The coachman brought the carriage to a halt. Irritated, Askik opened the door just far enough to put his head outside. It was drizzling. The man had got down from the box and was walking slowly toward a large roadside cross.

"Where are you off to?" Askik cried.

The coachman turned around and shrugged innocently. "*Ben*, to say my prayers."

"Come back here and keep going!"

But the man was already on his knees. Even an intendant would not have the gall to interrupt his prayers.

Beaten, Askik began to settle back in the cold carriage, and then decided to get out himself.

It was the last word in roadside crosses, life-size, painted white and topped by a pagoda-like roof; the dead Christ was painted gaudily in pink and red, wounds executed with an anatomist's eye. The old crosses, two round logs notched and nailed together, were disappearing. They were simply too crude.

"Get up," Askik growled, approaching the coachman. "You'll catch cold. Your horses can rest well enough without your prayers."

The coachman, mulish fellow, continued his devotions a minute or so more, then crossed himself and stood up with a groan.

"We ain't givin' enough heed to the horses, monsieur. They're good servants but we hafta let 'em catch their breath and have a pee now and then."

"How about you, Dumoutier," Askik enquired, pulling on his gloves, "are you a good servant?"

The coachman collected his wits, smelling a trap.

"Yes indeed, monsieur. You got no reason to complain about me?"

"No Dumoutier. Not yet."

The coachman hastened away. He relieved his bladder in the company of his horses.

Mist and rain blanketed the whole countryside. The ice on the river was rotting; huge black patches were spreading over its snowy surface. Perched on the riverbank was a pretty little fieldstone house. Gaily coloured curtains and geraniums brightened the windows and there were frozen dahlias leaning against the walls. The farmyard was a cheerful jumble: a tip-cart, two tiny storage sheds, a heap of manure, a small barn. That's the trouble with Quebec, Askik thought. A little fishing, a little farming, a little hunting. They use everything they get and produce nothing for export. Then they wonder why the English are ahead in everything. No, worse than that, they don't even wonder why.

"Dumoutier," he snapped "we're leaving!"

Dumoutier climbed back onto his box without further protest. He was anxious to be rid of this dangerous passenger.

Askik spent the rest of the journey stirring dark thoughts. When he recognized a village he had thought was already behind, he loosed a kick at the wall of the carriage. In fear, the coachman urged the horses forward at breakneck speed.

Askik had almost stopped thinking about Élisabeth. She was still there in the depths of his being, a dull ache that was fading gradually, but he never called up her memory. Sometimes a remaining pang of despair would overtake him, particularly at night, but compared to the pain he had felt at first, it was not much. He was getting over Élisabeth, though he knew he would never be the same again.

Eugène Sancy had waited long weeks before calling him to his office, and then had treated him generously, like a prodigal son. His government appointment had been approved but was not yet public knowledge; Vielleterre was weighing on him and he urgently needed to be relieved of the burden. Askik had refused at first but in the end gave in, worn down by Sancy's persistence. Sancy paid off the young man's debts and made him a present of an ageing pure-bred horse. Askik sold the horse, his furniture and the fisher coat.

A pair of red brick gateposts marked the entrance to Vielleterre. The forecourt, woods and house seemed bigger than when he had left. The day was ending and the wheels of the carriage broke great sheets of ice in the driveway. He gave a wry smile when he saw the little bench under the elm on which he had dreamed of a happy future at Élisabeth's side. How naïve! And now, how old and disillusioned he felt! He no longer expected anything of life; duty done was the only thing that still brought him a certain austere satisfaction.

The people of Vielleterre greeted him coldly. They were inconvenienced by his arrival. Vielleterre had developed a comfortable routine that left no place for a master. Watching the new intendant get out of the carriage, each worried about what this arrival could mean for the future.

The old foreman, Paradis, was an exception. He was waiting impatiently at the bottom of the steps. As soon as Askik had two feet on the ground of Vielleterre, Paradis seized his hand and cried, "I'm right glad to see you, monsieur!" It was not flattery, it was the truth. Paradis was profoundly grateful to be handing over his responsibility.

"I pushed the horses, Paradis," Askik said dispassionately. "See they're well looked after."

"It'll be done, monsieur."

"Then come and have dinner with me. Bring the accounts, ledgers, receipts, all the papers, everything."

The old man beamed. Rosalie bustled to the carriage, mumbling, "I'll take your bags, monsieur."

"There's just this one," Askik said, lifting out a small suitcase.

"We've got your usual room ready for you," Céline told him. She was saying a respectful *vous* to him now, which was new, but there was no respect in the way she looked at him. Seeing the look, Askik remembered that now he was merely an employee in this household.

"Tomorrow I'll move into the steward's room, near the office."

"Very good, monsieur."

The intendant shut himself in his room. When she recalled his dark expression and his drab clothes, Rosalie was now definitely afraid. The hired hands mumbled against him as they rubbed down the exhausted horses. Madame Paradis thought he was thinner and more "savage, like" than ever. Only Céline returned to her work as though nothing had happened; she had decided to make no change whatever in her habits.

The morning after his arrival, Askik sent all the men to the fields. There were grasses and willows growing in the drainage ditches; they all had to be dug out, which meant first chopping away the remaining crust of ice and snow. Each blow was delivered with an oath. Askik went to the site but wisely refrained from putting a hand to the work.

"We won't never do it without help," Paradis said, moving away from the men as they worked. "Our men're soft."

"The other ditches can wait till summer. This is the one that matters most. I'll go and hire men in the village."

Askik lifted his face to the wind, a south wind cooled by the snow but laden with the smell of wet earth.

"It smells good, doesn't it, Paradis? In the States the thaw has begun. Hey, isn't that the Dubois' shack down there? Are their cows still coming onto our land?"

"The Dubois're in the charnel house. Died durin' the winter. Far's I know, the cows took off t' the woods."

"Is the land for sale?"

"Ain't worth much..."

"I'll go and have a look anyway."

"You gonna clay this here land?" Paradis cocked his head toward the field.

"Why clay it?"

"The earth's tired. We only got eight bushels an acre last year. I thought we'd clay it 'n' let it rest this year."

"Fallowing's a waste. We'll sow it with alfalfa. That'll regenerate the soil and we'll have more hay for the animals. The more animals we have, the more manure we'll get and the richer the land will be. The English don't fallow any more and they produce more than we do."

"Well, they're smarter'n me, then," Paradis growled, "'cause the land don't rest when it works, far's I know."

"You've fallowed all your life, and you say yourself the land doesn't produce nowadays."

"Bad harvests happen."

"And good ones are planned. We have to rethink all our methods," Askik declared. "We exhaust the soil when we sow wheat all the time, we still throw manure in the river instead of using it to fertilize the land, our fields are flooded in spring and die of drought in summer..."

"We always had 'nough t' eat, anaways," Paradis interrupted testily.

Defiantly, the old man glared at Askik, jaw clenched, cap pulled down over his eyes. His was the indignation of ten generations of French Canadians who had always had enough to eat, had lived as their own small masters, and had died leaving their heirs the same little parcel of land they themselves had inherited. In the meantime, newcomers with larger ambitions had arrived and gathered everything else to themselves.

All of this Askik would have liked to explain to the hired men who kept taking a little rest after each handful of grass they dug out of the ditch, but they would have laughed at him. For him it was a much more attractive prospect to mount his handsome half-blooded horse and gallop off across country to the village.

"I'll send you some men," he called as he rode away.

The air was brisk and light. The big bay snorted with pleasure. He was Élisabeth's horse, but Élisabeth rarely came to Vielleterre and even more rarely went riding. Askik had immediately established a bond with the animal. It's my Métis blood, he told himself. After all, when he was a child his neighbours used to spend three-quarters of their time in the saddle. He would laugh aloud when he remembered their buffalo hunts. Still, he did not set much store by this past of his. How could one trust childhood impressions? And yet there were times when the countryside here seemed too plump, too docile, and then he would think nostalgically of the prairies with their scraggy growth. But not often.

9

The white, raw post-Easter light flooded through the windows. A *"truie"* or "sow," a little potbellied stove, purred contentedly in its corner. Now and then a piece of coal would fall through the grill into the pan below with a friendly plop. Paradis's accounts, tidied, licked into shape, were being reborn on new paper in a new-smelling ledger. The sun would progress steadily across the room. When it reached the mahogany filing cabinet, Rosalie would come in with tea and little cakes. Sometimes Askik would weary of all this orderliness and then would have Élisabeth's big bay saddled up and gallop away to the fields where there was nothing for him to do. He was surprised that he had to give so few orders. Everything was happening as though the mere presence of an intendant were enough to make things work. Appearing strict was the most important part of his job.

Paradis cleaned his boots on the bootscraper outside the door and entered without knocking. He seemed agitated.

"Joseph Lambert from the village is here. Says he bought our 'taters. Wants to load the whole lot in 'is wagon!"

"Let him do it. I sold the potatoes."

"But them's our seed 'taters!"

"Potatoes are being given away. They're not worth planting. We're not going to plant peas either. It doesn't pay."

"I got the best seed in the country, an' you go an' sell it t' the first asks fer it! What we gonna do this winter without 'taters or peas?"

"We'll buy them."

Paradis looked wounded. Buy what you can produce yourself? Depend on others for one's food? So why not bread and milk too? Why not go begging in the village after mass? Did this young fellow realize what he had done? How could he have sold his seed potatoes, his, Paradis's, after he'd spent all those hours and hours in the sun, picking out the best plants, purifying the strains? His potatoes were the envy of the whole county!

"So what *are* we gonna plant?"

"Hay. Oats. I'm going to buy milk cows. Set up a butter factory. The whole province is turning to dairy farming. It's time we did too."

"Butter! I don't know nothin' 'bout butter!"

"Don't worry, I'll find a man..."

Askik stopped. Paradis had turned grey. He was twisting his cap in his grubby fingers.

"Come on, Paradis," Askik said, softening his voice. "We can't go on this way: a few pigs, a handful of chickens, half a dozen half-dry cows, eight bushels of wheat to an acre. Vielleterre's going to ruin."

"I always done my best..."

"I know, I know, and you'll always have a place here. But times have changed. We can't just make do with taking care of ourselves any more."

"How 'bout Gendron?" Paradis demanded, fixing Askik with an accusing eye. "Gendron's always looked after the cows. What'm I gonna tell him?"

"Nothing. Send him to me."

Paradis paused, his hand on the door.

"You're goin' too fast, m'sieur. You hafta give people time to git used t' things."

"Vielleterre's got no time left, Paradis. If business doesn't improve by next spring, it might all have to be sold: land, house, cattle, everything."

Paradis was crushed by the verdict. Askik felt sincerely sorry for this old man who was confronting the harsh law of profit for the first time.

"You've lived here a long time, haven't you, Paradis?"

"I wuz born at Vielleterre, under the last seigneur. He wouldn't never have sold. Never!"

"Times change."

"But they ain't no better," the old man said as he left. "Sure ain't no better!"

"Lord, bless this earth..." The censer swung two or three times over the heads of the faithful and drops of water flashed briefly in the sunlight before disappearing in the furrows. The people resumed their walk, men first, women following. Aves faded one into the other, spoken in time with the footsteps on the soft earth.

What exactly are we praying for? Askik wondered. Surely we should get together on that. Are we asking for cool weather for the wheat or hot weather for the corn? Will God make it hail in other parishes? Will he keep lightning away from our stables? He hasn't done it in the past; why do we keep on about it?

No point asking the curé. He was striding ahead, forehead unfurrowed by any doubt. His golden chasuble flapped in the wind like a standard. The procession wound through all the roads in the parish, saying a prayer for every field. When it came to Vielleterre's land, Askik stopped sneering and prayed fervently. Just in case.

Once past his own domain, he became bored and began to hope for rain to put an end to the procession. Fat clouds were blowing in from across the river, throwing a patchwork of shadow over the fields. A moist wind set the big church banner clacking.

It was pussy willow time. The children plucked great handfuls from the growth in the ditches. The trees in the distance had a fuzzy green look. A robin raised its bright voice in competition with the people's mutterings.

Now and then Askik took advantage of a turn in the road to glance at Céline, who was behind among the women. She was praying methodically and earnestly, the way she mended sheets or cleaned raspberries. When she caught Askik looking at her she did not look away and pretend not to have noticed; she looked him straight in the eye in a way that was neither friendly nor interested.

What an icicle! Askik thought as he turned away. Still, his mind retained the look she had given him and the picture of her full, graceful figure.

Paradis was walking ahead of him, bareheaded, cap in hand. His old, scarred boots had been polished and he was wearing the black suit he had worn at his wedding. He bowed before each field and prayed that everyone without exception would have food and clothing throughout the year. A Christian may quarrel with his neighbours; he cannot wish them ill.

Some first drops of rain splattered on the rich brocade of the chasuble. The curé looked up at the sky. The clouds were thickening; the shower might last. He sounded the retreat. The crowd fell back to the Beauchemin barn. When there were still several hundred paces to go, the heavens opened with a torrential, hazing rain of a kind not yet seen that year. Shamelessly, the faithful stampeded toward the barn. The more dignified, like Paradis, arrived soaked to the skin.

With help from the *syndics*, the curé carefully removed the chasuble. An old housekeeper inspected the cloth and pronounced it safe and sound. The altar boys put the bucket of holy water and the tapers on a window ledge and the banner was propped against a beam; now everyone could simply wait for the shower to end. After some milling around, the sexes separated instinctively. The women talked about gardens and children; the men gathered at the barn door, watching the rain and wondering whether there was too much or not enough.

Askik remained outside the conversation. He had spotted Céline leaning against a post at the back of the barn. Her wet hair had come loose from its chignon and locks of it hung dripping about her cheeks. She too took no part in the conversation, and stood gazing vacantly at the straw about her feet. Her wet dress clung to her body, molding her full breasts even more than usual, despite the thick underwear she was wearing. She had no shawl to put about her. When he looked at her, Askik felt a rush of desire that astonished him. Gone the satisfactions of accountancy! His mouth went dry, his heart pounded against his ribs. He wanted Céline in a way he had never wanted Élisabeth. It was not love, but he burned to possess her. Every finger, every hair on her head was suddenly desirable. Her coldness only fanned his desire. Did other men want her too? How could they not? Even stark-naked she would not be more desirable. He looked away for fear she would look up and see him staring at her. He was certain everyone in the barn could read his thoughts from his face. He was about to go outside when he felt a iron grip on his arm.

"Monsieur Mercredi, I believe."

The priest was looking him full in the eyes. A short, broad-backed man, the son of a peasant and still a peasant himself. He did not introduce himself; his identity could be in no doubt.

"I heard you're takin' Vielleterre in hand and you got plans," he began. "What are they?"

It was a blunt question and he offered no apology for prying into other people's business. Everything going on in the parish was his business.

Askik said coldly, "It's no secret to anyone that I plan to start a butter factory..."

"Good, good! The soil's gettin' very poor. It's time our habitants learned sump'n new. You'll be a good example."

"It's more than example that's needed, Monsieur l'abbé," Askik replied loftily. "It's money."

"And perhaps your master'll be good enough to let us have some. But to get back to the point, you got men there, men who've been at Vielleterre all their lives..."

"And they'll stay..."

"Glad t' hear it," the priest interrupted in turn. He gripped Askik's arm tighter. "But that's not enough. Take away their pride and pay means nothin'."

"Monsieur l'abbé, with all due respect..."

"Now, now, now!" the priest admonished, raising a thick finger. "When people say that, they usually don't intend to show any."

Askik was becoming irritated. He was not used to being interrupted these days.

"Our employees," he said, "are accustomed to old methods that are not good enough now."

"They were good enough for quite a long time, Monsieur Mercredi. They didn't kill anybody. Teach yer men the new methods. Let 'em learn gradually. Be a father to 'em. If God gave you an edjercation, it was so you could share it."

"I'm sorry, I don't have time..."

"Take the time, Monsieur Mercredi. Men don't change jus' like that. Sometimes it takes a whole lifetime to undo one weeny sin, and you wanta put everything right overnight. What makes you do it, Monsieur Mercredi? What's pushin' you so?"

"Money, Monsieur le curé. There has to be a profit at the end of the year."

"A profit? What for? The land's paid for. You got plenty t' eat. If you don't make a profit his year, you'll make one next year."

This priest had no manners, he kept interrupting. Askik disliked his muttonchop sideburns, his exaggerated peasant accent, his arrogant stare that said, You may argue, but you will obey.

He felt his face redden, which brought his irritation to a head. "It's precisely that attitude, abbé, that keeps us on our knees before the English. That way we have of thinking small. Making do with our shoddy little lives, our shoddy little way of doing things."

An embarrassed silence fell over the crowd. People avoided looking at each other, shamed to hear such impertinence toward their curé. Askik himself sensed that he was putting himself in a bad light. To be silent, however, one has to be sure of oneself.

"As long as we look down on business, the English will run everything in Canada. As long as all we do is pray for good harvests instead of enriching the soil properly, we'll be buying their produce instead of selling ours. As long as we're satisfied with third class, first class will be for others!"

There were murmurs of displeasure in the crowd. Who was this Métis taking himself for? The curé, however, had not so much as flinched. When he spoke again, it was in the same quietly imperious and mocking tone.

"You're not from here, Monsieur Mercredi. Quebec is old. Its habitants are patient. Very patient. They're obedient, they're long-sufferin'.

If you start puttin' the stick to 'em, you're no better'n the English."

Well said! There was a buzz of satisfaction throughout the barn. No two ways about it, Monsieur le curé knew how to put a man in his place!

The rain had all but stopped. The banner emerged heroically under the grey clouds; pipes were pocketed; fervently, the aves began again. Askik observed that Céline was wearing a little smile when she came out of the barn.

Every farm has its rites; the hired men are their guardians. They do not like change. When the first milk cows arrived, Holsteins of Dutch origin, the men found them unlikable. When a purebred bull that had cost three hundred dollars followed, rumblings of rebellion began. No one at Vielleterre earned even a hundred dollars in a year. Now the men began making it a point of honour to coddle the half-dozen remaining Canadian cows and rough up the foreigners.

From this time on, Askik was obliged to rule by fear. The autumn ploughing had been badly done; lumps of earth as big as skulls lay all over. Askik ordered the fields harrowed and the stones removed before seeding; this was additional, unexpected work that drew grumbling from the men. They began to return from the fields with harnesses or harrow teeth broken. When it came time to sow the alfalfa, they complained that the fine seed jammed their mechanical seeders. Attempts at adjustment, so-called, led to the loss of considerable seed. After a few days, exhausted and drained of admonishments, Askik stopped losing his temper and kept an impassive face. The men chuckled and told each other they had mastered the Métis.

For Askik, the end of seeding was like a first prison leave. On the morning after the work ended, he woke with a deep sense of gratitude. He asked Paradis to keep the men busy with minor chores around the yard so he would be spared facing them so soon again.

He paid a visit to the butter factory building site to persuade himself that his efforts were not being entirely wasted. The framework was up and the maturation chambers and cooling vats were taking shape. The head builder, a stout, greying man who had built a dozen butter factories in the Townships, was pleased with the materials and delighted with the flow of water from the artesian well.

"You'll get butter as long as you've got milk," he declared.

Askik then saddled the bay himself, only too happy to do without the men, and galloped away. I'm like my father, he thought wryly. As soon as things get bad, I jump in the saddle and go.

The countryside was breathing contentment. Men and plants were happy to be done with winter, with Lent and the rogations, with stonegathering and seeding: happy to do nothing for a few weeks. Everywhere the harvests were beginning to sprout in the fields. Tiny plants, easy to distinguish up close, made great swaths of solid green from a distance. Birds vied noisily for nesting sites in the trees and reeds.

The first farm along the road belonged to a man named Lavergne. As he rode by the pasture, Askik counted three Canadian cows of Breton and Norman stock. Fine, fat animals. Strong, healthy calves. A promising prospect.

"Well!" the farmer exclaimed when he saw Askik. "This our neighbour come to visit? Yup, that's him!"

He was a young man, barely older than Askik, with a bushy black moustache. His forearm was muscular, heavily veined and as thick as a bear's leg, yet he did not try to crush Askik's hand as a bully would have done. Another man of around sixty came out of the barn, a straw hat on his head and a fork in his hand.

"Won't you come in?" the father said, taking a step toward the house.

"Thankyou," Askik replied, "but I've got other visits to make."

"What can we do fer you?" the son enquired.

"I'm hoping we can be of mutual service, in fact. I've come to buy your milk. I'm building a butter factory. I'll have my own herd of milk cows, but it won't be enough. As you know, there's no lack of markets abroad for our Canadian butter."

"Yeah..." said the son, scratching his chin. "Trouble is, I got six kids. They drink all our milk. I wouldn't have nothin' much to sell you."

"You're a good farmer. If you buy two or three more cows you'll have plenty of milk to sell. If you feed them well, you could let me have enough for three hundred pounds of butter a year. At ten cents a pound..."

"Hey, wait up there... we don't milk much past November. The hay runs out, y'know..."

"You planted potatoes this spring? Feed your cows potatoes. Boiled, of course. And your wheat. I can sell you a little forage too, and then you'll have milk all year round."

Lavergne frowned. Get up every morning to milk cows, winter as well as summer? If you couldn't rest in winter, what was the point of living on a farm?

"Yeah... buy cows..., make the barn bigger..., buy hay. All that's pretty expensive."

"But there's a sure return! It's not only the States that takes our butter, but England, Brazil... and they're even talking about India and Japan!"

The farmer scraped the ground with his foot. "Ruther not," he replied. "Thankyou anaways."

The older man behind him nodded agreement. Askik could not believe his ears. Rather not make money? This fellow Lavergne hardly seemed an imbecile.

"Think a bit, for heaven's sake! Wheat doesn't pay any more. The North West will soon be producing tons of it. I'm offering you a way to increase your income, make your farm bigger."

There was irritation now in Lavergne's voice. "It's two hundred years now my family bin livin' off this farm. You trying' to tell us how t' earn our livin'?"

A woman had come out of the house onto the stoop, a baby in her arms and two small children clutching at her skirts. Two older boys had stopped teasing the dog when they heard the tone of their father's voice change.

Askik remounted. Father and son Lavergne at once switched on their geniality again.

"Come back 'n' see us," the father said.

"Stop by Ferland's," the son added, "he's got cows, he has. Mebbe he'll like yer idea."

The next farm did not inspire confidence. The house and barn stood on a totally treeless plain, a case in which the French-Canadian peasant's aversion to trees had worked wonders. A half dozen cows, listless from the heat of the sun, were lying on their sides roasting. Their ribs were somewhat too visible. In the farmyard, a dog short on flesh but long in fang barked furiously at the end of a chain. A solitary hen scurried away under an outbuilding, the sole escapee from a forgotten slaughter. In a minute enclosure beside the barn, a yellow-eyed bull was foundering in manure.

Askik expected a second Dubois to appear; perhaps the first Dubois's ghost. Instead, a vigorous, freshly-shaven man of forty-odd approached. He was wearing a bright-coloured chequered shirt, trousers of excellent quality corduroy, and boots that were finer than Askik's.

"Looks t' me like Monsieur Mercredi," Ferland said, holding out a friendly hand. "C'm in, then!"

He took Askik into the parlour through the visitor's entrance. There were more surprises in store. The room was papered with expensive wallpaper; the sofa, in carved wood and brocade, rivalled the Sancys'. A large bevelled mirror reflected and augmented the daylight. A beautiful marquetry games table occupied the centre of the room.

"It's beautiful in your house!" Askik exclaimed. His optimism was renewed.

The farmer's chest swelled with satisfaction. His wife came in with a carafe of mulled wine. She was wearing a flowered dress; it was simple but pretty, and looked new.

"Here's t' you, Monsieur Mercredi!" The farmer knocked back a whole glassful.

"I see you're a prosperous man, Monsieur Ferland."

The other raised his hands, about to protest, but Askik cut him off. "I have a good business deal to propose to you, a chance to increase your income," he said, thinking that this time he was addressing a man of good sense. Ferland glanced uneasily at his wife but said nothing.

"I'm building a butter factory. I'm ready to buy your milk — at a good price. I'll look after the transport. If you increase your herd a bit, you can count on a good income, a secure future for your wife and children..."

"Have another glass, Monsieur Mercredi?" the man said, seizing the carafe. "Évelyne, bring some cake for monsieur."

"No thankyou, and please, no cake either. Think of the advantages if you convert to milk. Hay doesn't deplete the soil and stands up better to freezing and drought..."

"This 'un's my oldest!" the peasant cried as a tall adolescent entered, pushed in by his mother.

"Fine boy," Askik said. "The two of you could easily milk ten or a dozen cows. I pay ten cents a pound of butter, guaranteed, in good times and bad. Think of it. You won't ever be at the mercy of fluctuating wheat prices again..."

"Well, wheat, y'know, I don't sell so much o' that..."

"I'll guarantee to buy your surplus hay at market price. The demand is excellent in the States. I've ordered a hay baler..."

"Ah yes, handy thing, very handy..."

"And I might even start producing cheese this year..."

"Cheese!" the fellow exclaimed in a tone of great amazement. "Fancy that!"

"... which will increase the market for milk even more. As a businessman, you'll realize the kind of profit there is in this, I'm sure."

"Uh... yes," Ferland conceded with a little nod. "But... it's a lotta expense."

"Investment," Askik corrected.

"Ah yes, that's so, but... investment, that's money. Think o' it that way an' it looks pretty much like expense."

Askik gestured smilingly at the parlour's elegant furnishings. "How about all this? You must have bought all these things with money, didn't you?"

"Sure. That's what I mean."

"But you don't spend all your income on furnishings, do you? You put some of it into your farm. Well, what I'm suggesting is only that you reinvest part of your income so you can increase your production capacity."

Ferland said nothing.

"And if you can't buy six cows all at once," Askik continued, "start by buying three... or two... or one."

The teenaged boy had disappeared and the mother was bustling about the kitchen.

"Well, I'll think about it," Ferland exclaimed as if hoping to be heard on the next farm. "I sure will think about it. Another *petit coup* Monsieur Mercredi? Come on, one fer the road. No? Pity!"

Quebec etiquette requires a lot of merriment as a guest departs. Ferland was positively jolly, smiling, laughing, slapping his thighs until sweat came to his brow.

"I'm at Vielleterre every afernoon," Askik said. "Think over my suggestion carefully. Send your boy with a word for me."

"That I will, count on me!"

"Don't wait too long, though. I'm only going to take a certain amount of milk. Once I'm promised as much as I need, it'll be too late to change your mind."

"Ah yes, natcherly. That's only right."

"My compliments to Madame."

"Too kind!"

The bull had sunk up to its hocks. It stared apathetically at Askik as if to say, This time I'm letting myself sink all the way.

The same jovial indifference greeted Askik at every farm he visited. Everyone thought his plan an excellent idea but no one would give a commitment to sell him milk. Riding along the roads, he passed peasants in luxurious *calèches* drawn by pure-bred horses. The extravagance of farmhouse interiors surprised him more than once. In the barnyards, however, cows in varying stages of negect were all he saw.

He returned home after dark, wondering if the dairy industry was not already a lost cause in the Province of Quebec.

10

He was lonely. The farmhands destested him, Rosalie avoided him and Céline ignored him. Even the villagers were turning their backs to him since his altercation with the curé. He was casting about for a pretext to escape, an excuse for a visit to Montreal, when two letters arrived in quick succession.

The first was from Grandet. He was asking if there was work in the country for a criminalist.

On the second envelope, Askik recognized the fine, elegant handwriting of the Speaker, and saw with astonishment that the letter bore the postmark of a village on the North Shore.

> *Dear rustic,*
>
> *I can address you as "rustic" because the word derives from* rus, *meaning "country," and hence describes you and I both.*
>
> *I have taken the leap. I am a substitute teacher at a school for boys. I shall have a post in the autumn. I have repaired an old boat with my own hands. After school I go fishing on the river or scribble articles for the local newspaper.*
>
> *All the* mamans *hereabout are busy trying to find me a wife. They are rich peasants and I am a penniless aristocrat. Could one imagine a happier union?*
>
> *I am gradually being cured of my pedantry.*
>
> *De Meauville*
>
> *P.S. That unfortunate fellow who was looking for you last winter turned up again this spring. I understand he was positively disconsolate when he learned that you had left. I have*

this from Lecorbu, who, of course, obtained no useful information whatever.

Sourly, Askik put the letters away and thought no more about going to Montreal. What good would it do if there was no work to be had? This country has come to a pretty pass, he thought, when it relegates its honest, upright men to godforsaken holes and throws open its privileged places to opportunists. Which opportunists, Askik could not say, but he swore now to withdraw permanently from this society, read no more newspapers, cease following the political scene; to concern himself, in short, with nothing but his own little rural bailiwick, like de Meauville.

The closer he kept to Vielleterre, however, the more lonely he felt and the more a failure.

Spring did not last. At the beginning of June an oppressive heat settled in. Everywhere, the rains had left ponds and wetlands that bred huge clouds of mosquitoes. Horses died of fever and cattle stopped going out to pasture and day by day grew visibly thinner. In the evenings, the whole countryside reeked of smoke from mildewed hay being burned in barnyards to drive away the insects.

The masters suffered along with their animals. Babies were buried in every parish, having failed to survive sour milk, stagnant water, green fruit, rancid bacon and stale bread. Diarrhea was the maker of many angels in those years in Quebec. The little bodies were buried without ceremony beside great-grandparents halfway returned to dust.

The peasants sat on their small plots of stoney ground and once again cast their eyes at the factories of the United States where so many of their relatives already worked. Vermont and Maine haunted them in their beds and at their tables. They pictured a better and indeed idyllic life: ten short hours of work a day, fixed wages, a cute little house in a French-speaking village. Many gave Dame Fortune an ultimatum: this year, or I leave!

The exodus mentality even reached the farmhands of Vielleterre. They became insolent, contemptuous of their work, boastful of the skills they would deploy in a factory. When Askik reproached them for a poor job of hoeing, one of them, a hard-drinking fellow by the name of Beaudry, stuck a finger in the intendant's chest and demanded that he change his tone.

"Ya think I need *you* fer a livin'?" he snarled. "I could find me a job in a factory jis like that!" And he snapped his fingers to prove it.

Askik kept his head down and took such behavior without a word because he needed these men. When they went to the village, they boasted to all who would listen that they had "a nice, polite little intendant."

It was a stifling afternoon. Askik was about to desert his office, which faced west and after two in the afternoon heated up like an oven. Paradis came in, his face long with contrition. Because he thought it more honest, he delivered his bad news without excuse or beating around the bush.

"One o' the new cows is dead," he announced. "She got into the alfalfa and swole up."

Poor Paradis. Although he saw no merit in the big Holsteins, he was genuinely saddened. Askik, however, considered that he was the only one who cared. Black rage surged in his eyes. He was going to roar invectives but was so furious he could not utter a word. He strode out of the room without taking his straw hat off its peg. The hired men stopped talking when they saw him cross the barnyard. Paradis followed him.

From a distance the cow looked like a huge white flower blooming in the alfalfa field. It had succumbed in midfeast. Walking through the hay was difficult, for it was already high. Askik arrived first, heart thumping with effort and anger. Mechanically, he took note of the swollen flank, the popping eyes, the tongue covered with green froth. Also a small red wound between the ribs where Paradis had planted his knife in an effort to deflate the animal. There were flies clinging about her orifices.

"Where did she get in?" Askik asked.

Paradis pointed. A few minutes' walk brought them to the pasture. The rail fence was intact, everything was in order. Askik turned questioning eyes to Paradis.

"I put the rail back t' keep the rest o' the cows out," the old man said. "It's this 'un was on the ground." He put his hand on the top rail.

"It's not broken. How did it fall off?"

Paradis looked at the ground, abject and ill at ease.

"Who did it?"

"Dunnow," Paradis replied. "I had 'em hoein' the corn. One of 'em coulda come without me seein'."

Askik turned away. He had no desire to look at anyone now. Teeth clenched, he gazed at his herd of Holsteins in the distance. Low-down, ungrateful louts! Murderers!

"We'll come and bury it tonight," Paradis proffered gently. "A fine cow. A real shame."

"No," Askik replied in an expressionless voice. "Not tonight. Wait three or four days. Send the men to bury her then."

"*Mais voyons*," the old foreman objected patiently. "Three or four days in this heat? She'll stink!"

"Too bad for them!" Askik retorted. "Send them to do it Saturday. Not before."

"Don't do that, monsieur," Paradis begged. "We hafta start hayin' next week. I'm already short o' men. If you gotta punish 'em, wait till winter when threshin's done."

The heat! Askik felt dizzy, nauseous. What was he doing among these savages?

"All right then, do as you like!" he shot back in disgust, without turning.

The countryside was deserted. The birds and crickets were groggy with the heat. The galvanized church roof glistened in the distance like a mirage. Not a cloud, not a breath of wind. Even the poplars were at rest. Askik observed all this studiously, trying to convince himself that there was nothing else on his mind. The insolence of the hired men did not affect him, he told himself. The affairs of Vielleterre left him cold; he washed his hands of them. At the same time, however, another voice deep inside was saying, I'm going to crush them!

From the garden he heard the sound of women's voices laughing. Céline and Rosalie had set up a scarecow and were putting an old straw hat on its head. As soon as they saw Askik they stopped laughing. Rosalie looked alarmed. Even Céline glanced away. Were they all poking fun at him? Even Céline? Even Paradis?

"Look," Céline said with forced gaiety, "this is our new hired man."

Askik studied the silent scarecrow, a fright made of straw and ragged clothes.

"Is he good and obedient?"

"He does everything I ask him to," Céline replied.

"He's a very exceptional hired man, then."

"Ah, but I only ask him to do what he's able to."

"Nothing more?"

"Never."

"Can't he learn anything new?"

Céline gave the scarecrow a comical pout. "Oh... yes, but not very fast."

"You know they killed one of the new cows?"

Rosalie tiptoed away. Céline gave Askik a reproachful look.

"Why d'you say that? You don't know they killed it."

"Somebody took down the fence. It didn't happen all by itself."

Defeated, Céline let her shoulders droop.

"It was wrong," she conceded. "They shouldn'ta done it."

"They did, though, so what should I do about it?"

"You don't know who took the fence down?"

"No."

"Then don't do nothin'."

"Rosalie must know who did it. The men are always sniffing round her skirts. I could question her."

"She's afraid o' you enough already! They're all afraid. That's why they do dumb things."

She had bent to pick up pieces of string and cloth from around the scarecrow's feet. The movement triggered the memory of another, similar scene for Askik. He could see a little girl with dirty hair, picking up bones in a thicket.

"You remind me of someone."

"Who's that?"

"A little girl I knew a long time ago, when I was a child myself. Her manner was rather like yours. Her name was Mona, but we pronounced it Moun-na."

"She was a Métisse?"

"Yes. Does that shock you?"

"Not a bit. Madame Sancy says I gotta have Indian blood in me myself, 'cause o' my hair."

"Why are you letting me talk to you today?"

"Because you seem unhappy."

"Because you're sorry for me, then."

"To stop you doin' mean things."

"You think I'm mean?"

"The more alone you are, the worse you are."

"So you're not going to leave me alone any more?"

He gave a hard little snicker, thinking to make fun of himself, but Céline was already moving away toward the house; she did not reply. Once again, Askik could see Mona walking across a prairie in the mist; small, alone and indomitable.

11

The alfalfa was in flower. The hired men had swept out the hayloft. Askik was combing the countryside for reapers. He wanted skilled men capable of showing his own employees a thing or two. Every reaper vaunted his scythe and skillful wristwork; every one wanted top rates of pay. The greater a man's reputation, the more pay he commanded, for a good reaper sets the pace for all the others.

Askik barely slept a wink the night before the reaping. He wakened repeatedly, convinced he had heard rain on the roof. He dozed off toward morning and dreamed that a big herd of swollen cows had devastated his fields. Waking with a start, he leapt up and rushed to the window. The stars were pale but clearly visible; the sky was clear, the weather was still fine and dry.

Overjoyed, he ran downstairs four steps at a time. Women from the village were already busy in the kitchen. Céline was overseeing everything, directing everything, without appearing to be in charge.

The reapers who had spent the night in the barn were beginning to gather in the yard. Others were arriving on foot from neighbouring farms. A smell of pipe smoke already hung in the morning air. Scythes were being compared, some more renowned than their men; some were receiving light strokes with scythestones, allowing evaluation from their resonance.

Paradis was in command. When he judged the number sufficient, he gave the order to move off. On their way by the pasture, the men peered with curiosity at the Holstein cows.

Paradis disposed his reapers according to their strength, so that the best could readily be seen by the others. The sun was just coming over the horizon as the work began. Those who considered they had a reputation to defend advanced with broad, rhythmic strokes, watching their rivals out of the corners of their eyes. Paradis, who was no longer supple enough to handle a scythe, moved from row to row, judging the uniformity of the cut, slowing down the young and less experienced who might run out of steam if they went too fast.

"The day's gonna be long," he told them. "It's better to cut good than cut fast. Cut low, that's where the hay starts."

Like a mechanic going from one engine to another, he regulated the operation of his great machine. Before long, the sweep of the scythes through the growth became slower but more regular.

Pretty good, pretty good! Paradis said to himself as he trotted this way and that. Who's doin' best? Looks like young Lavergne. Fine lad! Fine work! A sheep 'd starve to death followin' 'im.

He became quite frisky with glee. It was exciting, the cool air, the dew, the workers all together here. He felt like a boy again. His old legs refused to keep still and his hands itched. He had brought his ancient scythe, just in case... in case another man broke his own, he had told himself. He spat on his scythestone and ran it lovingly along the edge of the blade.

"*Envoye le père!* Go grandad!" a reaper called when he saw Paradis join the work. A cheer rose from the men. Paradis's sight was hazy, but his hands and wrists rediscovered the movements he needed. A rich swath of alfalfa fell to the ground, stalks sliced clean at ground level. He went at it slowly, methodically, lapping the strokes of other scythes with his, leaving nothing standing. The youngsters could scythe for fame and glory; he did it for love. A right of seniority.

Once the initial burst of enthusiasm had passed, and excepting the pace-setters who would keep competing until the stars came out, most of the reapers began to find the time long. Now and then, field mice or other small animals would scurry away inches ahead of a blade. Near the pond, a reaper discovered a duck's nest. A flurry of mirth greeted a hare leaping a zigzag course among the men. These were shortlived diversions, however; the work itself seemed endless.

The sun began to beat down hard. The dew evaporated within an hour and then the scythes sliced less easily through the alfalfa. Now the men were stopping more ofen to sharpen their scythes. The cut stalks gave off a strong, sweet smell. Bees flew over the field in every direction, skimming the tops of the alfalfa still standing, hurrying to finish their harvest before the men finished theirs.

Askik had stayed at the farmyard all morning. It takes training to handle a scythe; sensibly, he had decided not to try his hand at it. He was longing to go to the fields but was afraid of looking absurd, walking around among the reapers with his hands in his pockets. He oversaw the milking and preparation of the hayloft, but these were getting done perfectly well without him. In the end, finding that he was in everybody's way, he shut himself up in his office where he could at least give the appearance of working. Yet shuffling papers did nothing to make him feel better. He thought about the young men out there reaping. They were the same age as he; they were skilled workers and had wives and families. He himself could do nothing with his hands and was entirely dependent on others for his subsistence. The fabulous stroke of luck that had plucked him from the prairie was beginning to look less like a boon. These habitants had accessible goals, artless pleasures, a simple faith. He, on the other hand, had never had an uncomplicated feeling. Never one of tenderness that was not coupled with irony, never a commitment untainted with doubt. All his resolutions melted away in scepticism. The habitants were right to despise him. He was rotten. A man adulterated by vainglorious pursuits.

Hating yourself can be rather satisfying. Askik was carrying his self-condemnation to new heights when Céline came and tapped on his window.

"Come on, we're goin' to the fields."

"I... er... have work to do here," he replied, gesturing vaguely at his papers.

"You're goin' to help us turn the hay. It's easy."

A south wind had risen. The hay was drying rapidly. Older women spread out across the field, testing the mown alfalfa by feel. The stems must be elastic enough to hold their leaves, but dry enough not to ferment in the hayloft.

At Céline's instigation, Askik found himself at the reins of a big wagon loaded with children. Every bump in the road set off a carillon of squeals that must have been heard for miles around. The mothers walked alongside, admonishing the little ones to hold on tight and not fall off under the wheels. Askik had hoped that Céline would ride on the wagon beside him, but she walked with the village girls. They were laughing merrily, exchanging stories that he could not hear. For all that, he was not displeased with his lot. From up there on the wagon, he could look around at the undulating, flowering sea he had created. If it had not been for him, this depleted soil would have been taxed once again to yield a poor, unsaleable crop of wheat. Instead, he had brought forth a rich green shag that stored up the sun's rays, injected nitrogen into the soil, and pervaded the countryside with its sweet smell. Again he calculated the amounts of butter and milk he was expecting. When he saw the bees buzzing about the field, he resolved to read up on apiculture over the winter, providing it was warranted by the price of honey.

His passion for planning had returned; he was no longer doubting his usefulness. Whether you want it or not, he said to himself as he looked at the women and children, whether your men go along with it or not, I'm going to make you rich. I'm going to teach you to save and make yourselves powerful. I'm bringing you better living conditions, even if you don't know it, so who cares if you despise me?

The party stopped in a small grove of trees that used to belong to the Dubois. The children flew off looking for wild strawberries. The women unpacked the midday meal, setting soup cauldrons, bags and jugs on the grass.

"Soup's ready!" a tall farm wife shouted, but the reapers kept working, heads down, displaying the supreme arrogance of males at work. Madame Paradis caught her husband's eye and beckoned scoldingly. Paradis straighted up, spoke a few words to his co-workers, and the work stopped.

"So how's it goin'?" the tall farm wife asked.

"Not bad, not bad," muttered an untalkative reaper. The men had been occupied with their own thoughts since dawn, and now were not readily finding their tongues. They arrived walking slowly, their rough cotton shirts soaked with sweat, their boots turned green by the alfalfa. They passed around jugs of cool water before sitting down on the grass in the shade.

"Fine harvest!" Paradis said to Askik. "There's spots where it's a bit thin; hafta sow closer next spring. Fine harvest, though."

"Will you get finished this week?"

"Long as the weather holds. Need more hands, though. If I was you, I'd go get reapers from t'other shore next summer."

"Next summer," Askik said, "we'll have mechanical reapers. Scything's all right for small areas, but to feed the herds I'm planning we'll have to double our hay production. We'll have to have machines for that."

Paradis said nothing. He leaned his scythe against a tree and went to join his wife. Stiffly, he let himself down onto the grass. He accepted his bowl of soup and hunk of bread without a word, but instead of eating he gazed miserably at the reapers who, like him, had dropped to the ground to rest under the trees.

"What's the matter, Auguste," said his wife, "ain't you hungry?"

"I ain't so sorry I'm old, wife," he said. "I lived my life at the right time. I thank the good Lord fer it."

His wife kept looking at him, waiting for an explanation.

"You see them young 'uns," he continued, indicating a group of teenage boys. "It's their first scythin'. They're tryin' hard to learn, but it won't do them no good. There's gonna be machines to take their place."

"Young folks like machines."

"That they do," Paradis sighed, dunking a piece of bread, "but I'm glad I knowed it t'other way."

As Askik sat down beside Céline, he thought he heard smothered giggles from the village girls. Céline showed no embarrassment. No great pleasure either. She served him soup and salt pork, like the reapers. Askik felt rather ill at ease to be eating the workers' meal when he had spent the day sitting around, but enjoyment of the food soon got the better of his scruples.

"The men say it's a good harvest," Céline remarked. "You can be proud."

"Why? I didn't grow it. Or reap it."

"That's not your place," Céline replied with the good sense that brooks no argument. "You study, and you decide. That's your work."

Askik gestured toward the resting reapers. "The others don't believe much in my work," he said. "They think ideas just come into my head ready for use, without the slightest effort on my part."

Céline could not reply. She too had very little idea what Askik's work consisted of. She could barely read and write. When she was old enough to have started school, the peasants had burned down the village school so as not to have to pay school taxes. She imagined that an educated man emerged from classical college fully formed, having assimilated once and for all whatever knowledge he needed. Like a cake recipe one never forgets. In any case, she was well aware that peasants do not like to be managed by people who work. Idleness is the proof of superiority that they demand of a master, be he curé or intendant. They can poke fun at literate people, even hate them, but for all that they expect masters to live like masters. Askik was the only one to find it inappropriate for him to be sharing the soup prepared for the workers. All this, Céline could not explain to him.

Askik was not surprised at the young woman's silence. She was not a voluble talker anyway. He thought she was beautiful in her coarse cotton work dress, sitting under a young poplar tree. He felt in love with her and was not conscious of the gulf separating them.

How strange it is! he thought. This is the life I've always longed for, the one that even this morning I thought I'd never find. The fields, the sun, the farmwork, a gracious, simple woman by my side. De Meauville is so right! Why do I need the wear and tear of the city? What do I care for opulent carriages, salons and courtrooms? Élisabeth was pretty; she bewitched me. But Céline is good; she has transformed me. It's true, I'm not the same any more. I'm gradually getting over my cynicism. I think I too am going to become a good person.

"Well, Monsieur Lavergne!" Céline exclaimed, seeing the young farmer approach.

Lavergne squatted in front of Askik, his straw hat in his hand. Askik envied him his fine moustache, his virile, handsome face.

"Have you changed your mind about my offer?" he asked. Lavergne seemed embarrassed.

"No, I thought about it pretty good, but I ain't the kind to be a milk farmer. Ain't got it in me. No, I've come t' ask your advice. You're a lawyer, I think. An old aunt of my wife's died without no will. I'm wonderin' if we got a right to part o' what she left."

Because he was becoming a good person, Askik repressed his impatience and helped Lavergne perceive the multitude of old aunts, young aunts, nephews and cousins still living and breathing besides his wife. In conclusion, he advised him to give up hoping for an inheritance, and not to throw away money going to court.

No sooner had Lavergne departed than a second habitant came to replace him. This one was squabbling with his neighbour over a fence line. A third complained of a municipal bridge in disrepair. A fourth, of a water source polluted by a manure pile. Half the county came. Each had a secret grievance, a thorn of injustice in his hide. When the habitants quarrelled with their neighbours, the disputes could go on for years. When they came into conflict with those stronger than they, however, they had only one recourse: to give in and be quiet. They knew nothing of laws, could not read, and signed their names with crosses. How could they stand up for themselves under such conditions? In this single hour at midday, Askik promised to arbitrate a boundary dispute, write to the Minister of Roads, and speak to the secretary of the parish council. The farmers thanked him politely but not effusively. They probably thought it natural that Askik should come to their aid. He had received an education, had been reading and idling while they had been working. Every privilege has its price. Even an habitant can demand certain services of an intendant.

The men took up their scythes again and the women and older childen began turning the new-mown hay with short wooden forks to ensure uniform drying. Askik took part in this and found the task pleasant at first. The alfalfa scent and the singing of crickets delighted him; he felt he was one with the earth and the peasantry. After an hour he began to want some diversion. His back hurt; he was not used to working bent over. After two hours, he was wishing he were back in his office. He was bored to death with the monotony of the work. He marvelled to see these tireless women turning and piling the hay with unflagging attention. How could they stay interested in such a mindless task? The sun must surely have stopped moving in its course; the day would never end. At six o'clock came another break for refreshment, then the work continued until dusk. The horses were brought and the hay cut in the first hours of the day was loaded onto the wagons. When the wagons were full, the women shouldered their forks and set off for home. Askik would have liked to heave a sigh of relief but could not muster the strength. His back and shoulders were stiff and his hands were raw from the coarse-grained handle of the fork. In future, he promised himself, he would have more respect for the division of tasks between habitants and "lettered folk."

12

"Not so rough, Rosalie! You're makin' bread, not bricks!"

The fat girl muttered something that might have been an oath. When she was in a bad temper she let her muscles express it, in this case at the expense of the dough she was kneading in the bottom of the dough box.

"There's some days you're like a thistle," Céline told her. "It's hard to know how to take you."

"Well, don't take me at all!" Rosalie bellowed. "Jis lemme alone."

Madame Paradis heaved a long sigh. Rosalie's moods were beyond understanding; you just had to let them pass. The old lady brought her knitting close to her eyes to count the stitches. Céline was shelling peas at the big kitchen table.

"So it's certain the Sancy's ain't comin' back this summer?" Madame Paradis asked.

"That's right," Céline replied, "they're stayin' in Ottawa. Alexis got the letter yesterday."

"So you're callin' 'im Alexis now!" Rosalie taunted, thinking to touch a sore point. Céline paid no attention.

"A pity," Madame Paradis continued. "I like when the house fills up a bit."

"Ottawa's a long way and Monsieur must be busy."

"Well, I'd like better for 'em to come back anaways. It'd be a nice change for us. If y'ask me, Monsieur Sancy's gonna end up sellin' Vielleterre."

Rosalie rose up in anger.

"An' what's gonna happen t' us then?"

"Ah, when it comes to that, my girl..." Madame Paradis raised her hands toward Heaven, and so doing lost the stitch she was counting. She had to recount the row before asking, "You ain't had no word from Mademoiselle Élisabeth?"

"No, nothin'."

Madame Paradis smiled at her knitting needles. "She was always so pretty, so sweet, my Élisabeth. I practic'ly brought 'er up, y'know." She sighed, concluding, "I hope I live long enough to see 'er married."

"I know somebody won't be so pleased," Rosalie said.

The women worked in silence for a time, each following the train of her own thoughts. Flies slapped against the screen door. A dragonfly flew around the porch clicking its wings, then went its way.

"Well now, is that my Auguste down there at th' end of the yard?" Madame Paradis said, looking out the window. "Rosalie, you got good eyes, can you see?"

"It's him. He's with Monsieur Mercredi."

"Ah, that one! I'm wonderin' what more he'll be up to. Since he come, my Auguste ain't had a minute's peace. Barns, a factory, hay an' what all..."

"But if Vielleterre gets richer the Sancys won't so likely sell it," Céline interrupted.

"Hmmf! We'll see 'bout that!"

There was another silence during which Rosalie glanced back and forth between Céline and Madame Paradis. It had been bothering her plenty long enough. Why shouldn't she know? Boldened by the presence of a third woman, she decided to get it off her chest.

"About Monsieur Mercredi," she said to Céline, "d'you like 'im?"

Madame Paradis' eyes lit up. Good question, but the fat girl was going about it the wrong way. Madame Paradis tried it a little more tactfully.

"Mark my words, Céline," she said in her most maternal voice, "Monsieur Mercredi's a fine-lookin' man. He's young, educated, got a future. I heard tell he'll only be one season at Vielleterre. After that, who knows? He could go far!"

"I can see ya in Ottawa, Céline, can't you?"

Like hunters who have planted their bait and now only have to wait, the two women watched Céline in silence. Any reply would do. Admission or denial, it hardly mattered; their minds were made up.

Céline kept shelling her peas in total indifference.

Madame Paradis repressed an exclamation of annoyance. The girl could be so stubborn!

"If y' ask me, he's a good catch. He's a Métis, but he's perfectly presentable. And then, my girl you ain't so young no more."

"Monsieur le curé says jiss about all Canadian families got Indian blood in 'em," Rosalie offered encouragingly.

"Well, not all," Madame Paradis corrected. "It ain't important, but I know all the Paradis're descended direct from seigneurs in France."

"Us too," Rosalie affirmed.

"But that don't make us no better," Madame Paradis conceded. "We all know what fine, strong little things Métis children are."

"That's what you'd expect!" Rosalie exclaimed. "When you cross two breeds o' cats, you always get better kittens."

The old lady's face reddened. She tolerated clumsiness but not impropriety.

"Come, come, girl, we don't talk 'bout men an' animals like they was the same."

"Well, they're made the same way!"

"Yes but there's things we just don't say!"

"Well, look at Monsieur Mercredi. He's a healthy, fine lookin' man. That's proof there's good things about crossin'."

Madame Paradis impaled her balls of wool on her kniting needles and got to her feet.

"All this time my Auguste's supper's not gettin' made," she said crisply.

She banged the screen door twice to dislodge the flies before leaving.

"You're goin' about it right if you wanta stay single, Céline, my girl," she said from outside. "You're goin' about it right!"

Céline gave her a vacant smile but kept on shelling her peas. In the kitchen, the only sound now was the dough box feet tapping on the floor. With her face bathed in sweat and her arms bright red, Rosalie kneaded harder and harder until she could keep it in no longer.

"So d'ya like 'im or dontcha?" she burst out.

Céline disposed of the pods, picked up the bowl of peas and went to the sink. On the way by, she glanced inside the dough box.

"Looks like old plaster," she said.

She picked up a broom and put it in its corner, then a dishcloth and tossed it back in the sink. All this gabble! She felt discontented and, for the first time in years, indecisive. Had she made the right choice? The kitchen seemed small and dirty. Incurably dirty. Even the house, this great vessel that she used to pilot with such pleasure, no longer appealed to her. Vielleterre; what was it? A collection of empty rooms, scented sheets and furniture to be preserved for masters who were never there.

She went to the door and leaned against the frame, looking into the yard the way a fisherman casts a line into an unpromising river: in case something might happen.

Nothing was happening. Madame Paradis was home by now. Her husband was rattling buckets in the dairy. The hired men had already hightailed out of the barn, in haste to begin their Saturday night in the village, drink till they were sick and come home nursing broken teeth.

When she was a small child, Céline had decided she would never take a husband. The spectacle of her cowed, humiliated mother had taught her that one does not live to be old when at the mercy of another. Could she, however, have chosen the wrong occupation? Always doing other people's housework, having only Rosalie for company — was this the best she could do?

I should have been a nun, she said to herself for the hundredth time. There's room for strong women in the orders. I could have finished my education and worked in a school or hospital. Maybe even been a principal or hospital director. Who's going to give lessons to a woman of my age, though? They'd put me in the kitchen. I'd be peeling potatoes for a hundred instead of six. A lot further ahead I'd be!

She went to the rocking chair by the window. She sat in it clasping her knees, as her mother used to do when trying to escape from the present into memories of her chidhood.

She was only my age, Céline thought with amazement. She was old and broken, but she was only my age!

Was she going to be angry all over again with this woman who had been too weak to protect her? No. Surprisingly, no. In this quagmire of apathy she was in, not even anger could struggle to the surface. Neither anger nor joy; only the window, the yard, and the maple tree across the way.

A man was striding briskly out of the yard; Askik was going to visit his new factory.

There's another that's never happy, Céline thought. Why? Maybe we were all put together wrong when we were children, like half-risen bread. For each of us, some ingredient left out. Rosalie would have loved to be beautiful. I didn't have the father I needed. And Alexis... what was it he didn't have?

Rosalie swung her large mass around, hands on her hips.

"I'm goin' up to my room. I ain't feelin' good." She spoke in her most truculent voice, but her eyes betrayed fear. She was lying.

"All right, Rosalie," Céline replied gently. "Go and get some rest. I'll watch the bread."

Rosalie left the room, as much relieved as surprised, convincing herself that she really was a little under the weather.

Céline stayed a while in the rocking chair. Evening was approaching. The big kitchen was filling with shadows. The cricket in the pantry began his twilight song. The bread was baking without rising.

With her chin on her knees and her eyes closed, she tried to imagine a dark night. A vast city. And in the middle of the city, a Métis child clinging to a wrought-iron gate, waiting for daylight in order to discover that he had been abandoned.

13

What to do of a Sunday when mass has been said and lunch is over? Askik had settled into the armchair in his room with an English novel on his lap and a cup of tea at his elbow. Grandet had sent him the book, worrying that his friend was moldering in the country. It was a thick Gothic tale of adventure, very much in fashion. Askik had resolved to read a chapter a day. He had also planned to look over some judicial reports and after supper write letters. Instead of these things, he was drowsing.

The house was sleeping with him. Céline was spending the afternoon with her aunt in the village. The hired men were getting over their hangovers. Paradis had not been seen all day.

The impassive Ithaca clock sounded the hours; the English knight's adventures were not advancing an inch. Chide though he might, his mind was refusing to cooperate. On page eighteen, a lady-in-waiting had just fainted; in his whole life, Askik had never seen a woman collapse in a faint.

It was already late when, disgusted with himself, he picked up his hunting rifle and went out. A small yellow dog had been lying under the steps and now ran out, dragging its belly and peeing in excitement.

"Don't try and humbug me," Askik growled. "I know you. You'll have all the rabbits in the parish on the run, the way you did last time."

The mutt thumped the ground happily with its tail as if to say, No I won't, I've changed, and without waiting to be invited, streaked across the yard like a bullet, heading for the fields.

"Might as well stay home now," Askik grumbled, but he followed anyway. Anything rather than work.

The meadows and woods were sodden with rain. The hemlock woods in the distance were veiled in mist. Askik buttoned his jacket all the way to the neck, surprised to find it so cold. The hay was growing vigorously; the second crop was going to be as rich as the first. The wheat was turning yellow prematurely, aged by weeks of heat, but Askik did not care; wheat was cheap.

He crossed a stone fence through which large oaks were growing and then was on Dubois land. No one had wanted this small rocky field; left to itself, the earth had grown a bewildering mixture of wheat, rocks and weeds. The small dog plunged ahead like an habitué of the place. He raced in exuberant circles, barking madly, flushing game that he alone could see.

At the bottom of the field was a rotting haystack half-eaten by deer. Dubois had done his haying but had been unable to harvest his wheat. So illness had struck him down in late summer. The grain had ripened on the stalk and fallen; the man had remained powerless at home.

Askik recognized the dismal avenue leading to the house, the tall elms, the wheel tracks overgrown with grasses. Was it the cloudy sky, the close weather? The trees looked dark and resentful. You didn't come when it was time, they were saying, so why are you bothering us now? Rank lambs-quarters were growing in front of the door of the shack. The door was ajar. Askik hesitated. He almost expected to find the Dubois' corpses inside, but all there was was the most ordinary stuff. The few objects of any value had been removed. A rickety table was leaning against a wall, a chair with seat stove in was overturned on the floor. The canvas had been taken off the windows and a cloak of dust covered everything.

Behind the farm buildings the woods began. A lumber skid road wound upward through the trees, avoiding the steepest inclines. Poplar, maple and ash still held sway, but here and there massed clumps of spruce trees had already made an appearance.

Askik crossed the crest of the hill, where the road ended. The small yellow dog had disappeared. Good riddance. Askik checked his gun and struck out through the woods. He had long ago dismissed the teaching of the Ojibway, who pretend indifference in order to deceive the game. Not even the most simple-minded rabbit would be deceived about his intentions. Finger crooked around the trigger, eyes probing under every tree, he hunted with murderous intensity, like a Montréaler.

The woods did not last. The trees covered no more than the rocky summit of the hill; the more fertile flanks had been largely cleared. The meadows, square or meandering depending on the richness of the soil or accidents of topography, climbed unevenly to meet the edge of the trees. Askik had just disturbed a herd of sheep when he heard the crackling of a wood fire. He came to a long, passage-shaped clearing. At its far end, barely visible in the darkess of the woods, a small man was throwing branches onto a bonfire; the flames were flickering at the bottom, held in by the green wood and humidity. Askik put his gun over his shoulder and walked toward the stranger, thinking to talk a bit and pass the time.

The man was dragging a small tree to the fire. He stood straight when he heard footsteps.

"Paradis!" Askik exclaimed.

"I reckon that's me," the foreman replied, heaving the tree onto the fire.

"What are you doing here?"

Paradis smiled mischievously, a rare occurrence with him.

"How d'ya mean? I'm home here."

"Home? Have you bought the Dubois farm?"

"*Pantoutte!* Dubois' is t'other side o' the mountain. This here's mine."

"Oh. I didn't know you had land."

"Ain't had it long. Bought it from the neighbour. He keeps and eye on it for me. Them's my sheep you just scared."

Paradis sat down on an upturned tree root with his hands on his thighs and watched his fire burn.

"I'm makin' a road," he said, "so I can come get firewood."

"What's the point? There's no shortage of wood at Vielleterre."

Paradis looked embarrassed, almost contrite.

"Well, y'see, I'm gonna build me a little house come spring, down there by the village road."

His eyes pleaded for indulgence, but Askik, caught short by the news, could only see the inconvenience this was going to cause him.

"You're leaving Vielleterre?" he demanded reproachfully.

Paradis hung his head. Yes, he was letting people down. Yet it had not been easy to turn his back on Vielleterre, on his parents who had died there and the seigneurs who had entrusted its care to them. But the young man would not understand all this.

"Y'see," he said softly, "I lived all my life on somebody else's land. I promised myself I'd know what it was like bein' on my own land, in my own house, one day before I died. I been waitin' a long time fer it."

All of this was touching a raw nerve with Askik. He was anticipating Eugène Sancy's displeasure on hearing of this departure.

"You're doing it because of me, aren't you?"

"*Pantoutte, pantoutte, voyons.* I knowed things was gonna change long before you come. I ain't agin it. You're bringin' in machines, cows, you're gonna make butter... That's good, but it ain't for me no more. It's time I leave them things fer others."

"Yes, but how are you going to manage here?"

"I'll have a cow, a few sheep, a garden..."

"I'm not talking about that," Askik said testily. "You're not young any more, or your wife either. And you don't have children. In five or ten years, who'll take care of you?"

"Ah, when it comes to that..." The old man spread his hands wide.

"That's no answer."

"There ain't many answers in this life."

"You're not going to have me believe you haven't thought about it, or you'd rather not think about it."

"The good Lord didn't give us no children. It's up to him to look after us."

"He didn't look after the Dubois."

"How d'you know?"

"I went to see them last winter, because you asked me to, I remind you. I didn't get the feeling the good Lord was keeping their accounts. Or else he was a bad intendant."

"Don't blaspheme, my boy."

"Well, how about you, it's Sunday and you're working."

"All I'm doing's burnin'. It's the fire does all the work."

"At Vielleterre you'd be taken care of."

"I got no doubts 'bout that, no doubts at all," Paradis replied placidly.

"So?"

So? Paradis spread his hands wide again. So he was going, that was all.

"Don't you trust me?" Askik demanded.

This time Paradis could not resist a smile. Trust him? Do you turn your back to a big bull calf? Do you trust young folks? He had to reply, however, had to save this moody young man from himself.

"It ain't just to be ornery," he said. "Could be I got a few more years to live, but you... I'd be surprised to see you here much longer."

"What d'you mean? I do a good job here."

"Ah, that you do, but I figger you won't be workin' long for other folks. Too much education, no patience, that don't make a good employee."

Askik said nothing. How could he deny it? He himself sensed that his situation was becoming intolerable. A feeling that he was wasting his time gnawed at him night and day. Surely he was called to greater things... but what? Should he return to Montreal, to go dredging through the prisons like Grandet? Or take a cue from de Meauville and stay in Saint-Aimé, teach and write there, win the confidence of the habitants and defend their interests? It worried him constantly. He had opened his heart to no one lest his aspirations be taken for arrogance. In his own mind, however, his humility was not in question; he was convinced that all he sought was an opportunity to serve. Yet *how* was he going to serve?

Had the old man been pondering this? Has he guessed my discontent, Askik wondered; has he discovered the cure for it? Appearances are deceptive. These old habitants know more than they let on. But if he has advice to give me, why hasn't he said anything? Is he waiting for me to ask him?

"Perhaps in fact I ought to leave Vielleterre," he ventured.

"You got plenty o' time," the old man said. "Ain't no need to hurry."

"I could go back to Montreal and do court work, perhaps even open my own office."

Paradis nodded slowly.

"Or else settle in the country... to practice law or teach. There isn't much education among the habitants. I could help them, I could defend their interests."

Another nod.

"Later, after a few years, I might serve as an alderman, or member of parliament, say."

Paradis nodded again, gravely as if considering each of these possibilities. He said nothing, however.

"So what do you suggest I do?"

"Well, all o' that's good."

"Yes, but what should I do, stay or leave?"

"One or t'other's good."

"But which should I choose?"

Paradis gave a shrug. "Don't matter none," he said.

Heartless old codger! When you've got one foot in the grave, career choices don't matter much, of course. Whatever they say, Askik thought, there's nothing rarer than a wise old man. Men live and die selfish; age makes no difference. Still, he had come close to believing in Paradis and his old-time Christian ways.

"Damn, it's cold," Askik muttered, pulling up the collar of his coat.

"Ah, the north wind always brings cold weather."

"But this is August!"

Paradis spread his hands. So?

The flames were becoming brighter, more orange as the daylight faded.

"Well, I think I'd better go on home," Askik said, getting to his feet.

"Take the road," Paradis said, pointing to the path he had cleared through the woods.

"No, it's shorter over the mountain."

"It'll be dark soon. You'll git lost."

"No, no, I've got plenty of time."

Perhaps Paradis had been right. Night was gathering. The pastures were grey marshes in which sheep melted away. The top of the hill had been swallowed in fog. It was as black as a wolf's lair in the woods. The dark welled up between the roots and mounted into the branches. For a time Askik thought he might have to turn back, but he found the Dubois' trail without difficulty; so easily he was disappointed, in fact. It had been a very humdrum day after all.

The woods were silent in this cold, damp weather. All Askik could hear were his own footsteps, muffled on the grass, hollow on culverts across the trail. His thoughts raced far ahead of him, paying no heed to these monotonous woods. In his mind, his outing was already over.

Suddenly an explosion of wings. A grey shadow. *Take care! Take care! Take care!* A bluejay flapped away, its hoarse cries echoing through the far corners of the woods. Only a jay. If it had turned out to be a partridge, Askik thought, he would certainly have died of fright. Some hunter!

The Dubois' pond was the colour of lead. Askik walked quickly down the avenue of great elms and at last was on the village road. He was relieved to be here; this road belonged to everyone.

The wind swept despotically over the countryside, trailing shreds of mist snatched from the distant river. Night was settling in. A wild, excessive night. A night for staying home, sipping punch and now and then taking a look at judicial reports. The telegraph wires moaned plaintively, like souls in agony beseeching prayers.

Between two gusts of wind, a faint pattering like rain dripping onto sand at first, nothing more. Askik stood still the better to hear. There was more out there than just the wind in the grass. There it was again, louder, more insistent: pat-a-pat, pat-a-pat, pat-a-pat. He was hearing footsteps, animal footsteps, coming toward him. He stared into the darkness, his gun over his shoulder. He only remembered the weapon at the last minute when with shining eyes and mouth open the small yellow dog bowled into his legs.

Now he heard a cautious voice out there in the darkness. "Dou-dou, Dou-dou, where are you? Come back!"

"Céline?"

There was a moment of startled silence, then the voice said hesitantly, "Alexis, is that you?"

They were in such a hurry to meet that they nearly collided in the middle of the road. The small yellow dog jumped and barked joyfully all around them, as though he had taken a lot of trouble to organize this meeting.

"Oh my, I'm glad to see you!" Céline exclaimed. "Dou-dou, be quiet!"

"Why?" Askik asked jauntily. "Were you afraid? There's nothing to be afraid of."

"Well, I like it better now you're here, anyways."

They turned toward the house again, walking side by side but not arm in arm. Céline set a rapid pace, arms crossed under her shawl.

"I was at my aunt's in the village," she explained. "I forgot what time it was. It got dark so fast..."

"I went hunting on the other side of the mountain, behind the Dubois'. I didn't get anything, but I made an interesting discovery. Paradis has bought a farm over there."

"Yes, I know."

"Oh..."

They walked on for a time in silence, then Askik spoke again.

"Who found the Dubois last winter?"

Céline shuddered. "Why d'you have to talk about the Dubois tonight?"

"Surely you don't believe in ghosts!" Askik taunted.

"Not me," Céline affirmed in hushed voice, "but my grandmother seen some."

Strange reasoning, Askik thought.

"Was it Paradis who discovered the bodies?" he asked in a more serious voice.

"What bodies?"

"The Dubois', of course."

"The Dubois died in the Hospice of Sainte-Anne. It was their lungs did it."

"You mean they didn't die at home?"

"Why d'you have to shout?" Céline whispered. She glanced about uneasily. "No, they didn't die at home. Where'd you get them ideas?"

"Well... no, I must have misunderstood. I stopped by their house a little while ago..."

Céline looked at him anxiously. "You saw ghosts?"

"No, of course not. You think Dubois would come back to that filthy old shack?"

"Don't say that!" Céline admonished in a whisper. "They was poor and they suffered plenty. You musn't make fun o' the dead."

"You said you hadn't seen any ghosts yourself?" Askik pursued.

"Not me, but people I know..." She was walking briskly, head erect, knees beating energetically against the long skirt of her dress. Her expression said, Don't make me get into that.

"So tell me about it."

"I better not."

"That's because you haven't got anything to say."

"My aunt's husband came back three years in a row," she said defiantly. "Always the twelfth of December, the day he died. The clock in the *grand-chambre* would stop at eight o'clock sharp, the time he'd started feelin' bad, and start up again at eleven, the time it was when he died. Every year it happened, my aunt had masses sung for his soul to go to its rest. The fourth year he didn't come back, he'd got out of purgatory."

Askik had begun to feel uneasy. His conscience was crowded with hastily recited rosaries and neglected confessions. He was sorry now to be in such poor standing. Most of all, he was sorry he had got Céline started on this subject. She shared the fascination of humble folk for the lugubrious — weeping spirits, dead bodies miraculously preserved...

Delighted to be sensing reaction on Askik's part and frightening herself as well, Céline continued in a half-whisper.

"My mother's father lived at Saint-Georges-des-Terres on t'other side of the river. In winter it was him used to heat the church. Whenever there was morning mass, he'd get up in the middle o' the night to go light the furnace. One night, walkin' through the village, he saw a nun diggin' in the garden behind the convent. She was hoein'!"

She looked at Askik with eyes big and round with wonder.

"Well, is that all?" Askik said. "That's your story? A nun digging in a garden? That's scary stuff, all right!"

"It was winter!" Céline protested. "The middle of winter, in the snow! My grandfather always made fun of the nuns; crows, he called them. When he saw this nun diggin' in the snow, he went closer to tease her a bit, but soon's he got inside the garden, she raised her hand like this..." — she raised one hand in ghostly slow motion — "then she disappeared."

Here she paused for dramatic effect, but Askik was careful not to encourage her.

"Pépère didn't scare that easy," she continued, "but still! He went to wake up Monsieur le curé and they come back to the convent together. There was the nun, hoein' in the snow in the same place. Once in a while she'd bend over, like she was huntin' for somethin'. When the men went closer, she stood up and showed them her hand, then she disappeared. There weren't no marks in the snow..."

She looked up to see what effect she was having; finding that Askik was suitably impressed, she delivered the key to the riddle.

"When they was gettin' their garden goin' that spring, the nuns found a silver ring, the kind nuns wear. An old woman in the village told about a nun, years and years before, who'd lost her ring workin' in the garden and had looked an' looked for it an' never found it. The curé took this ring and buried it in the nuns' plot in the cemetery, then nobody never saw that nun in the garden no more. And my grandfather never made fun of the nuns no more."

The moon was illuminating a patch of billowy cloud. Someone else would have seen a snow-covered garden there; Askik thrust the thought aside. He tried to find something lighthearted to say and gave up. It was really not worth showing off for a woman who was doing her best to frighten you.

"At Sainte-Marthe," Céline pursued, "there's a man without a head walks on the beach on stormy nights. They say..."

"You don't really believe those silly things, do you?"

Céline bent her head. She hated this superior tone that Askik put on at times. She was uneducated but she was not stupid.

"In the North West, don't people never see ghosts?" she retorted.

Askik pretended not to have heard. Ghosts? In the North West a man could meet a departed ancestor three times a day and not make a big thing of it. But there were also the mahtsé-manito, the evil spirits, it was true. Strange how all this was coming to mind.

Céline, having watched him thinking these things, gave him a quizzical smile. "You ain't a wee bit afraid o' dead people yourself?"

"They say the dead are afraid, too."

She hunched her shoulders. "Oh, come on, now."

"It's true. Sound, light or a mask can frighten them. Even a White can scare them off, they say."

With a look of disbelief, Céline burst out laughing.

"Whites," Askik explained, "are scary things when you're not used to them."

"Here, maybe it's the opposite," Céline said. "Maybe a Canadian ghost can be scared by a Métis."

"And well it might be! Imagine some poor, unsuspecting Québécois ghost going for a walk on his own stamping ground and meeting up with a big, ugly Métis in the middle of the night. How awful!"

Céline laughed heartily. Dou-dou, who had been dragging his feet for some time, pricked up his ears, wagged his tail and then went back to plodding along half asleep behind them.

Céline put a hand on Askik's arm. "I don't think you're ugly," she told him, "and if I was the ghost, I'd feel perfectly safe."

"You disappoint me," Askik replied with a nervous laugh. "I though I was scarier than that."

She turned her face away as she slipped her arm though his. "Not scary at all," she murmured, shyly in spite of herself.

14

The next morning Askik wrote to Eugène Sancy suggesting he buy the Dubois farm. Hemlock bark was rich in tannin and was selling for seven dollars a cord. From this alone, Askik could pay for the land. This was only the beginning, however. He proposed to set up a pig farm on the Dubois farm. The pigs would be fed at little cost on wheat and skim milk from the butter factory, they would be distant enough not to foul the air at Vielleterre, and the Dubois shack could house a full-time employee. Without having to part with a cent, the seigneury would have more land and a new source of income.

Askik was proud of his letter. It was terse, matter-of-fact and precise. It had the incisiveness of a Napoleon writing, "If you are not on the march for Naples within two hours, you will be shot." This was the way he liked to be: clearheaded, decisive. Like an English industrialist directing his branch operations and ships with telegrams to right and left. Buy this. Rig that ship. Set sail. And yet, when he looked out the window and saw the sleepy farm and the gloomy forest in the distance, he wondered again what had to happen before fate removed him from this dead end.

He opened his office door, put his head out into the corridor and shouted, "Rosalie!"

It was a long time before the fat girl appeared, eyes half closed, face bright red and one cheek bearing the marks of bedsheet creases.

"Here's a letter for Monsieur Sancy," Askik told her crisply. "Give it to one of the men and have him take it to the village. Post-haste."

"Eh?"

"At once."

"Yes, monsieur."

She ran out of the house, waving the letter like a flag and yelling the name of her favourite hired man. In those days a letter for the master still inspired respect.

Askik went out too. The wind was catching the clouds broadside and breaking them up. The heat was sucking up masses of evaporation. Dou-dou lay in the shade of the dahlias; he thumped his tail twice but did not bother getting up. Workmen were putting the final touches to a big ventilated shed which was to house the second haying. The hammer blows were muffled by the humidity in the air.

With consummate sloth, a hired man was stacking leftover lumber. "Where's Paradis?" Askik asked him, hiding his irritation.

"D'ya think I oughta know?" the other replied, using the *tu* pronoun never addressed to one's betters. At once he raised frightened eyes, realizing he had gone too far. He was an adolescent with a greyish, downy chin. When he was with the older men he was a cocky fellow, but alone, face to face with the intendant, he was less sure of himself.

"Go and get him," Askik ordered. "Tell him to come and see me behind the barn."

In the bull paddock, the heat and humidity was paroxysmal. The mud, trampled and churned by the animals and enriched two feet deep with dung, gave off a staggering stench of ammonia. A cart was tilted on its rear end, its slats coated with dried manure.

Paradis arrived, his boots covered with mud.

"Is that the only cart we've got?" Askik asked him.

"There's another 'un by the wood pile, but it's in bad shape."

"Can you repair it?"

"I reckon so, but why bother? This'n's enough."

"Our neighbours aren't using their manure. I've seen big piles of it along the road. I'll pay them fifty cents a cartload. Our men can go and get it in their free time. Have them dump it at the edge of the fields; we'll spread it when we plow."

Paradis scratched his chin. "They won't like it."

"Too bad for them," Askik said as he walked away.

He felt powerful and determined. The men needed management because they did not know what was good for them. He imagined them twenty years from now saying, Monsieur Mercredi was tough and demanding, but things really worked back then!

Life moves in strange ways... Askik had spent part of the night under the great elm, in the very spot where, the previous winter, he had dreamed of living happily ever after with Élisabeth.

How could I have been so miserable over that woman? he wondered. Of course, I didn't understand a thing about love then. I wanted emotion, I wanted to win, and I wanted passion. I was living under the same roof as my real source of happiness and didn't know it. How could I guess that true love is calm and humble, that it doesn't inflame desire but soothes it? That it can be as simple as two souls exchanging confidences on a country road in bad weather?

In short, he had decided he was going to marry Céline, move to the village, open an office, and buy land. He was not aspiring to parliament any more. That was not the kind of society his wife-to-be was suited for, he recognized. No, he would stay in the country, befittingly, and use his money to raise up his less fortunate compatriots; by renting them his land inexpensively, for instance. He had resigned himself to his lot. He was being denied the highest echelons, but his sons would reach them. He had come up too fast in the world. Families aren't made over in a single generation. My father was a hunter, he said to himself; I'm a farmer; my sons will be statesmen.

The great house of Vielleterre seemed to be approving gravely. The dark bricks, the sharp-pointed gables, the high chimneys looked down on him kindly as if to say, We're made of the same stuff; we deserve each other.

Céline was setting the table in the pergola by the garden.

"I thought we'd have breakfast outdoors," she told him with a smile.

"Where's Rosalie?"

"In bed. She's feeling sick."

They looked at each other, groping for words, a little embarrassed that their ruse was so transparent. Céline gave a little smile and went back to the kitchen.

It was cool, almost cold under the ivy roof overhead. Every now and then a warm, moist breeze blew in from outside. Eugène Sancy had had the pergola built after seeing others at colleagues' estates. Very English-country-manor.

Céline returned carrying a tray.

"You were up early this mornin'," she said. "I heard you go out."

"I didn't get much sleep. How about you?"

She laughed. "After all those ghost stories I thought I wouldn't sleep a wink, but no, I slept very well."

Askik felt a little resentful. Would he always be the only one to stay awake? Céline was serving the food. She has lovely manners, he thought. Not manners copied from others but an instinctive, thoughtful grace. As if each movement deserves to be considered and deliberate.

They sat at the table together like husband and wife meeting between tasks and sharing a meal in silence. She was the first to push her plate away. With her elbows on the table and her chin in her hands, she gazed out at the fields in the distance.

"Alfalfa's so beautiful. No one else but you would find a hay crop that flowers, Alexis."

"I must confess the flowers had nothing to do with my choice."

"Never mind, it's pretty."

"How long have you been living here, Céline?"

"Me? Twelve years. Why?"

"Have you never thought of leaving?"

"I'm happy here."

"Happy enough to stay?"

Céline was ill at ease. What could she tell him? That she had vowed never to take a husband but was feeling her determination weakening? How could he be asking her such a question? Was he asking her to marry him? If so, why not say it? She was not sure she would accept, but she had the right to hear him ask.

"Where d'you suppose I'd go?" she retorted, putting the ball back in his court.

Like a silly fellow who has ventured too far out on the ice and suddenly feels it buckling, Askik stopped short. He was terror-stricken. Two words more and there would be no turning back. Yet he was being silly. He was sure of himself; his decision had been made. Why not ask her right now to marry him? He had not courted her, it was true, but what of it? This was something that should happen. They were not adolescents, they had both got over romantic love. They suited each other, and as a beginning, that was a lot. Why not come out with it?

But the young woman's total composure unnerved him. She was not blushing, not crumpling the tablecloth, and her eyes were dry. She sat perfectly still, her head slightly bent to spare him her gaze. This was not the way he imagined a young woman waiting for the words that would make her happy ever after. It was all far too prosaic.

"Well, I don't really know," he said finally. "You could get a job in a big house in Montreal, or work in a bank..."

She looked at him with a touch of amusement. Askik felt a wave of shame. What a coward he was! But all was not lost, there was still plenty of time. His intentions had not changed; all he was waiting for was the right moment to speak up.

They finished the meal in silence. Céline was pouring coffee when the man who had been sent to the village with Askik's letter approached.

"There's the mail," he said, slapping a bundle of letters and papers down on the table. He looked at Céline and Askik with a leer and said, "Yer lookin' comfortable, my little sparrows. Make yerselves at home."

He went away laughing. Askik vowed to sack him. Céline paid no attention.

Agricultural bulletins, parliamentary debates (which Askik no longer read), a devotional book for Madame Paradis and — miraculous! — a letter from de Meauville!

When he saw de Meauville's elegant, extravagant handwriting, Askik burst irresistibly into laughter. Just thinking about the Speaker was enough to put him in a good mood. He tore the envelope open with one stroke of a knife, unfolded the letter and read avidly, tossing out fragments for Céline.

"He's a regular teacher... He's bought a house. It's tiny, he says... Well! Gives evening lessons to the habitants. Teaching them to read... Oh no! No! I don't believe it!" He laughed so boisterously, so exuberantly that Céline could not keep from laughing too.

"What is it?" she pleaded. "Alexis, come on, tell me!"

"He's a *marguillier*, a churchwarden!" Askik exlaimed, weeping with laughter. "The curé appointed him to the parish council. Imagine! De Meauville a marguillier!" And he dissolved into gales of laughter.

"Let's see now, what else does he say? Goes fishing, I knew that already... has adopted an old dog, that's a change from his rat... and... oh, de Meauville, you devil! He's kept the best for last!" Askik rose to his feet, his eyes shining with excitement.

Céline put a hand on his arm, happy to see him so happy. "What is it, Alexis? Tell me."

"They're coming here!" Askik cried. "De Meauville and Grandet. They're going to visit us! They're coming to see us!"

Overjoyed, he smiled and laughed both at once, beaming like a small boy who has just won a race at a church picnic. The eternal malcontent had flown, the intendant had vanished. Céline was amazed to be discovering another Alexis, and for the first time, perhaps, felt something more than friendship for him.

15

"Brother de Meauville, you're joking!"

"Not in the least. Get in."

Grandet disdainfully eyed the big brown rowboat rocking gently at the end of the wharf. "Is this all you could find?"

"What were you expecting, for goodness' sake?" de Meauville retorted as he stepped into the boat himself.

"Oh, I don't know. A steamer. A sailboat if necessary. But this cockleshell..."

"There's no steamer crossing on this part of the river. Look and see for yourself, the other shore's just a stone's throw. This will do very nicely. And I'll wager our pilot isn't making his first crossing."

The pilot, a young peasant with strong brown arms, grinned from ear to ear. In all his sixteen years, he had never seen anything remotely like Grandet. The lawyer was wearing an exquisite pearl grey suit with gloves and hat to match, a dark coat draped artistically about his shoulders, and a gold chain looped across his stomach. He turned his pince-nez up at the river and then down at the boat, and with nervous fingers twisted a graceful, silver-headed cane with increasing rapidity.

"Grandet, time's a-wasting and I'm getting older..."

"That's the trouble, de Meauville, it's an agreeable thing to get older. I've been really counting on it."

"Your Wolseley ascended the Nile in boats hardly bigger than this, and there were Arabs all over the place."

"Sudanis. But then, you don't read the newspapers." Grandet heaved a sigh, looked back toward shore in hope of sighting more civilized transport. Finally, delicately, he stepped down into the boat.

"There isn't too much current?"

The boy laughed loud and long and the sound rolled away across the perfectly smooth surface of the water. The massive shores of the St. Lawrence were tinged pink by the rising sun. From both shores came a dull tinkling of sheeps' bells. Cows with swollen udders bawled at barn doors. A church bell was sounding matins.

"Where are the cocks?" Grandet growled. "I thought there were supposed to be cocks crowing at dawn. Isn't that part of country mythology?"

"Perhaps they're asleep," de Meauville said archly.

"Well then, they're smarter than we."

"They don't have to cross the river; the water's calmer at this hour."

"Well... I must admit the view's not lacking a certain charm."

"You get more and more English every day," de Meauville laughed. "Half your sentences are negatives."

"You're exaggerating. Is this what your adopted home is like?"

"Not exactly, no. The river's wider there, the shores more rocky, and inland it's less cultivated, wilder."

"You did well to meet me here, then. You're a pioneering hero, de Meauville. I don't envy you, though."

"Why? Country life might suit you to a T."

"Allow me to doubt that," Grandet retorted, studying the silver head of his cane.

The oars sliced cleanly into the river and the black water raced by on either side of the boat without foaming. A steeple, houses and a wharf were coming into view on the far shore.

"Is that where we're going?" Grandet asked. "Is that where Mercredi's waiting for us?" Watching the approach of dry land made him feel more confident.

"I doubt he'll be there at this hour. We'll have to wait a while for him. Long enough to have breakfast."

"Capital idea!" The exclamation was in English. "I'd love an omelette *aux fines herbes!*"

The boy guffawed, then apologetically rowed harder than ever.

That's the way I should have been, de Meauville thought, watching the boy as he worked. I've never been strong and brown and handsome. I've never been young. I should have read less and rowed more.

He watched the approaching shore come alive, the dark woods and green meadows and little farm buildings with their walls washed pink by the dawning day. Dogs barked as their masters trudged toward their barns. A breeze was rising, ruffling the surface of the water. Thank God I'm now part of this miracle, he thought; I finally woke up.

"Here we are, coming safely to port!" he said aloud.

"Good heavens! We could have turned around and gone back and I wouldn't have been the wiser." He turned to the boy. "Are all your villages exactly alike?"

"No, monsieur," the adolescent replied. "Some's less alike than others."

"Oh, I see."

An old man was waiting at the foot of the wharf beside a calèche drawn by a big black horse. He greeted the travellers politely.

"Messieurs de Meauville and Grandet? My name's Auguste Paradis. Monsieur Mercredi sent me. I'm to take you to Vielleterre."

"Excellent!" Grandet said as he handed him his travelling bag. "But tell me, my good man, is there an inn in the village where we might breakfast?"

"Breakfast's waitin' for you at Vielleterre. We'll be there in half an hour."

"I'm a little surprised that Alexis isn't here to meet us himself," said de Meauville.

"It's hayin' time," Paradis said laconically, as if to say, And I've really got better things to do, too.

The big black was Paradis' favourite horse. He had a trot that was neither graceful nor rapid but very powerful. He trotted up the hill from the river, through the village and onto the flat without a single change in pace.

"Fine horse," de Meauville remarked, looking for an opening in Paradis' reserve. "This animal knows you. Unless I'm much mistaken, you're the one who trained him."

Paradis could not repress a smile. "Yes, monsieur, I trained 'im. And 'is mother too."

"It shows. Are we already on your land?"

"No, monsieur, it's along a ways. In the old days all this belonged to the seigneury, but since '54 it's bin the *censitaires*, the tenants that's the owners."

"Still, the seigneury has a lot of land, doesn't it?"

"Our seigneur was a smart man. He bought land back from the tenants. When the Sancys come, they bought more. An' Monsieur Mercredi's talkin' about buyin' more again. He wants t' build a pig barn."

"Oh dear," Grandet said with genuine distress.

"Them's my feelins," Paradis rejoined, turning morose again.

Grandet pursed his lips disdainfully as he watched the fields go by. He knew nothing about work in the fields and was glad of it.

"What are they doing over there?" he asked, pointing to a group of workers.

"They're mowing wheat," de Meauville replied.

"But it's still green!"

"That's so it won't beat down in the field. Ripened wheat is easily blown flat. When they cut it green, they lose less."

"The grain can't be as good."

"Of course."

The calèche came to the foot of a hill. Paradis pointed with his whip and announced tersely, "That there's Vielleterre."

Grandet whistled in admiration. The main part of the house was clearly of English inspiration: dark walls, latticed windows, high, pointed dormers. A lower wing with more roof than walls was more like a French-Canadian house, but this wing too had been dressed up with brick and wood, which gave it a rather hybrid look.

What a gloomy house! de Meauville thought as they approached. Even the grounds had a sinister look. A one-armed plaster Saint Francis, crumbling away from humidity, stared blindly into the trees, waiting for birds that never came. Blood-red cannas flowered profusely in the circular bed in front of the house.

To Grandet's indignation, the calèche continued on past the main entrance and stopped at the door to the summer kitchen. De Meauville jumped to the ground before the vehicle came to a stop, seized Askik by the shoulders and kissed him on both cheeks. Grandet descended with more dignity and put all his affection into a handshake.

Askik was speechless for a minute.

"How you've changed!" he blurted finally.

It was only true for one of them, in fact. Grandet, always something of a dandy, was now positively elegant. He breathed prosperity and confidence. Yet he was still the same old Grandet.

De Meauville, however, was unrecognizable. The Speaker had perished from desertion on the North Shore; the man who survived him had short-cropped hair, tanned skin and a simple manner of dress. Eating three meals a day and sleeping in a warm bed had been good for him. He had put on thirty pounds and his tall frame was no longer ungainly.

"Can I go?" Paradis enquired perfunctorily, then clacked the reins without waiting for the reply.

"Farewell, Man of Few Words," Grandet murmured, "I shall miss you."

"I've put you in the summer kitchen," Askik said, picking up their bags.

Grandet looked keenly disappointed. "We're not going to sleep in the house?"

Askik stopped short, embarrassed. He was only an employee. His guests had no right to the masters' quarters. De Meauville was about to intervene when Céline, who had been standing back, stepped forward.

"We thought you'd be more comfortable in the summer kitchen," she said. "It's cooler there."

Grandet acquiesced with a chivalrous bow, giving up all thought of protest. He was not good at talking to women.

"This is Céline Robitaille," Askik said. He was going to add, ...my fiancée, but it was not exactly true. His two friends understood this anyway, he told himself.

He helped his guests put away their coats and bags, then led them to the pergola where breakfast was waiting. The coolness of the night was just beginning to dissipate. The reapers in the distance seemed to be dancing on a sea of green.

"Wheat?" Grandet asked.

"Hay," Askik replied.

For a good ten minutes, Grandet proffered no further sound while the two famished travellers did justice to their plates of bacon and eggs cooked in maple syrup, pausing now and then to munch fat slices of buttered toast piled high with wild cherry jam.

De Meauville finally pushed his plate away. "Is that coffee in that pot?" he asked. "I'd gladly have some. Coffee's a very French-Canadian phenomenon. Our ancestors drank it under the French régime, did you know? It was the English who got us drinking tea, and now we're rediscovering coffee from the Americans. Alexis, didn't you tell me one day that the American Indians are very fond of coffee?"

"That's true, while the tribes north of the border only drink tea."

"Must depend who your enemies are," de Meauville concluded.

Grandet poured himself a cup of amber darjeeling. "As far as I'm concerned you can have your tobacco oil," he declared. "It wasn't worth colonizing India and pushing the bounds of Empire to the foot of the Himalayas if we were going to drink grasshopper juice ever after."

"Right you are!" de Meauville declared loudly, tossing the remains of his coffee over the hedge. "A little patriotism here, sacrédié! Tea, please!"

"Hooray!"

Céline burst out laughing. It had been a long time since Vielleterre had heard such humour.

"By the way, how is the Empire?" Askik enquired obligingly.

Grandet sighed and put his cup in its saucer. "I'd swear I was visiting monks," he said. "How could you be so ignorant of what's going on in the world?"

"It's a contract," de Meauville replied. "I leave the world alone and the world stays off my back."

"Well, it's wrong, because we're all involved. Particularly you, Alexis, because..."

"Wolseley again?"

"The Adjutant-General, Baron Wolseley," Grandet corrected. "His friend, General Gordon, is under siege in Khartoum... you do know that, don't you? No? Ah, I don't believe it! Men of feeling everywhere are distraught over the fate of this great hero; even the ladies are giving teas in his honour, while you..."

Grandet's hands fell limply to his sides and a look of resignation came over his face. Then he continued his elucidation more rapidly, as if to say, Might as well get it over with, since it's beyond you.

"If the contemptible Gladstone will part with his tuppence — that's what the expedition would add to the income tax — if he finally heeds the cry from the heart of every man, woman and child in the Empire shouting in chorus, 'save Gordon!' and 'To Khartoum!'; if (I'm summarizing) a relief expedition is dispatched to the Sudan, there is no doubt that this self-same expedition will be commanded by Sir Garnet."

"Conqueror of Egypt, confidant of Gordon, and your benefactor," added de Meauville, leaning toward Askik.

"Thank you, I realized that."

Grandet poured himself another cup of tea and then, remembering himself, offered some to Céline.

"Won't you have some, mademoiselle?"

The young woman, who had been sitting at the table without breakfasting, declined with a broad smile. Her eyes were sparkling. She thought Grandet the most amusing thing in the world. It had been a long, long time since she had enjoyed herself so thoroughly.

"By the way, Alexis," de Meauville spoke up, "it's not entirely true that I never read newspapers — it seems Riel is back in the North West. The Métis went to Montana and brought him back. They have grievances to air, they say. Some people are predicting another rebellion."

"Oh, I'd be surprised," interrupted Grandet with an air of authority. "The Métis haven't forgotten the drubbing they got last time."

De Meauville gave a sarcastic smile. "Drubbing? There wasn't a single shot fired!"

"The Métis thought they were safe out there on their faraway prairies. By his mere presence, Wolseley showed them that they weren't out of reach of the authorities."

De Meauville laughed. "Grandet, you're a soldier at heart. I'm surprised you never joined one of those expeditions you talk about all the time."

Grandet flushed with pleasure. A soldier at heart? Yes, rather... Perhaps even a commanding officer. He had pictured himself many a time in a gold-braided scarlet tunic, white and blond in a sea of hostile black faces, holding firm beneath a Union Jack riddled with bullet and arrow holes. He would have given a lot to be in Gordon's shoes.

"It could still happen," he said modestly.

"On condition it happens on this continent," de Meauville bantered. "You don't take well to water-borne travel."

"Oh, what a liar! Shame on you! Are you alluding to that crossing in a sieve you just inflicted on me? Ah, my friends, you should have seen the craft."

The two travellers, sparring and scolding mutually, then undertook to recount the voyage in question, each from his own perspective. Céline laughed until she was gasping.

In this cheery little company bubbling with youthful good cheer, Rosalie appeared, dropping like a surly bomb.

"There's them has a good time, an' there's them that works," said the fat girl, planting herself behind Céline.

The smile vanished from Céline's face. "I'm comin'," she said. "Go wait for me in the kitchen,"

"We bin waitin' a long time arreddy in the kitchen."

"I'm comin'!" Céline shouted, her face ugly with anger. She could feel all that delicious gaiety dissolving inside her. Then tears sprang to her eyes; she was ashamed to have made a display of coarseness in front of the visitors. For the first time, she was measuring how morose and untalkative the people of Vielleterre were. What killjoys, those hard workers, those slaves to duty! Even Alexis had only occasionally and briefly smiled as he listened to the debate between his friends.

Askik had expected his companions to congratulate him on his choice of bride once Céline had left for the kitchen, but de Meauville murmured only "Poor girl..." and Grandet tucked into a cold piece of toast and said as he ate, "It's pleasant here."

The sun was seeking them through the ivy overhead. A soft breeze brought them the scent of new-mown hay.

"It's charming," de Meauville agreed, "but I understand why Alexis doesn't want to stay."

"What?" Grandet exclaimed, rousing from a post-prandial reverie. "Of course he's going to stay! It's splendid!"

"Yes, but it all belongs to someone else. It's beautiful, I'll admit. Big house, lovely garden, fine tableware. It's not like Alexis, though. It doesn't suit him."

"Rubbish! It suits him perfectly! God knows, our poor friend's had little enough comfort and dignity in his life..."

"It's not comfort, it's luxury," de Meauville retorted heatedly. "And what is dignity? Manners. A way of putting oneself above life..."

"Oh, come on! You were that way inclined yourself!"

"Affectation, I tell you!"

"Well, you can't just wash your hands of your past like that! For goodness' sake, Alexis, you haven't said a word! Have you nothing to say? This concerns you, after all."

Askik seemed out of sorts. He glanced absently at his friends and said in an offhand manner, "I agree with de Meauville. I should leave."

"Very well," Grandet cried with a sly grin, "but why?"

"Because this land doesn't belong to me."

"But you hope to own land one day. Perhaps even this land?"

"Of course."

"You see?" Grandet concluded with a gesture of triumph. "Our friend's not indifferent to refinement and order. You have to admit it, de Meauville, you were wrong."

"Hearing us talk," de Meauville grumbled, "I'll even admit to being surprised we aren't all millionaires."

Suddenly the friends were slightly uncomfortable. For the first time, they were conscious of sitting at a rich man's table, using his forks and soiling his tablecloth.

Askik put down his napkin. "I have to go out to the fields. May I leave you for a while?" He did not invite his friends to go with him for fear the peasants might raise their hackles at the sight of these idle tourists.

"Certainly," said Grandet, "I think I'm going to have a little nap."

"And I," said de Meauville, "shall take a walk in your grounds. Your Saint Francis looks lonesome."

Askik was out of sorts and it surprised him. He had looked forward to this meeting with his friends, had been impatient for them to arrive and had amassed a quantity of colourful local stories and jokes to tell them. Yet he was discontented. Although he barely dared admit it to himself, he was already resenting the visit for upsetting his schedule and holding him back from his work. He was displeased with Céline for having replied in such a childish way to Rosalie, displeased with Grandet and de Meauville for showing no interest in the farming operations he was managing or the plans he was working out.

Still, perhaps he had expected too much. The first moments of reunions never ring the right notes. Everyone is in too much of a hurry to talk about himself and make an impression. It takes time for each to begin behaving naturally with the other again.

It will be better tonight, he told himself as he saddled up the big bay.

Although there was not far to go, in irritation and inattention he spurred his mount to a gallop at once and arrived in no time. The bay had barely found his breath when he felt the bit against the roof of his mouth. Angry to be interrupted just as he hit a satisfying stride, he began to snort and circle, chewing on the bit. Askik reponded by jerking the reins, which only made things worse.

How is it that bad things happen at the worst moments, when one is least prepared to cope with them? It took Askik time to grasp the extent of the fiasco. In some places, a scythe had dug into the ground, even upturning roots; in others, it had cut six inches from the ground, merely beheading the alfalfa and leaving the rich stalks standing. The field looked ragged, pockmarked, as if struck by huge hailstones. Some of the harvest was irrevocably damaged.

Askik savagely spurred the horse and galloped toward the reapers at the other end of the field. He saw Paradis step away from the group and headed straight for him. He reined in the horse in mid-stride a few feet from the old man, who did not even flinch.

"Who?" he hissed.

Paradis looked glum, downcast. "Our men."

"Why?"

"The manure."

"How about the other men?"

"They're workin' pretty well. Like you can imagine, they ain't seen a good example, though."

Now Askik found his full voice again. "Why didn't you call me?" he shouted.

Paradis' face flushed deep red. "'Cause I had enough o' whinin' like a baby every time one of 'em does sump'n stupid! I'll come back later with a sickle."

Askik yanked brutally on the reins. The bay spun about, almost lost his footing and with terror in his eyes charged toward the reapers. Beaudry kept on working calmly, without looking up, and when the horse was almost on top off him, swung his sickle wide toward the animal's legs. The horse whinnied in terror and shied, almost throwing Askik to the ground.

"Oh, sorry," the reaper said, looking up with big, round, innocent eyes. "Mustn't come up on a fella like that, M'sieur Mercredi. I coulda hurt yer horse, there."

All at once Askik's rage vanished. He was ashamed of losing his temper, ashamed of having mistreated his horse. He sat up straight in the saddle, returned the gaze and spoke in a calm voice. "You're working very badly today, my friend."

"Yeah?" The man was throwing derisive glances at his comrades. "I ain't noticed, m'sieur."

"Perhaps you're tired."

"Well... mebbe, yes."

"I think you need rest," Askik said in a flat voice. "Go home and rest."

The man kept smiling with the corners of his mouth but in his eyes there was now a look of worry.

"Howzzat, m'sieur? We ain't done yet."

"Leave your scythe. Go home and lie down."

"Well, if you say..." Beaudry shrugged and with a little chuckle glanced knowingly at his companions. The others, however, had put their heads down and were working diligently.

"No, no," Askik said to the other hired hands. "You too, go home and rest. You're all tired."

The men looked nervously at one another. They collected their belongings from the edge of the field and eventually straggled off toward the farm buildings, laughing wanly and shouting a joke or two at their fellow parishioners, who did not respond.

The big bay trembled, still frightened but docile. The scythes were now leaving a short, clean, uniform stubble. With relief, the remaining men were rediscovering the monotony of workmanlike reaping. Paradis looked up at him gratefully but Askik pretended not to have seen. He felt alone and unhappy, like a disciplinary master patrolling an unruly class at school. He tethered the bay in a shady poplar grove and brought it some alfalfa to make amends. Then he took a scythe left by one of the departed men and went about the field going over places that had been particularly badly mown.

He worked this way until evening, silent and solitary, keeping apart from the others. When Paradis sent a child to bring him water and bread at noon, he drank several cups of water one after the other and immediately picked up his scythe again. His black thoughts began to fall away from him like scales; his mind was emptying. Soon, all he had left were aches and pains, sunburn and the monotonous singing of crickets. When the time came to go home, he found that his hand would barely open, it was so used to being folded around the scythe handle. He turned the bay over to a boy from the village and walked home.

As he cut across the garden, he could hear laughter and voices. Grandet, in his pearl grey suit and a straw boater, was sitting on the small bench under the elm and holding a newspaper up to the light of the setting sun. De Meauville and Céline were walking side by side along the tree-lined driveway among the lengthening shadows. The young woman's clear laughter rang through the surrounding woods, falling silent when the couple disappeared in zones of shadow.

"I do believe," Grandet said with a wink, "that de Meauville has made a conquest."

Pale nocturnal moths clustered on the screens of the summer kitchen. The light from the oil lamp on the table fell on the remains of a meal, open books and half-empty glasses.

"Lord, it gets dark in the country," Grandet muttered. "I'd forgotten what it was like to live without gas."

His two friends smiled but said nothing.

A piercing scream came from outside. Grandet gave such a start that he banged his knees on the skirt of the table.

"It's nothing," Askik said, "just a fox calling his mate. He must have killed a mouse or a young bird."

A look of distress crossed Grandet's face. Never, oh never more would he venture off the Island of Montreal!

Silence fell again. Askik was thinking about the poems he had just listened to, which had reawakened his taste for serious reading. Grandet was secretly despairing for his pearl grey trousers, so ill-suited to summer kitchens. De Meauville had been inattentive, almost bad-tempered all evening and had mellowed only latterly. On several occasions Askik had looked up to discover him looking long and hard at him. Twice or three times, de Meauville had seemed to be on the point of speaking but apparently changed his mind, turning his head to the window instead.

The warm night throbbed with a thousand signs and signals. Nighthawks and owls exchanged calls in the woods. Crickets crouching low among the grasses rubbed their forewings, unwittingly alerting sharp-toothed field mice. Grass snakes slithered silently among the cabbages, devouring mantises, toads and caterpillars. All around the summer kitchen there was watching, prowling, dying, while inside, the humans with their feeble vision could only listen and surmise.

"Well, the man of few words," Grandet murmured on seeing Paradis emerge from the night. Although all three sets of eyes inside were fixed on him, Paradis knocked politely at the door before coming in. Askik drew up a chair for him.

"A little caribou, Monsieur Paradis?"

For a moment the old man seemed undecided, then accepted the chair and the glass of fortified wine.

"To yours, messieurs!"

He sipped his wine respectfully, then produced his tobacco pouch. Once his pipe was lit, he began the long stream of pleasant, empty chatter that an habitant can spin out indefinitely when the situation calls for sociability.

"We got a fine harvest," he said with a look of satisfaction. "Real fine."

"In spite of our men," Askik rejoined. "What did they do this afternoon?"

Paradis hesitated, embarassed.

"They're my friends," Askik said, "you can be frank in front of them."

"Well, they did what you told 'em to do. Nothin'. I hope it don't last too long."

"Were you able to carry on?"

"With help from a few boys from the village."

"Hire them. We'll soon have enough cows to need men regularly round the yard."

"What about our own men?"

"Have them cart manure for a few more days. Then I'll sack them."

"Hey now!" the old man burst out. "I'm gonna need them men fer the harvest!"

"Not at all." There was an angry glint in Askik's eyes. "I've put up with those good-for-nothings long enough already. I've ordered a machine..."

"A mower? We'll need even more men..."

"It'll be better than that: a reaper-binder. We might be the first in Quebec to have one. With that, we won't need anyone. And when we've done the harvesting at Vielleterre, we'll do the rounds of the parish, renting it out to the habitants. It'll bring in double its price. I'll drive it myself if I have to."

"There's folks ain't gonna like that," Paradis said at last.

"I know the ones who aren't going to like it," Askik replied. "We won't have to put up with them for long."

"It ain't just the hired hands. The habitants like comin' to do the harvest at Vielleterre. It puts a bit o' money in their pockets."

"All they have to do is sell me their milk. I pay cash."

"It ain't the same thing."

"Indeed not. The harvest at Vieilleterre is over in a few weeks. Raising dairy cows means work all year round. They'll have to get used to that. You see," Askik said turning to his two friends, "the Canadian habitant has got into bad habits. Nature has spoiled him. When he settled here, the land gave forty bushels an acre. Now it only gives five. The habitants don't fertilize their land or drain it, and always sow the same thing. From the very first, they got used to working only in summer and lived by hunting in winter. Today when the land gives nothing and there's no more game, no more woods, and less fish, Baptiste wonders why he's poor. So he just resigns himself to living poorly; it takes less effort and makes him look like a Christian."

"You take a rather black view," de Meauville objected gently.

"You think I'm exaggerating? Let's face it. Who controls our trade, courts and government? What language is spoken in all the offices?"

"Everyone agrees that there's injustice..."

"There's no injustice. We've got what we deserve. If our country people were educated, our produce would be in great demand abroad. Our butter would be less watery, our cheddar would be aged better, and we'd have cornered the bacon market long ago. Our peasants would be prosperous. Instead of keeping their children cooped up on stoney farms, they'd be sending them to agricultural colleges or making merchants of them. They wouldn't have to pack up and go to the States in order to eat. And at long last there'd be somebody to stand up to the priests!"

There was an embarrassed silence, as always happens when passion accompanies the proffering of truths. Out of courtesy, Grandet made an effort to answer Askik's thinking.

"But don't you see, Alexis, it's a vicious circle. Without rights, there's no prosperity. Without prosperity, there are no rights. How can we get to the top if our language isn't even recognized? What do you think, de Meauville?"

De Meauville made a face. He looked up at the moth-covered screen as if thinking of flying out the window.

"Our language, our faith, our rights," he said with a sigh of disgust. "Lord, it's tiresome being an oppressed people! Always whipping up our indignation, always testing our loyalty!" And he added derisively:

Chafing 'neath the yoke of a foreign race,
Their hearts filled with pride they still embrace
*Their memories of France, which naught will erase.**

"That's Crémazie!" Grandet protested. "He wasn't afraid of bold talk, but still, Crémazie..."

"A third-rate poet who lived with his nose in his navel," de Meauville said scornfully. "A fine hero, fine specimen of our intellectuals. We go into raptures over France, we dream of a French-Canadian people that's more heroic, more French — more like us. If only there'd been more of us fighting at Saint-Denis, if only the habitant had been less worried for his land and shekels! Is our habitant going to put himself out for a flag, a country, national pride? Not on your life! Does he want them? Not even that! We call on him to stand up and resist, and what he does is lie down in the mud. D'you suppose he suspects there's less in it for him than for educated folk? Could it be he doesn't even like us?"

"And you, monsieur," Grandet said, turning to Paradis. "What do you think?"

"Ah... I reckon... you're right," he stammered, stuffing his tobacco pouch back in his trouser pocket, "but mornin' comes early this time o' year, though the nights is growin' longer arreddy. Time I was gettin' to bed." He stood up. "So g'night t'you," he said. "Sleep well."

His footsteps could be heard on the gravel before being muffled in the grass. De Meauville repressed a strong urge to laugh; he seemed to have recovered his good humour at long last.

"Oh yes, I got a lot from my cucumbers this year, but look... all the lettuce is bolted. It's Alexis had blood an' offal put in this corner o' the garden last autumn. He read that it's good for vegetables. It's good, but too much is as bad as none at all."

Her face all smiles beneath her big straw hat, Céline was moving from row to row, showing de Meauville her garden. She barely gave the humble carrots and onions a glance, praised the cabbages as she passed, and knelt down by the strawberry patch.

"There's plants from two years ago here," she said. "D'you see the

---

*Octave Crémazie, "Le vieux soldat canadien."

old roots? I covered them up with sheep manure last winter. Alexis wanted to pull them out, but I knew my plants'd bear another year. You always hafta pick strawberries when the dew's down," she continued in all seriousness, "and it always has to be the same person pickin'." She smiled triumphantly as she handed him a strawberry. "See?"

The strawberry was sweet and juicy, but to de Meauville not nearly as sweet as that smile. He too knelt down while she, sitting back on her heels, put her hands on her apron with an air of satisfaction.

"You know a lot about plants, don't you, Céline?"

"After maman died I swore I'd never have a garden. It was too hard work. Then when I come here I got to like it bit by bit. It's Madame Paradis showed me what to do. Each plant's got things it likes and things it don't. It'd be too borin' without that."

"How old were you when you came here?"

"Twelve. I didn't do much first off. I washed dishes, made beds."

"And today you run everything here."

"Yes, but it ain't like it was. There was lots more people before."

For a few minutes there was silence, distancing them. Then, looking up from under her hat she asked, "How 'bout you... where are you from?"

"D'you know where Rimouski is? We started there. My father had no head for business. He moved to Montreal, took up with a phony Scottish noble, invested in a scheme to import bananas, and lost every penny. The Scot came out none the worse, but we stayed poor. Luckily, there are still royalists around... The Sulpicians couldn't bear seeing a nobleman's son stay illiterate all his life. I spent twelve years at their college, nine years drinking and writing poetry, and now I'm a teacher on the North Shore."

He stopped, dismayed at his unintended tone of irony when he meant to be totally sincere.

"Cynicism," he added softly with an apologetic smile, "is the mark of long years of education."

"I think you're lucky. I'd love to of gone to school!"

"What for? They don't teach you to cover strawberries at school."

The young woman bridled. "I'd like to know 'bout more than just my corner o' the garden. Know what goes on in other places. Read the newspapers, and books."

"Why?" de Meauville insisted. "The world is filled with idiocy."

At once he was sorry he had said this. Anger flashed in Céline's eyes.

"D'you think the habitants like bein' ignorant?" she demanded. "They elect men who steal from them and lie to them every chance they get. They know it, but what d'you expect them to do 'bout it? They don't know how to talk in public, don't know the laws and can't write letters. So they make up their minds they won't say nothin' even when they know they're right. Oh yes, they pooh-pooh the educated folk, but d'you really think they don't envy them? They're afraid of the shabbiest little teacher or the lowest little office worker."

De Meauville drew in his head as though caught in an icy rain shower.

"I'd like to get letters from my friends, an' read the Gospel myself," Céline continued, "but it's all I can do to figure out a few recipes... There's more t'life than just strawberries!"

Poor de Meauville. He was accustomed to disparaging his education the better to extol the simple life of the peasants. He had all the fervour of a convert; everything in his past he saw as bad, and everything in his reincarnation as good. Returning to a less black-and-white view was going to be upsetting. Recognizing that one has been cosseted by life, after all, entails certain responsibilities.

"Forgive me, Céline. I'm behaving like a spoiled child. You're right. I've been very lucky."

Céline stood up. "We better work a bit," she said, "afore Rosalie gets after us."

"Yes, ma'am."

"First, twist this rag round your knees, then it won't hurt so much. Here's your basket. You take this row" (she designated a long row of string beans) "an' I'll take the next."

Around the vegetable garden was a little hedge which attracted the birds and a fence to keep the cows out. Grandet came and leaned on this fence, a folded newspaper under his arm. He was still wearing the same rumpled pearl grey suit, for if his infant fortune permitted elegance, it did not yet allow variety.

De Meauville was on all fours among the beans. "You should come and join us, Grandet," he called. "It'll do you good."

"What good should I expect such exercise to do me?" the other asked with polite ennui.

Céline could not keep from laughing.

"How many times have you read that newspaper since we arrived?" de Meauville shot back. "Five times or six?"

Grandet kept a dignified silence. How could he explain that this paper was his only link with his own world? These three days in the country had seemed an eternity. Not a single new idea, not the least little emergency for excitement. He had fallen into a total void. The countryside bored him to death. The country people exasperated him with their slownesss. Even this young woman, this Céline, drove him to despair. Pleasant, yes. In her way. But that homespun skirt, those short fingers covered with scratches, and that straw hat! She was not ugly, which would be excusable. She was common. And in the country, people make do with common. In thirty years, Grandet thought, this woman would still dress the same way and would still be picking beans. How long it took to fill a pail with beans! he thought with extreme irritation. When Céline finally straightened up and carried the beans to the kitchen, he had to make a supreme effort not to fling himself on his friend. Instead, he folded his paper, put it under his arm and walked decorously across the vegetable garden, being careful not to step on the plants because they were considered important.

"I want to leave," he said bluntly.

"What? Don't you like it here?"

"My dear de Meauville, I'm bored *to death.*"

"You were impressed with the house, though."

"It isn't as big as I thought at first. In open country, any hovel looks important. It's a pretentious little house, in fact. No real taste. We were going to stay a few days; we have done so. We intended to pay a brief visit to our friend Mercredi; it's been accomplished. And to be frank with you, he doesn't seem enchanted to have us."

"He does seem rather distant."

"Distant? Yesterday he spent the day in the fields. And today?"

"I think he's in the village. He's taking delivery of a new machine."

"He's avoiding us, for God's sake!"

"He's *evading* us. I don't think he's really resigned to living here. Our being here forces him to reconsider everything. The fact is, he envies you, Grandet."

"Me?" Grandet was clearly pleased.

"Yes, or rather, the kind of life you lead."

"So it's agreed? We'll leave tomorrow at first light?"

De Meauville seemed uncertain. With his head on one side, he looked at the basket Céline had left between the rows to mark where she had been.

"All right," he said, "we'll leave tomorrow. We'll tell Alexis at supper."

They waited a very long time for him. The cows had been turned back out to pasture, the reapers had come in from the fields, and still no

Askik. Every so often a boy would run down to the road, shade his eyes with his hand, and call with an air of importance, "I don't see 'im."

Céline put the dinner in the oven and went to join de Meauville on the driveway in front of the house. Grandet went back to his spot under the elm. He heard his friend tell Céline that he was leaving in the morning. The couple moved away, speaking low. Grandet realized from the serious tone of their voices that their relationship was advancing by leaps and bounds. Embarrassed, he went to check for the hundredth time that his shirts were folded and his bag closed and ready.

The moon was rising over the still-green fields when they heard, far away at first, the strangest racket imaginable: a cacophony of wood, iron and sheet metal, squealing, banging and clashing in chorus. The horses entered the yard with their nostrils flaring, eyes wide and ears laid back. Behind them, jolting and groaning, came an ungainly assemblage that looked like a huge, wind-battered bird.

Paradis quietly swore an oath of astonishment: "Ça parle au sorcier!..." His wife ventured to the door of her house and no farther. The hired hands approached with deep suspicion graven on their faces. Even Grandet came to examine the machine, wearing an expression of mild amusement.

Askik was following on the big bay. He jumped exuberantly from the saddle with a grin from ear to ear.

"What d'you say about this? It's the first in Quebec, perhaps in Canada!" He laughed. "It took us all day to get it in working order. You see, when you take it on roads you have to turn the table so it doesn't take too much room. See this wheel?" He bent and pointed under the machine. "It's removable. Oh my, the time it took us to figure that one out! The blacksmith's still scratching his head. Ha ha ha! Otherwise, it's simplicity itself. The grain is cut, rolled, bound and tossed out onto the field."

He burst out laughing again. A machine playfully tossing around bundles of grain: a whimsically charming idea, it seemed to him.

A more striking contrast than that in the faces gathered around the machine would be difficult to imagine. The young people — de Meauville, Grandet, Céline and the stable boys — had been infected with Askik's enthusiasm. They fingered the machine and laughed and exclaimed over the marvellous complexity of the gearing. The hired hands' faces were black and malevolent; their hard, deeply lined features captured the evening shadows and appeared the blacker for it. Paradis ran his hand over the frail wooden blades, then approached Askik and spoke to him very quietly.

"Have it put right up beside my house. I don't sleep much. I'll watch it. Tomorrow I'll let the men go, but fer tonight we better be careful."

As was his custom, he did not wait for a reply but went to the jittery horses and led them slowly toward his house, talking to them soothingly.

"Well, brother Mercredi," Grandet said, "you've made the last supper very late."

"What? You're leaving?"

"I'm afraid so. I'm not earning my living reading the paper in the garden."

Askik showed no displeasure at the news. Perhaps his delight in acquiring the new machine was all-absorbing, or perhaps the departure suited him. The three friends sat down at table in the summer kitchen.

Excited over his purchase, Askik kept his guests laughing for a good quarter of an hour by imitating the bewildered faces of the villagers at the sight of the machine. With help from the wine, he could feel the reserve that had been standing between him and his friends dissipate. All was as it had been before. Better, for Askik was discovering considerable affection for Grandet, whom he had never genuinely liked.

And yet, however tenderly he regarded his friends, he could not help thinking that one day he would go farther than they. You, de Meauville, will be happy, he said to himself. I can see you in thirty years, a teacher, an endearing old bachelor, a mite eccentric but much loved in your little town. Grandet, you try hard and you keep the pot boiling, you speak English and do the rounds of the salons, but I don't think you'll reach your goal, which I sense to be a glorious one. You'll be a prosperous lawyer, no more than that; a big fisherman catching little fish. To go beyond that, to really make a mark, you have to innovate, be audacious enough to buy a reaper-binder, create needs and implant them in others.

When Céline came in with the meal, Askik suggested that she dine with them, but she avoided his gaze and returned quickly to the kitchen.

"À la compagnie!" Grandet cried, raising his glass. The prospect of having access to fresh news the next day had restored and enlivened him. His beaming face radiated friendship. What a marvellous fellow! thought Askik; how could I not have seen it before?

There ensued a rollicking conversation between the two. They talked pigs and Boers, Gatling guns and manure. They talked endlessly about their pet likes and dislikes and offered each other tons of advice.

De Meauville meanwhile, seemed pinched and ill at ease, and remained silent. The two others, caught up in good cheer, did not notice.

When the lights went out in the big house, when the whip-poorwill had finished singing for the night, Grandet took out his gold watch, snapped open the spring cover, and exclaimed in surprise, "Half past midnight! Good heavens! We have to be up in a few hours!"

"Then it's not worth going to bed!" Askik rejoined. "Let's open another bottle. Let's stay up till morning."

"Oh, no, no, no!" Grandet protested. "Can you picture what state I'd be in tomorrow night at the Richelieu? No, I'm going to bed." He seized Askik's hand between both of his and with tears in his eyes said, "I don't remember ever having spent a pleasanter evening. Thankyou for having us, my friend. A delightful stay that I shall not soon forget. Thankyou!"

Putting aside his English reserve, he kissed Askik solemnly on both cheeks before teetering out the door. Once out in the darkness he turned about and cried, "Hey, I'm supposed to be sleeping here! It's you who has to leave, Mercredi!"

Askik bid good night to his friends and went out into the yard. He was not sleepy. The very thought of shutting himself up in his little room made him shudder. He needed the stars and the wind on which to pour out his overflowing happiness. The reaper-binder, snug against Paradis' house, looked at him lovingly, its beautiful white wood blades glowing softly in the moonlight. Let a single hired man lay a finger on it and I'll kill him! he swore to himself.

A tall, powerful man emerged from the night.

"De Meauville!" Askik exclaimed after a moment of surprise. "What are you doing here? Aren't you going to bed?" He could barely see de Meauville's face, but sensed seriousness and perhaps sorrow in it.

"I wanted to talk to you, Alexis." His calm voice had a curious ring. "Let's move way from the house, could we?"

"Let's go to the driveway."

"No, not there. What's on this side?"

"The pasture."

"Let's go there."

They climbed a rail fence and began walking. The cows lay peacefully chewing the cud, their coats silky and blue in the light of the moon and stars.

"When I was little I loved seeing cows at night," Askik said. "They were comforting."

"Alexis, I've only been here a few days..."

"It's been too short. You're used to the country, you should stay a bit longer. I understand why Grandet wants to go; he stifles away from the city. There's no hurry for you, though."

De Meauville sighed. "In a few minutes," he said, "you're going to be asking me to leave."

"Impossible!"

"Something's happened that I didn't anticipate. Otherwise I wouldn't have come. I was happy; I wasn't asking for anything more."

"For heaven's sake, de Meauville, what are you talking about?"

The wave of good feelings that had engulfed Askik was beginning to recede, uncovering a suspicion that he could not yet name.

De Meauville was groping for words. "The worst of it is that nothing's certain. I'm going to wreck your happiness for something that might not lead anywhere."

"My happiness?" Askik gave a nervous little laugh. "I don't worry much about my happiness. I've got other fish to fry."

"Well, I worry about it," de Meauville said with another sigh. "I know having no family, no ties, has been hard on you, but — no, why deny it? I'd hoped, coming here, to find you happy and settled. And now I'm the one who's going to undo it all. Still, I swear to you, Alexis, if I could give her up, leave her knowing for certain that things would work out between you..."

"Céline..."

Askik had murmured her name even before thinking it. It was not a question, it was a statement: he was betrayed.

De Meauville did not excuse himself. What would be the point? He was distraught over the unhappy state of affairs, but he had not created it. He could curse fate for arranging things so badly, but he could not fight it; neither he nor Céline could command their feelings. When they had first spoken, when they had first looked at each other, each had recognized in the other a need they had not known existed. Before, he had hoped for nothing more from life because he thought he wanted nothing more, but he had discovered with dismay that there was still immense happiness for him to assimilate, and it was going to happen at his best friend's expense. How can one beg forgiveness for an injustice one does not intend to redress?

Askik felt neither anger nor bitterness. Had he lost something, was he more alone than ever? He felt confused, unsettled, as if about to begin drifting again. He had thought he had found a safe haven. His moorings were being cut. That was all. He felt a little resentful, weary; if truth be told, he was nursing the bitter satisfaction of feeling sorry for himself. Tears stung his eyes, a sign that part of him was already hurting from a leaden weight of torpor, and the pain would soon spread.

He turned from his friend and went into the house.

A fine, persistent rain was giving goose pimples to the St. Lawrence. A small clutch of people huddled with its baggage in a shelter at the foot of the wharf. Askik and Céline had stayed in the calèche, beneath its streaming roof. Céline was wearing a black straw hat and grey hooded cloak which made her look like a little old woman. A yellow suitcase waited at her feet. She sat staring upriver.

In Askik's mind, that look in her eyes redeemed her. They shone so brightly with barely-contained hope and love that the inelegance, the dowdiness of her attire quite vanished.

"Don't worry," Askik told her, "it'll be here soon."

She gave him an absent-minded smile and returned to her vigil. The horse was trying to nibble grass through its bit. Askik got out and slipped the bit out of its mouth. The rain murmured pleasantly as it fell on the road. Fat drops gathered on the horse's oily coat.

"There 'tis!" a child's voice called.

The ship emerged from the mist and spray, shrouded in its own vapours. Céline twisted her gloves nervously.

"I never been on the water before," she said with a faint laugh.

"You won't feel anything at all. And it's very safe."

"Yes, but how d'you know when to get off?"

"It will be announced, don't worry."

The excitement died down among the waiting travellers; the ship was still a long way off. A sick child was lying on a stetcher among the baggage. His frail arms moved restlessly over the covers and his head turned back and forth on the pillow. The mother was bickering with the older children, peppering her husband with questions, filling the air around her with fears and exhortations.

Céline gazed at the child. "They're taking 'im to the Hospice of Sainte-Anne," she said. "I wouldn't be brave enough to work with sick people like that."

"But the job de Meauville's found for you is in a hospital, isn't it?"

"A hospital, not a hospice. And anyways," she added with embarrassment, "I might not be there long."

A handful of passengers was visible, defying the rain on the forward deck. Peasants.

"You know," Céline said, reddening a little more, "you mustn't think that..."

"What?"

"That I don't care for you."

"You'd given me the impression that you cared for me. A bit."

"We was left alone too much at Vielleterre. We never saw nobody."

"Meaning you could be interested in me as long as there wasn't anybody else?"

Céline sighed in exasperation. "You're so hard, Alexis. Why d'you insist on everything goin' the way you imagine it? God's got to have something to do with it once in a while."

"No, you have to know what you want."

"How about that child," Céline replied, turning her eyes to the shelter, "don't he know what he wants? What difference does it make?"

Vexed, Askik kept silent. All these words, pending the last.

The children squealed for joy as they watched the steamer approach. The paddle wheels stopped turning, creating a silence that was even more impressive than the churning of the water. Smoke swirled around the smokestack and down to the shelter and the waiting travellers. A baby screamed deafeningly.

Céline gave Askik a look of desperation. "Alexis," she said, "don't make yourself miserable. Write to us. Come and see us. Don't stay alone!"

"I'll miss you," he said simply.

"Oh Alexis, we're going to miss you too!"

She kissed him, sobbing. He felt her damp, heavy hair against his cheek and for the first time was genuinely heartsick to think that he was never going to see this young woman again. At last he was free to grieve intensely for her, independently of his frustrated appetites or wounded pride.

"You have to board," he said gently. She broke away from him, putting her gloves to her eyes. He picked up her yellow suitcase and walked with her to the wharf. He was about to express his parting wishes for her when events once again intervened.

The stretcher was being carried aboard. The child was twisting and turning more distressfully than ever, trying to look back at the crowd. At the foot of the gangway, the mother talked faster and faster, on the brink of hysteria.

"We tried to keep 'im, y'know," she said, looking all around her. "We wanted to keep 'im at home, but it's so hard. He dirties all the time. Then I got other little 'uns too. But he's just as nice as the rest, my baby is. Just as good as the rest, y'know."

"It's all right, mother," the husband said soothingly, "it's all right."

She, however, glared at him and began to lament in a broken voice, "The hospice ain't no life fer a little fella, not with all them old folks, no life at all!"

The husband made a long face and hung his head. Céline touched the woman's shoulder; the woman gave her a bewildered, half-crazed look.

"Don't worry, madame, I'll look after your little one till he gets to Sainte-Anne."

The woman grasped her hand with frightening intensity. "Oh, how good you are, mademoiselle! You understand, even if nobody else don't. He ain't no animal, he's got all 'is wits. I wanted to keep 'im at home, but how could I? The Virgin will make it up to you, mademoiselle. Oh, you're so kind!"

The stretcher had reached the top of the gangway; the sailors were turning it awkwardly into the narrow passage. The child gave a gutteral wail of alarm to have lost sight of the wharf. Céline ran up the gangway after him and disappeared into the ship. Askik was left standing at the bottom, a word of farewell on his lips.

He returned to the calèche. He put the bit back in the horse's mouth, drove up the hill and stopped when he reached the open country on the heights just outside the village. The ship had reached the middle of the river. There was no one on deck.

She'll spend all day looking after that child and won't see a thing of her first water voyage, he said to himself. She's a stubborn one, that Céline!

The grass was washed clean, the dust on the road well-flattened, and still the drizzle continued out of pure obstinacy. The horse gave a snort; Askik set him walking again.

16

The men had left, as surly as beaten dogs watching for their moment of revenge. Beaudry had established himself at the village tavern and was holding court from morning till night. The resentments he vented were always the same, and there were always listeners. Mere days before harvesting, the habitants were learning that there would be no work at Vielleterre that year, and hence no cash in hand for the winter. For those who lived meagerly, the loss was serious.

"Did Sancy *père* hafta have a machine fer the harvestin'?" Beaudry shouted. "Is the grain gonna taste any better? So what's the machine gonna do? Save money? D'ya think it cost the Métis less'n he paid you?"

"No!" chorused two or three men, biting hard on their pipes.

"Yes!" Beaudry contradicted, perplexing his listeners. "His machine cost 'im less, 'cause it's you gonna pay fer it! When the mowin' at Vielleterre's done, he's gonna rent it to you to do yer own fields with."

"If'n he bring 'is machine t' me, I'll show 'im what he can do with it!"

"He ain't never gonna put foot on my land, I tell you, not never!"

"Don't talk too fast, *le père*," Beaudry retorted, levelling a finger at the last speaker. "You say the Métis won't never put foot on your land? He already bought the Dubois'. Yourn's next door, ain't it?"

The habitant was a sturdy fellow with drooping moustaches. A shadow of worry crossed his face. "So what?" he demanded. "He still can't make me sell."

"But what d'you live on, *mon bon monsieur?*" Beaudry cast a mocking eye over his audience before finishing. "No more work at Vielleterre, that's no more money. What you gonna do? Sell milk? Beef? Wheat? The Métis's got ten times what you got. You think you gonna compete with him? No, no, no," he chanted, returning his gaze to the last speaker, "he's gonna get your land, fella. He's gonna get all 'e wants."

Checkers pieces stopped clacking on their boards. Spitoons stopped ringing. The taverner's oil lamp shone on hard faces with deep, shadowy creases, on rough shirts and grimy hands.

"It ain't gonna be like that."

"It's two hundred years we bin here."

"We can still live off'n our own farms. Long as nobody don't want too much."

"Anahow, things was a deal sight better when Sancy was lookin' after it all hisself."

"His little Métis's gone an' got everythin' upside down."

"Even Auguste Paradis lost his job!" cried another. "Didn'tcha know? The Métis kicked 'im out. He's s'posed to go in the spring."

A wind of anger swept over the men.

"It ain't right! It's us belongs here!"

"It's the Métis gotta go!"

"To hear 'im talk, ain't nobody but him knows how to work the land."

"He tried to tell me how to do my ploughin'!"

"Ain't just the land he bin ploughin'," said Beaudry, laughing coarsely. "Didn'tcha tell me Céline's took off t' th' North Shore? Over there, o' course, one brown baby more or less..."

The men shared a knowing chuckle. All of them, at one time or another, had undressed Vielleterre's toothsome housekeeper in their heads.

"Send a savage to school an' he's still a savage. I wouldn't let 'im round my daughters!"

"When they c'n get their paws on a white woman..."

"That's what they like best!"

"D'you blame 'em? Their own women ain't used to washin'."

"An' Céline filled up a dress pretty good!" cried a tipsy little fellow.

"Well, now she's gone, it's the fat one's turn t' git laid," another bellowed.

The men laughed heartily, forgetting briefly that they were afraid for their farms. With eyes lit up and sneers on their lips, they challenged Beaudry to confirm that Indian women, with whom he had boasted of sleeping, turned into wild, sensual animals at the first caress from a White. Of all the myths born of the meeting of the two races, this is the most persistent. However, since it is recognized with the same degree of certainly that no white woman can be attracted to an Indian, they wondered what pleasure Céline could have found with her Métis. In which case, the possibility of rape could not be excluded.

"Well, now, all that don't fix your problem," Beaudry concluded.

"I say we oughtta go see Monsieur le curé," said a farmer better dressed than the others. "He knows Sancy. He'll write a letter to 'im in Ottawa. We're good parishioners, good sons o' the church; I think our curé owes us that."

"That's talkin'!"

"All right!"

The next day was Sunday. Very early, a note was sent to the presbytery. After mass, while the parishioners waited on the church steps with the serious faces appropriate to such an initiative, their delegates entered the sacristy, scraping their boots and clearing their throats. Monsieur le curé was expecting them.

By day it was still summer, but the nights already belonged to autumn. A crisp cold fell from the shivering stars. The country was feeling frost in the air.

Unable to bear the big, silent house, Askik had fled to the fields. He had lit a small fire in the upper pasture, and with his back against a fence post was contemplating the country spread out beneath the half-moon, those woods and meadows stretching all the way to the distant, invisible river. At times he thought he could hear the river's murmur as it slipped along between its giant banks, which of course was impossible. In his thoughts he followed the water's flow as it passed villages and farms, snagged on piers, tossed boats, and kept on flowing all the way to the faraway land where no light shines and wolves and bears live all alone in their pitch-black forests.

A grey shadow was approaching up the hill. From its uneven gait and its way of putting out a steadying hand to the fence, Askik recognized Paradis. The old man had seen the fire and, suspecting dirty work on the part of the men, had come to investigate. He showed no surprise to see Askik.

"What you burnin'?"

"Wood. And dry dung."

"Thought it smelled funny."

Paradis went to the trouble of sitting down on the damp grass, which required considerable effort and placed him in the vexing position of having to get back up later.

"In the old days the Métis nearly always burned buffalo dung for heat," Askik explained.

"They liked it better'n wood?"

"There wasn't any wood on the prairies."

Paradis sat thinking about this. He tried to imagine the St. Lawrence valley without trees. He left the meadows, the villages, the mists, but eradicated every last bush. The prairie, he concluded, must be a deathly dreary place. He was too polite to say so.

"Gonna freeze t'night if y'ask me."

"Have you ever been outside Lower Canada, Paradis?"

"Me, monsieur? Never."

"Didn't you ever think about it?"

"I thought about it now 'n then... back in them days when the Company was recruitin' voyageurs." And after a pause he added a confession: "I'da bin homesick up there in the Terres d'En Haut, far away from the country."

The moon had cloaked the church steeple in silvery light. A dog in the distance barked once, twice, then stopped, cowed by the answering icy silence. Askik shivered in his coat.

The country is here, Askik thought. Old Canada. The late, lamented, beloved New France. Virgin forests, stone fences, nets on the beaches, graveyards full of ancestors. My ancestors. Joseph and Baptiste immortal, stubborn and silent, as Canadian as pumpkins. Everything I love with all my heart but will never want me as part of it.

Askik did not say these things. Paradis did not hear them; he sat peacefully smoking his pipe, having learned to savour transient pleasures. His old eyes roamed over the landscape; each islet of trees, each fence-ringed meadow, each farmhouse with its darkened windows stirred a memory. Not all of them good ones, far from it. Good ones of weddings and new year's celebrations mingled with the spectres of famine and cholera and the ghosts of travellers frozen to death and babies dead from colic.

Askik tossed some last sticks on the fire; a shower of sparks flew up toward the stars, surrounding the old man with a light like a halo.

You're blessed, Paradis, Askik thought. You belong to this place and no other. But where is my place? Here? All I have to do is disturb things a bit and people remember I'm half Indian. The North West? I have the tastes and needs of a White now. Congratulations, fathers! Well done, teachers! It looks as though you succeeded with me!

The craziest thing, Paradis thought as he pursued his meditations, is if I got to do it all again I'd make the same mistakes. I like you fine now, Dubois, but if you came back we'd end up fightin' again just like before. You and yer damn cows!

Might it be that there isn't anything for me to do in this world? Askik wondered. No place, no mission, no destiny? Has it all been a gruesome joke, then? So there wasn't a reason I was born a Métis after all. It was just pure chance that brought me to the Sancys'. There'll be no end because the journey never did have any purpose from the very beginning.

By now the cow dung was yielding only a tiny blue flame. Paradis gave a surprised groan. While he was wool gathering, the cold had crept down his shirt collar and now was gnawing between his shoulder blades. His chilled legs creaked as they straightened. Or rather, as he hoisted himself to his feet, holding to the rails of the fence.

"Try'n not git old, boy," he growled.

Askik remained sitting, shoulders hunched.

"Monsieur Mercredi, it's time t' git t' bed. If you wanta start the wheat tomorra an' then rent the machine..."

"They don't want the machine," Askik interruped gloomily. "I've done the rounds of the farms. Nobody wants to rent the machine."

"Bunch o' lunkheads!" Paradis grumbled, rubbing his lower back. "Sounds like Beaudry's doin'. They'll end up seein' you was right, though."

"No, I was wrong."

"Whazzat? Them cattle'd starve to death afore they'd change their ways. You do right to let 'em feel the prod once in a while."

"You don't understand what I'm saying," Askik replied in a weary voice. "The habitants would have accepted those changes from you. They won't from me. As long as I show I'm grateful, as long as I tell them quaint stories, they'll be pleased with me, but the minute I try to exercise a little influence, they hate me. Dolts and charlatans can aspire to positions of authority, but I can't. There's not a drunkard in Quebec who isn't my superior. To Canadians, I am and always will be a savage."

Paradis blinked his eyes, silently cursing his failing vision. The flames were dying and he could no longer see his intendant's face. "What's that got to do with it?" he said.

"I'm not one of yours. I don't belong in this country."

"If ever'body that's got Indian blood talked like you, there wouldn't be nobody left in Lower Canada."

"I wasn't born in Lower Canada."

"Well, yer here now!" Paradis retorted, turning and setting off for home and bed. Some men, as they age, are touched by the anxious introspections of youth. Not Paradis.

Seconds later, Askik looked up with a wry little smile. "Funny," he said, "I've heard that before. Would you have an old Sioux in your family, Paradis?"

Too late. The old foreman was already hobbling down the hill, listening only to his own creaks and groans. Askik stamped out the remaining embers and hurried off to catch up with him.

The following days were the best Askik had known at Vielleterre. From morning till night he lived on the reaper-binder. When one team of horses became exhausted, he had another brought and pushed on until dark. He discovered a new kind of fatigue entirely associated with the machine. The metal seat mounted on a flexible iron strap pounded his rear to a pulp. His back screamed from spending hours on end without support. The constant vibration from his toes to the roots of his hair quietly but surely sapped his strength.

It had taken a whole morning to get the horses used to walking at a steady pace so as not to jam the cutting blade, and to the infernal noise of the turning gears. But what a marvel the machine was! It did ten times, twenty times more work in a day than a whole gang of reapers and binders. All Paradis and the stable boys had to do was follow on foot, loading the firmly-tied sheaves which never came apart on the wagon.

The village road, which was normally deserted, was full of vehicles going by as if by chance. The drivers, although they did not dare stop, slowed their horses and turned on their seats to study the marvellous contraption as it cut through broad swaths of the golden wheat. On arriving in the village, each made his report.

"They've finished the Souricière field."

"They can't of! I went by yestiddy an' they'd only jus' started."

"They've finished, I tell ya!"

Quarrels broke out and those reporting were called liars or dupes. Lacking more concrete argument, most insisted that for every boon there is a price to pay. The machine worked fast, granted, but how could the blades and rollers not mangle the ears of wheat?

To get it out of their systems, a small group invaded La Souricière at twilight. They bent over the stubble, scratched at the ground among the stems, picked up a lost grain of wheat here and there. They scoured the field from one end to the other until the eldest of them declared what was obvious.

"There ain't enough left t' feed one hen!"

It was true. The machine harvested cleanly and well. The men went home when darkness fell, silently calculating what they would save in time and effort by having the machine mow their fields.

The next day they arrived at Vielleterre one after the other, always alone and always in a hurry to be gone. They asked for Paradis and settled the rental terms with him. They left by the side roads, avoiding the village. Those who had already harvested their wheat while green kicked themselves for it.

Despite their small number, Paradis, the stable boys and Askik fittingly saluted the last sheaf. In the field, they drank to it with rum, dressed it up with a straw hat and a coloured shawl, enthroned it on top of the wagonload, then escorted it home, shouting loudly. When they had put this last load away, they sat down to a feast in the barnyard.

Their table was an assemblage of trestles and boards and their chairs were crates and barrels. In the bowls before them they found fennel-stuffed chicken, potatoes, ears of corn, green peas and turnips. Over it they poured thick gravy, and with hands still dirty and faces covered with dust, did joyous honour to the excellent fare. Rosalie, radiant with pride, kept running between the table and the kitchen. The gravy was smooth, the bread soft and the chicken succulent. Since Céline's departure, Rosalie had discovered competence and skill to a degree unsuspected even to herself. Being alone and responsible was all she had needed to find pleasure in her work.

Fat grey clouds had drawn across the sky. The wind was turning cold.

"Good time to be finished," Paradis said. "It's gonna rain for sure."

"As long as it doesn't rain too hard," Askik rejoined, "so I'll have time to do our neighbours' fields."

"And while you're at it, me 'n the boys 'll dig up the 'taters."

There was an embarrassed silence. Madame Paradis leaned toward her husband and whispered a few words.

"Eh?" the old man exclaimed with a look of bewilderment. "What am I talkin' about? That's right, there ain't no more 'taters! I'm gettin' old for sure, talkin' though my hat."

He laughed at himself so gaily that the boys could not help doing likewise. Askik felt a twinge of pain to see his old comrade's mind beginning to wander. Madame Paradis, however, had gone back to her meal as if nothing had happened. When you've worked so hard all your life that you've worn yourself out, she seemed to be saying, there's no shame if one's thoughts stray a bit with fatigue.

They had come to the raspberry pudding when they spotted a vehicle in the distance, approaching from the village.

"Another customer for the machine," Askik predicted. "Perhaps I'd better get out of sight."

"No," said the boys, who had stood up the better to see. "There's a coachman," they declared with excitement. No one in the village had a coachman, not even Monsieur le curé.

Shortly afterward, an elegant victoria drawn by two purebred horses pulled into the yard. A man in a suit and top hat was sitting like a ramrod in the back, with a cane between his knees and his hands folded over its head. He opened the door himself and descended stiffly but imperiously.

"It's Monsieur Hubert!" Rosalie cried, in a twinkling of an eye losing her self-confidence.

Without a single glance toward the people sitting in the yard, Cousin Hubert walked up the front steps of the house and went inside. Madame Paradis and Rosalie flew off to the kitchen, carrying away the tea and apple fritters they had just placed on the table. The men and boys were left alone with their empty plates, feeling vaguely humiliated.

A few minutes later, Askik was summoned to the drawing room. The tea had been transferred to a silver teapot and the fritters now occupied a fine porcelain basket. One of them, half eaten, reposed on a starched linen napkin. Cousin Hubert had laid his gloves and cane on the sofa beside him. He had not allowed his coat to be taken away, but had thrown it himself over the back of a loveseat. Clearly, he was not staying. He looked tired and out of sorts. When he saw Askik enter, he made a slight face and put down his cup.

"I'd invite you to sit down," he said without rising, "but with the way you're dressed I'd fear for my aunt's furniture."

"I can stand."

"Good, it won't be for long. You've made a fine mess of things, Mercredi. Half the county is up in arms against you. D'you know how many voters there are in this parish alone?"

"They hate me, but they admit I'm right."

"Expenses have attained unheard-of proportions."

"Revenues too."

"You've been organizing little parties for your friends. That servant — what's her name again?"

"Céline."

"Got herself pregnant by one of your guests."

"That's not true!"

"But she's gone?"

"Yes."

"For that, my aunt will never forgive you."

Hubert allowed a brief silence to weigh. His scornful eyes added, Do I have to tell you?

Askik spared him the trouble.

"I'm dismissed?" he asked in an expressionless voice.

"Yes."

"I'll leave tomorrow."

"You'll leave today." Hubert held out an envelope. "My uncle instructed me to give you this sum. Do me the favour of accepting it and sparing us both an altercation."

Askik took the envelope without a word.

"You must understand," Hubert continued, "that this puts an end to all connection between you and the Sancys. For reasons that I do not question, my uncle gave you an education and a position. You have abused his kindness. Expect nothing more. Is this well understood?"

Askik made no reply.

"That's all," Hubert said as he picked up his gloves and cane.

On the way out, Askik encountered Beaudry, who was standing near the carriage with his arms crossed, sniggering.

"Is this your new intendant?" Askik asked; he too had an urge to laugh.

"Monsieur Beaudry," Cousin Hubert replied, "will oversee the farm's operations until the new intendant arrives."

A flash of sardonic humour caught Askik by surprise. Since he was only a lowly Métis, he asked with exaggerated servility, "Would you let me ride with you to the village? I could sit with the coachman..."

"Sorry, Mercredi," Cousin Hubert replied as he closed the carriage door behind him, "you've already taken me rather far out of my way."

"One last word, then," Askik said, speaking seriously now. "Paradis has bought a farm on the other side of the mountain. He's not strong enough to grow crops on it. If Vielleterre could sell him a few cows and some hay, cheap..."

Hubert leaned toward him slightly, very slightly. "Do you take yourself for the only charitable soul in the world, Mercredi? Monsieur Paradis has served our family honourably for many years. My uncle will see to his needs."

"Thank you."

"Don't thank me, you have nothing to do with it. On, driver!"

The carriage took off, spewing dirt and sand. Askik and Beaudry were left face to face.

"I suppose there's no point asking for a vehicle to take me to the village," Askik said ironically.

In reply, Beaudry gave an unpleasant nasal laugh and spat tobacco.

When he left the yard with his bag in his hand and a coat thrown over his shoulder, Askik did not once look back at the big house. He kept his eyes fixed on the horizon just visible at the end of the driveway. He had a mind to travel, to go and keep going for miles and miles without ever arriving anywhere.

Like papa, he thought. Exactly like papa.

At the end of the driveway, hidden by the trees, Paradis was waiting for him. The old man held out his scrawny hand.

"Mustn't let it git you down, lad," he said. "Ever'thin' works out in the end."

"Anyway, as you say, it doesn't matter,"

The old face showed a toothless smile. "Well, pretty close," he acknowledged.

"We had a fine party today."

"A fine harvest, mighty fine! I'll remember it the rest o' my days."

Askik held the bony little body close against his. When they separated, Paradis bowed his head to hide the tears in his eyes.

"Goodbye, Paradis. I don't think we'll see each other again."

"We will sooner'n you think," the old man retorted after clearing his throat. "You ain't immortal no more'n me."

Askik reached the river at nightfall. The stagecoach was not due until morning. He settled down on the front stoop of an old spinster's house. The poor lady was so horrified to see a savage on her steps that she slept no more than he did all night.

The day that dawned was grey, windy and cold. In places, there was sleet driving into the river.

The stagecoach was dirty and badly sprung. Each time Askik dozed off, the vehicle gave him a mighty whack on the back of the head. He resigned himself to staying awake.

A faded note pinned to the coach wall announced to the ladies and gentlemen aboard that newspapers had been provided for their comfort and enjoyment. Askik rummaged under the seats and unearthed some tattered, yellowed remnants several months old. As the coach was entering the outskirts of Montreal, he read an editorial in a major daily which bore below it, in the manner customary with French editorials, the name of its author, "Étienne Prosy, Editor-in-Chief." By now nothing surprised him any more.

PART FOUR

The Prairie

1

Grandet could hardly believe his good fortune. He hurriedly took off his coat, threw aside his gloves and scarf and pulled off his boots, all without once taking his eyes off the package he had laid on the table.

The scissors! The scissors!

He ran to his desk, a handsome piece with at least twenty drawers and other pull-outs. He opened and closed drawers, muddled their contents, scattered papers that had been carefully sorted by name, filing date or crime.

Ah, the letter opener! A handsome little dagger bearing the royal family's coat of arms, but no sharper than a butter knife. Grandet sawed long and feverishly at the string around the package, and finally, triumph! — it parted.

He forced himself to take a moment's pause. His heart was thumping and his mouth was dry. Then with trembling fingers he undid the package and, holding his breath, removed the paper.

He had not been dreaming. It was true. A warm, dizzying joy enfolded him, a joy the like of which he had never felt before. In the package, against a black cloth background, glowed a white enamel Maltese cross surmounted by a crown and bearing the number 65 in bold figures. Like a father gingerly lifting his firstborn, Grandet unfolded the sash and laid it reverently on the sofa. Then the tunic, black as coal, banded with braid in swirls across the chest and with the high collar he had always dreamed of. The very dignified trousers. And underneath the rest — behold! — boots of fine, gleaming black leather.

He undressed, letting his expensive rags fall where they might, and solemnly donned his new clothes, the way a bride tries on her white dress. For verily, Grandet was changing condition. When all was ready, collar hooked, belt buckled, bandolier properly in place, he opened a hatbox and took out a plumed shako. Then, holding his breath once more, he went and stood before the mirror.

He almost fainted. Elzéar Grandet, barrister and solicitor, was no more. In his place stood an officer with broad shoulders, full chest, and a powerful and imperial bearing. The tailor had done his work well.

"At last, at last, at last!" he murmured. "I knew I was born to bear arms."

There are turning points in life when a man hears destiny calling his name. Thereupon, all his previous sufferings take on meaning and purpose. How can one keep from shedding a tear or two at such moments?

Joy gave way to panic. There were still three long hours before the regimental dinner — and he had already creased his trousers, had he not? Cursing his foolhardiness, he undressed again, put on a dressing gown and pulled the bell cord. In a twinkling there was a chambermaid at the door, a girl of twelve, the landlord's daughter.

"Have this uniform pressed," Grandet ordered. "No, wait! It's not you who'll be doing the pressing, is it?"

"Oh no, monsieur," the girl replied, "it's Madame Trudel."

"How old is she?"

"She's very old, monsieur."

"She should know what's she's doing then. She's not senile, is she? She can still see? All right, take it away. But tell her to be careful!" he cried, his voice a falsetto. "I have to wear this uniform for a very, very important occasion!"

He felt his stomach knot with nervousness. "And have some wine brought up. No — brandy!"

His state of nerves infected the chambermaid and she took the uniform and ran. Grandet collapsed on the sofa. I won't live to see it! I'll surely die before seven o'clock!

He survived, however. He had to. The sub-lieutenant's commission had cost him an arm and a leg. He had contributed generously to the conservative party's election coffers, had paid assiduous court to the officers of the batallion, even attended their ladies' teaparties. He had lost count of the lunches he had bought at the Éthier for the batallion commandant. And all he had got was a wretched little sub-lieutenancy! Damned unappreciative, these military men could be!

But now it was done. He was in. None too soon, either. In a few weeks, he thought, the recruiting offices would be deluged, and then it would be goodbye to commissions. The newspapers were proclaiming an imminent declaration of war between England and Russia. Hostilities would surely begin any day. He had combed all the bookstores, pillaged all the reading rooms, and had amassed a wealth of information on the coming conflict which, in Montreal, he alone must possess. He knew the rivers and mountain ranges of Afghanistan by heart, had even practiced locating towns and villages on an unmarked map. Lacking information on the combat methods of the Muslim mountain tribesmen, he had also devised his own infantry tactics adapted to the rocky crags and wadis of the region. He would return a general or he would not return at all.

He sat as straight as a bayonet in the open carriage that took him to the regiment. His breath blew back in his face, frosting his spectacles so that he could not see a thing. His cheeks turned purple and froze, and he suffered the tortures of a martyr with his ears left bare to the elements by the dashing shako. Able to bear it no longer, he thrust his face under the driver's seat. The coachman, a bear of a man covered in hair and wool, turned with a broad smile.

"You a mite cold, *mon pauv' monsieur?*"

The officers were dining at the Richelieu. With rifles at the slope, two militiamen were stamping back and forth on the steps of the hotel. As soon as they perceived Grandet's plumed headware, they stiffened and saluted. Enchanting! Grandet thawed out in an antechamer while the hotel staff wiped his spectacles and brushed and straightened his plumes. And then, with his shako pressed to his heart, he made a dignified entrance. When he recognized the batallion colours — *Nunquam retrorsum* — he was so moved he could have wept.

"Ah, here's our new man!" Colonel Ouimet exclaimed.

"Bravo!"

The officers were having a final pre-dinner drink. Colonel Aldéric Ouimet, wealthy landowner, distinguished barrister and solicitor, Member of Parliament, took Grandet's arm and introduced him to his brothers in arms.

"Captain Giroux, Sub-Lieutenant Grandet."

"Captain."

"Sub-Lieutenant."

"Lieutenant Destroismaisons, Sub-Lieutenant Grandet."

"Lieutenant."

"Sub-Lieutenant."

Grandet exchanged manly handshakes and brotherly eye-to-eye looks. He was overcome by the immediate liking his fellow officers were demonstrating. He moved about in a cloud of cigar smoke, took in the succession of black tunics and mutton-chop sideburns, and despaired of remembering all those names. He was therefore startled to find himself suddenly face-to-face with a pale, blond young man in a bottle-green uniform whose presence jarred in this gathering.

"Here's a guest," Colonel Ouimet offered. "Lieutenant Robert Simpson of the Queen's Own Rifles of Toronto."

"How do you do," said Grandet, disappointed not to be the only one with a place of honour that evening.

"We've already met, I believe," the young Englishman said pleasantly. "You're a friend of Alexis Mercredi, are you not?"

"To tell the truth, I don't see much of him any more..."

"We'll talk again later, I hope..."

The hotel majordomo was moving about among the officers, discreetly inviting them to take their places at table. Colonel Ouimet left the room and the officers stood at attention behind their chairs. When there was complete silence, the colonel came back in, took his place at the head of the table, crossed himself and said grace. Then, raising his glass, he added "Messieurs, the Queen!"

"The Queen!" shouted all the others.

Grandet was displeased to find himself opposite Lieutenant Simpson. Not that he had anything against the man, but any reminder of his past life seemed an intrusion. He was anxious to immerse himself totally in his new military condition, and here was Simpson insisting on drawing him back from it.

"Have you been in the militia long?" Simpson asked.

"It's... rather recent."

"Ah, I didn't think you had a military air about you."

Grandet was cut to the quick. "Of course, out of uniform..." he stammered.

"Don't be upset," Simpson rejoined soothingly, "A man can find himself under arms without really liking it."

"Is that your case?" Grandet retorted, beginning to feel vicious.

Simpson smiled amiably. "My family has a warlike bent," he said. "Military service is a tradition with us. And a requirement," he added with a wince. He leaned toward Grandet and whispered, "I thought I had found a soul mate, but I see you're a soldier to the core. Forgive me."

Grandet could think of nothing to say in reply and concentrated his attention on his turbot with mousseline sauce. After a time, seeing that Grandet's neigbours were paying no attention to him, Simpson politely relaunched the conversation.

"So you've not heard from your friend Mercredi for some time?"

"Not for quite a while, no."

"I don't see him at the courthouse any more."

"He's not pleading any more."

"Oh? What does he live on then?"

"Perhaps he has investments."

"A remarkable fellow, don't you think?"

Grandet hesitated. What was remarkable about scuttling one's chances of success? The situation called for polite noncommittal, however. "Yes, quite remarkable," he said.

Simpson sensed his reticence. He had decided to hold his peace when a captain at the other end of the table presented him with a challenge.

"So, Lieutenant, are the Queen's Own Rifles ready to fight for the country's honour?"

Simpson gave a vague smile. "Is the country's honour in danger?"

The captain held his knife and fork suspended over his plate, speechless for a minute. Then he uttered a resounding "Ha!" and for the benefit of those around him, exclaimed, "What about Afghanistan?"

"I can't see in what way that conflict puts our country's honour at stake, monsieur."

To tell the truth, nor could the captain. He had never probed beyond the headlines for an understanding of the subject. To him, the interminable exchange of diplomatic notes between London and St. Petersburg were a crashing bore. Neverthless, he uttered a magnificent growl and declared with very French grandiloquence:

"It's not up to us soldiers to judge when honour is at stake, monsieur. It's up to us to defend it."

There was a rumble of approval. Grandet glowed with pride.

"To return to my question," the rotund captain continued, elated with the effect he was having, "are the Queen's Own Rifles ready to fight for the country's honour or aren't they?"

Simpson's smile was more congenial by the minute. "The Queen's Own are always ready to fight," he said. "No questions asked."

Since his final words were in English and most of the diners did not understand, the reply was taken as satisfactory. The conversation now turned to Afghanistan and Grandet thought his chance to shine had come. To his dismay, however, most of his fellow-officers did not think there would be any Canadian intervention in Afghanistan. No, they said, in case of war the Canadian militia would more likely be called on to relieve British regulars. In Jamaica, for example. Grandet's plans were thus reduced to dust. How could he become a general in a peaceful rum-producing colony? He had the poor taste to press his point.

"Excuse, me," he said, "but I've read up a bit on this subject. The Indian army is strong, I grant you, but Afghanistan is a difficult country to hold. We would not be underfoot there. Remember the retreat from Khabul; from an army of sixteen thousand, one single survivor. The savagery of the mountain tribes mustn't be underestimated. Remember how the diabolical Gilzhais hacked up the English prisoners and paraded their body parts on the ends of sticks!"

A number of the diners now looked alarmed. They were shopkeepers, shipowners and lawyers; family men for the most part. Parading, bearing the standard to church on the Feast of Saint Michael, attending regimental dinners once a month, these were pleasant pastimes. Fighting diabolical what's-their-names was not on their program. They glanced at each other uneasily. Might they be called to active service? And where did this dreadful little whipper-snapper come from? Who had let him into the batallion?

The conversation was steered back to neutral ground. The French were taking a licking in Tonkin. Here, at least, Canada's honour was not at stake. The meal ended with liqueurs in quantities left to the diners' discretion. Grandet exercised none at all. Midway through the evening, he was obliged to disappear and bring up part of his initiation dinner. He felt nauseated, debased, and disgusted with this batallion that did not want to die.

In order to see oneself as one really is, one needs to catch sight of oneself unexpectedly in some unfamiliar mirror or shop window. As he left his cubicle, Grandet caught sight of himself in the washroom mirror. He saw a tall, lanky fellow with sparse hair and face drained of colour; his shoulders were tiny in spite of the padding; his chest looked like a child's. He nearly wept with frustration. Command is not offered to weaklings. God had put the heart of a conquering hero in a scarecrow's body.

He nearly collided with Simpson on his way out of the men's room. Simpson looked at him with concern.

"D'you not feel well?" he asked. "I could take you home..."

Grandet flared up indignantly. "There's no need," he snapped. "Where's Mercredi? D'you know?"

"Again! You're very interested in poor Mercredi," Grandet said disdainfully. He leaned against the wall, his face ashen. "Why are you looking for him?"

"I don't like disappearances. I went and talked to his old landlady on Rue Saint-Paul; he hadn't been back. Or to his office either. I understood he was going to ask his former teacher, Monsieur Prosy, for a job; Prosy hasn't seen him. So where is he?"

"I don't know. At the Muses perhaps." Grandet saw Simpson raise his eyebrows and explained. "That's a dockside tavern. A word of advice: change your clothes if you go to the Muses. Military men aren't welcome there, especially English military men."

"D'you know any habitués there? Could you give me some names?"

"You've got your nerve," Grandet hissed. Then he looked up at the other and, distrust vying with nausea in his eyes, asked again, "Why are you looking for him?"

"Because I'm rich and I've nothing better to do than look out for my friends," Simpson bantered, then in a more serious tone he added, "besides, I'm not the only one looking for him."

"Ah, so that's it!" Grandet breathed. "A creditor!"

"Oh no! No one as important as that."

"Who, then?"

"Shhh!" Simpson whispered, his eyes twinkling. "Professional secret..."

Grandet was looking more woeful by the minute. He had lowered one buttock into a pedestal ashtray which was preventing him from slithering to the floor.

"In fact," he said, "if you're going by Sherbrooke Street, I'll accept your offer... You know, those oysters..."

"Could teach the Gilzhais a thing or two, I know. I avoid them like the plague, dear fellow. Like the plague!"

Askik was not so far away. He was residing in Verdun, slightly upriver, on the premises of Ernest Mathieu, "Carter, Brick-Maker, Purveyor of Hay & Construction Materials." Mathieu's property occupied three acres of waterfront. His enormous yard was cluttered with carts, haystacks, manure piles and stacks of bricks and lumber. From morning till night it was a constant bustle of heavy conveyances and contractors' carriages coming and going.

Old man Mathieu had a single passion, percherons, and a single hate, accounting. To give himself more time for the first and liberate himself of the second, he had agreed to rent his garret to Askik, who in exchange would look after his paperwork. At first Mathieu had not been sure whether he should turn his accounts over to a Métis, but the newcomer did his job so well and asked for so little pay that soon the other merchants of the neighbourhood were arriving with ledgers in hand. The Métis had more than one string to his bow, besides; it was quickly learned that he was conversant with the law and could draw up contracts and petitions and, better still, knew how to get around an occasional tax.

Unfortunately, he was not very industrious. It was not easy to get him to accept an assignment. Even before morning was over, he might be seen leaving on foot in the direction of the mountain and would not return until nightfall. At other times he would be seen on the river; he kept a canoe hidden behind Mathieu's gravel piles. He could push off at any time without a word to anyone and not be back until the following morning. It was believed that he spent the night in the woods on the other side of the river beyond Ste. Anne. He had lost two canoes in the rapids but, with the skill of an otter, had escaped himself unscathed. On Sundays he could be found at the Caughnawaga reserve across the river, watching the Indians' lacrosse games. However, no one seemed ever to have seen him downtown in Montreal. He stayed by himself, talked little to anyone, and discouraged overtures by the curious. Old man Mathieu left him alone and the village eventually did likewise.

Mathieu's garret was huge and, like the rest of the house, reeked of horse. The smell of percherons had permeated the furniture, curtains, clothing and even the walls. Askik very quickly became oblivious to it. His garret contained a desk, a wooden bed, a chair (with a horsehair seat) and an iron stove that heated red-hot. The corners of the room had been taken over by paddles and ropes, an axe, three hunting rifles, fishing lines, a net and a hodgepodge of dust-covered tools. Hare and fox pelts hung from the tie-beams. Light entered from the south through two dormers, whose windows looked out on the stable.

It was here that Askik spent the winter. He would rise after the sun, work on his clients' accounts in the morning and then go out and stretch his legs. In the evenings he read novels by the light of an oil lamp.

When he tired of reading, he would escape. To Quebec by train, to Sherbrooke by stagecoach. But most often he would rent a broken-down carriole and roam the roads of the Laurentians and the Ottawa Valley. He loved the spruce forests, the log coaching inns, the snow-covered roads leading to crude pioneer villages. Their simplicity soothed him. He would sleep on benches in taverns or on the floor in a colonist's house. He had only to knock and he was taken in; the impoverished colonists never missed an opportunity to earn a few cents for food and lodging. The children, raised in the wilds without ever seeing an Indian, would open their eyes wide at the sight of Askik Mercredi. The master of the house would get up several times during the night, supposedly to stoke the stove but really to make sure the Métis did not make off with the dishes. In a house at La Petite Nation on the Ottawa River, a narrow band of lime was dusted around his pallet because everyone knows that Indians are infested with fleas. In another house the owner shut himself in his bedroom with an axe. Everywhere, people were surprised at the smell of horse that accompanied the stranger.

Nevertheless, when severe weather obliged him to stay several days in the same place, the habitants soon became accustomed to having him around. What an astonishing creature this Métis was! He spoke educated French and could help the children with their readers or write letters dictated to him by the parents. He gave good advice on land clearing and farm husbandry. He even cured a sick cow or two. In the evenings he would entertain half the village with astonishing stories, most of them about the faraway Pays d'En-Haut. Farmers offered to take him on as a hand and a curé wanted to hire him as a teacher, but the Métis would leave as mysteriously as he had come. No one was surprised; everyone knows Indians can't stay long in one place.

Askik himself did not understand this extraordinary wayfaring among places and people. He travelled aimlessly, simply for the pleasure of setting off each time. He paid no heed to either expense or danger. He lost a horse in a raging snowstorm and had to spend the night in a snowbank. The dead mare cost him dearly, another blow to his already diminished savings. But he absolved himself with a wry reflexion: everybody knows Indians can't save money.

When spring arrived, his purse was empty. Though not particularly worried by this, he considered finding some small employment to enable him to buy a new canoe. He resumed his excursions to the mountain while waiting for the ice to break up on the river and the roads to become passable.

It had rained during the night. There was a hard, porous crust on the snow. Invisible seepings of water were awakening the soil, sapping the snowdrifts and combining into noisy, busy little streams bounding down the mountain's slopes. Flocks of chickadees flitted from twig to twig, twittering their usual din, undisputed masters of the woods, although robins, thrushes and vireos could not be far behind. Above Mount Royal, the wild geese were already stringing out their long formations.

Askik was puffing hard when he arrived at the top of the mountain. A winter spent reading novels and riding about in a carriole surely softens a man.

The clouds had not moved all night. Then in the morning, like a regiment that has received the order to advance, they raced eastward, grey and dark underneath, brilliant above. Salvos of wind blew holes of blue in them, giving the city shortlived patches of brightness. Beams of sunlight flashed between clouds or struck the ground in this neighbourhood or that. The grey streets were full of people going about their business and oblivious to the heroic engagement taking place above their heads.

Getting away from oneself makes for the best possible holiday. For Askik, the mold of the consciencious student — discipline, self-denial, guilt, forethought — had collapsed in the wake of failure. His rigorous training had not brought the promised rewards either of position or prestige. Since his customs and convictions had proven groundless, they foundered of their own accord. For the first time in his life he was free to do nothing because the future no longer beckoned. Now he would spend hours listening to the pattering of rain, the rolling of thunder that comes with spring, the soughing of wind in the branches. He would spend all day doing nothing, and come home at night tired, satisfied, fulfilled, a condition he had never known in twenty years of striving and hustle.

Not that he had total peace of mind, for part of himself kept stubbornly seeking order, purpose, a goal, and the passage of days sometimes caused him bitter pangs of remorse. However, since nothing in him any longer justified these cares, they passed like spent bullets, whining but doing no harm.

The fine weather was making the squirrels skittish. Heedless of anything or anyone, they scuttled about between their nests and their caches. Askik never tired of watching them. They reminded him of Numeo, who admired their boldness, and, reaching back further still in his memory, the chipmunk hunts he had joined on the outskirts of the Métis summer camps. Strange. These childhood memories, which for so many years he had thought fantastic and improbable, were now returning with convincing clarity. In his sleep at night, he was rediscovering the faces and ways of his playmates of those days. He saw them without particular kindness, without missing them in the least, but simply as they were when he had left them. As if the long years of study and solitude had turned to smoke. As if nothing had happened since his childhood. He had begun again to dream. Not the agitated, disjointed dreams of an office worker, but long, slow dreams that he remembered when he woke and that stayed with him part of the day.

It was late when he came in from the woods. Mathieu had gone to bed. In the kitchen, the only light came from a crack in the woodburning stove. As he groped for the candle that he kept near the door, he felt paper wrinkling under his fingers. He lit the candle, brought the envelope near the flame and read, "Alexis Mercredi, *avocat*, care of Monsieur Ernest Mathieu, Verdun."

A gravelly voice spoke from the darkness. "You seen yer letter?"

Mathieu approached in nightshirt and slovenly old slippers. The smell of percheron, already strong in the room, redoubled. The old man leaned shamelessly over the note that Askik was unfolding and read along with him, "Come and see me at the paper. Urgent. I have a proposal for you. Prosy."

Mathieu was disappointed. "Don't say much," he grumbled, then after a minute looked up with wide, shrewd eyes and added, "So yer a lawyer..."

"I was."

"Cré-taque!" Mathieu exclaimed softly, wagging his head slowly. Impossible to know whether he had learned this movement from his horses or had taught it to them. "Which paper?" he demanded.

"L'Époque."

"Ah no, that one I don't read. No good stories."

Mathieu was a devotee of serialized novels. He liked them syrupy.

For him a good story had to have a French marquise, a château and an ill-treated little girl. He had been following *Le Supplice d'une femme* in the daily press all winter — a tale of a young woman's multiple sufferings — and considered it a masterpiece. His only other cultural pursuit was reading the "Commercial Difficulties" column, snickering as he did.

He had reached his bedroom door when he turned and spoke again. "Didja bring me some partridge?"

"No, I wasn't hunting."

"Too bad," the old man growled, heading back to his bed, "I sure do like a bird on Sunday."

"Is it Sunday tomorow?" Askik said as he put the letter in his pocket. "The paper will be closed, then."

"Mebbe not. Things is all upside down in the city these days."

"What's going on?"

Askik heard the bedsprings creak under his landlord's weight.

"Oh, don't rightly know," the gruff voice said. "There's a war, I think."

Then, turning to his own thoughts, the old man gave a long, drawn-out snort. "A lawyer, *crétaque!*"

3

It was early when Askik arrived in Montreal. No doubt about it, the country was at war. One would have thought it had rained Union Jacks overnight. There were Union Jacks on flagpoles, at windows and on lamposts. Many merchants were displaying engravings of Queen Victoria and the Prince of Wales in their shop windows. Others featured portraits of a sad young man with an angelic face in the manner of Sir Walter Scott, framed in black crepe: evidently some dear departed. Churches were decked with regimental colours; plumed bandsmen were setting up camp on church steps and preparing to startle little old ladies arriving for first mass.

Askik gave up thought of breakfast and pushed on to the office of *L'Époque*. He was put off by all this uproar. He wanted to get back to his mountain and its solitary pathways at the first opportunity.

The paper was on a war footing. Typographers paced the corridors waiting for copy, reporters arrived at the run, messenger boys scurried away through the streets to the telegraph bureau.

A harassed editor put his head out of an office and, across a large room that was really rather quiet, bellowed at the top of his lungs, "Has the 65th got its marching orders?"

No one bothered to look up. "Not yet," replied an anonymous voice.

The editor flung back to his desk and sat with his head in his hands, chewing ferociously on a pencil.

"Could you tell me which is Étienne Prosy's office?" Askik asked him.

"Eh?" the editor cried with a start.

"Étienne Prosy..."

"That way!"

Prosy had an office enclosed in glass at the end of the room. He caught sight of Askik and raised his arms in a gesture of impatience.

"At last! Come in!"

It was more an order than an invitation. Askik remembered the time when Prosy had pulled his ears. The editor-in-chief's eyes were red and his face grey. There was a nervous twitch in his right eyelid. His shirt was not very clean.

"You look tired out," Askik commented.

"I haven't slept since Friday," Prosy offered in explanation, tilting back in his chair.

"Friday?"

"That's when the mobilization order came. The 65th should get its departure order any minute. I've called you..."

A piercing ring filled the room. Prosy lifted both feet off the ground as if a powerful spring under his chair seat had just released. He grabbed a black tube from a large box attached to the wall, put his face to a hole in the box and yelled, "Hello!" He nodded once or twice, bellowed "No!" and put the tube back in place."

"What's that?" Askik asked.

"A telephone. Listen carefully. We're covering all the usual things — ceremonies, masses, speeches, all that kind of thing. All the papers are going to have that, though. I want more. I've arranged to have a militiaman followed by one of our correspondents on the day of departure. You can imagine how it will be: the last family meal, sisters crying, father fighting back his tears as he embraces his only son, tearful goodbyes at the station... I'm going to call it 'A Mother's Farewell'; how d'you like it? I'll have three artists — three! — at the station. It'll be drawn from life. No imagination needed!"

He paused and nervously lit a small white cylinder.

"What's that?"

"A cigarette. Listen to me, now. We'll have reports by telegram during the campaign. Like everybody else. Page One. Every day. Hourly... What? What is it?"

A tall, languid young man was knocking on the glass; he put his head inside the office and announced with a smirk, "The regimental tailor says it won't be before Tuesday."

"The tailor!" Prosy replied indignantly. "Surely it isn't the tailor who's going to give the marching order!"

"Can't leave without their pants," the reporter observed with imperturbable irony.

"All right, do me a paragraph. We'll stick it in somewhere."

Prosy paced around his office like a caged rat, his hands held to his temples and despair in his eyes.

Askik's desire to leave was getting stronger by the minute.

"Where was I?" Prosy resumed. "Ah yes, the telegrams. No. What was it then? The correspondent. That's it..." He perched on the corner of his desk, facing Askik. "We're going to send out a correspondent," he explained, "Lemercier, my best. I don't want him to send me back the usual kind of prattle, though — General This, Major That... Yes, yes, we'll have all that, but I want more. I want colour. Local customs, interviews, anecdotes, you follow me? All the papers are sending correspondents; they'll all attach themselves to headquarters and that's where they'll stay. What else can they do? They don't know the country and they're scared stiff of the enemy. But *L'Époque's* correspondent... ah, *L'Époque's* correpondent," he repeated as if inspired, "will be different! He's going to move around on his own. He's going to talk to the locals. In their own language. Because, of all the papers, *L'Époque* will be the only one to give its correspondent a guide. Exactly, a guide!"

The editor with the pencil came in without knocking. He was holding a telegram and looked distraught.

"The Royal Grenadiers are leaving tomorrow."

"And the 65th?"

"Still nothing."

Prosy might have been struck with apoplexy. His hands dropped to his sides, his head fell back, and between his pale lips passed a sepulchral voice saying, "So the *Toronto Globe* will be the first on the scene."

"Looks like it," the editor said with profound sympathy, and added charitably but without real conviction, "We could send our correspondent to Toronto to go with the Second Batallion."

390

Prosy dropped into his chair. "Our readers would never forgive us." Then, reviving somewhat, he said, "We'll arrange something. Thankyou..."

An oppressive silence filled the room. Prosy sat staring dreamily at the glass walls.

"Ottawa was never going to let a French-Canadian regiment leave first, of course," he muttered. Then he sat up straight in his chair. "Well!" he declared, and turned to Askik. "Don't worry," he said, "our plan holds. We won't be the first there, but we'll do it in depth. I was saying... on the morning they leave, I'll take the serial novel off the front page. It's risky, I know, but the event should carry it off. On page two," he said, raising his hands to make a square, "we'll have pictures of the correspondent and his guide. Backgound material on both. Our readers will see from the outset that we're better equipped to cover the campaign. Our circulation will soar. Guaranteed!"

Prosy paused and bestowed a warm, kindly gaze on his former pupil.

"And you," he said, "will be famous."

Askik frowned. "Me?"

A look of consternation crossed Prosy's face. "Has another paper already approached you? You haven't given any undertakings, I hope! How much do you want?"

"Thankyou, but..."

"Surely you're not angling for the highest bid, putting the squeeze on your old teacher!"

Askik stood up. "I don't want to be a guide," he snapped. "That's what you're proposing, isn't it? It's a ridiculous idea. I don't see what use I'd be out there."

Prosy now understood that his plan was safe, that the other papers had not yet thought of Askik. He was so happy he began to laugh softly, almost sobbing with relief. The tension! In these dark times when black clouds of danger and threat hung over the country, men of courage lived fast and intensely.

"What d'you mean, what use?" he gasped, still laughing. "You're a natural for this work, dear fellow! You're ideal! You know the terrain, the customs, the language..."

The truth hit Askik like a bolt of lightning. He struck his forehead and exclaimed, "Oh, I see! There's been a mistake. You've confused me with somebody else. It's my friend Grandet who's the great expert on Afghanistan, not me."

"Afghanistan? I'm talking about the North West, my friend."

Prosy stopped short, amazed at the stunned look that came over Askik's face.

"For heaven's sake, can it be?" he asked, his laugh now incredulous. Then incredulity turned to wonder and he leaned across the desk. "It's hard to believe," he said gently. "Where the devil have you been hiding? Verdun's not the moon. How could you not know?"

Askik said nothing. He wanted to remain impassive, but powerful emotions were tugging at his face. His eyes begged for clarification even if his mouth remained resolutely closed.

Prosy was enjoying this unexpected little drama to the full. "The Métis have begun a rebellion, my friend! The North West is on fire!"

He ducked under his desk, rummaged frantically in a stack of papers and resurfaced with the Saturday edition.

"See for yourself. Read this. The Mounted Police have been defeated at Duck Lake. Battleford is under siege. The Crees and Sioux are on the warpath. Riel is leading the insurgents. All of Canada is under arms. And you, while all this has been going on..." He stopped, speechless. "Don't you talk to anybody?" he blurted at last.

Askik bent over the paper. His eyes were swimming and all he could make out was one headline: "Insurrection in the North West." He had no desire to read more. What did this insurrection have to do with him anyway? He had heard nothing from the North West for fifteen years. So a handful of Métis had killed some policemen on the Saskatchewan River. What of it? He had never even been anywhere near there. Was he afraid for his parents? No, he had to admit to himself. What was distressing him was not the news of the insurrection but the prospect, the odious prospect, of going back. For he knew deep down that in the end he would accept Prosy's offer. He was going to draw a line through fifteen years of effort and go home in the same condition he had left in: a penniless nobody.

Deep down, in some dark fold of his being, the great man was girding for a last desperate fight, although in Askik's estimation his chance of success was nil. The old dreams had been badly breached; it was time to haul down the flag. Askik would go home, partly because he was homesick but mostly because he had been beaten and there was no point struggling any longer. Once a savage, always a savage.

"I'll think about it," he told Prosy, getting to his feet.

"You'll do no such thing!" cried Prosy, horrified. "The batallion could get its orders ten minutes from now, or some time tonight, or tomorrow. No, no, no! Here's what you're going to do. You're going to go back to Verdun, you're going to pack your things, pay your bills, etcetera. At two o'clock you're going to go and meet Lemercier at the Bonsecours Market House; he's covering the drill. From then on you're not going to let him out of your sight. Bonsecours Market House, two o'clock! Have you got a watch? Here, take mine. Give it back to me before you leave."

Askik had his hand on the door knob. "Who's the man in the picture in the shop windows? The one in mourning frames?"

Prosy gave a sour little laugh. "Thomas Scott. Riel had him shot in '69."

"I think I remember Scott. He didn't look like that."

"He wasn't a martyr then."

Le père Mathieu received his accountant's resignation without a word. Askik thought his departure would be an inconvenience and went as far as offering his hunting rifle to make amends, but the old man refused.

"Waddya think I'd do with it? Can't see anaways." And back he went to the stable to fuss over his beloved pecherons while Askik gathered his belongings.

As he left the garret, Askik looked back one last time at his books and furs. He felt a pang of regret. So this was how it was all ending. Poor garret. So humble, so unpolished. And yet, he thought, I was almost happy here. The old man will probably close up this room. In thirty years I might come back and find everything the way I'm leaving it. "Bah!" he said as he clattered down the stairs. "I'm getting sentimental!"

He came out into the yard with his winter coat on and his bag on his back. The spring thaw had turned the ground around the house into a morass. He sloshed over to the stable.

"*Au revoir, le père!*" he called, putting his head through the open door.

"Yer off to war, boy?" said a voice from the storeroom.

"I'm going to the North West," Askik called.

"Well, kill two 'r three fer me!"

"Two or three what?"

"Whajja mean? Ain't we warrin' the English?"

Montreal was dreaming of glory and nothing but. The talk in the shops, bars and schools was about fusiliers, grenadiers and riflemen, and woe betide the uninformed. Attendance at militia drills had become solid proof of patriotism. Happy the man with haggard face in the morning who could say, "Phew! I was at the drill all evening!"

There were discordant voices, of course. A crowd of fifty or so citizens gathered at the Hôtel Rivard on Rue Saint-Gabriel to show support for the Métis. Certain newspapers also let it be known that the Métis might even have valid grievances, but hastened to add that nothing justified resorting to arms.

Quebec was embarking on this campaign with its conscience not entirely clear, but the delight of finally having its own little war outweighed by far the moral discomfiture. England had India, Germany had West Africa, France had Tonkin. Christians the world over were making glorious war. It was only right that Canada should have its North West.

A huge crowd was jamming Rue Saint-Paul and all around Bonsecours Market House, pressing up to the doors, where frantic soldiers were trying to hold back the mass of curious humanity. There were so many people inside that the parading militiamen were having difficulty manoeuvring. Despairing of being heard by the guards, Askik waited and passed beneath the rifle barrels with a surge from the crowd.

He was immediately sorry. The doorway to the hall was like the funnel of a meat grinder. Once started he could not retreat, and the farther he went the tighter the crush became. He was pressed so hard against his neighbours it was hard to beathe. Protests were voiced from ahead.

"No more room!"

"We'll suffocate!"

"Close the doors!"

And still more newcomers were absorbed by that compact crowd. In spite of the huge windows, a haze of tobacco smoke darkened the hall. Askik could see rifle barrels moving in formation. He tried to push through to the front but furious faces turned to him, teeth bared.

"Git back fer crissakes!

"Whojja think y'are?"

"We was here first!"

A military figure approached with an air of extreme annoyance. "*L'Époque?*" he cried on hearing Askik's explanation. "Why aren't you with the journalists, then? Follow me." And he forged through the crowd calling imperiously, "Make way! Make way!" In obedience, the onlookers, who worshipped anything in uniform that week, squeezed tighter, some even holding out their arms the better to compress their neighbours. What would they not do for their country?

Askik found himself out on the parade floor with a small clutch of privileged folk who were being spared the jostling. Those in fine clothes were the dignitaries. Those armed with pencils and notebooks were the reporters. The first are rarely found without the second.

There was an anomaly amid this collection of dark coats and notepads, however. Askik immediately noticed a baby-faced reporter who stood head and shoulders above all around him. A colossus with the airs of a ballerina, wearing a beige serge topcoat, a jaunty brown fedora and delicate spectacles. The giant was taking no notes; he did not even seem interested in the drill. He was talking volubly to his neighbour, who lacked the courage to ask him to shut up. Of the whole group, he was the most outlandish and furthermore knew it and was enjoying it. His eye caught Askik's and he strode forward, holding out a huge paw.

"Maître Mercredi? De-lighted! Arthur Lemercier at your service!"

Askik smiled in spite of himself. "No," he replied, "if I understood Prosy correctly, I'm supposed to be at your service."

"I don't accept subordinates," the journalist declared with a flourish, "only partners. We'll be colleagues or nothing!"

"Colleagues, then."

"May I call you Alexis?"

"Askik."

Lemercier opened his eyes wide. "Char-ming! En-chan-ting!" he exclaimed in a high-pitched voice. "I *do* get the feeling we're going to work well together! Thank God the Weasel found you!"

"The Weasel?"

"Oh!" Lemercier placed his fingers over his lips. "I shouldn't have... I believe Prosy's your friend. I haven't offended you, have I?"

"No, no. 'The Weasel' suits him perfectly. A very clever, very ferocious animal."

Lemercier clapped a hand on Askik's shoulder, threw back his head and burst into a squeaky laugh. "I *do* get the feeling we're going to have fun! We're so un-a-like!"

A gust of cold air swept over the crowd. The tobacco smoke swirled overhead. The great main doors had just been opened. The soldiers of the 65th came to attention at one side of the drill floor. From outdoors in the street came the strains of a brass band and L'Harmonie de Montréal marched in playing with all its might, followed by three hundred red tunics. The crowd roared with delight.

"The Victoria Rifles!" Lemercier cried.

The two batallions, the red and the black, were now face-to-face.

Their commanding officers came forward, saluted and shook hands. Renewed cheering. Tears sprang to many an eye to see these two regiments, one English and one French, joining hands in a common cause.

A low podium draped in red and black had been set up at one end of the hall. His Honour Mayor Beaugrand mounted it and waited for silence.

"Citizens! Allow me to express the satisfaction I feel to see our English and French compatriots come together in brotherhood as they do today..."

Wild applause greeted these words, as if the onlookers were hoping to prolong the new harmony with the vigour of their clapping.

"Worthy and valiant descendants of Wolfe and Montcalm, Brock and de Salaberry, you bring to your combined endeavour the *élan* of the French and the tenacity of the English!"

Now the crowd's enthusiasm knew no bounds. Some wiped away tears while others blew their noses. English and French Canadians love to bestow the benefit of their national virtues on each other.

The mayor raised his hands and continued his speech. "You are about to receive the baptism of fire. Go, and return to us covered in glory. Hail to the brave!"

After the ringing calls comes discipline. The Assistant Adjutant General of the region, Colonel Harwood, mounted the podium next. The crowd became serious and resolute. Colonel Harwood reminded the volunteers that they were now on active service and hence subject to the Queen's Regulations, hence liable to severe penalties for any undisciplined behaviour. He quoted Lamartine: "An army that questions orders is like a hand that presumes to think."

In the ranks, the recruits hardened their beardless jaws and swore to march to the death before questioning the least directive. They were students and salesmen, sons of respectable papas. Most had never slept away from home; in their imaginations they were savouring the wounds they would bring back from the war.

In the farthest rear, in 8th Company, Grandet stood as stiffly motionless as possible. His muscles ached but he refused to relax them. His body, his soul, his life henceforth belonged to his country. From now on he would not allow himself to complain or indulge in self-pity. He was a fighting man, totally at the service of his nation. Elzéar Grandet no longer existed for himself. He would endure small discomforts in preparation for major sufferings. He was pleased with himself at long last.

Colonel Harwood was too down-to-earth to succeed as well as the mayor had done. Still, he did manage to raise the temperature slightly as his speech drew to its conclusion.

"The life of a soldier demands endless sacrifice," he cried. "If it falls to your lot to meet the enemy, I have no doubt that you will consider it all in a day's work, and will go into battle shouting at the top of your lungs, Vive la Canadienne!"

Instantly, the colonel was given a fine example of lung power. He stepped down, bowled over by the cheering, and fell into the arms of Mayor Beaugrand, who was never one to miss an opportunity.

The crowd began to disperse. Lemercier took Askik by the arm. "Let's go and see how the take has been," he said.

They entered a small office where half a dozen men in uniform were going through files or putting away clothes.

"Eighteen today," said an officer, seeing the reporter approach.

"Counting those two?" Lemercier pointed to two boys being enrolled.

"That's right."

The adolescents were each picking up an armful of newly issued equipment: boots, moccasins, mess gear, oilcloth coat, ammunition bag, blankets, comb and soap. The break would be total; henceforth they owed nothing more to the lives they had led before. Everything down to the last button now came from the government.

"That's all for today," Lemercier announced, turning to Askik. "My holds are full. Back to port."

"What are you going to write?" Askik asked as they bounded down the steps of the market building.

"That the troops are moving better. Ranks tighter, soldiers bright-eyed and bushy-tailed. A few speech quotes. I'll have to see."

Lemercier's walk was so rapid that he was passing carts going in the same direction, rounding puddles in the street with his arms extended like a skater.

"Are they ready to fight?"

Lemercier stopped short and looked at Askik like a delighted teacher. "Ex-cel-lent question! You know, nobody knows." He set off again at his headlong pace. "The trouble is," he said, "nobody in Canada knows anything about fighting. There's no army, only a handful of career soldiers who've never been under fire, a few British officers having a soft time of it, and militiamen who haven't even finished school yet."

"Are they well armed?"

"Oh no... no. Old Sniders: muzzle-loaders converted to breech-loaders. Long, heavy. An enormous bullet. Very effective point-blank. Otherwise..."

"Well then," Askik said, stopping in his turn, "it's going to be a disaster!"

Lemercier kept walking, hands held away from his body, head tilted slightly back the better to appreciate the smell of spring thaw in the air. "A disaster?" he shot back cheerfully. "Perhaps, but I'd be surprised. Life doesn't have the keen sense of calamity you do."

"Nevertheless," Askik said, catching up with him, "I remember two or three incidents in my childhood that I could really call calamitous."

"Ah, you're going to tell me about those!" Lemercier said as if savouring the prospect.

The Richelieu had been turned into a barracks. Camp cots blocked all the passages. Soldiers in undress uniform were polishing boots or reading newspapers. In a small room previously reserved for private parties, notaries were providing their services free of charge to officers anxious to write their wills. This was where Askik met Grandet. The sub-lieutenant had a new manner, bluff and virile, which did not suit him.

"Delighted to see you, Mercredi," he said.

It was not true. His first impulse on seeing Askik had been to avoid him. It was not a convenient meeting. How he longed to be far, far away from all his old acquaintances!

"Were you at the drill?" he asked, just to have something to say. "The batallion's beginning to look like a seasoned old unit, don't you think?"

"They say you're poorly armed."

"Tut, tut! The government has placed an order in England for ten thousand Martini-Henrys and fifteen million rounds of ammunition. Fifteen million, my friend!"

"That's a lot for ten thousand Métis," Askik allowed.

Grandet flushed slightly. "There are also... the Indians," he stammered, "and then the government will certainly put some munitions in reserve in case of, er, future incidents... But while we're on the subject, is it true the Métis are armed with Winchester repeaters?"

"I don't know. They didn't have them twenty years ago."

"Nobody had them twenty years ago."

"Of course, if they've got Winchesters..."

"Ah, yes..." Grandet had a distant look in his eyes for a minute. His hands instinctively moved over his thin chest.

"Have you heard from de Meauville?" Askik asked to draw him away from the dark thoughts he was having.

Grandet's face reddened. His fingers closed nervously over his turk's head buttons.

"De Meauville? He tried to find you and tell you... but... well, we didn't know where you were. In winter, you know..."

"He's married?"

Grandet sighed with relief. "Not yet. Next month."

"They're happy?"

"Happier than you or I will ever be."

"That's what I think too."

"Will you dine with us?" Grandet asked solicitously. "I can get authorisation."

"Thankyou, no, I'm going back to the paper. I'm attached to *L'Époque*."

"I know, I was told that. Oh, Mercredi, before you go: do you remember the lawyer Robert Simpson? He went back to rejoin the Second Batallion. He left a letter for you, but I'm sorry, I have it at home."

"There's no hurry. You can give it to me another time. When you leave, perhaps."

"Oh yes, when we leave!" Grandet exclaimed, brightening at the thought. "It surely won't be long now!"

4

They waited another two days, in fact. They still had no field caps or boots. Meanwhile, Askik paced the corridors of *L'Époque*. He was feeling depressed, had no desire either to read or go out, and was having to force himself to eat. He had begun to think he might not be leaving at all; from the incoming telegrams, it sounded as though the rebellion was petering out and the 65th might be demobilized. He waited for each telegraph boy, each telephone call. He had resigned himself to returning to the North West and now hated the thought of having to choose a future for himself.

Then suddenly the marching orders were given: Thursday, ten o'clock, the C.P.R. station. Viau Brothers, the bakers, received an order for a thousand loaves of bread. The caterer Napoléon Bourassa promised eight hundred pounds of hams and roasts. The caps and boots were issued at long last. Forty-five tents and a thousand blankets were discovered in a warehouse on Île Sainte-Hélène. A train of colonist cars, emptied of immigrants, was standing in the station with a coal tender full to the brim.

At *L'Époque* too, all was in place. Prosy held a final council of war on the eve of the departure. He was pale and trembling with fatigue and yet had never been stronger. He delivered directives like slaps of a hand. The reporters stiffened under the onslaught and did not argue. Even the oldest caught themselves respecting this ferocious Weasel who was forcing them to do new things, do the unheard-of. With his sleeves rolled up and his tall body leaning across his papers, he pounded the table with his bony hand.

"Colour! Colour! Colour! I want feeling! I want warmth!"

Once the meeting was over, he collapsed into his chair. He had played his cards and could only wait now for destiny to play hers.

Askik and Lemercier stopped at the accountant's to pick up their advances. Lemercier was dancing with glee; he spent money on reflex and was always short.

"You're coming to the Richelieu?" he asked. "The mayor's giving a punch party for the officers. Oh yes, do come! Please! So you'll join me? We're on, then. See you shortly, dear fellow!"

Prosy, left alone in the editing room, rubbed his bloodshot eyes.

"So, Askik," he said, putting his glasses back on, "here we are again. It must be ordained somewhere that I shall always preside at your departures. Astonishing how far we've come, though. Who would have said, twenty years ago, that I would become a newspaper publisher, and you…"

He hesitated, not knowing quite where to place Askik on fate's chess board. The Métis looked at him steadily with his impassive, unfathomable eyes. Strange, Prosy thought, that twenty years of living among us has not rid him of that… look. Like a deer watching for your next movement. There's defiance in it, implying fear, but also a kind of indifference. A fatalism. What is he thinking right now? Is he happy? Unhappy? Or does he not even know himself, like those wolf-children found in the jungle who have no idea who they are? Lord, can it be as hard as all that to shake loose of his Indian soul? So we haven't yet finished our work with these poor people…

He rose and warmly shook his former pupil's hand. "Bon voyage, Askik," he said. "May God keep you. Don't forget everything you've learned from us." Ah, there now, he thought, he's smiling at last. They're touching in their own way.

"Au revoir, Monsieur," Askik said. "No, I won't forget any of it. Count on me."

Tears came readily to Prosy these days. He was almost overcome with emotion.

It's a shame, he thought as he watched Askik leave; so few people recognize what fine if simple people these courageous Métis are. There are so many racists! He resolved to write an editorial about it some day. Or why not a book? *My Life Among the Métis*...

The Richelieu was in a festive mood. Toast after toast was being drunk. Dignitaries and officers were having punch and refreshments together, while the enlisted men wandered from room to room holding glasses of lemonade, their eyes wide with wonder. For some, this was their first night away from the paternal hearth. They could hardly believe they were really here, walking about as they pleased in the brilliantly illuminated salons of this hotel.

"Mercredi! Mercredi! Yoohoo!" Grandet raised his long arm and waved, standing on tiptoe. In three strides he crossed the room and caught up with Askik. He had drunk too much and was giggling like a schoolgirl.

"I'm so happy to see you!" he exclaimed. "What a magnificent party! The ladies are lacking, of course, but what does that matter for a pair of old bachelors like us, eh? This is a rare moment in our lives, Mercredi. A precious moment! I've never known a better group of men. Stout lads! Good lads! Our commanding officers are like fathers to us. I'd die for them!"

The fervour of self-sacrifice glowed in his face.

A new attack of giggles seized him. "I was going to forget again," he cried. "Oh, la la, where'd I put it? Aha! At last, here it is." He produced a creased envelope and handed it to Askik. "It's Simpson's letter. Better late than never! May I pour you a punch?"

Askik opened the envelope while Grandet went for the punch. The sub-lieutenant must have spilled some already on his uniform; a corner of the envelope was damp and smelled of rum. The writing was still legible, however.

Dear Mercredi,

I am giving this letter to your friend Grandet in the hope that he will see your shortly.

You will forgive me for meddling in your personal affairs; a word or two will explain.

Our firm occasionally takes prosecutions for the crown. While working up a case against a merchant accused of receiving stolen goods, I went to the city prison to question a material witness, Charles Delorme, alias Bidou, who was serving a sentence for breaking and entering.

When I had finished the interrogation, to my great surprise this Bidou asked me if I knew you. He said he met you sixteen years ago. You were arriving from the North West and he was the carter who took you from Lachine to Montreal. He said he had tried to meet you last winter and had set a time and place, but while he was waiting for you he was discovered and arrested by the police.

This fellow claims to know one of your benefactors of days gone by, a friend of his who has fallen on hard times. When last heard of, your benefactor was living at La Jolie Pinte, a tavern near the docks. His name is Urbain Lafortune.

I was going to verify these facts when my regiment was mobilised. I advise you to be extremely cautious. This Bidou is a villain; I have no doubt that your friend Lafortune is one also.

Cordially,
Robert Simpson

Grandet was making his way unsteadily back through the crowd, a glass in each hand.

"I propose a toast between friends," he said. "Wh... What are you doing?"

Askik had taken both glasses from him and put them on a window sill. "Can you be away from here for a few hours?" he asked. "I might need your uniform. Get your coat, then. I'll find a calèche."

Minutes later they were spanking through the streets of Montreal. The stone buildings gave way to warehouses, the warehouses to wooden houses, the houses to shacks. The driver was uneasy and made his horse

402

move along at a brisk trot despite the city restriction. He pulled up before a low, evil-looking tavern without a sign. Mercredi jumped to the ground. Grandet, sobered up by the cool air, followed more cautiously.

"Wait for us here," Askik said to the driver.

"No, môssieur," the other replied, "I ain't gonna wait here! Pay me so I can go."

He took the money with an air of disdain. These elegant debauchers trailing round in the gutter revolted him. There were better places than this in Montreal to go wenching in.

"Be brave," Askik said as he pushed open the door of the tavern. A hostile silence greeted them. In the smokey, poorly lit, low-ceilinged room, the newcomers made out a couple of dozen men and women. The most striking thing about La Jolie Pinte was its smell, a combination of outhouse and grilled meat. Grandet thought he was about to bring up Mayor Beaugrand's excellent punch but restrained himself, sensing that he would pay for it dearly.

"I'm looking for Urbain Lafortune," Askik told the tavernkeeper, an animal with arms as big as thighs. The man looked balefully at the uniform; Grandet felt himself shrink.

"What you want 'im fer?" the tavernkeeper asked with a curl of the lip.

"He's an old friend and I've heard he's in a bad way."

"The police is pretty hard up if they gotta hire fags an' savages," someone in the room piped up, drawing a round of coarse, provocative laughter from the drinkers. Grandet felt his cheeks burn; he could not bear being ridiculed.

"Anaways," the tavernkeeper said, "Lafortune ain't here no more."

"They took 'im to th' hospice," his wife cried with a wave of her hand that added, Now get out of here!

"Which hospice?"

The tavernkeeper was losing patience. "How should I know, fer crissakes?" he barked. "He's prob'ly dead by now."

Askik and Grandet were obliged now to set out on foot, make inquiries of a half dozen calèche drivers gathered about a brazier, and take a calèche to the nearest hospice. The puddles were freezing over and the wheels of the calèche skidded on patches of hardened snow. It was past midnight when they stopped before a tall, yellow-brick building surrounded by an iron fence.

"Mercredi," Grandet begged, "it's more than high time I got back. We're leaving tomorow!"

"One minute more. They won't want to let me in at this hour and you can explain to them. Open up your coat so they'll see your uniform better."

Despite the late hour, a nun came to the door almost immediately. She was a tiny woman; she opened the door barely a crack and peeked out at them.

Grandet turned on the chivalry. "Good evening sister. I'm so sorry to disturb you at this late hour. I am Major Elzéar Grandet, 8th Company, 65th Mont-Royal Batallion. This man is... an interpreter attached to our regiment. He's leaving in a few hours for the North West and might never return to our city. He wants to say a last goodbye to an old friend, Urbain Lafortune."

"Why didn't he come during visiting hours?" the nun said in the mousy voice that postulants acquire when they join an order.

"It was only today that he learned that this old friend was still alive."

The nun hesitated. Grandet poured it on some more.

"Sister, this man is going to war. He's putting his life in danger for the nation."

"But you say he's an interpreter."

"He's a Métis. In the eyes of his people, he's therefore a traitor. If he's captured, he'll suffer the same fate as our saintly Fathers Lebeuf and Jogues."

The nun's eyes widened; in the chapel, as it happened, there was a picture of the saintly fathers being burned at the stake.

"Come in," she said, stepping aside.

Askik entered while Grandet fled. The nun led Askik across the parlour and started up a narrow staircase.

"Your friend's name again?" she enquired softly.

They came out on the third floor in a huge room with steel columns. Askik could make out four rows of beds in which there were bodies under white blankets. For the second time that night, he was assailed by a suffocating stench. If a single sleeper's exhalations can sour the air in a room, the misery of fifty women, old, incontinent and ravaged by illness, can fill it completely. Combined with the smell of remedies, chamber pots, musty sheets and the strong disinfectant soap used to scrub the floor, it created an unbearable fug.

The floorboards creaked under their feet. A plaintive voice rose from a dark corner. "Sister... sister...!"

The nun walked straight on with rapid though silent footsteps, diffusing as she passed only some faint light and the soft clicking of her rosary. The circle of light from her lantern fell on the sick for fractions of seconds. Some of the bodies lay still, tiny and sunken into their mattresses. Others lifted frail, twisted arms. A woman sobbed in a bed with barred sides, repeating over and over, "J'ai mal... j'ai mal...," as if endlessly surprised to be in such pain. When she saw the nun bend over her, she blurted in a stifled voice, "I don't wanna die! I don't wanna die!"

The nun opened a door and let Askik through to a passageway. In the dimly-lit pharmacy, an aged sister was rocking in a chair and telling her rosary. She smiled respectfully at Askik.

"This way," the younger sister said, opening another door. "This is the men's ward."

This second dormitory was more silent than the first. The harsh breathing of the sleepers was audible on all sides. Once in a while, someone would utter a name or a protest. Were these men seeing their wives, their children, their own houses in their dreams? Only one short step more and they would be full-time wraiths.

The nun led Askik to the far end of the room, beside some big windows.

"He loves to look at the river," she said, "that's why we put him here." She lit a candle and placed it on the bedside table. "I won't light the gas so as not to wake the others," she added. "If you need anything, ask at the pharmacy."

She brought him a chair and disappeared.

Askik had no trouble recognizing the old voyageur. He had not changed much. His skin was like brittle parchment and his hollow cheeks were streaked with tiny blue veins, but the hawk-like beak and high forehead had endured. He quivered as he slept; his lips and eyelids trembled; his heavily-veined, bony hands clutched the blanket under his chin. Askik blew out the candle so as not to disturb him.

He could see better without it. The beds seemed to go on and on, like a reflexion endlessly repeated between two mirrors. The window muntins cast dark crosses on the sleepers. From time to time a nun would flit among the beds like a shadow.

It was around midnight, when sleepers sink into their deepest being, wage battles in their dreams and live the dark underside of their lives without astonishment. Askik, being awake, could have only the memories that conscious life permits. This dormitory reminded him of the college, his school in Montreal. He could see the pupils coming back from days at home with scarves knitted by their mothers, boxes of goodies and brand new books. What he got, every spring and fall, were clothes bought cheaply by the fathers, their cost reimbursed from Vielleterre. He was always dressed in dark colours because, as everyone knows, savages lean to garish colours. The other children asked their parents for skates, hoops and sleds; he could ask for nothing because what he had received already was too much. He remembered the long nights beside the pampered little white boys, when the least memory of the Red River would hurt so much that he thought it was going to choke him. And then gradually he had got used to it all; routine finally brought him to heel. In the end he had believed his teachers' promises: work and you will succeed; shine and you will be accepted.

His case, however, was one of mistaken identity as the jurists say; the "you" of the promises meant his classmates, not him. For him, a different destiny was envisaged. He was expected to return to the North West to assist in the work of the civilizers. No one ever expected him to succeed in Quebec. You may allow a pauper to warm his hands at your fire but you do not give him the keys to your house. The French Canadian may be charitable to his colourful Métis cousins, but he likes the line between benfactor and protégé to remain clearcut. If the protégé learns to provide for himself, well and good, but let him keep his sights low and above all not compete with his saviours. All this went without saying; Askik had been the last to recognize it, that was all.

It's crazy, he thought; I'll have spent my first and last nights in Montreal wide awake. In between, I think I never woke up at all.

He stared at the little body in the bed; a sharp hip bone poked up the covers. Images from the past came unbidden: Lafortune building his canoe in a cabin too small to allow its removal... Lafortune in the mud and mosquitoes of the Savane Portage... Lafortune laughing with glee to have hoodwinked the English colonel... Yet these represented the merest sliver of his entire life. What about the rest?

Askik was roused by whisperings from the pharmacy. Day was about to dawn. The low sky stretched unbroken all the way to Longueuil; beyond, nothing was visible. The lights of the harbourfront burned a bright, ridiculous blue; Askik disliked electricity already.

"What happened, Lafortune?" he murmured. "You couldn't wait to get back to Canada. You had savings. Who fleeced you? The old codger who picked you up that first night? Bidou? If we'd known it would all end the way it has, we'd both have stayed in St. Boniface. I was right that last morning of our journey; I should have gone back with Numeo.

You and I have a talent for messing up our lives. You were hunting for the past and I the future. What a pair of hunters! What a crazy idea!"

A grey light was spreading through the room. Askik watched a large crucifix with a lenten shroud appear at the far end. It's Holy Thursday, he thought mechanically. The day of goodbyes.

The patients were waking. Some gazed at him gloomily while waiting for their morning porridge. Others resumed their silent contemplation of the ceiling which the night had interrupted; a tin ceiling embossed with complex designs in which a mind could lose itself for a time.

The ageing nun he had seen briefly in the pharmacy was approaching with heavy step.

"It's seven o'clock, *mon bon monsieur*," she said in a kindly voice. "Your regiment's leaving in a few hours, I think."

Askik was surprised that news of the rebellion had filtered through to such a place as this. It must have shown in his eyes.

"Our patients read the newspapers," the nun explained with a smile. Then she looked down at Lafortune and added, "He's not going to wake up. It's been a month since he was last conscious. It won't be long now."

"What had happened to him before he came here?"

"Oh, he wasn't talking much even then, monsieur. As soon as he came into this room he asked to be where he could see the river. That's about all. Sometimes he'd say something about wanting to go back up the St. Lawrence, I don't know where to. It was already too late, much too late..."

Askik thought, I know where he wanted to go.

The nun had placed a hand on the old voyageur's bald pate and was gazing at him with the tenderness of an elder sister. For her too, it was beginning to be late. Her manners and speech were those of the old Canadian families. A seigneur's daughter perhaps, who had been too plain to find a husband but in her caring order had acquired unfading beauty. Lafortune drooled a little on his pillow; the nun wiped up the drool with her handkerchief.

Askik was horrified. How can she live amid such misery? he wondered. He remembered the advance he had received the evening before at the office of *L'Époque*. He put his hand in his pocket and placed a roll of bills in the astonished nun's hand.

"For you and your patients," he stammered.

The nun took his hand and closed it on the bills. Her fingers were soft and strong.

"Keep your money, young man," she said. "Your friend doesn't need it any more. You're disturbed by what you saw during the night? Tell yourself that this is reality. When you're out there chasing after your appetites, that's when you're dreaming. People who've spent their whole lives dreaming wake up here."

"Well, anyway," Askik mumbled, feeling foolish, "you're very kind to look after these patients."

Did the old woman have to restrain a flash of annoyance? There was no sign of it. Her yellowed eyes betrayed only that gentleness and patience whose limits had been endlessly repressed.

After a time she said, "You're going to war, aren't you? Try not to kill anyone."

She walked away with her heavy step, her rosary beating an ancient measure against her thigh.

As he crossed through the parlour, Askik met the little nun who had let him in the night before. Although her face was drawn with fatigue, by light of day she turned out to be astonishingly young.

"We'll pray for you, monsieur," she said in her piping little voice.

5

Ten thousand people were waiting at the Canadian Pacific station. The regiment had difficulty reaching the platform. More than once, soldiers were separated from their comrades by the jostling of the crowd. Finally they were all standing in formation before the railway cars, which were festooned with Union Jacks. Colonel Harwood mounted the podium, called for silence and the crowd complied; it was in fashion to show respect for officers. The only sound was the puffing of steam from the locomotive.

"Soldiers!" cried the Adjutant General in his genteel English-accented French. "Today civil war is raging in our Canada. Each of us is allowed his own opinion regarding the rights of the Métis. Each of us is allowed to seek redress of his grievances, but this does not warrant civil war, and it is your duty to go out and fight those who are fomenting revolt..."

Meanwhile, the journalists were being boarded at the back of the train. Lemercier was splendidly attired: a long raccoon coat, fur hat and riding boots.

"Don't you think you're going to be hot?" asked a correspondent from France, winking at the other reporters.

"Why should I?" Lemercier replied, laughing.

"The climate is continental on the plains," cried the Frenchman. "The summers are torrid, *mon vieux*! Your colleagues are dressed much more lightly, you can see that."

There was an obliging titter among the group. The correspondents were busy putting away their bags and scarves. Lemercier turned to Askik with an look of disappointment.

"Keep your coat," Askik advised him.

The Parisian took off his handsome green chequered gabardine coat, threw his tweed bowler in the luggage rack and, unfolding a newspaper, settled himself as comfortably as he could on one of the wooden seats.

"*Ah ben dis-don'*," he exclaimed, "we're not travelling First Class!"

"Officers, soldiers of the 65th!" Colonel Harwood was declaiming. "I bid you au revoir! Return to us soon covered in laurels, and you will be a credit to your country and your nationality!"

How gratifying to hear this from an *Angliche*! Thunderous cheers dislodged the pigeons sheltering beneath the station roof.

The soldiers boarded the train. A blast of the whistle. A burst of steam. A clang of couplings. Two or three elegantly dressed young ladies, in full view at the front of the crowd, chose this moment to faint. Solicitous arms caught them up and finely gloved hands proffered smelling salts. At the back of the crowd near the doors, a young laundress collapsed on the floor and struck her forehead. She was immediately hustled outside and regained consciousness in tears on the station steps.

The train picked up speed. The officers went from car to car distributing cigars and comradely slaps on the back to their fellows.

"Now we can breathe at last," the soldiers said, a mite weary of their admirers despite all. They began intoning songs befitting the occasion and barely noticed a river flitting past under the steel wheels; they had left the Island of Montreal. Excited, they now crowded about the windows to watch the snow-covered villages and farms go by. Everything was new and memorable in their eyes.

Snow and darkness soon closed off the view. Lamps were lit, little stoves were stoked and the colonist cars began to look like genteel, swaying clubrooms filled with golden youth. The journalists wandered through the train, introducing themselves to the soldiers, receiving confidences, taking notes.

"I was born in Varennes. My father's a notary. He ran for parliament in the last election. Perhaps you know him..."

"I'm in rhetoric at the Collège de Montréal. I'm thinking of entering seminary, devoting myself to God, but first I want to do this service for my country..."

The young are so deeply convinced of their importance that the militiamen seemed to consider it entirely natural to talk about themselves to the journalists. With flattering attention, the reporters noted their past, their dreams, their ambitions, in case one of the braggarts should be killed. Alive, a self-important adolescent is tiresome; dead, he is sublime.

Among the reporters, Lemercier was once again an exception to the rule. He was playing poker with the officers and losing repeatedly. He was about to play a particularly weak hand when the train wheels squealed deafeningly, slowed abruptly and then stopped. The soldiers, the provisions and (thank God!) the cards were all hurled forward. A paymaster landed in Lermercier's lap and Lemercier took advantage of the opportunity to drop his hand.

The soldiers picked themselves up and straightened their tunics.

"What's going on?"

"Go and ask in the car ahead."

"Maybe there's something on the track."

"A cow..."

"Or a bear!"

No one knew anything in the other cars. The stop dragged on. It couldn't be a bear unless it was a bear with monumental nerve. Voices could be heard outside.

"Shhh! Put out the lamps so we can see what's going on out there."

The car was now in darkness and the soldiers pressed about the windows. They saw a huge grey forest of enormous evergreens whose arms were laden with snow, and officers walking up and down beside the track, talking and looking preoccupied. Snow was falling heavily and the wind was rising. The volunteers felt a delicious thrill. Was it already time to do battle? They could see shadows emerging from the woods behind the train.

"Hey, chaps!" shouted a recruit returning from another car. "The batallion's been recalled. The rebellion's over!"

"Damn fool! Is that why they're walking 'round in the woods?"

"Shut up, so we can hear what they're saying!"

They could hear only snatches, however. As the officers passed they looked up blankly and seemed surprised at the excitement of the troops. The locomotive blew its whistle and the train started up again. Disappointed, the volunteers went back to their places.

Journalists were dispatched to get the news. They returned ten minutes later, laughing their heads off.

"You won't believe it... somebody deserted!"

The news unleashed a tempest in the car. Every man was on his feet with cries of indignation; every man wanted to know the coward's name.

"Wait, you haven't heard the best of it! When he saw we were past the last village, our hero put on his cap and coat, held his haversack over his head and went head first out the window."

"Can't be true! A bully-boy!"

"There's a head start for you!"

The reporter had more to recount.

"The officers in the car were such dimwits they took a while to sound the alarm. The fellow's tracks were plain to see in the snow, but he'd taken off like a hare. Anyway, he's thought to have family on the south shore. There won't be any trouble finding him."

"Good riddance!"

"It's his company commander who'll catch it," the journalist continued. "Sub-Lieutenant Grandet, if you please, did a bit too much partying last night and today in his weakened condition wasn't able to stop the escape." In an aside behind a cupped hand, he added, "Of course, he couldn't have done much about it anyway, but somebody has to be the goat."

A generous laugh denoted broad agreement with this judgment.

An officer entered the car. "Curfew, gentlemen!" he barked. "Put out the lights now, please. It's going to be a long trip. Get some sleep and build up your strength."

How could anyone sleep in these swaying, jolting cars, on these hard wooden seats specially designed to pulverize tailbones?

In the baggage rack, one of the militiamen found a crumpled pamphlet with a picture of a luxury passenger liner afloat on big, strange letters.

411

"Looks like Greek," said his seat-mate.

"It's Arabic!" retorted another with firm conviction.

"No, no!" one in his final year of classical college said scornfully. "That's the Cyrillic alphabet. It's Russian or Ukrainian, and that's an immigration pamphlet. Haven't you ever been down to the port in Quebec City? People like that are coming in in droves. Canadians won't be in charge in this country much longer, I tell you."

"Well," the proponent of Arabic said, "if they came all the way across the ocean to get here, riding in this car must have been a disappointment."

"How much more of this have we got? It goes on and on!"

"Ten days, my friend!"

Askik woke with a start, his mind confused and his back sore from the wooden seat. The train was braking. Station lights were blinding him. He had the awful impression that they had turned around and were arriving back in Montreal. He heard voices behind him.

"Where are we?"

"Ottawa."

Élisabeth! Askik thought, and was surprised at the immediacy of his reaction. He never thought about her any more these days.

It was one o'clock in the morning. Despite a snowstorm, a small group of French Canadians had gathered at the station and were bravely waving flags.

"Vive le 65ᵉ! Vive Montréal!"

The soldiers strained at the frosted windows to open them. The people handed up cups of hot tea and a variety of goodies.

"The journey hasn't been too hard for you?"

"We're making the best of it, madame."

"Gallant lads!"

Askik searched the crowd with quickened pulse. Would she be there? Suddenly he saw the Honorable Eugène Sancy — his predecessor had finally departed this earth in the course of the winter — shaking hands with Colonel Ouimet. His heart skipped a beat. Élisabeth... but she was nowhere to be seen. Sancy mounted a small flag-draped podium. No question about it, Askik thought, he's a handsome man; a little short, but just the right degree of corpulence, and a silver-white mane, clean features, powerful gestures. He'll go far, old man Sancy, if he can manage not to get too venal.

Sancy, it must be said, had realized that the wind direction was uncertain, that the Métis question could blow back in the government's face. He was beginning to hedge his bets, speaking of the Métis as misguided friends rather than enemies.

He had barely launched his panegyric to the Canadian troops when the locomotive gave a resounding Phoooff! and pulled out of the station.

"What's this?" the soldiers cried. "We're not getting off?"

"They've forgotten Colonel Ouimet!"

Twenty minutes later the train was braking again.

"Riel's going to have time to die of old age," Lemercier observed.

"Ev'rybody off!" a railwayman called, passing along the train outside. "Supper's ready!"

"What neck of the woods is this?" Lemercier asked of him.

"Carleton, monsieur. Our good Ottawa ladies have made ya a bite t'eat."

The men trooped into a little hall where ladies armed with big serving spoons were standing duty behind steaming caldrons. Alerted by some premonition, Askik stayed in the shadow by the door. He looked guardedly about the room and indeed Élisabeth was there. The cabinet minister's daughter would not for the world have missed such an occasion.

She was moving about between the tables, teapot in hand, pausing here and there to exchange a few words with the troops. Other young ladies were there too, but the men had eyes only for her. A queen, you might say, playing at serving her subjects. Moving in aristocratic circles had accustomed her to other tastes, other manners; she had given up the showy, beribboned clothes and hairnets that Askik had adored on her. The bronze-coloured dress she was wearing would have been severe on any other woman of her age; on her, the simplicity of the cut brought out the sensuousness of her body and face. Her golden hair was caught up in a soft twist. A solitary diamond had been nestled in it just over her left ear, at the last minute, one could imagine. There was enough naturalness in her beauty to raise a man's hopes, enough majesty to take his breath away. She had the poised and gracious manner of supremely beautiful and therefore supremely powerful women.

Was Askik going to cross the room in his rough boots and old coat, his hair cut with a knife, and offer her a brown hand? He would have been as embarrassed as she.

The railwayman was coming in behind him, knocking the snow off his boots on the door sill. "It's blowin', it's blowin'," he cried, then, seeing Askik, "Howzzat? Y' ain't goin' in t'eat? Gwan, gwan in!"

413

"Thanks, I'm not hungry..."

"That don't matter none, gwan in, I tell ya!"

His noisy goodwill was attracting attention. Élisabeth gathered that one of the volunteers had stayed at the door, too shy to come all the way in; these recruits were so young! She set out to rescue him. This was precisely the kind of situation she excelled in; she would gather up the shy young man, take him gently by the arm and lead him forward with his envious comrades looking on.

Askik turned around in the half-open doorway, one foot in the snow, the railwayman still holding him by the sleeve. He and she looked each other full in the eyes. She neither looked away nor gave any sign of recognition. It was only barely that Askik read a shadow of amused severity in her face, like a mother wondering what new devilment her child has been up to. Her slightly scolding gaze said, You know very well you have no business here.

Askik left.

The storm was blowing itself out. Small snowdrifts, powdery, sugar-like, blocked the streets. Fine, hard little snowflakes swirled around the gas streetlamps. The station looked deserted. The locomotive was hissing peacefully at the end of its siding while the crewmen warmed themselves by the stove in the stationmaster's office. The only human presence was a small shadow walking beside the train; it was Grandet. With his hands in his pockets, he was turning this way and that, angrily kicking pieces of coal fallen from the tender. Askik felt sorry for him.

"The desertion's caused you problems, hasn't it?"

"Hummph!

"You couldn't have stopped it, though..."

"Of course not!" Grandet snapped, barely containing himself. "And now we've got a sick man on board. All in my company. I suppose I'm responsible for that too!"

"Well, when you're an officer..."

"Officer? Ha!" Grandet took aim at a walnut-sized clinker and sent it spinning. "Do you know a lot of sub-lieutenants in this battalion?" he cried in exasperation. "The rank was created specially for me! I'd paid too much not to get a commission, but their graces, the officers, didn't want a newcomer in their august club. We'll see when the test comes which of us has the stuff of an officer!"

The locomotive was emitting sparks. It was Grandet who should be breathing fire, Askik thought. In his present state he would have relished throwing himself before the enemy's guns.

Askik was cold and hungry. "Let's get on the train, shall we?" he suggested. "There are sure to be some sandwiches left from this afternoon."

"You're lucky." Grandet growled. "You're going home, back to your people. Good for you. No more folderol, a nice peaceful existence far from all these aggravations. Sometimes I long to do as you're doing; find some quiet little village, a hamlet far away somewhere, like de Meauville." He was being unusually familiar, addressing Askik as *tu*. It was a measure of his despondency.

"What's stopping you?" Askik asked, having guessed what the answer would be.

"'Alas, it is not given to all men. God is the arm, chance the sling, a man the stone. Try to resist once thrown into the air!'" Then, a little sheepishly, "That's Victor Hugo."

"The lament of the chosen, yes, I know the passage. The burden of having been chosen by destiny. But it's wrong. Nobody's chosen, there are only vain, selfish people pushing to get ahead of everybody else. It's to them we owe this obscene little war."

They were back in the press car. Askik stoked the fire. Grandet unearthed a box of food.

"Listen, Mercredi, you want to be governed by humble people who have no ambitions? Where are you going to find them? Not among the working class, I hope. My chamber maid is twelve years old and already she's putting on airs. Don't forget the parable of the talents. The poor aren't going to make the economy go round, and simpletons aren't going to make government work. So what are you going to do? Forbid able people to take pride in their competence? I'd take a frankly conceited Sancy any day over some hypocrite who pretends he's just another humble, unassuming man of the people."

"Well then, what about the best of us, like de Meauville? Those who have no ambition. What should they do, run away? Withdraw from the world?"

"You say de Meauville but it's yourself you're thinking of. Yes, de Meauville can hide, love his wife, work in his garden. It won't last. Like it or not, he'll end up being principal of his school, or mayor, or member of parliament, because he has the talent for it and we can never entirely escape our responsibilities. You're confusing peaceableness and lack of courage."

"You were the one who was sighing for a peaceful life a minute ago."

"I know," Grandet replied, sighing anew. "I let myself be tempted sometimes, but I know that way is closed to me. I wouldn't last three days without ambition. I'd die of boredom."

"So what are your ambitions? Dare you say it out loud with someone listening?"

A bitter smile twisted Grandet's lips. "It all boils down to birth, Mercredi," he said harshly. "If I were British and big and handsome, I'd be Wellington or I'd be dead. I could hope for anything. But I'm French-Canadian and scrawny and ugly, so my ambitions are crackpot."

He leaned his forehead on the window and gazed absently outside. The railwayman was returning from the dining hall. A fat little man in overalls. When he opened the door to the stationmaster's office he gave a hearty burst of laughter. Inside, the men sitting smoking by the stove turned their heads and looked at him disdainfully but tolerantly.

"Look, there's our railwayman," Grandet said. "Mouth full of smutty jokes and flasks of cheap gin in his pockets. His accent makes everybody laugh so he lays it on. He's the station clown, and it's as such that the English workers let him hang round with them. I bet he even brags to his children about being their friend."

"We're a conquered people..."

"We're a degenerate people. Put on some more coal, I'm freezing. Here come our worthy volunteers, returning with their bellies full. We shall see what they're capable of."

6

The journey continued without further interruption until morning. Unlike his companions, Askik had no trouble falling asleep; even eight hours later, it took effort to rouse and he opened his eyes to the pale, envious faces of the others.

"Old Indian trick," he explained.

The mercury was falling steadily. At Matawa, the soldiers bought woollen socks. The French correspondent, taking Askik's advice, bought himself a warm hooded parka. He was disappointed not to find one of buckskin with fringes and beaded embroidery, but was pleased with his purchase nevertheless: a Hudson Bay capote, creamy white with bands of colour. He completed his outfit with a tuque and a voyageur sash. Except for his fine patent-leather boots, he might have passed for a prosperous trapper.

The day went on for ever. The little locomotive wound its way between huge rocks, huffed and puffed up steep grades, ploughed a channel through deep snow. It passed farflung villages perched on the rocky shores of icebound lakes with their backs to the boreal forest, which seemed to be trying to push all these rough dwellings into the water. Between the villages, boredom. Hours and hours of spruces and pines, rocks and lakes. Enough lakes to make you sick of them for the rest of your life. There were even lakes staggered one above another on the sides of hills, staircase fashion, as if the country had been specifically designed to contain them all. The numbing monotony played on the militiamen's nerves. The farther they went, the lower their spirits sank. Was this what Canada was like? Were wastes like these really worth fighting for?

Conversation had dried up. The men were trying to avoid each other, to the extent that this is possible among sixty men in a railway car. They read, wrote letters, or just sat heavyheartedly watching the day wear away. For the first time, perhaps, they were thinking that they might not return, might never again see stone churches, green meadows or Quebec-style houses; might die far, far away in a hateful land, for a cause that did not concern them.

The train ran all night long. Its headlight caused green, startled eyes to glow in the forest. Shadowy deer crossed the track now and then and the engine driver could never be sure if they had been real or he had dreamed them. The moon sailed along in his right side window. He turned to his fireman.

"It's gonna be cold!" he shouted. "The wolves are gonna howl!"

The fireman just smiled through the coal dust caked on his face. He was in a hurry to get to Biscotasing and to bed.

The new day dawned over the same grey and green forest. One gets used to anything, however, even boredom. The soldiers spent a more peaceful day.

Lemercier played game after game of whist and lost with a regularity which itself was aggravating. The journalists by now were thoroughly tired of each other and were either reading or dreaming of being somewhere else. Their little group was divided in two: those who had managed to sleep more or less, and those who had not slept a wink since leaving Montreal. The latter were near panic because the end of this phase of the journey was approaching, and no one had said when the battalion would next be sleeping under cover. The non-sleepers had thirty-six hours of nervous irritation under their skin and not a hint of relief in sight.

"We'll do as the Eskimos do," Lemercier taunted them. "When you really can't keep up any longer — not before, I insist — we'll leave you with a little food and a match or two. That way you can have your choice between freezing and starving to death. Hee, hee, hee!"

A third camp formed: those who could no longer abide Lemercier's laugh.

"Just a few hours more, boys," the officers called as they passed. But morning wore away, afternoon gave way to evening, and evening, in its hatefully predictable fashion, yielded to night. The train advanced at caterpillar speed; the hastily completed new track was unstable. The men, no longer able to sit still, were looking daggers at one another for no reason and avoiding talk in order to avoid picking fights. And then finally, when no one believed it would ever happen, the travellers heard the locomotive begin to slow down. Noses were pressed against the windows, but snowbanks as high as the cars blocked the view.

"This is it!"

The brakes squealed. Huge bonfires were burning at the foot of the hill, sixty-five feet below. The train came to a stop. For a moment a strange silence spread through the cars.

"Unload in orderly fashion! Don't forget anything! Form ranks below the embankment!"

"Third Company, to the horses!"

The soldiers scrambled down the hill, sliding, running, shouting like schoolboys let out of school. Even the officers laughed at their antics. In no time the volunteers were in orderly ranks, smiling and cheerful, fatigue and boredom forgotten. At last they were discovering the North West of the story books. Those huge spruce bonfires, crackling and spewing sparks, the stars over the black forest, those rough-looking trappers and coureurs de bois in picturesque dress staring at them through the flames. Some even had dark skin!

The horses came out of their cars snorting and prancing; they too had endured a long emprisonment.

"First Company, march!"

The soldiers squeezed into rough wooden boxes on runners, twelve to a sleigh, their haversacks at their feet. They pulled up their collars and covered their ears with their hands. The most perspicacious wrapped scarves around their necks. They had left Montreal in April and now were back in midwinter.

"Hey, is it winter all year long out here?"

The horses started off. If there had been sleigh bells, the ride would have been a truly festive occasion. The volunteers sang, vied

418

musically between one sleigh and the next, hopped out from time to time to run in the tracks and warm up their feet. Three hours later, they came to a Canadian Pacific construction camp. The soldiers, by now chilled to the bone, thought they had reached the next railhead and prepared cheerfully to climb back aboard a train. They were invited instead to eat and warm up.

They crowded around the bonfires, jigged about to warm their feet, nibbled at canned corned beef, to which they were not unaccustomed.

"Isn't this where the railway starts again?"

"Ask the lieutenant."

"The lieutenant doesn't know any more than we do, pal."

"Hey, Théberge, you speak English. Go and ask how far before we get to the next train."

"And who'm I supposed to ask?"

"Well, that Indian over there."

"Because you think he speaks English?"

"Well then, the railway workers in that tent."

Théberge tore himself away from the fire and ran for the tent. He returned more slowly, a stunned look on his face.

"Eight hours," he said.

"What!" the volunteers cried. "Eight hours in a sleigh? We'll freeze! Are you fooling us?"

But Théberge had edged as close as he could to the flames and was absorbing heat with his coat open.

"They're going to kill us."

"My feet are still frozen," moaned a lad with a deathly pale face.

"Take your boots off and put your feet near the fire," Askik told him. "They'll never get warm through your boots. You've got moccasins, put them on. Have you got tuques?

"Not yet but they're supposed to be coming. Fine organization, I tell you!"

"Put something on your heads. A blanket, a towel, anything. When your head's warm your body feels better too."

They took his advice. The battalion soon looked like a troop of bedouins. The officers considered objecting, then let it go.

"*En route!*"

Huddling together in the jolting box sleighs, the soldiers dozed or sat stamping their feet. Those who were starting a third sleepless night spent the time musing over their short lives. The road was a rough trail over which the railway track would be laid and was full of humps and holes. Heads bumped together and one sleigh turned over, throwing a dozen men into the snow. The deep, silent forest weighed on the travellers like a curse. The mind's eye of each kept seeing familiar streets, pretty cul-de-sacs all enclosed in stone, well-behaved gardens where each bush had its proper place. These city-dwellers had spent their lives where the farthest they could see was the next building; to them there was something obscene about this profligacy of rocks and trees. When they saw a campfire in the woods, they remembered that in Quebec at this moment the faithful were lighting tapers for the Easter vigil.

When they reached the railhead at Dog Lake, the sun had been up for some time. The men of the Queen's Own had passed this way the previous week and had named the spot Camp Desolation. The Montrealers pitched two huge tents but spent the day outside by the fires, grumbling.

"What are we waiting for?"

"Colonel Ouimet. He stayed behind in Algoma."

"So there wasn't any point in moving all night."

"'Fraid not."

"What about tonight?"

"We leave as soon as Colonel Ouimet gets here."

"That's the militia for you! We hang around all day when it's nice and warm and travel at night when it's freezing cold!"

The fears were borne out. The colonel arrived in camp in late afternoon, issued tuques and blankets, and then ordered immediate boarding. The men climbed onto flatcars to which rough plank walls had been nailed. They wrapped themselves in their blankets and lay down on straw. The train had not been moving twenty minutes before they were up again, half-frozen and huddling together. Now their tribulations were really beginning. Weakened by hunger and fatigue, their bodies were not producing enough heat to make their clothing warm.

The Parisian correspondent crouched in the straw, his face twisted with pain, vainly kneading the toes of his boots. When Askik came and knelt beside him, however, he looked up with a satirical twinkle.

"*Eh bien, mon pote,*" he said, "I'm going to strike a fine figure on the Champs-Élysées. Without my toes I'm going to be pitching like an old ship."

"Your boots are too tight," Askik said. "Take them off. I've got some extra moccasins." He rummaged in his bag. "Here, stuff straw inside them."

"*Dites-don',* you carry a whole shoe shop round with you!"

"When I was small, we never travelled in winter without two or three pairs of moccasins."

The Frenchman beat his hands together and repressed a grimace. "You know, I'd never have believed I could hurt so much."

"As long as it hurts, the blood's circulating."

"You're a tough one, you are!"

"No, all of us here are soft. The Indians and trappers live all winter in the cold and don't think anything of it."

Lemercier was hopping about, uttering heartfelt curses. His anger was generating as much warmth as the exercise.

"To think the equipment's travelling in comfort through the States... Why the owl eyes? Didn't you know? That's the way most of the munitions go. There aren't any gaps in the railway system there."

"*Et nous alors,*" the Parisian said indignantly, "they could have sent us with the cartridges, *non?*"

"Don't be naïve!" Lemercier was hopping a lively rigadoon, gasping his reply. "Of course they could have. The Americans wouldn't have minded..., but our Canadian Pacific... is bankrupt...; this line has ruined it. The government can't subsidize the company... without getting the public... up in arms..., so it's paying it... to bring out the troops... Only natural, isn't it?"

"You're all loonies in this country!" the Frenchman wailed, curling himself up in a ball.

The sun was rising, pale and watery, as they reached the shores of Lake Superior. The men quickly scrambled off the flatcars. The assistant surgeon came and counted the frozen fingers, ears and noses. After a shot of rum and breakfast of salt pork taken by a warm fire, they found themselves again tramping through snow.

"In line of column, march!"

This was their first sight of the Great Lake of the Ojibways. The glistening crust of ice and snow stretched away for perhaps ten miles, then disappeared in dense fog produced by heavy clouds of vapour rising in spirals from the middle of the lake, where the water does not freeze. The battalion marched on the lake beside the rocky shore. The towering rocks were gleaming wet, for their snowy caps were beginning to melt. The men untied their scarves and unbuttoned their coats.

"Ah, I like this better already," the Frenchman said.

They covered twenty-five miles in ten hours, stopping only once to eat some bannock and cheese. When soaked, bannock is palatable enough; dry, it can choke a person.

A train was waiting at the end of the march. Flatcars again, this time not even with walls. The soldiers sat in the straw without any protection at all. An hour after departure it began to rain hard, a freezing precipitation that was part rain, part sleet. Still, a miracle awaited them when they got off at Jackfish Bay, where they could stretch out in heated sheds and sleep all night on dry ground near stoves. Conditions which they would have considered only just bearable four days earlier now seemed the height of luxury.

They were wakened well before dawn. The rain had stopped. Pipon had regained the upper hand. The journey could continue. The wet snow was coated with a breakable crust of ice. A biting wind blew from the forest. That day, the battalion covered a hundred and fifty miles, by sleigh, on foot, on flatcars and again on foot. From four in the morning until midnight, the men were driving their legs or beating their bodies with their arms.

At nightfall they scrambled down the rocky shore of the lake, marched twelve miles in pitch darkness on the ice of Thunder Bay and were singing when they arrived at Red Rock. When they boarded the train, they whooped and laughed in disbelief; Pullman cars had been sent for them. Damask curtains, soft velvets, dark mirrors, polished woodwork. These scions of bourgeois families no longer knew what to do with such comforts. They flopped into the club chairs and began snoring like steam pumps.

They travelled for another thirty-six hours, this time without leaving their little palaces on wheels. No one was complaining now about the landscape, which had not changed.

At Port Arthur they were greeted by an enthusiastic crowd waving flags.

"This is more civilized!" the enchanted soldiers exclaimed. The officers were whisked away to an official dinner with the mayor and aldermen. The journalists all raced on foot to the telegraph office. Askik had neither notebook nor uniform, and therefore was of no interest to anyone; he was free to wander at leisure through the streets of the village.

The wind was laden with moisture. The snow had the damp shimmer that announces a thaw. The air was still cold but surfaces exposed to the sun were warm. Two black birds flew across the bay; were they ravens or crows? Ravens stay for the winter but crows leave and stay away until the cold is past. Askik listened; crows.

Lemercier arrived at a brisk walk, his coat open and hair blowing in the breeze. He seemed mightily pleased with himself.

"*L'Époque* has been served!" he declared. "What a magnificent day! What a pretty little town! The mountain on one side, the bay on the other. I'd live here with pleasure — for a day or two. Have you been here before, Askik?"

"Sixteen years ago. The Kaministiquia River empties into the bay near here. That's where we met Wolseley's troops."

"Well, this is a great day for you, Askik. We get to the Red River after this leg. *Sacrédié*! To think of coming home after so long away!" Lemercier paused, then added, "Well, you don't exactly seem overjoyed."

"The Red River Métis have scattered. I don't expect to find any family."

"You don't want to see where you spent your childhood?"

"When I left, there was a fort and a few shacks. Today there's a city. I won't feel any more at home than you will."

When they returned to the station an hour later, they found the battalion in a fever of excitement. Officers were hurrying this way and that and the men were checking their equipment or talking in small groups. Askik caught Sub-Lieutenant Grandet's eye and Grandet descended on him like a hawk after a mouse.

"D'you know what's happened? The news came from Ottawa by telegraph. A massacre! In northern Saskatchewan. The Crees have wiped out a whole village of Whites! They killed two missionaries. They carried off two women. God knows what's happened to the poor things!" The confirmed bachelor sounded close to tears in contemplation of the horrible fate facing the poor things. "Poor *young* things," he added with a shudder. He took a big breath and said, "We've received our orders. We're going to push on to Calgary. We'll pursue those dastardly Crees and give them a thrashing they won't soon forget."

Thereupon he took his leave, a requisition order in his hand; the officers were short of honey for their tea.

"What d'you think, worthy Chingachgook," Lemercier said, "will our young tourists catch up with the dastardly Crees?"

"No, unless it's because the Crees find them."

"That's what I was thinking. And if the 65th is being sent to Calgary, it's to get them away from the Métis and the real theatre of operations, of course. The government doesn't trust the French

Canadians any more than they do the Indians. Hmmm... We'll have to rethink our plans, Askik. A change of course looks imperative..."

They travelled all that day and all night. It was particularly quiet in the cars. The volunteers might strut and swagger before portly mayors and matrons bearing little iced cakes, but now they knew that their hour of trial was approaching. The chaplain moved along the aisles hearing Easter confessions.

The sun rose over a snow-covered marshland as vast as an ocean; reeds, willows and poplar thickets as far as the eye could see. Once in a while a clump of conifers. The boreal forest was petering out; the prairie was taking over. For the first time in a week the men were seeing something other than forest. They were relieved, like a man who breathes more easily once he has unbuttoned his vest. Around seven o'clock the first houses of Winnipeg came into sight. Askik saw nothing familar and felt quite disoriented. They crossed the Red River and entered the station.

The soldiers descended from the train amid applause, smiling like seasoned old entertainers.

Askik escaped. I was right, he thought as he emerged on the street, I don't recognize a thing. Large stone buildings stood on either side of a very wide boulevard, a vestige of the old days when ox-drawn carts would take a great deal of room avoiding mud puddles. Now there were light carriages, freight wagons and horse-drawn streetcars vying for space on paving that was hard, clean and dry.

Winnipeg had appeared overnight, like a mushroom. Brought into the world by the railway, suckled by speculators, nourished by immigration. Some fifty languages were spoken here. Canada was anxious to populate its hinterland as quickly as possible to keep it out of American hands. Thousands of Scandinavians, Germans, Russians, Irish, Dutch, Poles and even Americans were flooding out to the Canadian prairies; all comers were accepted as long as they were white. The hordes of Chinese imported to help build the railway were once again undesirables.

Yet the West was still almost empty. The Minister of the Interior had not yet tapped the gigantic reservoir of suffering humanity in eastern Europe. In their ancestral villages, Ruthenians, Roumanians and Ukrainians were barely keeping body and soul together; sometimes they considered striking out to South America, but as yet had no inkling of the gruelling adventure that was to land them on Canadian prairies as glacial as their steppes.

However, when Askik was leaving Winnipeg station that morning, the recruitment of new Canadians had not yet achieved such a degree of refinement. Most of the immigrants were unmarried males seeking their fortune. The result was as might be expected: five times as many bordellos as churches. Before long, well-bred people would be demanding alcohol prohibition and denial of voting rights for these foreigners who could not control themselves and multiplied like rats in a garret.

The well-bred people lived in houses of brick or stone, true luxury on the prairies, on the other side of the world from the station. Here, elegant carriages passed through wrought iron gates, briefly disturbing the tranquillity of the neighbourhood. At the end of the street, abject, ruined, reviled and almost hidden from view, was the old fort. Askik had to smile in spite of himself at the rotting walls and loopholes so incongruously ensconced amid such luxury.

The ferry between Winnipeg and St. Boniface was as bad as ever. The two communities, English and French, apparently did not feel the need to be joined by a bridge.

Like the ferry, the French side had remained faithful to its past. Houses of sawn lumber had replaced the log cabins. In the distance, Askik could see some large, domed buildings, no doubt colleges or convents, but the rest was where it had always been: the Grey Nuns' convent, the bishop's palace, and the humble cathedral, at present topped with an undistinguished bell tower. Askik was stunned to find the cathedral so small and seedy-looking.

Another broad street led away toward the prairie, tracing more or less the path he had followed between home and school. The little farmhouses had given way to big wooden houses with peaked roofs and gingerbread gables. There were lilacs and rosebushes slumbering under shelters of burlap and straw.

My Uncle Raoul must live here, Askik thought.

There was now a small bridge across the Seine. Lafortune's cabin had disappeared, turned into firewood. Askik walked quickly through the little wood by the river and found himself in the fields.

The prairie of old was no more. There was the same treeless land, the same expanse, but now it was black, ploughed soil that showed between the patches of melting snow. The tall, playful grasses had been turned over and buried. A wetiko could never be imagined roaming these wheatfields. Or a Métis.

That was what was missing. Of the old French Métis colony, nothing remained but the Frenchness, reinforced by the arrival of settlers from Quebec. The Métis element had gone, taking its tchipayuk with it. The place now had the docile, industrious, rather pale face of its new masters.

Askik struck out through the fields, skirting mudholes. He crossed a small coulee (was this the fearsome ravine of his childhood?) and kept going, heading for his old house.

He had no trouble finding the Mercredi cabin. It was still intact, too far away and too rotted for anyone to bother taking it down for firewood. What men scorned, the land was reclaiming. Bit by bit, as ordained by successive freezes and thaws, the little house was sinking, lopsided, into the prairie. The roof had collapsed under the snow, the door was disintegrating somewhere in the grass. And yet it was curiously appealing, like an old woman with sunny memories chuckling tenderly at everything.

Askik too laughed to see the splintered cornices where the crying spirits had wailed so pitifully on stormy nights. He almost expected to see the wetiko come out of the coulee with arms dangling and a sheepish look, like a good-natured, overgrown child, trying to tell him he was sorry; those nights when I used to chase you, it was just in fun you know...

Bright, puffy clouds were arriving from the south with warm winds and wild geese in pursuit. Here and there the sun was trying out its warm new rays. Liquid diamonds trickled out of the snow. Passing through the little ring of poplars around the house, Askik discovered a swath of sky-blue pasqueflowers blooming cheerfully in the vestiges of snow. The long, dreary months were done for. He felt such a youthful, intense joy that he very nearly shouted a *Hai!* loud enough to wake his old mouchoum. A gift of youth from the scene of his youth; the last thing he would have expected! Perhaps after all he had been wrong to leave the prairies. Still, he was not really sorry.

He pressed on, running till breathless now, eargerly seeking traces of his people. He followed the course of the Seine, finding ruined shelters, bits of fencing, paths leading down to the water. Soon through the oak branches he saw the roof of Mona's house. He slowed his pace, wearied by the weight of the mud clinging to his boots. When he entered the little yard he felt his heart leap: the house was lived in. A beaten path led to the door. There was glass in the windows. The roof was being kept in repair.

For a moment Askik dared go no closer. He was seeing a little girl coming out from behind the house, wearing a blue hooded cape and holding a big bundle of sticks; her cheeks were dirty and her eyes wide with curiosity. He imagined the door opening and expected to see a grown-up Mona there, a woman and mother in her turn, surrounded by little ones. Oh, what wonderful stories they would have to tell each other! How she would laugh at his blighted hopes! But the door stayed closed. There was no little girl in a blue hooded cape. No bundle of sticks. No new beginning. Only compassionate whisperings from the oaks.

He knocked at the door. His knocks resounded inside and no one came to answer. He peered through the window and saw a table, a chair, a few books and some garden tools. This was not so much a dwelling as a storage place; the retreat of some old bachelor with a fondness for fresh vegetables. He retraced his steps across the yard, not sad, not disappointed, but a mite in love with a little girl who no longer existed.

7

There were gloomy patrons in Winnipeg's taverns. The militiamen had taken the opportunity to renew their supply of newspapers. They had cause to regret it. Aspersions were being cast on the 65th in the English papers: the French Canadian militiamen were deserting in droves, throwing themselves under the wheels of locomotives rather than fight, crying like babies on frosty nights, and, of course, daily drinking themselves into oblivion.

"Oh dear," Lemercier said, "we've fallen from grace again in our compatriots' esteem."

"We oughtta switch enemies if y' ask me," muttered Captain Provost, the same officer who, back in Montreal, would brook no discussion of honour.

"It's a misunderstanding!" Grandet insisted, his face as white as his enamel cross. "We're fighting for the same cause! We're brothers in arms!"

The portly captain laughed scornfully.

"Misunderstandings there are, enough and to spare," Lemercier pronounced. This time he was reading a French-language paper.

"What's up now?"

"What's up is that public opinion in Montreal is changing camps. A hundred demonstrators... letters to the editor... Nothing much yet,"

Lemercier concluded, looking up. "The banners are still up, but trust an old reporter's nose — the public is changing its mind. It's coming over to the Métis side."

"*Ben, bout de la marde!* If that don't beat all!" Provost growled, then finished off a foamy beer.

"Hey-ho!" the Parisian exclaimed, suddenly perking up. "If a civil war breaks out, a real one I mean, *franco-anglo*, you're going to look pretty silly, up to your ears out here among the *Angliches!*"

He drew a barrage of glares.

"Chingachgook!" Lemercier squawked, seeing Askik come in. "You found us!"

Askik made a face. "It wasn't hard," he said. "All I had to do was find the tavern the least number of steps away from the station."

"Chief talk straight. You eagle eye!" Lemercier intoned, accompanying his words with musical-comedy gestures. "Chief not get mad. Chief see this." And he spread the paper open for Askik.

"*L'Époque?* It got here before we did?"

"Paper come American choo-choo. Quick like flash. Cost like hell."

"Liar like you," Askik muttered, looking at page two of the paper.

There, face-to-face, contemplating each other across their frames, were portraits of Arthur Lemercier, war correspondent, and Askik Mercredi, Métis guide. Lemercier had the firm jaw and piercing eyes of the crusty newspaperman of tradition. Askik was even more impressive; slightly wavy hair falling to his shoulders, complexion darker than his coat, which was fringed and glass-bead embroidered; on his head a wolf-skin hat and across his chest a bandolier that could have held a tomahawk as easily as a water canteen.

"That's the kind of coat I was looking for," the Frenchman remarked.

From the biographical sketch beside the drawing, Askik learned that he had been born of a Canadian seigneur father and a Sioux mother, had received an impeccable education in St. Boniface and had spent his life fighting Indians and reading *L'Époque*.

"Is this stuff going to sell?" Askik asked.

"Like booze on Sunday!" Lemercier hooted, then dissolved in tears with that silly laugh of his.

At half past three, the battalion bouncers came and emptied the taverns of soldiers. It was observed with satisfaction that only two of the men were too drunk to walk. When the train left, the station was virtually empty.

428

The prairies were a disappointment for the soldiers. They saw a few scattered houses near the rivers, then nothing; a flat, white, empty land unfurled its vastness all the way to the sky. For the first time in their lives, they were seeing the pristine curve of the planet. Like an immense billiard ball. The clouds emerged directly from the horizon; the blue-black sky rose up and up to infinity. There was no scenery here; only a platform for the observation of the firmament, which occupied four-fifths of the landscape.

Askik could see the amaranth being tossed by the wind, the prairie chickens rising in fan formation, the humps of prairie poking through the melting snow, hairy and brown like old buffalo. The soldiers could see nothing but emptiness. Even cultivated, even squared off with roads and fences, to them this country was deathly boring. They thanked God for bringing them into the world elsewhere.

The train was moving faster. The spanking new railway line had been laid straight as a die, which to the soldiers was the last straw. They went to sleep with stomachs full of beer and gas.

Lemercier put his hand on Askik's shoulder and shook him gently. "Get ready to get off," he whispered. "Gently does it so the others don't suspect anything."

While he quietly gathered his belongings, Askik kept glancing outside. It was not quite daylight yet. A chalky moon was fading over the rolling prairie.

"Follow me," Lemercier whispered.

They went to the back of the car near the door and out of sight of their colleagues.

"They'll think we're in another car," Lemercier explained in a low voice.

"Where are we going?"

"We're getting off at Qu'Appelle. I found out some things in Winnipeg. Our expedition won't amount to anything. It'll provide some light comedy for the townsfolk of Calgary, nothing more. Headquarters would send the 65th to Mars if it could, just to be rid of it. Meanwhile, Middleton's marching on Batoche. That's where all the action will be. The Royal Grenadiers are at Qu'Appelle. They're going to join Middleton and we'll follow them."

"Have you got authorization?"

"My dear Askik, you must learn that administrations are governed by the rule of the least risk. Granting an authorization entails responsibility; refusing it involves none. *Ergo*, the authorization would be refused."

The train was slowing down. Grey wooden shacks flew by the window and the car shuddered over a switch. Lemercier pressed the doorhandle as the brakes screeched.

"Now!" he said softly. They descended onto the gravel, gently closed the door behind them and ran doubled over to the rear of the train, then shot across an open space and flattened themselves against the wall of a shed. Lemercier was spluttering with laughter and effort.

"Hee, hee, hee! I'd give a lot to see their faces in half an hour!"

Here the prairie folded down into a wide valley choked with woods and riddled with coulees. The snow on the plateaus above was turning bright orange from the rising sun. A kildeer called "too-wit, too-wit" as it flew over the still-frozen marshes.

"Are they getting ready to leave?" Lemercier asked.

"Not yet, they're filling the tender."

"We have to find out where the Grenadiers are camped. After that, I'm as hungry as a bear, aren't you?"

They slipped like a pair of cats between two coal storage sheds.

"That must be the immigration office," Lemercier said, pointing to a shed with windows. "No officials in sight? Let's go!"

A man in a cap and boots was sitting on the steps of the office, watching them approach with a friendly eye. Lemercier walked straight up to him.

"Excuse me sair, whair are de soljairs?"

The other kept staring in the same friendly way and said nothing.

Lemercier tried again. "D'you speak French, then? No? Well, what the hell do you speak?"

The stranger uttered some civilities in a language full of trills and hisses.

"It's incredible!" Lemercier exclaimed with a burst of laughter. "They don't teach them either English or French before sending them here! It'll be a fine mess pretty soon, I can tell you."

The railway workers were stowing the water pipe and coming down off the tender.

"Ho, Mistair!" Lemercier cried, seeing an old man walking toward the stables. "Whair are de Grenadairs, pleez?"

The locomotive emitted a noisy puff of smoke. The old man

turned to Lemercier with an expression of perplexity. The reporter was dumbfounded. "There's nobody but immigrants here!"

"No, mossieur," the old Métis said, "if you'd talked French I woulda understood ya."

The locomotive gave an initial huff. The driving rods began to move. The couplings clanged in quick succession.

"*Mon bon monsieur*," Lemercier cried, thinking with glee of his hoodwinked colleagues, "can you tell us, please, where the Royal Grenadiers are camped?"

"Them's which ones, the Reds or Blacks?"

"The Reds."

"Gone."

"Eh?" The smile froze on the big reporter's face.

"Day before yesterday," the Métis said helpfully.

"Askik!" Lemercier yelled. "The train!"

If one has never seen a bear — huge, lumbering and seemingly slothful — streaking through the woods like a bird on the wing, one could never imagine Lemercier running after a train. The railwaymen saw the charge of what looked like a buffalo in cat fur and instinctively made way. Lemercier grasped the handrail of the last car, flung his bag on the platform above, then wondered what to do next. The ties were flying by at dizzying speed under his feet; the train was already moving too fast for him to jump aboard.

Meanwhile, Askik was catching up with the car on the other side. He threw his bag on first, clung bodily to the handrail and hoisted himself on board. He slid across the platform on his stomach. The train was gaining speed. Lemercier, crimson-faced, legs splayed, looked at him with eyes wide as if to say, Do something!

"Put your other hand on the rail!" Askik shouted.

"Can't!" Lemercier gasped.

Askik grabbed him by the fur collar and, straining every last muscle, heaved him aboard like a great codfish. They collapsed together on the floor of the car. That's it, Askik thought, you can only muster an effort like that once in a lifetime. My muscles will all tear apart next time.

Lemercier lay with his hands on his ribs, breathing big gulps of air with whistling sounds.

"What are we going to do now?" Askik asked.

"Catch up with the Queen's Own. Swift Current."

They left their coats and bags and went back to their seats. No one had noticed they were gone.

"We're approaching Regina, capital of the North West Territories," the Frenchman announced, shaking out a big map. Lemercier sat down behind him, craned his neck and silently counted the stops to their destination.

Grande Coulee, Pense, Belle-Plaine, Moose Jaw; at each station, Lemercier folded the corner of a page in his book. Near the end of the afternoon he made a discreet recount, caught Askik's eye and solemnly nodded his head. Askik went to his post at the back of the car. Five minutes later Lemercier, pretending stiffness in his legs, came to join him.

They stepped off the train without haste, picked up their belongings and calmly climbed the station fence. This time there was no mistake. Some fifty tents had been pitched on the prairie. A giant Union Jack was flapping in the wind. The two hundred and fifty soldiers were gathered outside the camp, a green patch against the brown prairie. They were either silent or talking in hushed tones. It could have been a burial.

As Askik and Lemercier approached the group, they saw a short cannon with its barrel turned toward a pond which was still half frozen over. A duck was nervously patrolling the open water, keeping near the bank on the far side. Total silence fell over the group. A man in a blue uniform slowly placed his hand on a lever near the breech and with a confidant air suddenly pulled it.

There was a mighty roar that made the soldiers jump and a wall of water rose from the pond. The duck shot out of the spray like a stone from a sling and flew away over the prairie, skimming the ground.

"Son of a gun!" the American soldier said. "Missed!" It was surprising to hear him over the prolonged rolling of the detonation.

"Have to adjust the sights," the American explained with an apologetic smile.

The militiamen responded with nervous little laughs. What an inhuman weapon! What luck to have it on our side!

"Three cheers for Lieutenant Howard!"

The technical advisor bowed modestly and raised his hands. "It's all in the design, gentlemen. Twelve hundred shots a minute, providing you can activate it fast enough!"

The soldiers crowded around the Gatling gun, bestowing smiles on its master, Lieutenant Arthur L. Howard, 2nd Regiment, Connecticut

National Guard. He was already very popular with Canadian troops. In point of fact, an American can elicit admiration in his northern neighbours without much effort. Friendship with the United States is very important to Canadians, who consider it the next best thing to being American.

"'Ow manny gonns do you 'ave lak dis?" Lemercier asked with spectacular boldness. The militiamen made mortified faces. Did the Frenchies have to come all the way out here to embarrass them? Lieutenant Howard replied seriously and courteously, however, so as not to discomfort his Canadian colleagues. A real gentleman.

Askik had not taken ten paces toward the camp before he came face-to-face with a stupified Simpson.

"Good Lord! What are you...? I didn't know you were coming!"

Askik replied with a broad smile. "Mee needair. That uniform suits you, Simpson."

"Nonsense, I look like a green bean in it." Simpson took Askik by the arm and led him in the opposite direction from the camp. "Have you lost your head, Mercredi?" he whispered. "We're at war with the Métis and you go and pick a time like this to come home!"

"But I don't look like a Métis," Askik objected, unbuttoning his lawyer's topcoat, "see?" He had put on a collar and tie. The tie was rather narrow and rather frayed but no less a tie for all that. Simpson burst out laughing.

"You're stark raving mad! Have you got a tent, a cart? How are you going to keep up with us? Well, never mind, we'll find a way. Did Grandet give you my letter? How is our sub-lieutenant, by the way?"

"He's on that train," Askik said, pointing to the plume of smoke disappearing over the prairie.

"Oh dear, what a mess! Did you meet that Lafortune? No, don't tell me now. This evening. I have to rejoin my company. We leave at dawn."

Simpson stopped and gave Askik a long, puzzled look. The wind lifted a lock of blond hair. His eyes were such a striking china blue that it did not even occur to Askik to envy him.

"I think it's fabulous that you're here, Mercredi. I don't know what it means. I have a funny feeling about it."

"It means nothing. Not-ting!"

Lemercier returned, leafing over the pages of a notebook in which he had recorded the Gatling gun's firing characteristics.

"Ah, there you are, Mercredi," he said absently. "What have you found out?"

"The battalion's leaving tomorrow. At dawn. We might get a place in the carts."

"Excellent! You're doing well for a beginner. Here's what I've gleaned myself. We're marching on Battleford, which is under siege by Poundmaker's Crees. We're marching, you'll have noticed I said, because there are no carts. If the Saskatchewan River is high we'll go three-quarters of the way by boat. If it's low we'll go by the soles of our boots. And I must add with regret that the shots fired this afternoon may be the only ones we get to hear. It doesn't look as if the Crees are going to fight; they haven't made any real effort to take Battleford."

That evening Simpson listened carefully to the story of Urbain Lafortune. He asked probing questions about the ways of the voyageurs, ignoring the whines and mutterings of his brothers-in-arms over having to hear French spoken.

The wind blew all night, spreading heavy flakes of snow. The inexperienced sentries were jumpy; a shrub at the edge of camp narrowly missed being shot to shreds each time there was a change of watch. In the morning the angry troops tore it up by the roots.

Camp was struck in the early hours. There were twenty-five miles between here and the Saskatchewan River. It was a monotonous, desert-like land that the battalion crossed. Just an occasional bush to rest the eye. Land peeled bare and left jagged. There was gravel underfoot beneath the snow. Once in a while, one of the soldiers would run to the crest of a hill, hoping to see something different beyond. He would return more discouraged than ever, having seen only an endless succession of hills half-covered with snow.

Approaching the river at the end of the day, the column descended into a deep gorge with woods on either side. The sun threw long, fantastic shadows. The place was tailor-made for ambush.

"Like rats in a barrel," a recruit murmured.

"My God, what's that?"

Stones, ashes, bits of charred wood. The soldiers shivered in excitement. The remains of an Indian campsite! A child's corpse, wrapped in blankets and placed in a tree, caused a sensation. Hair rose on the backs of necks and in his soul each volunteer heard the fatal shot that flew from the underbrush and struck him full in the chest. For all that, the battalion reached the police post on the south bank of the Saskatchewan without incident. The men arrived dead-tired and footsore, rather proud of their adventure in the ravine and full of contempt for the savages who had missed such superb opportunities to massacre them.

The next day was foggy and cold. The river was low and only one steamboat had been able to navigate across the shoals. The boat plied laboriously back and forth between the two shores, ferrying equipment and supplies to the north side. The troops would have to do the remaining two hundred and forty miles to Battleford on foot.

While waiting to cross the river, some of the men passed the time doing their laundry or combing the banks of the river for petrified wood. Others amused themselves shooting revolvers at the buffalo skulls lying about on the ground. The shots made short, dull sounds, quickly carried off by the wind.

In late afternoon a running battle between crows and vultures passed over the camp. The crows had the upper hand. Smaller, more agile, they rolled and dove, pecking at their much bigger rivals. The vultures pulled in their heads, wobbled clumsily on their broad, stiff wings and took what the crows were giving them. Simpson and Mercredi, who were walking on the prairie while they waited, watched the aerial combat, shading their eyes with their hands.

"Perhaps it's an omen," Simpson said. "What do you think? We're a lot like those vultures, aren't we? We're heavy, slow and clumsy. Our adversaries are agile and quick. I think it augurs ill for us."

"I'd be surprised," Askik said. "The crows are busy but the vultures keep on going in spite of it. And if they find carrion, it'll be the vultures, not the crows, who'll fill their bellies. Once they're on the ground, they're the ones that will have the advantage. If it's an omen, it's a bad one for the Métis."

"A pity," Simpson said, letting his hand fall.

Askik laughed. "You're hoping for a defeat?"

Simpson looked at him with deadly serious china blue eyes. "Don't you think defeats bring us back to essentials, Mercredi, while successes only steer us away from them? It's true for individuals, and I think it's true for nations too."

"That's a very original idea."

"Oh, very original. There certainly aren't more than two or three million of us who've thought of it. I don't believe it's in Canada's interests to win this war. Don't you see what's going on in this country, this orgy of self-satisfaction? We're infected with ourselves, Mercredi, and it'll be worse still if we win a victory here. We'll become hardened racists because we'll think we're chosen by Providence. Canada will be blinded by this for a hundred years; its true mission will be poked away and forgotten."

"And what is its true mission?" Askik asked banteringly.

"To be a haven, a refuge for all races on earth."

Askik pursed his lips but said nothing.

"I know, I know," Simpson said quickly, "all this is close to indecent, coming from me. I belong to the privileged camp, while yours is doubly cursed because it's both French and Indian. I know I've got it easy and these noble thoughts don't cost me much. I can't change what I was born, but Mercredi, I can't go through life believing nothing's ever going to change. I love my country. I believe it's going to be a great and benevolent country."

This time Askik could not hold back a mocking smile. "Yes, but who's going to want your country, Simpson? The Indians? They're sorry the Whites ever came and dream of the days when they were alone. The French wish the English had never come, too. The English despise both the Indians and the French, and look on the immigrants as a blemish. Each group self-righteously hates the others and would rather have the country to itself. So tell me, Simpson, who are your real compatriots?"

"People of goodwill," Simpson replied without a shadow of a smile. "People who are willing to accept me as one of them."

Askik burst out laughing. "That's your definition of a Canadian? A man of goodwill?"

"What else do you and I have in common, apart from this land we're standing on?"

"Ah, you assume this land is yours, but by what right? Did the Indians turn it over to you?"

"Who turned it over to the Indians? Didn't you tell me the Crees and Sauteaux drove out other tribes who were here before them? And I won't say anything about the Métis..."

"My ancestors occupied this land for thousands of years!"

"And you for barely twenty-five years. Like me. I didn't choose to be born English, or you Métis. Do you have more rights on this planet than I do?"

"How come I have less?"

"Ah, there's the problem! Today's problem. Current, not historical. We're two human beings who have the right to be treated the same way. *That's* our ancestral right. It's the same for all of us."

"Excuse me, Simpson. When this big bruiser comes into your

house and says, The earth doesn't belong to anyone, I have as much right to your house as you do, do you make room for him? Even when your descendants have lived here for a thousand years, they'll still be intruders from the Indians' perspective."

"Well then, perhaps we should ask the Indians to give us refuge."

"Too late. There's the request going off now." Askik cocked his head toward the river, where the soldiers were loading cannons and Gatling guns on the steamboat. "That's how the Hairy Faces ask for hospitality."

"I know the evidence is against me, Mercredi," Simpson replied sadly, "but I'm convinced that some day we'll all have the same ancestors, we'll all have French, Métis, English and Indian blood in us. Then we won't be able to attack anyone without attacking a part of ourselves."

"So we'll be one big happy Canadian family?"

"There'll be no separate peoples any more."

"You're right, it'll take a hundred years for others to see things your way."

"I hope not," Simpson said. "I'd like to live in a tolerant country for a little while. If only to see..."

"Don't you hear the soldiers curse when we speak French? D'you think their attitude will ever change as long as they live?"

"That's ignorance. Ignorance can be rectified."

"It's hatred," Askik corrected him. "Hatred dies with the hater."

"So according to you there's no hope?"

"Not for the crows."

"I can't live that way."

"That's your guilty conscience talking," Askik retorted. "If you woke up and found yourself with the shoe on the other foot, you'd end up accepting it."

"How can you take these things so lightly?"

"Force of habit. Look, they're tying up the boat again. Too much wind. We're going to have the cannons for bedmates."

"I hope we get slaughtered..."

"Oppressor's reflex, Simpson. And besides, there'd be too much justice in it."

8

They stayed two more days on the Saskatchewan, pinned down by the wind. The soldiers, fed up with their daily fare of beans and bannock, grumbled resentfully, for the officers were dining on canned tongue and ham. At night, while the troops shivered in their tents, the gentlemen officers were discreetly drinking in theirs.

On the morning of the departure, the batallion wakened to a new layer of snow. There was a coating of ice in the water buckets.

On the other side of the Saskatchewan, morale rose for a time. The batallion was now in enemy territory. No more evening concerts. No more solitary walks on the prairie. At night, the equipment wagons were drawn up in a defensive circle around the camp. Standing guard was now an adventure. All night long the sentries announced their "All's well!" in strong, vibrant voices. In the morning, the soldiers were surprised to find everyone still alive.

The enthusiasm did not last; the prairie soon wore it down. The march was boring and difficult. The ground was fairly dry, but the coulees were full of water and snow, veritable traps. In the salt marshes, the soldiers sank up to their calves. They were bitterly disappointed. In the tales of their childhood the prairies were overrun with game and savages lurked behind every bush. They had seen no bison, no antelope, no elk. Nothing but prairie dogs and those interminable processions of wild geese trumpeting day and night.

Askik himself was surprised at the absence of game, although he knew that even when he was a boy one might not see any for several days on a march. He had learned of the disappearance of the buffalo through the newspapers but the chroniclers rarely bothered to identify its consequences. Since there were no more bison, the plains hunters quickly decimated the elk and pronghorn antelope. The wolves had not withstood the change either; deprived of their primary source of food, they had taken to prowling in alarming numbers around the human colonies, and then they too disappeared. This had been very hard on the rodents, which bore the ill-humour of wolves and coyotes alone in these years. Now, however, the prairie dogs and ground squirrels, being rid of their enemies, were having a marvellous heyday. They had turned the prairie into a colander. Horses and men were constantly stepping in their holes. The little prairie dogs barked insolently as the troops passed, not suspecting that other bipeds would soon come and settle on their land and poison them all.

In the end, little was left of the prairie of old — erratic boulders polished by thousands of buffalo with itchy hides; the wallows in which Moustous used to take his sand baths; bones and horns strewn everywhere in the brown grass. Even this last-named vestige was to disappear; with no buffalo to feed and clothe them, Métis and Indian families gathered up the bones to sell to fertilizer manufacturers in the United States.

Where exactly were the Indians? Not that the soldiers expected to see them. A savage, in their imagination, would never be standing straight up in plain view, but always crouching, hidden, invisible, waiting for a chance to put an arrow between someone's ribs. You don't see Indians, you get killed by them. It was vaguely disquieting to the militiamen that none of their number had yet died. An army returning without any dead is returning without proof of heroism.

Eleven days later, the batallion arrived opposite Battleford. The lower town had been devastated and the trading post flattened. On the far side of the Battle River, six hundred men, women and children had been living for a month and a half behind an undefendable palisade. Food was rationed out by the spoonful. The only way to get water was to go down to the river, providing target practice for Cree sharpshooters. Luckily, the Indians understood nothing whatever about telecommunications; it never occurred to them to cut the telegraph wire. The citizens of Battleford had filled their hours of captivity by peppering the country with plaintive telegrams badgering the prime minister, the governor and the newspapers; it was becoming urgent to liberate them, if only to shut them up.

Watching one's house burn and one's livestock roast while waiting forty days and forty nights for an attack that one cannot repulse leaves one in a perilous state of nerves. Like a cat beaten by a mouse, the inhabitants of Battleford were in haste to restore the natural order of things. Now the brown vermin would get a taste of White technology. The worthy citizens would have been happy just to have Lieutenant Howard's Gatling guns; the militiamen they did not need. Instead of launching an immediate offensive, Lieutenant-Colonel William Otter settled in at Battleford as if for the rest of his days, and he too began working the telegraph system. He asked headquarters for clarification. His orders had been to liberate Battleford; did this authorize him to undertake a punitive operation against the Indians? The citizens were outraged: ask for authorization to punish the savages? What was the Empire coming to?

While awaiting the moment of retribution, the citizens gave their rescuers an earful. They had learned some veritable horrors during their internment. First, they reported, Middleton had been beaten. Idiotically, in plain words, beaten. They had been wondering what the Métis were waiting for to annihilate his army of picnickers. Secondly, Fort Pitt had fallen into Big Bear's hands; the mounted police detachment had fled — on a raft, if you please! Thirdly, the savages were behaving like brutes. The winsome MacLean sisters had disappeared; their imbecile father had suggested they give themselves up to Big Bear. The poor lambs had been stripped naked and tied hand and foot and then the brutes had dislocated their hips the better to rape them. These stories were transmitted in low, emotion-charged voices by the men of Battleford, out of earshot of the women, who were too fragile to bear hearing them and who, furthermore, were circulating far better ones.

Askik thought these stories unlikely and said as much, drawing volleys of hate-filled glares. It was plain as the nose on your face which side this so-called guide was on. Two weeks in the open air had turned Askik even browner than before; he was like a bison among lambs. Malevolent looks followed him in the streets; lips parted in muttered oaths at the sight of him.

He left the village and never set foot there again. He established himself outside the camp and waited for Lemercier to come to him. Since hunting accidents occur all too easily, he did not go for walks.

Much later, he learned that the MacLean sisters had been found safe and sound after the rebellion, the Crees having more or less adopted them.

Lieutenant-Colonel Otter was no coward. He had been shot at by the Fenians and was not afraid of being shot at by the Crees. He was exasperated by Headquarters' indecisiveness but dared not act without authorization. He dipatched a stream of telegrams. At long last he received a reply that would do at a pinch; Major-General Middleton was suggesting that he send out reconnaissance patrols around Battleford. Scouts had located a camp of two hundred Crees and Assiniboines at Cutknife Creek. If he marched all night, Otter could surprise them at dawn.

Daylight was beginning to fade when the little expedition set out onto the prairie, flags fluttering in the wind, like a cruiser putting to sea.

440

Askik and Lemercier slipped in among the carters who were bringing up the rear.

The column marched for four hours straight but was obliged to stop once night had fallen. By now all hope of taking the Indians by surprise had evaporated; there were signal fires burning on the distant hills.

At eleven-thirty, a pale half-moon emerged from the prairie. There was fog in the heavens and on earth. The detachment resumed its march nevertheless, advancing with difficulty, almost blindly. When the trail dipped into a ravine or cut through a coppice, the column would halt and the colonel would order a reconnaissance. Intimidated by the darkess and the fact that the signal fires in the distance had been extinguished, the scouts proceded with redoubled caution, inch by inch, losing precious time. The sun was already rising by the time the detachment reached Cutknife Creek.

Here, it came upon the remains of a huge camp, abandoned in haste since many teepee poles had been left standing. Dead-tired and bitterly disappointed to have the excursion come to such an anticlimax, the men flopped to the ground here and there over the campsite. Meanwhile, the scouts beat the bushes on the other side of the coulee.

Lemercier subsided heavily beside a teepee skeleton. "I've botched it!" he said in a voice blank with despair. "I thought I was cleverer than others and I've made a mess of it all. If I'd stayed with the 65th, at least I'd have news of the regiment to report, but now..." He raised both fists to the sky and shouted, "What made me think this bunch of schoolboys could run Indians to ground? What am I going to write, Askik? It was the chance of a lifetime and I've botched it!"

He was inconsolable. Huddled in his big fur coat with his head in his hands, he looked like a grizzly that had blundered by mistake into the middle of the detachment. Askik felt a deep compassion for him and groped for a way to cheer him up.

"We could still go and join Middleton," he suggested. "Twenty years ago we would have needed a real guide, but today, with these trails..."

"Thanks, my friend, but it's too late!" Lemercier growled. "Middleton gave battle a week ago, so by now it's all over. I'm a ruined man — finished! I ought to take up teaching."

Askik put his fingers in the ashes of an old campfire. "Well, that's funny," he murmured.

Lemercier had to smile in spite of himself. "What is it, worthy

Chingachgook, are the ashes warm, showing that the enemy hasn't yet gone very far? If you put your ear to the ground, perhaps you might..."

"The ashes are wet," Askik interrupted. "It hasn't rained for three days. The Crees left this camp long before we left Battleford."

"And these conceited asses are patting themselves on the back because they think they just missed them! Just wait for my next paper, you clowns!"

"But three days ago the Crees weren't in any hurry. Why did they leave their teepee poles? They're hard to replace."

"Maybe they're planning to come back and get them."

"So they aren't far away at all."

"No, the scouts are coming back from across the creek. They haven't found anything over there. You know," Lemercier said wearily, "I'm getting to like this country There's something stark and basic about it. Take that hill out there ahead of us, for example, covered in rough grass, rising to the sky between two wooded coulees. It's... clean, austere. The sky, the earth. A black line between the two. Period, that's all. The way it is now, with the sun coming up, it's not what you'd call enchanting, but it's... heady. Yes, intoxicating."

"Seems we're pushing off. The colonel wants to have breakfast on your intoxicating hill."

Robert Simpson was approaching, a rifle slung over his shoulder and his face radiant.

"Askik! There you are at last! *C'est incroyable!* I've done a bit of a tour; there were two hundred tents here! Look." He opened his hand to show some broken arrow remnants. "I found these over there." He was as excited as a small boy on his first visit to the circus. "It's incredible, Askik, dazzling! To think they're living like this today, thumbing their noses at all the stuff we need if we're going to be happy. The independence! The strength of character! How I'd love to meet these men!"

"Me too," Lemercier remarked laconically. "Might it still be possible?"

"Oh, I'd be surprised," Simpson replied with a laugh. "We're going to have breakfast on the ridge, then look around a bit on the other side, then we'll head back. The men are exhausted."

An Indian trail led down to the creek. There was a treetrunk serving as a bridge, at which the soldiers lined up to cross one by one. No one wanted to wade in the icy water. The trees by the creek were in bud. A woodpecker drummed in the distance. A nuthatch was descending a treetrunk head first. The disillusioned soldiers were thinking of home.

"My hill's pretty, don't you think?" Lemercier said as he came out of the woods. Bright, puffy clouds were emerging from its crest. A breeze made hushing sounds in the dry grass. The detachment was straggling along lazily ahead, the soldiers walking in twos and threes. Some cattle were grazing on a hillside in the distance.

The first shots sounded ludicrous, hardly more fearsome than the tok-tok of the woodpecker. But then, in this open country, even the Gatling gun firing at top speed did not sound really alarming.

Lemercier turned to Askik with a look of confusion. Bullets whistled around them. Askik found himself face down on the ground even before thinking about it. He was surprised to hear birds still singing. His first thought, curiously, was of Rosalie's little cakes. The coulee to their left was filled with smokey haze. The Queen's Own were crawling to the edge of the coulee and raggedly returning the Indians' fire. A cry of "Stretcher!" rang out from the throng. Still, it seemed so disorganized, so unlike a real battle, that Askik had an urge to get up and walk off. There were even moments of silence while the combatants wondered what to do next. Lifting his head cautiously, Askik could see Cree and Assiniboine warriors running across clearings to positions in the wooded coulees. The Indians seemed hardly better prepared than the soldiers. But what about those signal fires the previous night?

The wagons had been drawn up in a laager in a depression midway along the hill. The cannons were being readied for action, although there seemed to be no clear target to fire at.

"Let's go and take a look at the battery," Lemercier said in a voice that was almost normal.

Keeping to the middle of the hill, well away from the flanking coulees, the two friends were able to cross the battlefield walking tall; the Indians hidden in the ravine beds could see the troops on the flanks of the hill, but anyone in the middle of the plateau was out of their sight. As they passed the laager, Askik and Lemercier saw three casualites tidily lined up one beside the next.

Battery B from Quebec was established on the crest of the hill. Most of the French-speaking men were sitting apart while the English officers bustled about two minuscule guns.

"What's up?" Lemercier asked of an artillery sergeant.

The sergeant spat in disgust. "Our guns ain't worth shit! Mounted Police eight pounders. The carriage wood's all rotten. Show cannons y'know. They musta left 'em out in the rain, 'long with their flag!"

The battery commander, Captain Rutherford, was hell-bent on loading the little howitzers in spite of all.

"What are you going to shoot at, though?" Lemercier asked.

The sergeant half rose from the ammunition case he was sitting on and pointed to some teepee poles showing beyond a wood, three thousand yards away. There appeared to be a huge, semi-circular village there.

"Hey!" Lemercier exclaimed. "Where did that village come from? Didn't the scouts see it?"

The sergeant's only reply was to spit a murky globule of saliva and tobacco.

The gun belched fire and tore itself off its carriage. A teepee in the distance blew apart. The camp had been evacuated, however. The officers retrieved the cannon and with heavy rope tied it onto its derelict mounting.

"That's goin' to a heap o' trouble just to blow up a tent," the sergeant observed. "Goddam *Angliches!*"

"You were at the head of the column," Lemercier pursued, "didn't anyone smell the trap?"

"Trap? There warn't no trap. We got to the top o' the hill, we seen them, they seen us, an' we all begun shootin'. Put that in yer paper an see who'll believe ya!"

Lieutenant-Colonel Otter and his aides were on horseback behind the battery. The colonel looked composed but concerned. His troops were encircled. The enemy were advancing up the slopes toward his firing lines. The site's configuration, the hour and the suddenness of the attack were all curiously reminiscent of the Battle of The Little Big Horn. Colonel Otter had thought of everything, except becoming the Canadian Custer. What was to be done about it? An advance was impossible. Retreat would be dangerous because of that cursed coulee to be crossed.

The sun rose higher and higher. Although the ground was still frozen, it was astonishingly warm on the plateau. The wounded were still flocking to the laager but in smaller numbers than at the start of the engagement. The volunteers had soon learned not to pop up to fire at blankets or hats held on the ends of a sticks. These damned Indians were treacherous, however. A militiaman could lie on his stomach behind a rock for half an hour without sign of life from the other side, then turn to answer a neighbour's comment and get a bullet in the temple. The enemy was invisible. The volunteers could pepper the woods with bullets, aiming by hunch, but since they never saw anything to shoot at they never saw what effect they were having.

444

Toward midafternoon, the Battleford riflemen and the Queen's Own launched an attack to clear their left rear flank. They drove the Crees out of the ravine, where at last they saw some enemy corpses, but had to beat a retreat, bringing back the body of one of their own. Captain Rutherford nearly killed them all with his support barrage. It was time to leave.

The wounded and cannons were evacuated first, and then slowly, cautiously, the withdrawal began; the detachment folded up like a pimpernel in the rain. A cannon placed on a slope on the far side more or less covered the manoeuvre. When they came to the water's edge, the soldiers, still at this hour loath to get their feet wet, once again queued up to cross the treetrunk bridge.

Lemercier took out his watch. "Noon already," he observed.

"A long breakfast," Askik said, laughing.

He caught a glimpse of the hate-filled face turning to him but did not see the rifle butt aimed at his ribs. Once again he found himself on the ground, nosedown in the rotted leaves. Everything was going black and he could not catch his breath. A kick landed on his right side and far, far away he heard a man's voice yell furiously, "Fuckin' breeds!" He also registered Lemercier's voice, shouting, then he quietly lost consciousness, thinking about that herd of cattle grazing on the hillside.

He came to a few minutes later with a taste of vomit in his mouth. He was sitting propped against a tree at the edge of a meadow. A blissful silence reigned over the world.

"There, he's coming round," Lemercier said, face bathed in sweat. He had carried Askik over a quarter of a mile. The detachment was beating a quick retreat to Battleford. "You've got a nasty bruise in the ribs," he said, "but nothing's broken as far as I can tell."

"Askik," Simpson said, "you'll have to stay away from the soldiers. They're in a foul mood. Don't go back to Battleford. We'll hide you outside the village. For a few days anyway."

"We can't stay here, though," the reporter said, "the Crees are crawling all over."

"What?" Simpson retorted with a bitter laugh. "We haven't struck terror into their hearts?" He was not usually given to sarcasm.

"They let us go," Lemercier said with a grunt as he helped Askik up. "Otherwise our carcases would be fertilizing that slope. I can't wait to see how our gallant officers are going to paint this fiasco."

Apathetically, the exhausted soldiers had begun the long return march. Although reasonably pleased to have been under fire, they were finding it hard to understand just what had happened. Lieutenant-Colonel Otter himself was trying to put order in his thoughts about the morning's events. Granted, he had let himself be taken by surprise, but the detachment had survived. He was bringing back six corpses, two men dying, and ten wounded. The number of enemy killed must be considerable, however, judging by the number of rounds fired. The more he thought about it, in fact, the more positive the outcome looked. His raw recruits had been ambushed, had held the Indians off for seven hours, and had retired in orderly fashion after inflicting heavy enough losses on the enemy to discourage them from following. All in all, a modest victory.

This interpretation would last until the trial of the insurgents, at which time another version of the battle came to light. There had been no ambush. Through negligence or contempt for their adversaries, the Indians had not posted lookouts around the camp. It was an old man, out walking alone before dawn, who had discovered the soldiers crossing the coulee and given the alarm. Thinking that they were being attacked, the Cree and Assiniboine warriors had rushed into the woods to stop the enemy and allow the women and children to flee.

When the soldiers began their withdrawal, the Indians' first inclination had been to cut off their retreat. It would have been so easy in the bushy ravine. The Cree chief Poundmaker, however, had persuaded them not to. With the enemy repulsed, he said, the village was safe; that was enough. Perhaps he too was thinking of the Battle of The Little Big Horn, and of the terrible reprisals inflicted on the victorious Sioux. The Indians let the soldiers leave, remaining sole masters of the territory. In Amerindian terms this was as good as total victory. Their casualties were six dead and three wounded.

The news of the battle, far from discouraging the neighbouring tribes, electrified them. The Canadian soldiers had suffered two defeats in quick succession. Perhaps at last the time had come to drive out the arrogant Palefaces. Prophets in the south had predicted an age of renewal. The Earth, they said, was going to roll up like a carpet, carrying off the Whites, their machines and their sicknesses like so many blemishing stains. Kitché-Manitou was going to reestablish the world as it used to be. Indians dead of smallpox would return from the Land of Souls, the buffalo and elk would return to the plains in great numbers, and the Whites would be no more than an unpleasant memory, a tale to be told to children on winter nights.

At the very moment when Colonel Otter was patting himself on the back for having knocked his Cree adversaries out of the picture, a party of Poundmaker's young braves was hurrying to Batoche, burning with hope and hatred. It was there that the next engagement was expected to take place.

Askik spent the night in a thicket on the outskirts of Battleford. Lemercier had lent him his fur coat to serve as tent, mattress and blanket. Askik woke just before daybreak, perishing with cold. His bed of dry grass had soaked up humidity from the ground; puddles around him were glazed with ice. Not daring to light a fire for fear of stirring up the countryside, he watched the day begin. He was hurting everywhere. The bruises to his stomach and ribs had spread during the night and the pain was radiating all over from his legs to his neck. Every movement required an effort: a foretaste of old age. And yet, as he shivered and winced, he could not resist an ironic chuckle.

I'd say I've handled my life masterfully, he mused. I'm twenty-five, penniless, sleep in ditches, and everyone wants to beat me up. Oh, maman, you'd be proud of your boy!

Perfidious flash of wit. It was supposed to make him smile, and it made his heart ache. Where was his family? All the time he had been away, he had imagined them happy because that was what suited him, but how could he be sure they had weathered the contempt of the newcomers?

A pale, unfriendly sun rose over a totally empty prairie. No more Blackfeet crouching in the ravines, no more Métis riding full tilt into seas of stampeding buffalo, no more water bearers laughing and joking on the homeward trail. The drums had fallen silent. Buffalo bones were being harvested and the bones of epidemic victims left in their place, pending the coming of the plough.

Lemercier arrived around midday, his face black with anger.

"Can you walk?" he demanded point-blank. "Good. We're leaving tomorrow for Batoche. I'll walk all the way if necessary. Can you imagine what happened? They refused to send my dispatch! They said they had better things to do than telegraph lies to a French newspaper. Lies!" The burly reporter was choking with indignation, breathing with difficulty. "I don't know what held me back; I nearly beat that idiot telegrapher to a pulp. A sickly little gnome, but what a prig! They've got it coming, I can tell you! Read this." He held out a some sheets of paper.

"This is your article? I like the title."

"A Calamitous Picnic, or Where not to Hold an Alfresco Breakfast," Lemercier recited. "Yes, I'm quite pleased with it. You can keep the article, it'll help you pass the time. Here, I've brought some food. I have to go back, I'm trying to dig up some horses. We'll leave at daybreak. Oh yes — whatever you do, stay out of sight. The neighbours are irritable."

Simpson came to shake Askik's hand late in the afternoon. He seemed weary and depressed but tried to conceal it beneath an affable exterior. He was one of those impeccably mannered men who consider it uncharitable to present an unsmiling face.

"I'll look forward to hearing from you," he told Askik. "I sense that I'm going to be bored here."

"You're not going after the Crees?"

"We're waiting. Middleton's marching on Batoche. If he defeats the Métis, the rebellion will be broken."

"You look exhausted."

"Two men died during the night. Head wounds."

They sat in silence for a long time, both too tired to gather their thoughts and try a new subject of conversation, both sore at heart not to have some small way of demonstrating friendship before parting. Before them was a young poplar with a bright, tender green halo. Both of them stared intently at it, saying nothing, as if hoping to draw some secret source of strength from it.

"I'm ashamed of what we're doing here," Simpson said finally. "We could have come into this country as friends, extending our hands."

"The Indians would have driven you off."

"No, in some ways they're more Christian than we are."

"Men are men, Simpson. You're a lawyer, you're paid to know that."

The other shrugged. "I'm no more lawyer than soldier, I'm afraid." Then, since Askik looked at him quizzically, he added, "I'm giving up the law. I'm not going to plead any more. It'll be a kindness to my clients, don't you think?"

"What are you going to do?"

Simpson now had a twinkle in his eye. He made an admission, watching Askik intently to see what effect it would have. "It's always

448

been my ambition to be... an historian," he said. "I want to write the history of the peoples of Canada."

"So that's why you wanted to know about Lafortune."

"I haven't been very honest, I realize."

"And this work is going to bring together the peoples of your great and benevolent country?"

"Prejudices are like bats. All you have to do is bring a little light to bear, and they'll fly away."

Askik laughed so hard he had pains in every one of his ribs. "You may know a lot about prejudice, Simpson, but you're no expert on bats."

"Oh dear, I was really counting on that analogy."

"I admire you. After all you've seen here, you still believe in this Canada of yours, don't you?"

"What's happening here is appalling. Oh, in world terms, it's nothing. A few dozen deaths, a mere incident. They do a much better job of killing in India or the Crimea. But Askik, the hatred, the contempt that are ingrained here! This ill-willed, unqualified rejection of others... And in people who are so normal, so humane in every other way..."

Simpson gave a little shudder. He sat in silent thought for a time, lips parted. Askik realized that he was contending with an old demon and did not disturb him.

"They'll notice you're not there," he said finally.

"You're right, I must go," Simpson sighed, but made no sign of moving. "Do you hate us for what we've done?"

"Collectively, I've often hated the English. Individually, it's not so easy."

"So that's the way we'll build our country, recruiting one person at a time."

"It's going to take a long while."

Simpson laughed. "Well, there are already two of us, that's a good start." He got to his feet, brushing off the seat of his trousers and straightening his cap. "Write to me," he said as he shook Askik's hand. "Since yesterday, we're going to be sticking pretty close to home."

9

"At last some warmth!" Lemercier exclaimed, lengthening his stride.

They were walking between the wheel tracks, where the ground was reasonably dry. The sloughs were now free of ice. There were still some old snowdrifts in the woods, but the prairie was entirely bare. A warm breeze blew from the south, smelling of earth and grass.

This road linked half a dozen newly surveyed Indian reserves. Askik and Lemercier kept passing wretched grey huts of squared logs. Tiny gardens enclosed in rail fences awaited seeding. Sometimes a bony cayuse watched them go by, munching on its dry grass. More rarely, they saw children, a woman or some old people.

Lemercier was disappointed. He himself looked more Indian than the Indians in the clothes he was wearing. Where were the graceful, barbaric teepees, the garb with fringes, the buckskin gaily embroidered with glass beads? The clothes the Indians wore were those of poor Whites and anything but picturesque: baggy shirts, trousers with shoulder straps and legs down to mid-calf, discordant colours. The women wore heavy boots, the old men ancient, feather-trimmed top hats. It was pathetic and absurd. Lemercier was ashamed for them.

"Have they already forgotten their traditional arts?"

"There are no skins for them to make clothes from any more," Askik told him.

"But these houses..."

"No buffalo, no teepees. There's canvas but it's expensive."

"Well, I realize they've had to change the way they live, but still, they could dress a bit better. And it doesn't cost the earth to whitewash a house."

Askik gave up. He himself was not sure he could grasp the depth of these people's bewilderment. When you have been nomadic for forty thousand years, when you have roamed the plains hunting the buffalo and escaped your refuse by moving on from one season to the next, being tied down to one little plot of ground must be disconcerting in the extreme. It must make things very, very hard, he thought. And yet he was not entirely right.

On reserves fortunate enough to have careful, farsighted chiefs and reasonably arable land, the Indians had converted readily to agriculture. Poundmaker himself cultivated potato fields that were the envy of white visitors. There was little equipment, however. The Indians did not handle the management of their lands themselves; in all things they were obliged to rely on an Indian Agent, who had a budget and guidelines and superiors. The native farmers had their wings clipped by red tape and budgetary restrictions at a critical time when what was needed was money and flexibility.

Askik and Lemercier took seven days to reach Batoche, which was far from making good time. They had not foreseen that most of the houses along their route would be abandoned, the white householders having fled to fortified settlements and the Indians to the prairie. The two travellers found any amount of shelter and firewood but had to make major detours in order to eat. As the days passed, Lemercier was in less and less hurry in any event. The rebellion was over, he had missed the principal engagements, and he had sent practically nothing to his paper. His reporting career was on the rocks, he said. He was resigned to it, even seemed to relish it. Returning to basics had given him back his youth. This long journey on foot through deserted country, these nights spent in barns and stables delighted him. He felt lazy and free.

He was a mite disappointed, then, on the evening of May 10 when they arrived at Gabriel's Crossing, to hear sounds of sporadic rifle and cannon fire.

The major general liked his comfort. With his sixtyish bearing, rotund form and drooping moustache, he looked like a self-satisfied walrus. Frederick Dobson Middleton had been a soldier for forty-three years. He had fought the Sepoys in India and had twice narrowly missed winning the Victoria Cross. He loved marmalades and fine meats and slept in the field, as at home, on a spring mattress, for which he made no apologies. In the morning he would wear field uniform, inspect the trenches and command operations. In the afternoon, after rising from his nap, he would don his dress uniform and do nothing more until the next morning. His officers considered him pompous, devious and grasping. He was nothing if not courageous, however, and enjoyed exposing himself unnecessarily to danger. At Fish Creek, his astrakhan cap had been knocked off by a Métis bullet and two aides-de-camp at his side had been wounded.

Nevertheless, Middleton was hesitating. His first encounter with the Métis at Fish Creek had been traumatizing. He had expected them to flee at first contact, but they had stayed and beaten him. At present, he believed them to be twice as numerous and twice as savage as they really were. His own troops filled him with scorn: drawing-room soldiers, mamas' boys who had come to smell the gunpowder before going back to their shop-counters. Only the volunteers from the West knew anything about fighting, and these knew nothing about obeying orders. A recipe for annihilation. This was why Middleton had stayed two weeks at Fish Creek with the Métis capital only a day's march away. This was why the major-general had camped for two days at the gates of Batoche without really joining battle. Lord Melgund, his aide, had mysteriously returned to Ottawa; it was said that he was there begging for British regulars to be sent out.

"That's Batoche?" Lemercier exclaimed. "That's the rebel capital?"

He had imagined something barbarous and fanciful, a grim redoubt, a ribald, bohemian town. Instead, he saw a village as neat as a pin in the midst of ploughed fields, with a pretty river flowing around it. True enough, the Crees and Assiniboines had set up their teepees on the other side, which redeemed the appearances somewhat, but the whole was so unlike a field of battle that even the artillerymen were being nonchalant. Long minutes might go by between one shot and the next. One kept expecting to see sowers in the fields and housewives in their gardens.

The general had ordered an entrenched camp built on the heights to the west of the village—a muddy square crammed with men and horses.

The Canadians were out of humour. They never saw the enemy and could only guess at the location of entrenchments in the woods and ravines defending the approaches to the village. Thus they had spent a whole afternoon firing at a black mass which could have been a redoubt and turned out to be a dead horse.

It was a war devoid of satisfaction. The Canadians lost men on every sortie and never saw any Métis killed. The soldiers were sniped at by day and by night were under fire that was more defiant than dangerous. Never the least opportunity to get one's blood up, never the pleasure of seeing one's shot strike home. Nerves became frayed, orders were disputed, the mess fare met with disdain. When a Canadian frets about what he eats, things are going badly indeed.

Askik fell into this bucket of bile like a mouse into a clowder of cats. He had barely set foot in the camp before a half-dozen uniforms descended on him and seized him by the scruff of the neck. Protest as he might, Lemercier's French accent only made things worse. The reporter truly believed for a time that his guide was going to be shot. Instead, he was taken to a sergeant, who handed him over to a lieutenant, who passed him off to a captain. He rapidly rose through the ranks this way and finally, for the second time in his life, found himself before a British commanding officer.

And what a commanding officer! Navy blue uniform with silver braid, glistening boots, starched, immaculately clean table napkin tucked under ample chin.

"Sorry to interrupt your meal, sir," said the last colonel to be stuck with Askik. "The men have arrested a Métis spy."

The major-general raised an indulgent hand.

"General," Lemercier implored, "dair eez a beeg mistek, verrie beeg."

He explained as best he could that he was a reporter, that Mercredi was his guide, a good Métis who had never killed anyone. As he pleaded for his friend, he gazed lovingly at the enormous steak the general was cutting into. The sight of that succulent offering intensified the pathetic tone of his voice; a number of officers present were touched.

The general was dining alone at a folding table. A carafe of wine awaited his pleasure. Bowls of pickles, potatoes, vegetables and canned fruit stood close to his plate. In the forty years he had been under arms, he could not remember having eaten so well while in action. This he owed to systematic pillaging of Métis farms on both sides of the Saskatchewan River.

The general raised a good-natured eye to the prisoner. "My wife is French, you know. My brother-in-law, Monsieur Doucet, will be our interpreter."

There followed a rambling interrogation which the general seemed to be conducting as a matter of form. Had they seen any Indian bands on their way here? Steamboats on the Saskatchewan? How was good old Ouimet?

"They don't seem very dangerous, colonel. Have them kept under guard tonight. It won't be for long."

Askik and Lemercier spent the night in a trench pretentiously named Fort Malakoff. They were sat against the wall of a connecting passage. Their two guards, volunteers of the 10th Batallion, seemed totally disillusioned and paid no attention to them. The Métis enemy too seemed to have lost interest; not a shot was fired all night. A magificently starry sky hung over the ramparts. The sentries could just see the roofs of the village in the distance.

"Seems we're going to attack tomorrow."

"Hmmmph!"

"What have we been waiting for to go after 'em?"

"For His Excellency to finish eating."

Recriminations of this kind were rampant in all the trenches. They passed from one man to another, returned magnified to their point of origin and began another round bolstered with even greater indignation. The men were tired of playing clay pigeon; it was time to shoot holes in Métis hides. What the devil was this English general waiting for? He had asked for British troops, said some. He was negotiating an armistice with the papist Riel, said others. He was a gouty old codger, a drunkard, a French Canadian sympathizer, everything, in short, but the kind of commanding officer these fine and gallant Canadians needed.

Sitting in his lair behind a cannon, General Middleton sensed the rising agitation around him and cared not a fig. So these tourists wanted to fight, did they? They took themselves for soldiers, did they? Well, why not let them fight? The general had drawn up a battle plan. He had no illusions as to his chance of success, but perhaps the militiamen needed to get their noses tweeked if only to find out the difference between an office clerk and a major-general who is a veteran of the Indian Mutiny. In any event, he wanted to probe the Métis defenses east of the village; here, he suspected, was the soft underbelly of the beast.

The following morning the troops breakfasted in a bustle of excitement. There was change afoot, something new in the air. And indeed, the cavalry units were given the order to mount.

"Here we go!" the soldiers cried, stuffing their pockets with bannock.

The cavalry paraded proudly just outside the camp. The major-general took the salute, saying in his heart, You wouldn't have lasted ten minutes against the Maoris, my lads!

The cavalry rode northward, taking a cannon and a Gatling gun. The infantry massed to the right of the enemy. Its mission was to perform a major flanking operation to bring it behind the village — into the soft underbelly. The plan was simple. The artillery and cavalry would open fire first. The Métis, thinking they were being attacked on the left, would move men from the right, thus opening the way for the infantry.

Unfortunately, the wind was blowing from the south. The sound of artillery fire failed to reach the infantry, which did not budge all morning. The mounted units attracted the full force of the Métis' fire and suffered heavy losses. In disgust, General Middleton ordered the buglers to sound a "retire" and went home to lunch.

There were pork chops on the menu and a jar of English chutney had just arrived from Ottawa; dear, Eugénie! The general sat down to table with mixed satisfaction and homesickness. Why should he wear himself out on campaigns as vapid as this when there were all those good things at home? Perhaps it was time he took his retirement. His pension would be small, true enough, but life in Canada was so inexpensive. And these French Canadian women were such thrifty housekeepers; real Normans! So how about retirement? He must discuss it with his brother-in-law. But first, his nap.

He was dreaming of being a gentleman farmer in tweeds and corduroys beside a river teeming with fish in some Quebec township when he was jolted awake by a flurry of rifle fire. A young artilleryman was perched on the cannon carriage.

"What's going on?" the general cried.

"We're charging, sir."

"Charging?" the general bellowed. "By whose order?"

The firing had begun on the left. A Métis sniper had wounded a Midlander. Furious, the militiamen had counterattacked. The excitement had spread to the Grenadiers and the neighbouring units. A rolling fire began all the way down the line. The soldiers were charging, bayonets fixed, led by officers who had prepared this in secret.

Monumental confusion reigned in the camp on the hill. The general mounted his horse and galloped out of camp. The men were leaping the ramparts; Midlanders, Grenadiers, Riflemen, scouts all ran to join the fray, uniforms of all colours mingled. What the hell did they need officers for?

The two volunteers guarding Askik and Lemercier kept looking despairingly over the parapet. Were they going to miss the final battle after coming so far? What would they tell their parents? I didn't get to fight because I was guarding an obese French Canadian and a Métis who blinked his eyes twice in an hour at most? They looked at each other questioningly, then both were gone over the parapet.

"Whoof!" Lemercier said. "I thought they were going to shoot us just to be rid of us."

The Métis were in flight. With their ammunition gone, they had taken to loading their rifles with nails and buttons. Whenever a Canadian bullet ploughed into the ground near them, they would dig it out and shoot it back. All this takes time, and time had run out.

When they came to the village, the soldiers instinctively took shelter behind the buildings. For a time it seemed as if the charge had run out of steam, but a hothead by the name of Jack French launched it anew by rushing out to meet the enemy. He broke down the door of a house, went upstairs to shoot from the window, and fell stone dead with a bullet in his heart.

The troops became immobilized again when the Gatling gun and cannons were brought up from the rear. At the first salvoes, the Métis scattered; by now they only had gravel to load in their guns. The Battle of Batoche was over.

"There won't be any novels written about it," Lemercier said as he and Askik walked down to the village.

He was wrong. Already the little battle was inflating into a big victory. After the staccato of actual shots came the rolling fire of dispatches. Throughout the mighty Canada, telegraph wires disseminated the news of the triumph.

At Batoche itself, the victors would have noisily celebrated their defeat of the enemy, but first, what enemy? Most of the soldiers had yet to see more than momentary shadows, silhouettes of men rendered shapeless by the woods and enlarged by imagination. They discovered what a Métis was really like when they saw the bodies; the rifle pits and houses held surprises for them. Beardless, barefoot youths lay here and there in the trenches beside old flintlock muskets. Joseph Ouellette, ninety-three, and Joseph Vandale, seventy-five, had both died at their posts. A girl of fourteen lay stiff, wearing an embroidered dress in a coffin in her parents' house, killed by an exploding cannon shell. The bodies had dark or pale complexions, hair cut short or braided Indian fashion, and were clothed in black or bright checks.

Like the other reporters, Lemercier telegraphed a detailed account of the sordid little bloodbath. For him, however, this was not enough. For three days in the pouring rain, he and Askik combed the banks of the Saskatchewan in search of refugees. Lemercier wanted to understand. He had witnessed an injustice and was presumptuous enough to want to put his finger on its source, to bring an explanation of it to those who would be reading his articles while eating their bread and jam after dinner.

There were Métis women and children crowded into damp grottos a few feet from the river. The children were coughing, and in every grotto there were bereaved women reciting the rosary while their elders murmured the funeral chants of the Crees.

The appearance of the two men frightened them at first, but their need to be comforted was so great that they accepted Askik's reassurances without discussion. On the strength of an outstretched hand they would have fallen into the crudest trap, so eager were they to believe that there were some who did not wish their death. Slowly, shyly, the questions came forth. Had the soldiers gone? Had their houses been burned? Had the pope excommunicated them? Askik was moved to be rediscovering the Métis ways, the eyes cast down in courtesy, the slow, deliberate gestures, the lilting speech of the women of his race. He was exasperated to understand them so poorly. He was suddenly learning that while the Métis dialect borrows extensively from French, its logic and rhythm are deeply Indian. Not only did he no longer really speak Cree, but he had lost the fluidity of thought that infuses order with intuition and rules and regulations with discernment. Whereas French had at first seemed finicky in its rigour, now his mother tongue seemed evanescent and imprecise.

In each grotto he asked after his parents; no one remembered them. From this first new contact with his people, he came away thoroughly bewildered.

"I'm not really anything at all any more," he said between puffs while climbing back up the bank of the Saskatchewan. Low, grimy clouds were raking the prairie and hanging raggedly about the black trees on the riverbanks, these riverbanks beneath which women and children huddled in misery. This must be the world's most dismal country, he thought.

In the days that followed, almost all the families of Batoche came back to the village. The men gave up their old guns, swearing they had acted under compulsion. The leaders were arrested and the others returned to their ploughs. Only a few diehards kept lying low in the ravines, hands constantly on their knives and humiliation in their hearts. They were much feared but seldom encountered.

And so, when Askik rounded a turn in a trail and came face-to-face with a heavily armed Métis, he thought his last hour had come. Lemercier had taken the steamboat to the telegraph post. The riverbank was deserted. Askik was alone. The other could shoot him down and disappear. There was something puzzling in the stranger's eyes, however; something like shyness, even affection. He was a young man, barely beyond adolescence, rather thin but tall. He was wearing a coarse cotton shirt, moccasins and an old, threadbare wool coat.

"*Tansé, Askik? Kekiskinimin na?*"

"*Mouats, kin… si… to… ta… tin,*" Askik replied, groping for the expression.

"Mikiki!" the other exclaimed, astonished not to be recognized. "Your… bro…ther," he added in French that was as laboured as Askik's Cree.

They closed the few steps between them and threw their arms about each other. This young giant was Mikiki? This elegant gentleman was Askik?

The younger brother broke the embrace. "*Astam outa,*" he said. He drew Askik toward the river, throwing backward glances. The soldiers could turn up here; they were poor marksmen but fired a lot of bullets.

He led Askik to a small clearing out of sight of both the prairie and the river. Here, he leaned his gun against a birch tree and lit a fire of twigs. There was a supply of wood, water and tea, but this was not a real camp. He must must be sleeping elsewhere.

"Where's Maman?" Askik asked. "*Tandé?*"

"At St. Laurent."

"That's no distance at all!" Askik exclaimed.

"No, the other St. Laurent, on Lake Manitoba," Mikiki corrected.

The brothers quickly established a code incorporating Cree, French, hand signs and drawings on the ground. Askik learned that his father was managing a small trading post in the North, the telegraph having rendered the profession of runner largely obsolete. Anita had returned to the South, discouraged with life in the Athabaska and lonesome for her people. She was working as a housekeeper for nuns at an Indian mission. Mikiki had been raised in the Athabaska, where he had learned Dogrib and lost his French. At fifteen he had become a boatman for the Company and then just a tracker, hauling boats through rapids from shore. After tracking several hundred boats from a swampy tracking trail, he had realized that he would not live to be old doing this and had fled. He had come south to the Métis villages of Saskatchewan in hope of finding a wife and a farm.

He had found Louis Riel, the prophet of the New Métis Nation, an inspired leader and founder of a purified church, who was dreaming of a Métis and Amerindian dominion. When he heard the prophet speak, Mikiki felt a deep and festering sore open wide in him. Everything he had received from the Whites — condescension, paternalism, scorn —

rose suddenly in his gullet. Oh, to take these arrogant, so-called bene-factors down a peg, show them that a Métis is a free, responsible man!

After the battle, he had taken to the bottom of a coulee and wept long and bitterly, making the mud fly with his fists. Why should the Métis be short of ammunition when they had no shortage of heart and courage? Why should the arrogant Whites with their infernal machines always win?

In the grottos by the Saskatchewan, to which he was bringing hare and squirrels, he had heard tell of a young Métis come from Canada with the soldiers. A hunch about this led him to watch the comings and goings at the camp, and he had easily recognized his brother. Like the rest of the Métis, he was not offended to see Askik among the enemy and did not hold it against him. A man's destiny can take him into many camps.

He finished by saying that he hoped Askik would stay in the North West, that they would be a family at last. He had missed having a family.

The tiny fire had begun to smoke and might give them away. Mikiki deftly cleared it to leave only dry twigs that burn clean without smoking, his calloused, knowing fingers flicking away the damp embers, rearranging the rest, fanning the flames. He handed his brother a steam-ing bowl of tea and then put out the fire. Sometimes, if he heard a suspi-cious snap or a bird flew too close, he would discreetly stretch his neck and scan the crest of the bank. He was alert and relaxed both at once, like the deer, who live and take rest in the midst of danger.

"*Kina?*" he asked, "You *coutan?*"

"Am I happy?"

"*Kewi kitsona?*"

"No, not married."

Mikiki looked shocked. Not married? "*Tché! Kikawi kikhow!*" he said disapprovingly. "You're old for that, brother!"

A partridge flew up with a noisy flapping of wings. Mikiki froze, eyes intent, hand reaching for his gun. Askik was angered to see this. No sooner had he found his brother than he was in danger of losing him to the soldiers; the Canadians took a dim view of these bold young men who kept roaming the woods instead of giving themselves up. Askik himself had little reason to count on kindness from most white men.

"Don't stay here," he told Mikiki. "*Awasse!* Get away! Go to Montana, you won't be alone there. I'll send for you in the Autumn. Here, take this. *Outsina.*"

Askik handed him what was left of his money. Mikiki took it, believing his brother to be rich, like all Canadians. He wanted to stay a while but Askik became assertive, insisting that he go at once. Finally Mikiki took his gun, embraced his brother and with a warm smile disappeared into the woods.

10

Scouts had brought word of a small party of Métis and Crees moving northward. Women and children and a few old men, probably going to join their men in the forest. General Middleton did not think it worth intervening. Lemercier, however, wanted to go and look. He rented horses for himself and his guide.

They rode all one morning without finding a trace of the fugitives. It hardly mattered; the air was fresh, there were pasqueflowers, prairie smoke, in bloom at the edge of the woods, the sun was radiant.

Lemercier had enjoyed his outing and now was ready to turn back. Near Batoche he had discovered a canny Métis woman who was selling him her hidden eggs and cheese at exorbitant prices; his head was filled with visions of a succulent omelet. Such a compulsive fellow, this Chingachgook! You'd think he was on the trail of his own parents.

"Askik!" he cried. "I'm dy-ing of hunger. For mer-cy's sake, let's go home!"

Askik, however, was already digging his heels into his horse's belly.

"Let's ask at that farm first," he called as he pulled away.

A small house of clay-daubed logs, a vertical-plank barn. Not a single hen or piglet. General Middleton was still eating royally.

A man came out of the house with a glowering face. When he saw another Métis coming toward him, too well-dressed and too well-mounted, he took him for one of those ambitious little punks who play the poodle for Whites. A sellout. His blood boiled and he ground his teeth quietly. He was a powerful man with a potbelly and greying beard. He had handed over his old muzzle loader to the soldiers but had held onto his Winchester. How could he go and get it without tipping off these two birds?

"Have you seen a group of women and children go by?" the poodle asked him.

"Mebbe," the farmer growled.

"What direction were they going?"

"Whajja want 'em for?"

"To see them, talk to them. My friend's a journalist..."

Suddenly the Métis' swarthy face lit up with delight. "A journalist?" he cried. "*Ben cré maudit!* Come down, come down off them horses, young sirs! I'm right honoured! Are you gonna put my name in the paper? How 'bout a bite o' partridge?"

"Ah now, for that, yes!" Lemercier replied as he dismounted.

"Sit yerselves down there in the sun," the man said, seating them together on a big tree-trunk lying in the yard. "I'll be right back. Willya take some jam with yer bread? Great!"

"What a charming man!" Lemercier said when he had gone. "The people here have kept their sense of hospitality. You'd think we were in Quebec."

In the far corner of his vegetable cellar, meanwhile, the charming man was digging with his hands in the fine sand covering his carrots, turnips and the Winchester. Tenderly, he exhumed the weapon, which was swathed in grease and rags. She had picked off more than one Canadian at Batoche, the rascal; it was time she woke up from her nap.

As he stealthily closed the trap door to the cellar, he heard the journalist outside holding forth on the basic humanity of the people of Saskatchewan. Suddenly the voice ceased. The farmer froze, afraid his game might be taking flight, and there he was, with his cartridges still buried in the flour. He suffered an eternity of anguish, then recovered his grin when he heard Lemercier's voice again.

"That's the oldest horse I ever did see!"

A piebald mare with a beard under her chin and a stub of a tail was limping slowly toward the stable. She had no hair at all on her shoulders, her haunches jutted up higher than her back, there were dark shadows between her ribs, and her knees were armoured with callouses. She was wearing neither halter nor hobble and seemed free to go where she pleased. It could not have been far. Sensing she was being watched, she stopped in the middle of the yard and turned great, inexpressive eyes to the visitors.

Askik could not help laughing. "Looks just like the Choquette horse!" he exclaimed.

"Whazzat?" bellowed the farmer just behind them. "You Jérôme Mercredi's boy?"

Askik and Lemercier jumped a mile. Lemercier turned in annoyance, his heart still thumping from the fright.

"What's the idea, scaring people like..."

He went as white as a sheet to find himself looking into the oily mouth of the Winchester. In great embarrassment, the farmer lowered the gun and stuck out a big hand to Askik.

"Ormidas Choquette," he stammered. "I knew yer father."

Lemercier seemed about to faint. "He was going to..." he muttered.

"I'm sorry," the man said, hanging his head, "I couldn'ta knowed."

Askik burst out laughing and the farmer followed suit with a loud, raucous guffaw, holding his belly with one hand and the gun with the other. The Choquette horse turned away and resumed her slow plod toward the stable. Yes, she had recognized the Mercredi kid. So?

"I bet there isn't even any partridge," Lemercier said heatedly.

"Ah, yer too right," the farmer admitted, still laughing.

"Have you seen a group of women and children?" Askik asked again."

"Yestiddy afternoon," Choquette gasped, wiping the tears out of his moustache.

"They were heading north?"

"West. They done a detour so's not to meet the soldiers. They're gonna cross over at Gariépy's crossin'. Hey, sump'n might interest ya, there's folks from The Fork with 'em. My respects to yer father."

Askik was already in the saddle.

"What's The Fork?" Lemercier called as they galloped full tilt out of the yard.

"The Red River," Askik replied. "They're my people."

Lemercier groaned. His stomach was complaining and his rear and spine had already been pounded to jelly.

"Askik! I can't take any more! I'm going back."

"See you tonight, then," Askik shouted without turning.

He continued alone, bending over the horse's neck, his knees pulled up to the animal's withers. The pounding of its hoofs mingled with the beating of his heart. Thank God the Métis had inherited their French-Canadian fathers' passion for horses! It was a good horse, a powerful beast, though a bit soft after a winter of idleness. When they came to the river, horse and rider turned north. Half an hour later they struck a trail which led to the water's edge.

"Cloudin' over," the ferryman said on the way down to the ferry. "*Wikimwan.* It's gonna rain. Ain't many folks crossin' no more since the troubles."

"But yesterday you took a group of Métis and Crees across. Which way did they go?"

"They gone west. Don't ask me where they're headin'. *Mouats nikiskenten. Tché!* Didn't even have no money to pay me. Ain't worth killin' yer horse, missieur, they ain't movin' fast. Got sick people. *Ahi! Nisikhats*, missieur, so go easy!"

He might have saved his breath. The ferry no sooner touched shore than Askik urged his horse to the same breakneck pace. He was keyed up as taut as the ferry cable.

The ferryman had been right, the fugitives had not gone far. Very soon, Askik was glimpsing the tops of teepees among the trees. Here the prairie formed a little bay in a small wood; this was where they were camping.

The camp looked so woebegone that Askik instinctively slowed his horse to a walk. He felt like turning back. The dirty canvas teepees were smoking beneath a grey sky. There were even some rectangular tents bought from the Whites. Wagons and travois were littered all over. Emaciated cayuses were cropping the new shoots of grass.

As he passed the tents, Askik could see women and children peeking out at him from behind barely opened flaps. Sometimes, not often, he saw a man sitting with his back turned by a fire. There were fires in all the tents but not the slightest whiff of cooking. Complete silence reigned, a sign that everyone in the camp knew he was there. He was uncomfortable. Each clop of his horse's hoofs, each squeak of his saddle sounded to him like an additional insult to these bereft people. What had he come here for? He recognized no one. He gently turned the horse's nose and headed back toward the prairie. He had been wrong to come.

He had already left the camp when a small boy of three or four came running out of the woods and, seeing the horse, stopped and stood still. He stared at Askik with that air of defiance mixed with fear that small children reserve for strangers. He was a sturdy little fellow with a round face and well-formed limbs. The stubborn chin was that of a future hotspur of the first order.

"His name's Ovide," a woman said, approaching.

Askik did not even have to turn around to recognize Mona. Her voice had not changed. It still had that almost unreal calmness that said with each inflexion, That's how things are, and that's how they're supposed to be.

"*Tansé*, Askik?" she said, smiling.

"You never used to smile when you were a little girl," Askik said as he dismounted.

The young woman laughed. "And you never rode like that, either."

They stopped and stood awkwardly face-to-face.

"Did you know I was coming?" Askik asked.

"Oh, come on!"

"You could predict things, back then."

"A bit, for a while. That passed."

She was taller than he had expected. Stronger too, and prettier. A rather wide face; her hair, gathered in two heavy braids, was almost brown and her slightly slanting eyes had acquired a twinkle with the years. She was holding a second child not more than a year old, who stared at Askik with big brown eyes.

"This one's Mathias," she said, hitching him up a bit. "He's named after his father. You remember Mathias Gauthier, who lost you on the prairie?"

"He's your husband?"

"He was. He's dead."

Askik thought back to all the dead bodies he had seen at Batoche. Could he have stepped over Mathias Gauthier without recognizing him?

Realizing what he must be thinking, Mona corrected the supposition. "He died last spring of consumption."

The baby gurgled cheerfully, as if contradicting what his mother was saying.

An embarrassed silence fell between them. Or rather, it was Askik who was embarrassed. Mona seemed just as serene and self-assured as ever. And as usual it was she who broke the silence.

"How about you, Askik?" she asked. "Did you become a great man?"

"No. My horse threw me. My gun blew up on me."

At that Mona began to laugh, but it was such a kind, warmhearted laugh that Askik would gladly have bungled another life just to hear it.

"You didn't have that sense of humour when you left," she said.

"Since those days I've made a lot of people laugh, believe me."

"And now?"

Askik shrugged. Unconsciously, his hand went up to the pommel of the saddle and his eyes checked the position of the stirrup. Mona's hands were brown and veined and strong. The texture of her clothes was coarse. She smelled of wood fire and humus. Could he live this way? He looked guiltily at her. She had such kind, patient eyes!

"We're going to St. Paul," she said. There are lots of Métis there. Maybe there'll even be a school for the children if we can find a teacher."

"I have to go," Askik said. "A friend's waiting for me at Batoche."

He remounted, then said, "Is it true you can't foresee the future any more?"

"When I was small and unhappy, there were times when I thought I could see things. Not any more."

Askik groped for some parting words. Once again she saved him from embarrassment.

"I'm glad you're back, Askik."

"Oh, I'm not sure I'll be staying," he protested.

"I know. I'm glad anyway."

The prairie was cold and grey and drizzly. Like that day seventeen years earlier when Mona had led him to a buffalo skeleton. For the first time, Askik was seeing the prairie as it was, unemotionally, with its demoralized hunters, illiterate children, squalid teepees, its little clans tottering on the brink of a baleful future. He thought of his fugitive brother, so proud of his strength and skill, who did not suspect how defenseless he was. He saw Mona's children again, with their huge Indian eyes. What did a Whites' future hold for them? Tuberculosis, alcohol, demeaning jobs? Perhaps Mona was right. Perhaps he could do something for them, and for others of his fellow Métis. But their destitution terrified him.

Angrily, he whipped at his horse. Drops of rain mixed with the tears he was trying to disown.

11

The soldiers of the 65th crowded against the rails of the ship, listening in silence to the sounds of battle reaching them from the heights. The crackling of rifle fire, the dull roar of cannons, the explosion of shells, more muffled still, roused uneasy feelings in them. Neither fear nor exhilaration; just vague anxieties; confused regrets. They had been waiting so long. For weeks and weeks, the batallion had twiddled its thumbs while its scouts frantically searched for Big Bear's warriors. At last the soldiers had them. The advance guard had engaged them. The militiamen were only waiting for the signal — a white flag on the hill — to disembark and join the battle.

A white shadow was floating now against the grey sky: the signal.

"What time is it?" asked Sergeant Charles Daoust, who was writing an account of the expedition.

"Five minutes to three," another replied.

The hour of the Passion, Grandet thought as he stood in the queue for the gangway. He was scrupulously taking stock of his own feelings. Was he afraid? No. Was he hoping to accomplish great things? No. What was he feeling, then? Indifference. Was this a defense against fear?

The chaplain stood before them, his crucifix in his hand. "Kneel, my sons, that I may bless you."

The soldiers knelt in the new grass, caps in hand, their guns upright at their sides. Grandet contemplated the heavy clouds covering the sky and raking the crests of the hills. Why did it have to be a grey day like this? It couldn't just be chance. And this young Oblate in his white surplice and purple stole against the grey prairie; was he aware how laughable it all was? What a strange ending, all the same.

"Fix bayonets! Quick march!"

Grandet did not see the countryside he was passing through: wooded ravines, sloughs, hillocks — the usual prairie panoply. All he saw was the endless column of black tunics.

So it's true, he thought, I'm going to die. I ought to pray, confess my sins to God, but what good would it do? I'm certainly not going to redeem the triviality of my life with this circus. To think I used to get excited over all this pompous claptrap! Flags, boots, left-right, left-right. Talk about sheep! And that great awkward lump of a chaplain trailing after us with his virgin-at-the-stake airs! I hope the Indians aren't the jackasses we are!

"Company, halt! Make camp!"

The men looked at each other in puzzlement. The shooting had stopped.

A soldier returning from the front brought them news. "The Indians had laid a trap for us," he told them. "We couldn't take them by assault. They're dug in on a butte behind a slough. Never mind, our cannons gave them a hot time of it. We're spending the night here."

"And tomorrow?"

"Back to Fort Pitt."

The soldiers feigned disappointment. Some were even genuinely disappointed. An officer of the Winnipeg Light Infantry passing by at this moment was surprised to see Grandet laughing.

"What's so funny?" the officer enquired, chortling already in anticipation of the joke he was about to hear.

Grandet smiled broadly at him and replied, "A more gullible fool than I there never was, brother."

Mystified and put out to be spoken to in French, the officer went on his way.

Montréal,
July 30, 1885

Dear Monsieur de Meauville,

My letter may surprise you. You do not know me but we have a friend in common. I thought you would like to have news of him.

I parted with Askik Mercredi — you know him as Alexis — three weeks ago at Battleford in Saskatchewan. Our party was about to travel by steamboat to Grand Rapids in Manitoba, and thence south by some dreadful boats down an interminable lake to Winnipeg. It was a nightmare; I shall spare you the details.

I saw Askik the evening before our departure. It had been hard on him to find his people in as dire circumstances as they are. He was taking hope again, however. He seemed like a man recovering from a long illness and thereby making sounder judgments regarding the importance of things. As we dined, he told me of a vision he had had as a child, something about a dead Indian and a wolf. I mention it in case it might mean something to you. For my own part, I was at a loss to understand it. I should add that our friend has lately been demonstrating a most peculiar sense of humour: rather dry, a bit facetious, very Métis.

We drank a last rum together and then, despite the lateness of the hour, he mounted his horse. As he left the village he turned around one last time to wave to me, and at that moment I felt I was looking at a happy man. When last I caught sight of him, he was riding hell-for-leather, bound for a village by the name of St. Paul in Alberta. God knows why.

Oh, I almost forgot — I met another of your acquaintances on the boat I mentioned, Sub-Lieutenant Elzéar Grandet. He says that he will soon be paying you a visit in your village and, for some reason that escapes me, considers that this will be an heroic accomplishment.

In closing, since people of wit must band together, I hope you will not hesitate to visit me when next you are in Montreal. Perhaps one of us will have heard from our brother Askik Mercredi.

A friend to be,
Arthur Lemercier,
Journalist.